Shojo Beat

NANA Vol.9

50-page bonus manga in the back!

Main Character

Contents

The Story of Nana

Nana "Hachi" Komatsu and Nana Osaki meet by chance on a train headed for Tokyo. Their personalities and the environments they grew up in are very different, but by fate or by chance, they meet again and become roommates...

Nana Osaki gets back together with her ex-boyfriend Ren, who she hasn't seen for more than a year. Ren's band Trapnest is wildly popular, and Nana is determined that Blast will keep up. A major label offers the band a temporary contract, and now Blast is busy practicing daily for their debut.

Hachi leaves Takumi for Nobu, and it's happily ever after until Hachi discovers she's pregnant. Takumi claims the baby, regardless of who the father really is. Hachi can't stand up to Takumi's manipulation or explain the real situation to Nobu, but she does decide to keep the baby. When Hachi tells Takumi her plans, he surprisingly proposes. Meanwhile, Nana, who's in even more shock than Nobu, runs to Yasu for advice and to vent. She calms down, but...

♥For the complete story, please check out *Nana*, volumes 1 - 8.
Available in bookstores everywhere!!

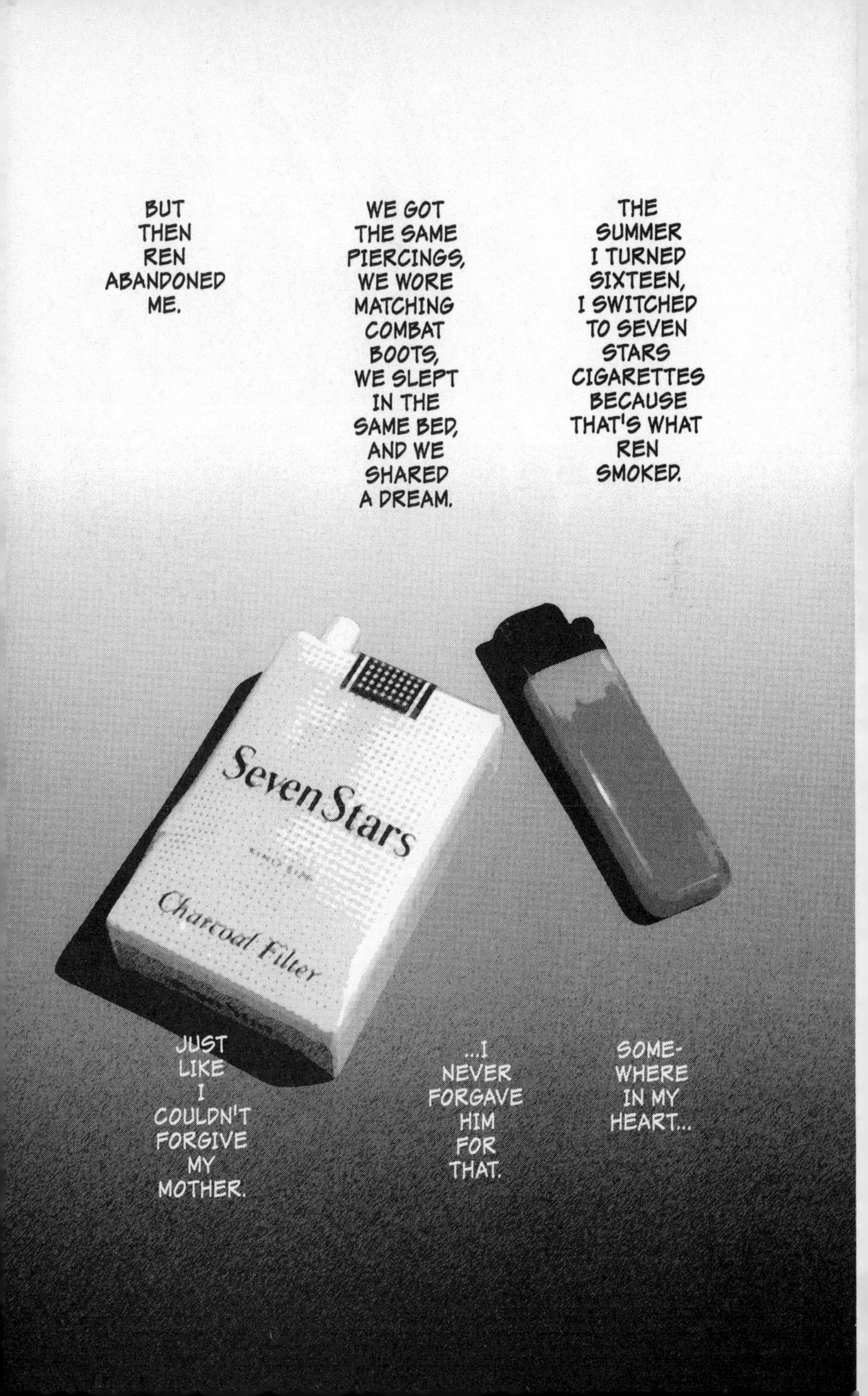
THE SUMMER I TURNED SIXTEEN, I SWITCHED TO SEVEN STARS CIGARETTES BECAUSE THAT'S WHAT REN SMOKED.
WE GOT THE SAME PIERCINGS, WE WORE MATCHING COMBAT BOOTS, WE SLEPT IN THE SAME BED, AND WE SHARED A DREAM.
BUT THEN REN ABANDONED ME.
SOME-WHERE IN MY HEART...
...I NEVER FORGAVE HIM FOR THAT.
JUST LIKE I COULDN'T FORGIVE MY MOTHER.
Seven Stars
Charcoal Filter

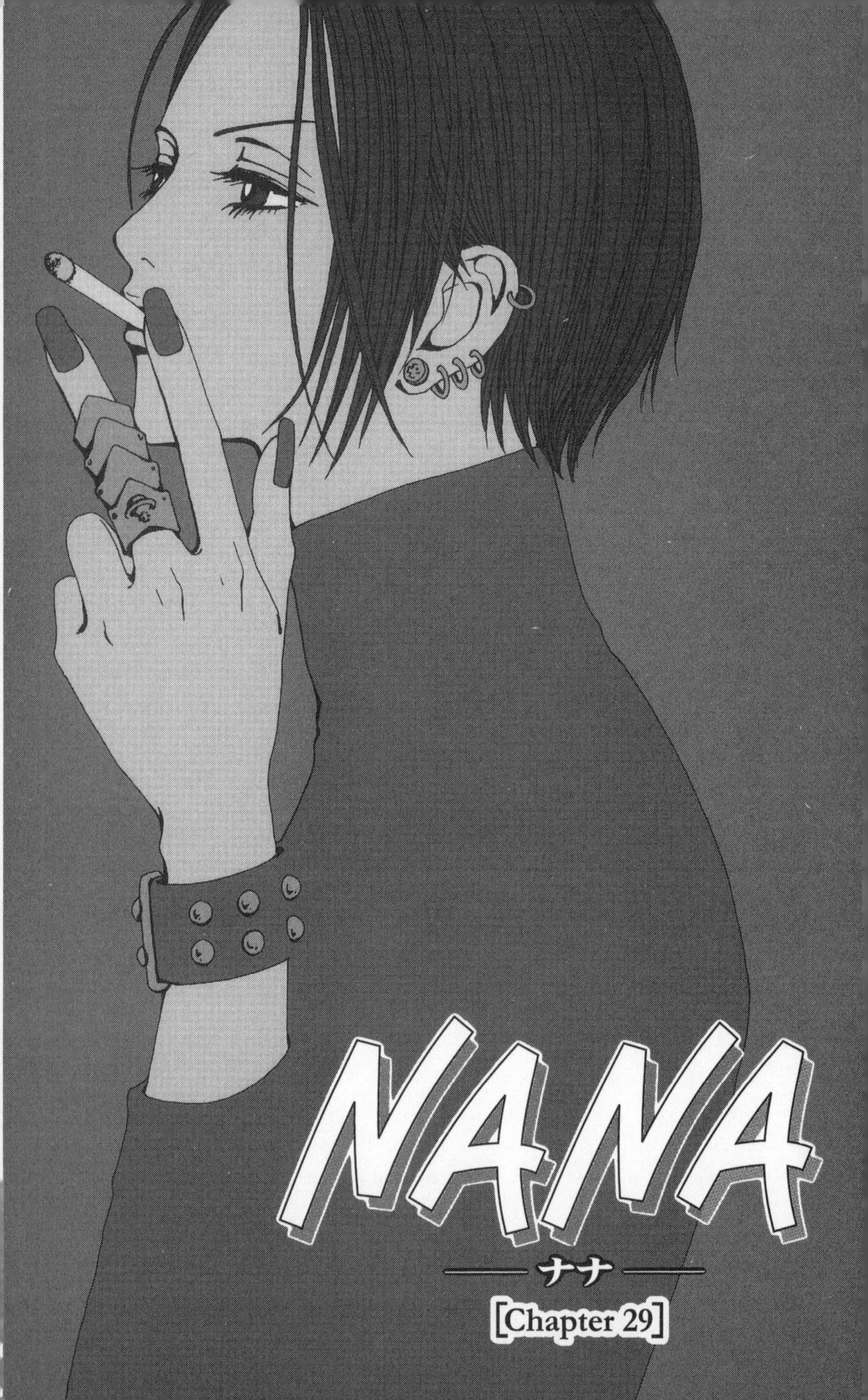
NANA
ナナ
[Chapter 29]

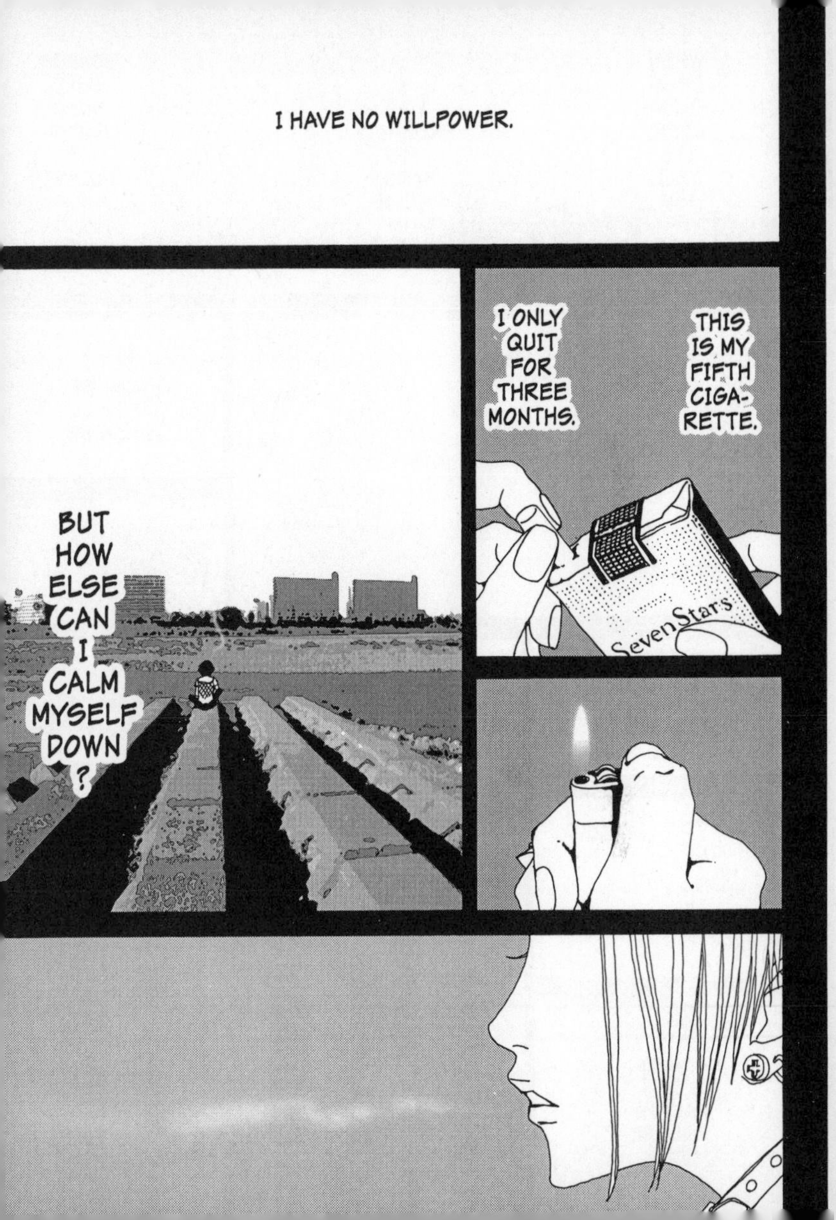
I HAVE NO WILLPOWER.
THIS IS MY FIFTH CIGARETTE.
I ONLY QUIT FOR THREE MONTHS.
Seven Stars
BUT HOW ELSE CAN I CALM MYSELF DOWN?

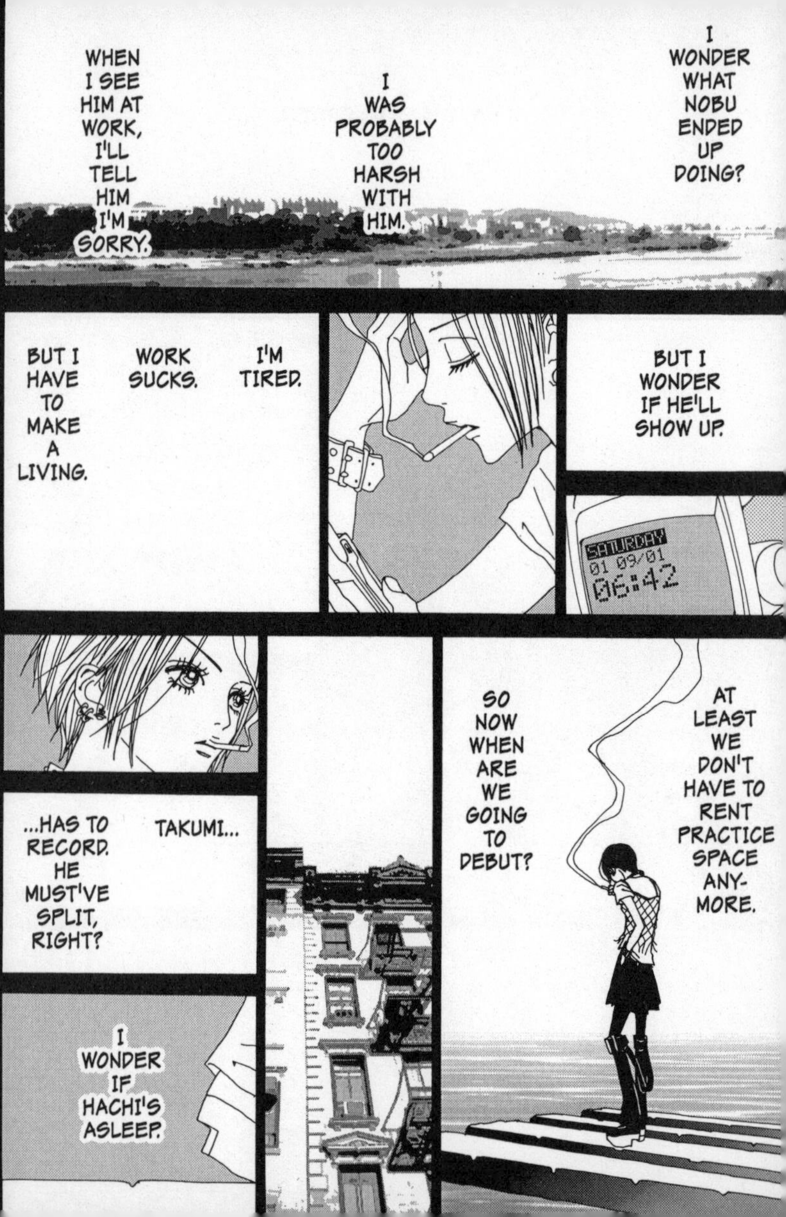
I WONDER WHAT NOBU ENDED UP DOING?
I WAS PROBABLY TOO HARSH WITH HIM.
WHEN I SEE HIM AT WORK, I'LL TELL HIM I'M SORRY.
BUT I WONDER IF HE'LL SHOW UP.
SATURDAY
01 09/01
06:42
I'M TIRED.
WORK SUCKS.
BUT I HAVE TO MAKE A LIVING.
AT LEAST WE DON'T HAVE TO RENT PRACTICE SPACE ANYMORE.
SO NOW WHEN ARE WE GOING TO DEBUT?
TAKUMI...
...HAS TO RECORD. HE MUST'VE SPLIT, RIGHT?
I WONDER IF HACHI'S ASLEEP.

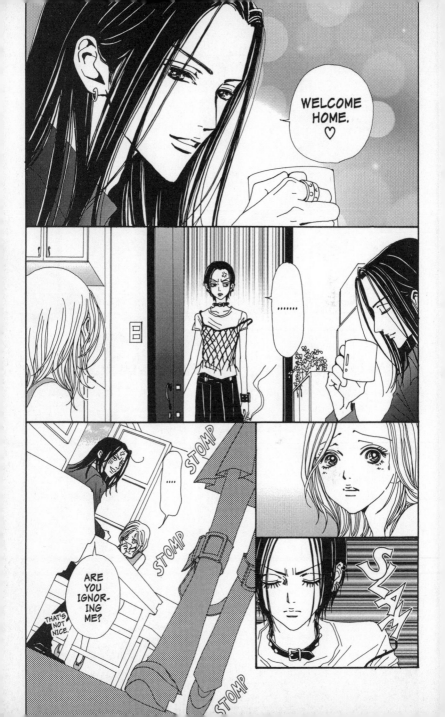

WELCOME HOME. ♡

......

....

ARE YOU IGNOR-ING ME?

THAT'S NOT NICE.

STOMP

STOMP

STOMP

STOMP

SLAM

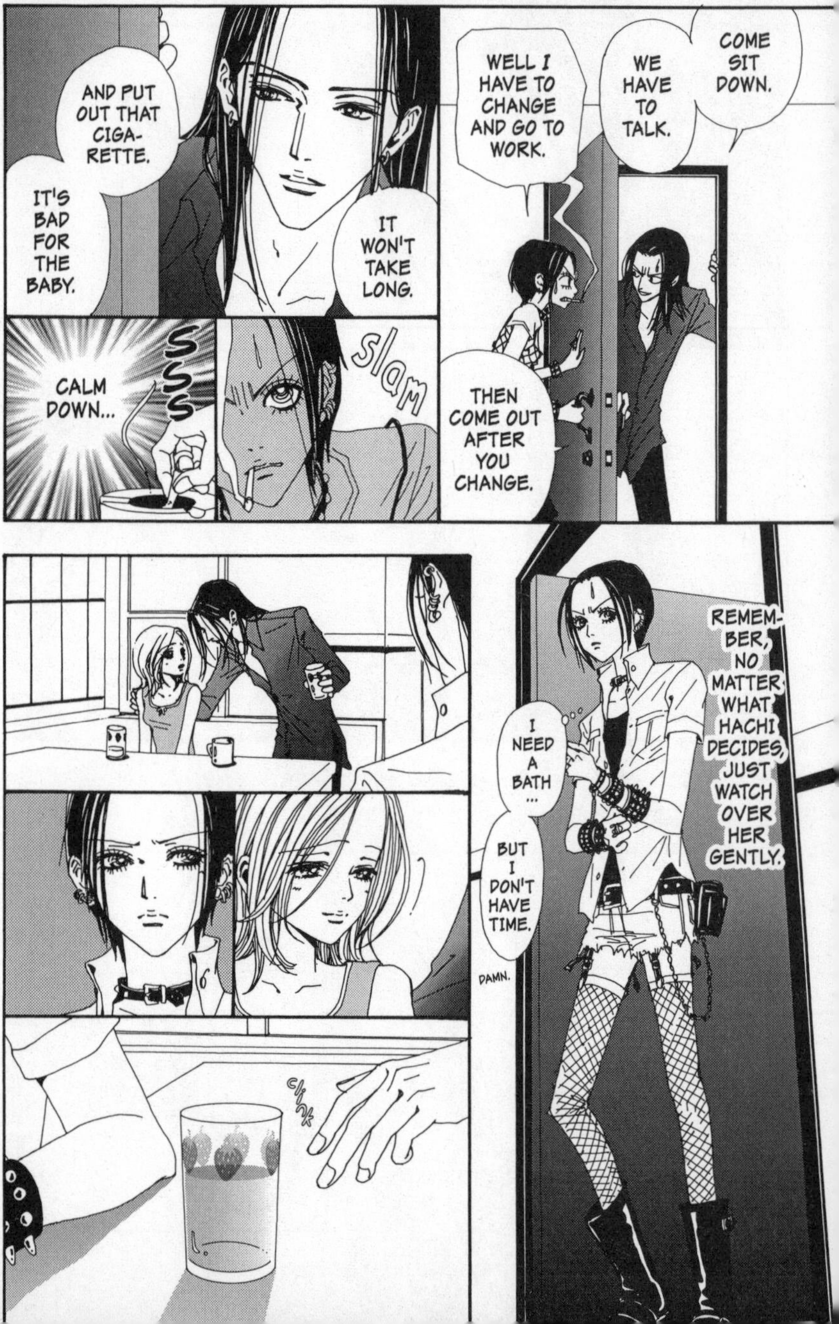
COME SIT DOWN.
WE HAVE TO TALK.
WELL I HAVE TO CHANGE AND GO TO WORK.
THEN COME OUT AFTER YOU CHANGE.
IT WON'T TAKE LONG.
AND PUT OUT THAT CIGA-RETTE.
IT'S BAD FOR THE BABY.
slam
SSS
CALM DOWN...
REMEM-BER, NO MATTER WHAT HACHI DECIDES, JUST WATCH OVER HER GENTLY.
I NEED A BATH...
BUT I DON'T HAVE TIME.
DAMN.
clink

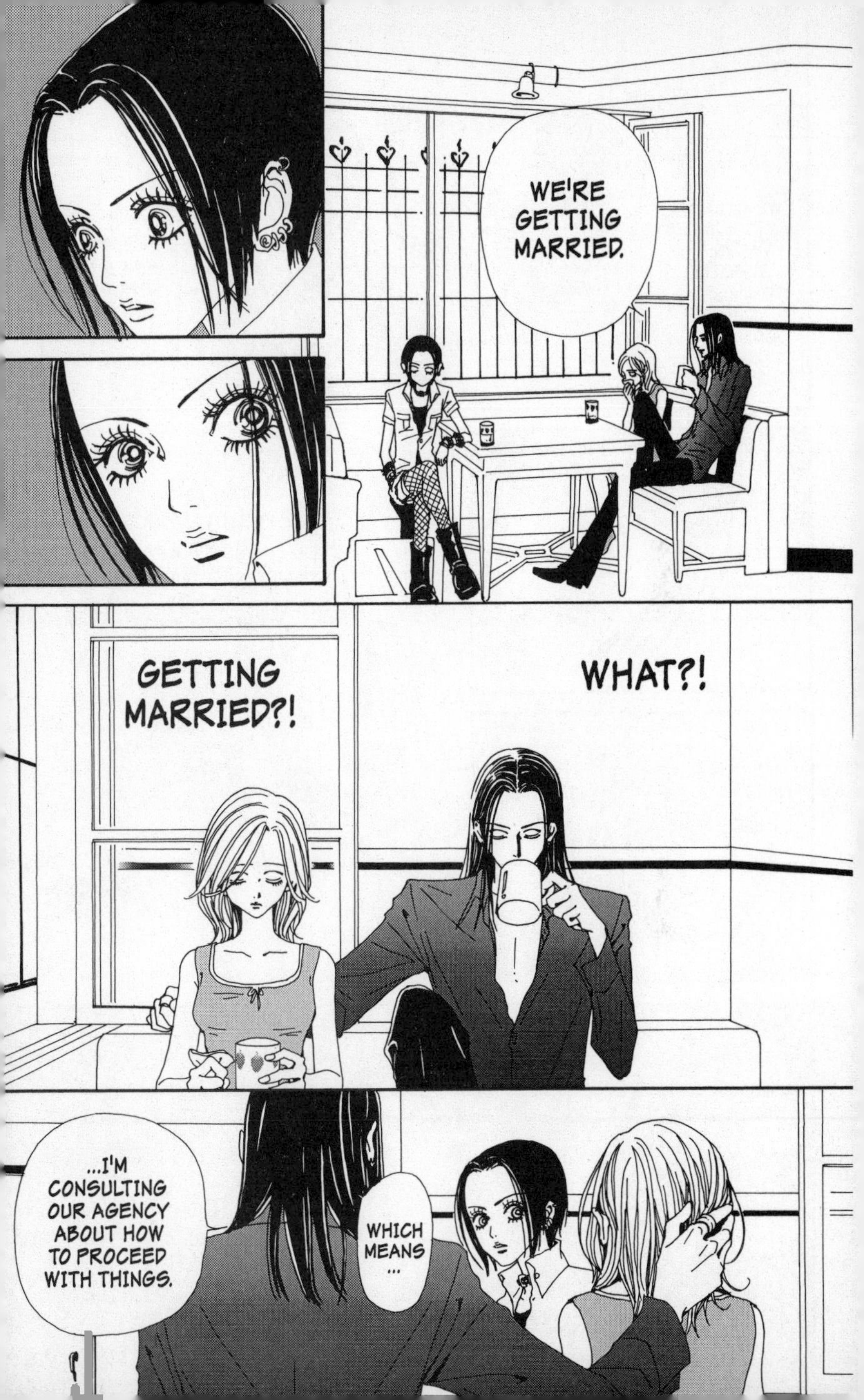
WE'RE GETTING MARRIED.
WHAT?!
GETTING MARRIED?!
WHICH MEANS ...
...I'M CONSULTING OUR AGENCY ABOUT HOW TO PROCEED WITH THINGS.

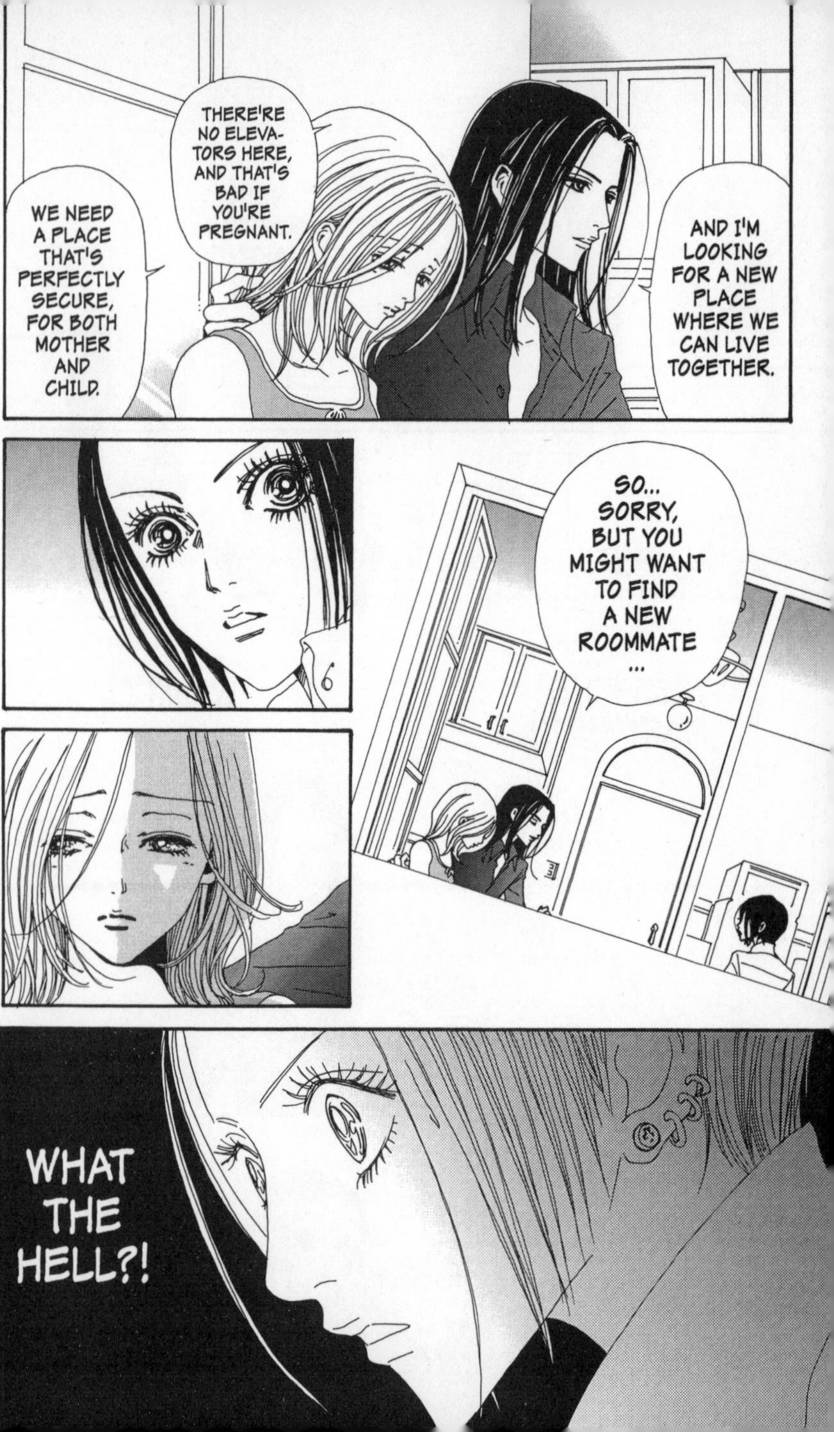
AND I'M LOOKING FOR A NEW PLACE WHERE WE CAN LIVE TOGETHER.
THERE'RE NO ELEVATORS HERE, AND THAT'S BAD IF YOU'RE PREGNANT.
WE NEED A PLACE THAT'S PERFECTLY SECURE, FOR BOTH MOTHER AND CHILD.
SO... SORRY, BUT YOU MIGHT WANT TO FIND A NEW ROOMMATE ...
WHAT THE HELL?!

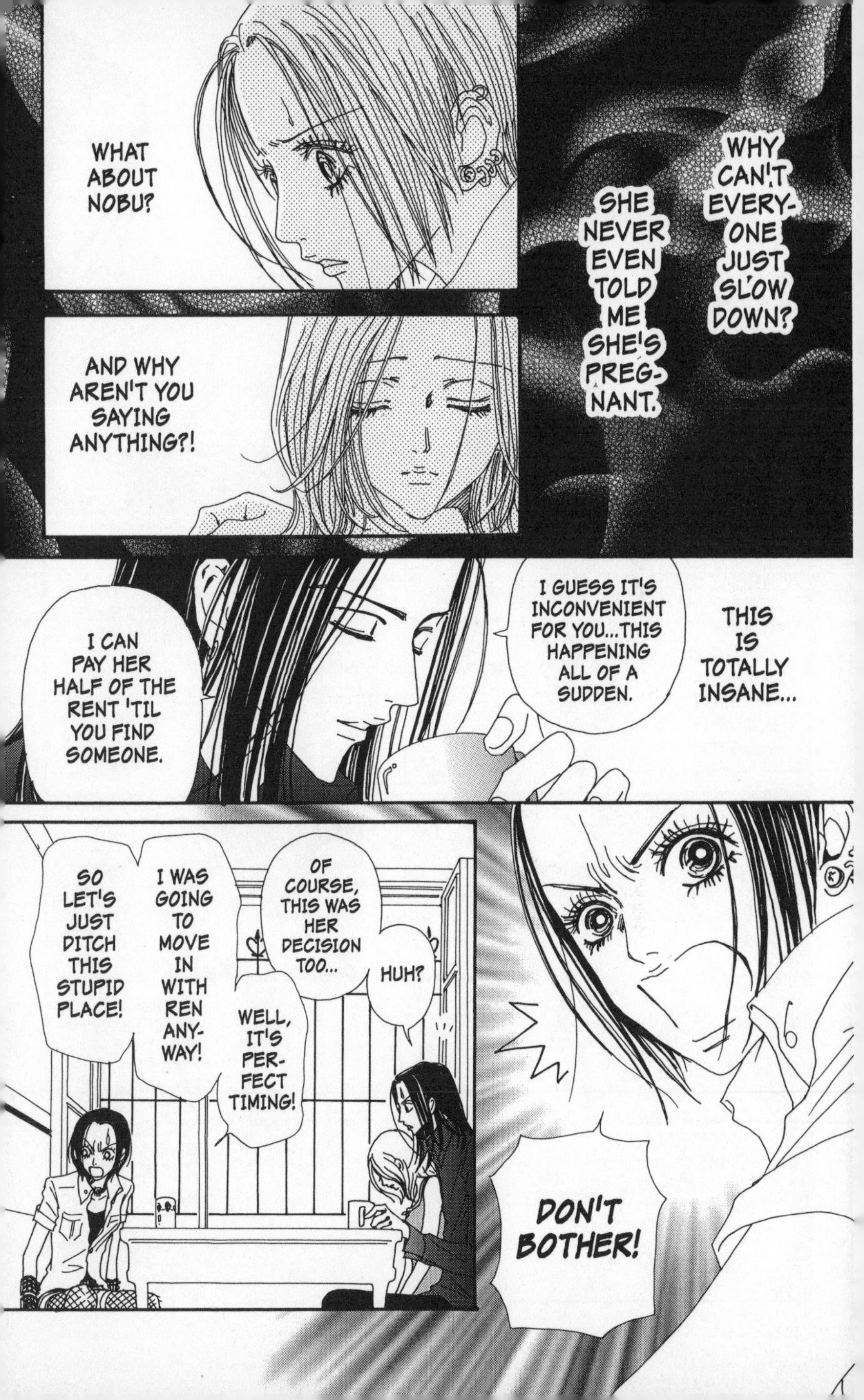
WHY CAN'T EVERYONE JUST SLOW DOWN?
SHE NEVER EVEN TOLD ME SHE'S PREGNANT.
WHAT ABOUT NOBU?
AND WHY AREN'T YOU SAYING ANYTHING?!
THIS IS TOTALLY INSANE...
I GUESS IT'S INCONVENIENT FOR YOU...THIS HAPPENING ALL OF A SUDDEN.
I CAN PAY HER HALF OF THE RENT 'TIL YOU FIND SOMEONE.
DON'T BOTHER!
OF COURSE, THIS WAS HER DECISION TOO...
HUH?
WELL, IT'S PERFECT TIMING!
I WAS GOING TO MOVE IN WITH REN ANYWAY!
SO LET'S JUST DITCH THIS STUPID PLACE!

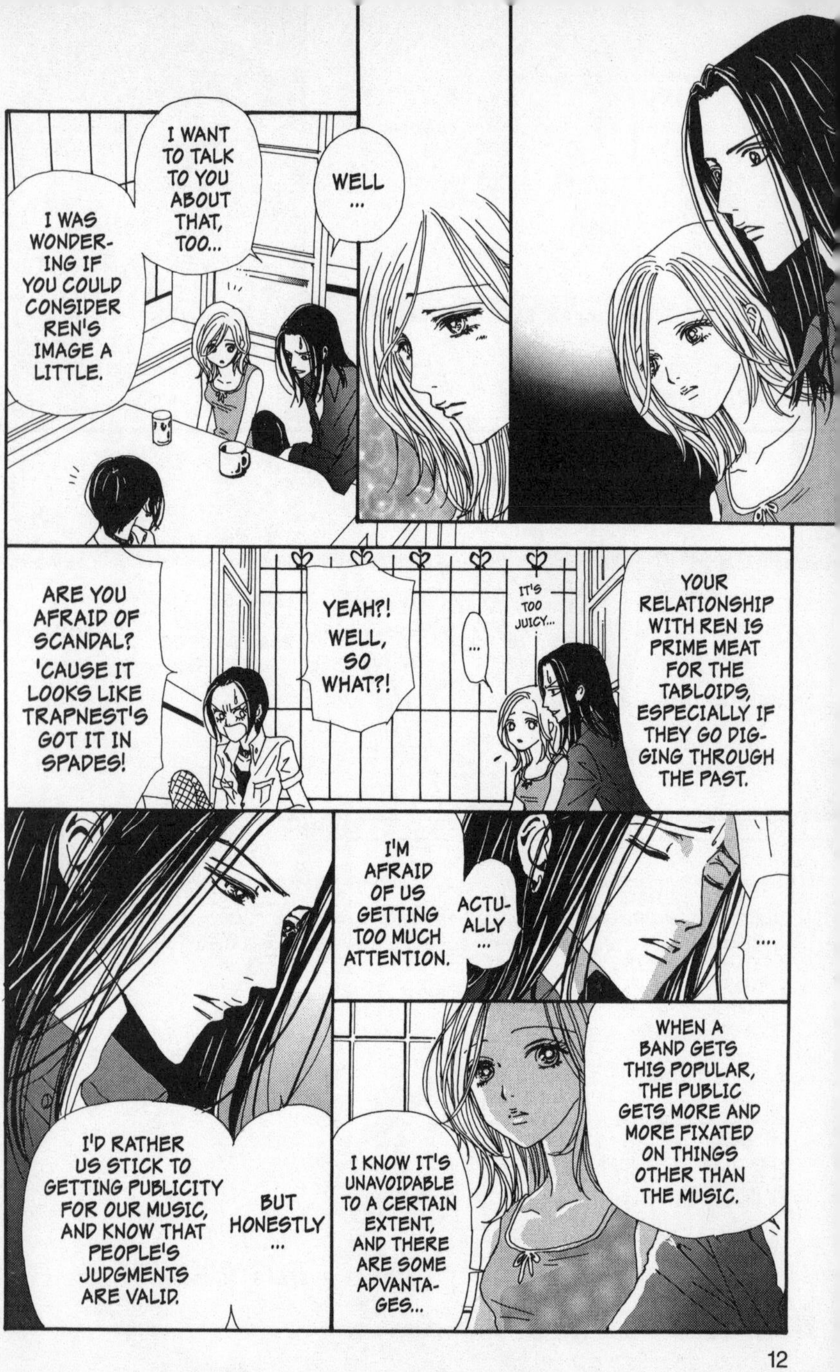
WELL ...
I WANT TO TALK TO YOU ABOUT THAT, TOO...
I WAS WONDER-ING IF YOU COULD CONSIDER REN'S IMAGE A LITTLE.
YOUR RELATIONSHIP WITH REN IS PRIME MEAT FOR THE TABLOIDS, ESPECIALLY IF THEY GO DIG-GING THROUGH THE PAST.
IT'S TOO JUICY...
...
YEAH?! WELL, SO WHAT?!
ARE YOU AFRAID OF SCANDAL? 'CAUSE IT LOOKS LIKE TRAPNEST'S GOT IT IN SPADES!
....
ACTU-ALLY ...
I'M AFRAID OF US GETTING TOO MUCH ATTENTION.
WHEN A BAND GETS THIS POPULAR, THE PUBLIC GETS MORE AND MORE FIXATED ON THINGS OTHER THAN THE MUSIC.
I KNOW IT'S UNAVOIDABLE TO A CERTAIN EXTENT, AND THERE ARE SOME ADVANTA-GES...
BUT HONESTLY ...
I'D RATHER US STICK TO GETTING PUBLICITY FOR OUR MUSIC, AND KNOW THAT PEOPLE'S JUDGMENTS ARE VALID.

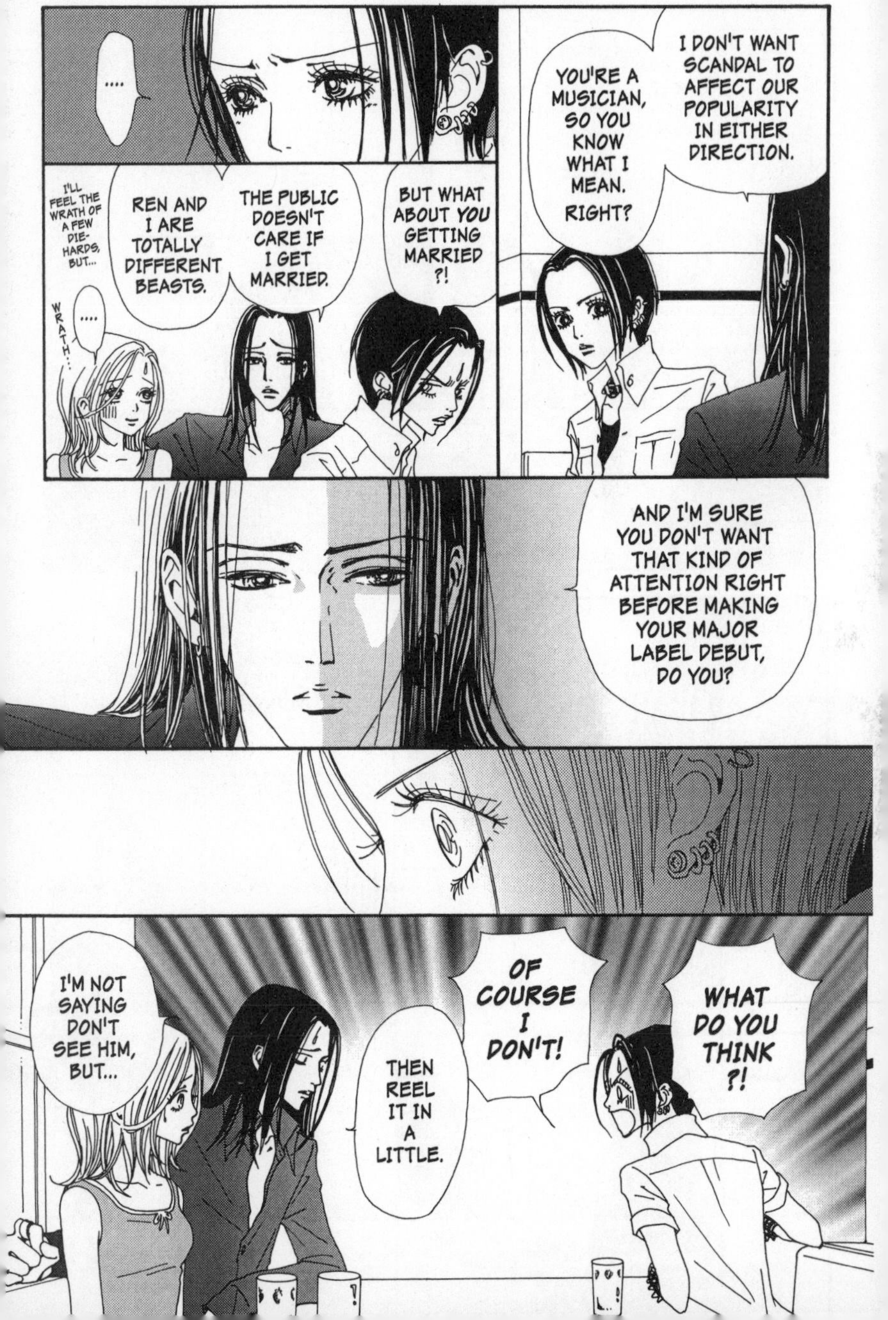

I DON'T WANT SCANDAL TO AFFECT OUR POPULARITY IN EITHER DIRECTION.
YOU'RE A MUSICIAN, SO YOU KNOW WHAT I MEAN. RIGHT?
....
BUT WHAT ABOUT YOU GETTING MARRIED?!
THE PUBLIC DOESN'T CARE IF I GET MARRIED.
REN AND I ARE TOTALLY DIFFERENT BEASTS.
I'LL FEEL THE WRATH OF A FEW DIE-HARDS, BUT...
....
WRATH...
AND I'M SURE YOU DON'T WANT THAT KIND OF ATTENTION RIGHT BEFORE MAKING YOUR MAJOR LABEL DEBUT, DO YOU?
WHAT DO YOU THINK?!
OF COURSE I DON'T!
THEN REEL IT IN A LITTLE.
I'M NOT SAYING DON'T SEE HIM, BUT...

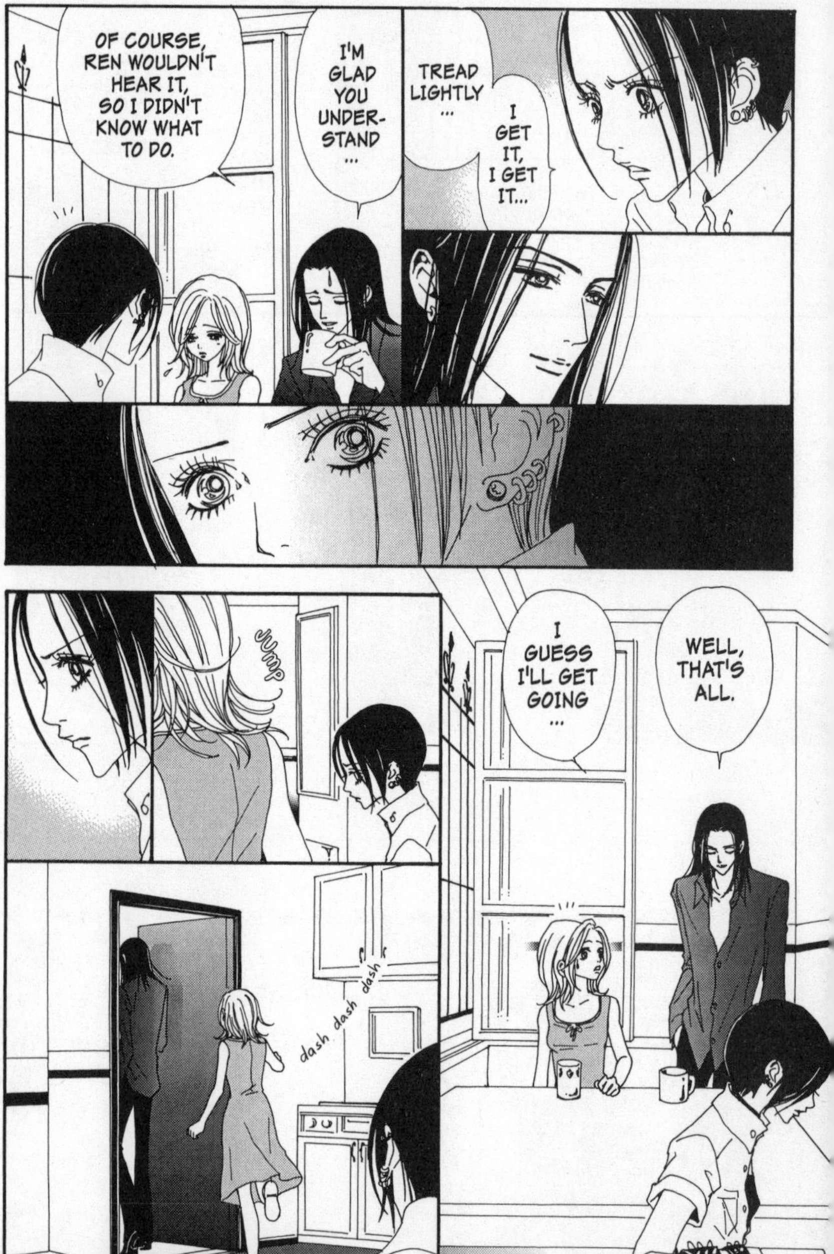
TREAD LIGHTLY ...
I GET IT, I GET IT...
I'M GLAD YOU UNDER-STAND ...
OF COURSE, REN WOULDN'T HEAR IT, SO I DIDN'T KNOW WHAT TO DO.
WELL, THAT'S ALL.
I GUESS I'LL GET GOING ...
JUMP
dash dash dash

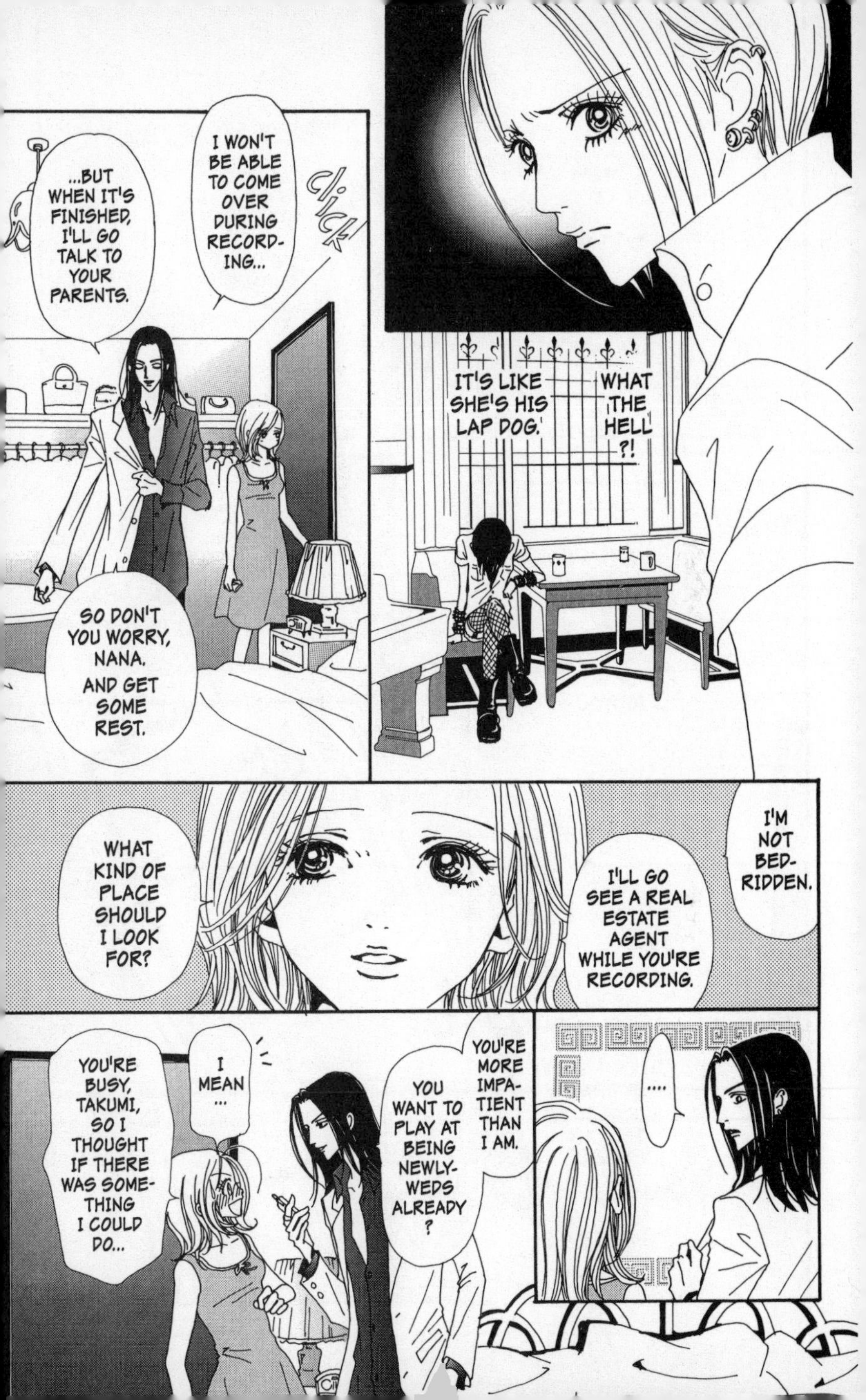
WHAT THE HELL?!
IT'S LIKE SHE'S HIS LAP DOG.
I WON'T BE ABLE TO COME OVER DURING RECORDING...
CLICK
...BUT WHEN IT'S FINISHED, I'LL GO TALK TO YOUR PARENTS.
SO DON'T YOU WORRY, NANA. AND GET SOME REST.
I'M NOT BEDRIDDEN.
I'LL GO SEE A REAL ESTATE AGENT WHILE YOU'RE RECORDING.
WHAT KIND OF PLACE SHOULD I LOOK FOR?
....
YOU'RE MORE IMPATIENT THAN I AM.
YOU WANT TO PLAY AT BEING NEWLYWEDS ALREADY?
I MEAN...
YOU'RE BUSY, TAKUMI, SO I THOUGHT IF THERE WAS SOMETHING I COULD DO...

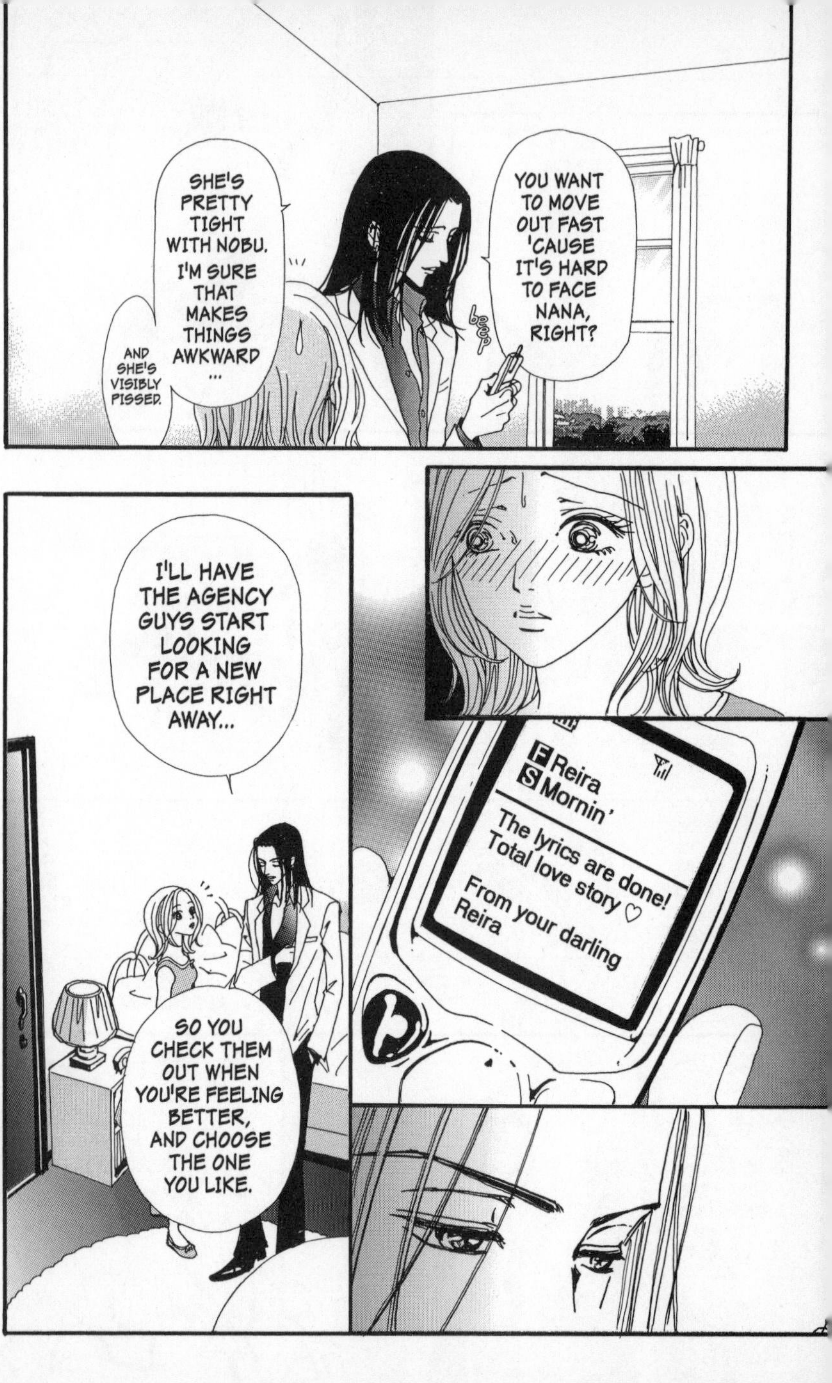
YOU WANT TO MOVE OUT FAST 'CAUSE IT'S HARD TO FACE NANA, RIGHT?
beep
SHE'S PRETTY TIGHT WITH NOBU. I'M SURE THAT MAKES THINGS AWKWARD ...
AND SHE'S VISIBLY PISSED.
F Reira
S Mornin'
The lyrics are done! Total love story ♡
From your darling Reira
I'LL HAVE THE AGENCY GUYS START LOOKING FOR A NEW PLACE RIGHT AWAY...
SO YOU CHECK THEM OUT WHEN YOU'RE FEELING BETTER, AND CHOOSE THE ONE YOU LIKE.

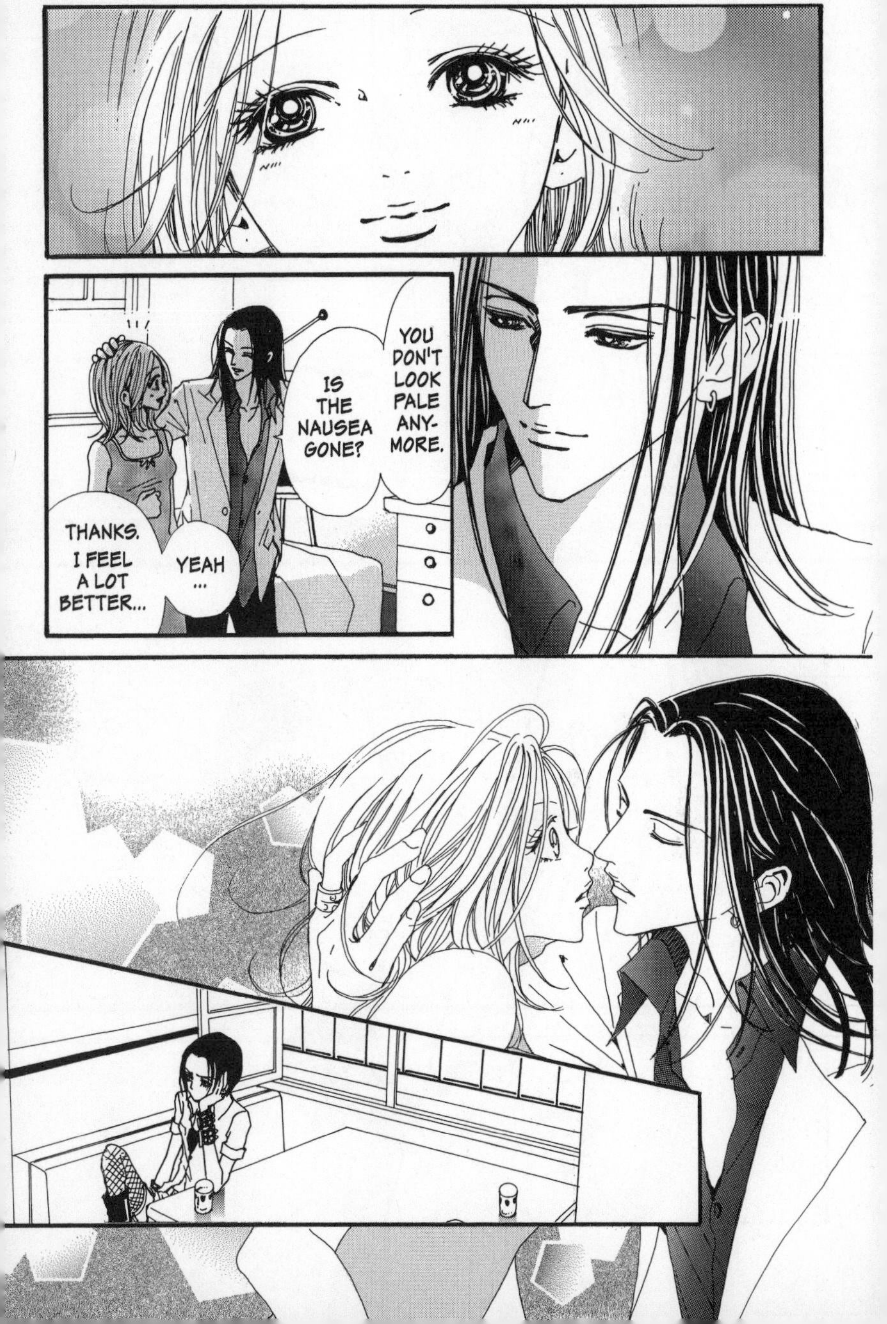
YOU DON'T LOOK PALE ANYMORE.
IS THE NAUSEA GONE?
YEAH...
THANKS. I FEEL A LOT BETTER...

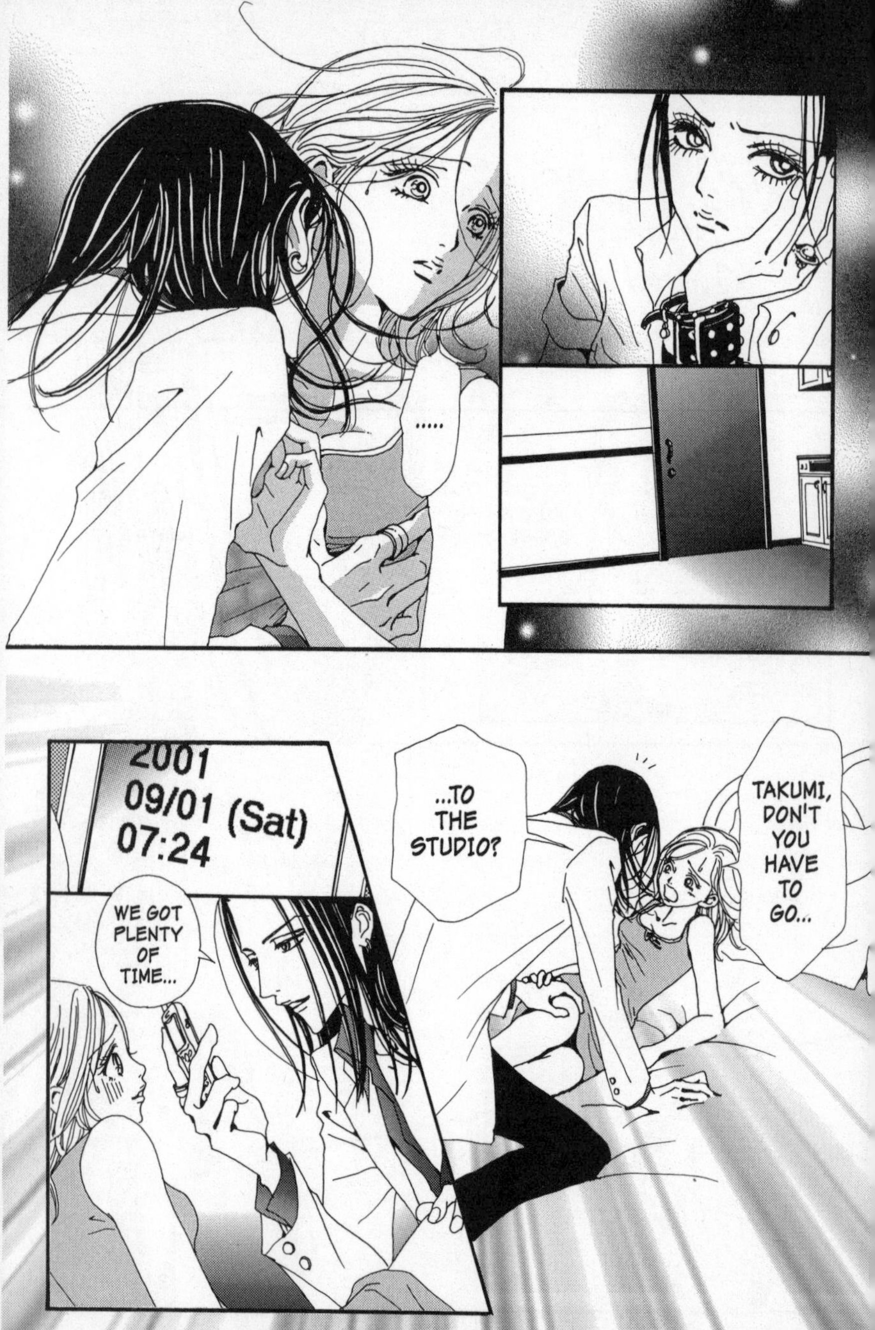
.....
TAKUMI, DON'T YOU HAVE TO GO...
...TO THE STUDIO?
2001 09/01 (Sat) 07:24
WE GOT PLENTY OF TIME...

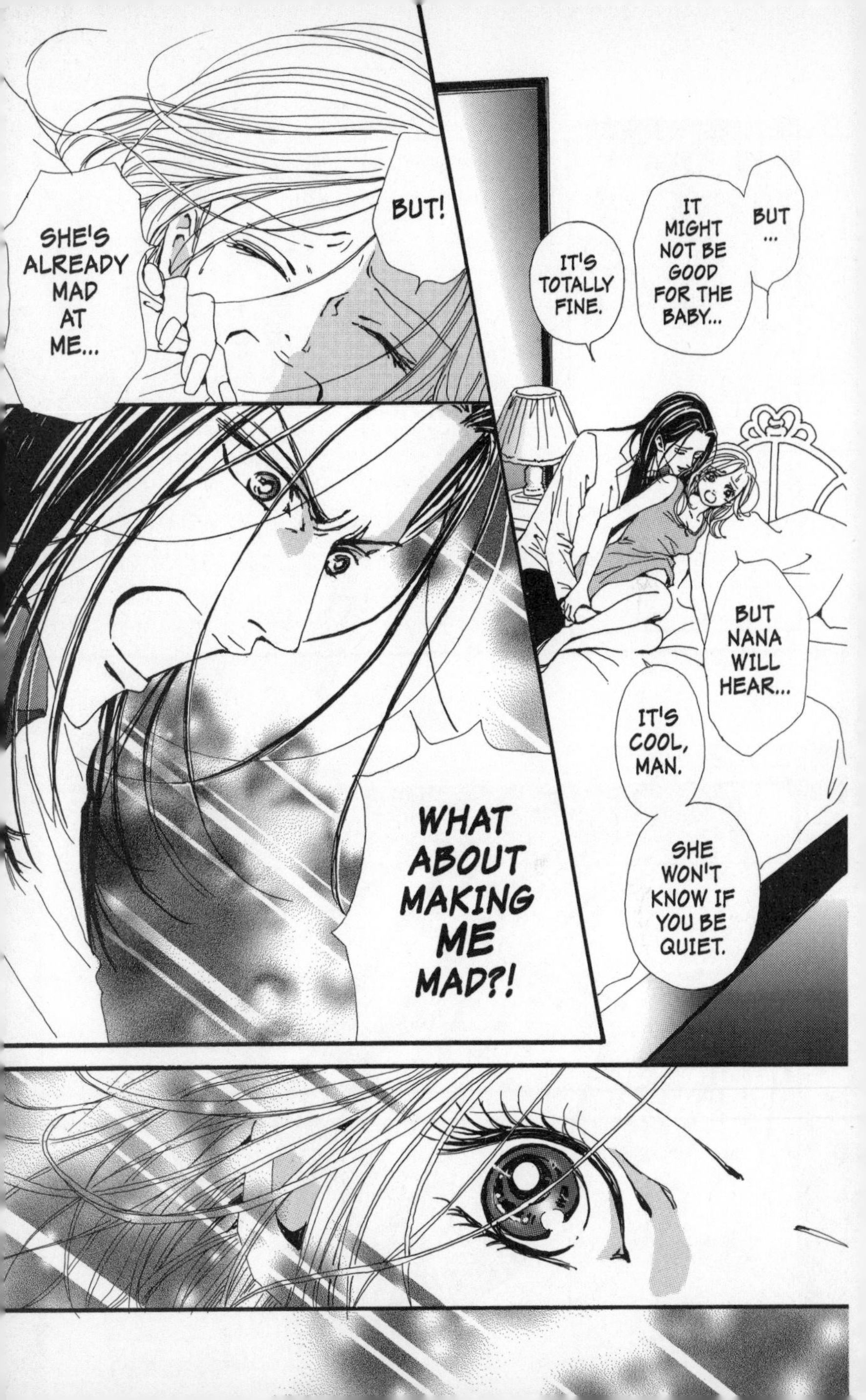
BUT...
IT MIGHT NOT BE GOOD FOR THE BABY...
IT'S TOTALLY FINE.
BUT NANA WILL HEAR...
IT'S COOL, MAN.
SHE WON'T KNOW IF YOU BE QUIET.
BUT!
SHE'S ALREADY MAD AT ME...
WHAT ABOUT MAKING ME MAD?!

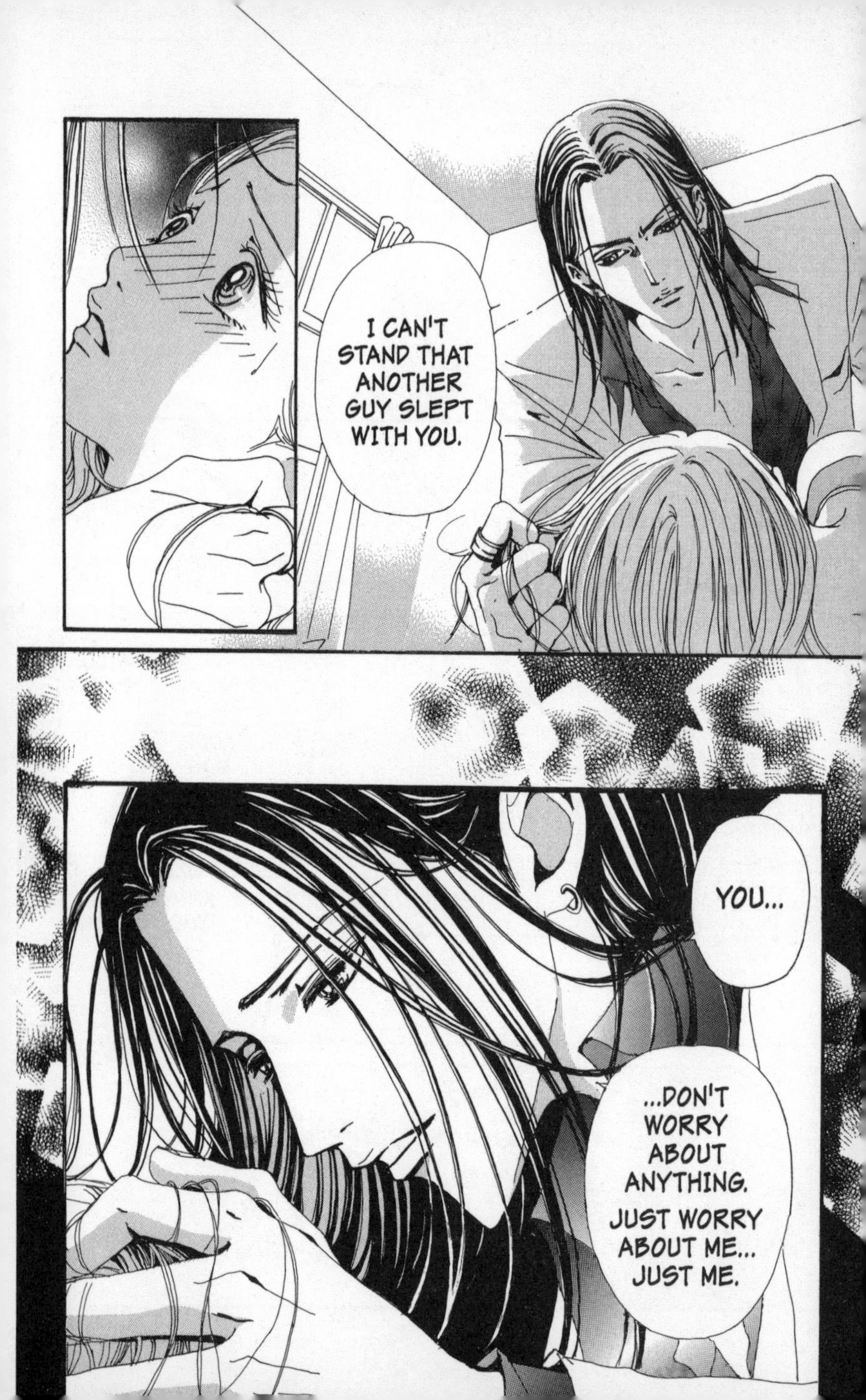
I CAN'T STAND THAT ANOTHER GUY SLEPT WITH YOU.
YOU...
...DON'T WORRY ABOUT ANYTHING.
JUST WORRY ABOUT ME... JUST ME.

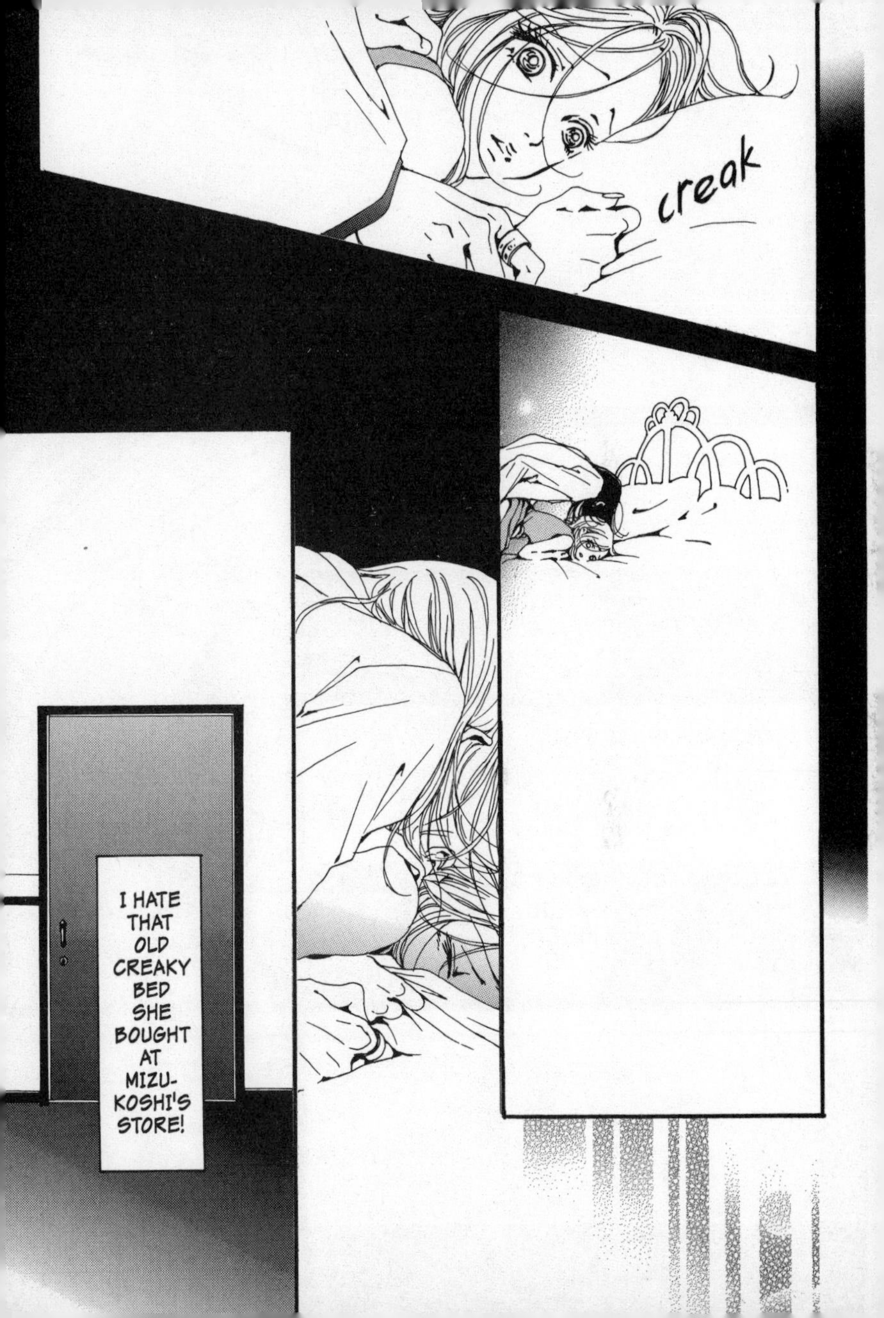
creak
I HATE THAT OLD CREAKY BED SHE BOUGHT AT MIZU-KOSHI'S STORE!

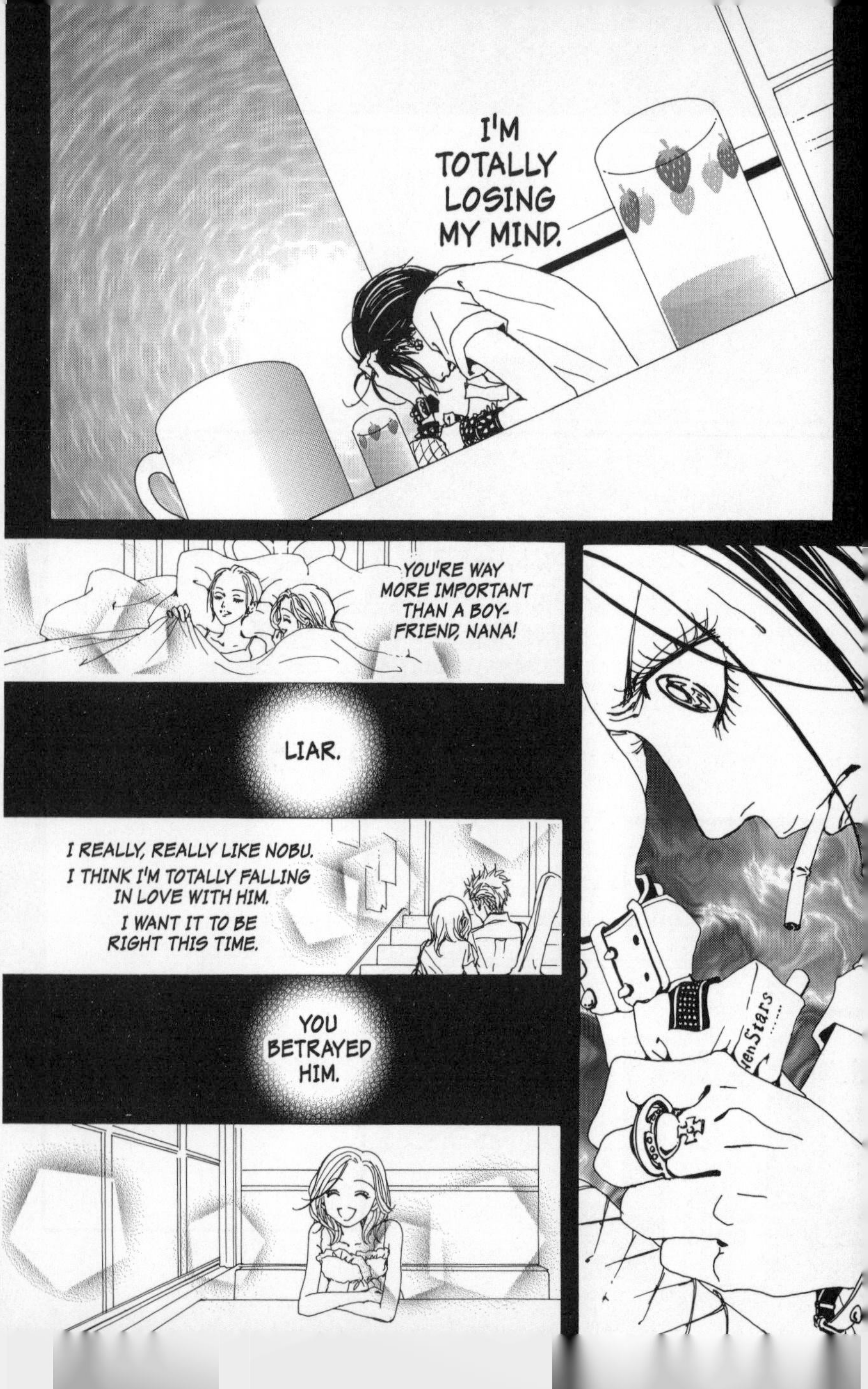
I'M TOTALLY LOSING MY MIND.
YOU'RE WAY MORE IMPORTANT THAN A BOY-FRIEND, NANA!
LIAR.
I REALLY, REALLY LIKE NOBU.
I THINK I'M TOTALLY FALLING IN LOVE WITH HIM.
I WANT IT TO BE RIGHT THIS TIME.
YOU BETRAYED HIM.

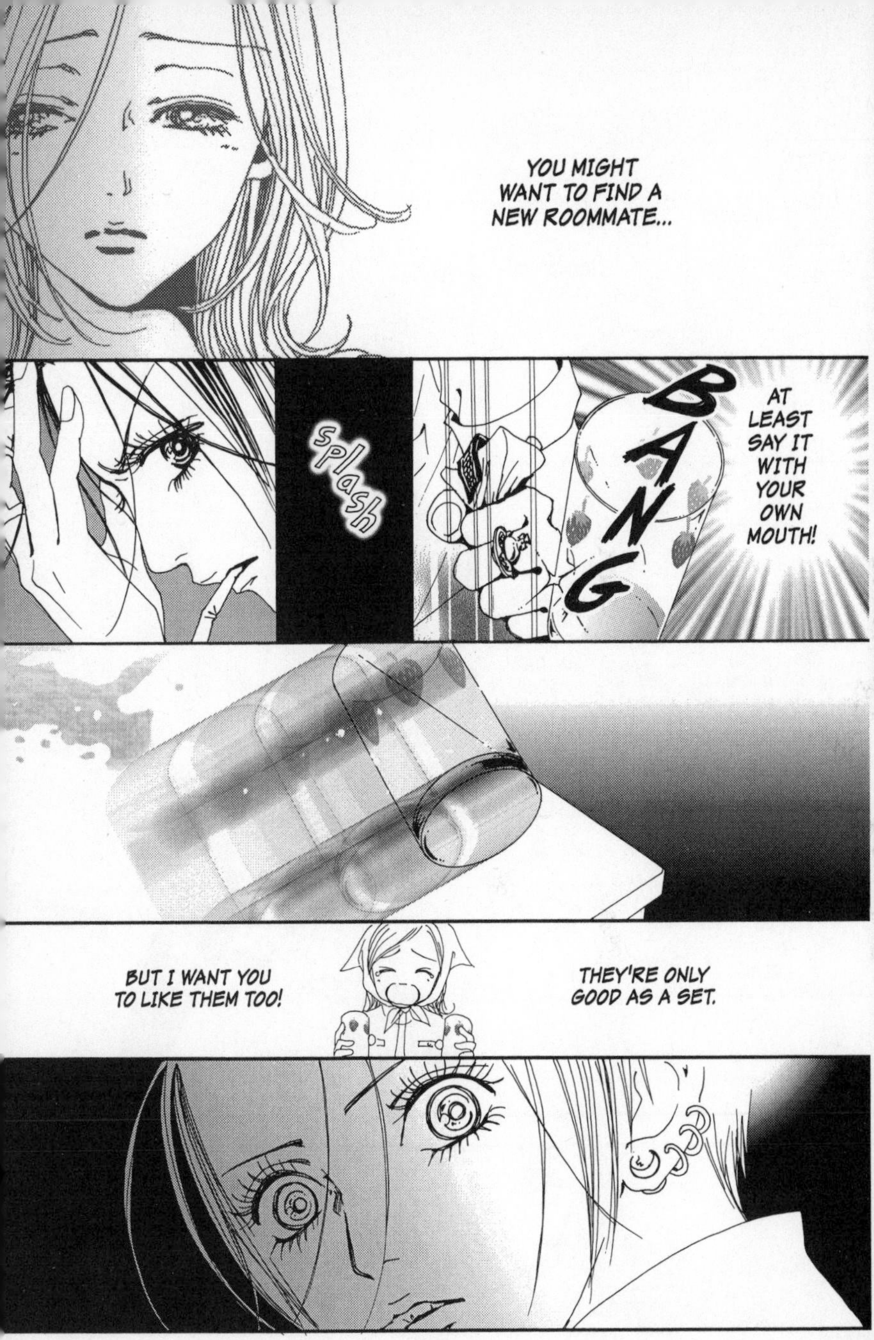
YOU MIGHT WANT TO FIND A NEW ROOMMATE...
BANG
AT LEAST SAY IT WITH YOUR OWN MOUTH!
splash
THEY'RE ONLY GOOD AS A SET.
BUT I WANT YOU TO LIKE THEM TOO!

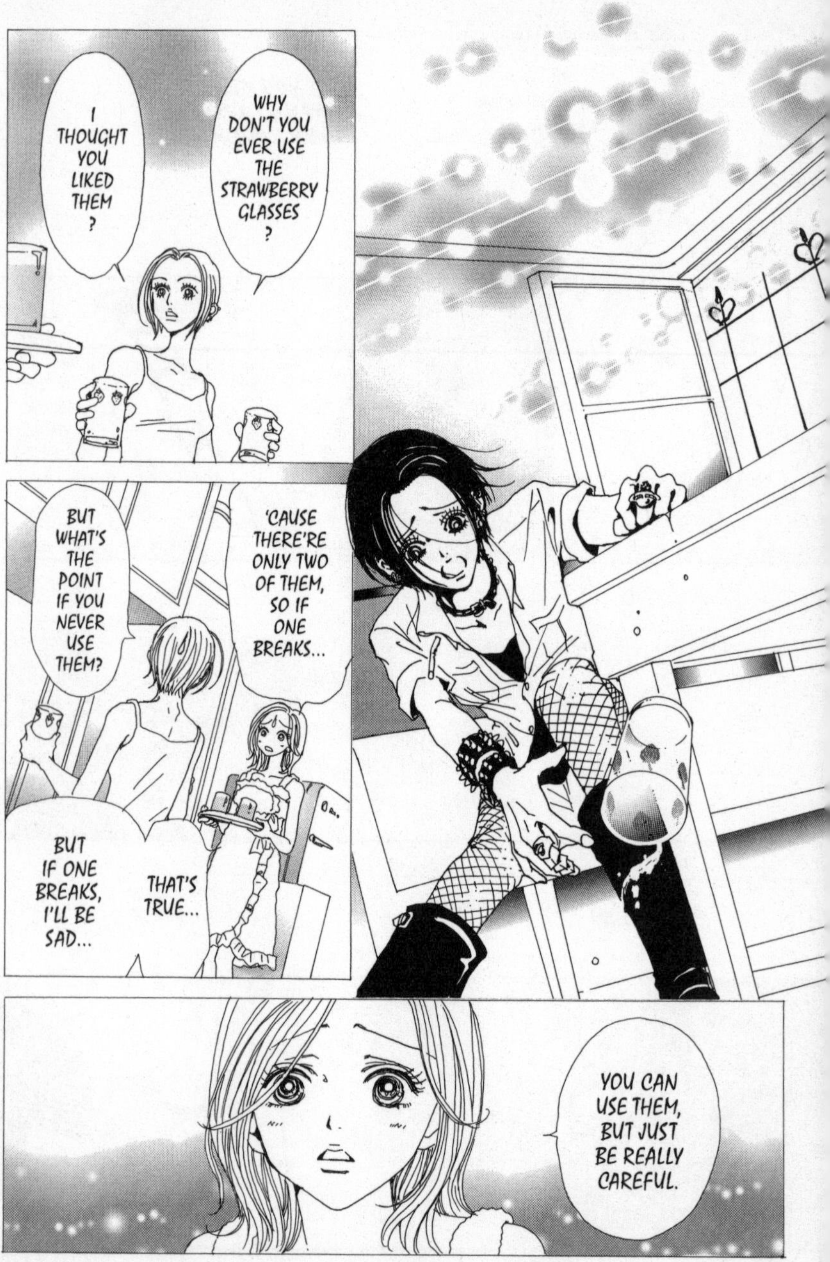
WHY DON'T YOU EVER USE THE STRAWBERRY GLASSES?
I THOUGHT YOU LIKED THEM?
'CAUSE THERE'RE ONLY TWO OF THEM, SO IF ONE BREAKS...
BUT WHAT'S THE POINT IF YOU NEVER USE THEM?
THAT'S TRUE...
BUT IF ONE BREAKS, I'LL BE SAD...
YOU CAN USE THEM, BUT JUST BE REALLY CAREFUL.

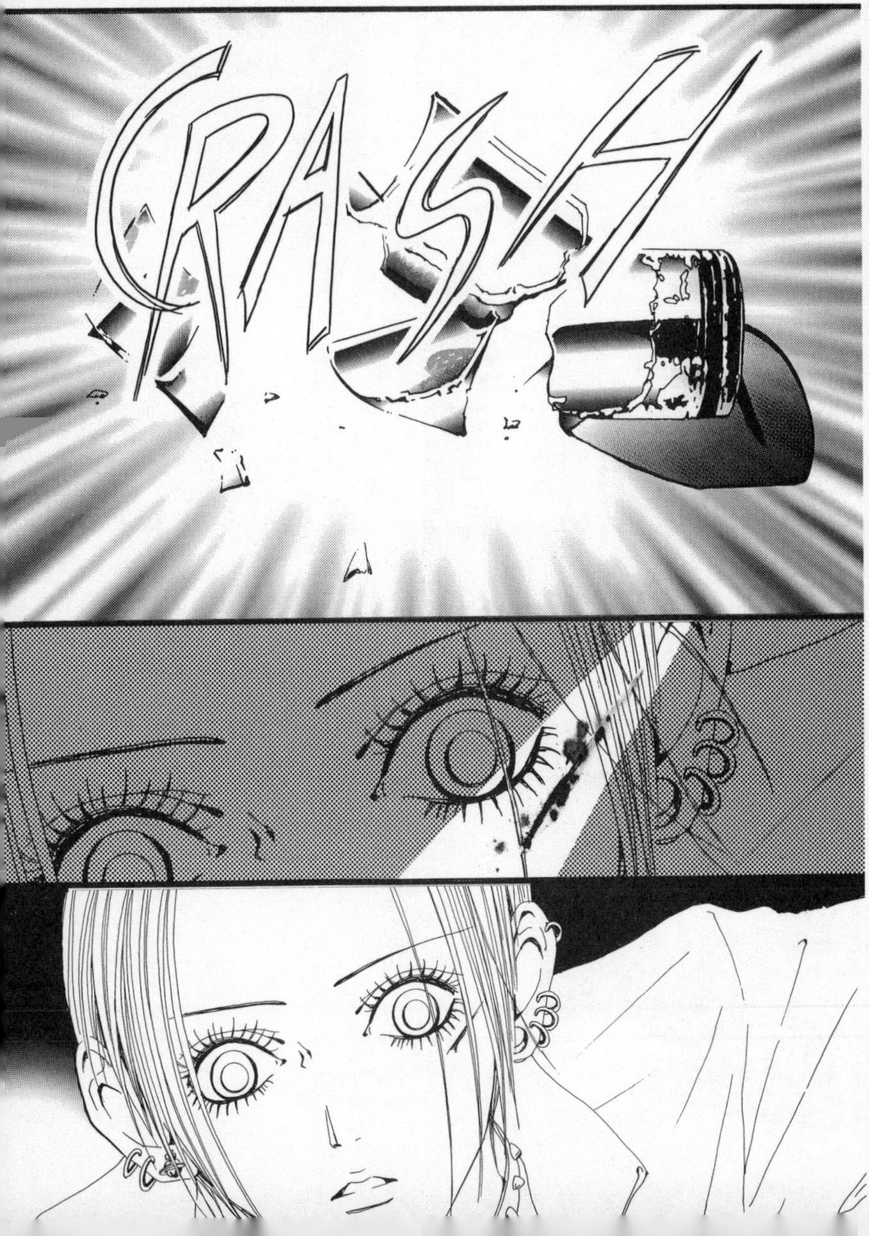
CRASH

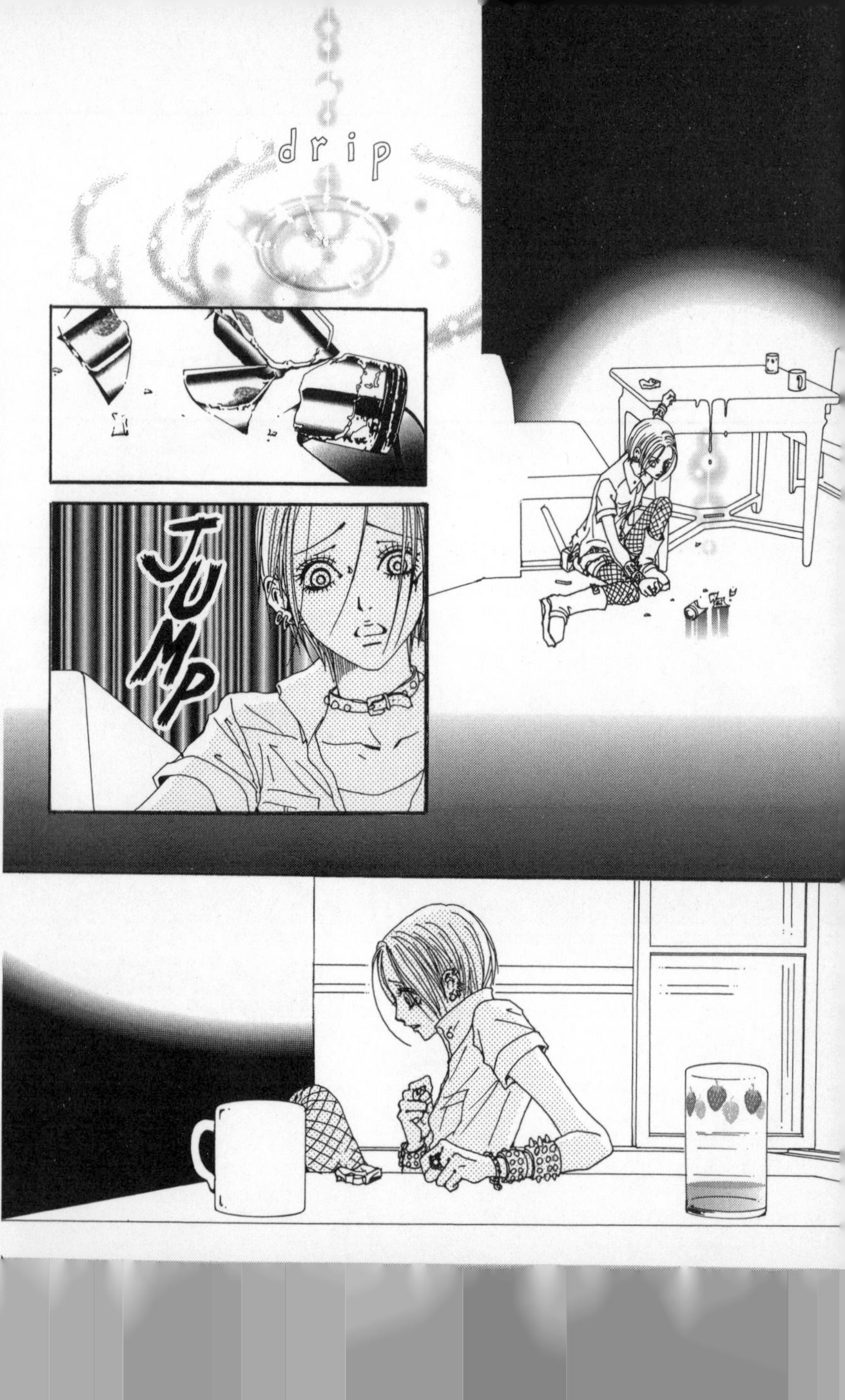
drip
JUMP

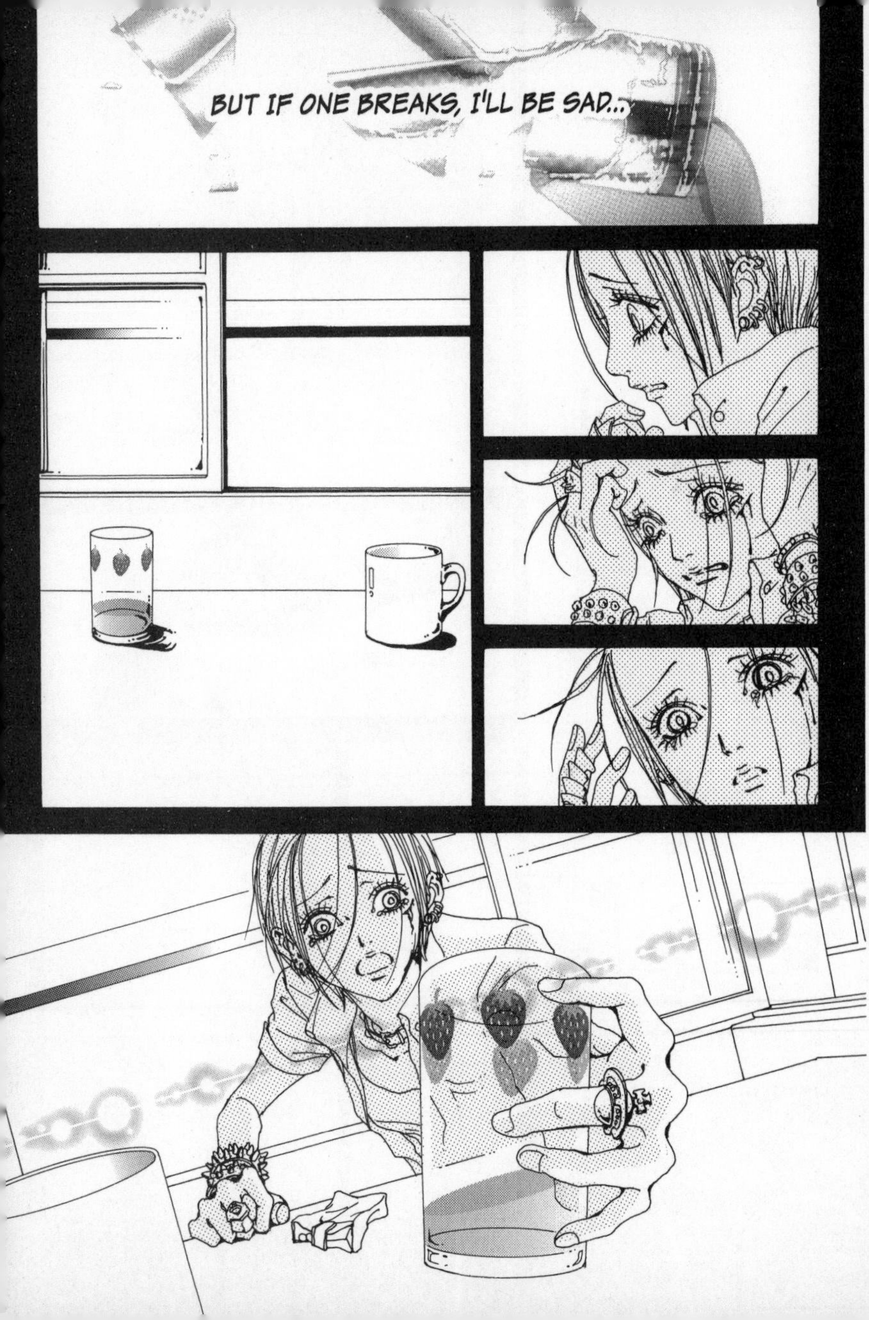
BUT IF ONE BREAKS, I'LL BE SAD...

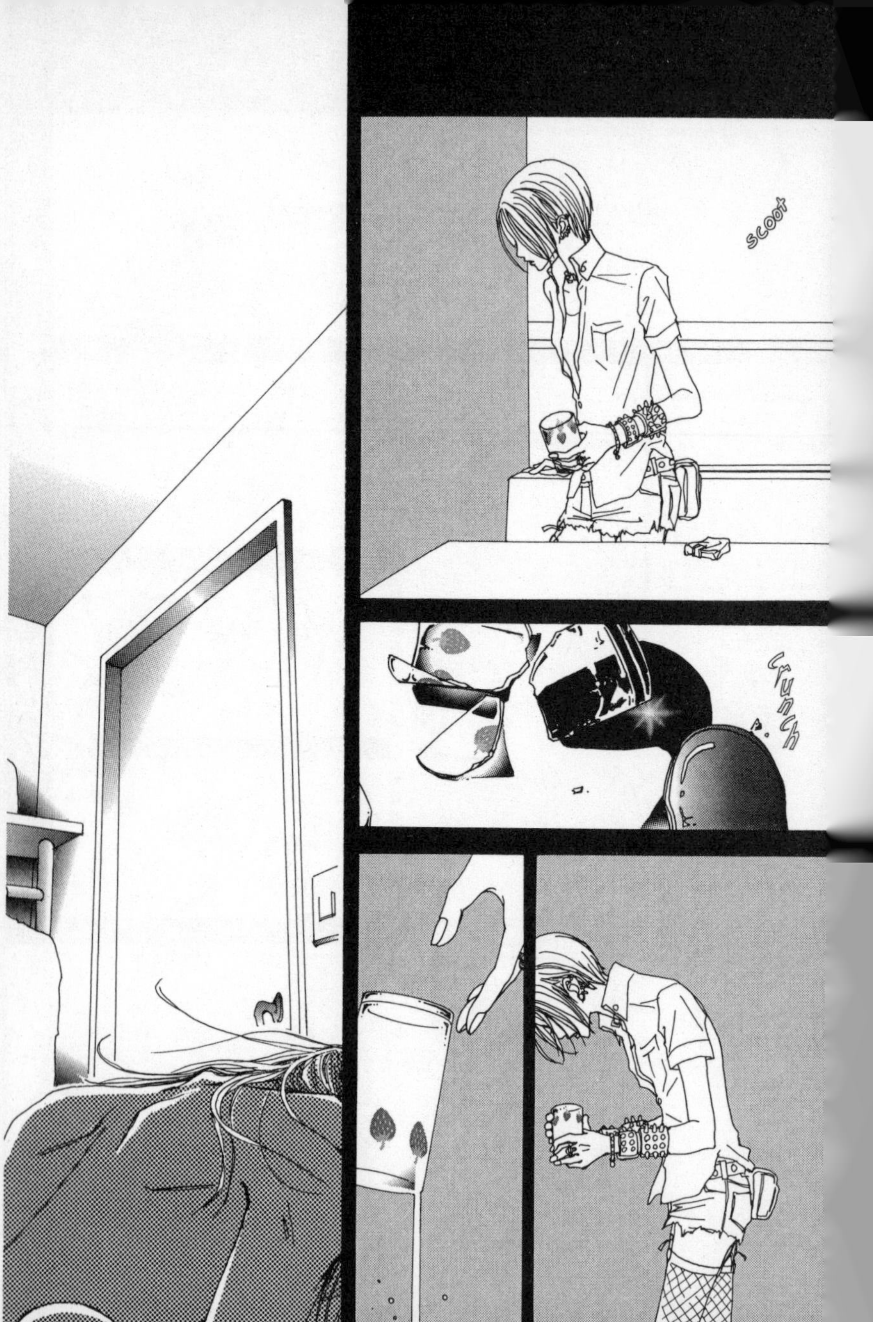
scoot
crunch

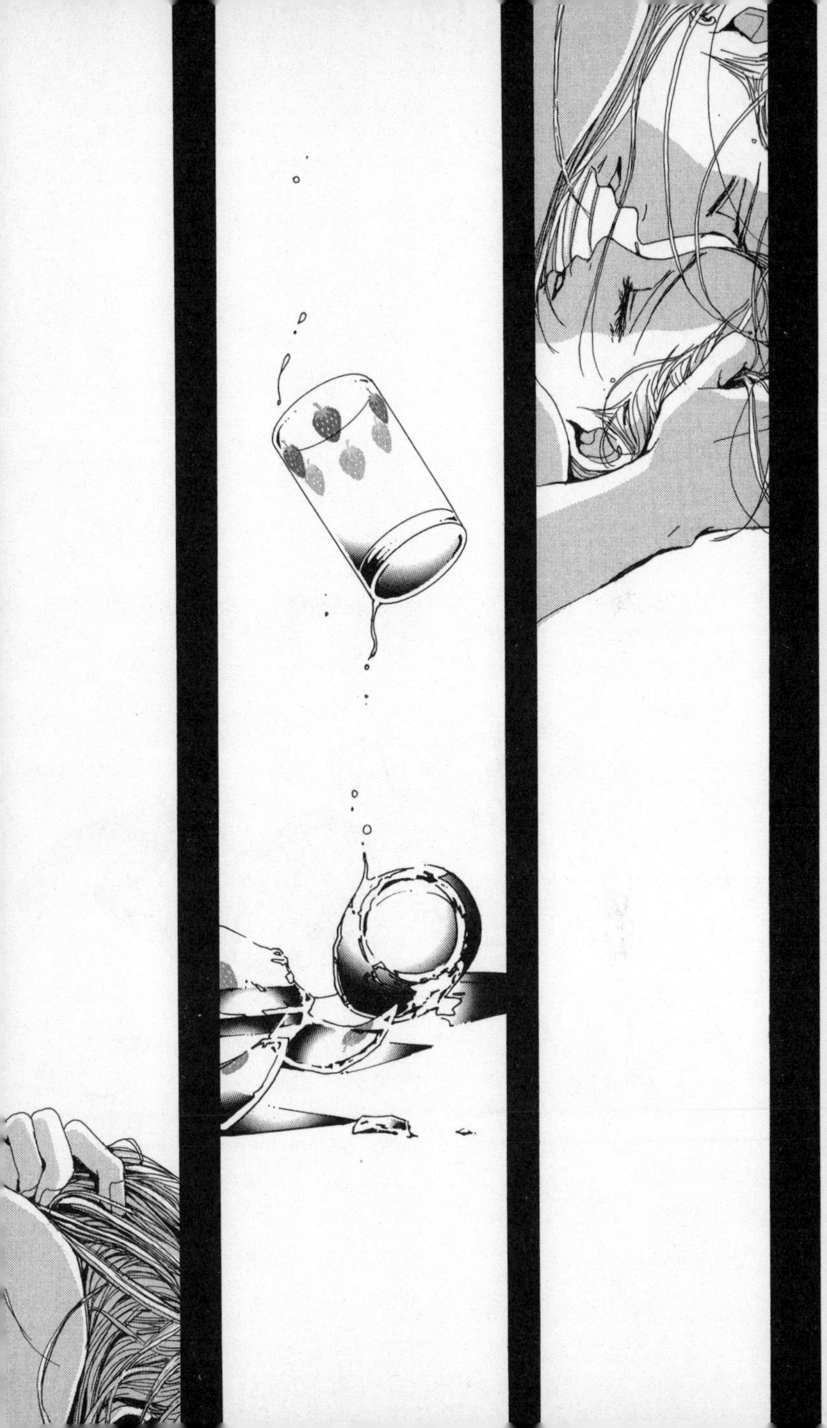

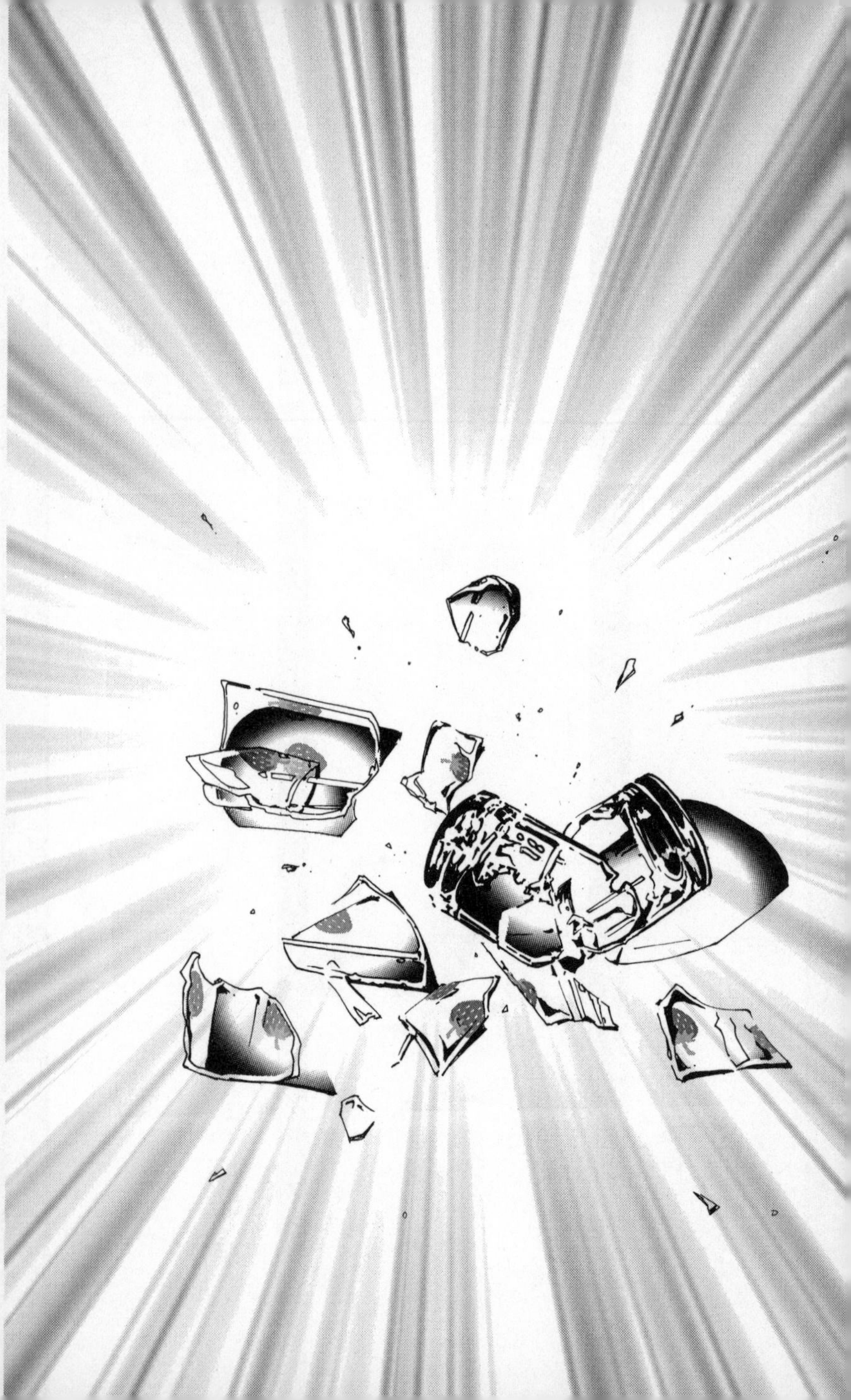

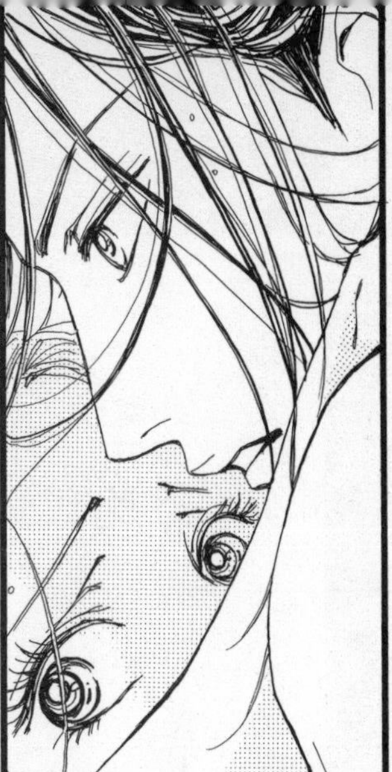

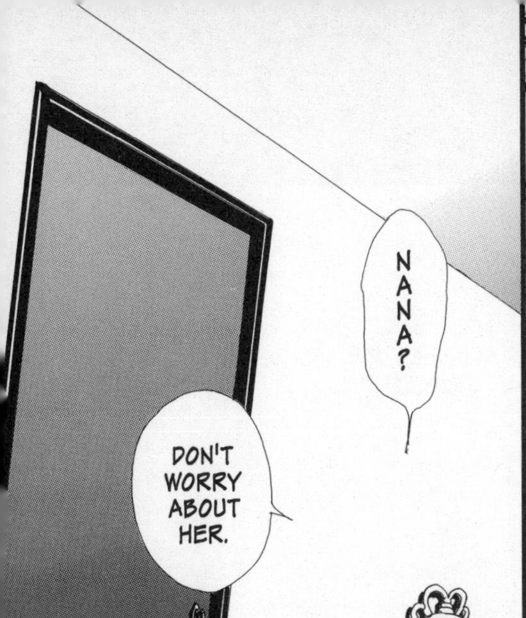
NANA?
DON'T WORRY ABOUT HER.

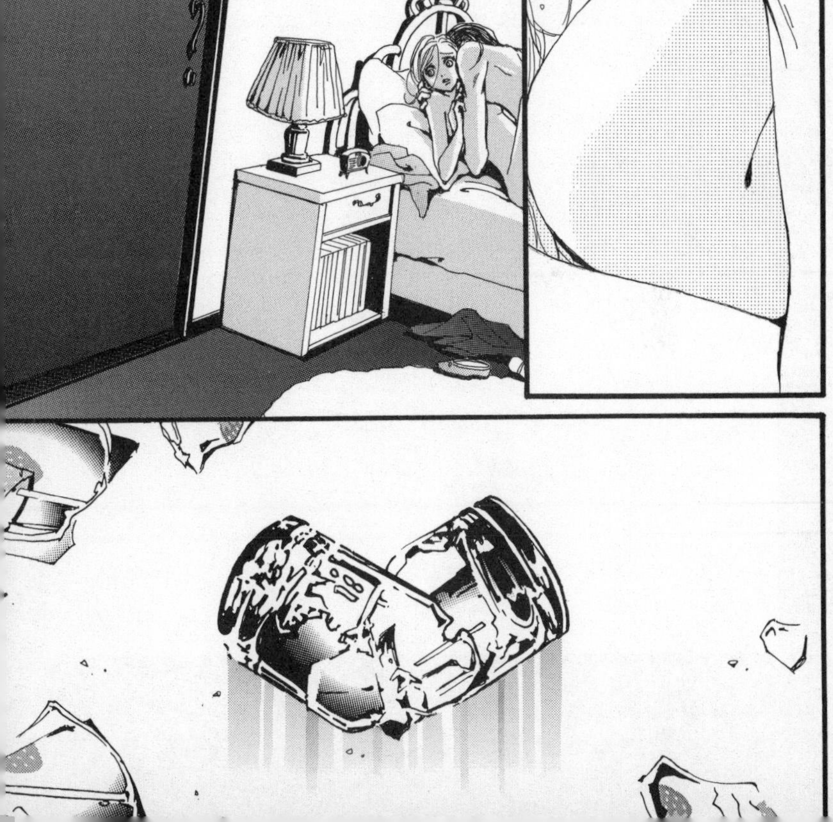

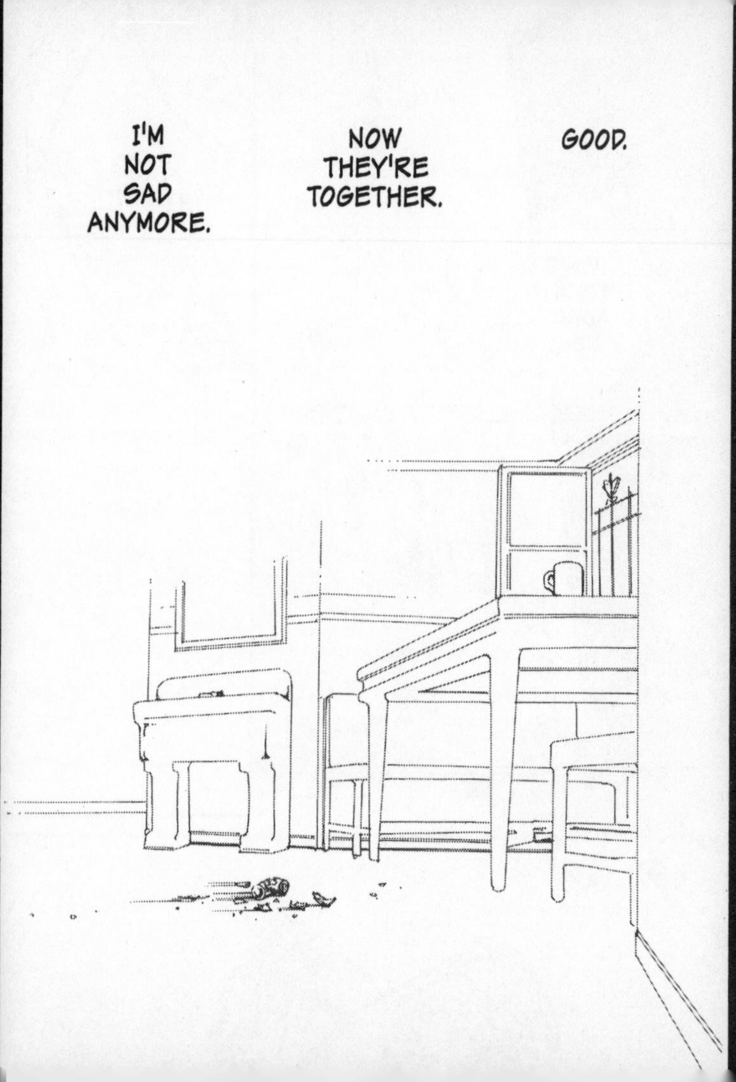
GOOD.
NOW THEY'RE TOGETHER.
I'M NOT SAD ANYMORE.

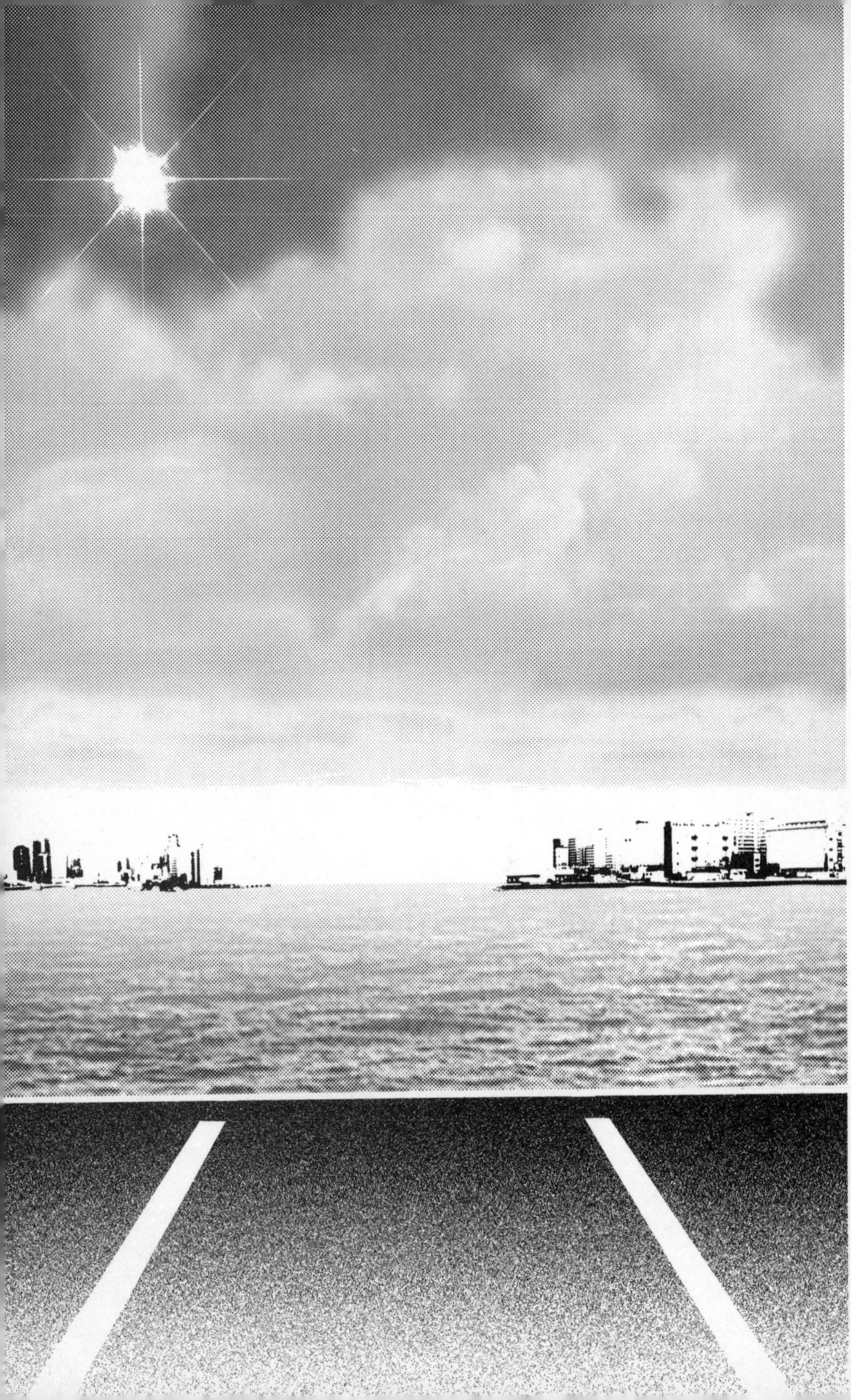

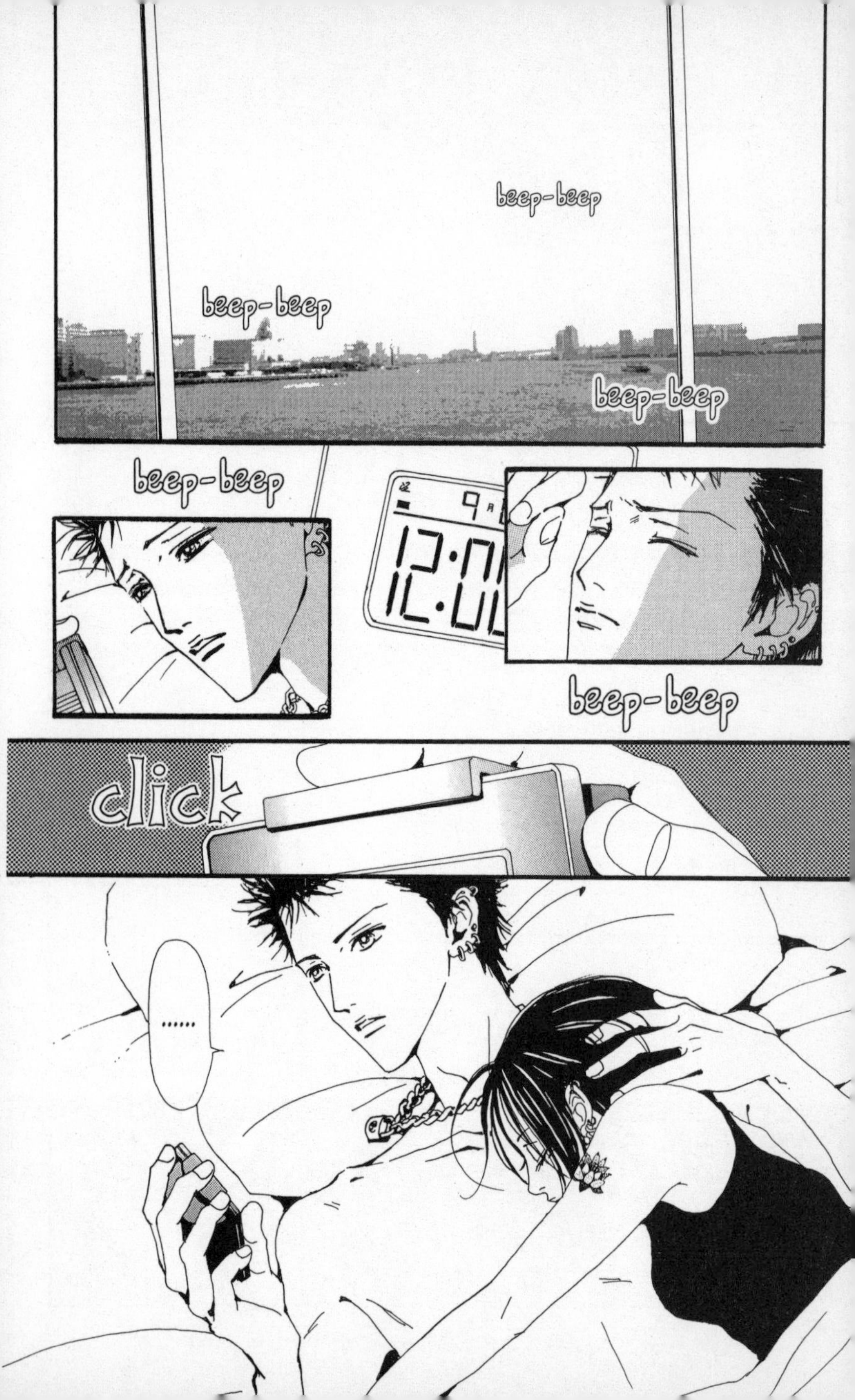
beep-beep
beep-beep
beep-beep
beep-beep
beep-beep
click
......

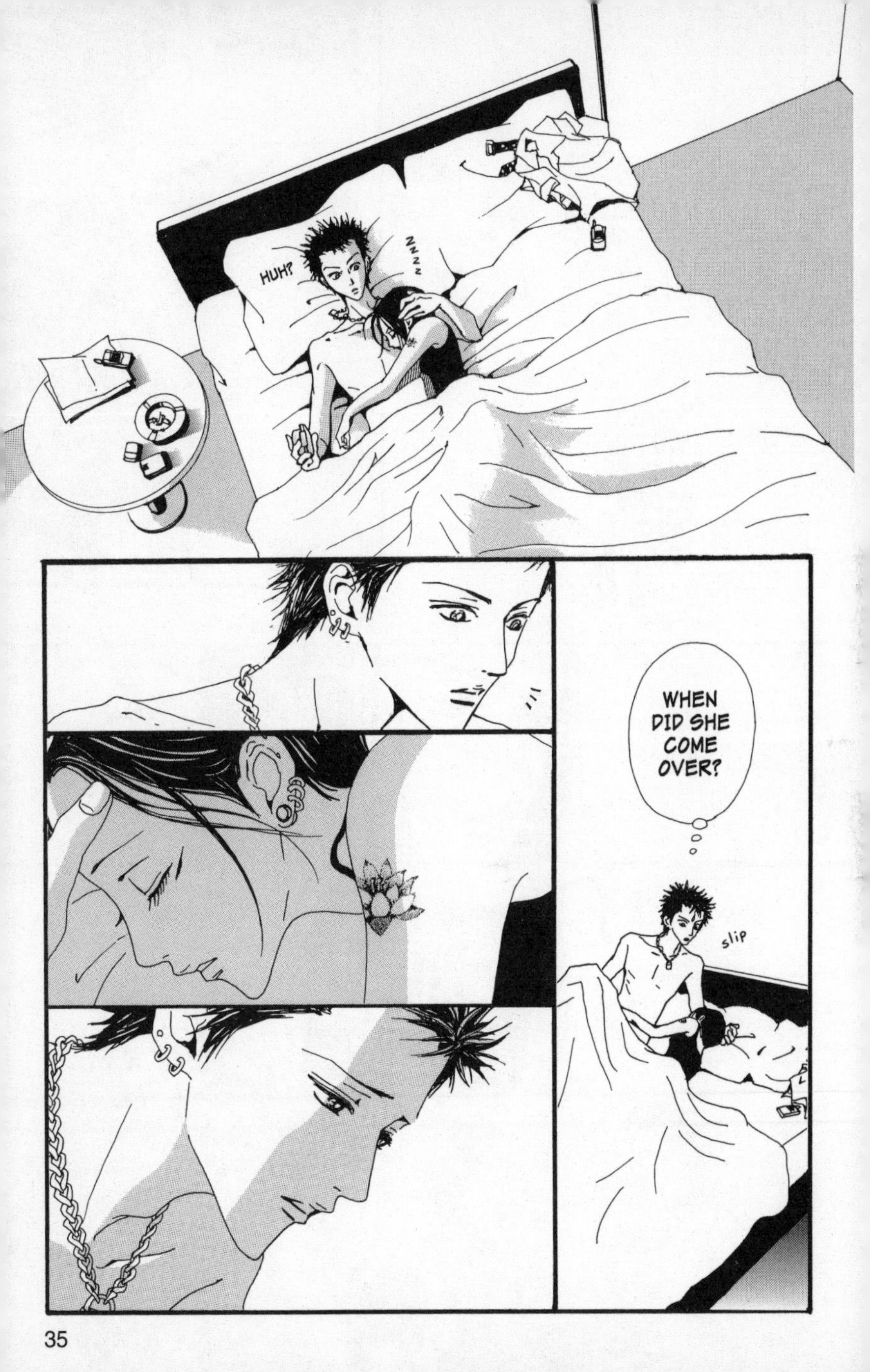
HUH?
ZZZZ
WHEN DID SHE COME OVER?
slip

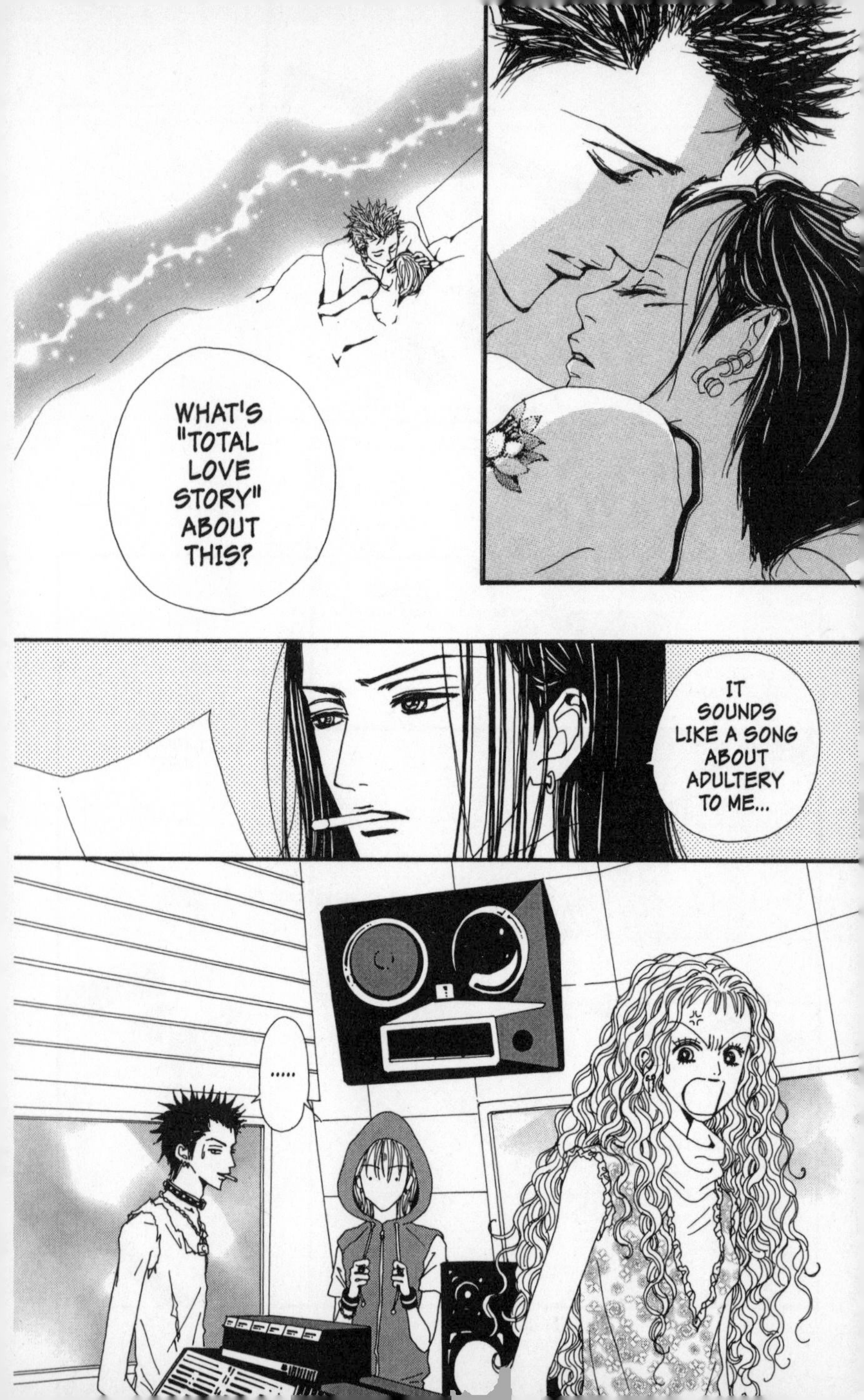
WHAT'S "TOTAL LOVE STORY" ABOUT THIS?
IT SOUNDS LIKE A SONG ABOUT ADULTERY TO ME...
.....

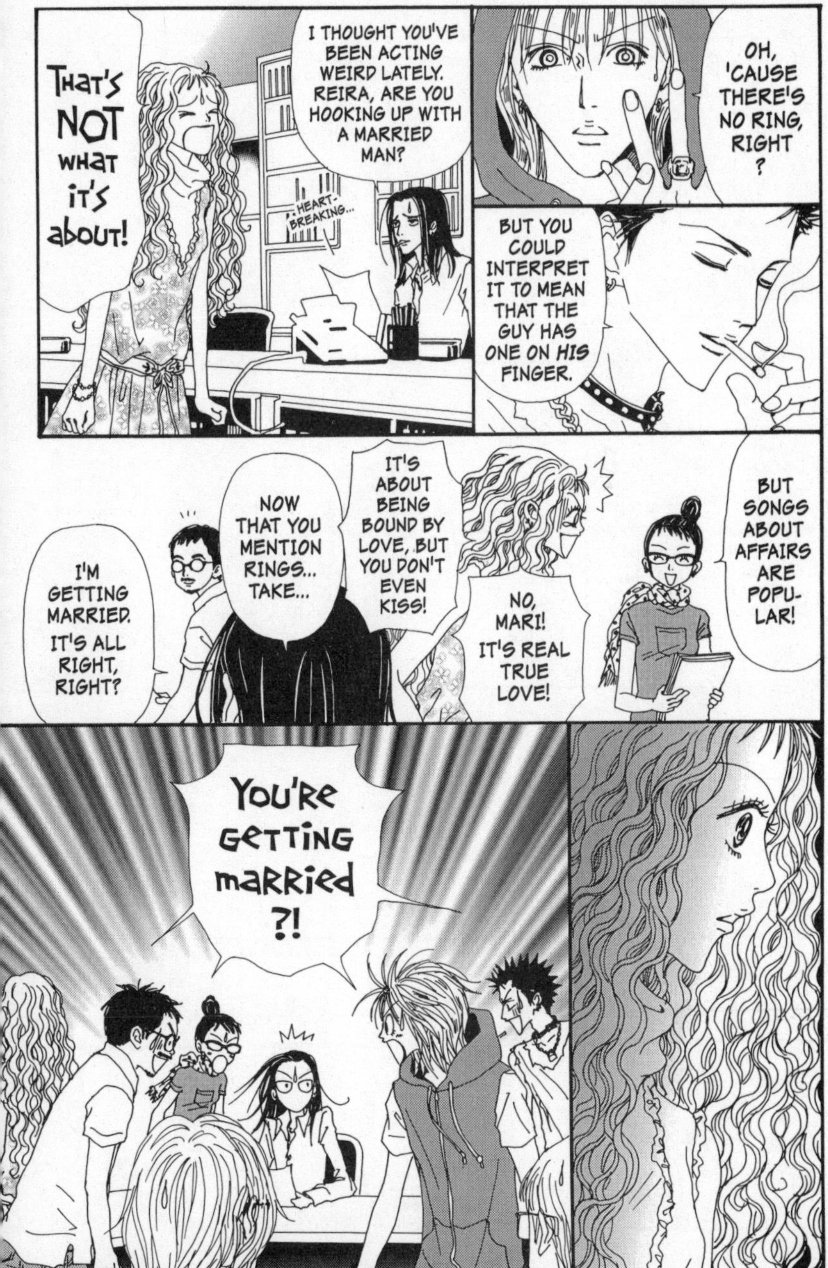
OH, 'CAUSE THERE'S NO RING, RIGHT?
BUT YOU COULD INTERPRET IT TO MEAN THAT THE GUY HAS ONE ON HIS FINGER.
I THOUGHT YOU'VE BEEN ACTING WEIRD LATELY. REIRA, ARE YOU HOOKING UP WITH A MARRIED MAN?
HEART-BREAKING...
THAT'S NOT what it's about!
BUT SONGS ABOUT AFFAIRS ARE POPULAR!
NO, MARI! IT'S REAL TRUE LOVE!
IT'S ABOUT BEING BOUND BY LOVE, BUT YOU DON'T EVEN KISS!
NOW THAT YOU MENTION RINGS... TAKE...
I'M GETTING MARRIED. IT'S ALL RIGHT, RIGHT?
You're getting married?!

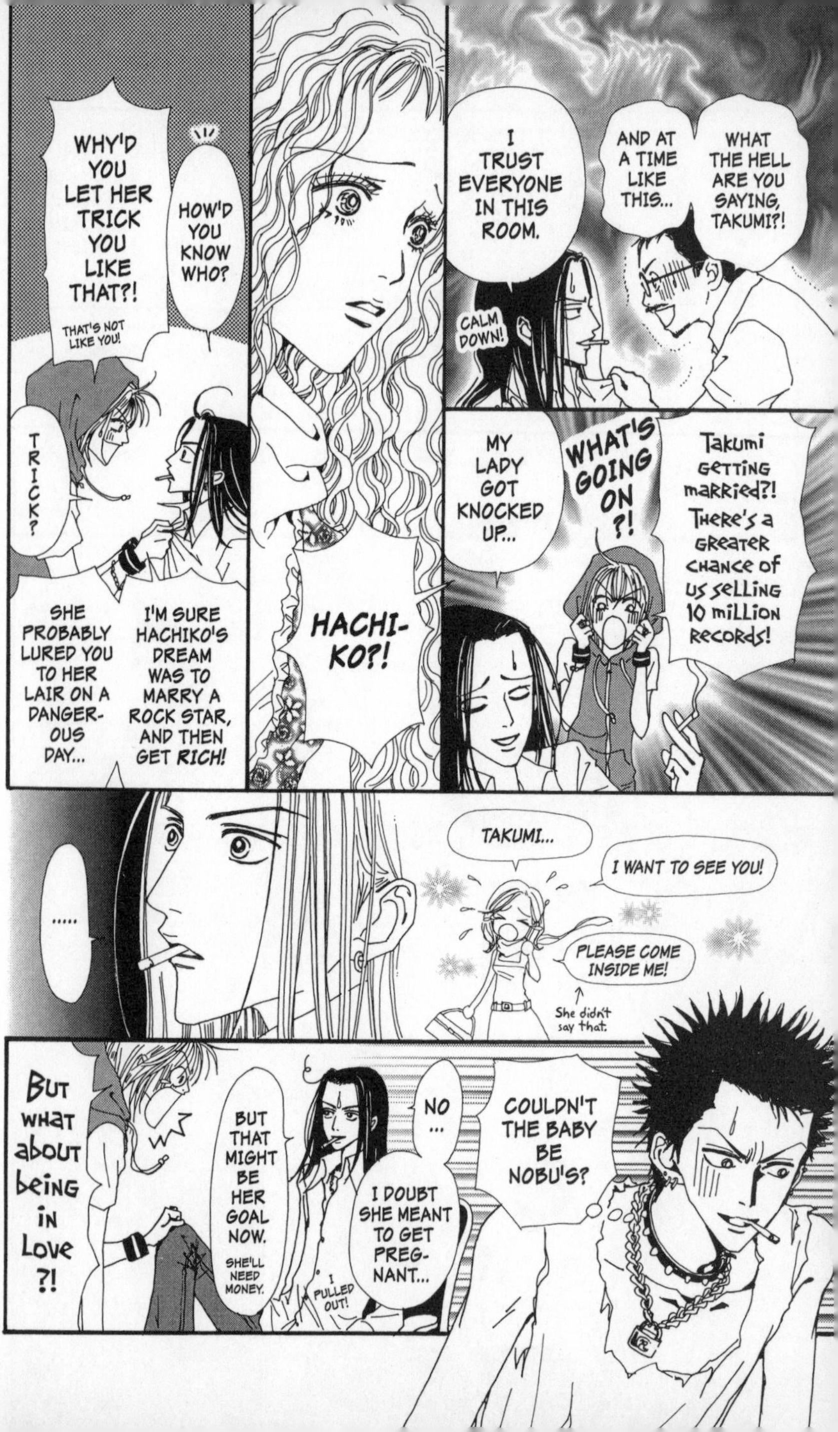
WHAT THE HELL ARE YOU SAYING, TAKUMI?!
AND AT A TIME LIKE THIS...
I TRUST EVERYONE IN THIS ROOM.
CALM DOWN!
Takumi getting married?! There's a greater chance of us selling 10 million records!
WHAT'S GOING ON?!
MY LADY GOT KNOCKED UP...
HACHI-KO?!
WHY'D YOU LET HER TRICK YOU LIKE THAT?!
THAT'S NOT LIKE YOU!
HOW'D YOU KNOW WHO?
TRICK?
I'M SURE HACHIKO'S DREAM WAS TO MARRY A ROCK STAR, AND THEN GET RICH!
SHE PROBABLY LURED YOU TO HER LAIR ON A DANGER-OUS DAY...
TAKUMI...
I WANT TO SEE YOU!
PLEASE COME INSIDE ME!
She didn't say that.
.....
COULDN'T THE BABY BE NOBU'S?
NO...
I DOUBT SHE MEANT TO GET PREG-NANT...
I PULLED OUT!
BUT THAT MIGHT BE HER GOAL NOW.
SHE'LL NEED MONEY.
But what about being in Love?!

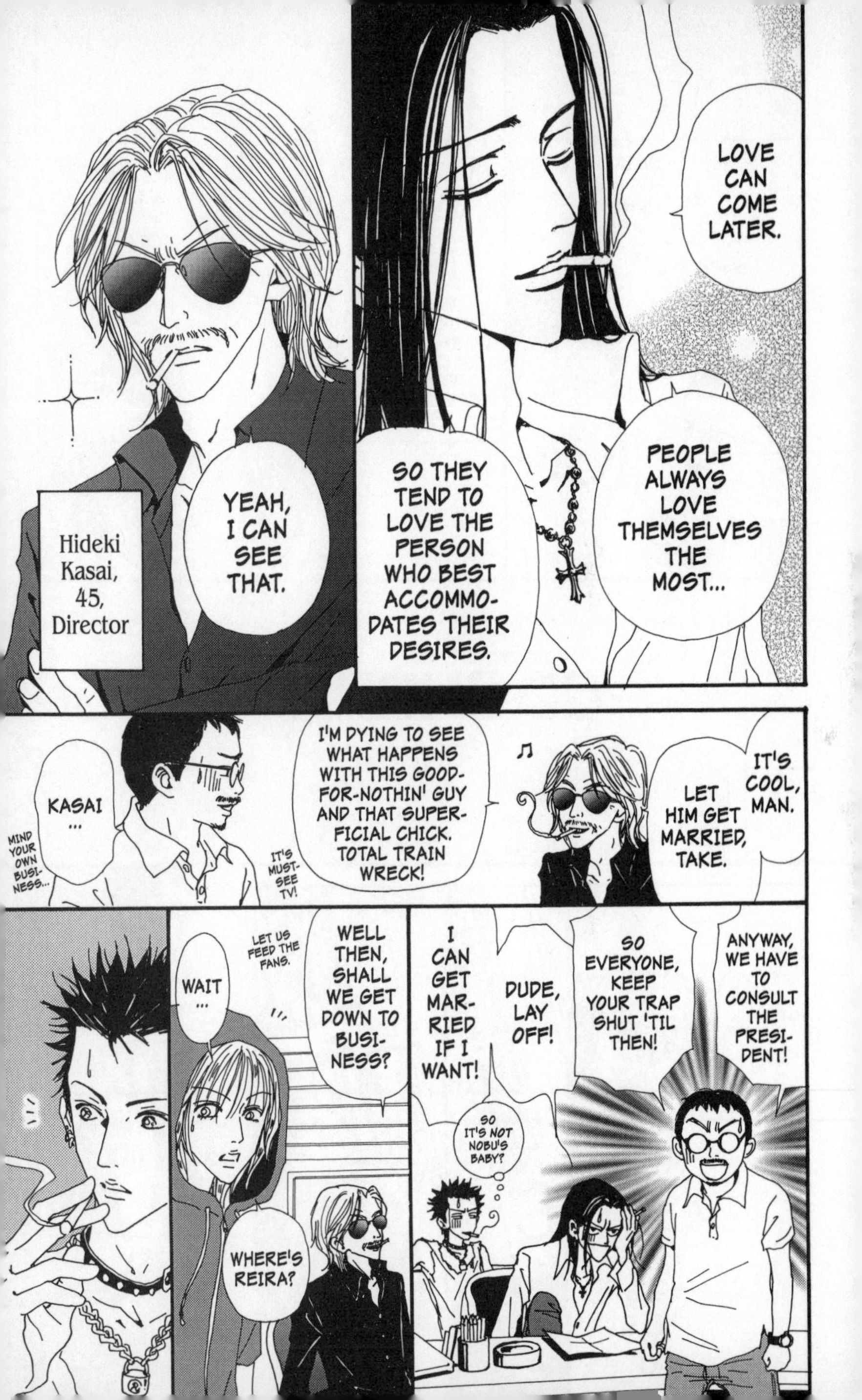
LOVE CAN COME LATER.
PEOPLE ALWAYS LOVE THEMSELVES THE MOST...
SO THEY TEND TO LOVE THE PERSON WHO BEST ACCOMMO-DATES THEIR DESIRES.
YEAH, I CAN SEE THAT.
Hideki Kasai, 45, Director
IT'S COOL, MAN.
LET HIM GET MARRIED, TAKE.
I'M DYING TO SEE WHAT HAPPENS WITH THIS GOOD-FOR-NOTHIN' GUY AND THAT SUPER-FICIAL CHICK. TOTAL TRAIN WRECK!
IT'S MUST-SEE TV!
KASAI...
MIND YOUR OWN BUSI-NESS...
ANYWAY, WE HAVE TO CONSULT THE PRESI-DENT!
SO EVERYONE, KEEP YOUR TRAP SHUT 'TIL THEN!
DUDE, LAY OFF!
I CAN GET MAR-RIED IF I WANT!
SO IT'S NOT NOBU'S BABY?
WELL THEN, SHALL WE GET DOWN TO BUSI-NESS?
LET US FEED THE FANS.
WAIT...
WHERE'S REIRA?

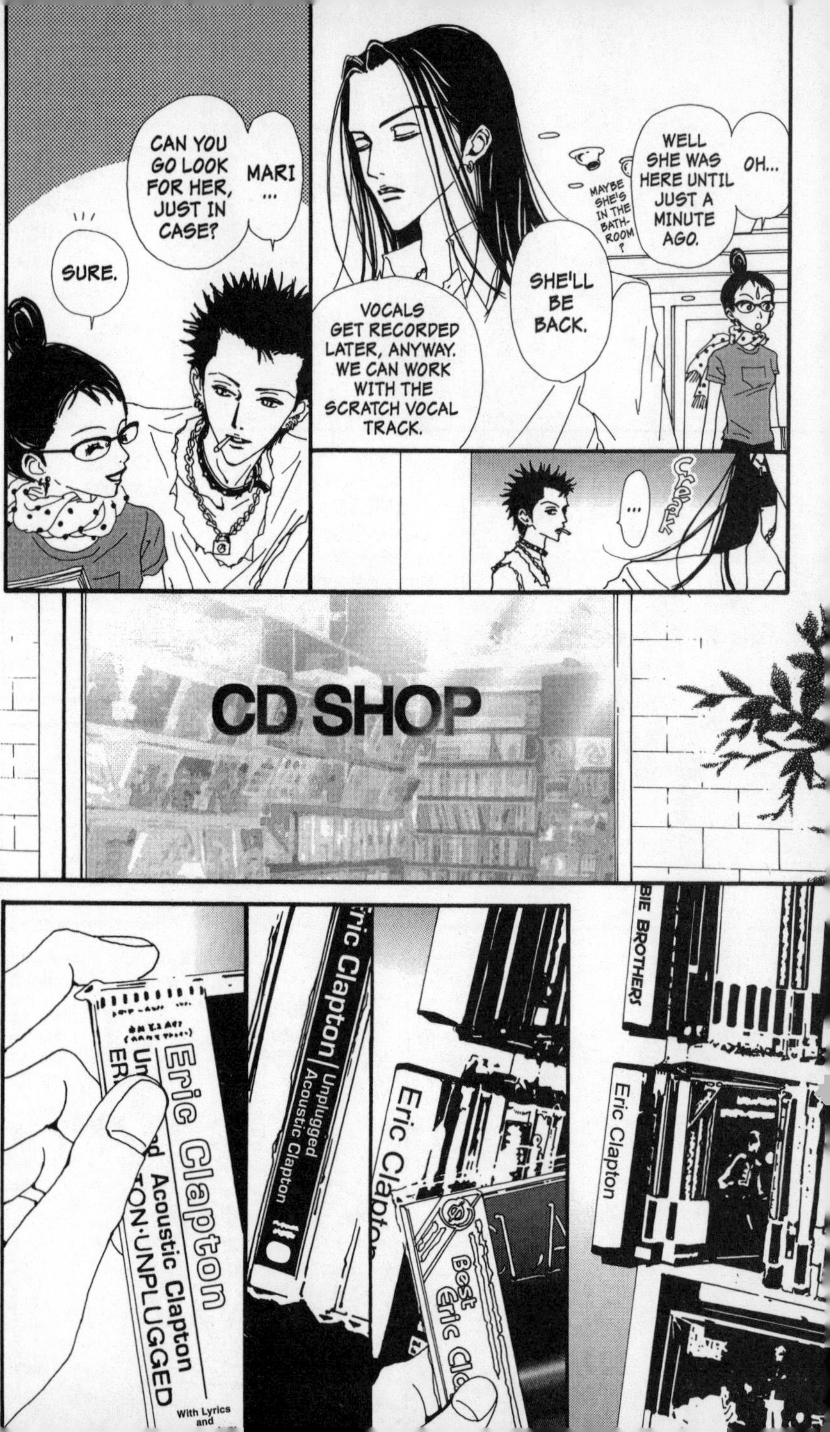
OH...
WELL SHE WAS HERE UNTIL JUST A MINUTE AGO.
MAYBE SHE'S IN THE BATH-ROOM?
SHE'LL BE BACK.
VOCALS GET RECORDED LATER, ANYWAY. WE CAN WORK WITH THE SCRATCH VOCAL TRACK.
CLANK
...
MARI ...
CAN YOU GO LOOK FOR HER, JUST IN CASE?
SURE.
CD SHOP
BIE BROTHERS
Eric Clapton
Eric Clapton
Best Eric Cl
Eric Clapton | Unplugged Acoustic Clapton
Eric Clapton
Acoustic Clapton
TON·UNPLUGGED
With Lyrics and

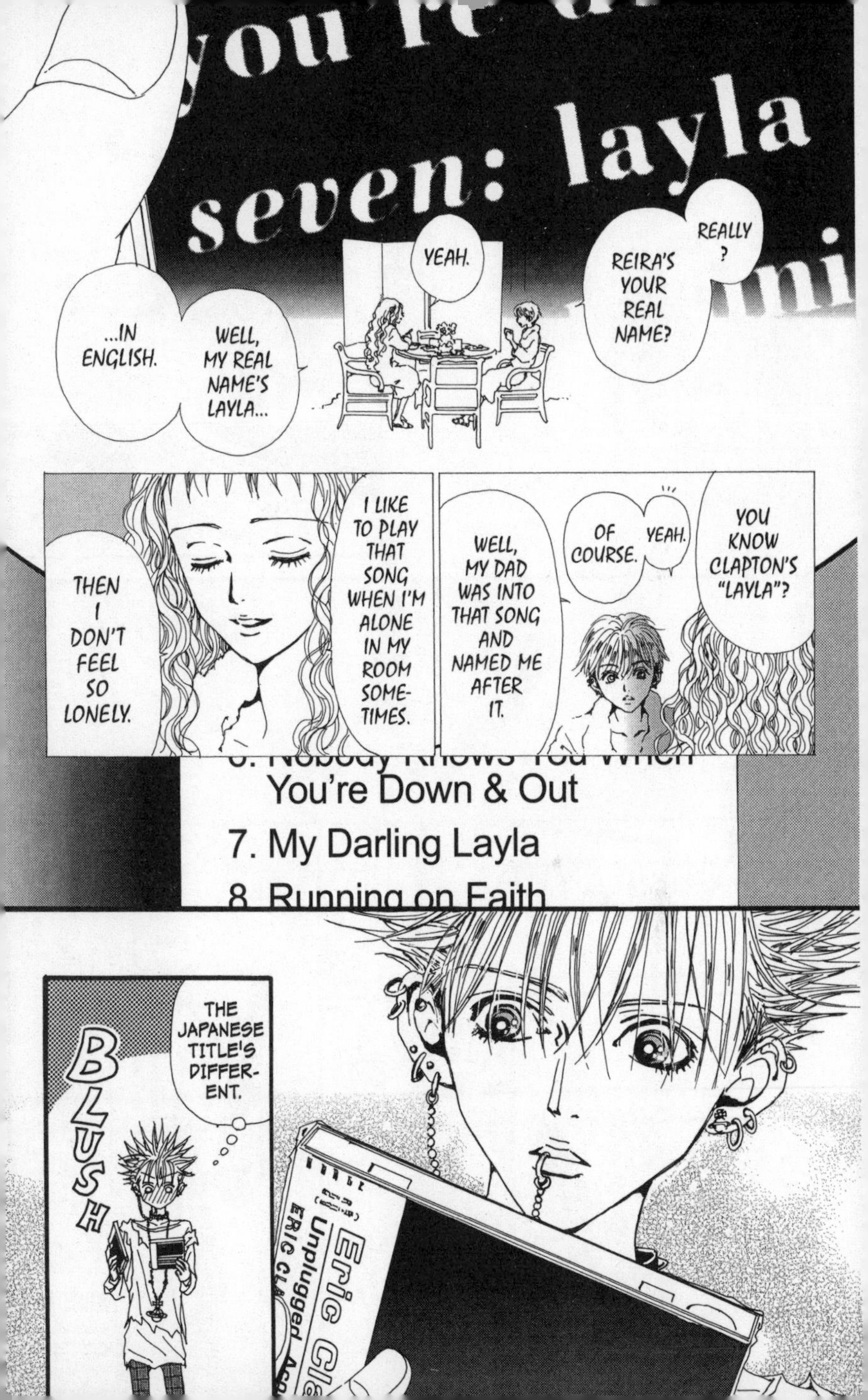
seven: layla
REALLY?
REIRA'S YOUR REAL NAME?
YEAH.
WELL, MY REAL NAME'S LAYLA...
...IN ENGLISH.
YOU KNOW CLAPTON'S "LAYLA"?
YEAH.
OF COURSE.
WELL, MY DAD WAS INTO THAT SONG AND NAMED ME AFTER IT.
I LIKE TO PLAY THAT SONG WHEN I'M ALONE IN MY ROOM SOMETIMES.
THEN I DON'T FEEL SO LONELY.
You're Down & Out
7. My Darling Layla
8. Running on Faith
THE JAPANESE TITLE'S DIFFERENT.
BLUSH
Unplugged

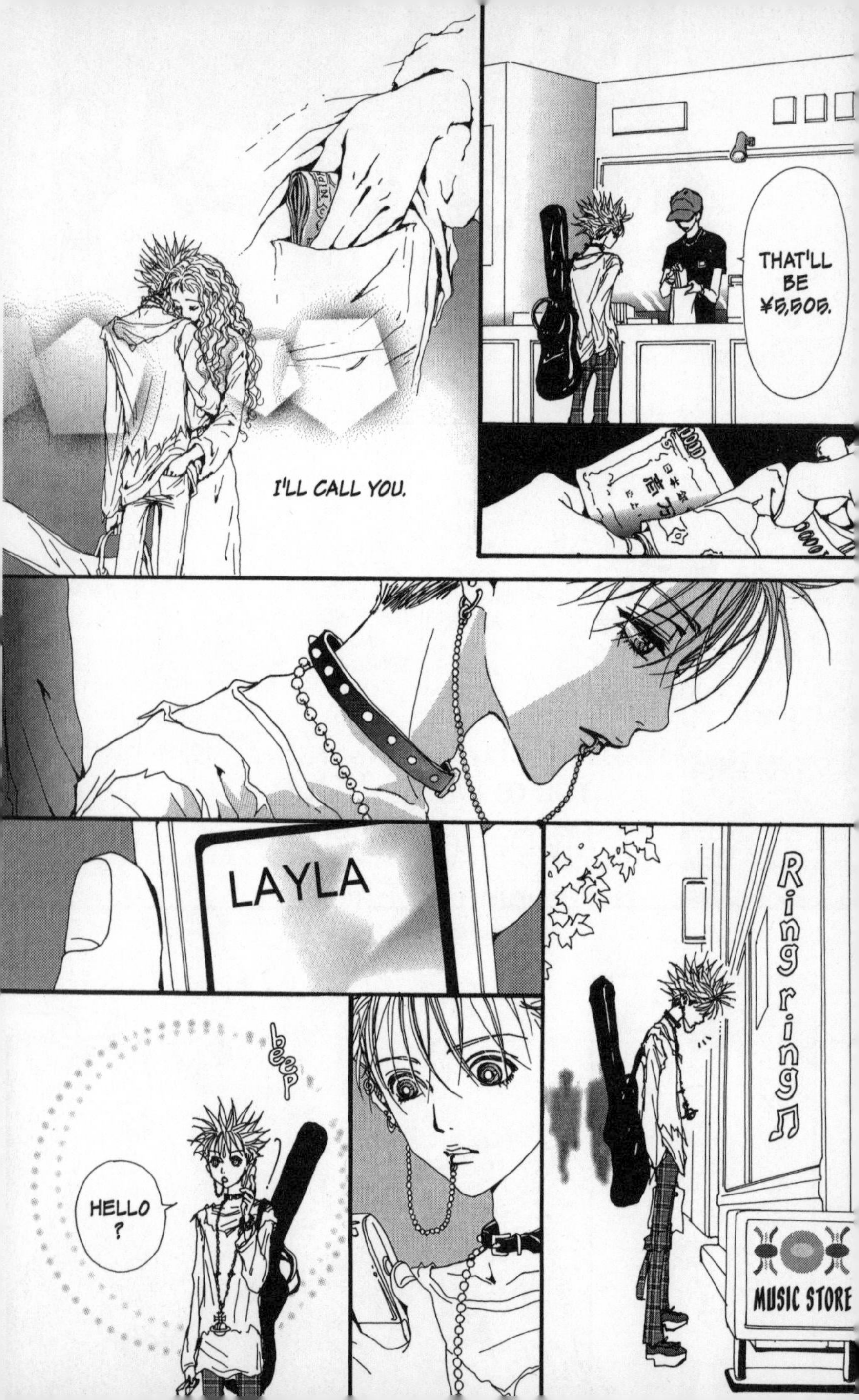
THAT'LL BE ¥5,505.
I'LL CALL YOU.
Ring ring♫
MUSIC STORE
LAYLA
beep
HELLO?

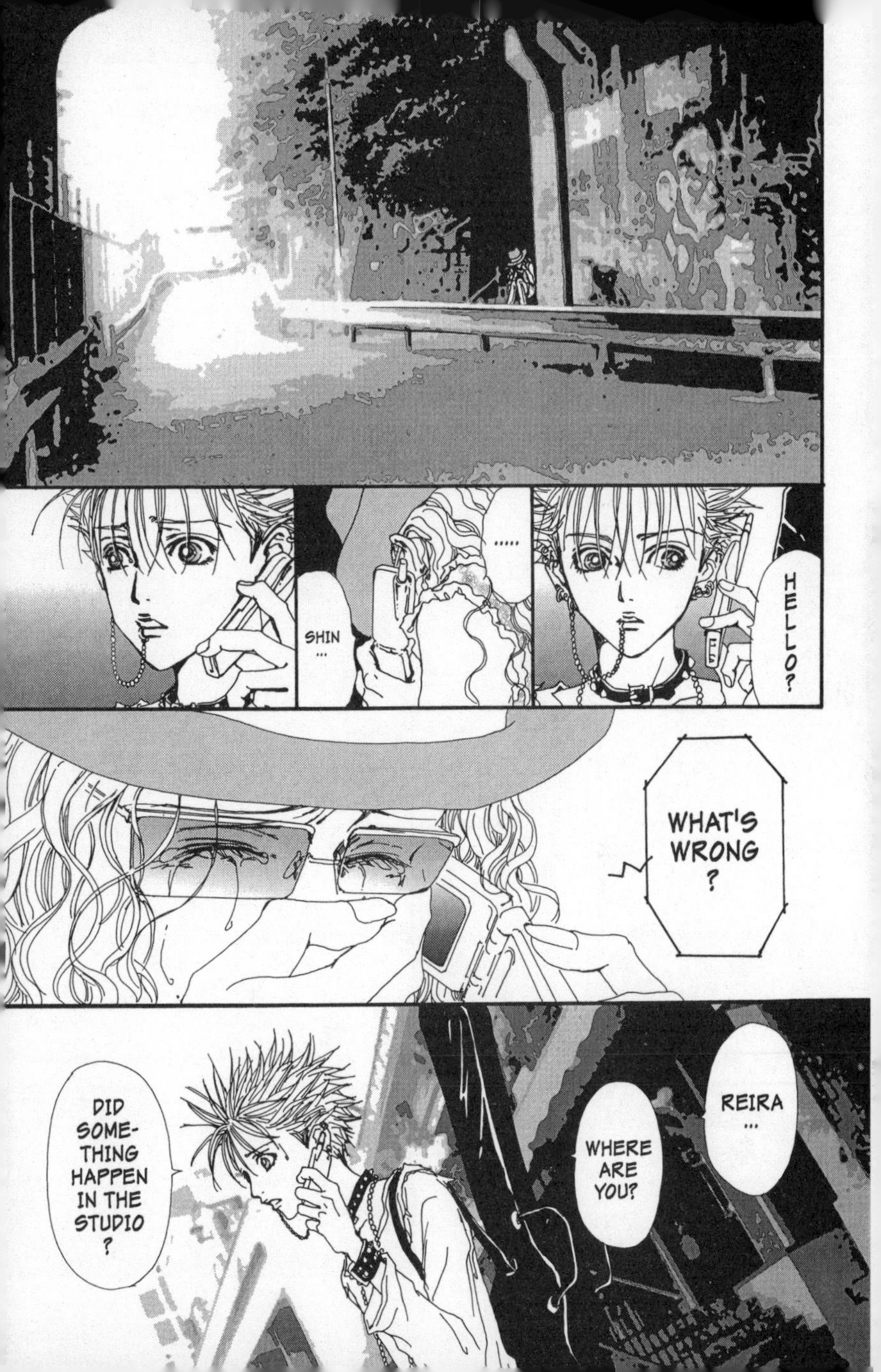
HELLO?
.....
SHIN ...
WHAT'S WRONG ?
REIRA ...
WHERE ARE YOU?
DID SOME-THING HAPPEN IN THE STUDIO ?

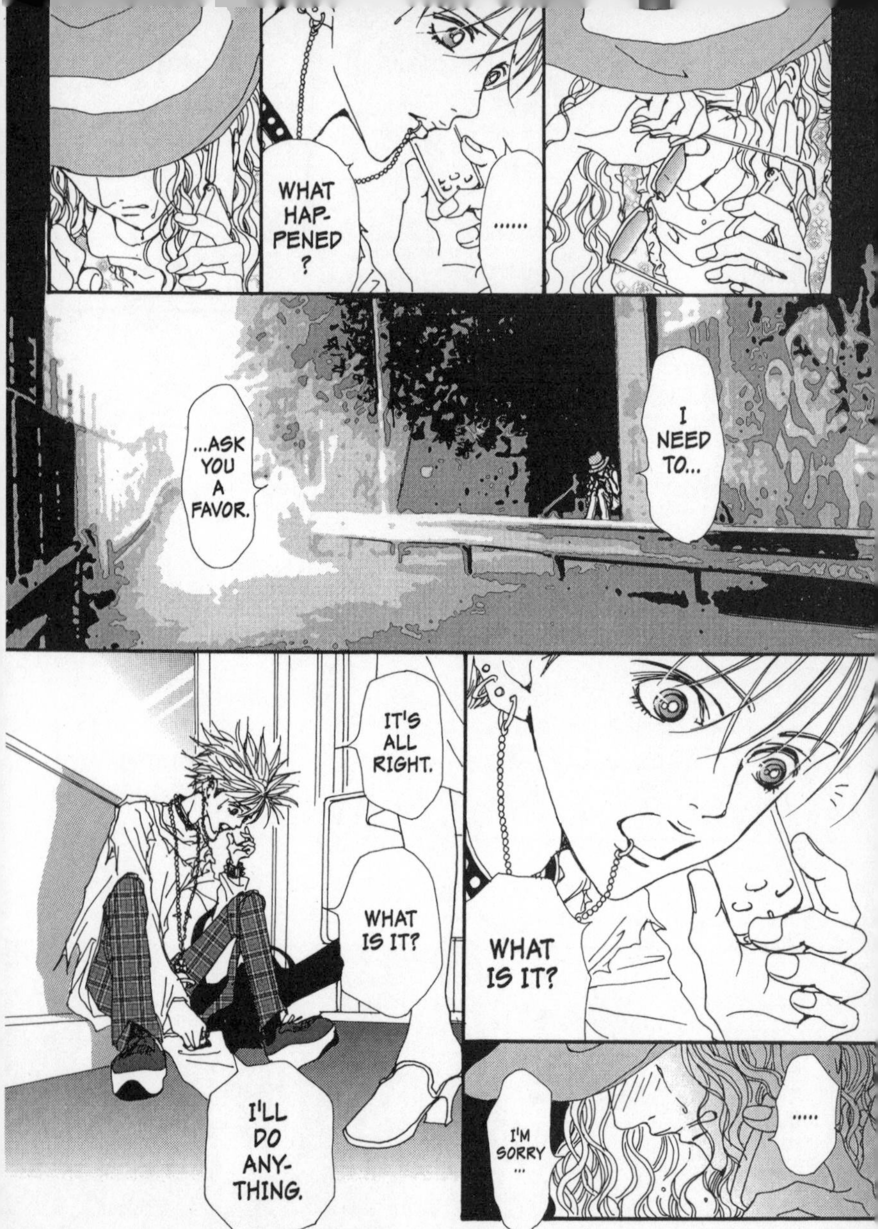
......
WHAT HAPPENED?
I NEED TO...
...ASK YOU A FAVOR.
WHAT IS IT?
.....
I'M SORRY...
IT'S ALL RIGHT.
WHAT IS IT?
I'LL DO ANYTHING.

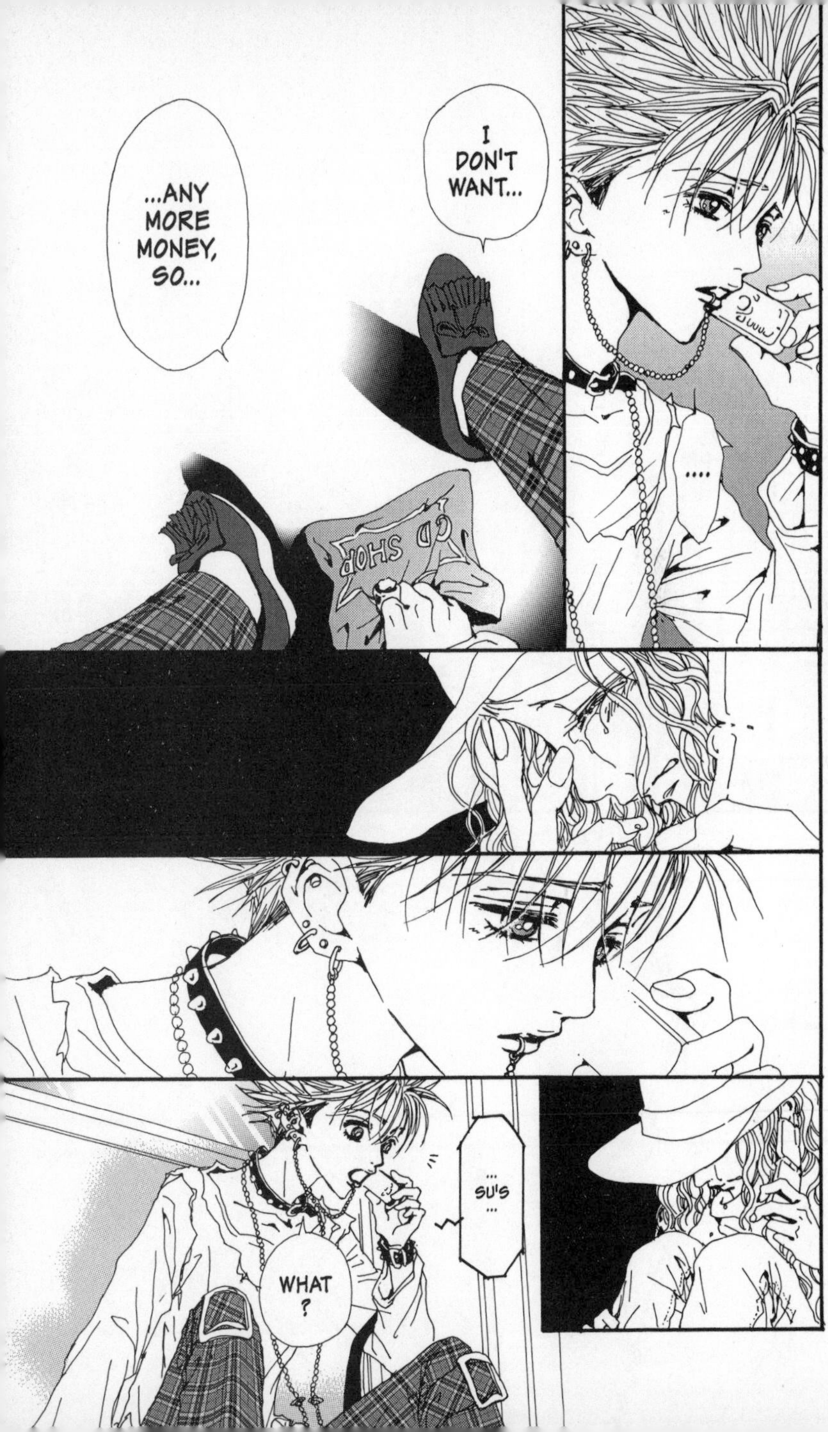
....
I DON'T WANT...
...ANY MORE MONEY, SO...
CD SHOP
...SU'S...
WHAT?

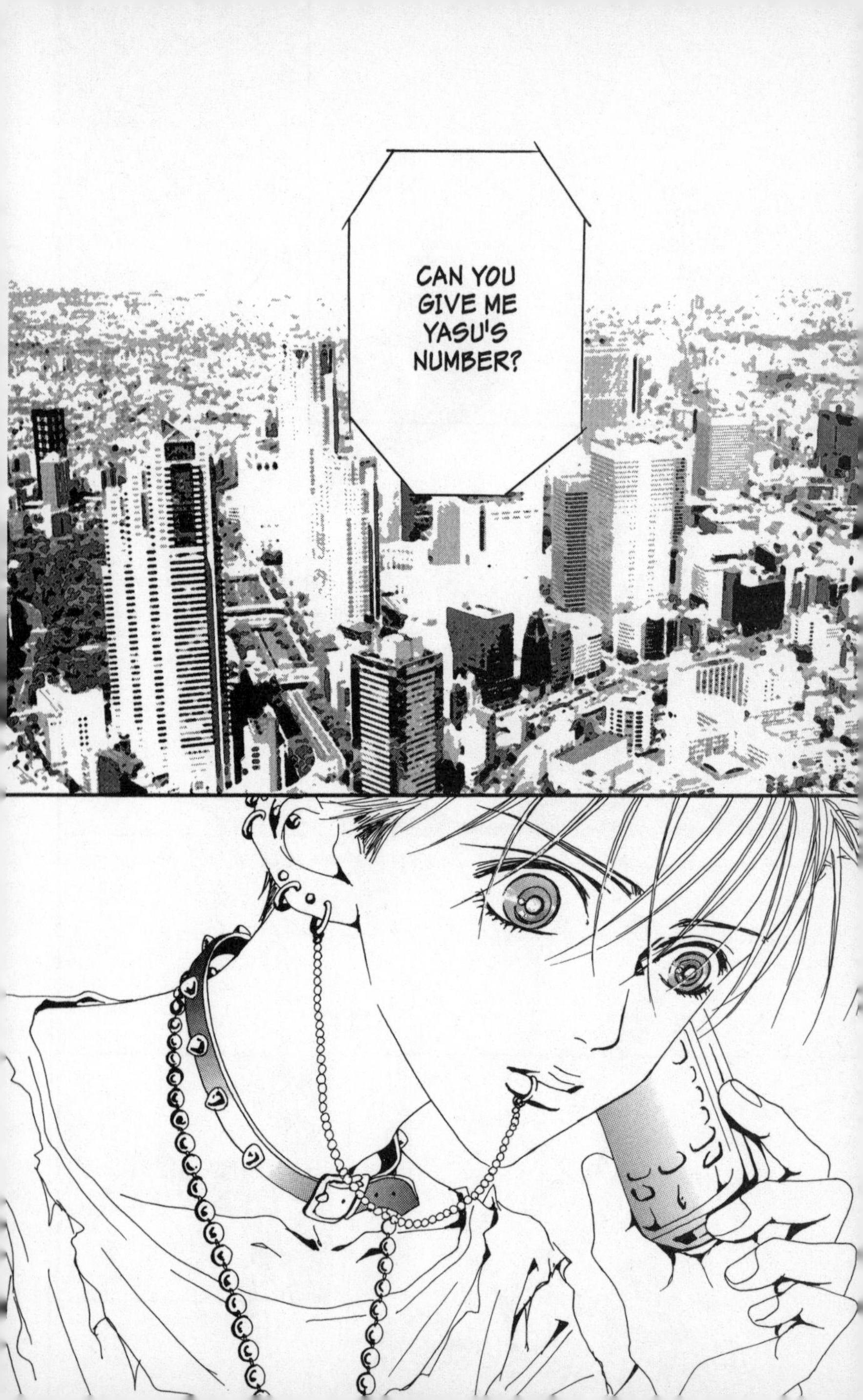
CAN YOU GIVE ME YASU'S NUMBER?

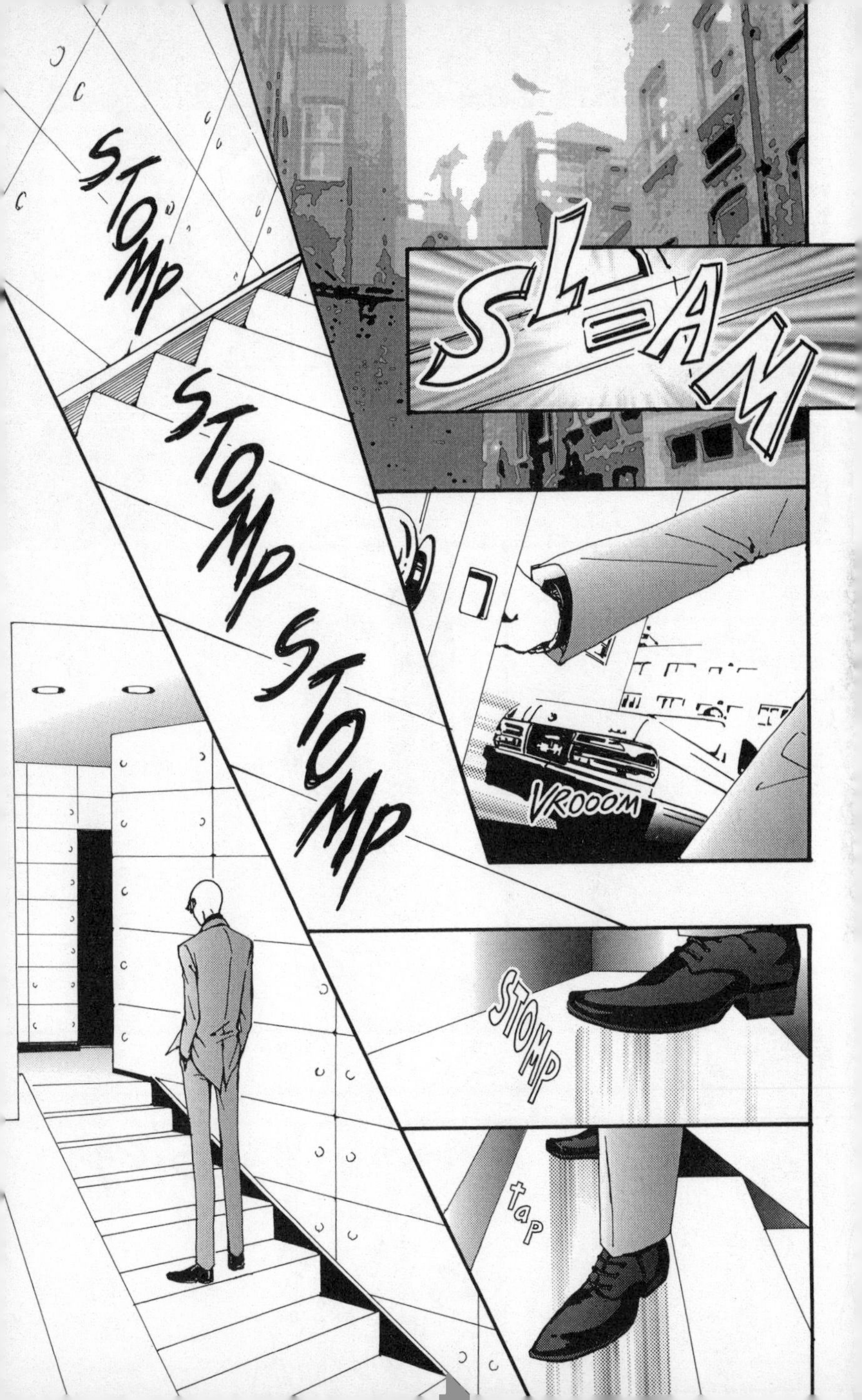
SLAM
VROOOM
STOMP
STOMP
STOMP
STOMP
STOMP
tap

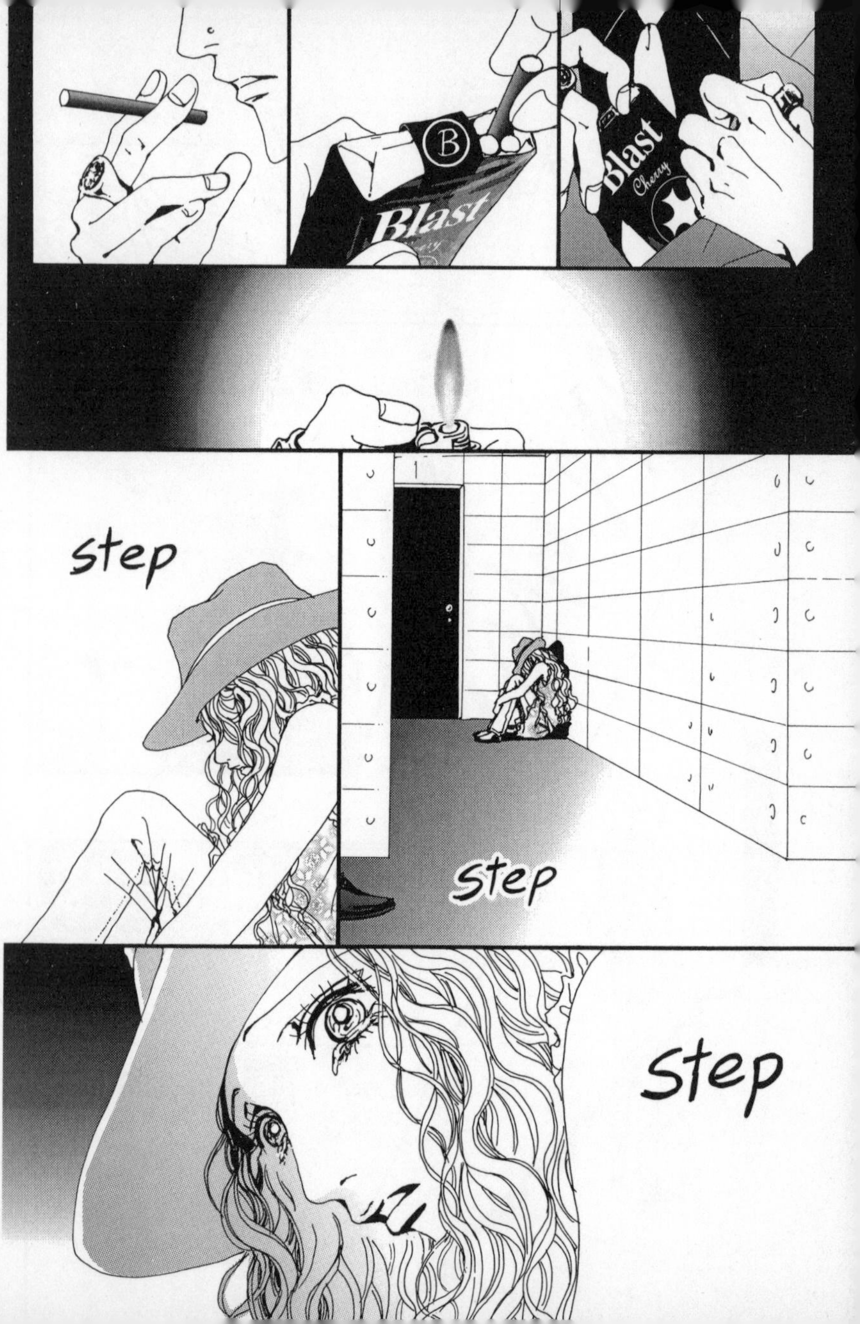
Blast
Cherry
B
Blast
step
step
Step

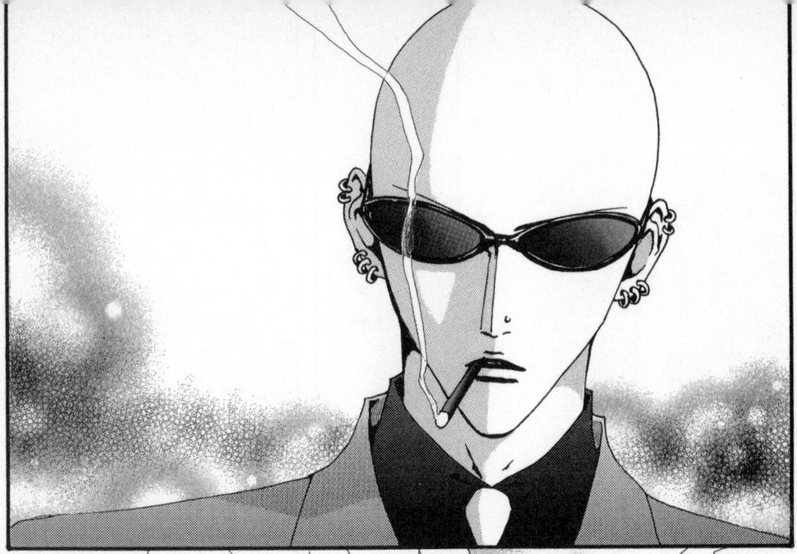
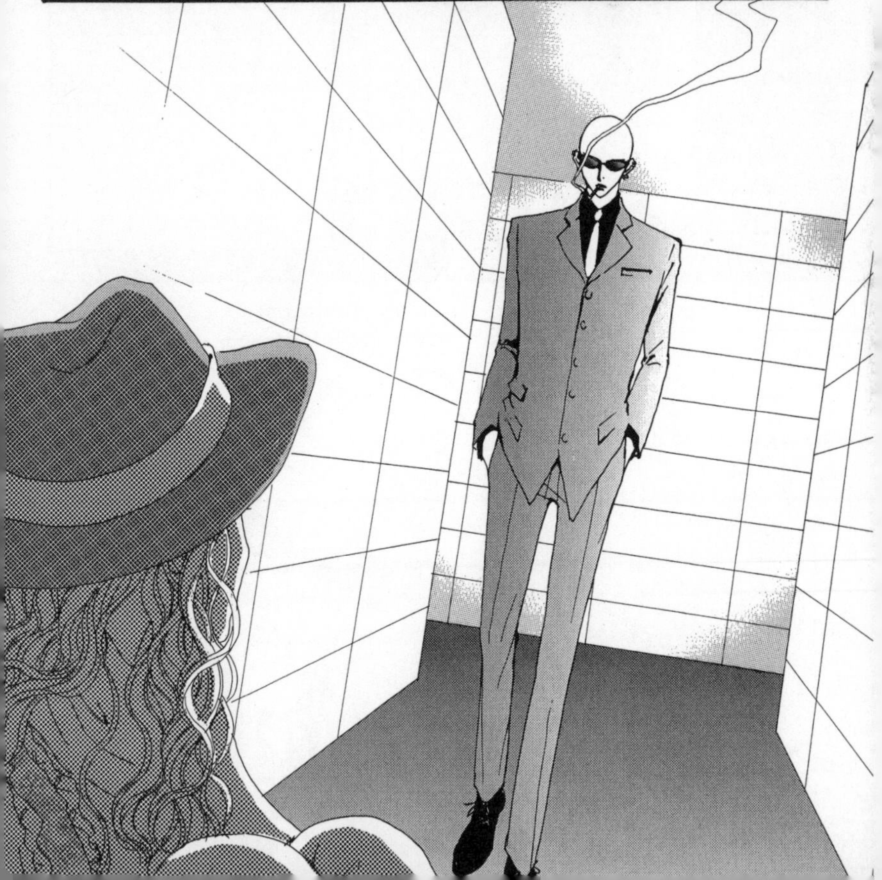

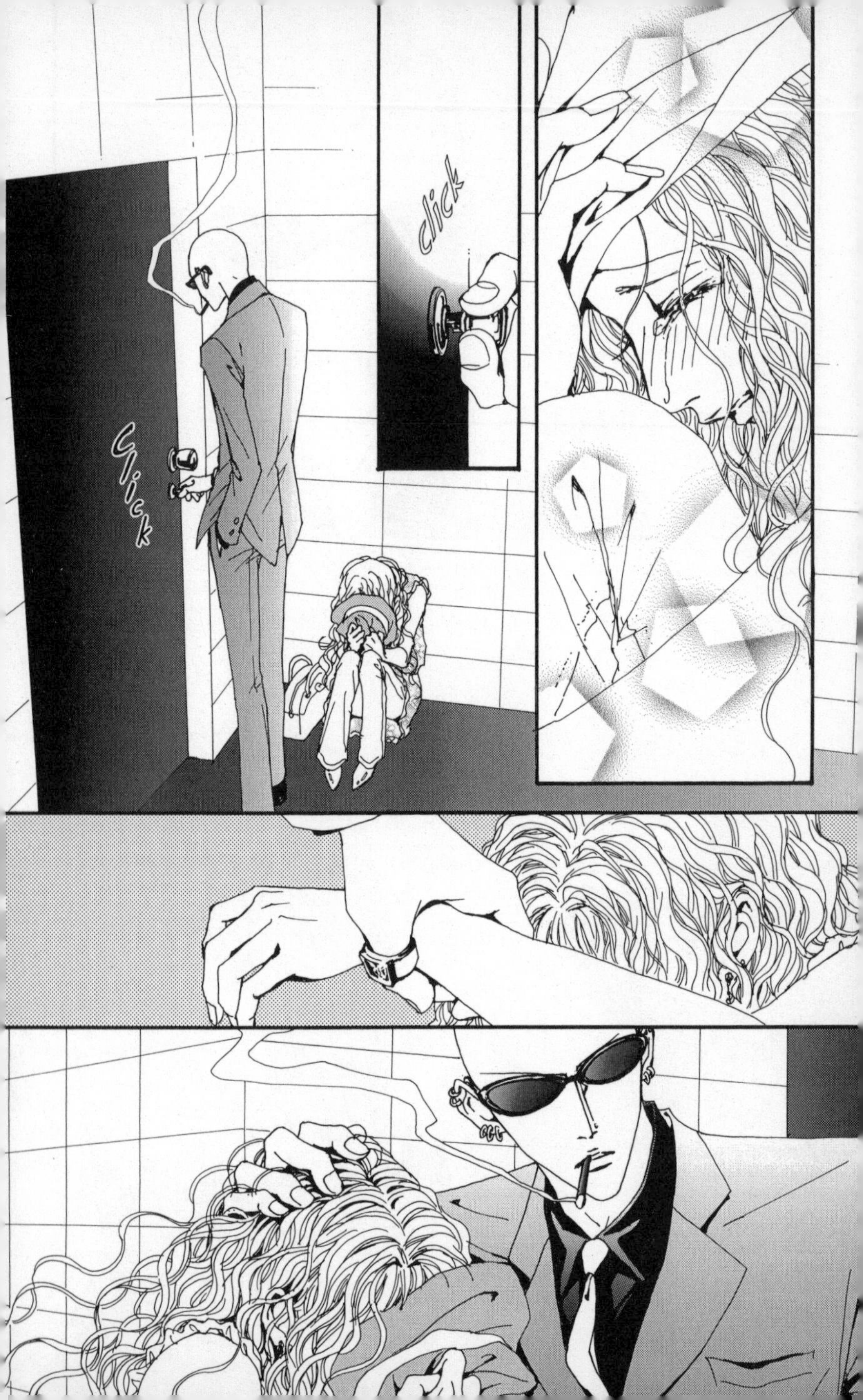
click
Click

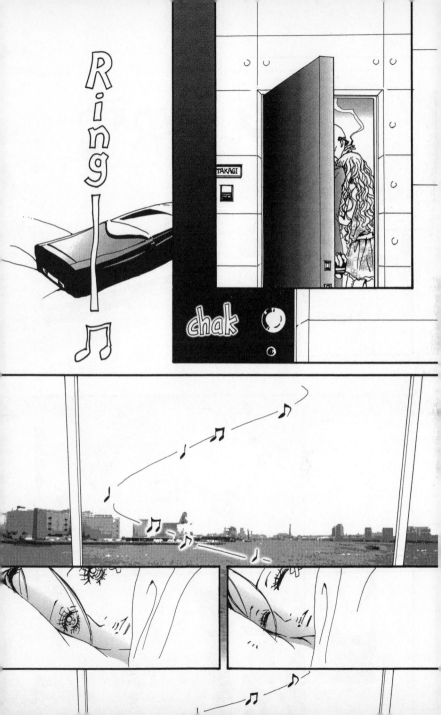
Ring

TAKAGI

chak

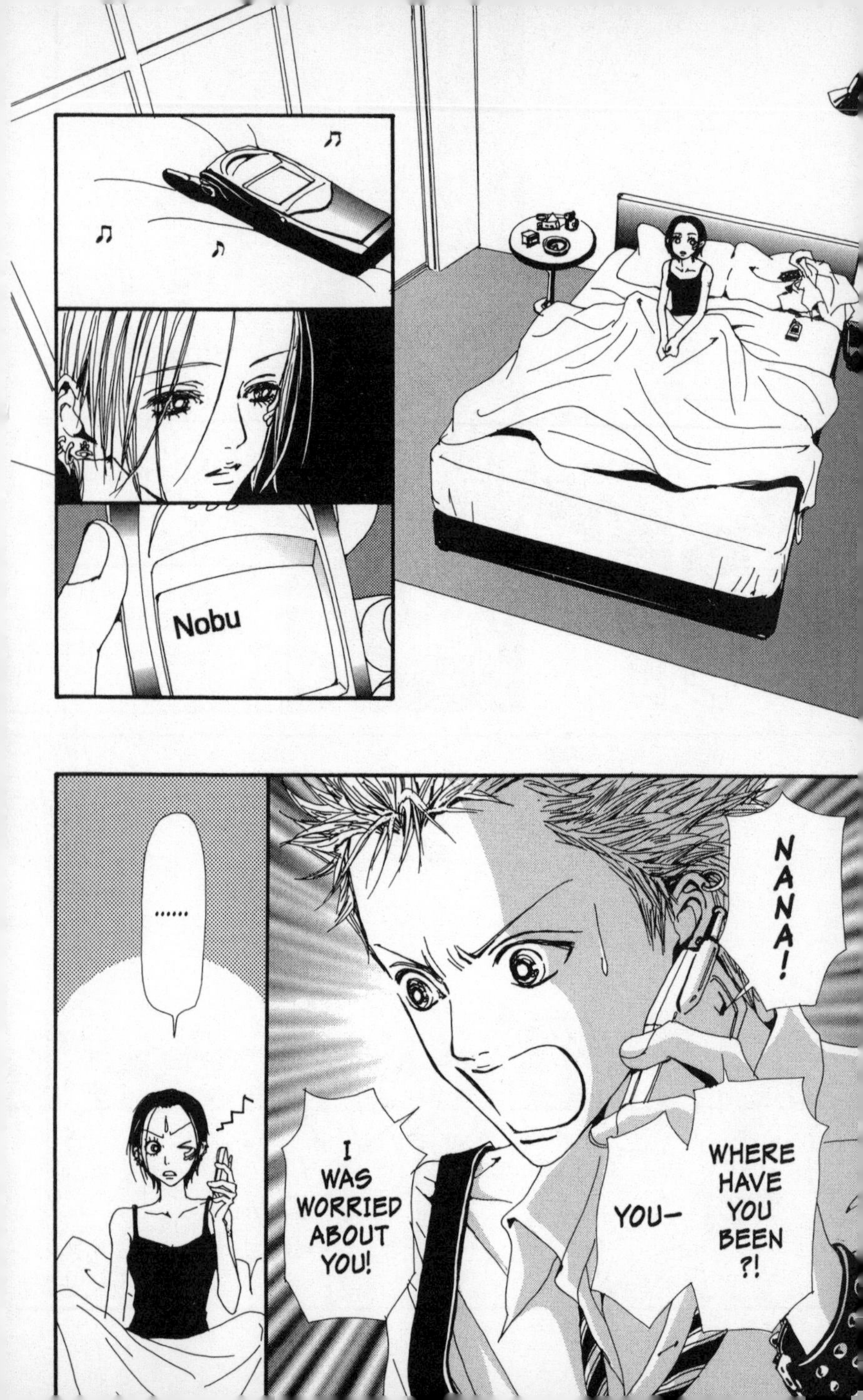
Nobu
NANA!
WHERE HAVE YOU BEEN?!
YOU—
I WAS WORRIED ABOUT YOU!
......

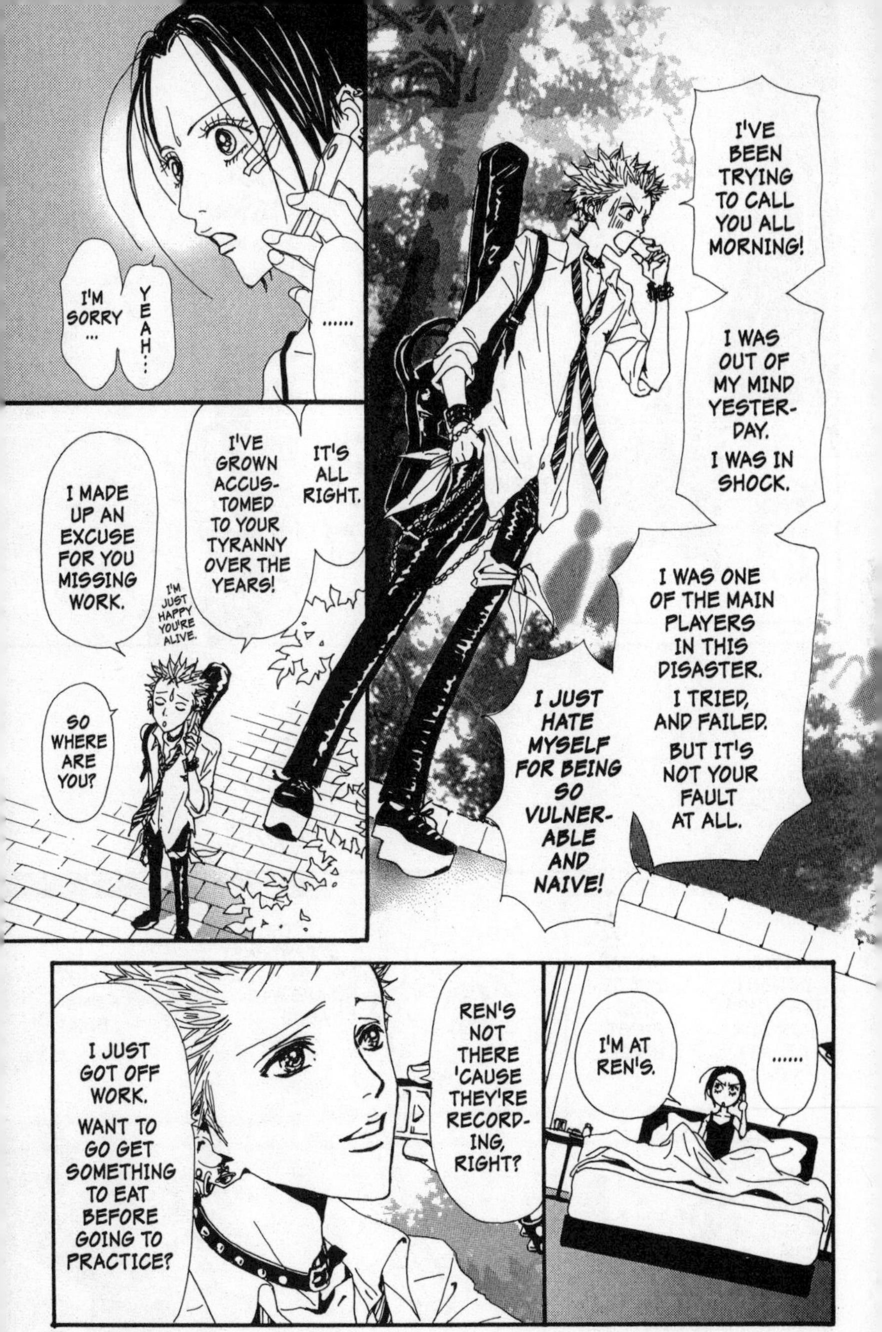

I'VE BEEN TRYING TO CALL YOU ALL MORNING!
I WAS OUT OF MY MIND YESTER-DAY.
I WAS IN SHOCK.
I WAS ONE OF THE MAIN PLAYERS IN THIS DISASTER.
I TRIED, AND FAILED.
BUT IT'S NOT YOUR FAULT AT ALL.
I JUST HATE MYSELF FOR BEING SO VULNER-ABLE AND NAIVE!
......
YEAH...
I'M SORRY...
IT'S ALL RIGHT.
I'VE GROWN ACCUS-TOMED TO YOUR TYRANNY OVER THE YEARS!
I'M JUST HAPPY YOU'RE ALIVE.
I MADE UP AN EXCUSE FOR YOU MISSING WORK.
SO WHERE ARE YOU?
......
I'M AT REN'S.
REN'S NOT THERE 'CAUSE THEY'RE RECORD-ING, RIGHT?
I JUST GOT OFF WORK.
WANT TO GO GET SOMETHING TO EAT BEFORE GOING TO PRACTICE?

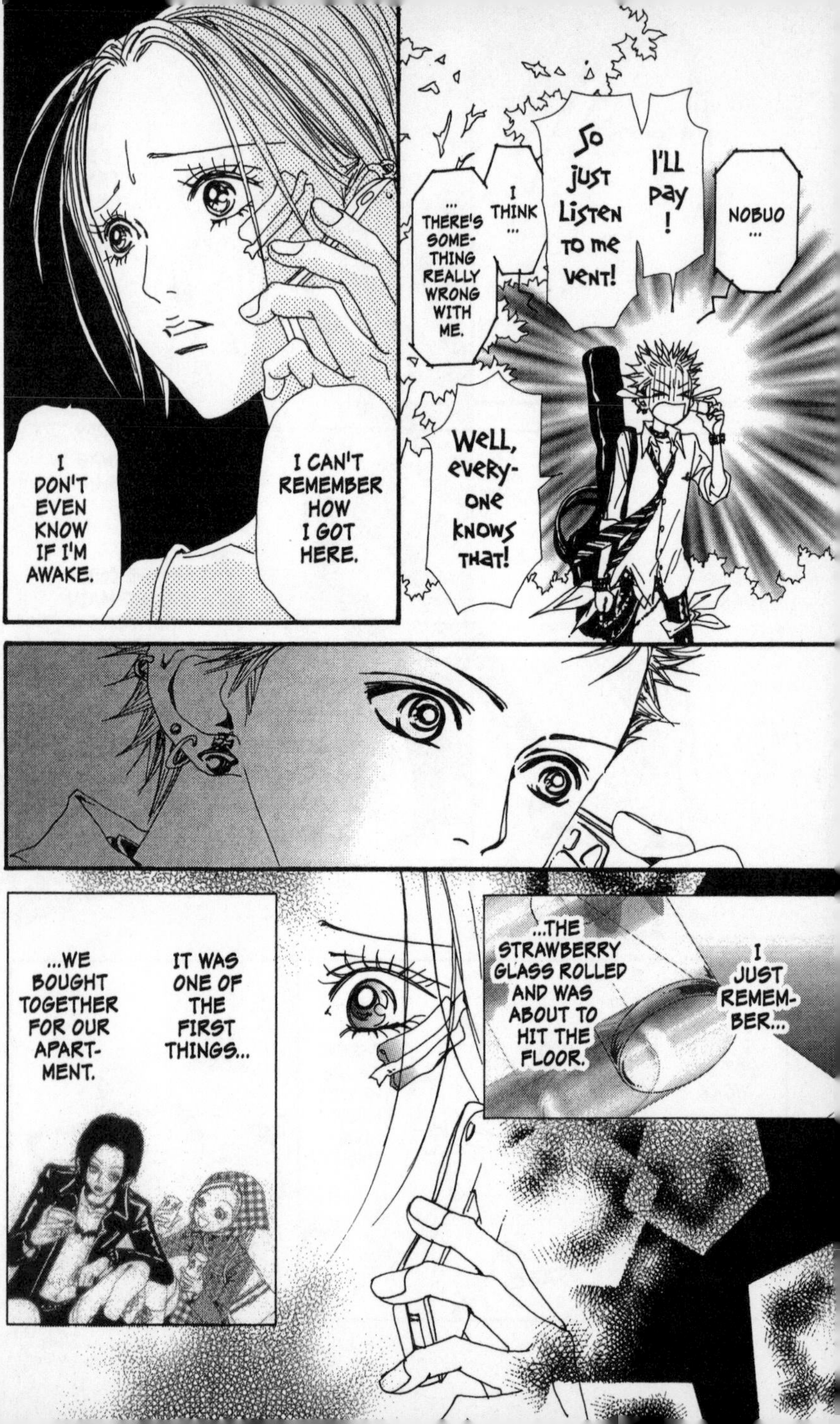
NOBUO ...
I'LL PAY!
SO JUST LISTEN TO ME VENT!
I THINK ...
... THERE'S SOME-THING REALLY WRONG WITH ME.
WELL, EVERY-ONE KNOWS THAT!
I CAN'T REMEMBER HOW I GOT HERE.
I DON'T EVEN KNOW IF I'M AWAKE.
I JUST REMEM-BER...
...THE STRAWBERRY GLASS ROLLED AND WAS ABOUT TO HIT THE FLOOR.
IT WAS ONE OF THE FIRST THINGS...
...WE BOUGHT TOGETHER FOR OUR APART-MENT.

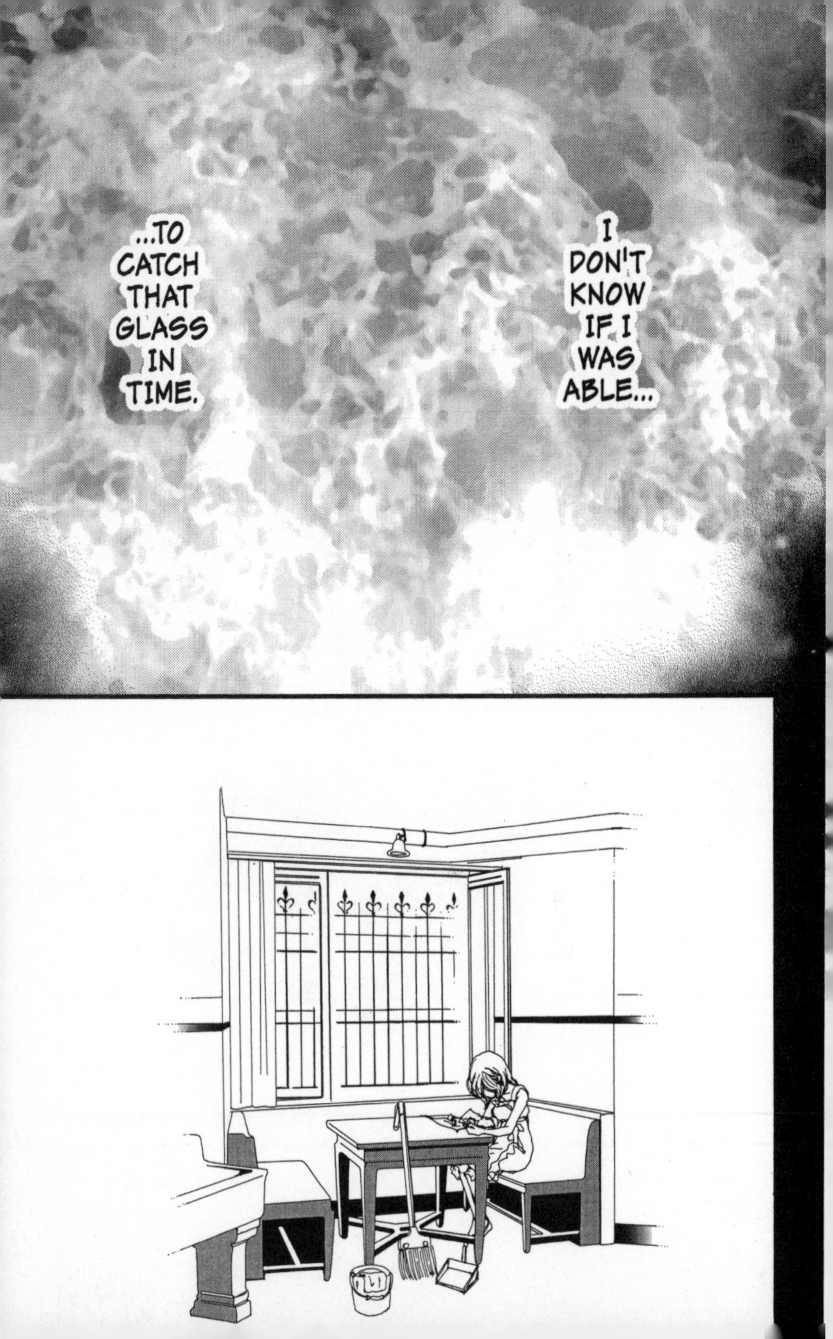
I DON'T KNOW IF I WAS ABLE...
...TO CATCH THAT GLASS IN TIME.

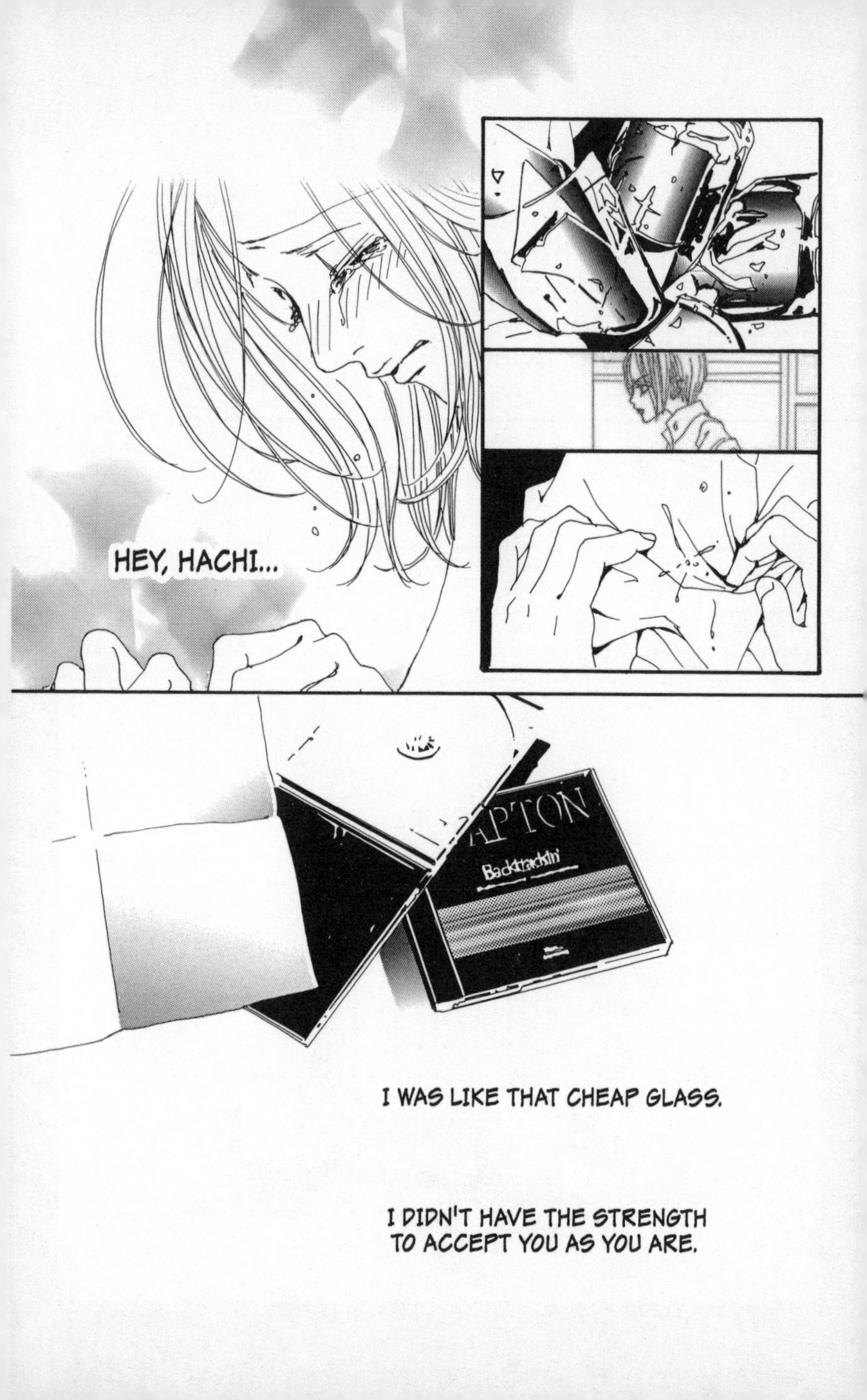
HEY, HACHI...
Backtrackin'
I WAS LIKE THAT CHEAP GLASS.
I DIDN'T HAVE THE STRENGTH
TO ACCEPT YOU AS YOU ARE.

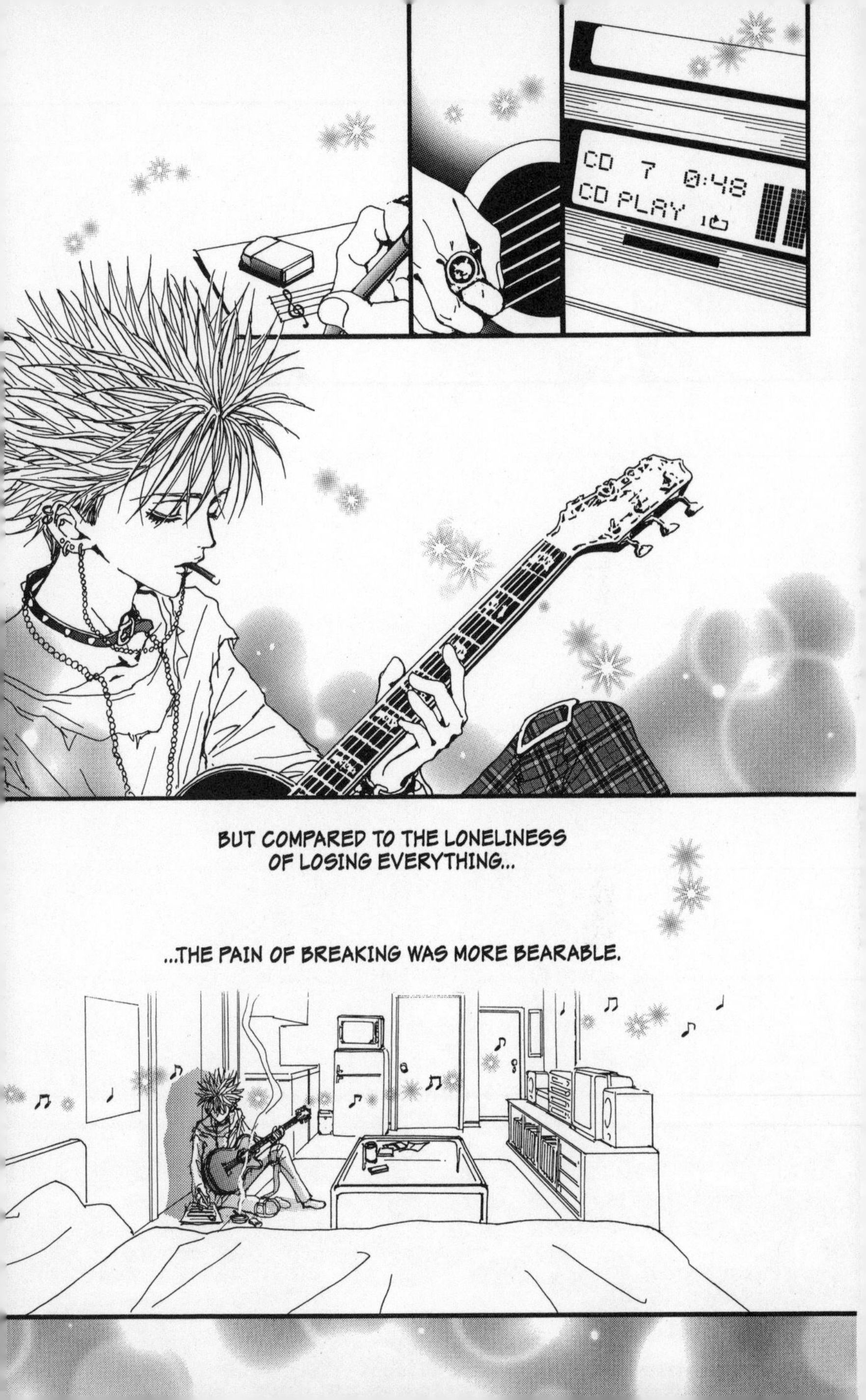
CD 7 0:48
CD PLAY
BUT COMPARED TO THE LONELINESS OF LOSING EVERYTHING...
...THE PAIN OF BREAKING WAS MORE BEARABLE.

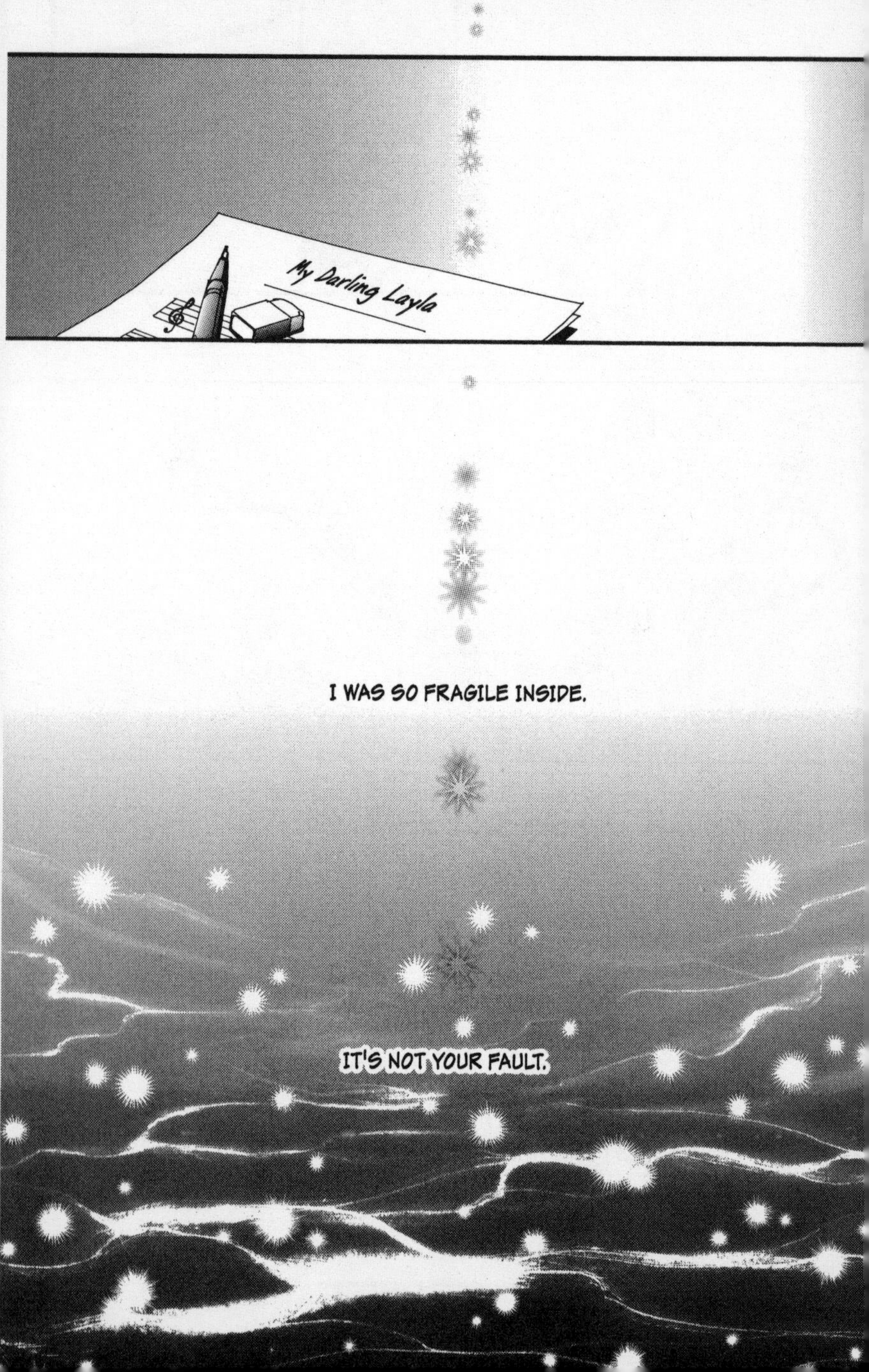
My Darling Layla
I WAS SO FRAGILE INSIDE.
IT'S NOT YOUR FAULT.

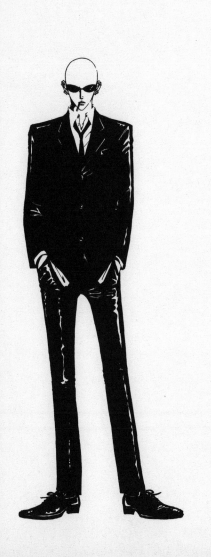

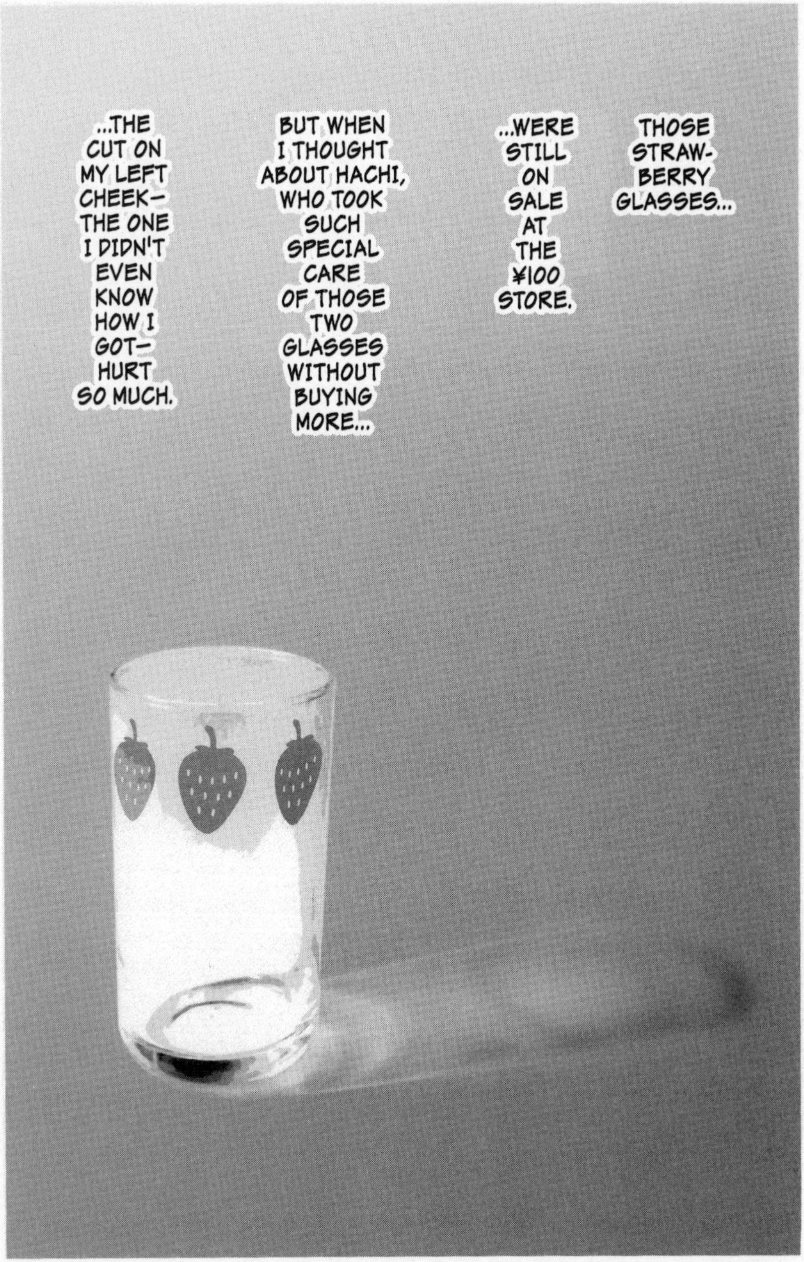
THOSE STRAW-BERRY GLASSES...
...WERE STILL ON SALE AT THE ¥100 STORE.
BUT WHEN I THOUGHT ABOUT HACHI, WHO TOOK SUCH SPECIAL CARE OF THOSE TWO GLASSES WITHOUT BUYING MORE...
...THE CUT ON MY LEFT CHEEK—THE ONE I DIDN'T EVEN KNOW HOW I GOT—HURT SO MUCH.

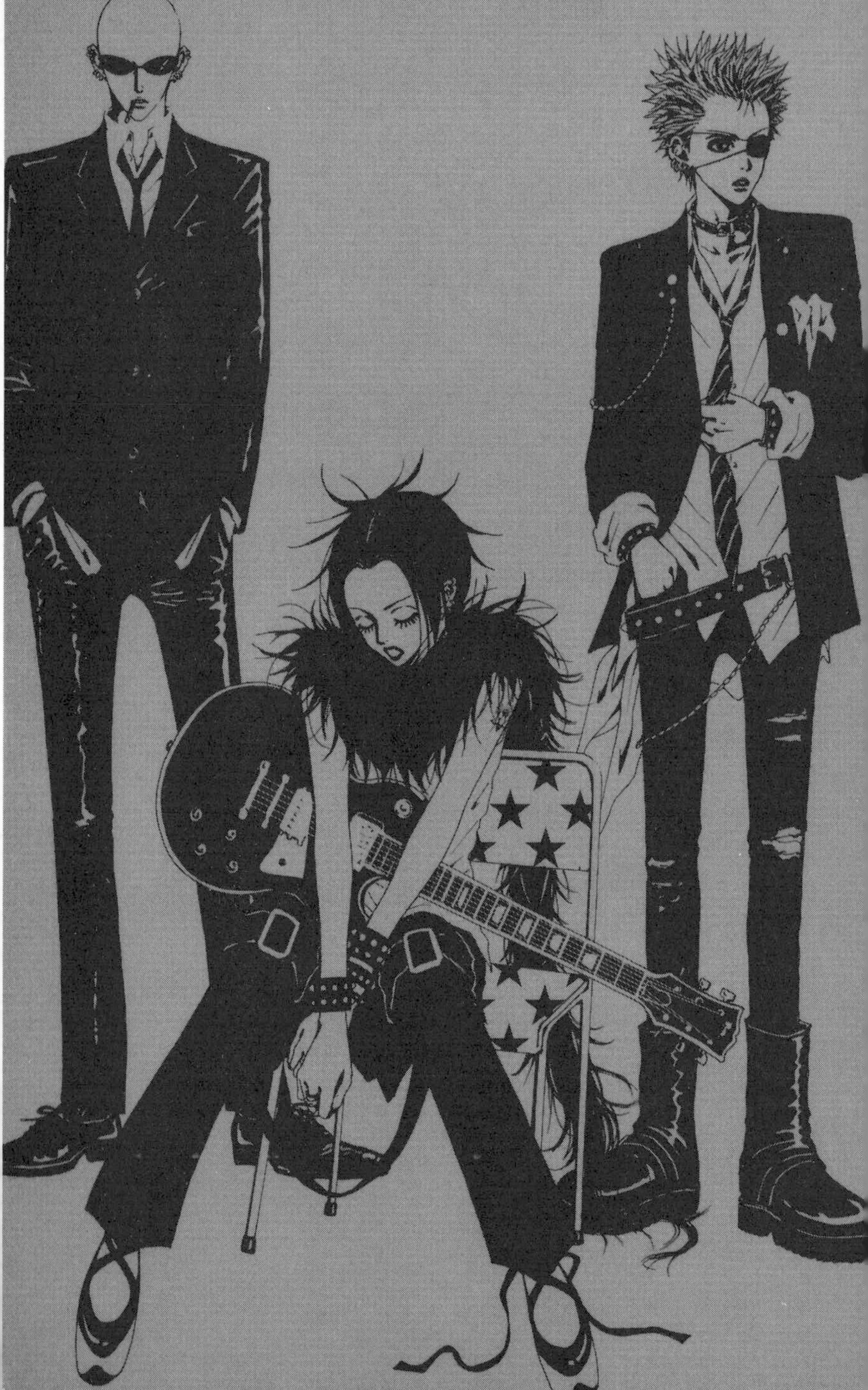

NANA™

ナナ

[Chapter 30]

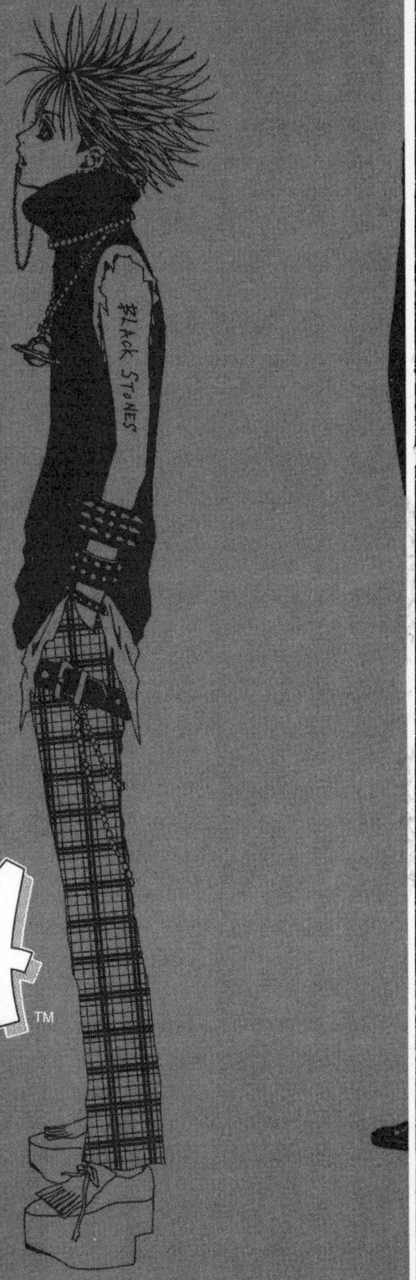
BLACK STONES

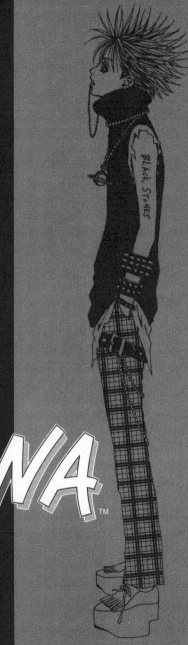

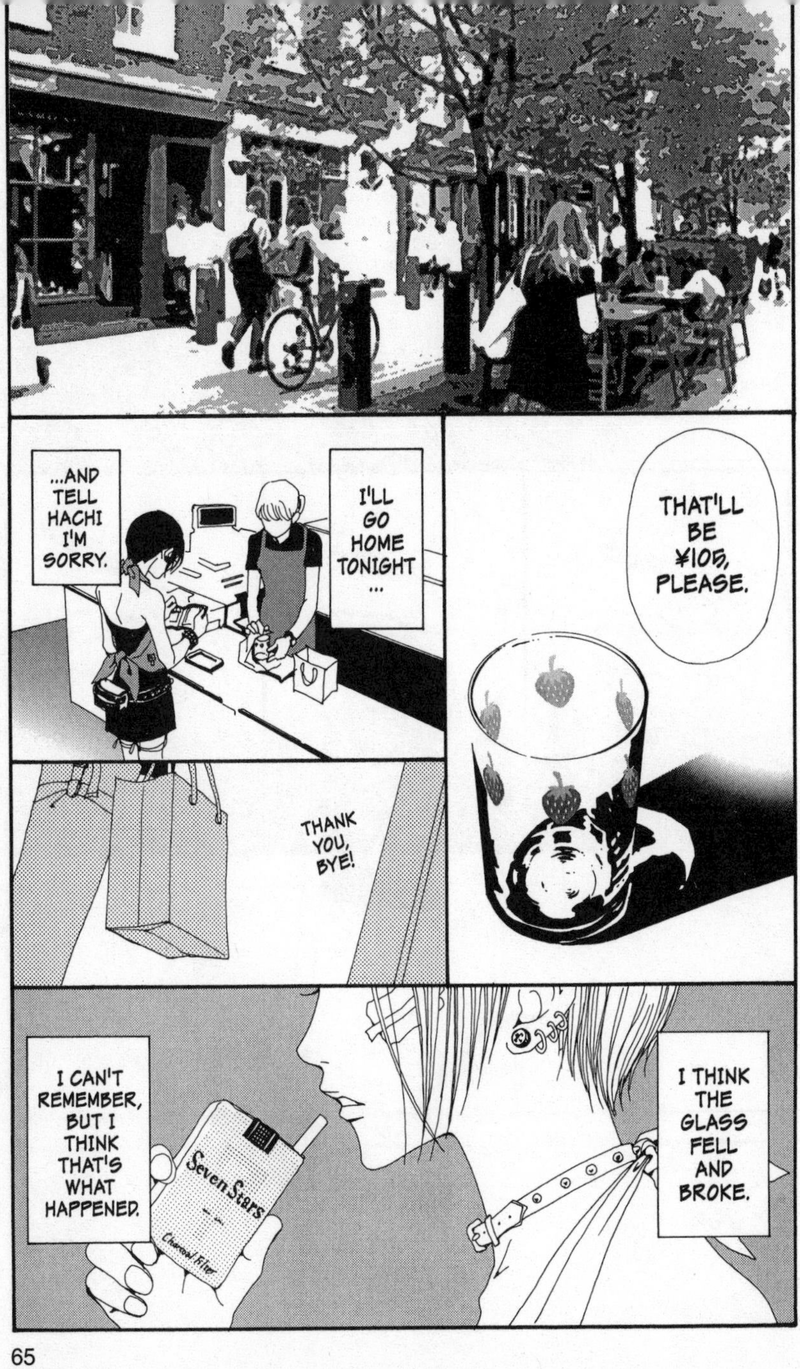
THAT'LL BE ¥105, PLEASE.
I'LL GO HOME TONIGHT...
...AND TELL HACHI I'M SORRY.
THANK YOU, BYE!
I THINK THE GLASS FELL AND BROKE.
Seven Stars
Charcoal Filter
I CAN'T REMEMBER, BUT I THINK THAT'S WHAT HAPPENED.

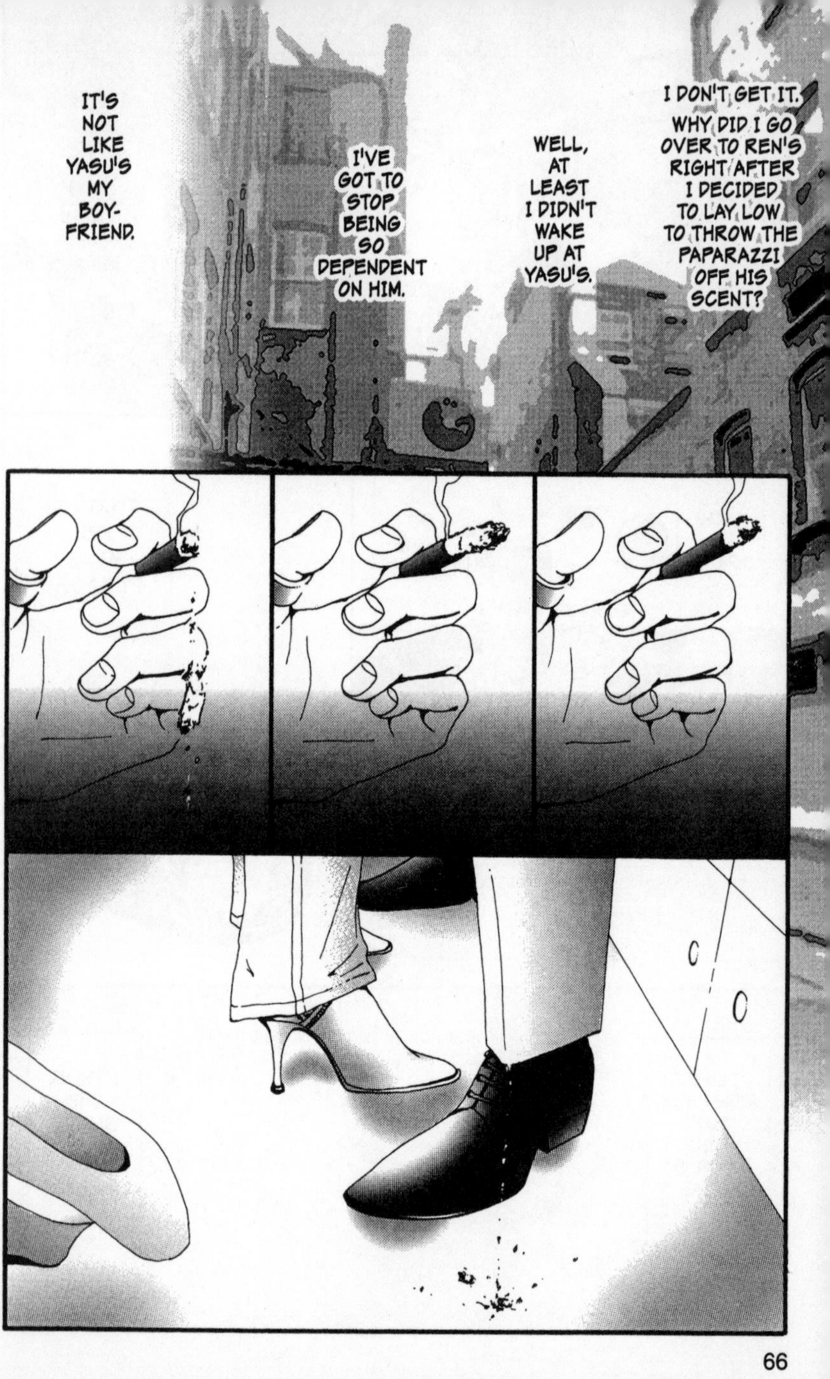
I DON'T GET IT.
WHY DID I GO OVER TO REN'S RIGHT AFTER I DECIDED TO LAY LOW TO THROW THE PAPARAZZI OFF HIS SCENT?
WELL, AT LEAST I DIDN'T WAKE UP AT YASU'S.
I'VE GOT TO STOP BEING SO DEPENDENT ON HIM.
IT'S NOT LIKE YASU'S MY BOY-FRIEND.

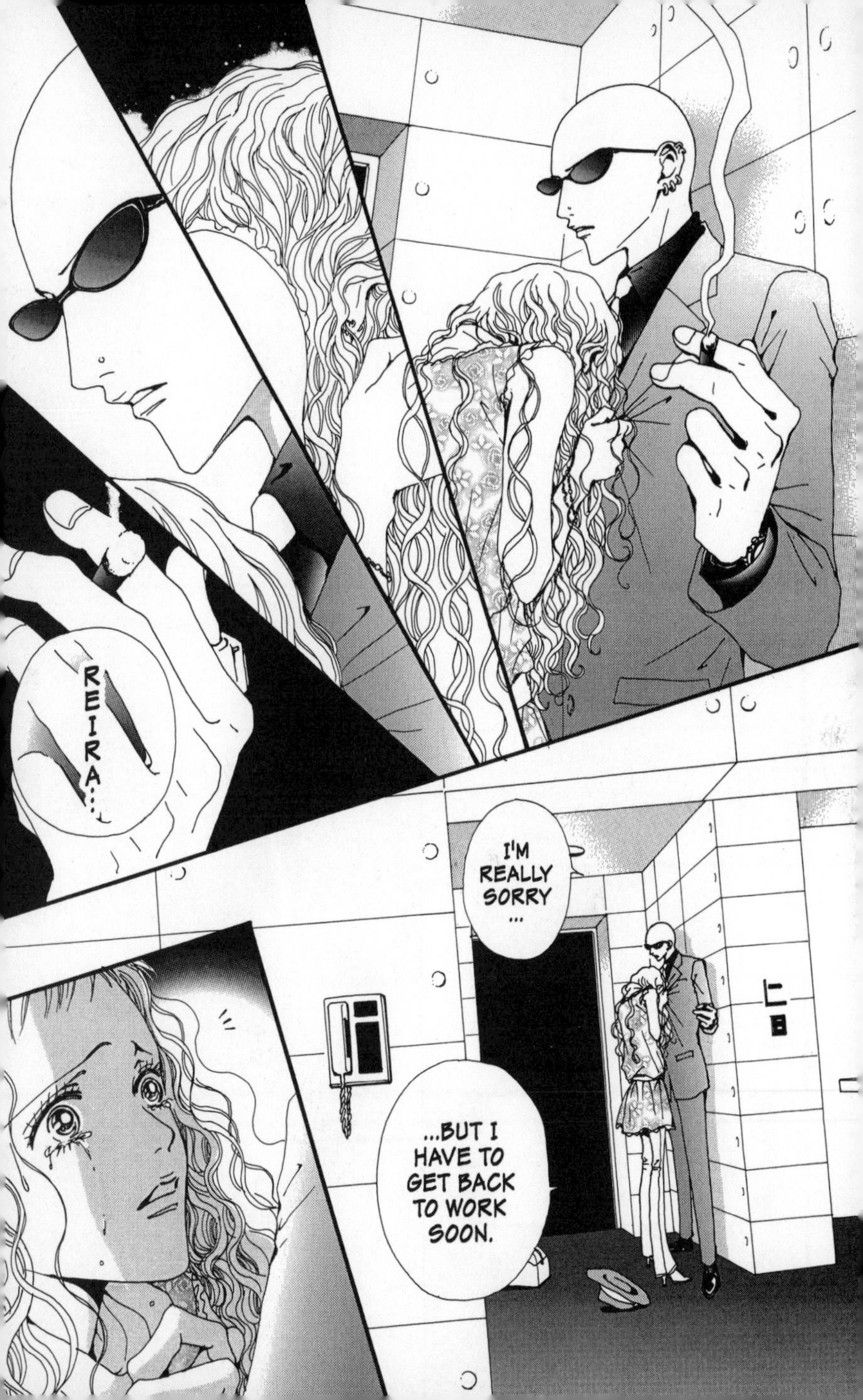
REIRA...
I'M REALLY SORRY...
...BUT I HAVE TO GET BACK TO WORK SOON.

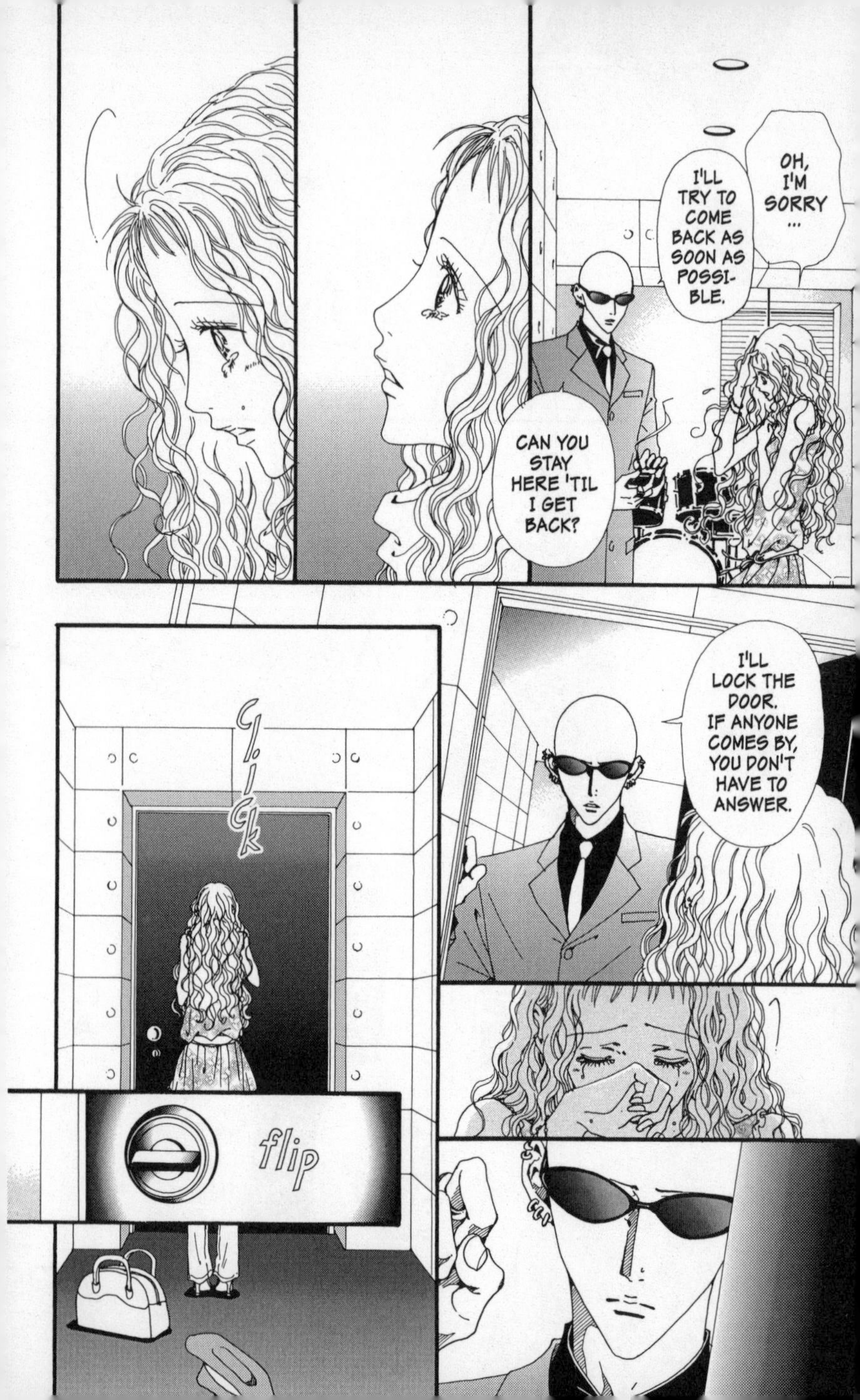
OH, I'M SORRY...
I'LL TRY TO COME BACK AS SOON AS POSSI-BLE.
CAN YOU STAY HERE 'TIL I GET BACK?
I'LL LOCK THE DOOR. IF ANYONE COMES BY, YOU DON'T HAVE TO ANSWER.
Click
flip

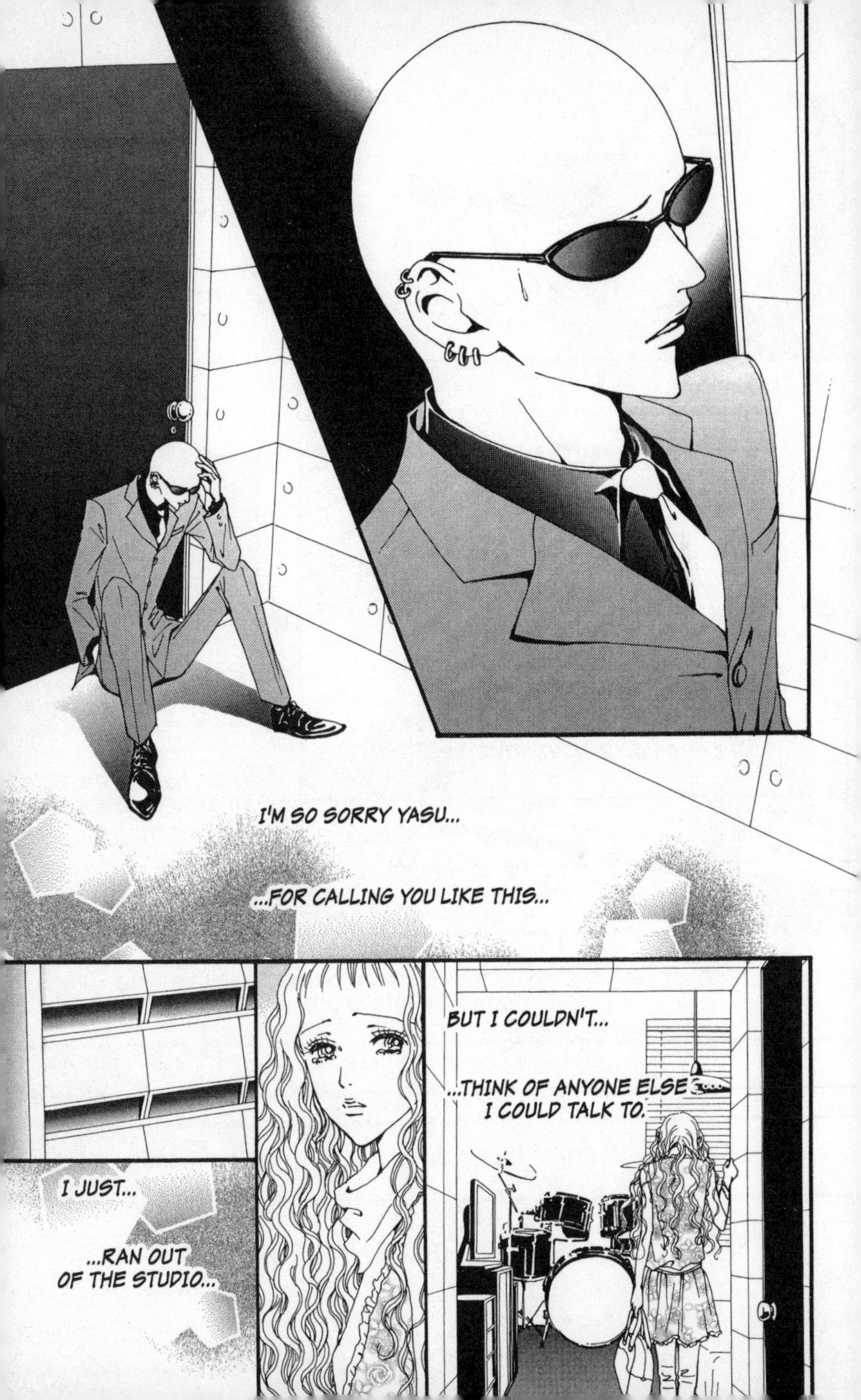
I'M SO SORRY YASU...
...FOR CALLING YOU LIKE THIS...
BUT I COULDN'T...
...THINK OF ANYONE ELSE I COULD TALK TO.
I JUST...
...RAN OUT OF THE STUDIO...

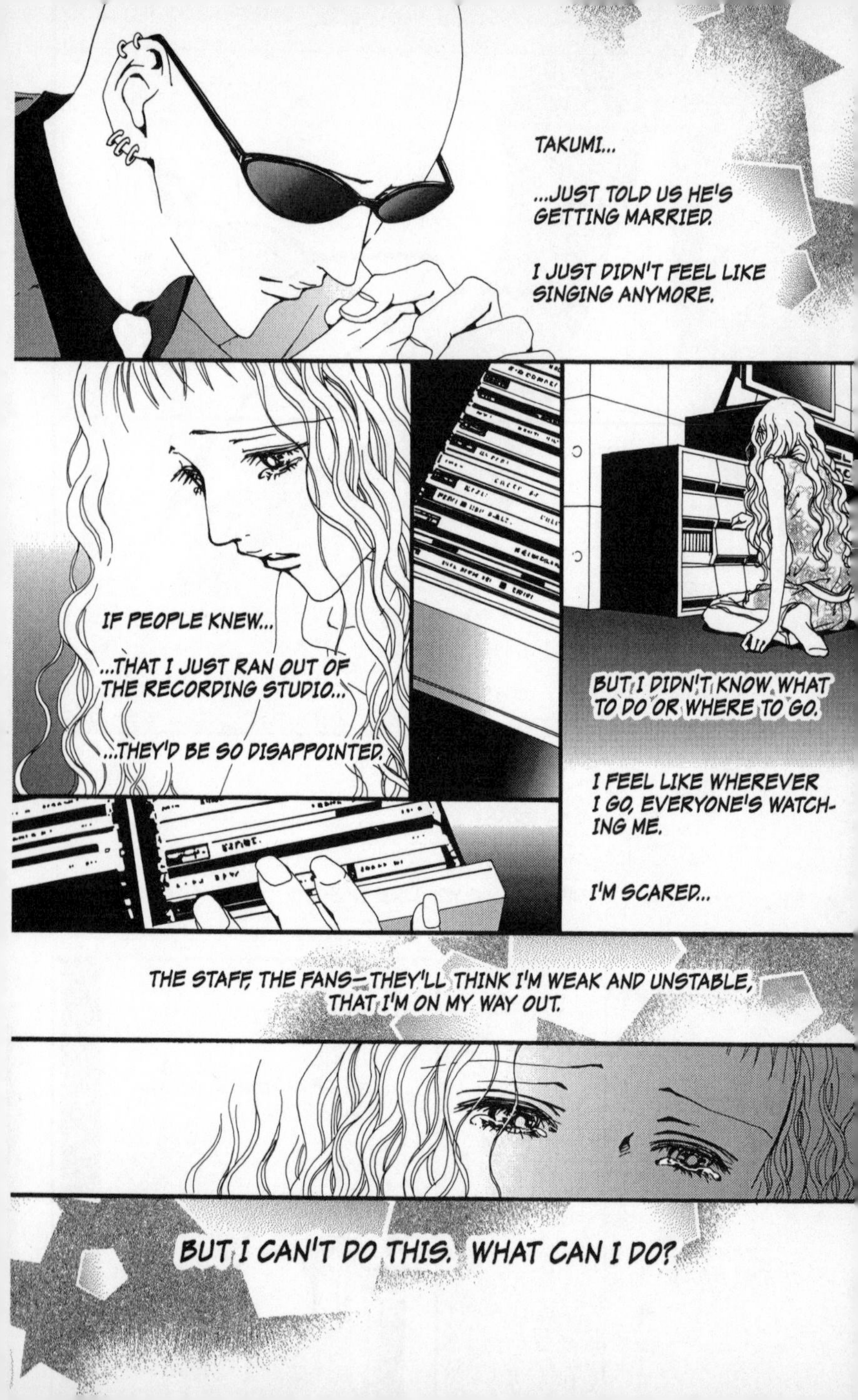

TAKUMI...
...JUST TOLD US HE'S GETTING MARRIED.
I JUST DIDN'T FEEL LIKE SINGING ANYMORE.
BUT I DIDN'T KNOW WHAT TO DO OR WHERE TO GO.
I FEEL LIKE WHEREVER I GO, EVERYONE'S WATCHING ME.
I'M SCARED...
IF PEOPLE KNEW...
...THAT I JUST RAN OUT OF THE RECORDING STUDIO...
...THEY'D BE SO DISAPPOINTED.
THE STAFF, THE FANS—THEY'LL THINK I'M WEAK AND UNSTABLE, THAT I'M ON MY WAY OUT.
BUT I CAN'T DO THIS. WHAT CAN I DO?

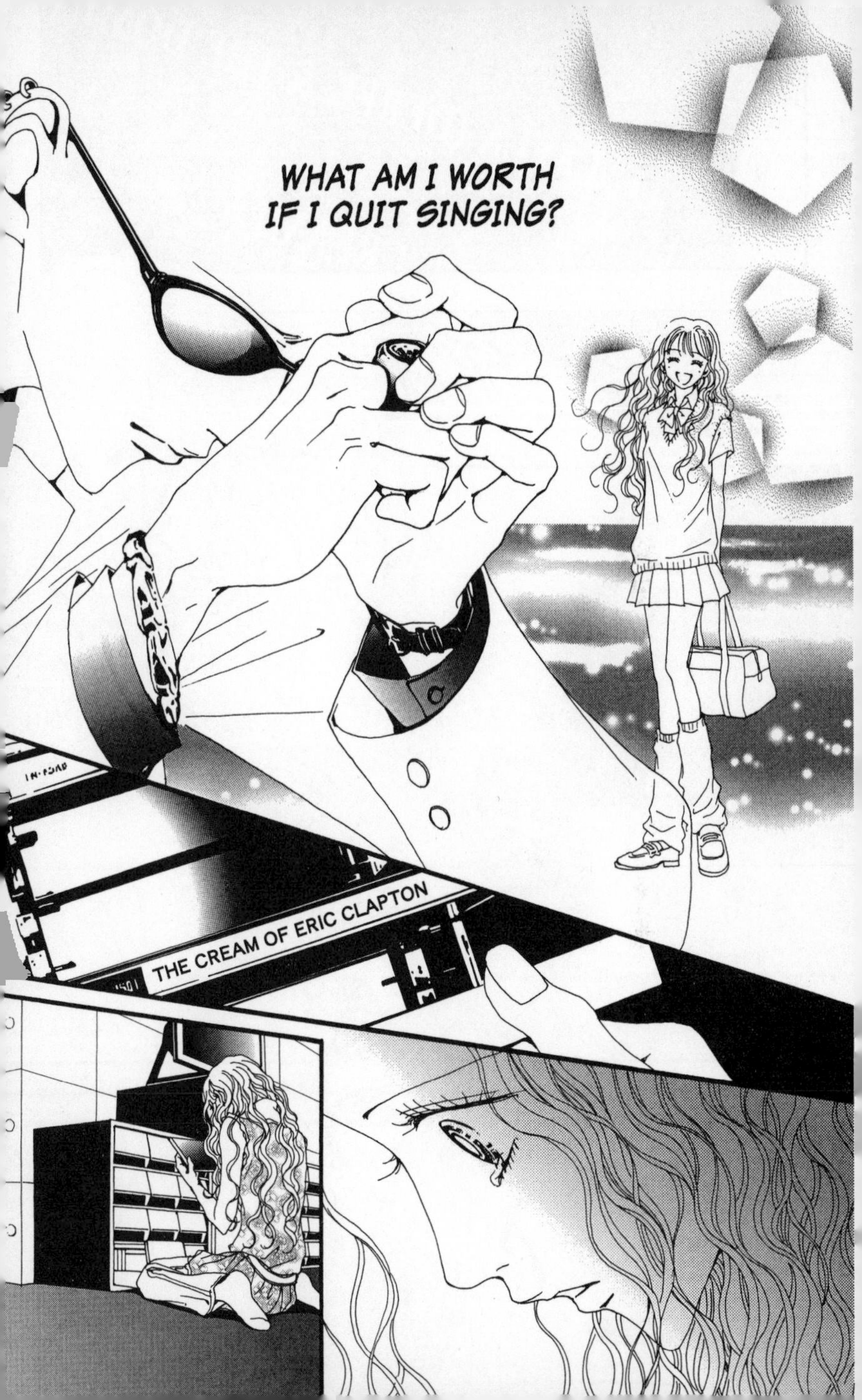
WHAT AM I WORTH
IF I QUIT SINGING?
THE CREAM OF ERIC CLAPTON

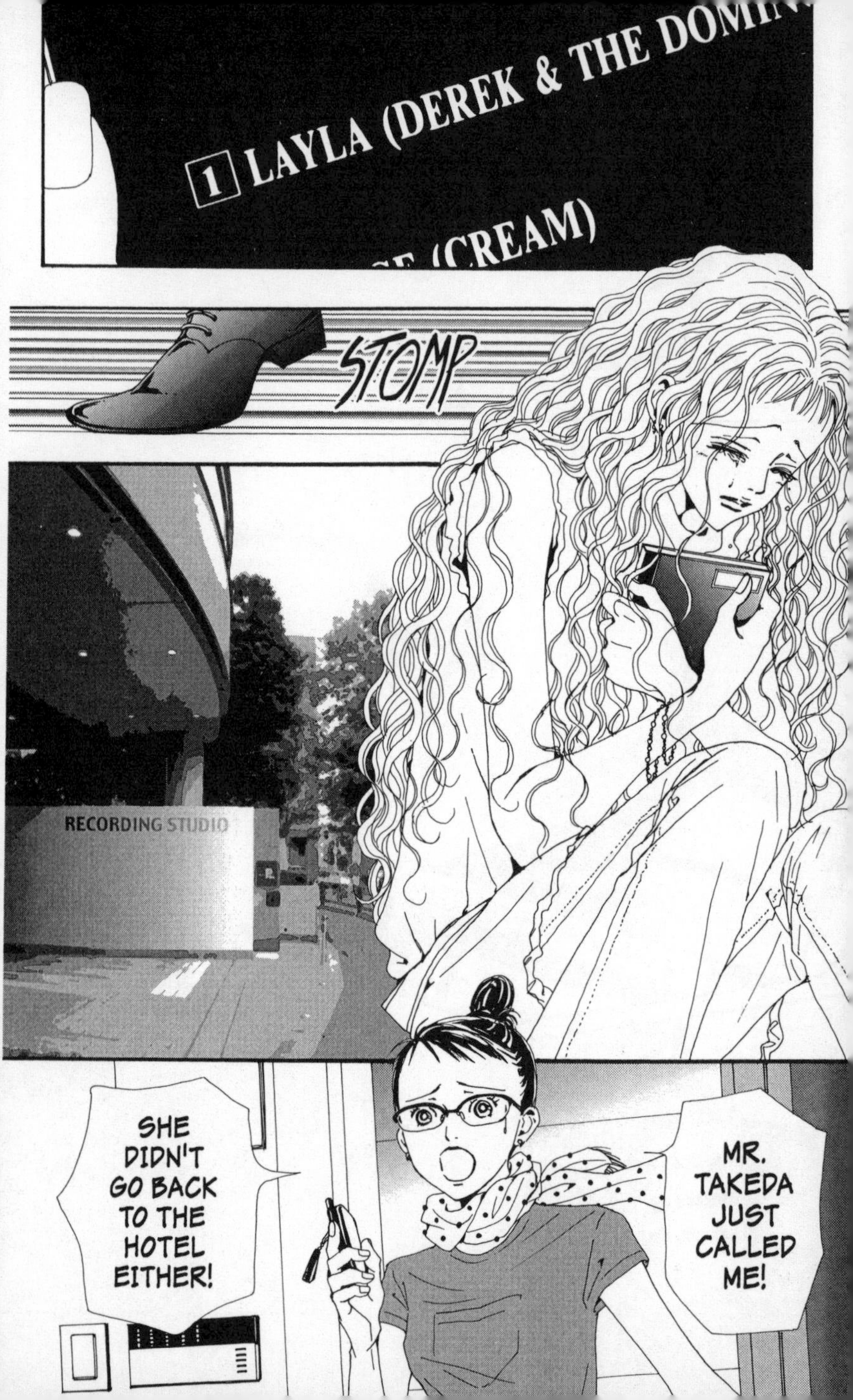
1 LAYLA (DEREK & THE DOMIN
(CREAM)
STOMP
RECORDING STUDIO
MR. TAKEDA JUST CALLED ME!
SHE DIDN'T GO BACK TO THE HOTEL EITHER!

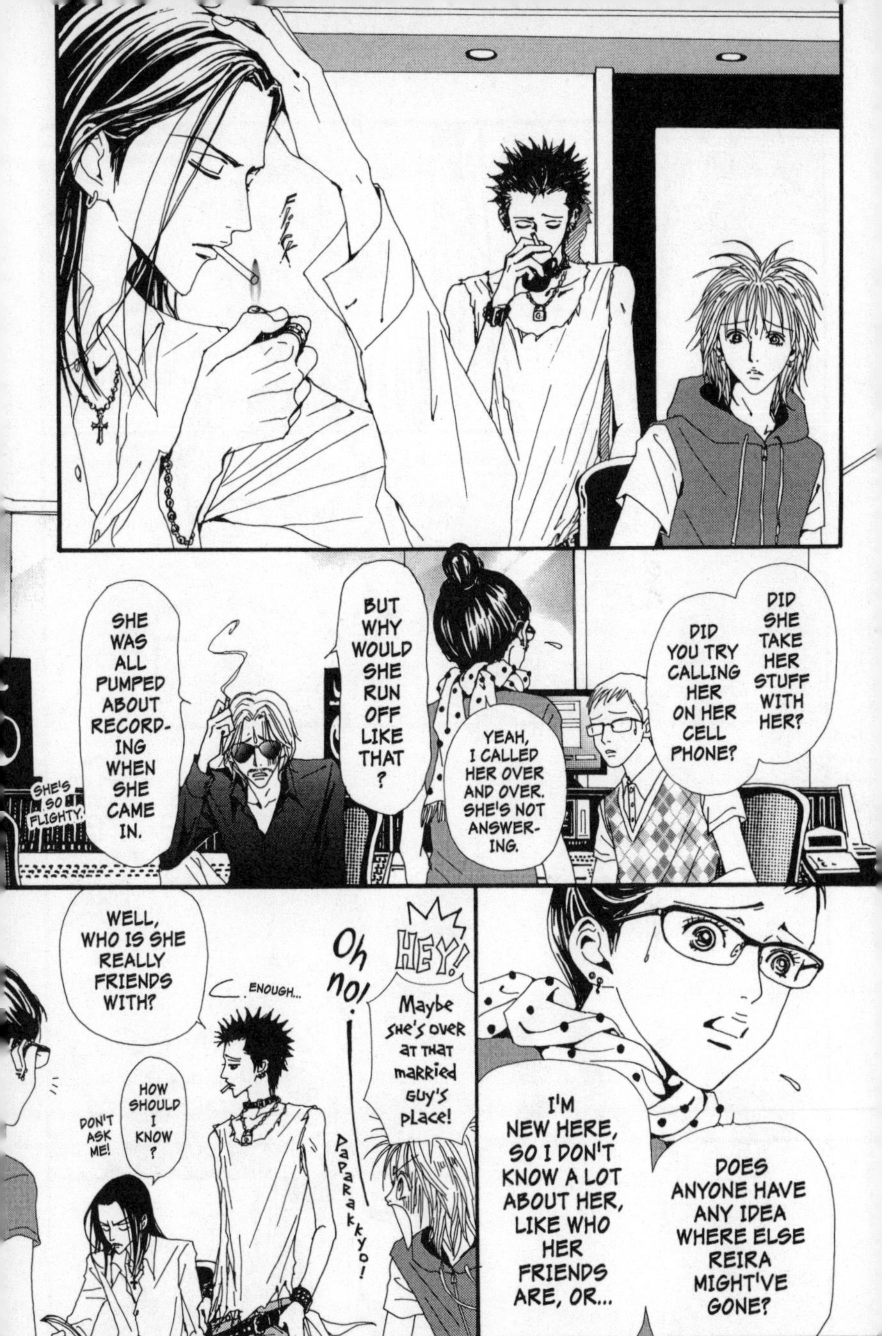
Flick
DID SHE TAKE HER STUFF WITH HER?
DID YOU TRY CALLING HER ON HER CELL PHONE?
YEAH, I CALLED HER OVER AND OVER. SHE'S NOT ANSWER-ING.
BUT WHY WOULD SHE RUN OFF LIKE THAT?
SHE WAS ALL PUMPED ABOUT RECORD-ING WHEN SHE CAME IN.
SHE'S SO FLIGHTY.
DOES ANYONE HAVE ANY IDEA WHERE ELSE REIRA MIGHT'VE GONE?
I'M NEW HERE, SO I DON'T KNOW A LOT ABOUT HER, LIKE WHO HER FRIENDS ARE, OR...
HEY!
Maybe she's over at that married guy's place!
Oh no!
Paparakkyo!
WELL, WHO IS SHE REALLY FRIENDS WITH?
...ENOUGH...
HOW SHOULD I KNOW?
DON'T ASK ME!

YEAH? SO WHAT?

BUT TAKUMI, DIDN'T YOU AND REIRA GROW UP TOGETHER?

SHOULD WE START RECORDING ANYWAY?

TAKUMI, WHAT DO WE DO?

....

HARSH...

YOU'RE REIRA'S ASSISTANT. DON'T WORRY ABOUT US. YOUR JOB IS TO TAKE CARE OF REIRA, ALL RIGHT?

JUST CHILL, MARI.

THAT PRINCESS NEEDS A LOT OF BABY-SITTING.

HOW CAN WE CONCENTRATE WHEN EVERYONE AROUND HERE'S FREAKING OUT?

WE CAN'T DO ANYTHING.

OH, I'M SORRY!

YEAH.

RIGHT.

twitch twitch twitch

74

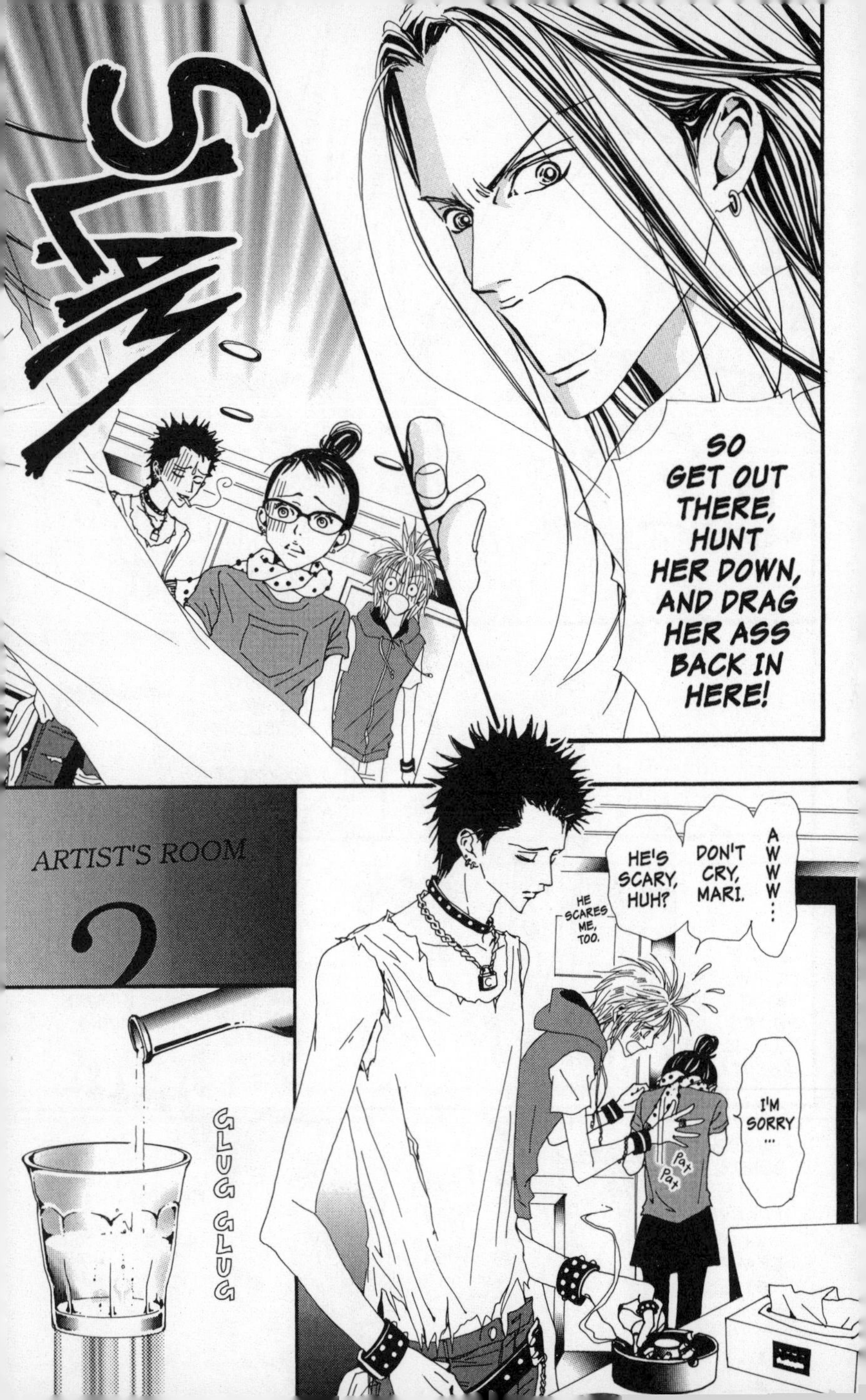
SLAM
SO GET OUT THERE, HUNT HER DOWN, AND DRAG HER ASS BACK IN HERE!
ARTIST'S ROOM 2
AWWW...
DON'T CRY, MARI.
HE'S SCARY, HUH?
HE SCARES ME, TOO.
I'M SORRY...
Pat Pat
GLUG GLUG

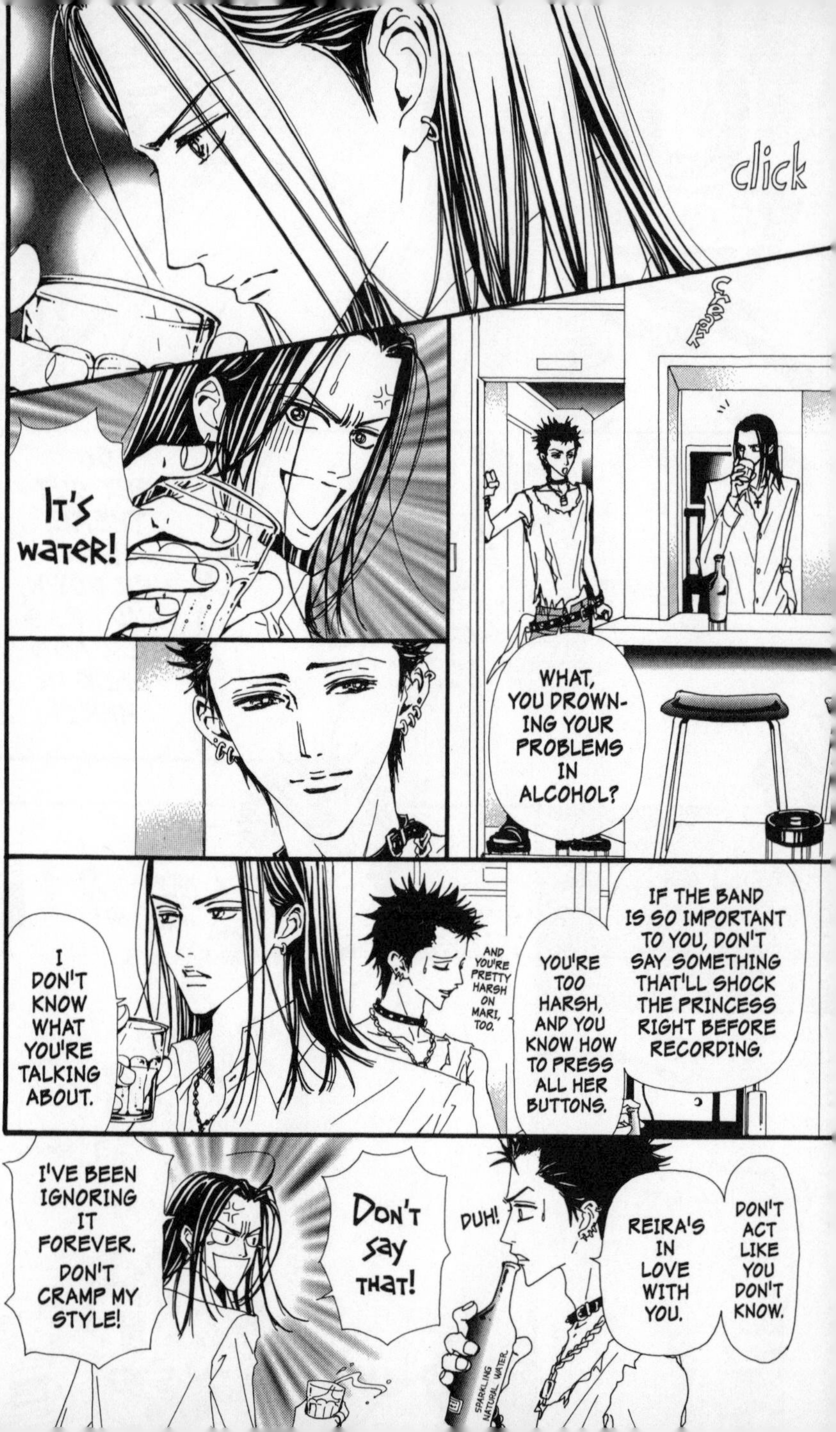
click
Creak
WHAT, YOU DROWNING YOUR PROBLEMS IN ALCOHOL?
It's water!
IF THE BAND IS SO IMPORTANT TO YOU, DON'T SAY SOMETHING THAT'LL SHOCK THE PRINCESS RIGHT BEFORE RECORDING.
YOU'RE TOO HARSH, AND YOU KNOW HOW TO PRESS ALL HER BUTTONS.
AND YOU'RE PRETTY HARSH ON MARI, TOO.
I DON'T KNOW WHAT YOU'RE TALKING ABOUT.
DON'T ACT LIKE YOU DON'T KNOW.
REIRA'S IN LOVE WITH YOU.
DUH!
SPARKLING NATURAL WATER
Don't say that!
I'VE BEEN IGNORING IT FOREVER. DON'T CRAMP MY STYLE!

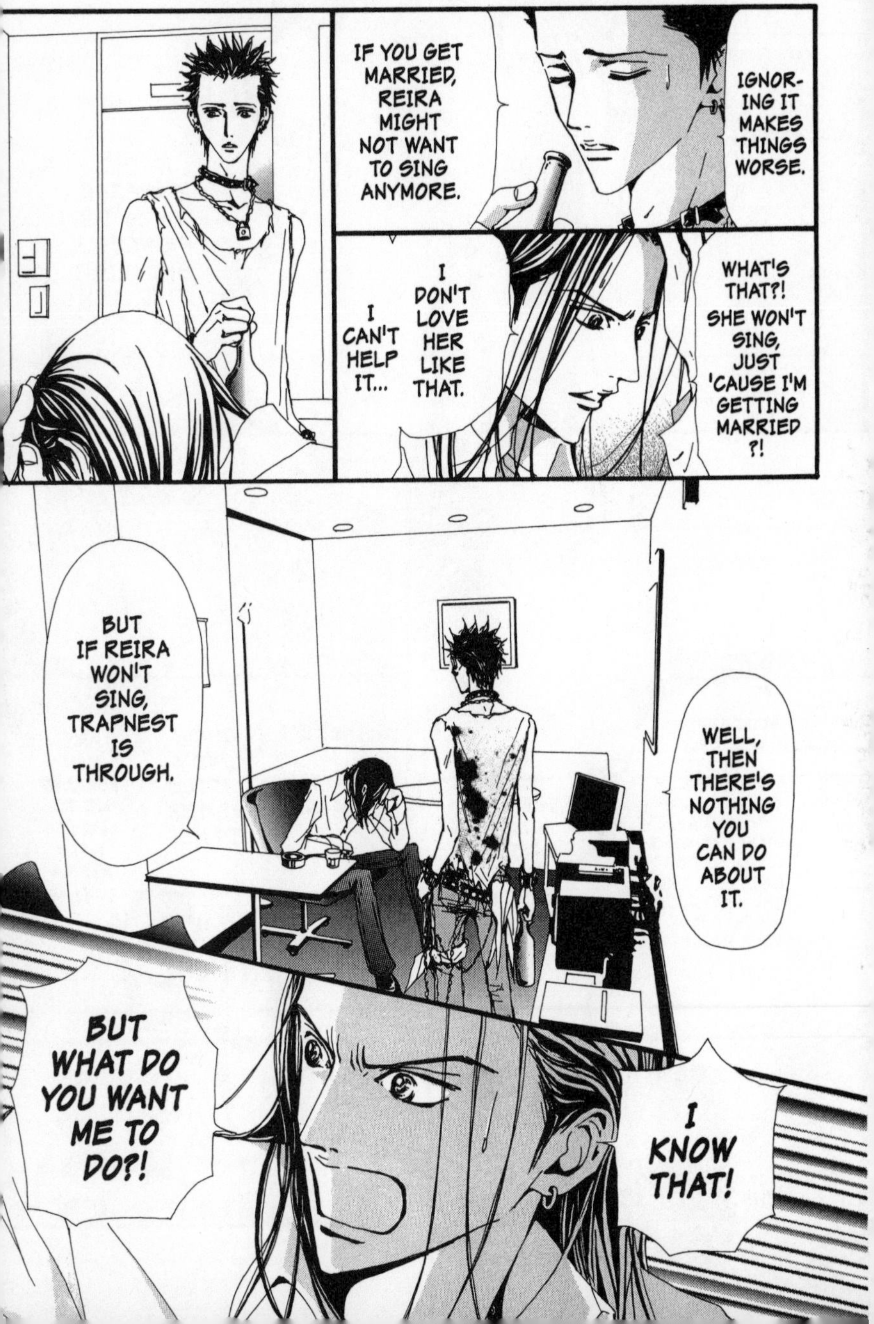
IGNORING IT MAKES THINGS WORSE.
IF YOU GET MARRIED, REIRA MIGHT NOT WANT TO SING ANYMORE.
WHAT'S THAT?! SHE WON'T SING, JUST 'CAUSE I'M GETTING MARRIED?!
I DON'T LOVE HER LIKE THAT.
I CAN'T HELP IT...
WELL, THEN THERE'S NOTHING YOU CAN DO ABOUT IT.
BUT IF REIRA WON'T SING, TRAPNEST IS THROUGH.
I KNOW THAT!
BUT WHAT DO YOU WANT ME TO DO?!

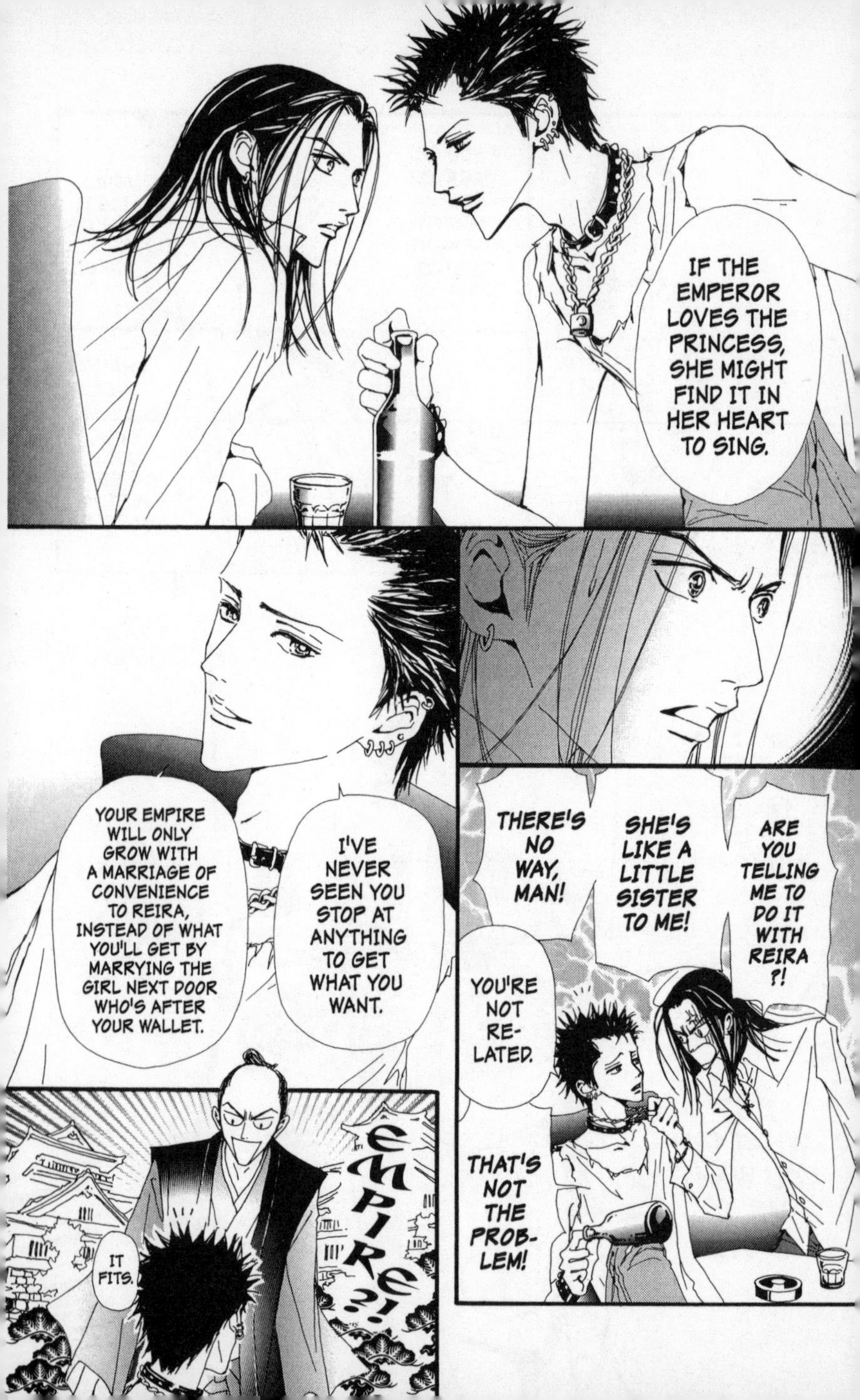
IF THE EMPEROR LOVES THE PRINCESS, SHE MIGHT FIND IT IN HER HEART TO SING.
I'VE NEVER SEEN YOU STOP AT ANYTHING TO GET WHAT YOU WANT.
YOUR EMPIRE WILL ONLY GROW WITH A MARRIAGE OF CONVENIENCE TO REIRA, INSTEAD OF WHAT YOU'LL GET BY MARRYING THE GIRL NEXT DOOR WHO'S AFTER YOUR WALLET.
EMPIRE?!
IT FITS.
ARE YOU TELLING ME TO DO IT WITH REIRA?!
SHE'S LIKE A LITTLE SISTER TO ME!
THERE'S NO WAY, MAN!
YOU'RE NOT RE-LATED.
THAT'S NOT THE PROB-LEM!

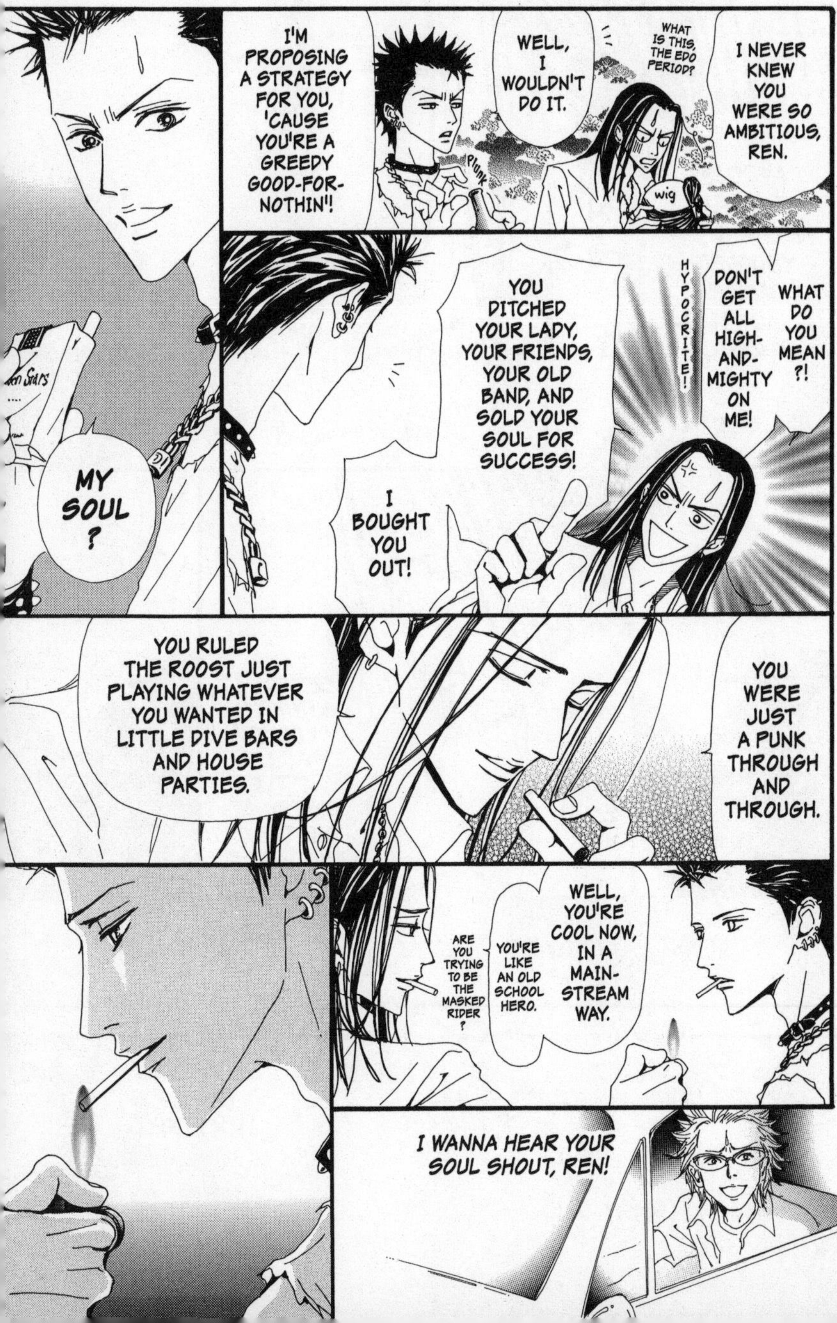
I NEVER KNEW YOU WERE SO AMBITIOUS, REN.
WHAT IS THIS, THE EDO PERIOD?
wig
WELL, I WOULDN'T DO IT.
Plunk
I'M PROPOSING A STRATEGY FOR YOU, 'CAUSE YOU'RE A GREEDY GOOD-FOR-NOTHIN'!
WHAT DO YOU MEAN?!
DON'T GET ALL HIGH-AND-MIGHTY ON ME!
HYPOCRITE!
YOU DITCHED YOUR LADY, YOUR FRIENDS, YOUR OLD BAND, AND SOLD YOUR SOUL FOR SUCCESS!
I BOUGHT YOU OUT!
MY SOUL?
YOU WERE JUST A PUNK THROUGH AND THROUGH.
YOU RULED THE ROOST JUST PLAYING WHATEVER YOU WANTED IN LITTLE DIVE BARS AND HOUSE PARTIES.
WELL, YOU'RE COOL NOW, IN A MAIN-STREAM WAY.
YOU'RE LIKE AN OLD SCHOOL HERO.
ARE YOU TRYING TO BE THE MASKED RIDER?
I WANNA HEAR YOUR SOUL SHOUT, REN!

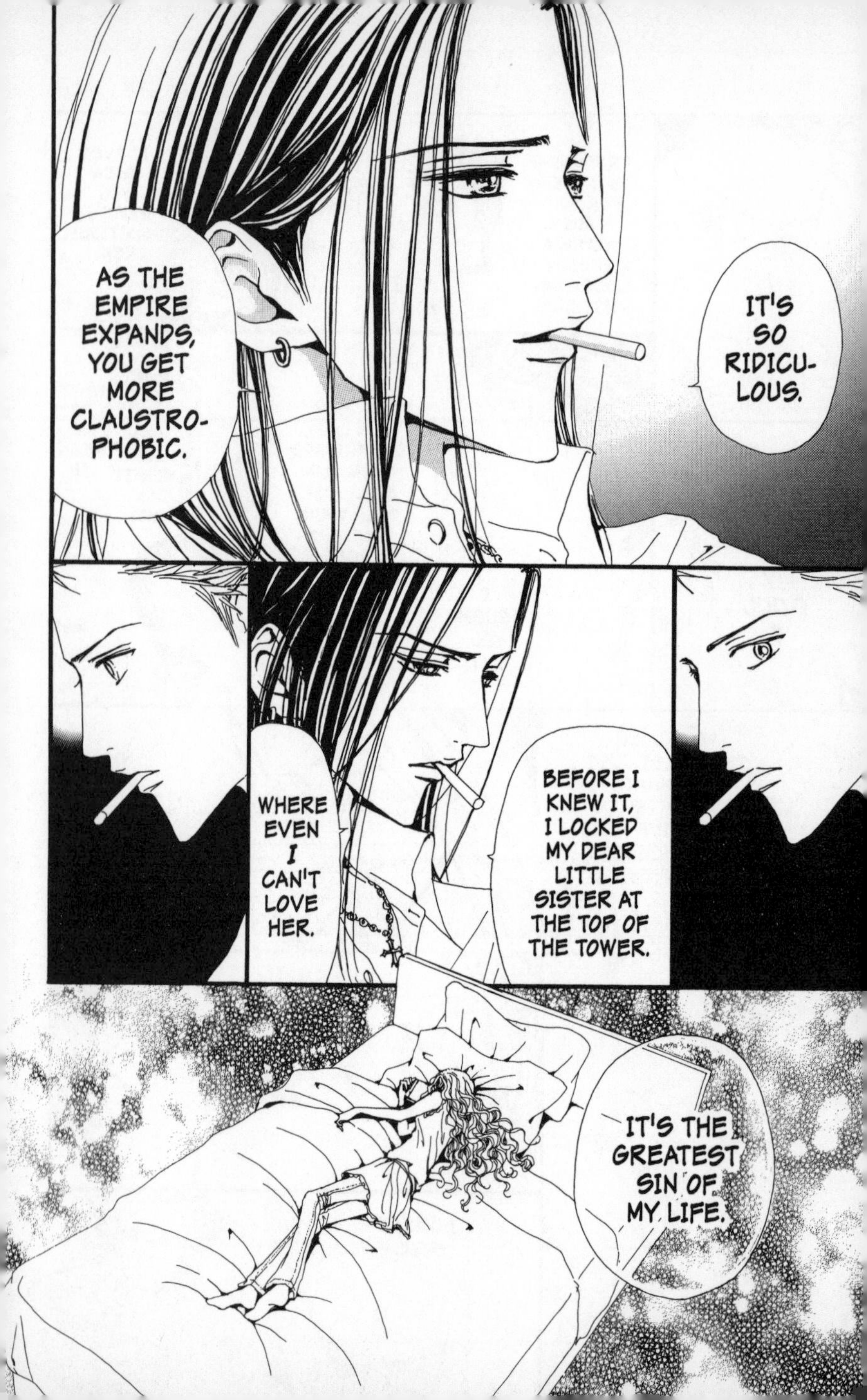
IT'S SO RIDICULOUS.
AS THE EMPIRE EXPANDS, YOU GET MORE CLAUSTROPHOBIC.
BEFORE I KNEW IT, I LOCKED MY DEAR LITTLE SISTER AT THE TOP OF THE TOWER.
WHERE EVEN *I* CAN'T LOVE HER.
IT'S THE GREATEST SIN OF MY LIFE.

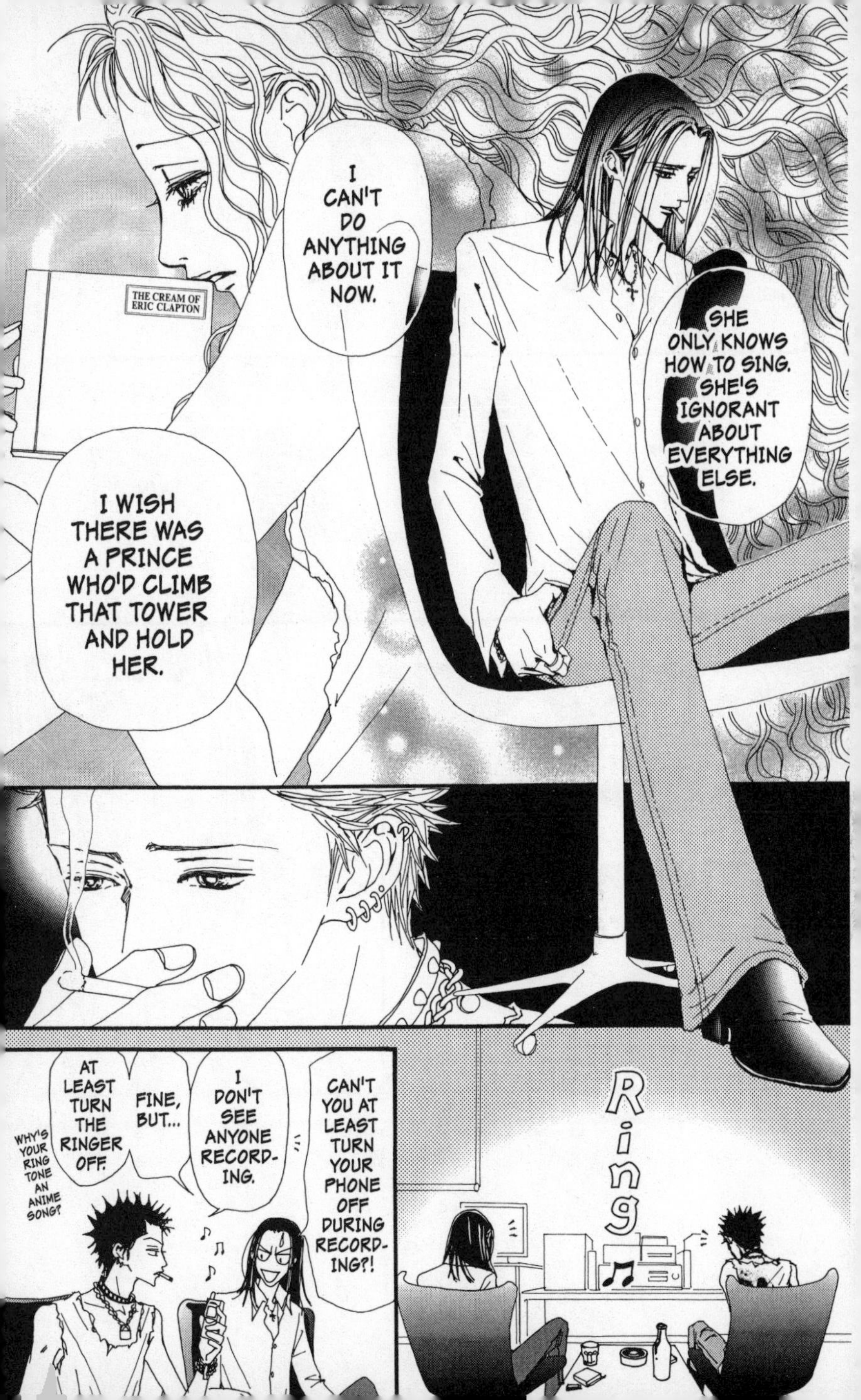
SHE ONLY KNOWS HOW TO SING. SHE'S IGNORANT ABOUT EVERYTHING ELSE.
I CAN'T DO ANYTHING ABOUT IT NOW.
THE CREAM OF ERIC CLAPTON
I WISH THERE WAS A PRINCE WHO'D CLIMB THAT TOWER AND HOLD HER.
Ring
CAN'T YOU AT LEAST TURN YOUR PHONE OFF DURING RECORDING?!
I DON'T SEE ANYONE RECORDING.
FINE, BUT...
AT LEAST TURN THE RINGER OFF.
WHY'S YOUR RING TONE AN ANIME SONG?

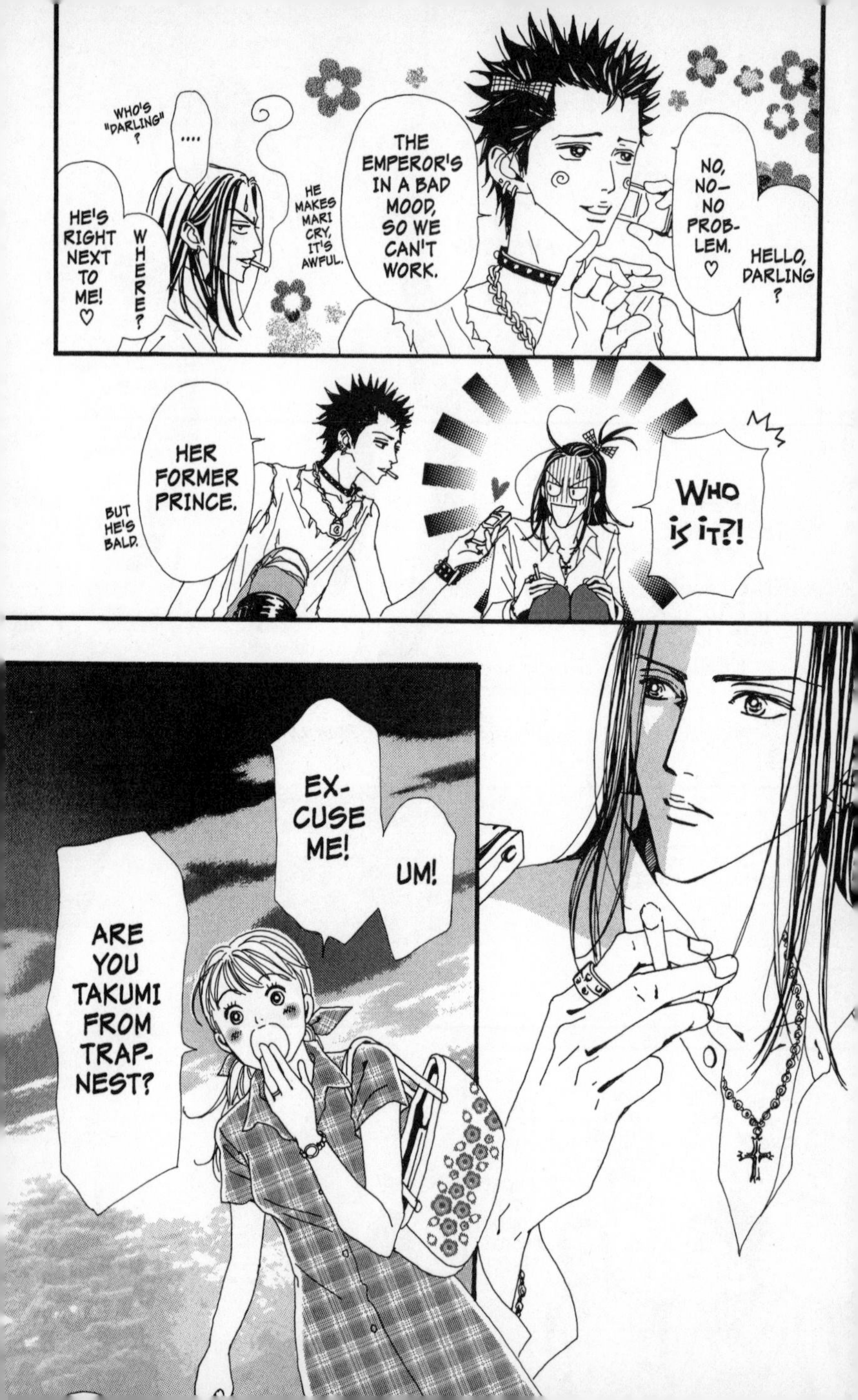
HELLO, DARLING?
NO, NO— NO PROB-LEM. ♡
THE EMPEROR'S IN A BAD MOOD, SO WE CAN'T WORK.
HE MAKES MARI CRY, IT'S AWFUL.
....
WHO'S "DARLING"?
WHERE?
HE'S RIGHT NEXT TO ME! ♡
WHO IS IT?!
HER FORMER PRINCE.
BUT HE'S BALD.
EX-CUSE ME!
UM!
ARE YOU TAKUMI FROM TRAP-NEST?

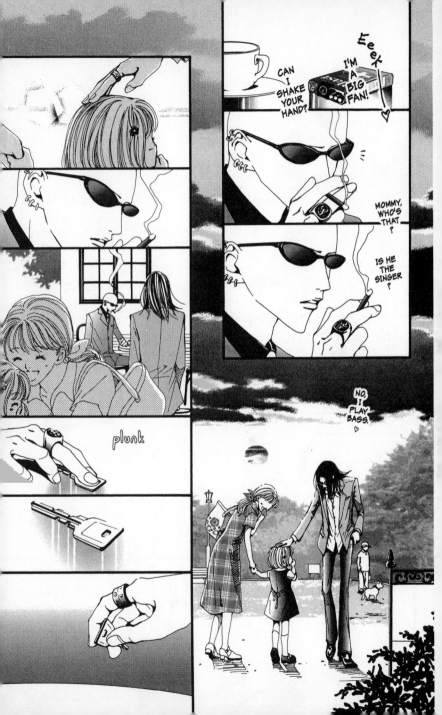

CAN I SHAKE YOUR HAND?

I'M A BIG FAN!

Eeek

MOMMY, WHO'S THAT?

IS HE THE SINGER?

plunk

NO, I PLAY BASS.

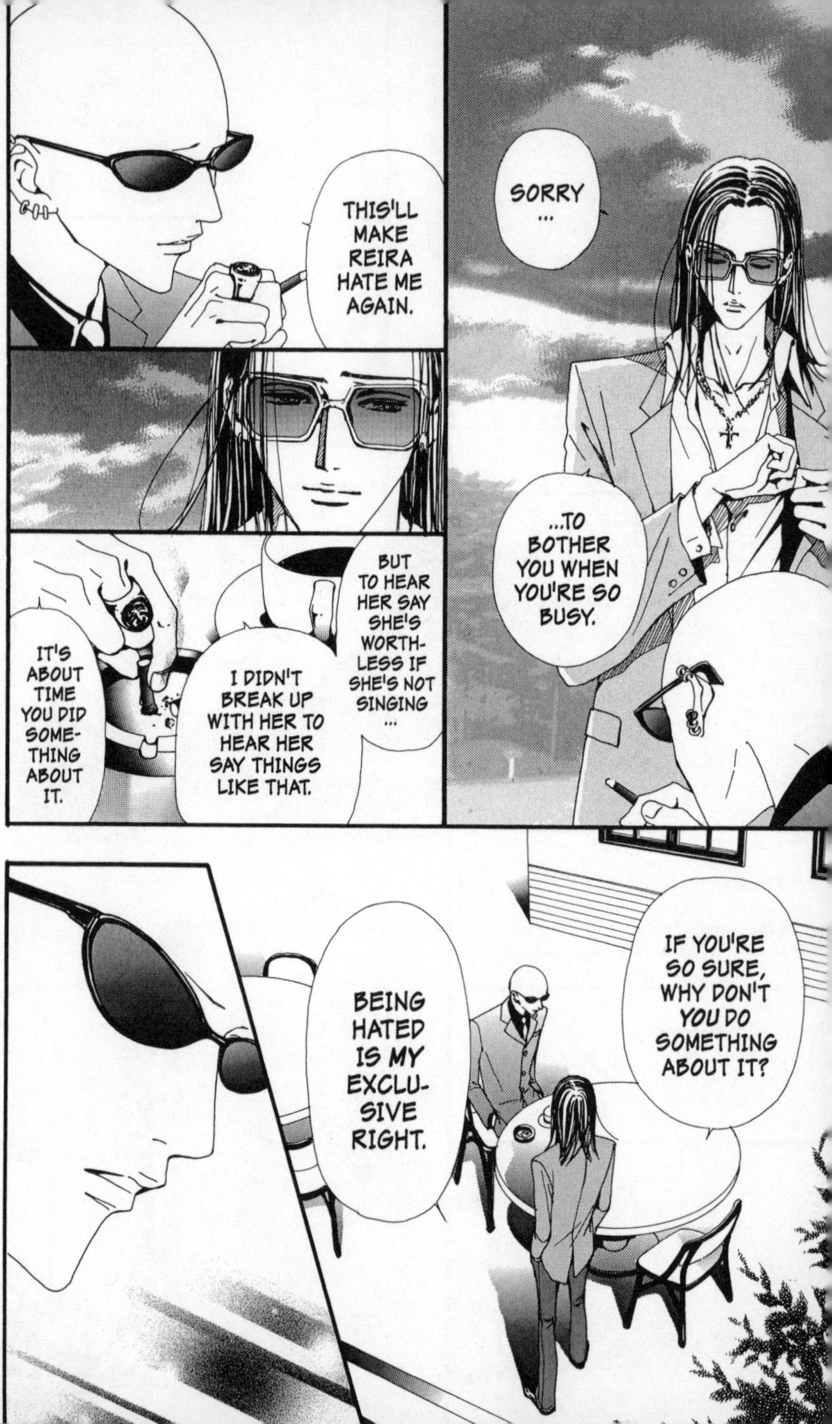
SORRY ...
...TO BOTHER YOU WHEN YOU'RE SO BUSY.
THIS'LL MAKE REIRA HATE ME AGAIN.
BUT TO HEAR HER SAY SHE'S WORTH-LESS IF SHE'S NOT SINGING ...
I DIDN'T BREAK UP WITH HER TO HEAR HER SAY THINGS LIKE THAT.
IT'S ABOUT TIME YOU DID SOME-THING ABOUT IT.
IF YOU'RE SO SURE, WHY DON'T YOU DO SOMETHING ABOUT IT?
BEING HATED IS MY EXCLU-SIVE RIGHT.

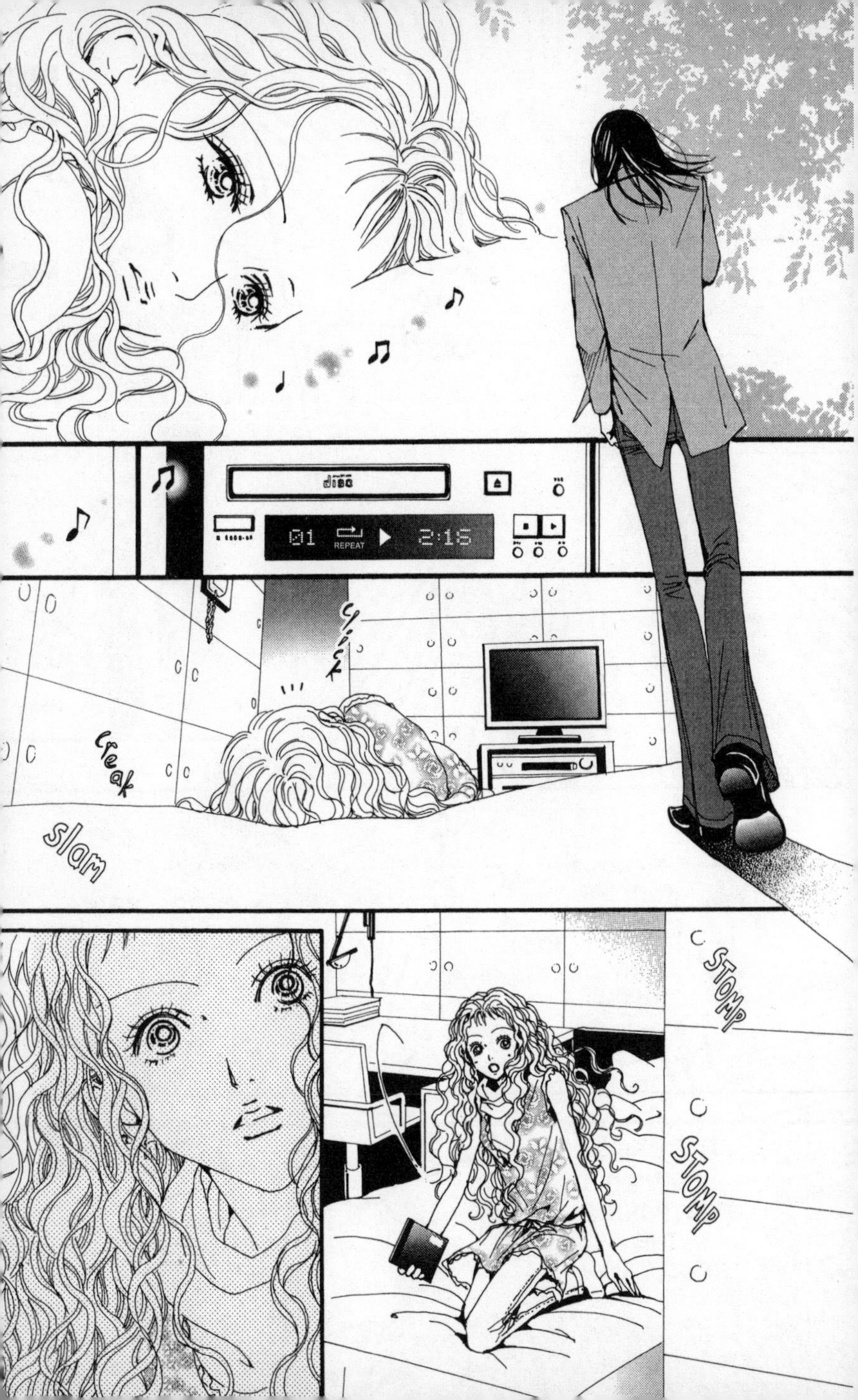
disc
01
REPEAT
2:16
clack
creak
slam
STOMP
STOMP

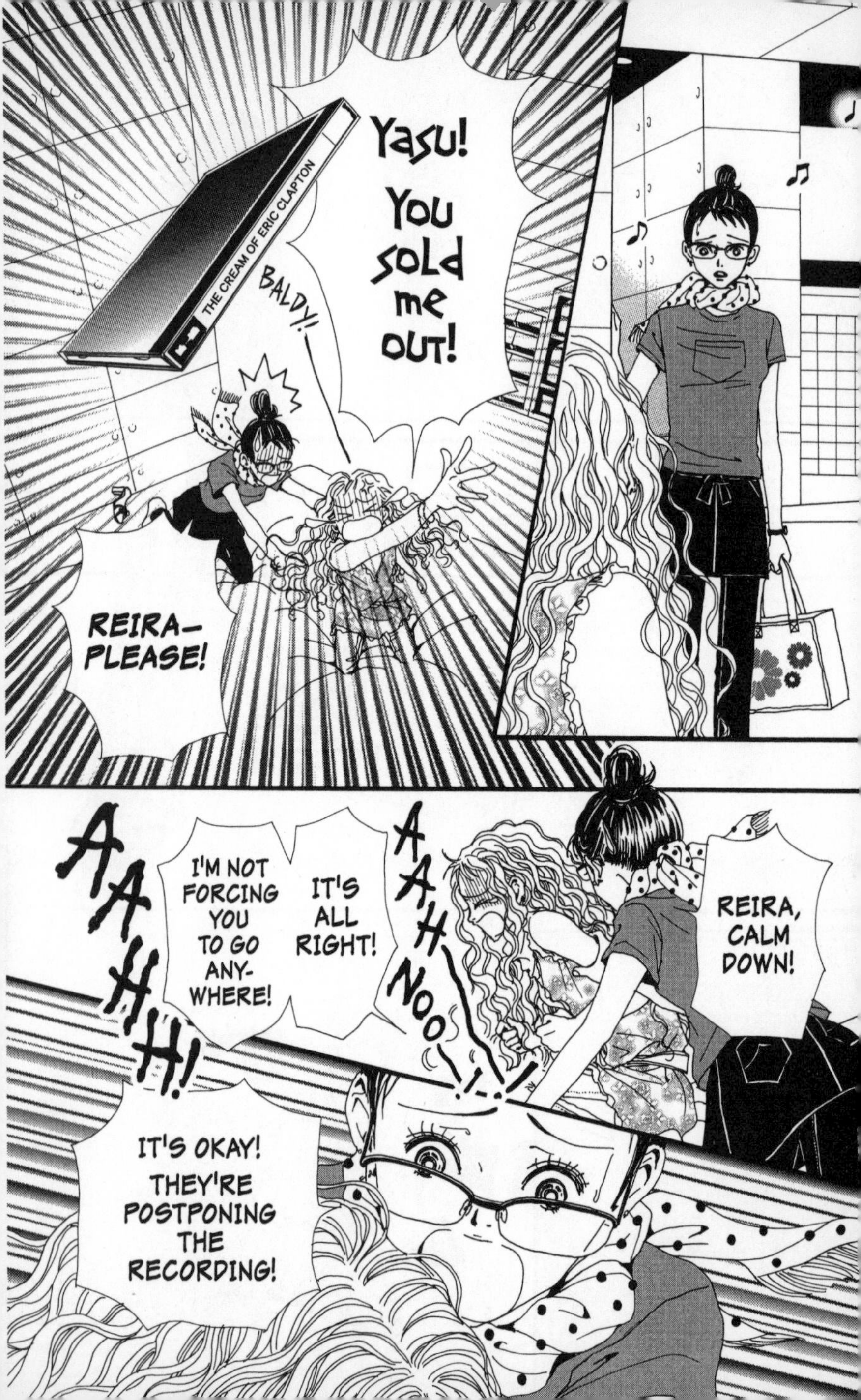
THE CREAM OF ERIC CLAPTON
YASU! YOU SOLD ME OUT!
BALDY!!
REIRA— PLEASE!
REIRA, CALM DOWN!
AAH NOO!!
IT'S ALL RIGHT!
I'M NOT FORCING YOU TO GO ANYWHERE!
AAAHHH!
IT'S OKAY! THEY'RE POSTPONING THE RECORDING!

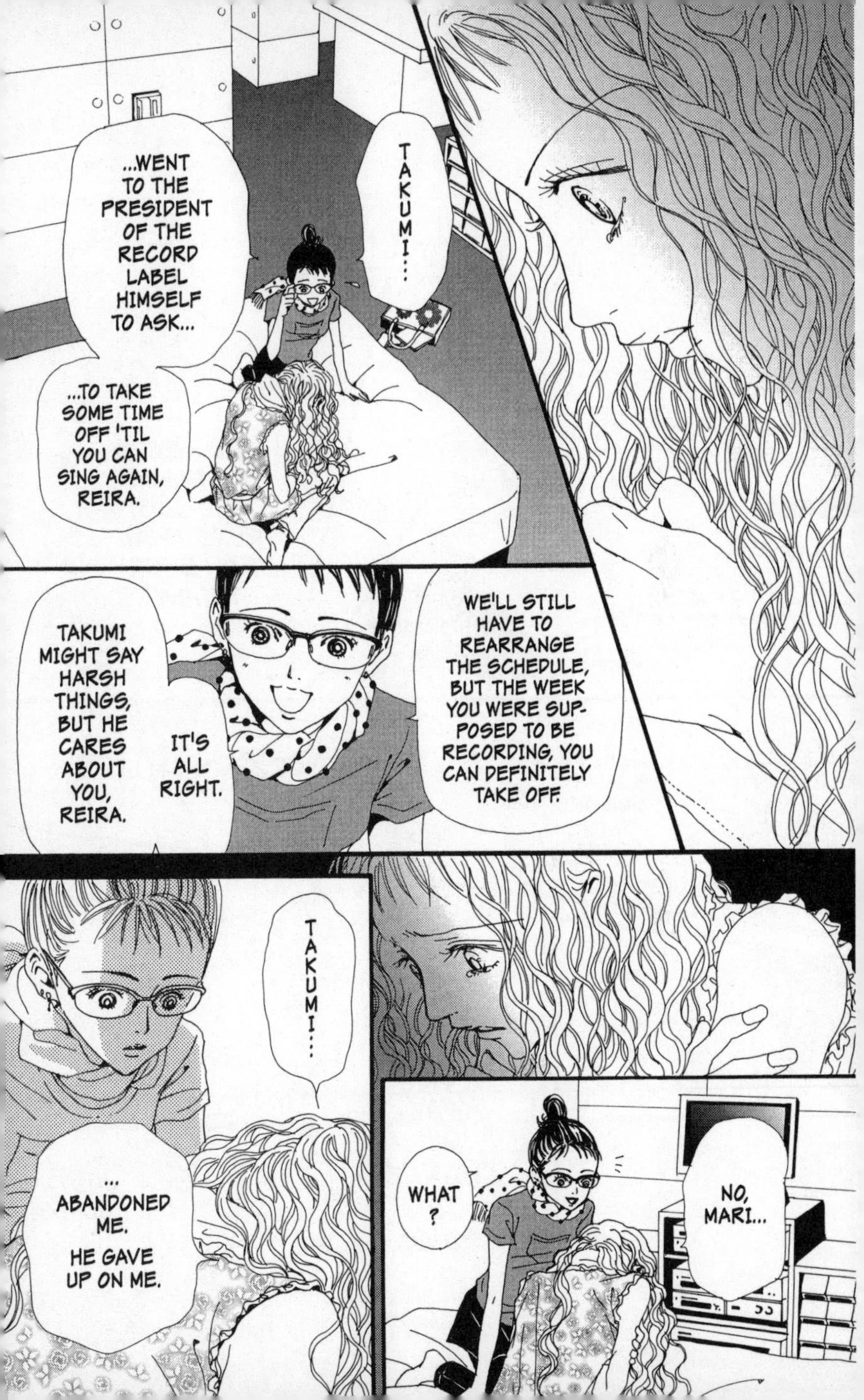
TAKUMI...
...WENT TO THE PRESIDENT OF THE RECORD LABEL HIMSELF TO ASK...
...TO TAKE SOME TIME OFF 'TIL YOU CAN SING AGAIN, REIRA.
WE'LL STILL HAVE TO REARRANGE THE SCHEDULE, BUT THE WEEK YOU WERE SUP-POSED TO BE RECORDING, YOU CAN DEFINITELY TAKE OFF.
IT'S ALL RIGHT.
TAKUMI MIGHT SAY HARSH THINGS, BUT HE CARES ABOUT YOU, REIRA.
NO, MARI...
WHAT?
TAKUMI...
...ABANDONED ME.
HE GAVE UP ON ME.

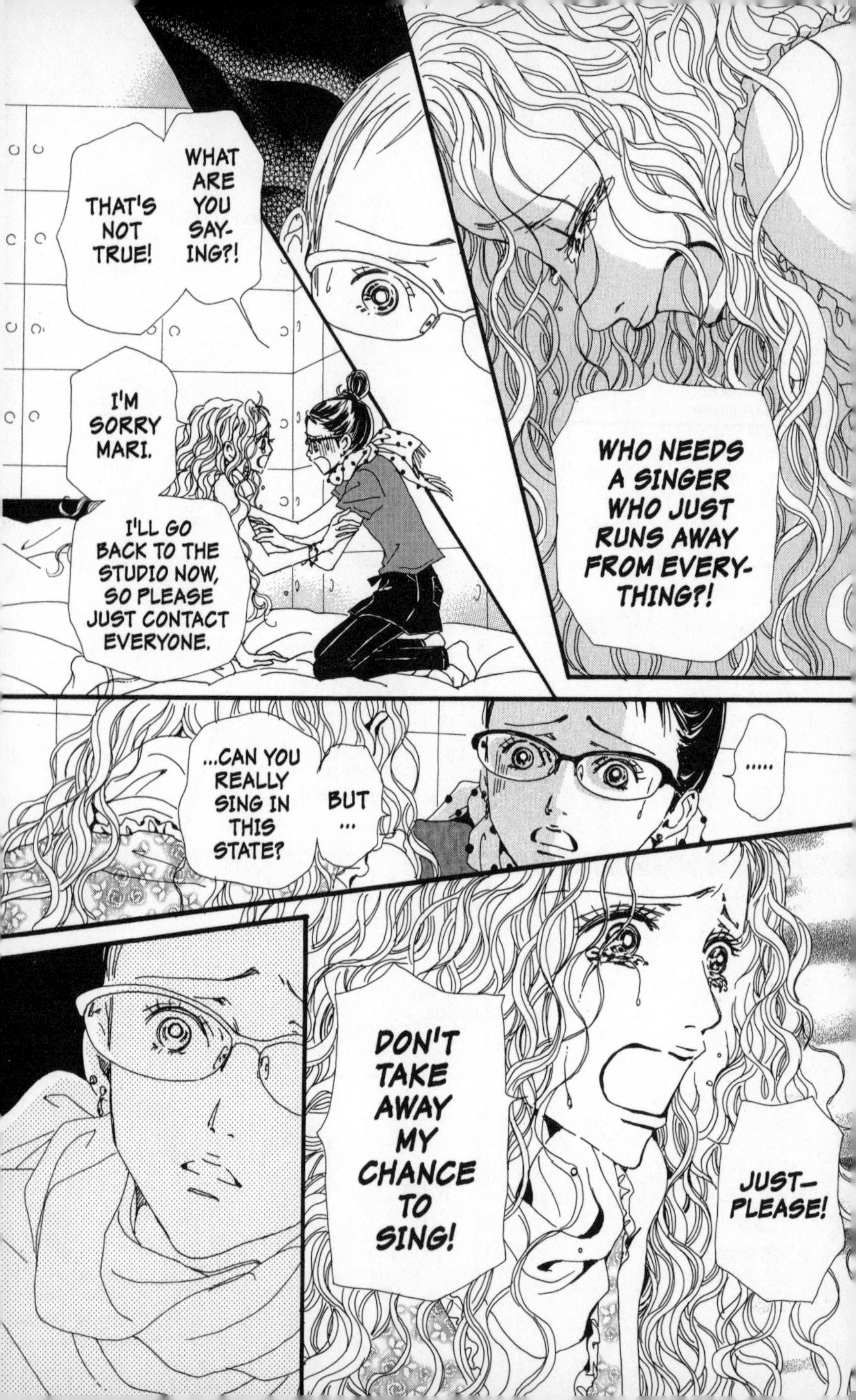
WHO NEEDS A SINGER WHO JUST RUNS AWAY FROM EVERY-THING?!
WHAT ARE YOU SAY-ING?!
THAT'S NOT TRUE!
I'M SORRY MARI.
I'LL GO BACK TO THE STUDIO NOW, SO PLEASE JUST CONTACT EVERYONE.
.....
BUT ...
...CAN YOU REALLY SING IN THIS STATE?
JUST— PLEASE!
DON'T TAKE AWAY MY CHANCE TO SING!

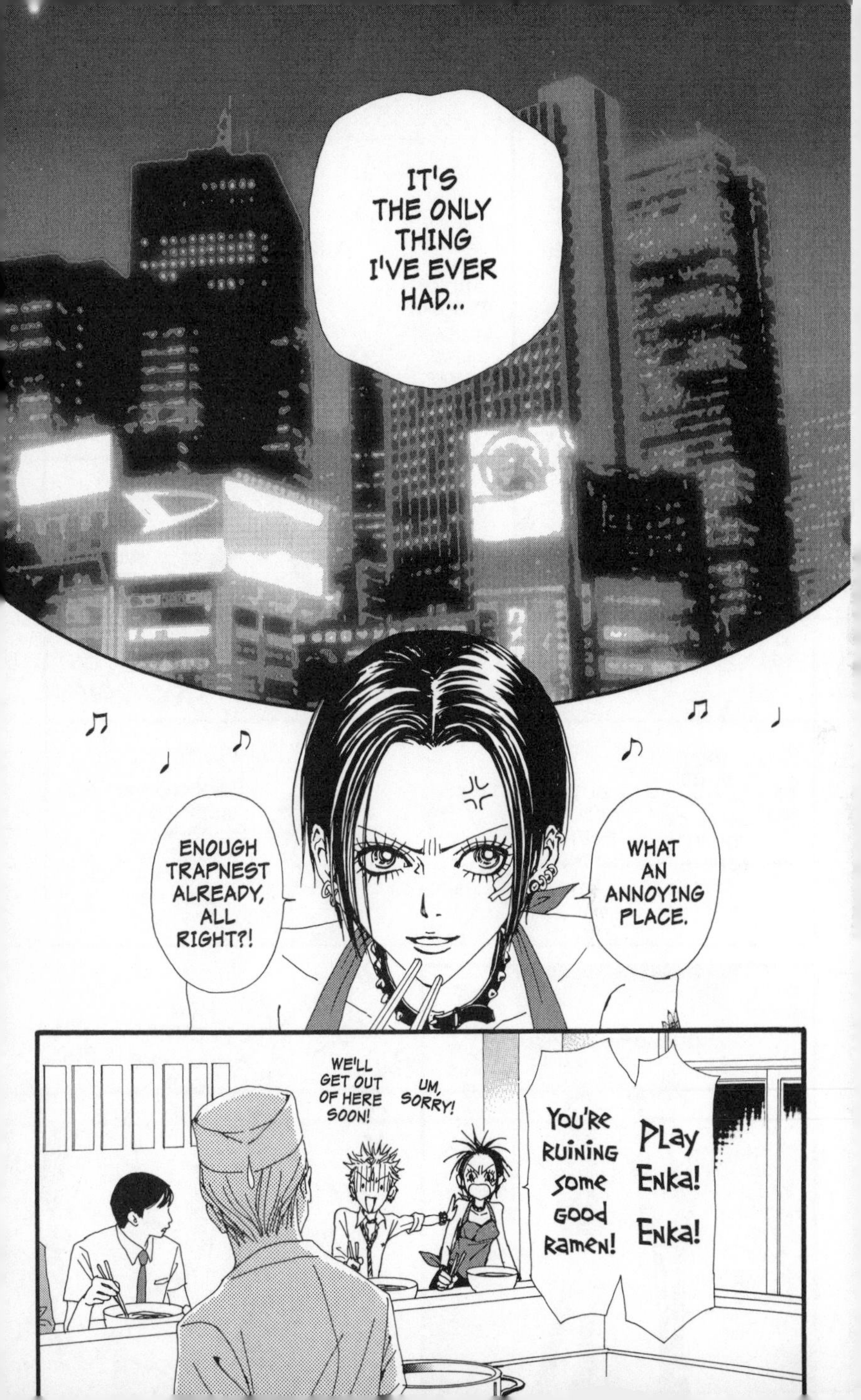
IT'S THE ONLY THING I'VE EVER HAD...
WHAT AN ANNOYING PLACE.
ENOUGH TRAPNEST ALREADY, ALL RIGHT?!
Play Enka! Enka!
You're ruining some good ramen!
UM, SORRY!
WE'LL GET OUT OF HERE SOON!

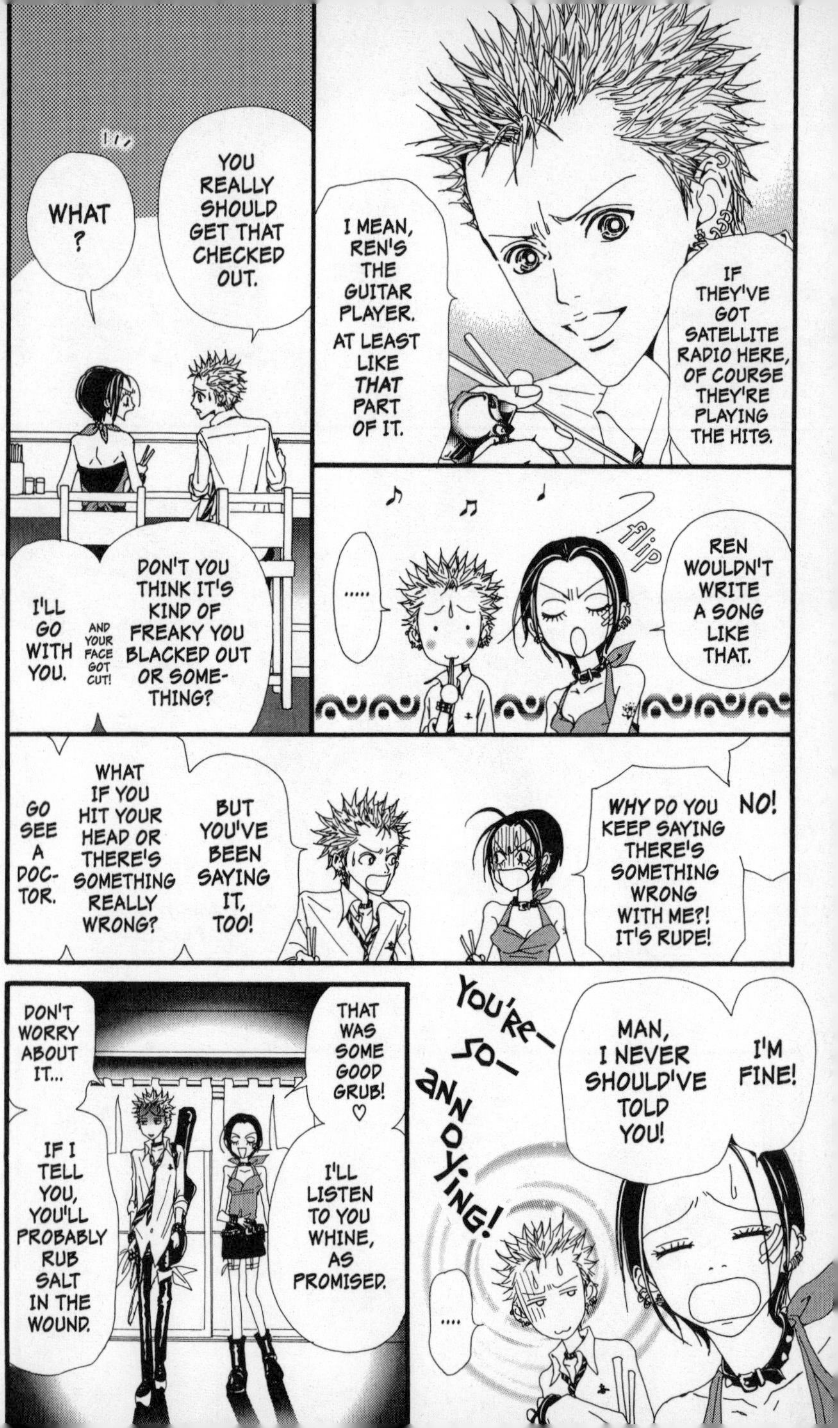
IF THEY'VE GOT SATELLITE RADIO HERE, OF COURSE THEY'RE PLAYING THE HITS.
I MEAN, REN'S THE GUITAR PLAYER. AT LEAST LIKE THAT PART OF IT.
REN WOULDN'T WRITE A SONG LIKE THAT.
flip
.....
YOU REALLY SHOULD GET THAT CHECKED OUT.
WHAT?
DON'T YOU THINK IT'S KIND OF FREAKY YOU BLACKED OUT OR SOME-THING?
AND YOUR FACE GOT CUT!
I'LL GO WITH YOU.
NO!
WHY DO YOU KEEP SAYING THERE'S SOMETHING WRONG WITH ME?! IT'S RUDE!
BUT YOU'VE BEEN SAYING IT, TOO!
WHAT IF YOU HIT YOUR HEAD OR THERE'S SOMETHING REALLY WRONG?
GO SEE A DOC-TOR.
I'M FINE!
MAN, I NEVER SHOULD'VE TOLD YOU!
YOU'RE-SO-ANNOYING!
....
THAT WAS SOME GOOD GRUB! ♡
I'LL LISTEN TO YOU WHINE, AS PROMISED.
DON'T WORRY ABOUT IT...
IF I TELL YOU, YOU'LL PROBABLY RUB SALT IN THE WOUND.

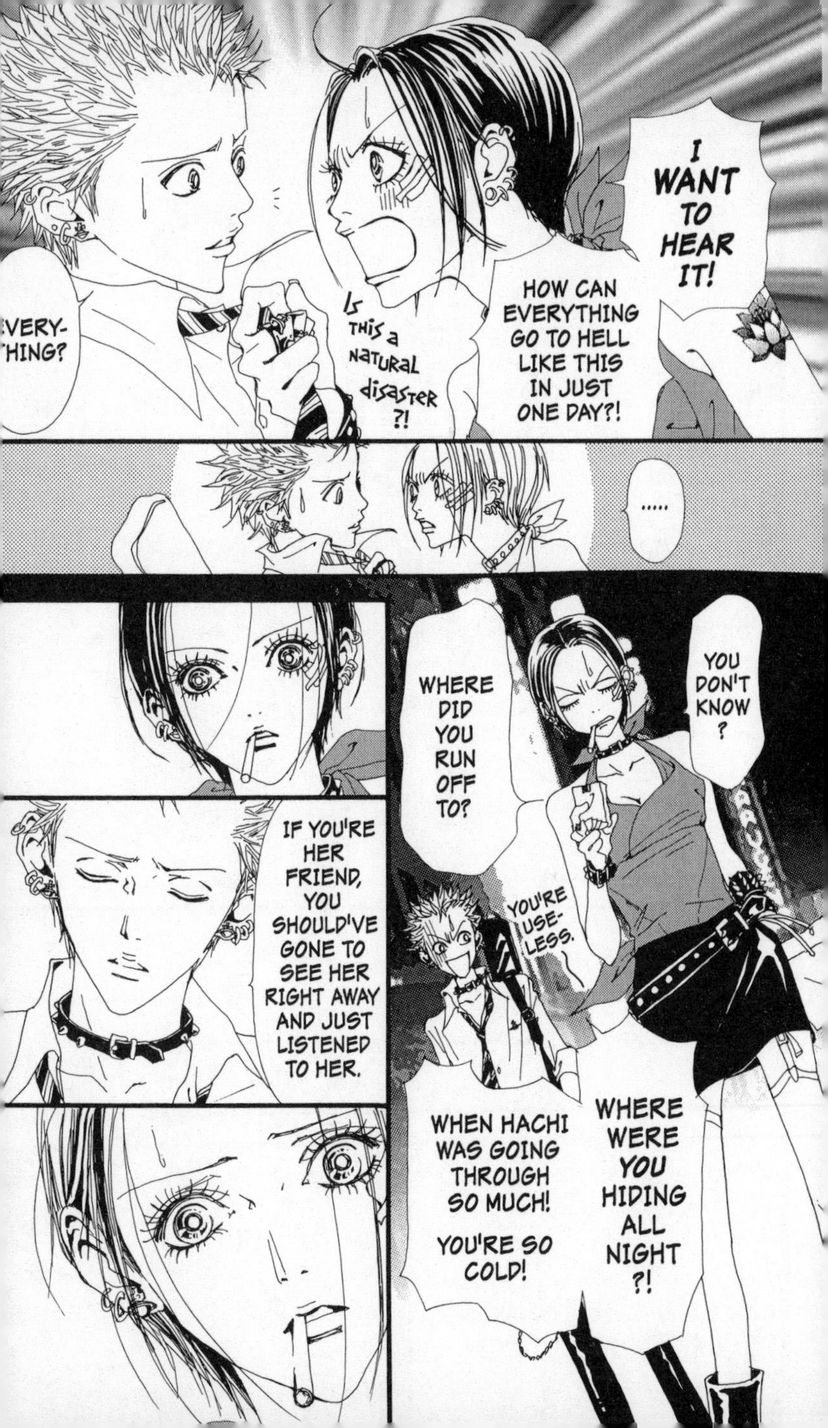
I WANT TO HEAR IT!
HOW CAN EVERYTHING GO TO HELL LIKE THIS IN JUST ONE DAY?!
Is this a natural disaster?!
VERY-THING?
.....
YOU DON'T KNOW?
WHERE DID YOU RUN OFF TO?
YOU'RE USE-LESS.
WHERE WERE YOU HIDING ALL NIGHT?!
WHEN HACHI WAS GOING THROUGH SO MUCH!
YOU'RE SO COLD!
IF YOU'RE HER FRIEND, YOU SHOULD'VE GONE TO SEE HER RIGHT AWAY AND JUST LISTENED TO HER.

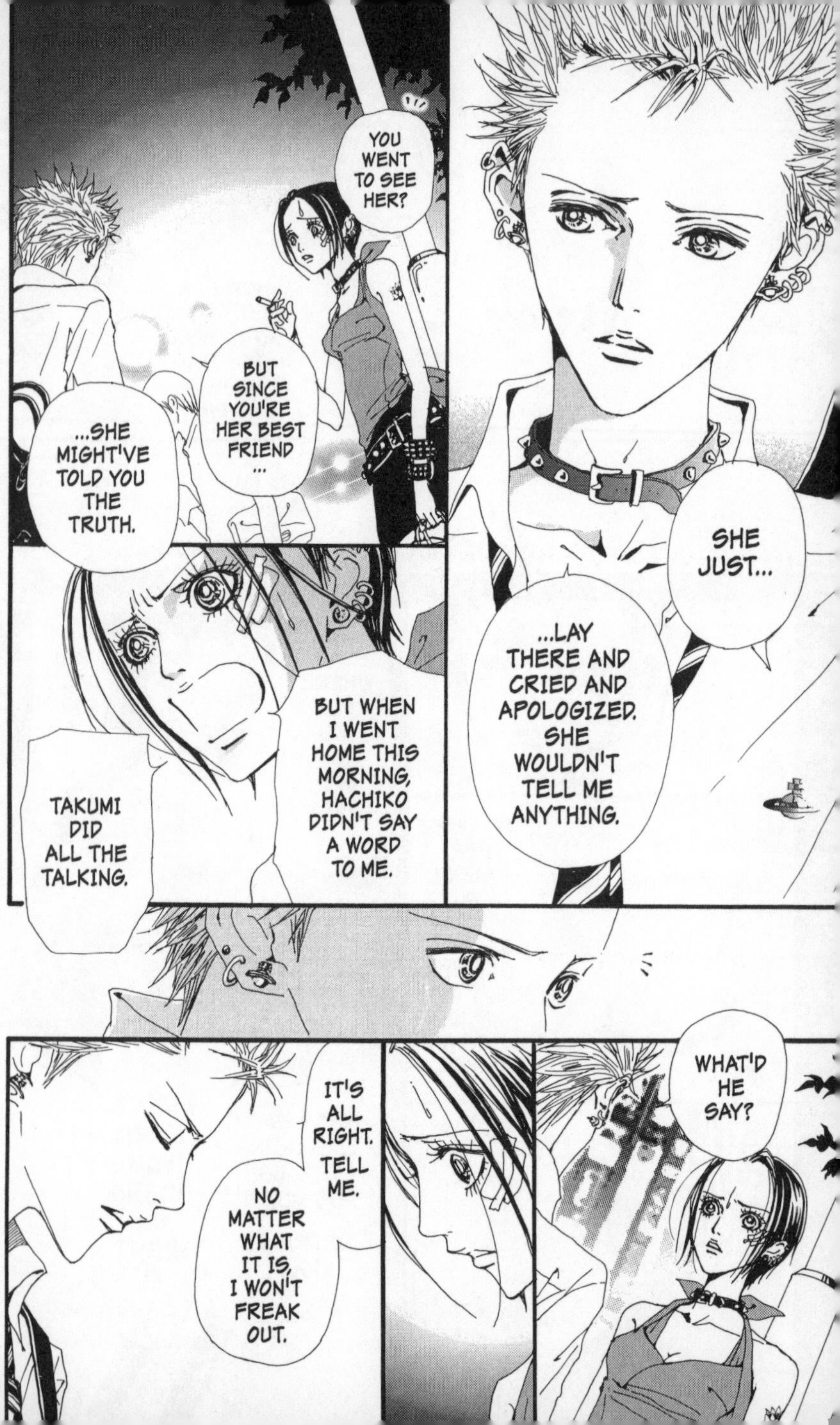
SHE JUST...
...LAY THERE AND CRIED AND APOLOGIZED. SHE WOULDN'T TELL ME ANYTHING.
YOU WENT TO SEE HER?
BUT SINCE YOU'RE HER BEST FRIEND ...
...SHE MIGHT'VE TOLD YOU THE TRUTH.
BUT WHEN I WENT HOME THIS MORNING, HACHIKO DIDN'T SAY A WORD TO ME.
TAKUMI DID ALL THE TALKING.
WHAT'D HE SAY?
IT'S ALL RIGHT. TELL ME.
NO MATTER WHAT IT IS, I WON'T FREAK OUT.

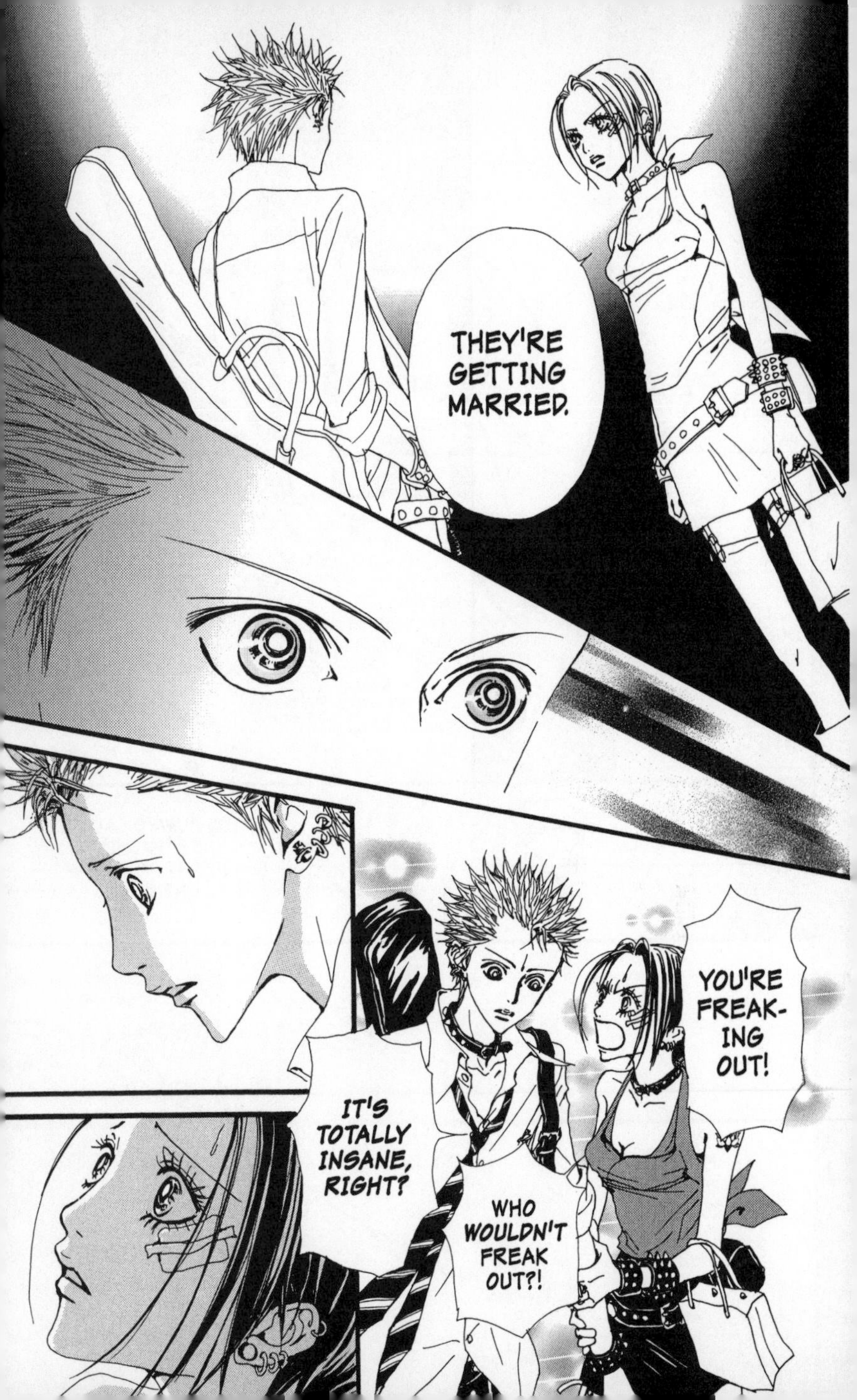
THEY'RE GETTING MARRIED.
YOU'RE FREAK-ING OUT!
WHO WOULDN'T FREAK OUT?!
IT'S TOTALLY INSANE, RIGHT?

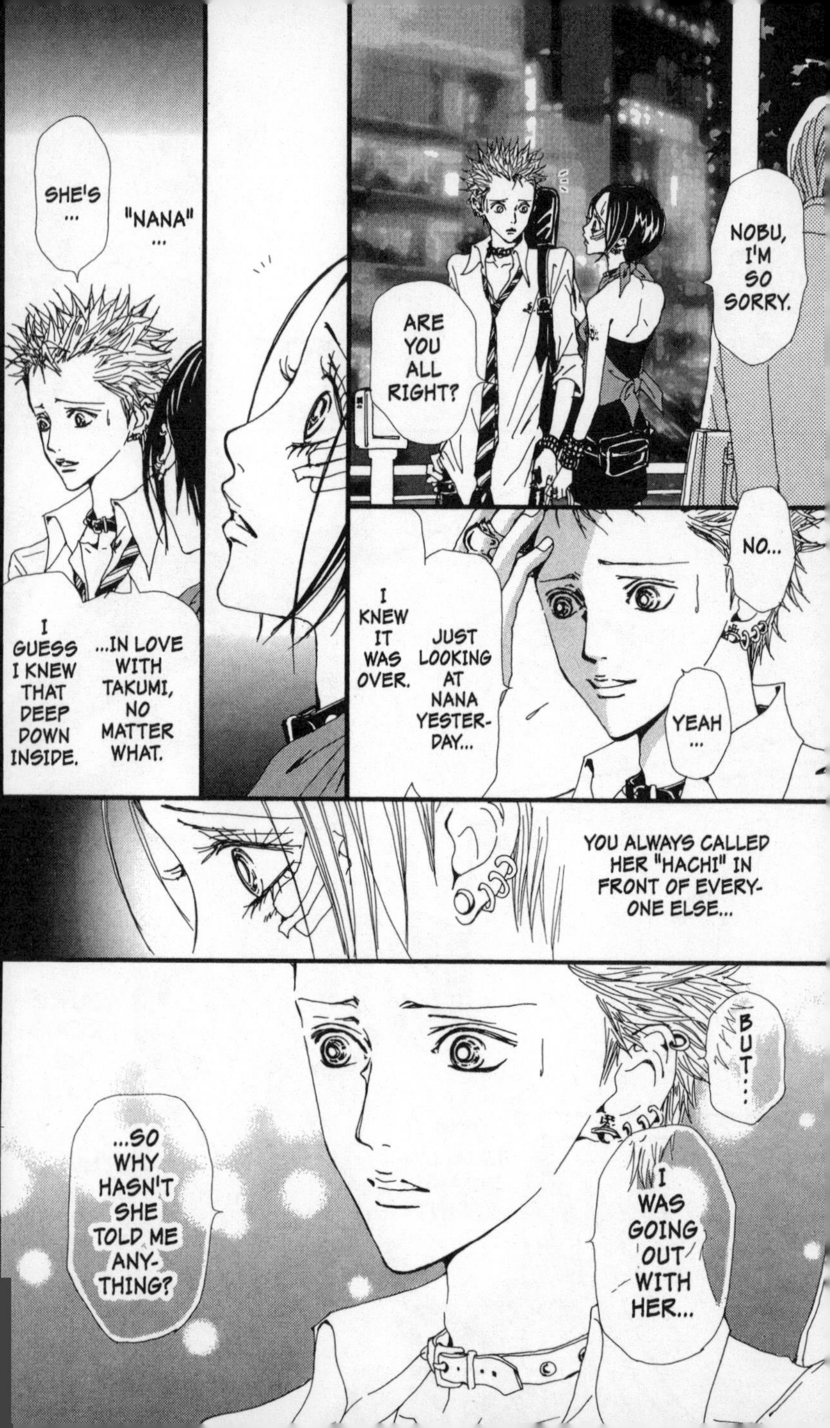
NOBU, I'M SO SORRY.
ARE YOU ALL RIGHT?
NO...
YEAH...
JUST LOOKING AT NANA YESTERDAY...
I KNEW IT WAS OVER.
SHE'S...
"NANA"...
...IN LOVE WITH TAKUMI, NO MATTER WHAT.
I GUESS I KNEW THAT DEEP DOWN INSIDE.
YOU ALWAYS CALLED HER "HACHI" IN FRONT OF EVERYONE ELSE...
BUT...
I WAS GOING OUT WITH HER...
...SO WHY HASN'T SHE TOLD ME ANYTHING?

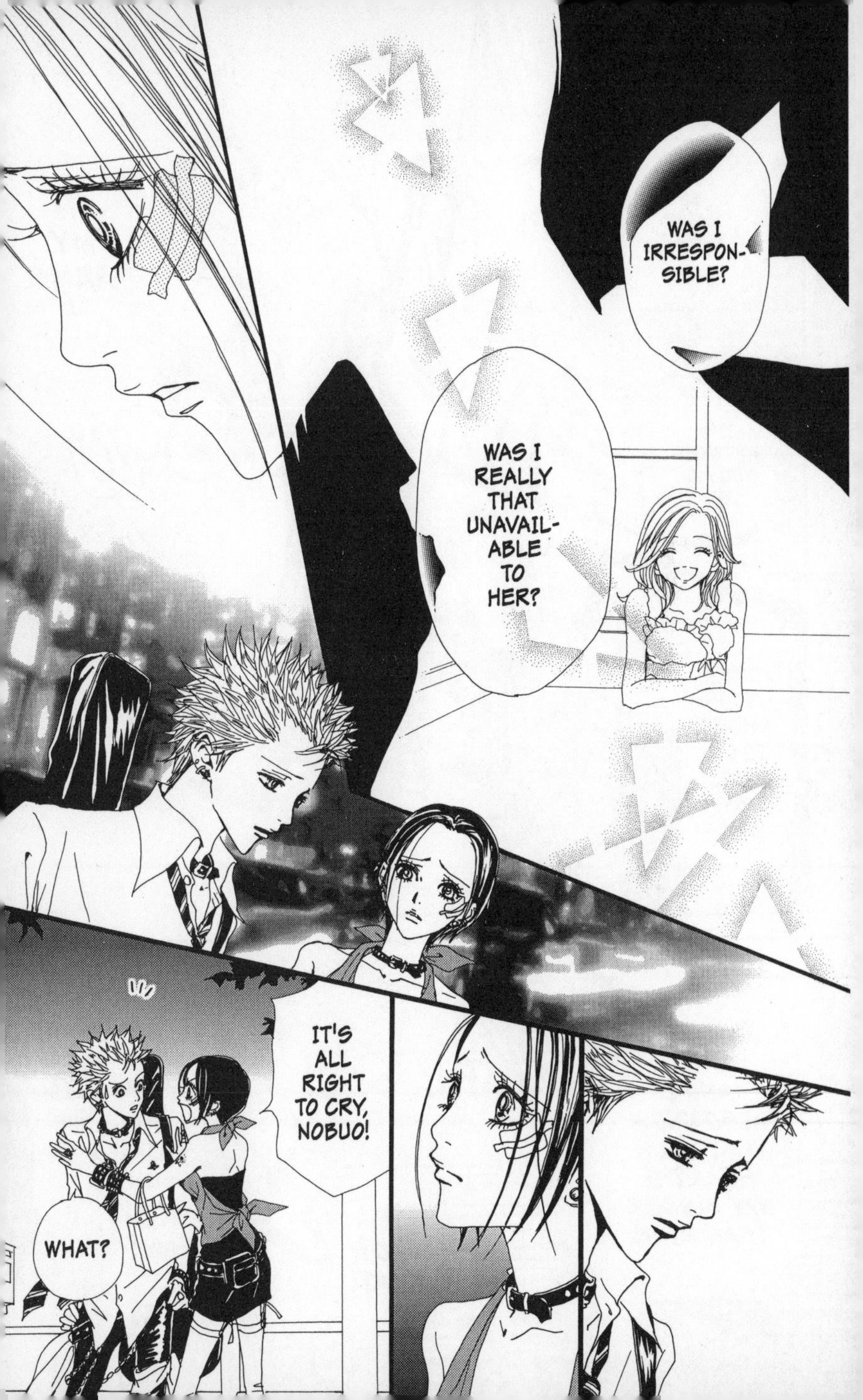
WAS I IRRESPONSIBLE?
WAS I REALLY THAT UNAVAILABLE TO HER?
IT'S ALL RIGHT TO CRY, NOBUO!
WHAT?

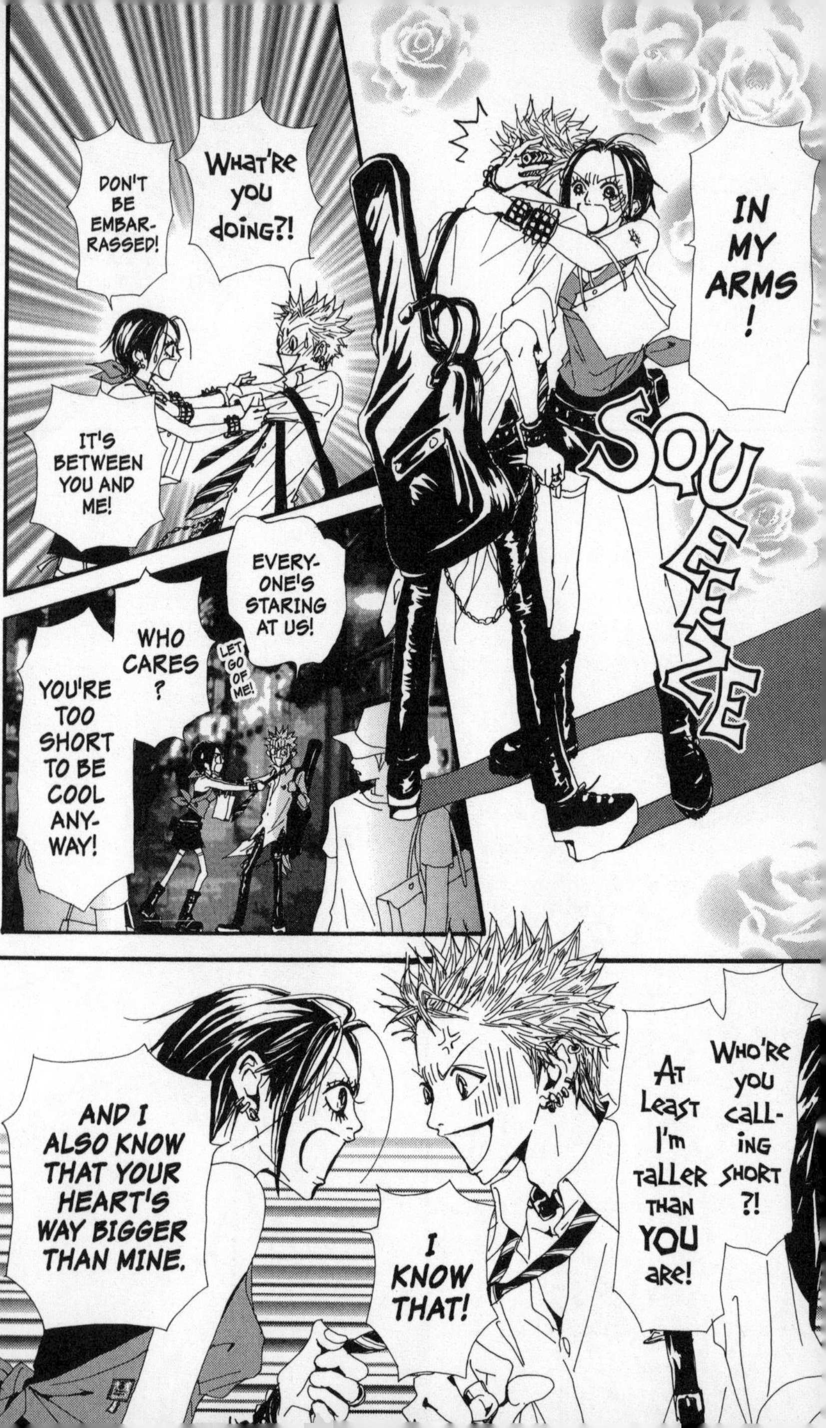
IN MY ARMS!
SQUEEZE
What're you doing?!
DON'T BE EMBARRASSED!
IT'S BETWEEN YOU AND ME!
EVERYONE'S STARING AT US!
LET GO OF ME!
WHO CARES?
YOU'RE TOO SHORT TO BE COOL ANYWAY!
Who're you calling short?!
At least I'm taller than YOU are!
I KNOW THAT!
AND I ALSO KNOW THAT YOUR HEART'S WAY BIGGER THAN MINE.

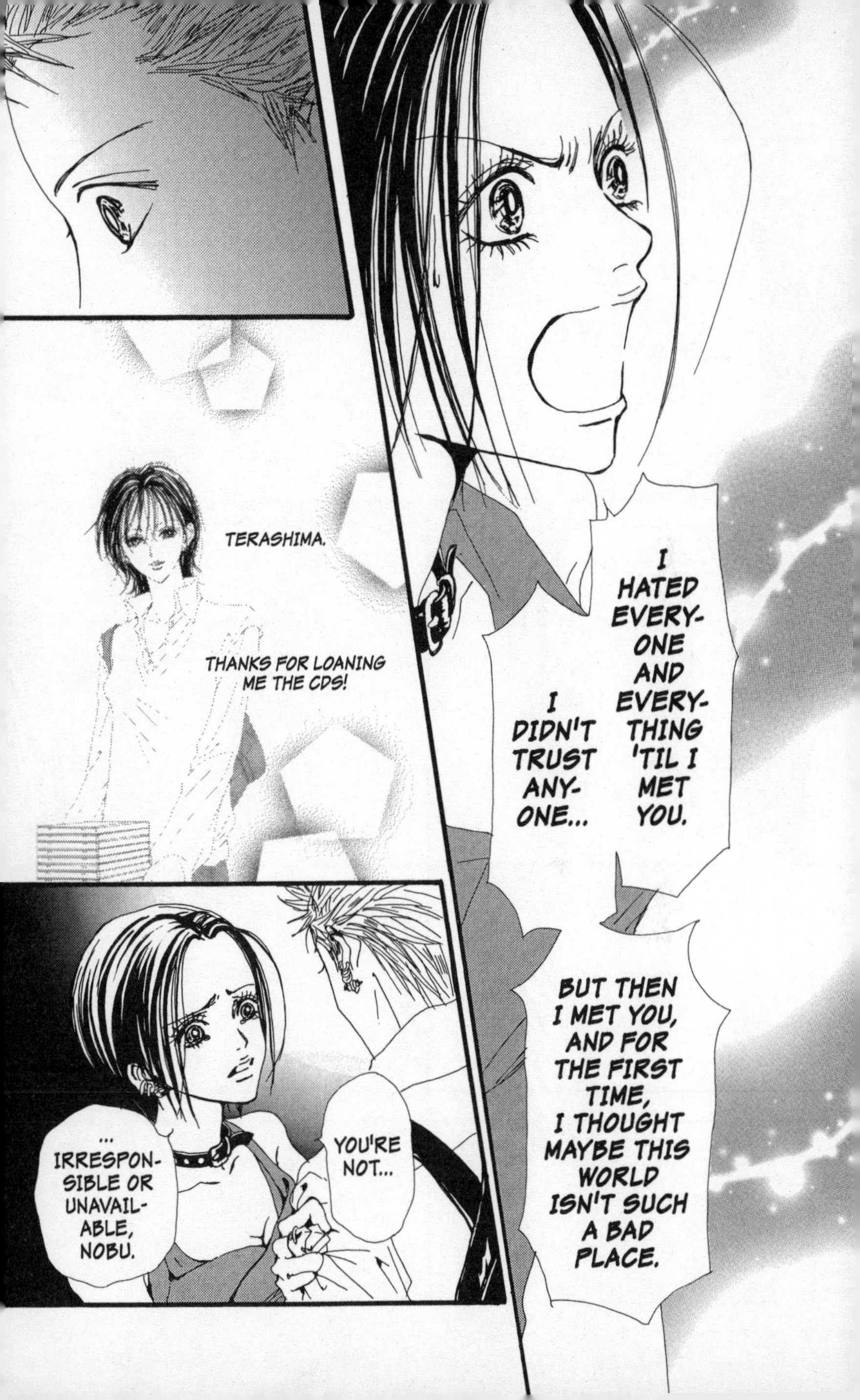
I DIDN'T TRUST ANYONE... I HATED EVERYONE AND EVERYTHING 'TIL I MET YOU.
BUT THEN I MET YOU, AND FOR THE FIRST TIME, I THOUGHT MAYBE THIS WORLD ISN'T SUCH A BAD PLACE.
TERASHIMA.
THANKS FOR LOANING ME THE CDS!
YOU'RE NOT...
...IRRESPONSIBLE OR UNAVAILABLE, NOBU.

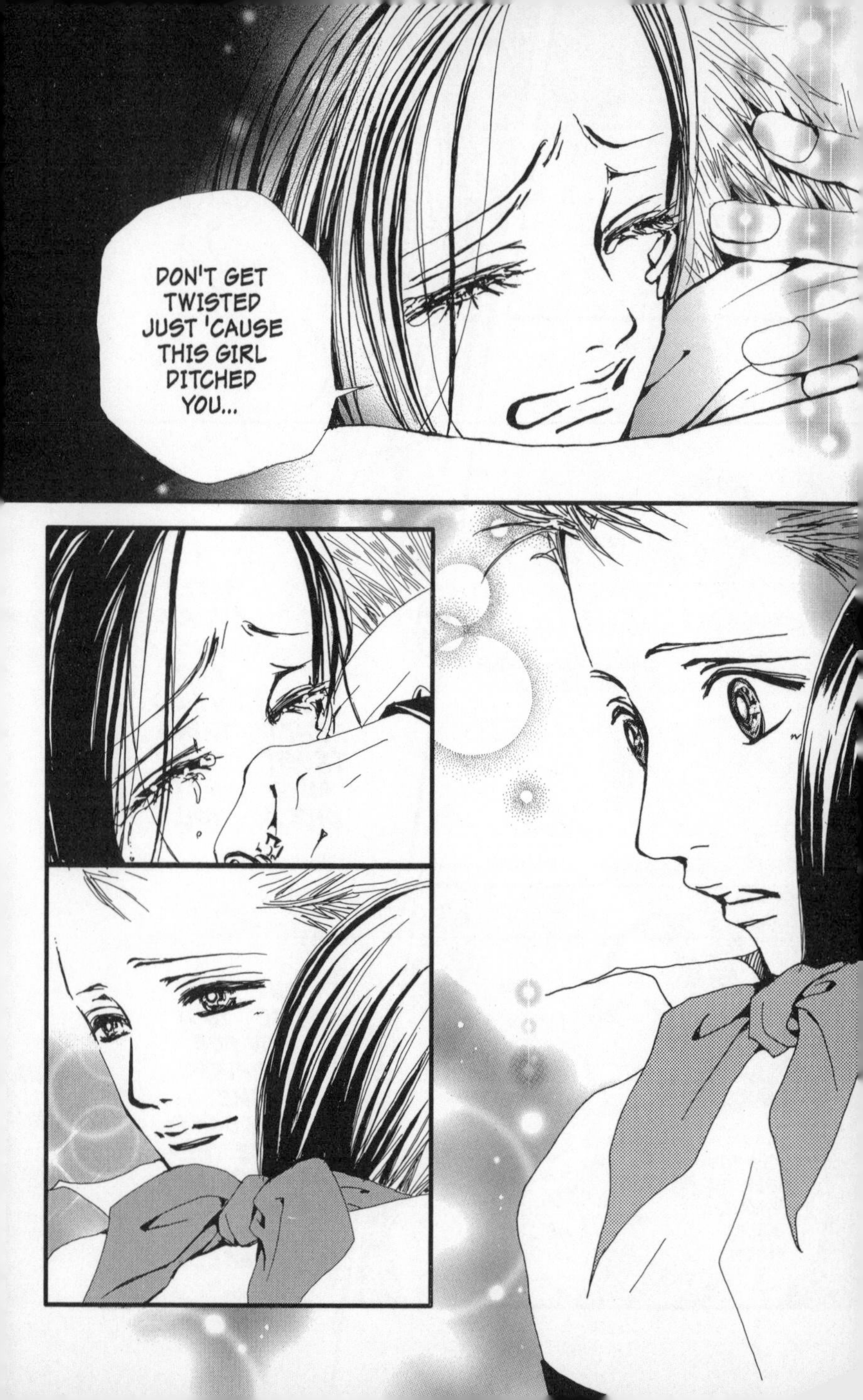
DON'T GET TWISTED JUST 'CAUSE THIS GIRL DITCHED YOU...

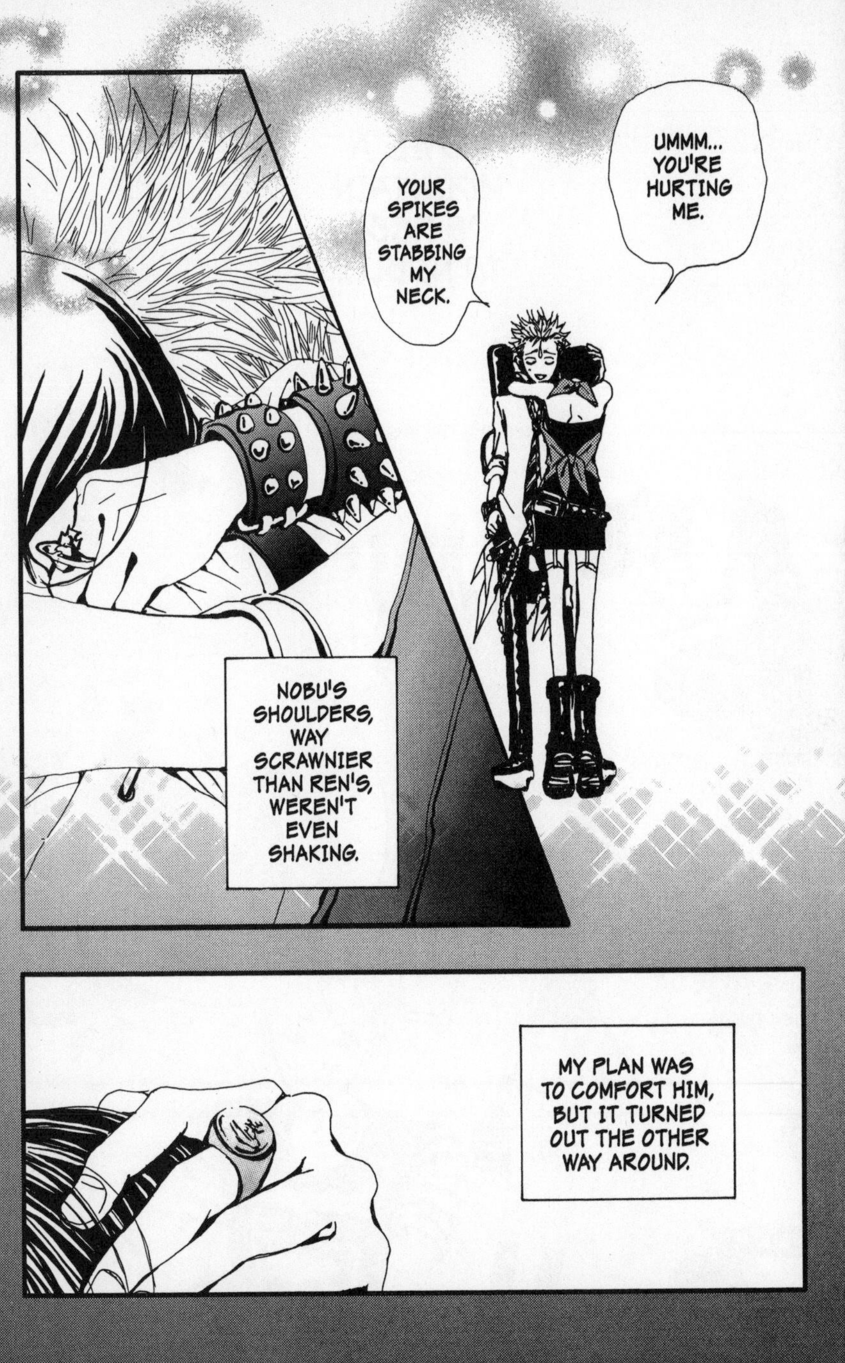
UMMM... YOU'RE HURTING ME.
YOUR SPIKES ARE STABBING MY NECK.
NOBU'S SHOULDERS, WAY SCRAWNIER THAN REN'S, WEREN'T EVEN SHAKING.
MY PLAN WAS TO COMFORT HIM, BUT IT TURNED OUT THE OTHER WAY AROUND.

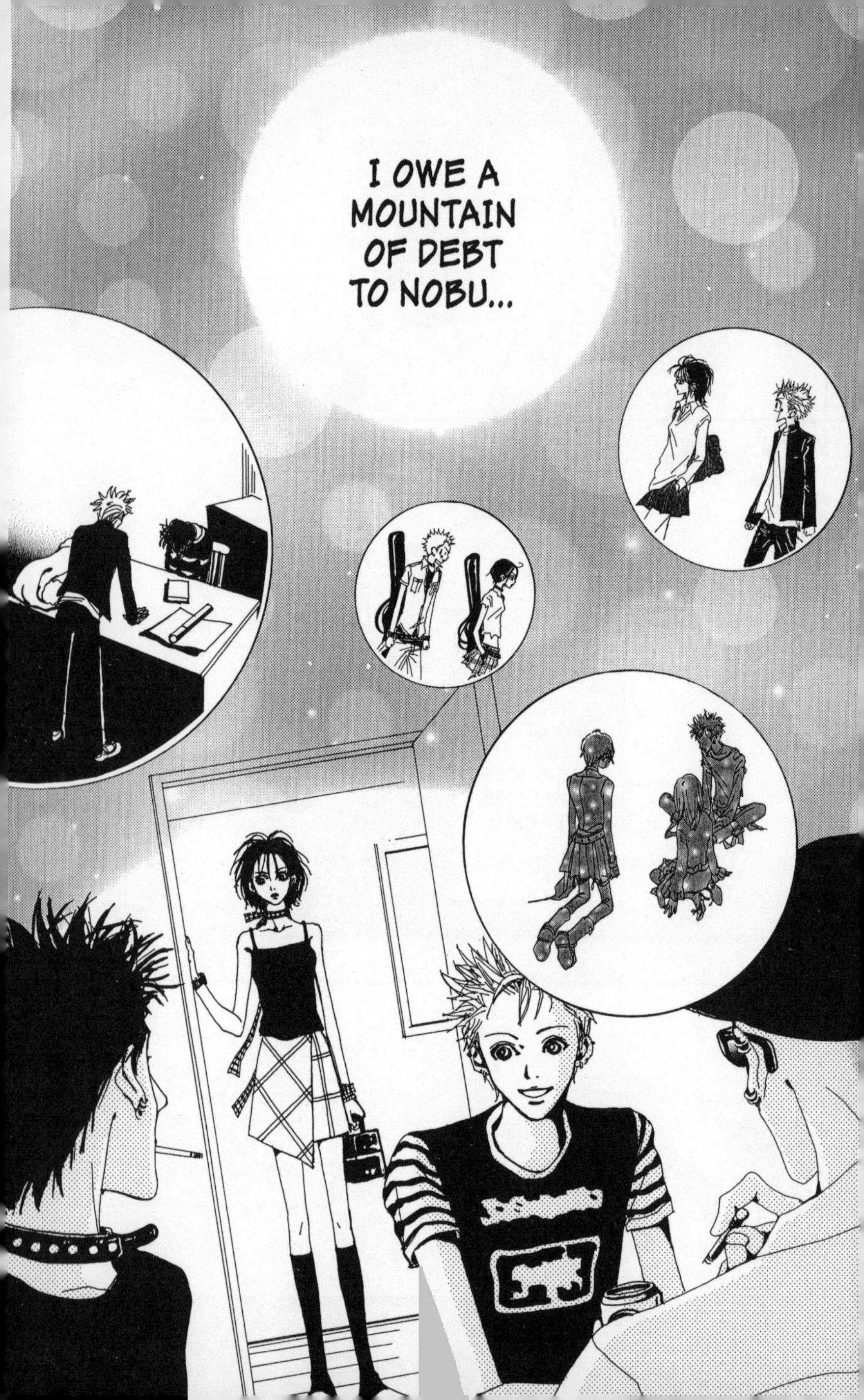
I OWE A MOUNTAIN OF DEBT TO NOBU...

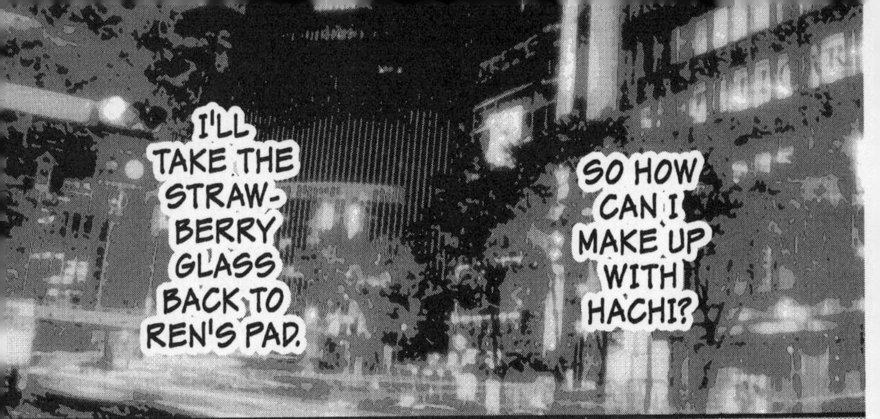
SO HOW CAN I MAKE UP WITH HACHI?
I'LL TAKE THE STRAW-BERRY GLASS BACK TO REN'S PAD.
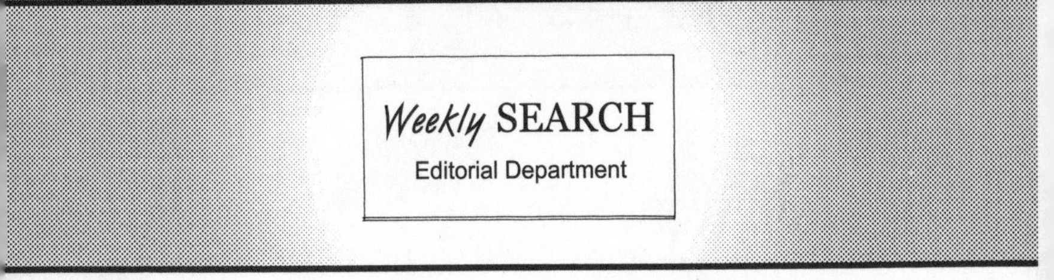
Weekly SEARCH
Editorial Department
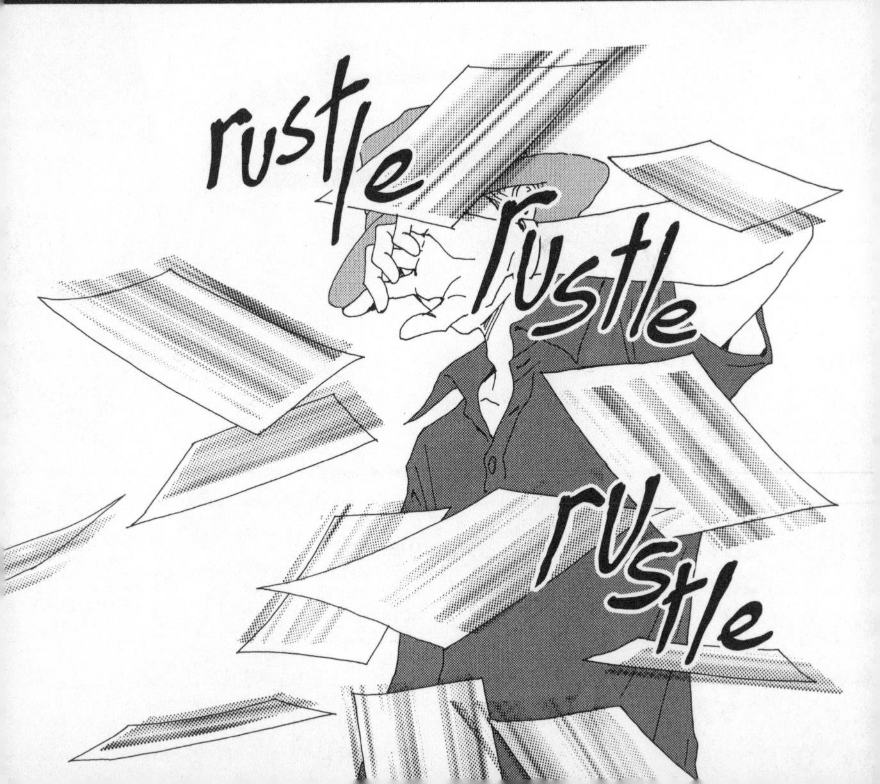
rustle
rustle
rustle

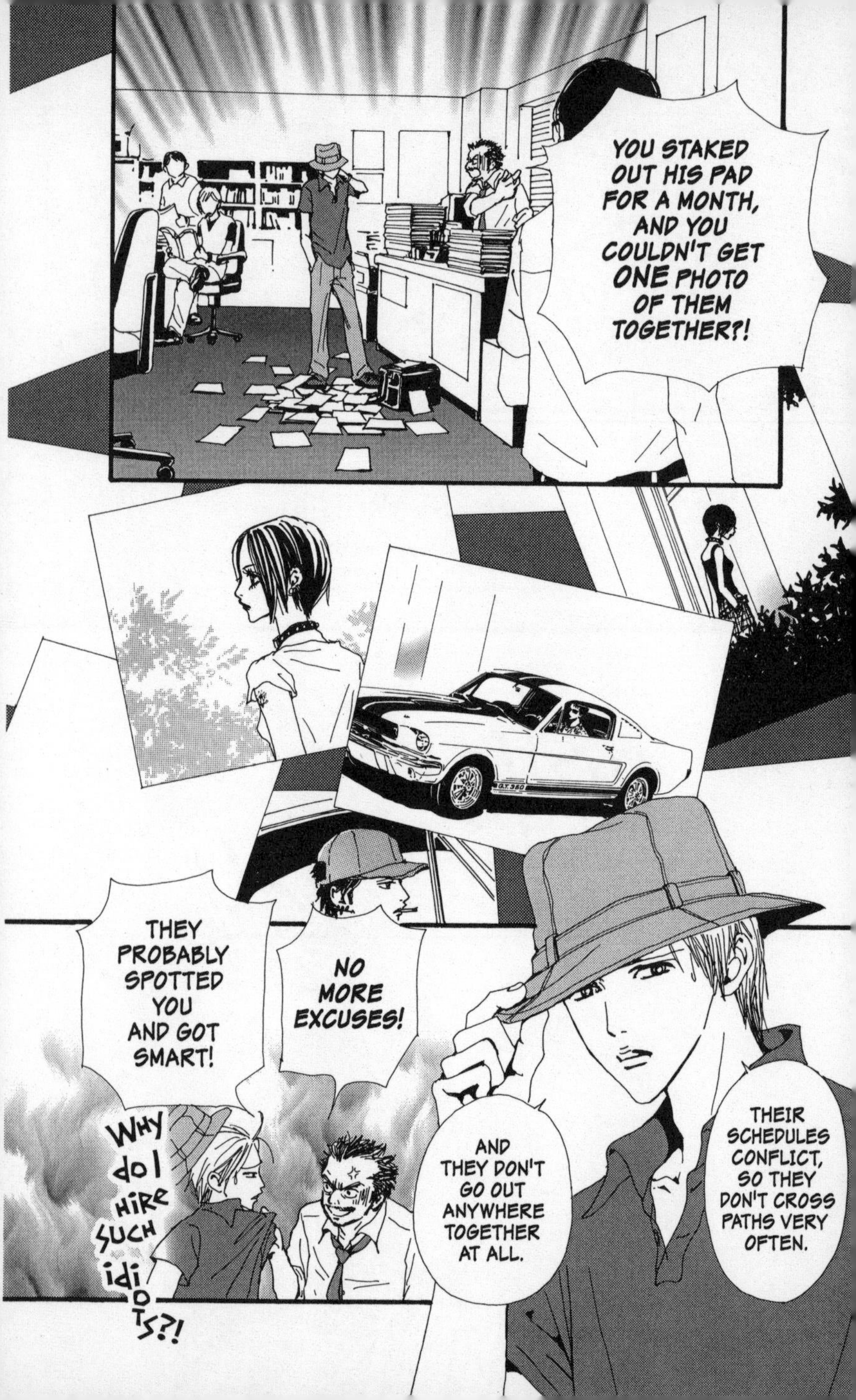
YOU STAKED OUT HIS PAD FOR A MONTH, AND YOU COULDN'T GET ONE PHOTO OF THEM TOGETHER?!
THEIR SCHEDULES CONFLICT, SO THEY DON'T CROSS PATHS VERY OFTEN.
AND THEY DON'T GO OUT ANYWHERE TOGETHER AT ALL.
NO MORE EXCUSES!
THEY PROBABLY SPOTTED YOU AND GOT SMART!
WHY DO I HIRE SUCH IDIOTS?!

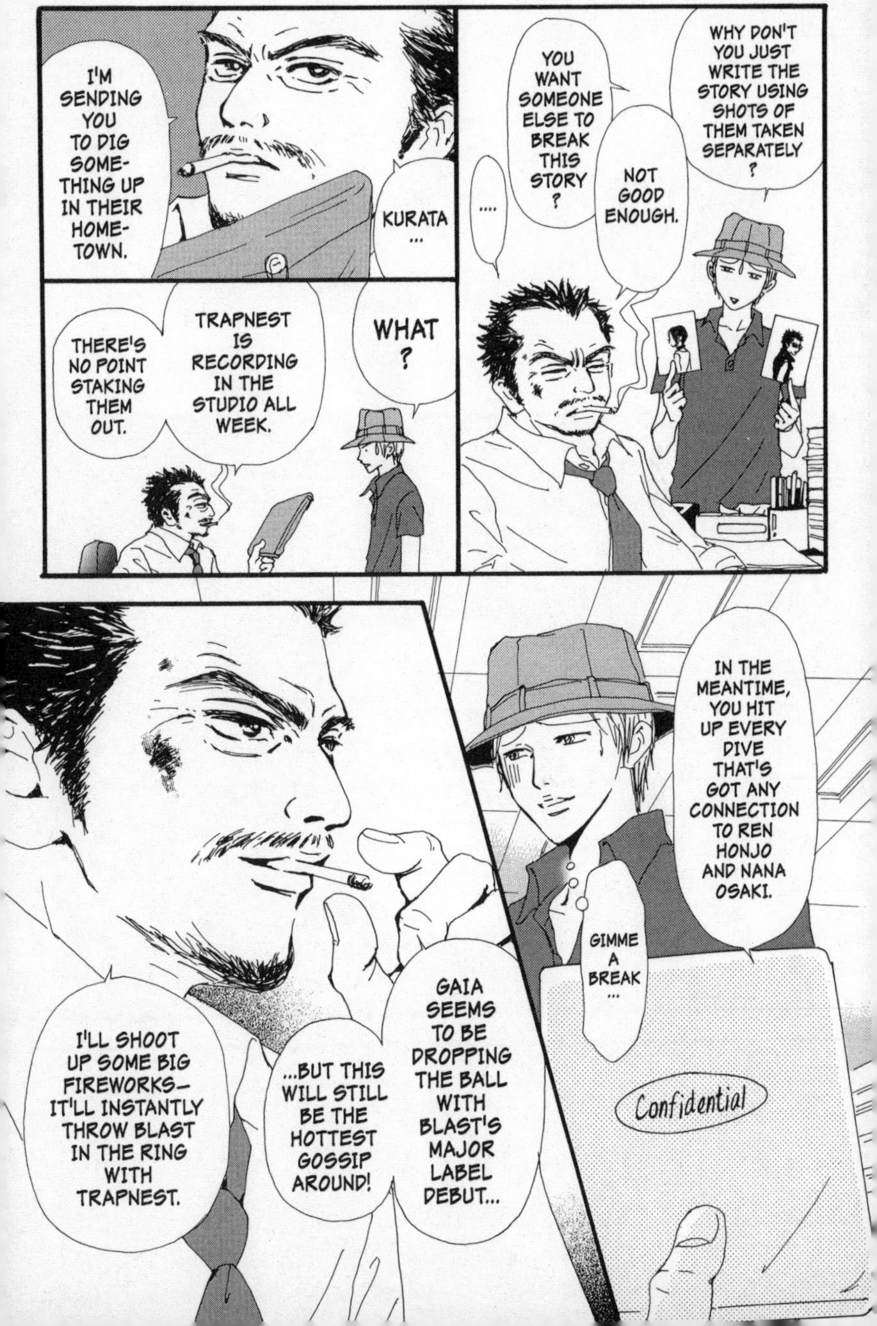
WHY DON'T YOU JUST WRITE THE STORY USING SHOTS OF THEM TAKEN SEPARATELY?
NOT GOOD ENOUGH.
YOU WANT SOMEONE ELSE TO BREAK THIS STORY?
....
KURATA...
I'M SENDING YOU TO DIG SOME-THING UP IN THEIR HOME-TOWN.
WHAT?
TRAPNEST IS RECORDING IN THE STUDIO ALL WEEK.
THERE'S NO POINT STAKING THEM OUT.
IN THE MEANTIME, YOU HIT UP EVERY DIVE THAT'S GOT ANY CONNECTION TO REN HONJO AND NANA OSAKI.
GIMME A BREAK...
Confidential
GAIA SEEMS TO BE DROPPING THE BALL WITH BLAST'S MAJOR LABEL DEBUT...
...BUT THIS WILL STILL BE THE HOTTEST GOSSIP AROUND!
I'LL SHOOT UP SOME BIG FIREWORKS— IT'LL INSTANTLY THROW BLAST IN THE RING WITH TRAPNEST.

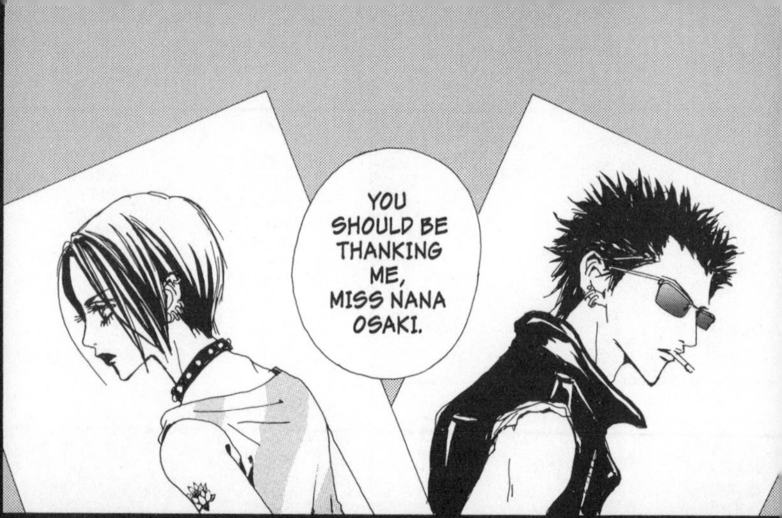
YOU SHOULD BE THANKING ME, MISS NANA OSAKI.
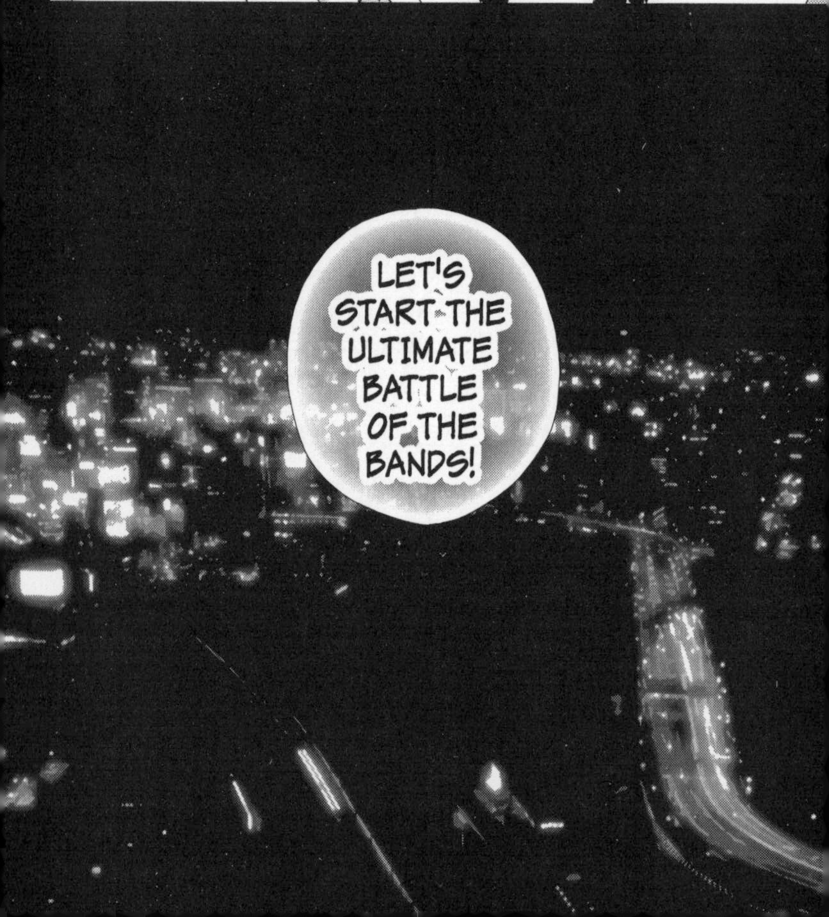
LET'S START THE ULTIMATE BATTLE OF THE BANDS!

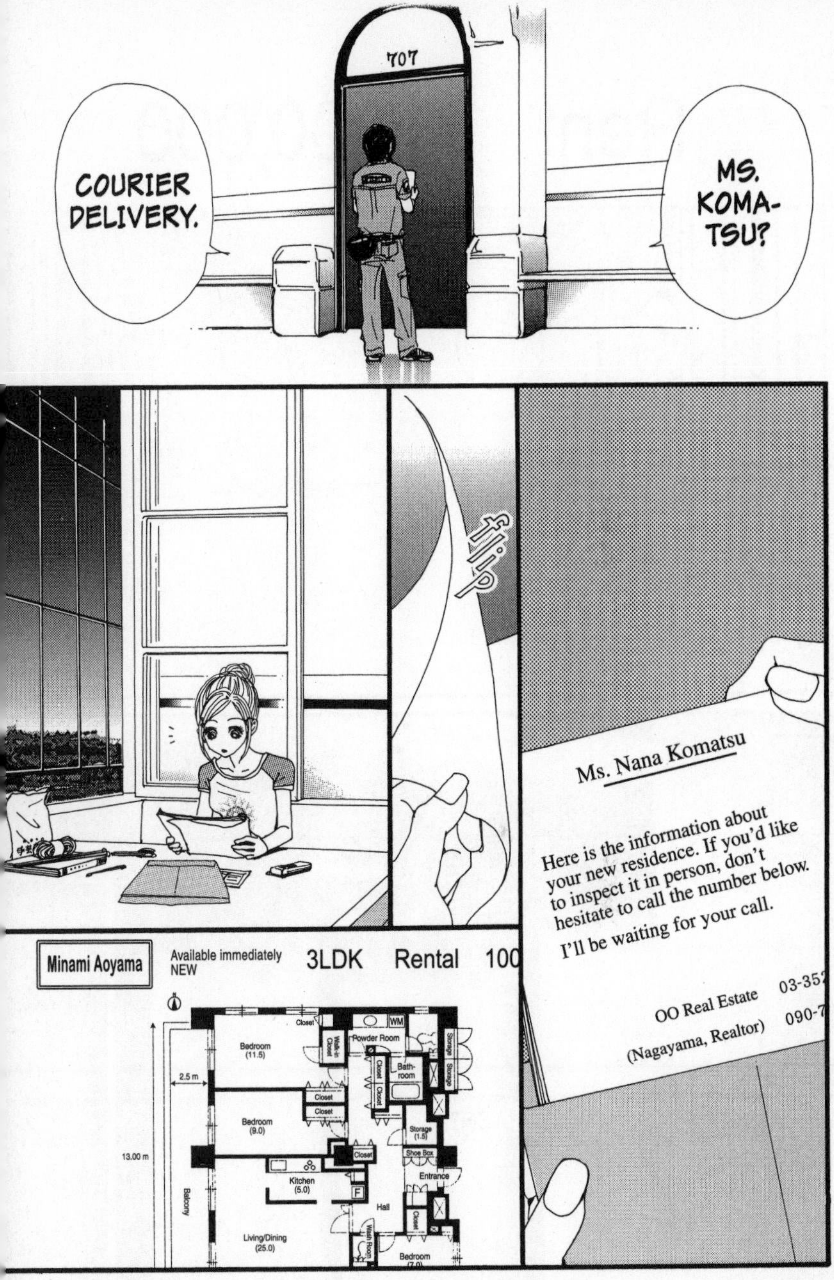
707
MS. KOMA-TSU?
COURIER DELIVERY.
Ms. Nana Komatsu
Here is the information about your new residence. If you'd like to inspect it in person, don't hesitate to call the number below.
I'll be waiting for your call.
OO Real Estate 03-352
(Nagayama, Realtor) 090-7
flip
Minami Aoyama
Available immediately
NEW
3LDK Rental 100
Closet
WM
Walk-in Closet
Powder Room
Storage
Storage
Bedroom (11.5)
2.5 m
Closet
Closet
Bath-room
Closet
Closet
Bedroom (9.0)
Storage (1.5)
13.00 m
Closet
Shoe Box
Kitchen (5.0)
Entrance
F
Balcony
Hall
Closet
Living/Dining (25.0)
Wash Room
Bedroom

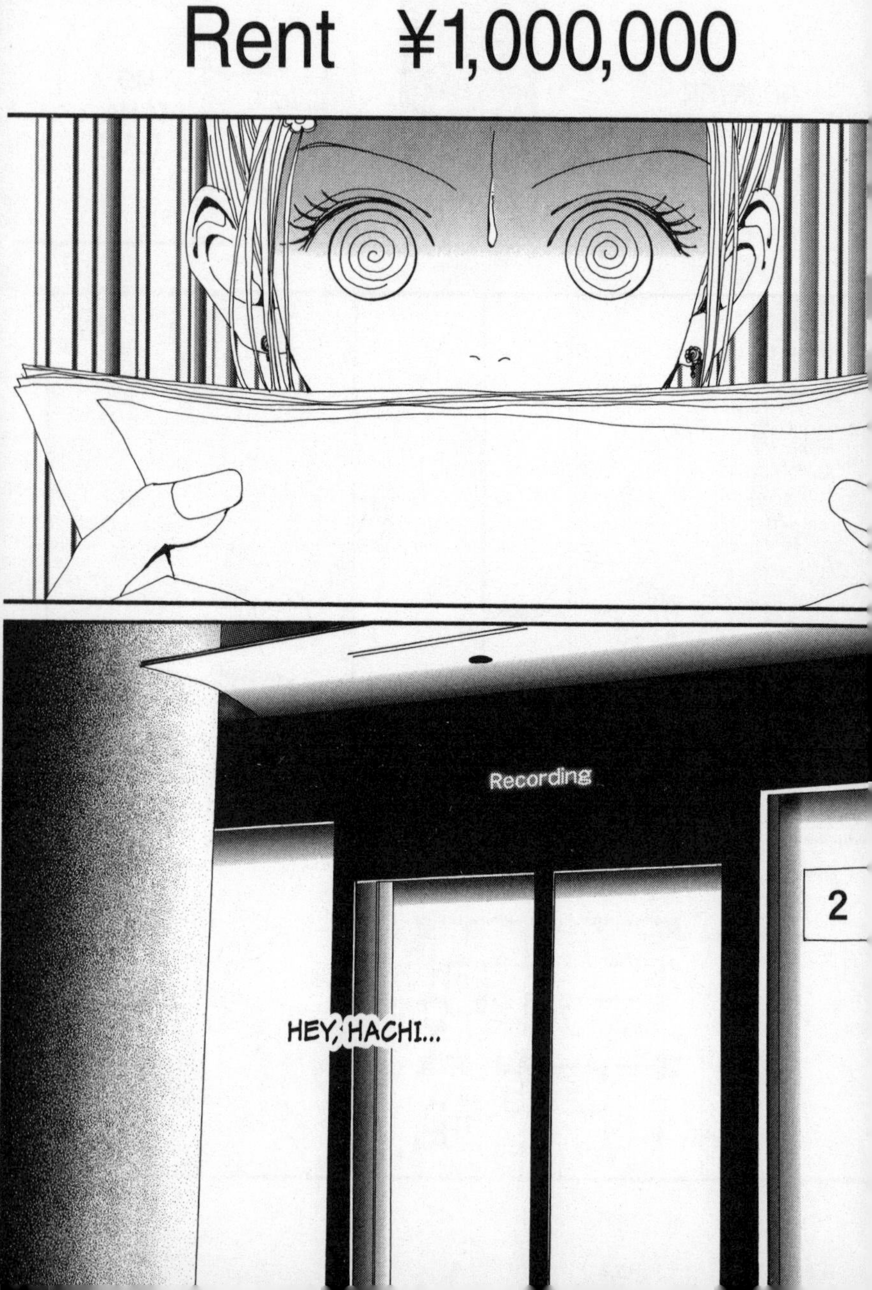
Rent ¥1,000,000
Recording
2
HEY, HACHI...

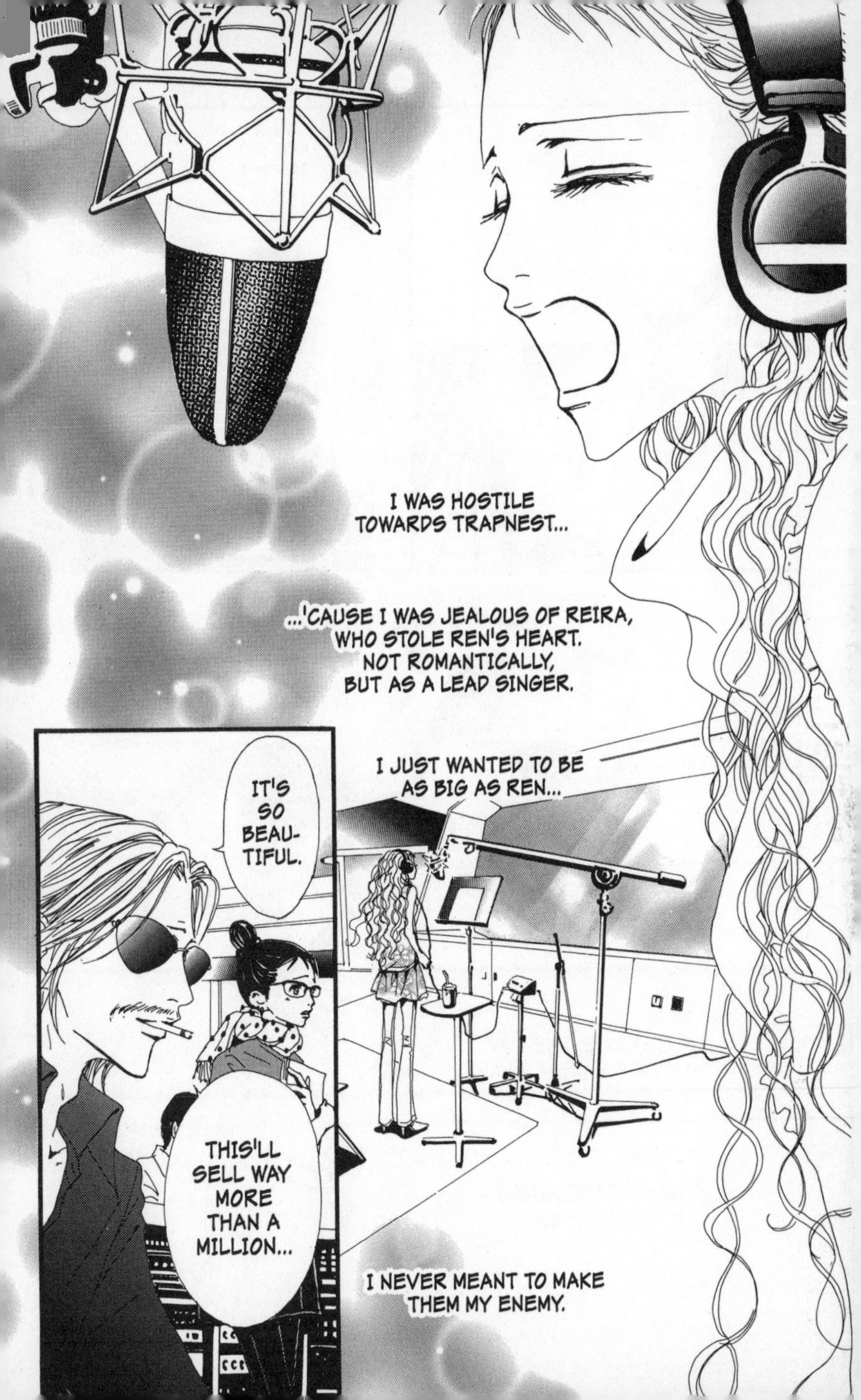
I WAS HOSTILE TOWARDS TRAPNEST...
...'CAUSE I WAS JEALOUS OF REIRA, WHO STOLE REN'S HEART. NOT ROMANTICALLY, BUT AS A LEAD SINGER.
I JUST WANTED TO BE AS BIG AS REN...
IT'S SO BEAU-TIFUL.
THIS'LL SELL WAY MORE THAN A MILLION...
I NEVER MEANT TO MAKE THEM MY ENEMY.

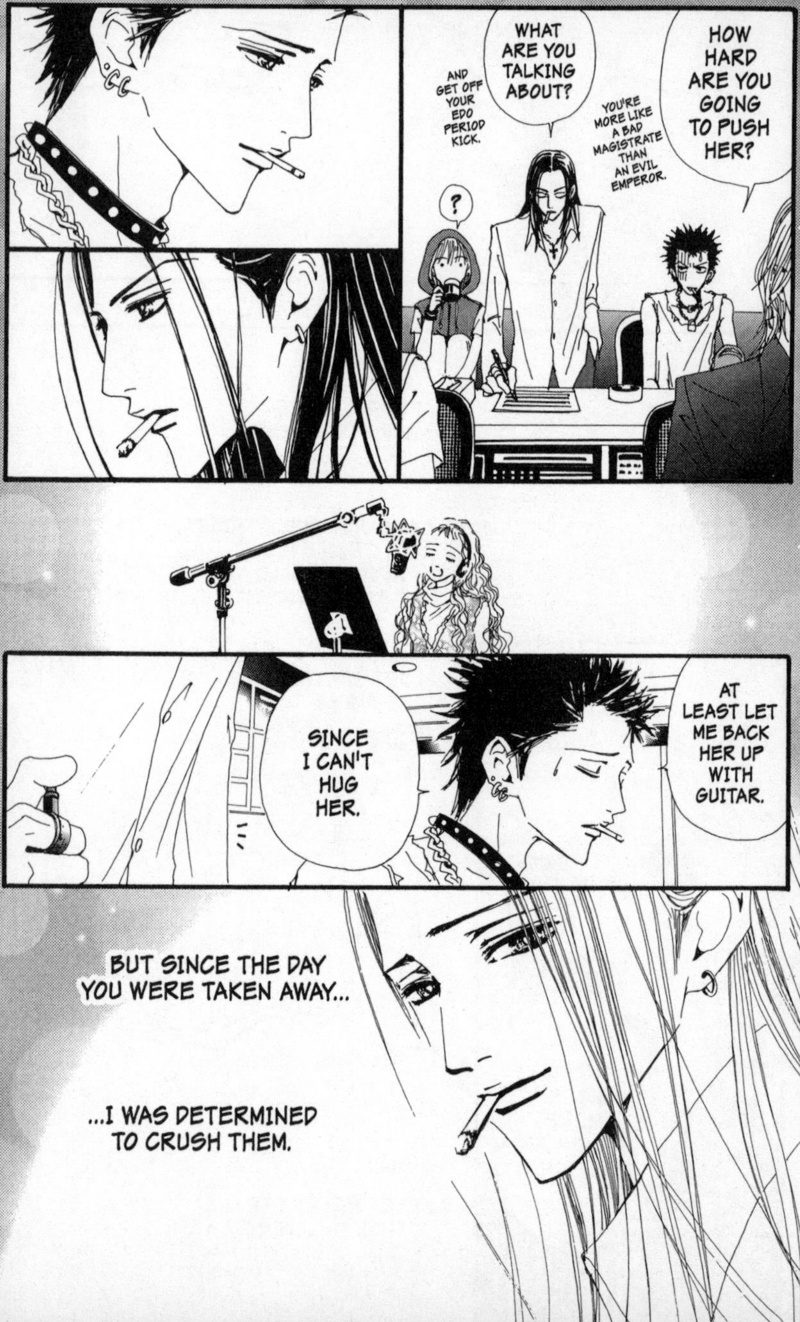
HOW HARD ARE YOU GOING TO PUSH HER?
YOU'RE MORE LIKE A BAD MAGISTRATE THAN AN EVIL EMPEROR.
WHAT ARE YOU TALKING ABOUT?
AND GET OFF YOUR EDO PERIOD KICK.
?
AT LEAST LET ME BACK HER UP WITH GUITAR.
SINCE I CAN'T HUG HER.
BUT SINCE THE DAY YOU WERE TAKEN AWAY...
...I WAS DETERMINED TO CRUSH THEM.

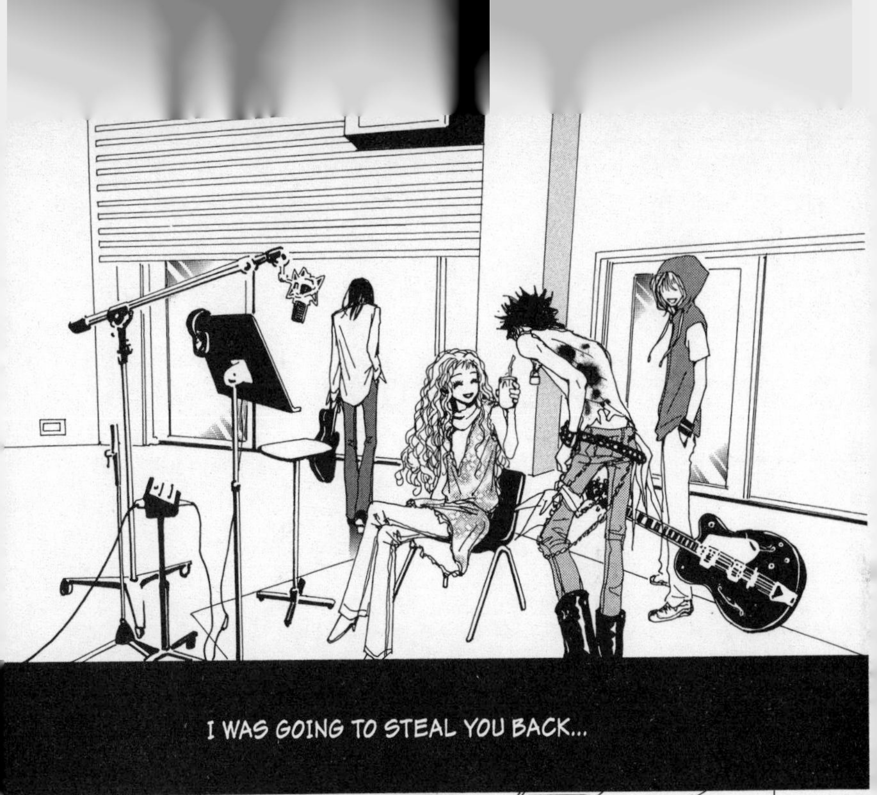

I WAS GOING TO STEAL YOU BACK...

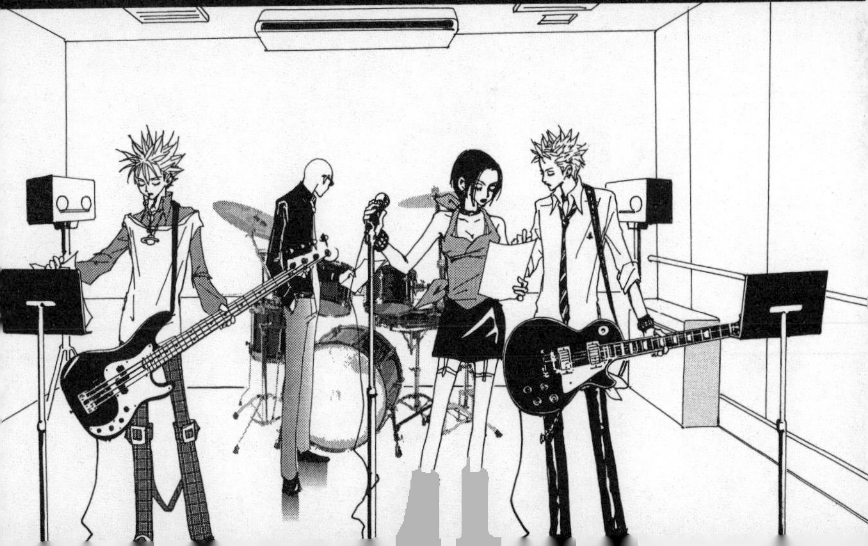

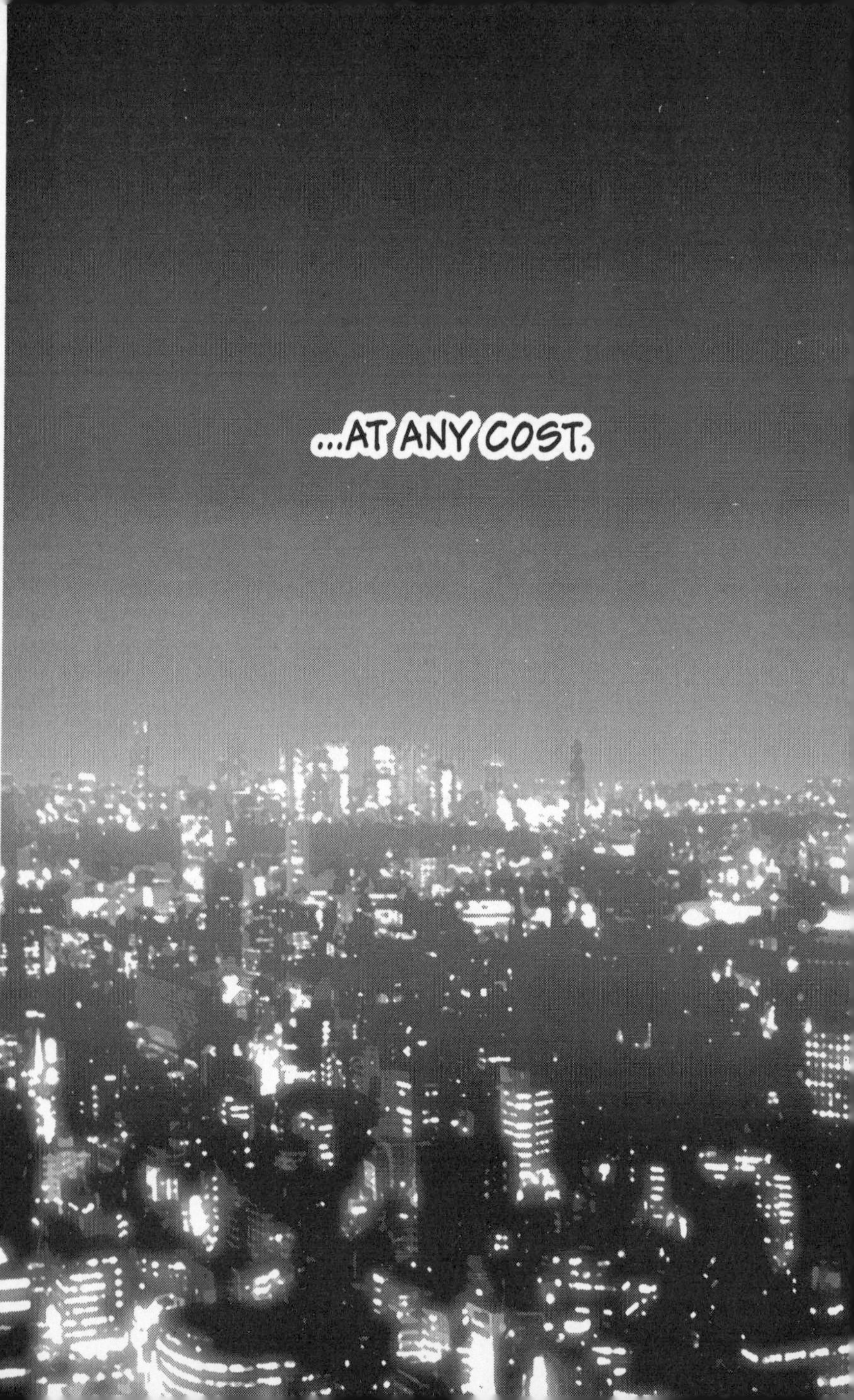
...AT ANY COST.

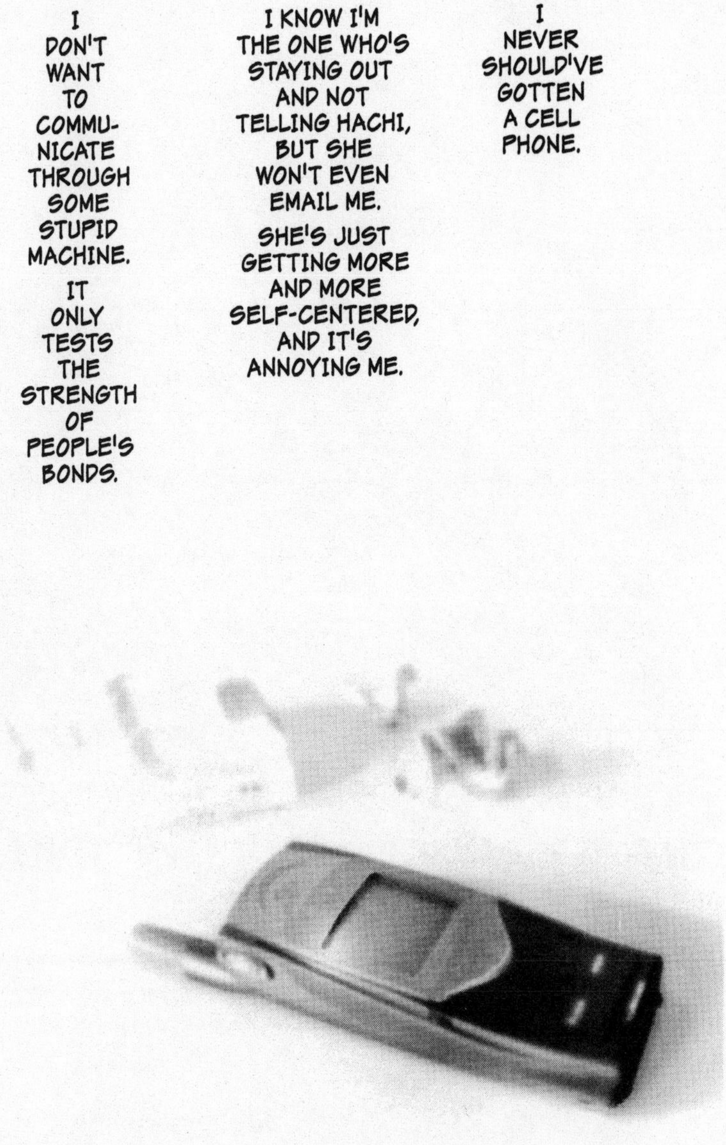
I NEVER SHOULD'VE GOTTEN A CELL PHONE.
I KNOW I'M THE ONE WHO'S STAYING OUT AND NOT TELLING HACHI, BUT SHE WON'T EVEN EMAIL ME.
SHE'S JUST GETTING MORE AND MORE SELF-CENTERED, AND IT'S ANNOYING ME.
I DON'T WANT TO COMMU-NICATE THROUGH SOME STUPID MACHINE.
IT ONLY TESTS THE STRENGTH OF PEOPLE'S BONDS.

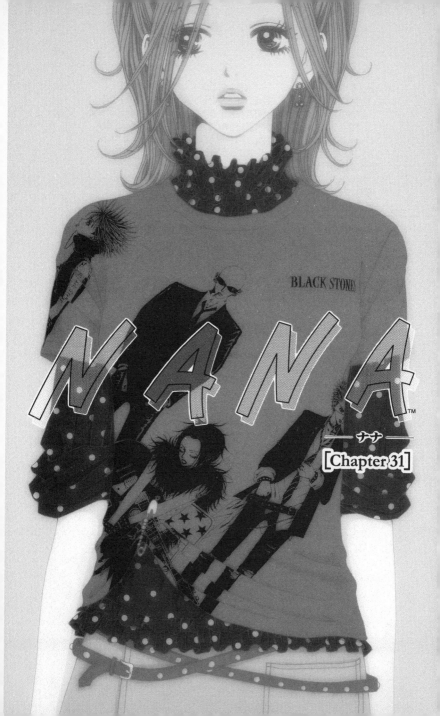

BLACK STONES

NANA™

ナナ

[Chapter 31]

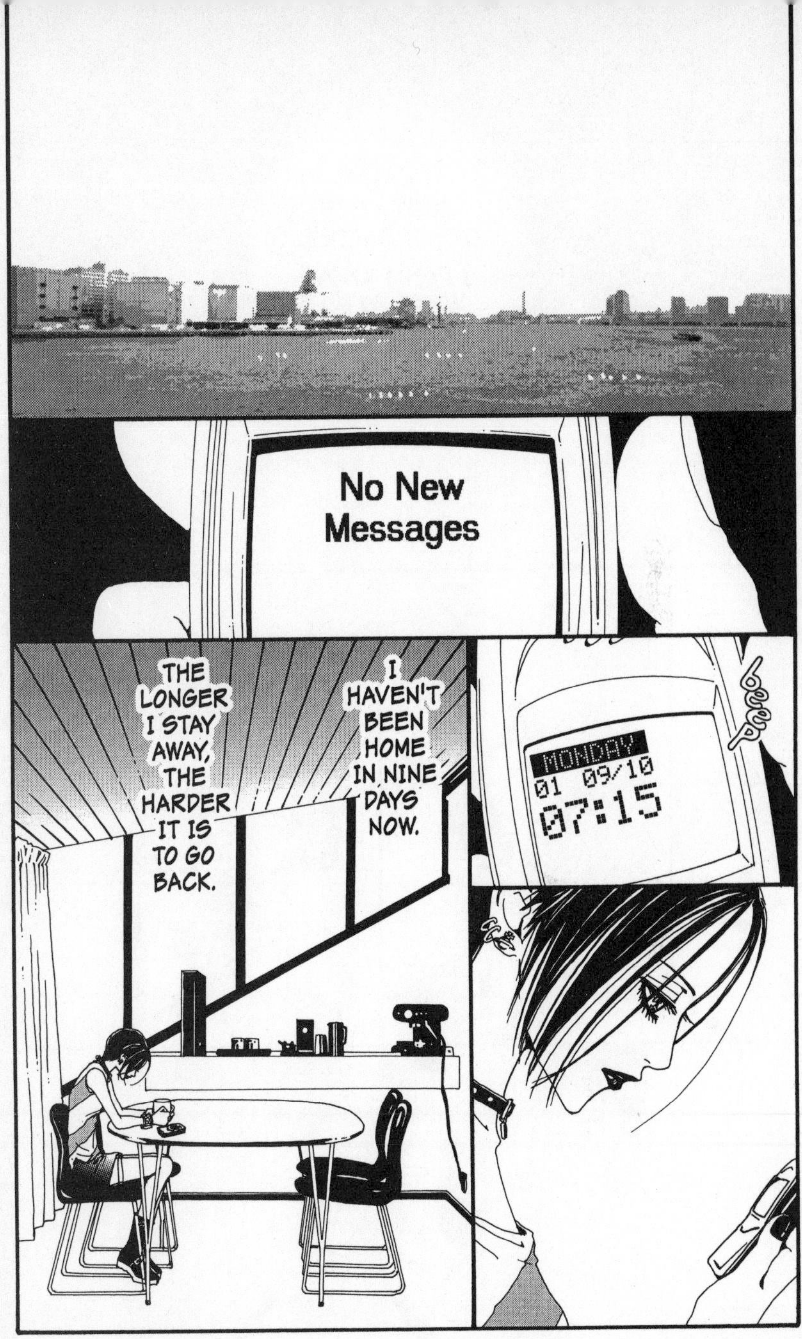
No New Messages
beep
MONDAY
01 09/10
07:15
I HAVEN'T BEEN HOME IN NINE DAYS NOW.
THE LONGER I STAY AWAY, THE HARDER IT IS TO GO BACK.

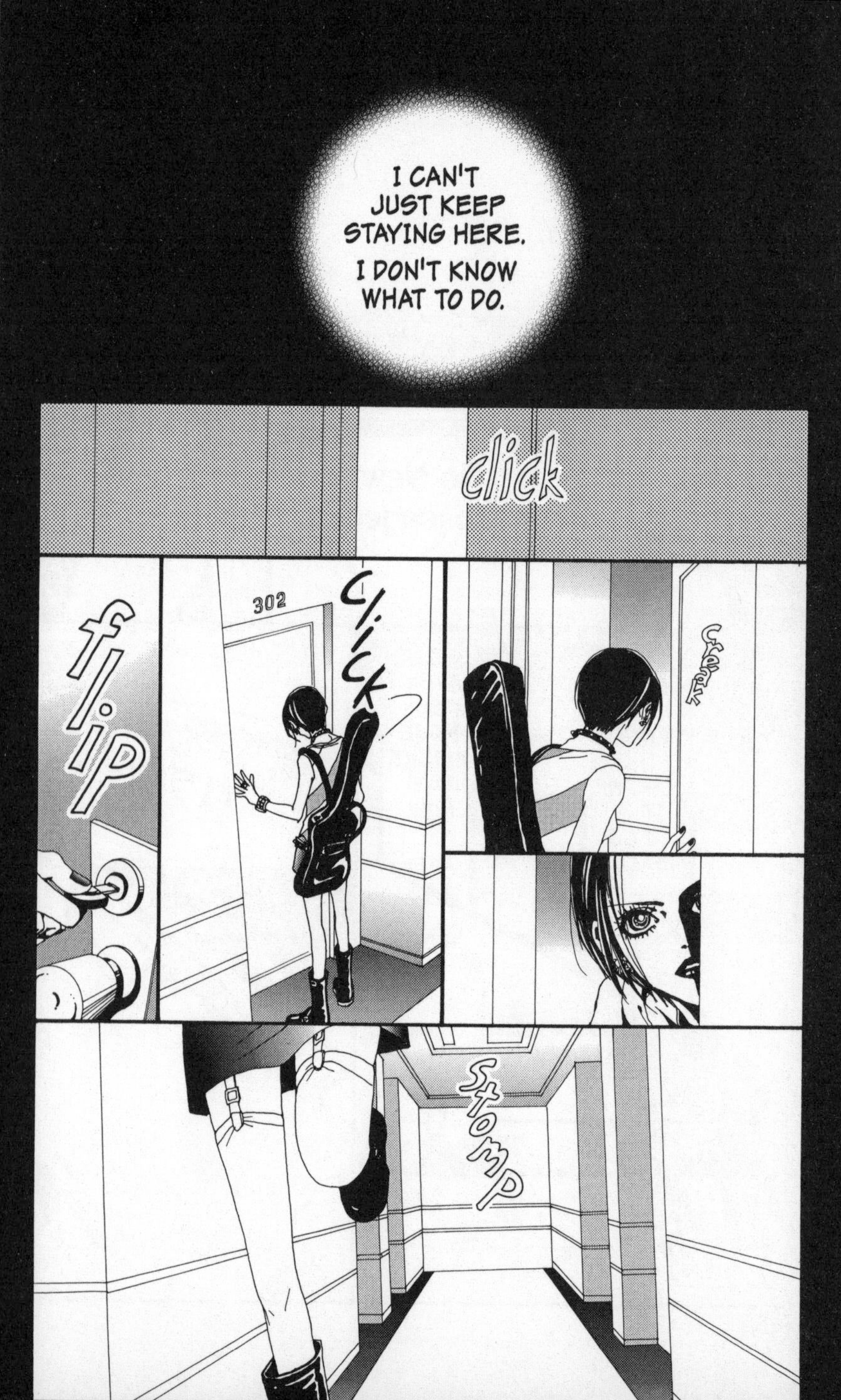
I CAN'T JUST KEEP STAYING HERE.
I DON'T KNOW WHAT TO DO.
click
creak
302
CLICK
flip
stomp

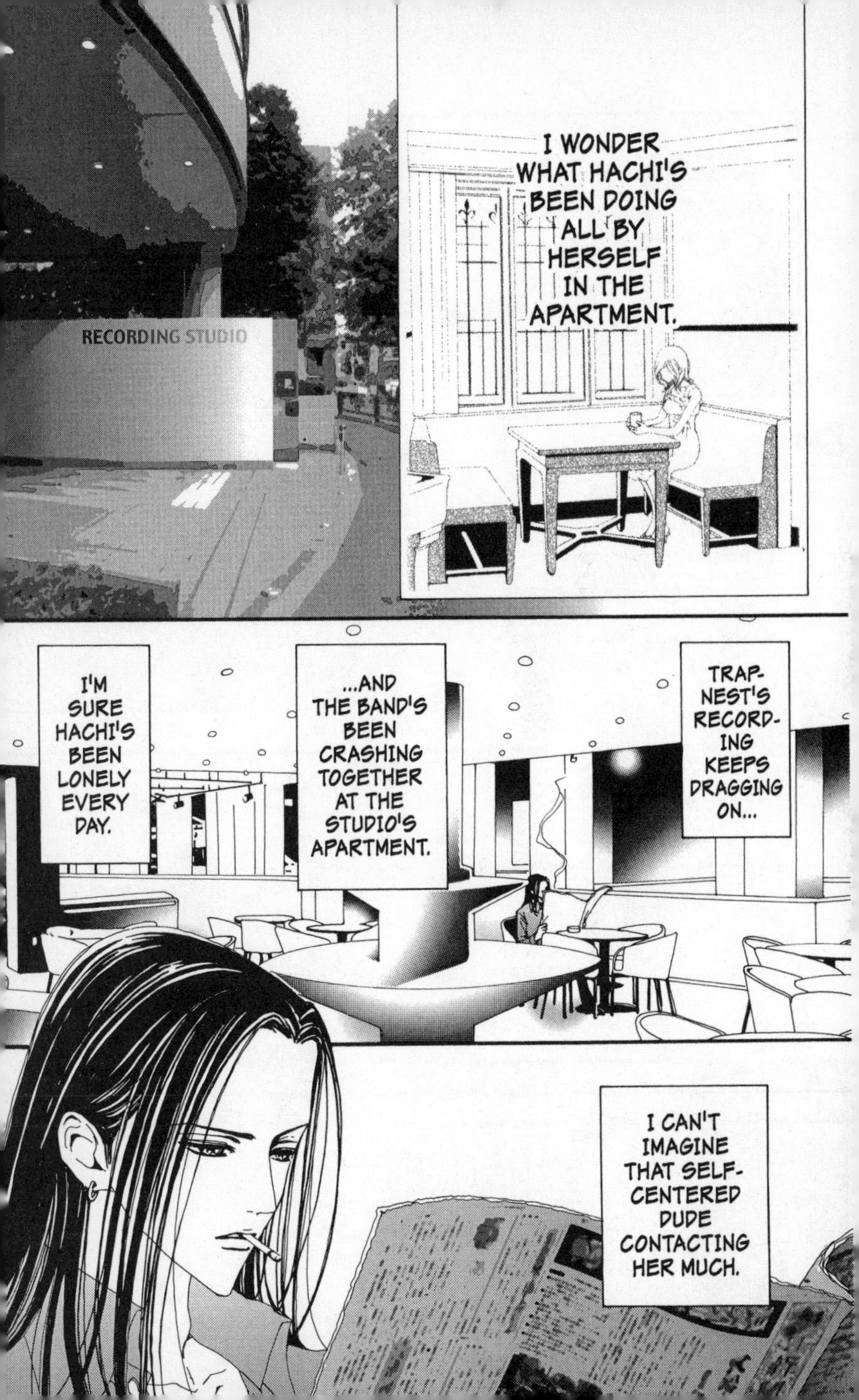
I WONDER WHAT HACHI'S BEEN DOING ALL BY HERSELF IN THE APARTMENT.
RECORDING STUDIO
TRAP-NEST'S RECORD-ING KEEPS DRAGGING ON...
...AND THE BAND'S BEEN CRASHING TOGETHER AT THE STUDIO'S APARTMENT.
I'M SURE HACHI'S BEEN LONELY EVERY DAY.
I CAN'T IMAGINE THAT SELF-CENTERED DUDE CONTACTING HER MUCH.

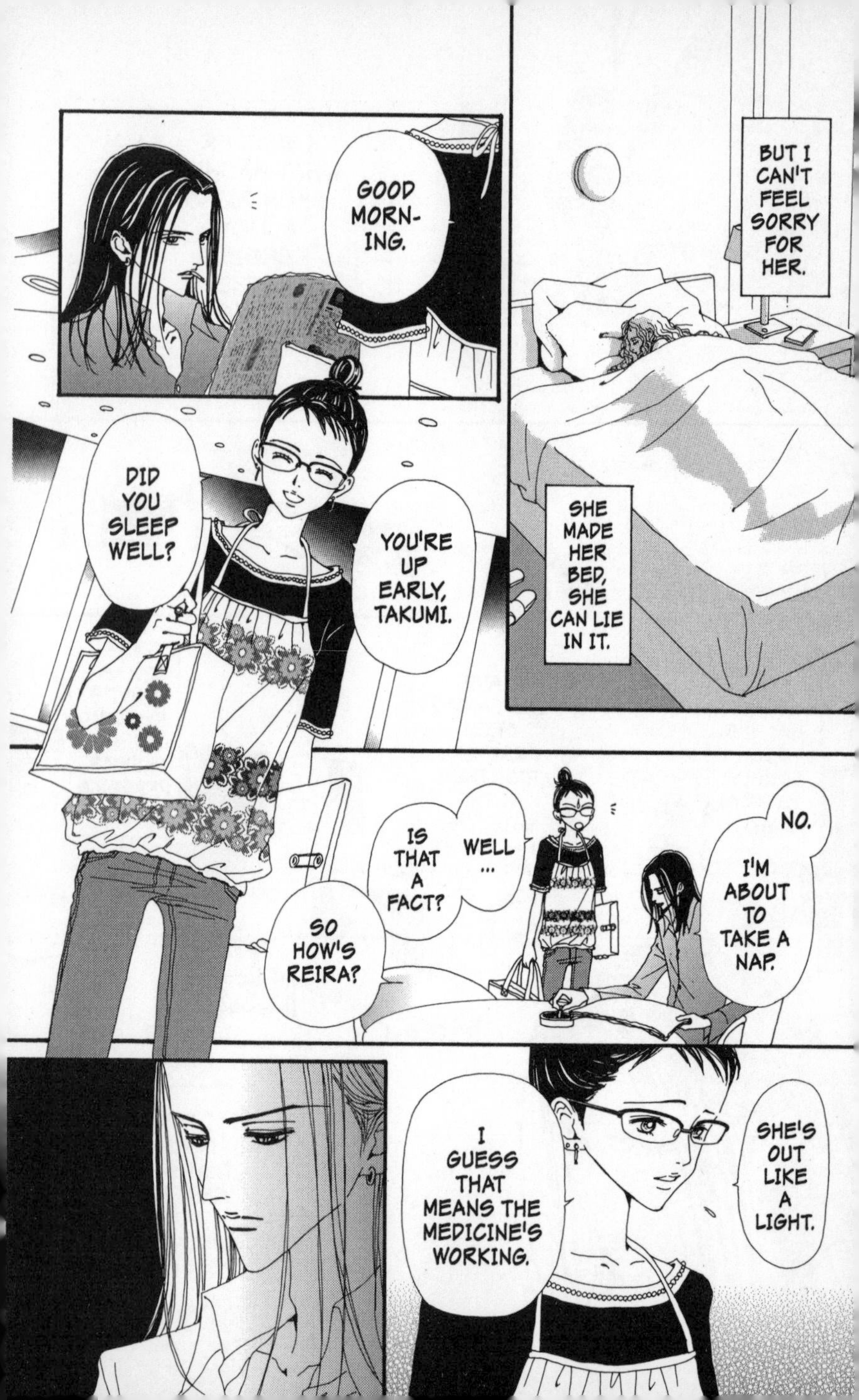
BUT I CAN'T FEEL SORRY FOR HER.
SHE MADE HER BED, SHE CAN LIE IN IT.
GOOD MORNING.
YOU'RE UP EARLY, TAKUMI.
DID YOU SLEEP WELL?
NO.
I'M ABOUT TO TAKE A NAP.
WELL...
IS THAT A FACT?
SO HOW'S REIRA?
SHE'S OUT LIKE A LIGHT.
I GUESS THAT MEANS THE MEDICINE'S WORKING.

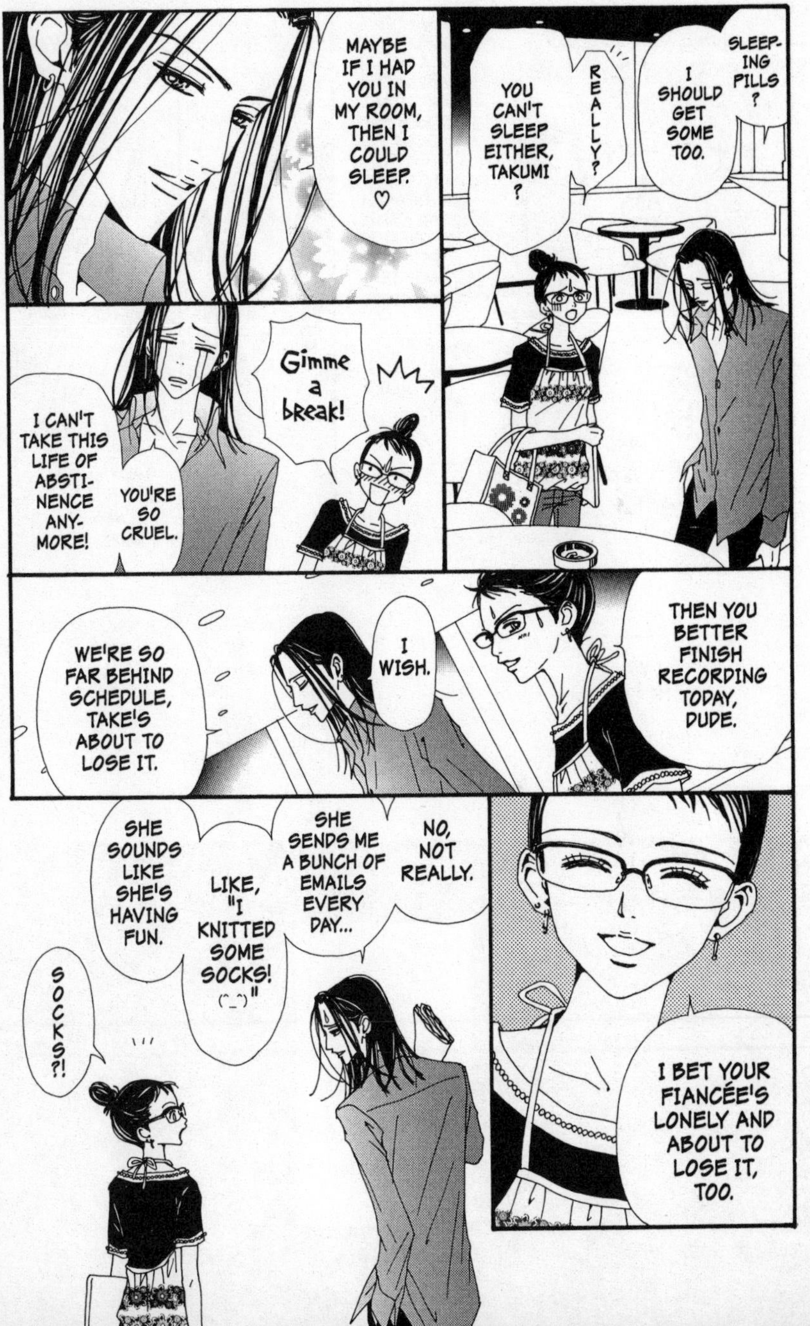
SLEEPING PILLS?
I SHOULD GET SOME TOO.
REALLY?
YOU CAN'T SLEEP EITHER, TAKUMI?
MAYBE IF I HAD YOU IN MY ROOM, THEN I COULD SLEEP. ♡
Gimme a break!
YOU'RE SO CRUEL.
I CAN'T TAKE THIS LIFE OF ABSTINENCE ANYMORE!
THEN YOU BETTER FINISH RECORDING TODAY, DUDE.
I WISH.
WE'RE SO FAR BEHIND SCHEDULE, TAKE'S ABOUT TO LOSE IT.
I BET YOUR FIANCÉE'S LONELY AND ABOUT TO LOSE IT, TOO.
NO, NOT REALLY.
SHE SENDS ME A BUNCH OF EMAILS EVERY DAY...
LIKE, "I KNITTED SOME SOCKS! (^_^)"
SHE SOUNDS LIKE SHE'S HAVING FUN.
SOCKS?!

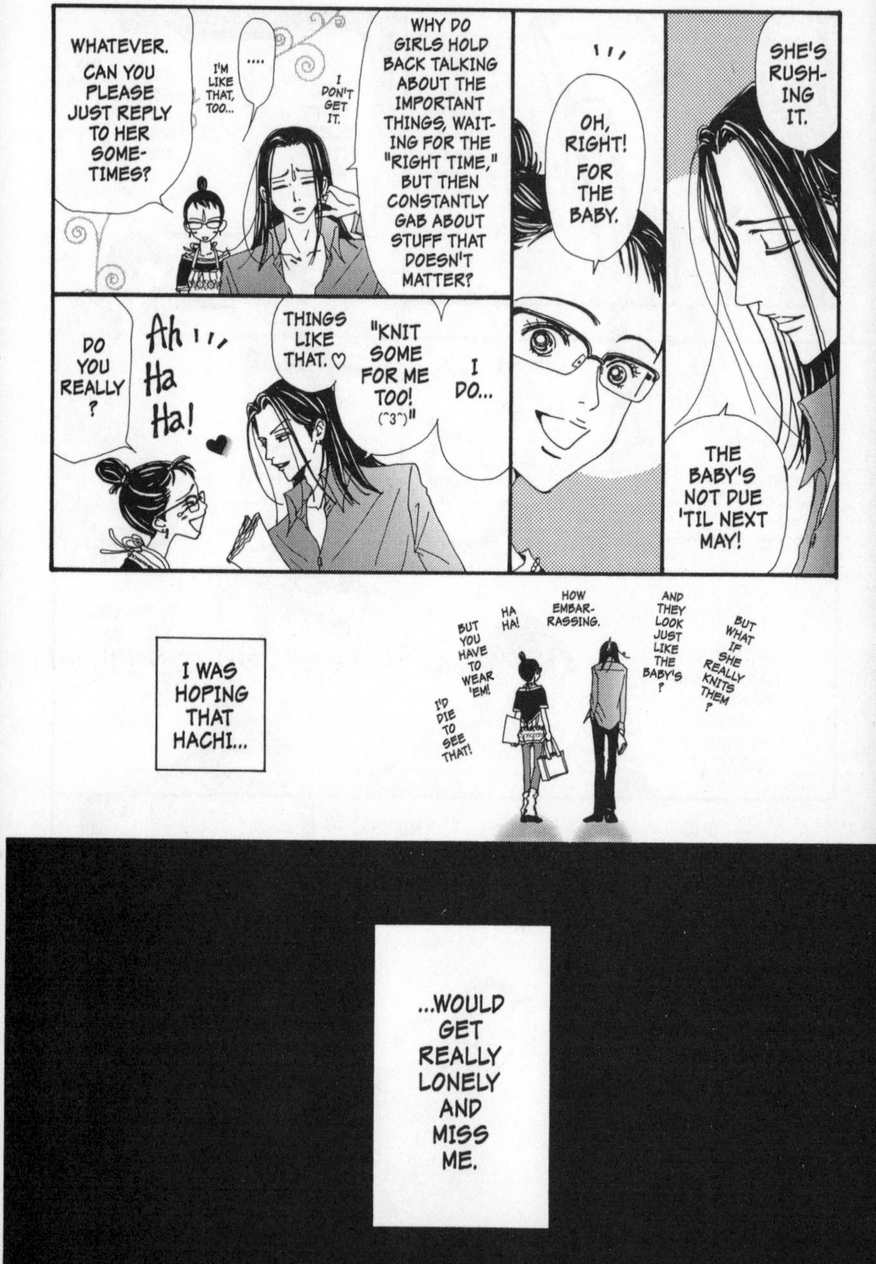
SHE'S RUSHING IT.
THE BABY'S NOT DUE 'TIL NEXT MAY!
OH, RIGHT! FOR THE BABY.
WHY DO GIRLS HOLD BACK TALKING ABOUT THE IMPORTANT THINGS, WAITING FOR THE "RIGHT TIME," BUT THEN CONSTANTLY GAB ABOUT STUFF THAT DOESN'T MATTER?
I DON'T GET IT.
....
I'M LIKE THAT, TOO...
WHATEVER. CAN YOU PLEASE JUST REPLY TO HER SOMETIMES?
I DO...
"KNIT SOME FOR ME TOO! (^3^)"
THINGS LIKE THAT. ♡
Ah Ha Ha!
DO YOU REALLY?
BUT WHAT IF SHE REALLY KNITS THEM?
AND THEY LOOK JUST LIKE THE BABY'S?
HOW EMBARRASSING.
HA HA!
BUT YOU HAVE TO WEAR 'EM!
I'D DIE TO SEE THAT!
I WAS HOPING THAT HACHI...
...WOULD GET REALLY LONELY AND MISS ME.

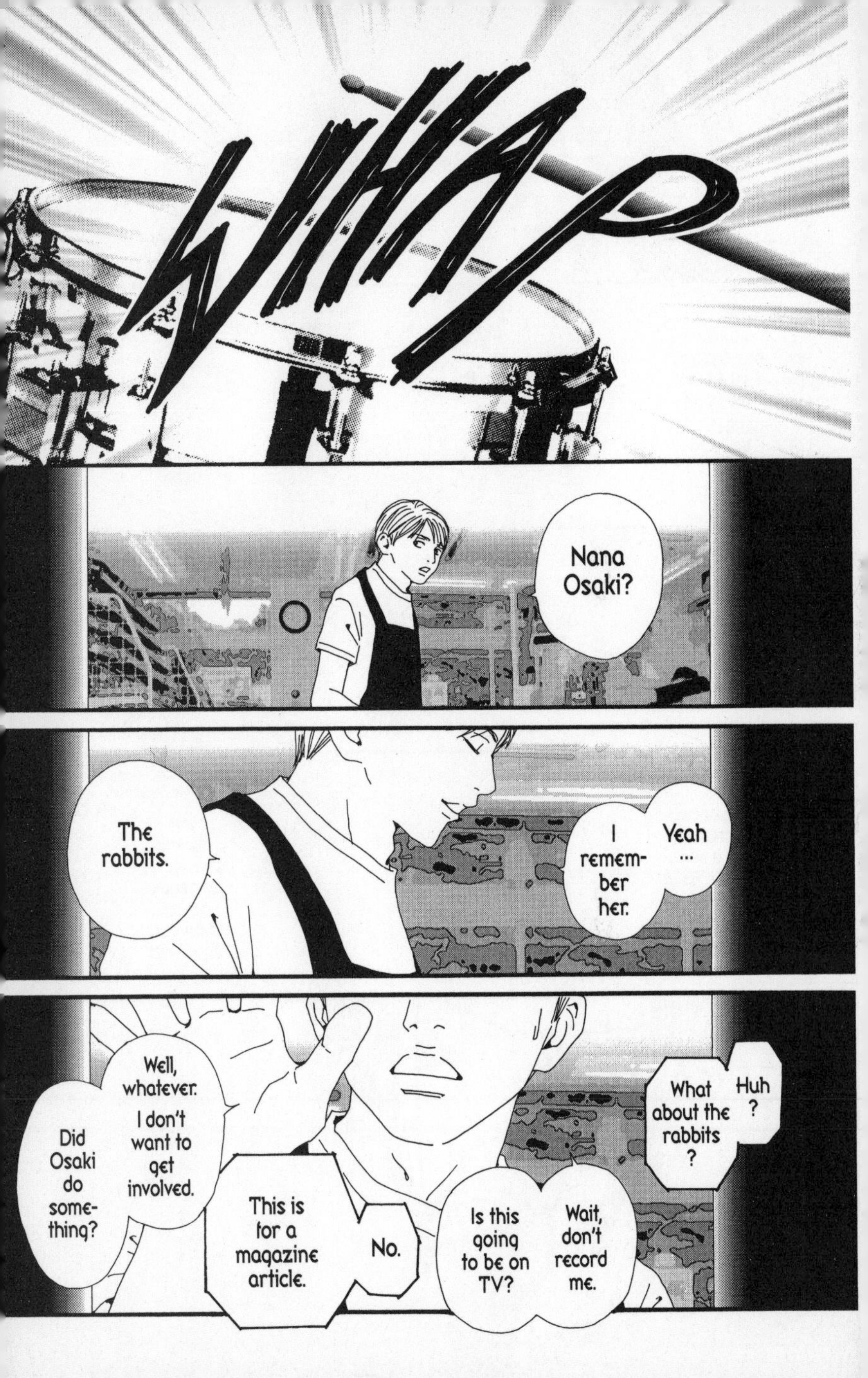
WHAP
Nana Osaki?
Yeah ...
I remember her.
The rabbits.
Huh?
What about the rabbits?
Wait, don't record me.
Is this going to be on TV?
No.
This is for a magazine article.
Well, whatever. I don't want to get involved.
Did Osaki do something?

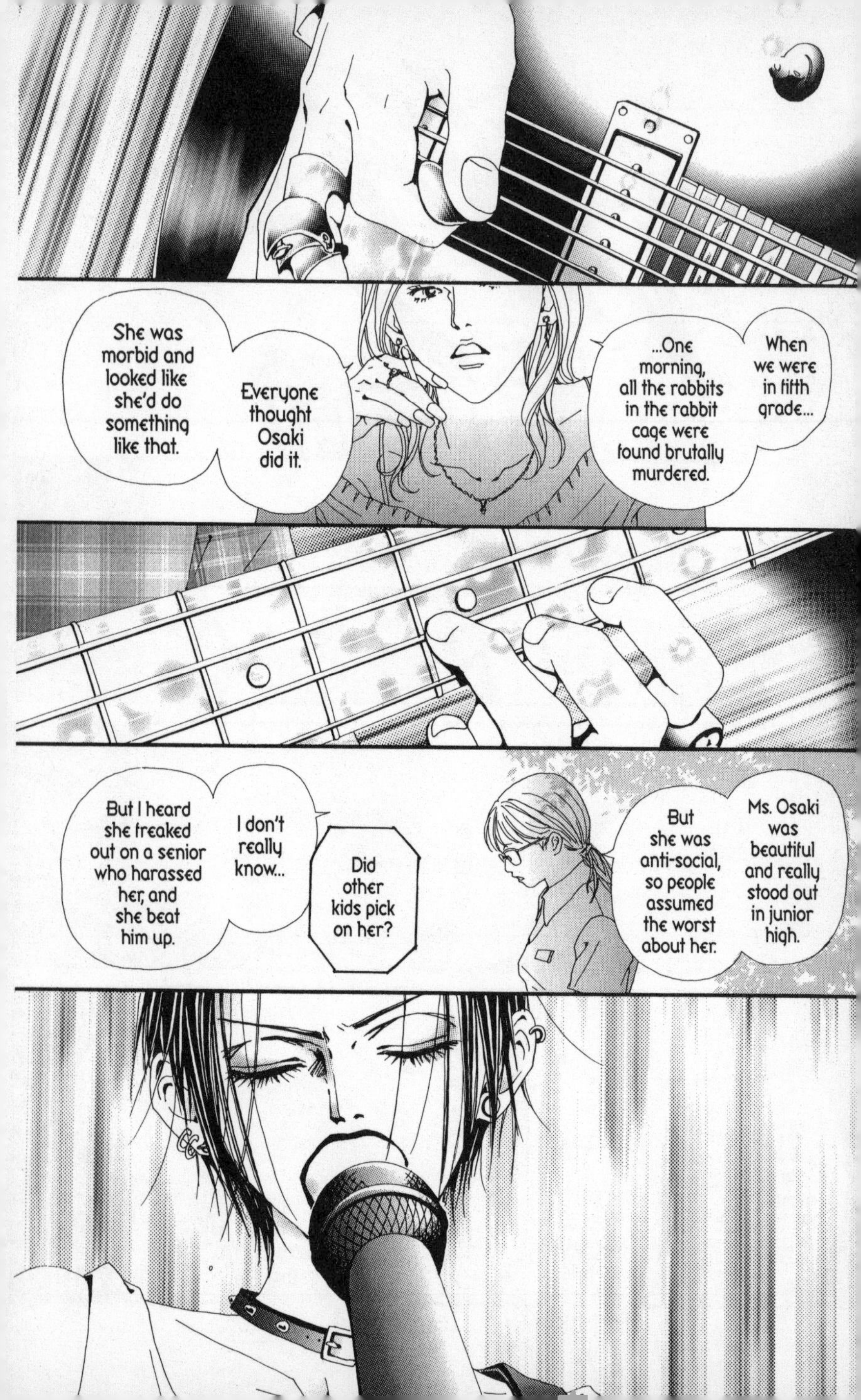
When we were in fifth grade...
...One morning, all the rabbits in the rabbit cage were found brutally murdered.
Everyone thought Osaki did it.
She was morbid and looked like she'd do something like that.
Ms. Osaki was beautiful and really stood out in junior high.
But she was anti-social, so people assumed the worst about her.
Did other kids pick on her?
I don't really know...
But I heard she freaked out on a senior who harassed her, and she beat him up.

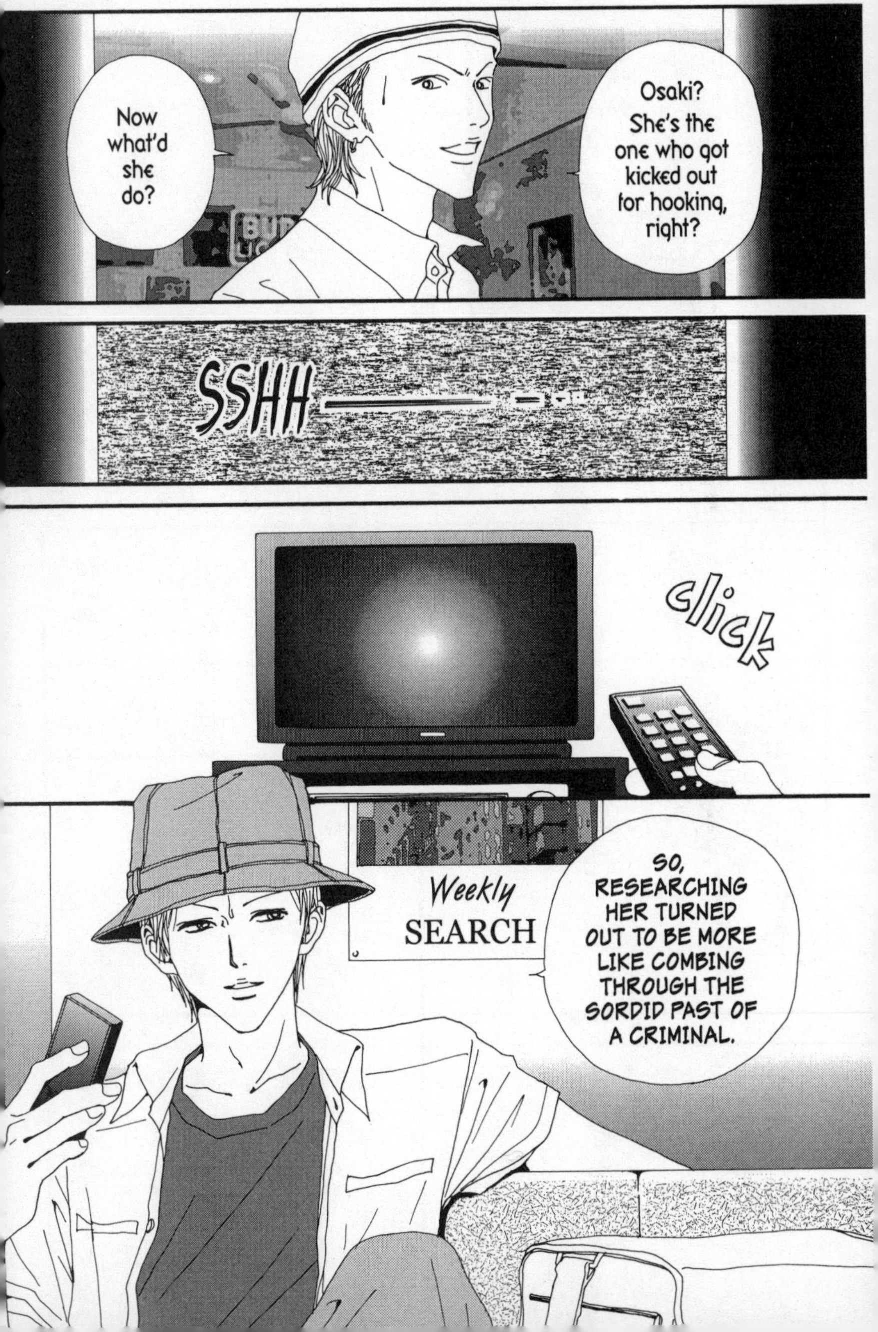
Osaki? She's the one who got kicked out for hooking, right?
Now what'd she do?
SSHH
click
SO, RESEARCHING HER TURNED OUT TO BE MORE LIKE COMBING THROUGH THE SORDID PAST OF A CRIMINAL.
Weekly SEARCH

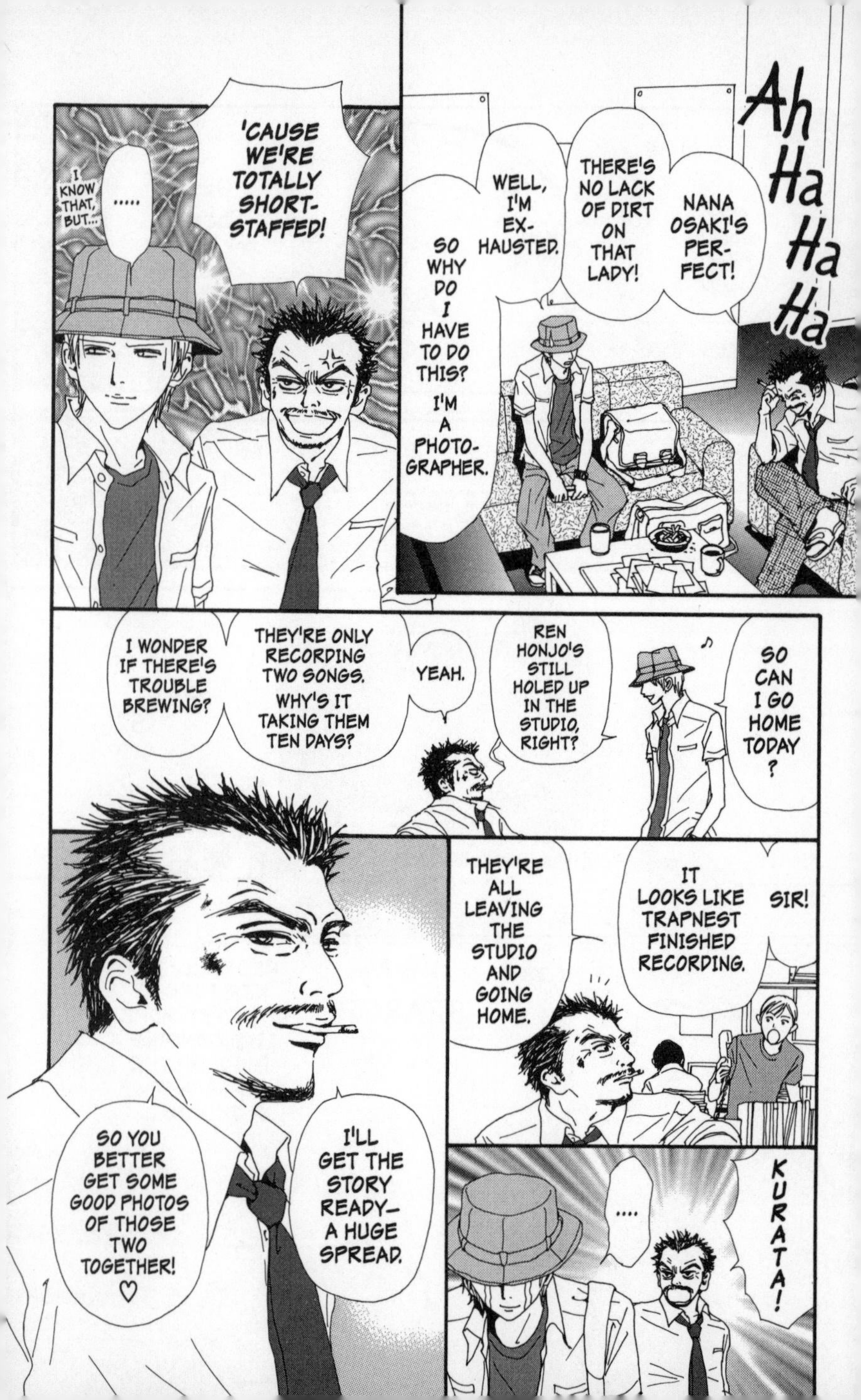
Ah Ha Ha Ha
NANA OSAKI'S PERFECT!
THERE'S NO LACK OF DIRT ON THAT LADY!
WELL, I'M EXHAUSTED.
SO WHY DO I HAVE TO DO THIS? I'M A PHOTOGRAPHER.
'CAUSE WE'RE TOTALLY SHORT-STAFFED!
.....
I KNOW THAT, BUT...
SO CAN I GO HOME TODAY?
REN HONJO'S STILL HOLED UP IN THE STUDIO, RIGHT?
YEAH.
THEY'RE ONLY RECORDING TWO SONGS. WHY'S IT TAKING THEM TEN DAYS?
I WONDER IF THERE'S TROUBLE BREWING?
SIR!
IT LOOKS LIKE TRAPNEST FINISHED RECORDING.
THEY'RE ALL LEAVING THE STUDIO AND GOING HOME.
KURATA!
....
I'LL GET THE STORY READY— A HUGE SPREAD.
SO YOU BETTER GET SOME GOOD PHOTOS OF THOSE TWO TOGETHER! ♡

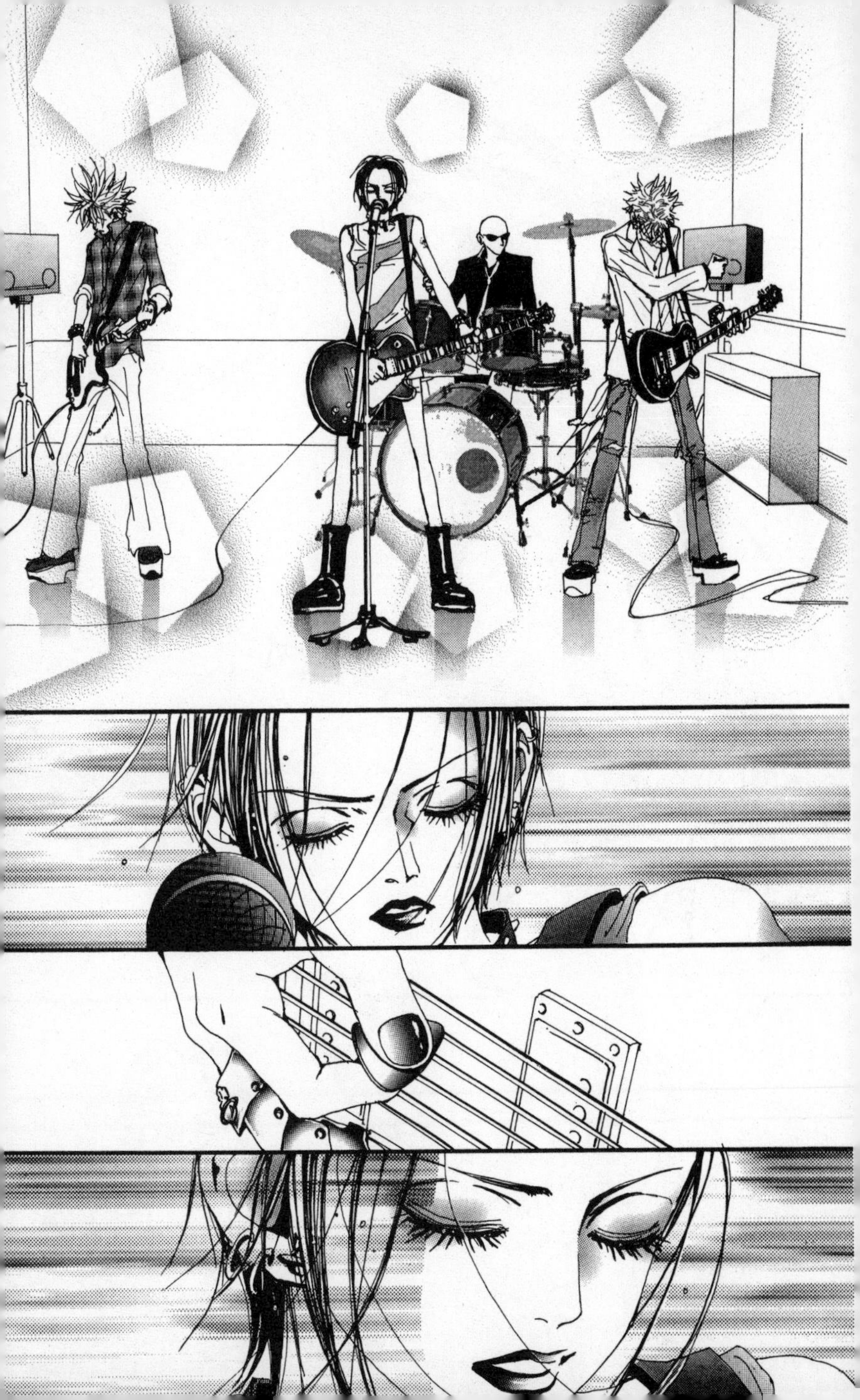

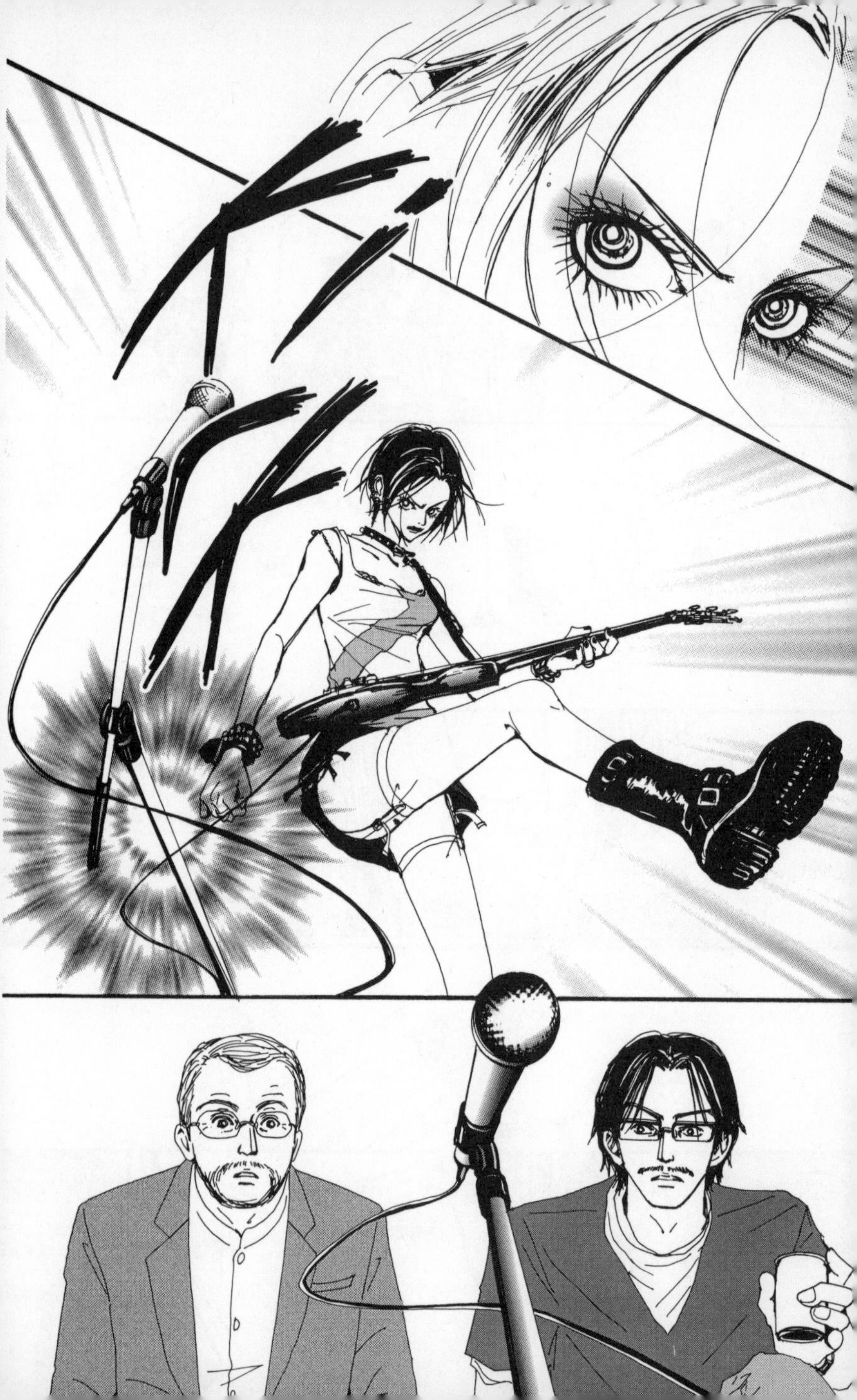

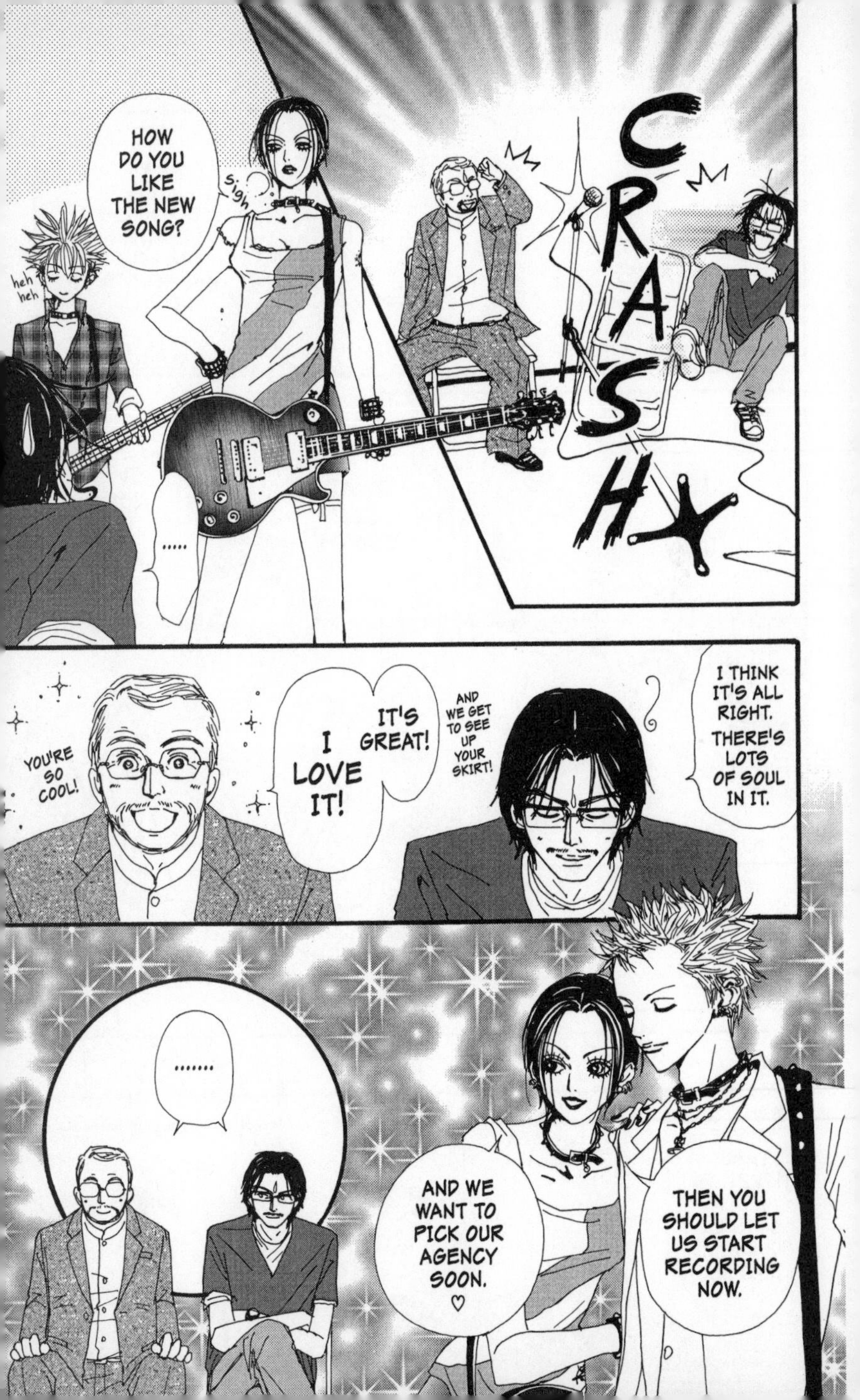
CRASH
HOW DO YOU LIKE THE NEW SONG?
sigh
heh heh
......
I THINK IT'S ALL RIGHT. THERE'S LOTS OF SOUL IN IT.
AND WE GET TO SEE UP YOUR SKIRT!
IT'S GREAT! I LOVE IT!
YOU'RE SO COOL!
THEN YOU SHOULD LET US START RECORDING NOW.
AND WE WANT TO PICK OUR AGENCY SOON. ♡
....

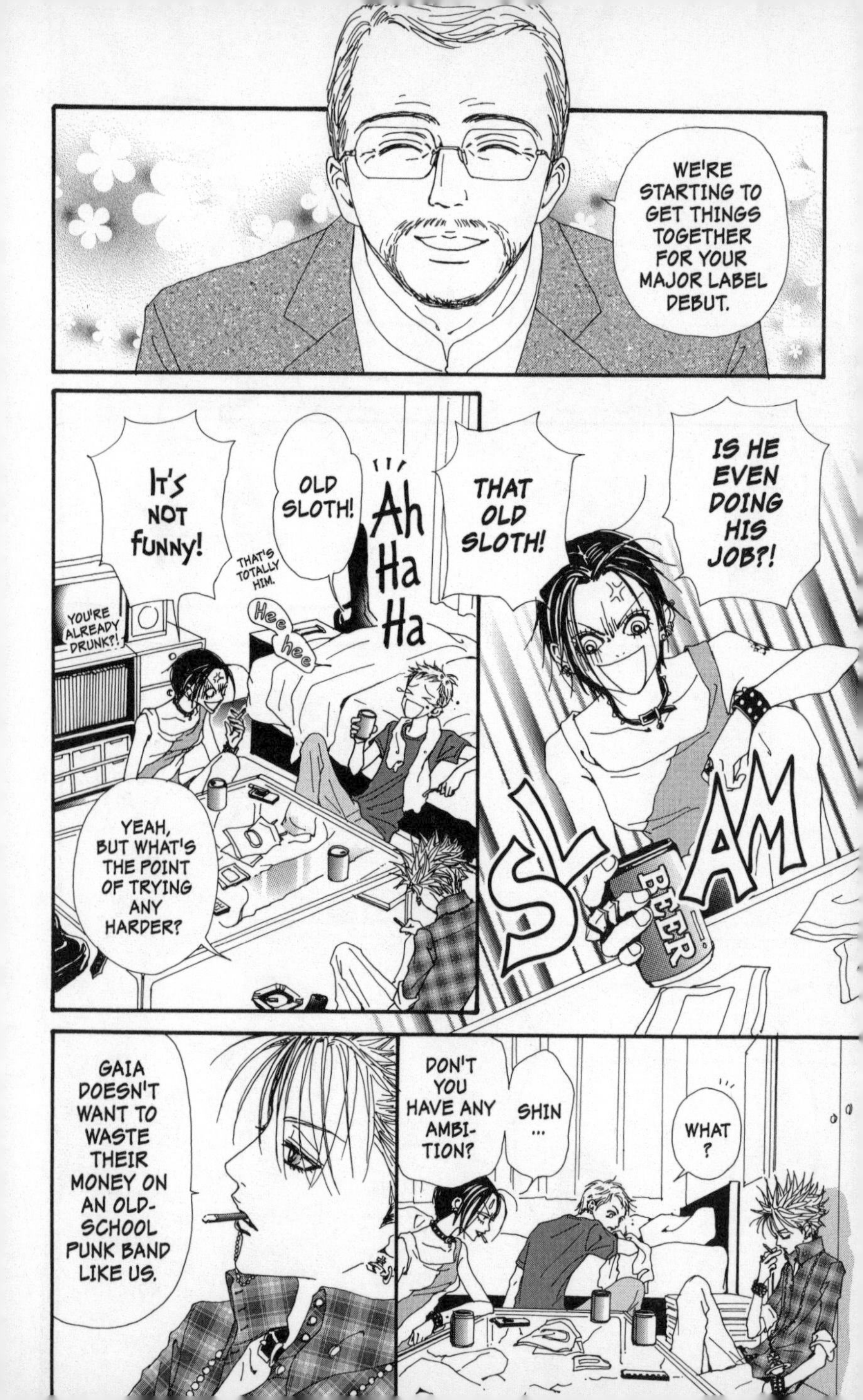
WE'RE STARTING TO GET THINGS TOGETHER FOR YOUR MAJOR LABEL DEBUT.
IS HE EVEN DOING HIS JOB?!
THAT OLD SLOTH!
SLAM
BEER
Ah Ha Ha
OLD SLOTH!
THAT'S TOTALLY HIM.
Hee hee
It's not funny!
YOU'RE ALREADY DRUNK?!
YEAH, BUT WHAT'S THE POINT OF TRYING ANY HARDER?
WHAT ?
SHIN ...
DON'T YOU HAVE ANY AMBITION?
GAIA DOESN'T WANT TO WASTE THEIR MONEY ON AN OLD-SCHOOL PUNK BAND LIKE US.

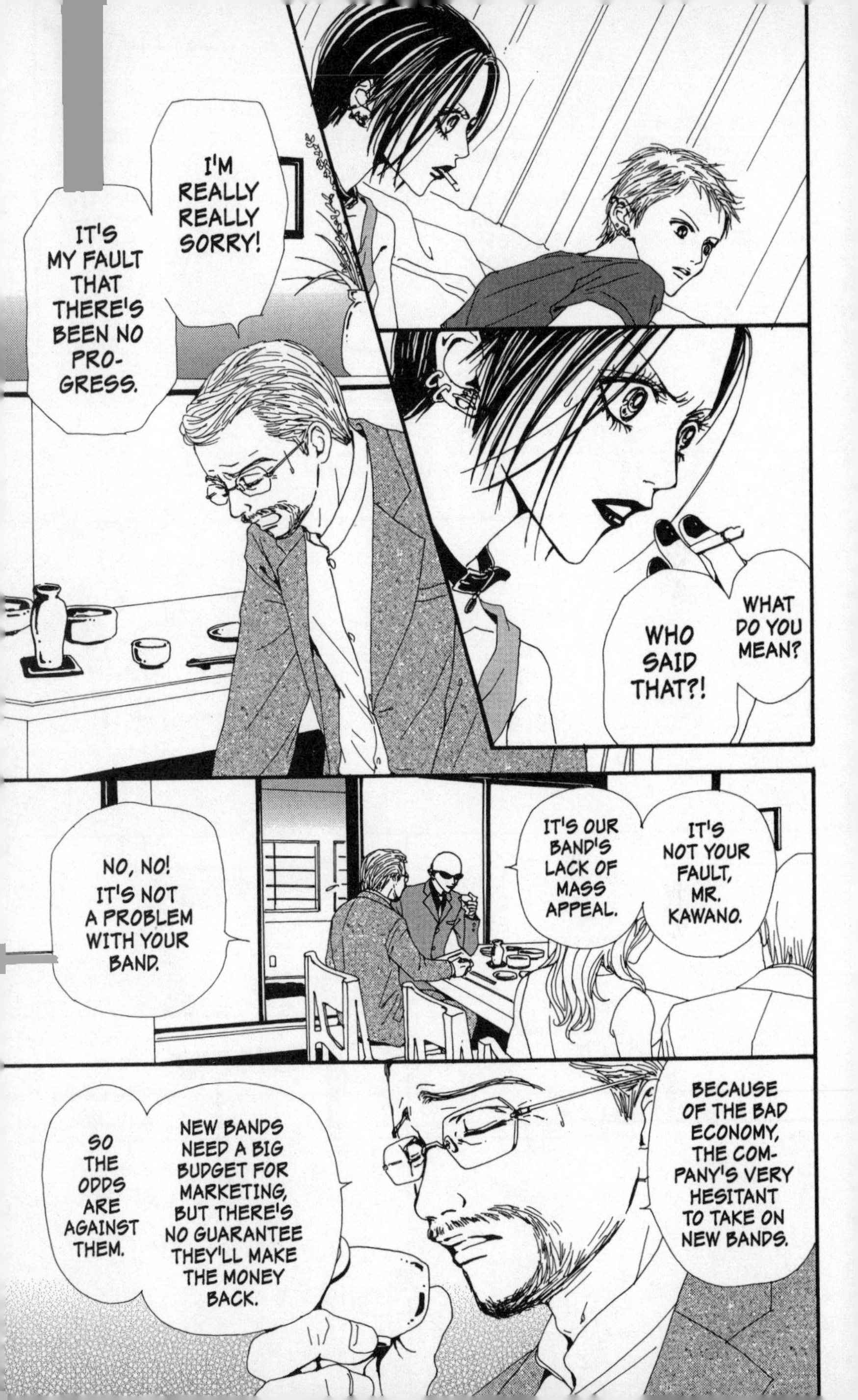
I'M REALLY REALLY SORRY!
IT'S MY FAULT THAT THERE'S BEEN NO PRO-GRESS.
WHAT DO YOU MEAN?
WHO SAID THAT?!
IT'S NOT YOUR FAULT, MR. KAWANO.
IT'S OUR BAND'S LACK OF MASS APPEAL.
NO, NO! IT'S NOT A PROBLEM WITH YOUR BAND.
BECAUSE OF THE BAD ECONOMY, THE COM-PANY'S VERY HESITANT TO TAKE ON NEW BANDS.
NEW BANDS NEED A BIG BUDGET FOR MARKETING, BUT THERE'S NO GUARANTEE THEY'LL MAKE THE MONEY BACK.
SO THE ODDS ARE AGAINST THEM.

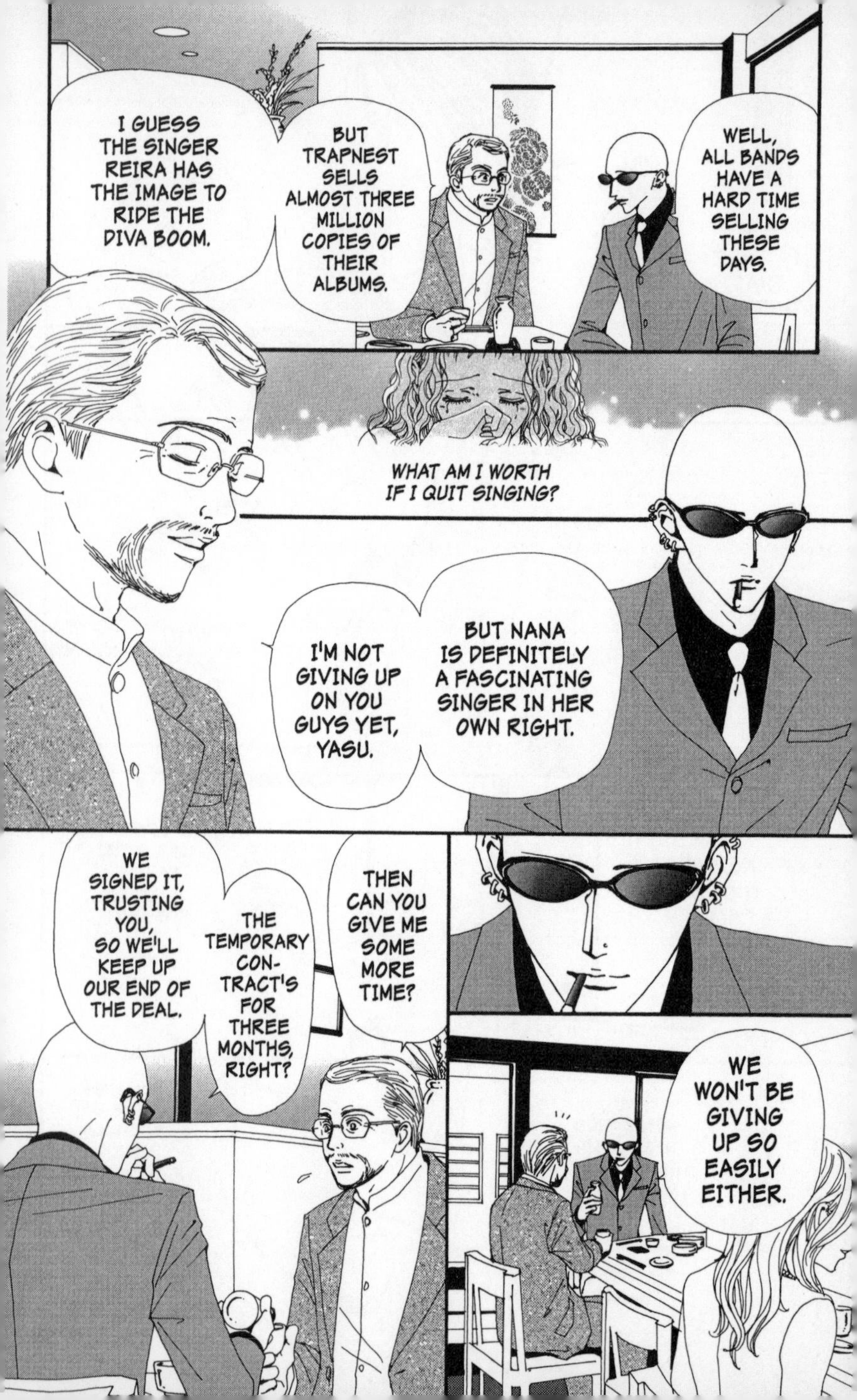
WELL, ALL BANDS HAVE A HARD TIME SELLING THESE DAYS.
BUT TRAPNEST SELLS ALMOST THREE MILLION COPIES OF THEIR ALBUMS.
I GUESS THE SINGER REIRA HAS THE IMAGE TO RIDE THE DIVA BOOM.
WHAT AM I WORTH IF I QUIT SINGING?
BUT NANA IS DEFINITELY A FASCINATING SINGER IN HER OWN RIGHT.
I'M NOT GIVING UP ON YOU GUYS YET, YASU.
WE WON'T BE GIVING UP SO EASILY EITHER.
THEN CAN YOU GIVE ME SOME MORE TIME?
THE TEMPORARY CON-TRACT'S FOR THREE MONTHS, RIGHT?
WE SIGNED IT, TRUSTING YOU, SO WE'LL KEEP UP OUR END OF THE DEAL.

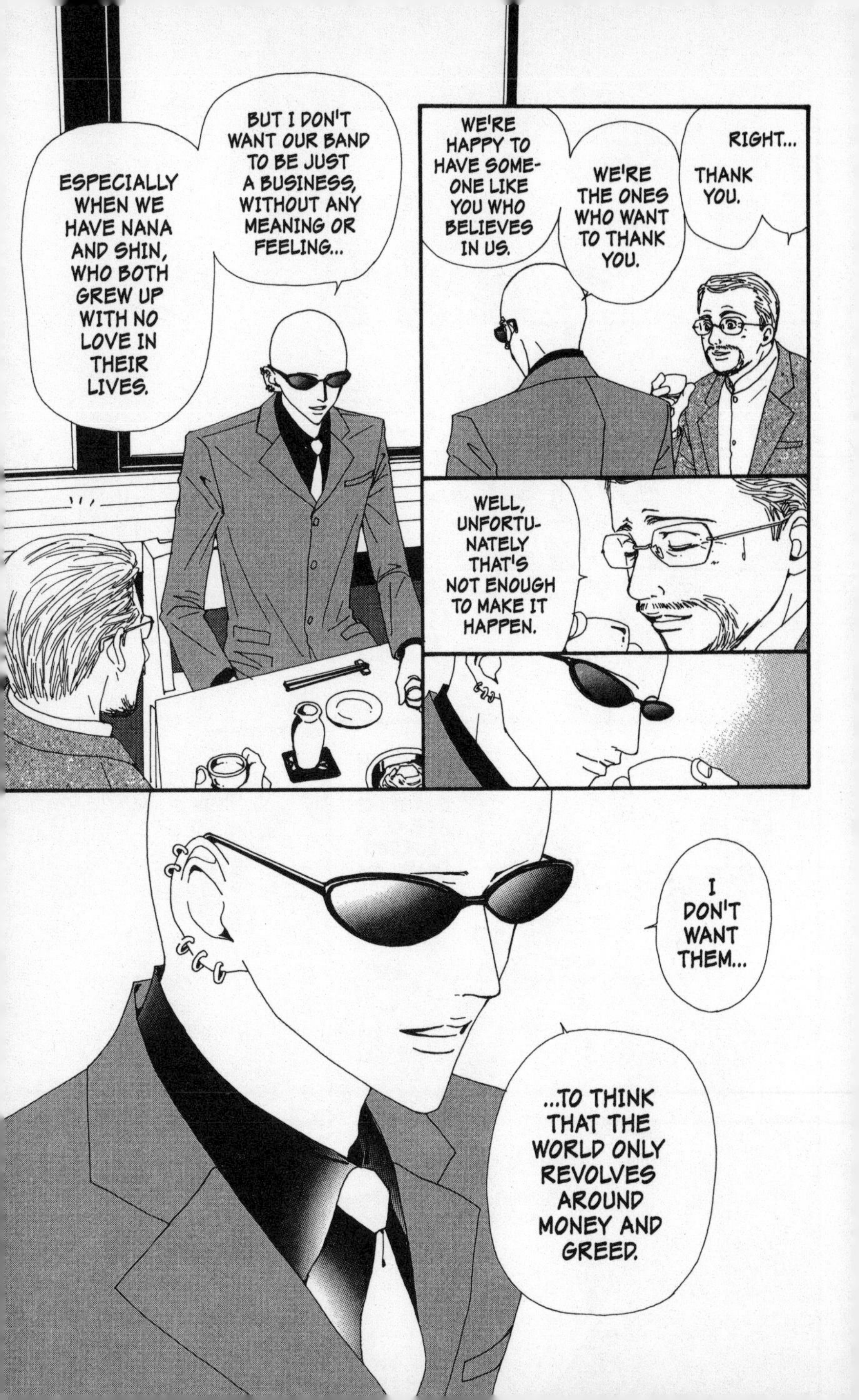
RIGHT... THANK YOU.
WE'RE THE ONES WHO WANT TO THANK YOU.
WE'RE HAPPY TO HAVE SOME-ONE LIKE YOU WHO BELIEVES IN US.
WELL, UNFORTU-NATELY THAT'S NOT ENOUGH TO MAKE IT HAPPEN.
BUT I DON'T WANT OUR BAND TO BE JUST A BUSINESS, WITHOUT ANY MEANING OR FEELING...
ESPECIALLY WHEN WE HAVE NANA AND SHIN, WHO BOTH GREW UP WITH NO LOVE IN THEIR LIVES.
I DON'T WANT THEM...
...TO THINK THAT THE WORLD ONLY REVOLVES AROUND MONEY AND GREED.

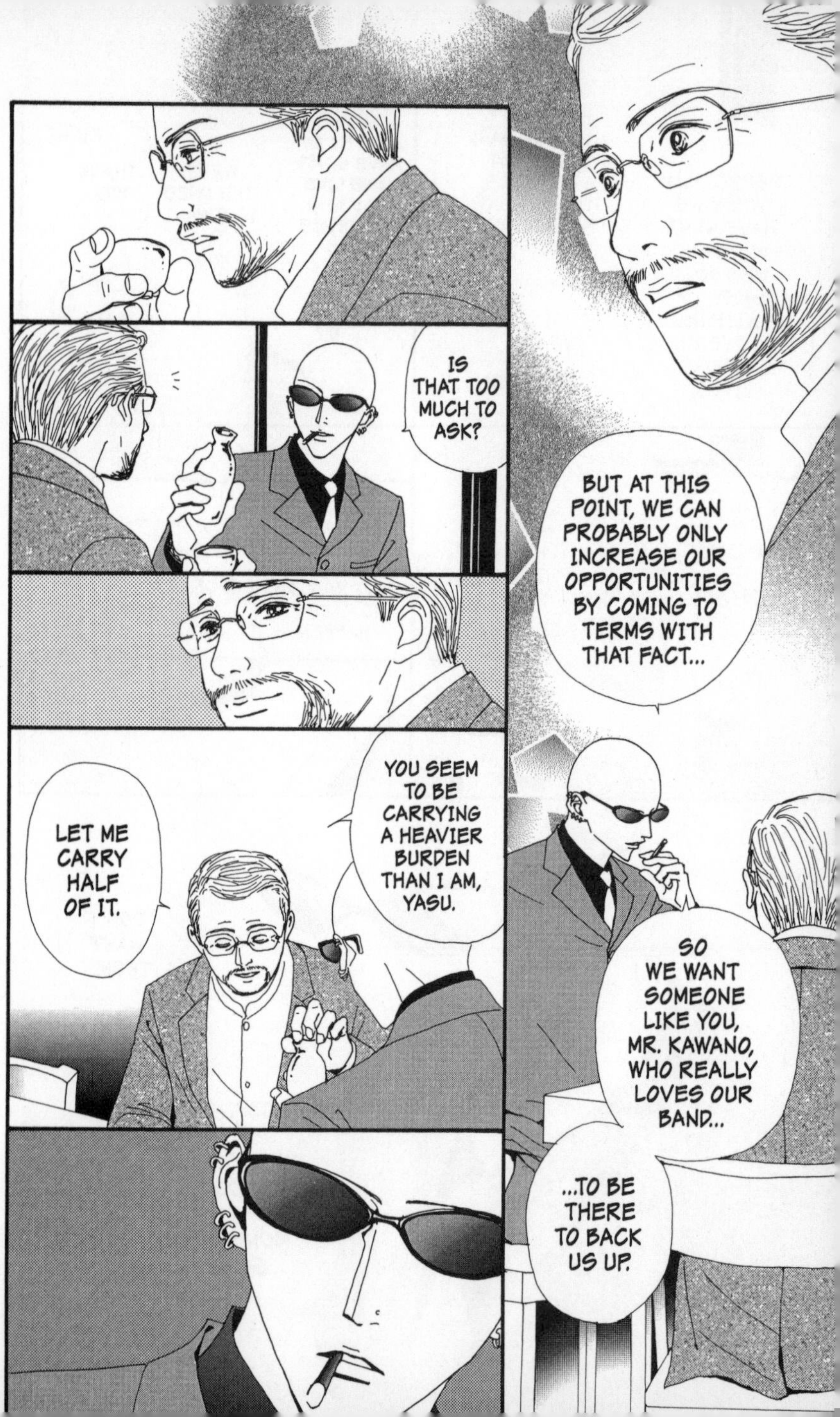
BUT AT THIS POINT, WE CAN PROBABLY ONLY INCREASE OUR OPPORTUNITIES BY COMING TO TERMS WITH THAT FACT...
SO WE WANT SOMEONE LIKE YOU, MR. KAWANO, WHO REALLY LOVES OUR BAND...
...TO BE THERE TO BACK US UP.
IS THAT TOO MUCH TO ASK?
YOU SEEM TO BE CARRYING A HEAVIER BURDEN THAN I AM, YASU.
LET ME CARRY HALF OF IT.

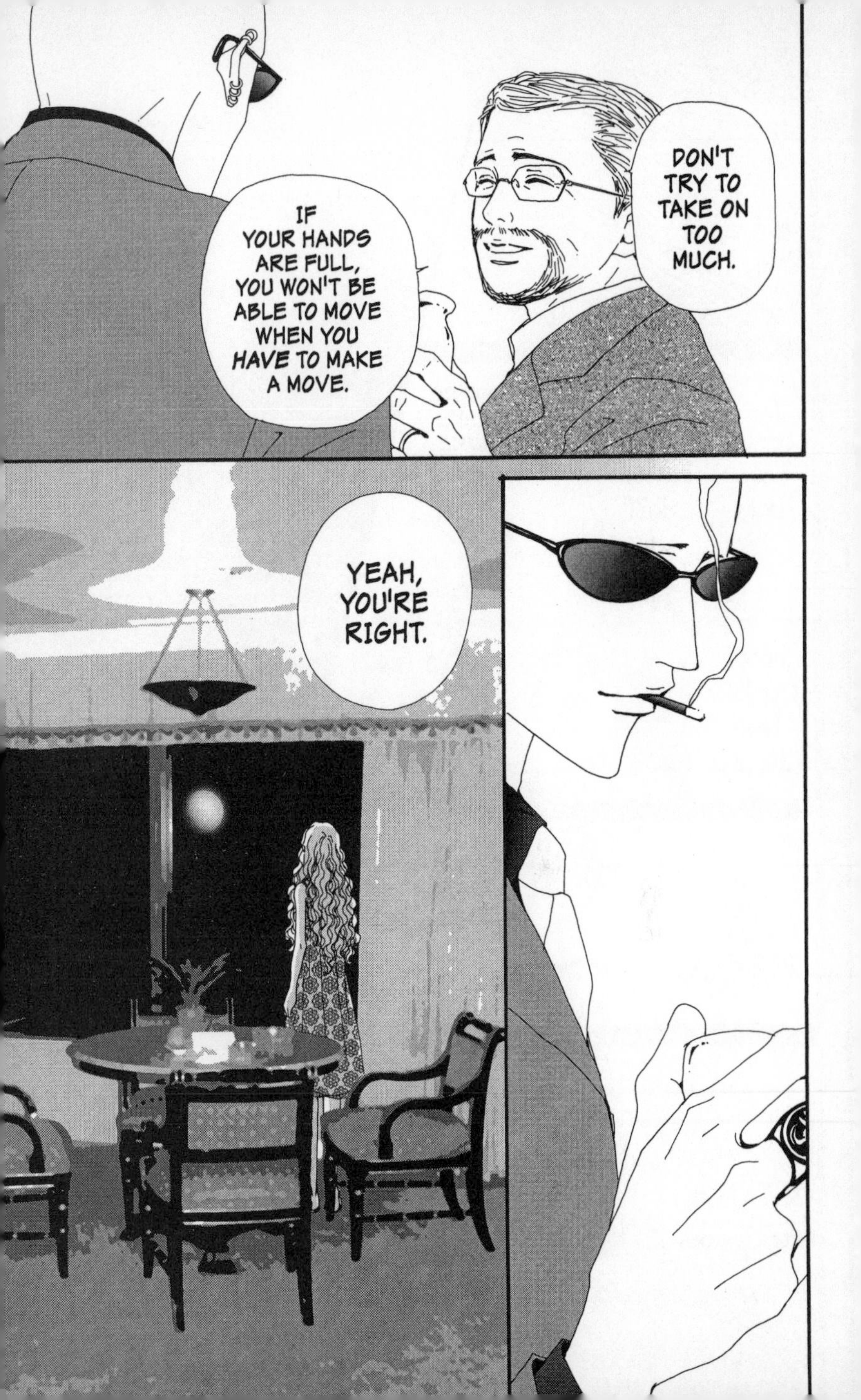
DON'T TRY TO TAKE ON TOO MUCH.
IF YOUR HANDS ARE FULL, YOU WON'T BE ABLE TO MOVE WHEN YOU *HAVE* TO MAKE A MOVE.
YEAH, YOU'RE RIGHT.

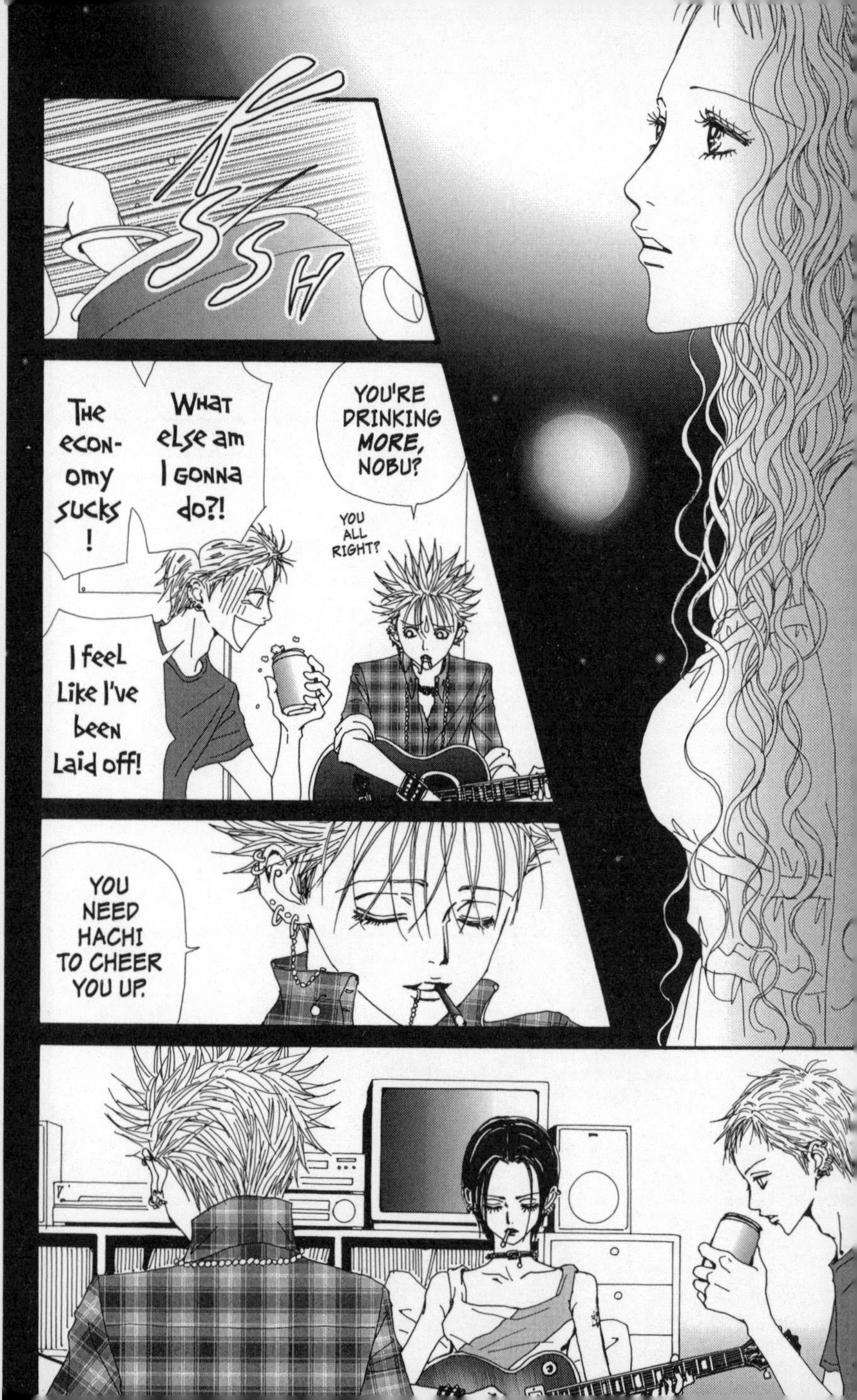
HSSH
YOU'RE DRINKING MORE, NOBU?
YOU ALL RIGHT?
WHAT eLse am I GONNA do?!
The econ-omy sucks!
I feeL Like I've been Laid off!
YOU NEED HACHI TO CHEER YOU UP.

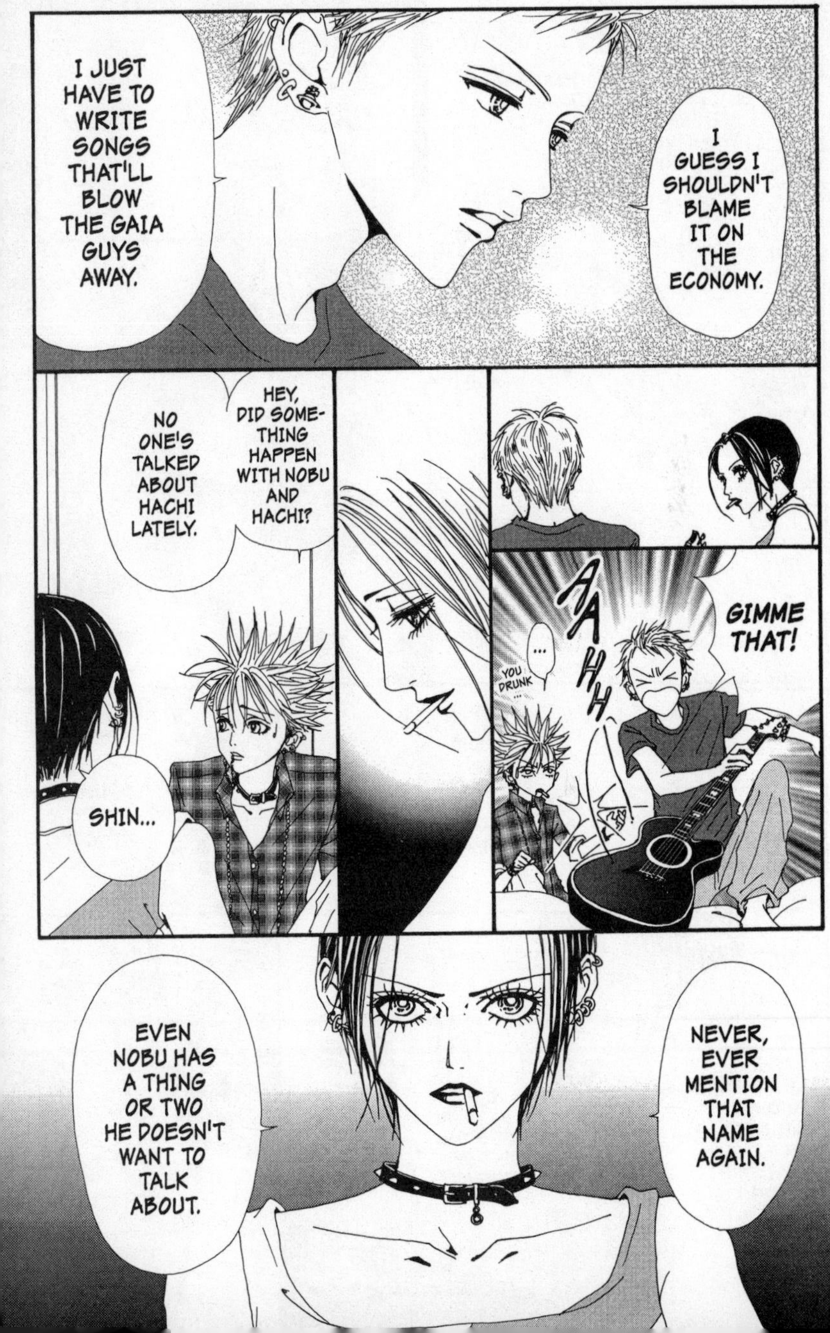
I GUESS I SHOULDN'T BLAME IT ON THE ECONOMY.
I JUST HAVE TO WRITE SONGS THAT'LL BLOW THE GAIA GUYS AWAY.
GIMME THAT!
AAHHH
...
YOU DRUNK...
HEY, DID SOME-THING HAPPEN WITH NOBU AND HACHI?
NO ONE'S TALKED ABOUT HACHI LATELY.
SHIN...
NEVER, EVER MENTION THAT NAME AGAIN.
EVEN NOBU HAS A THING OR TWO HE DOESN'T WANT TO TALK ABOUT.

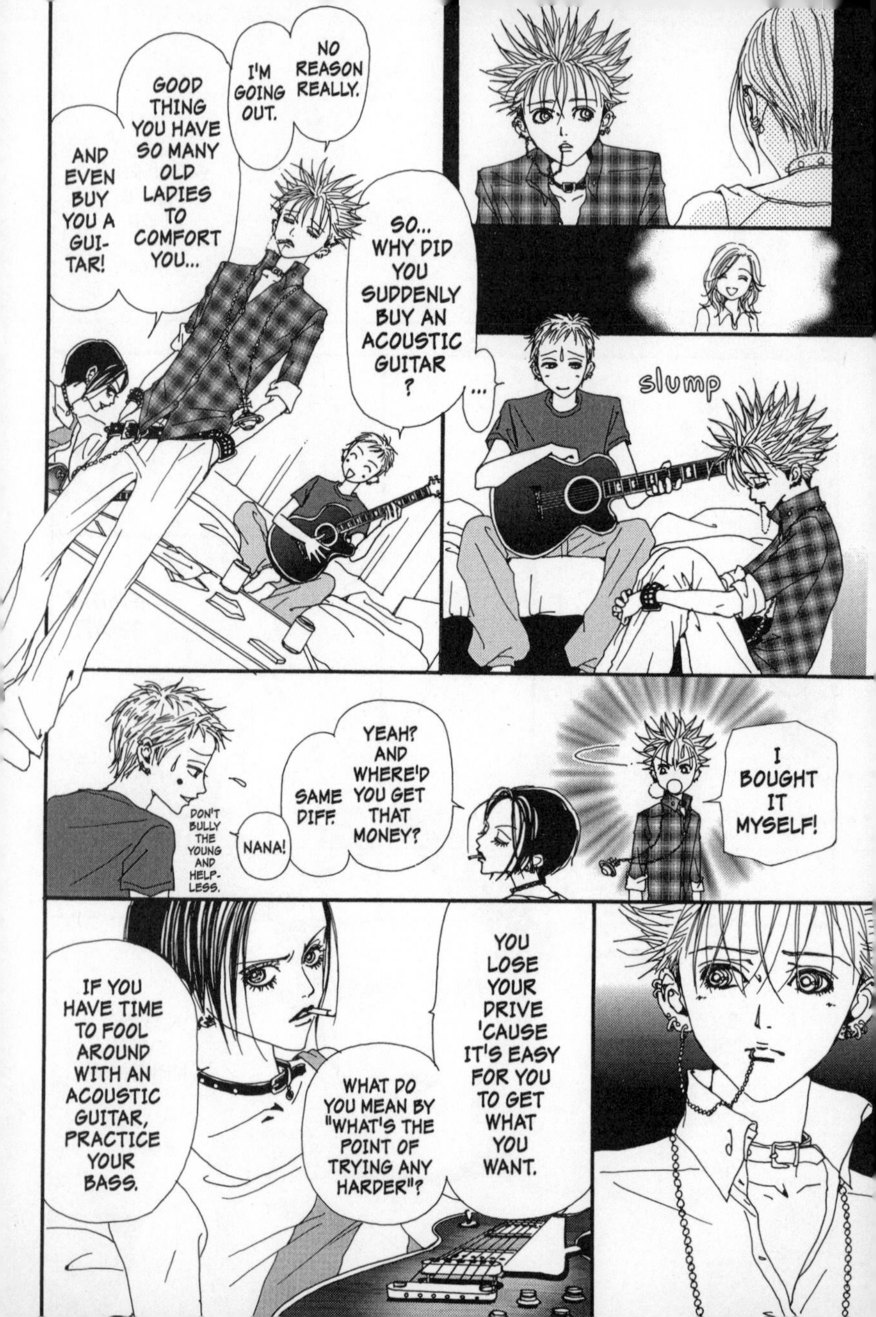
slump
...
NO REASON REALLY.
I'M GOING OUT.
GOOD THING YOU HAVE SO MANY OLD LADIES TO COMFORT YOU...
AND EVEN BUY YOU A GUI-TAR!
SO... WHY DID YOU SUDDENLY BUY AN ACOUSTIC GUITAR?
I BOUGHT IT MYSELF!
YEAH? AND WHERE'D YOU GET THAT MONEY?
SAME DIFF.
NANA!
DON'T BULLY THE YOUNG AND HELP-LESS.
YOU LOSE YOUR DRIVE 'CAUSE IT'S EASY FOR YOU TO GET WHAT YOU WANT.
WHAT DO YOU MEAN BY "WHAT'S THE POINT OF TRYING ANY HARDER"?
IF YOU HAVE TIME TO FOOL AROUND WITH AN ACOUSTIC GUITAR, PRACTICE YOUR BASS.

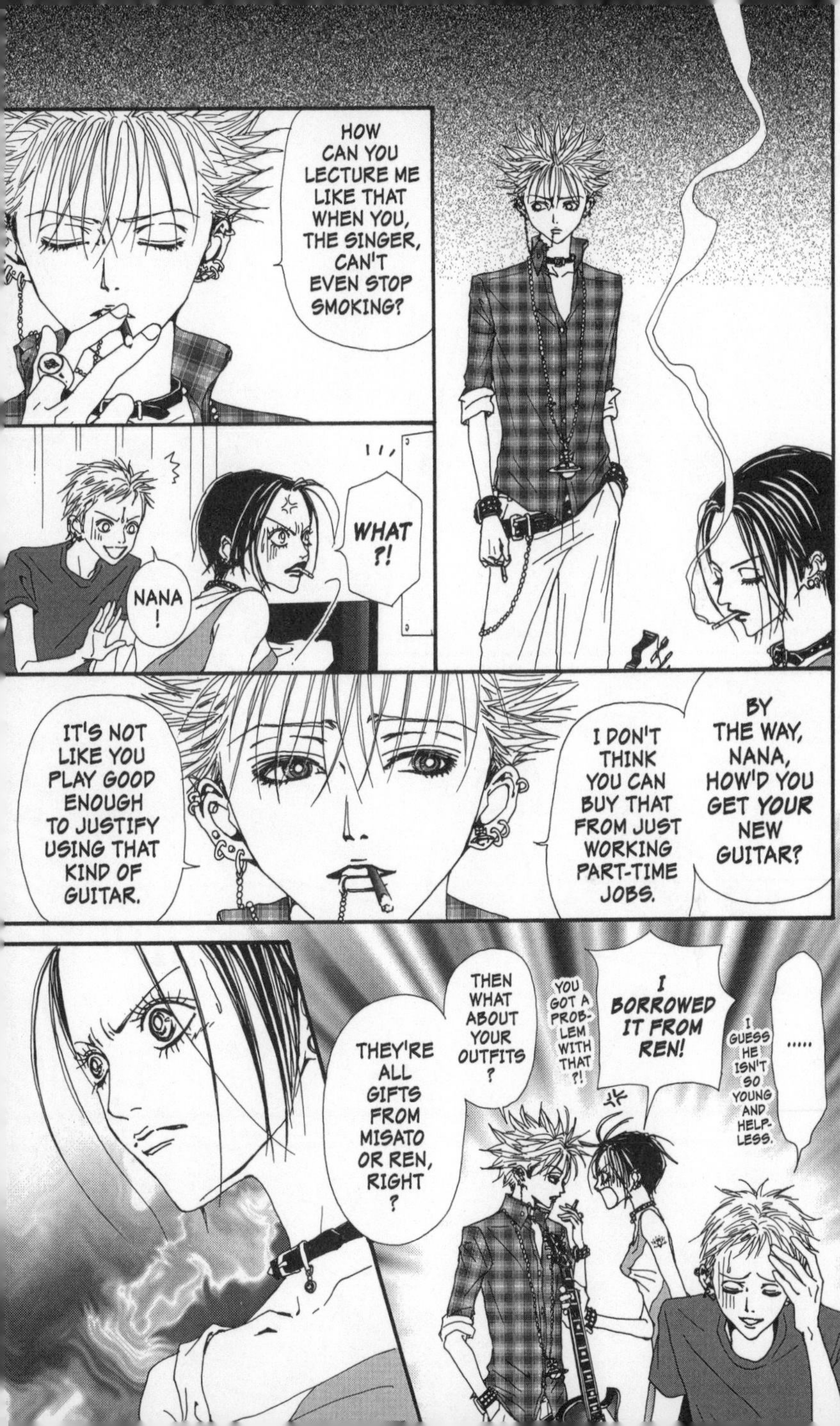
HOW CAN YOU LECTURE ME LIKE THAT WHEN YOU, THE SINGER, CAN'T EVEN STOP SMOKING?
WHAT ?!
NANA !
BY THE WAY, NANA, HOW'D YOU GET YOUR NEW GUITAR?
I DON'T THINK YOU CAN BUY THAT FROM JUST WORKING PART-TIME JOBS.
IT'S NOT LIKE YOU PLAY GOOD ENOUGH TO JUSTIFY USING THAT KIND OF GUITAR.
.....
I GUESS HE ISN'T SO YOUNG AND HELP-LESS.
I BORROWED IT FROM REN!
YOU GOT A PROB-LEM WITH THAT ?!
THEN WHAT ABOUT YOUR OUTFITS ?
THEY'RE ALL GIFTS FROM MISATO OR REN, RIGHT ?

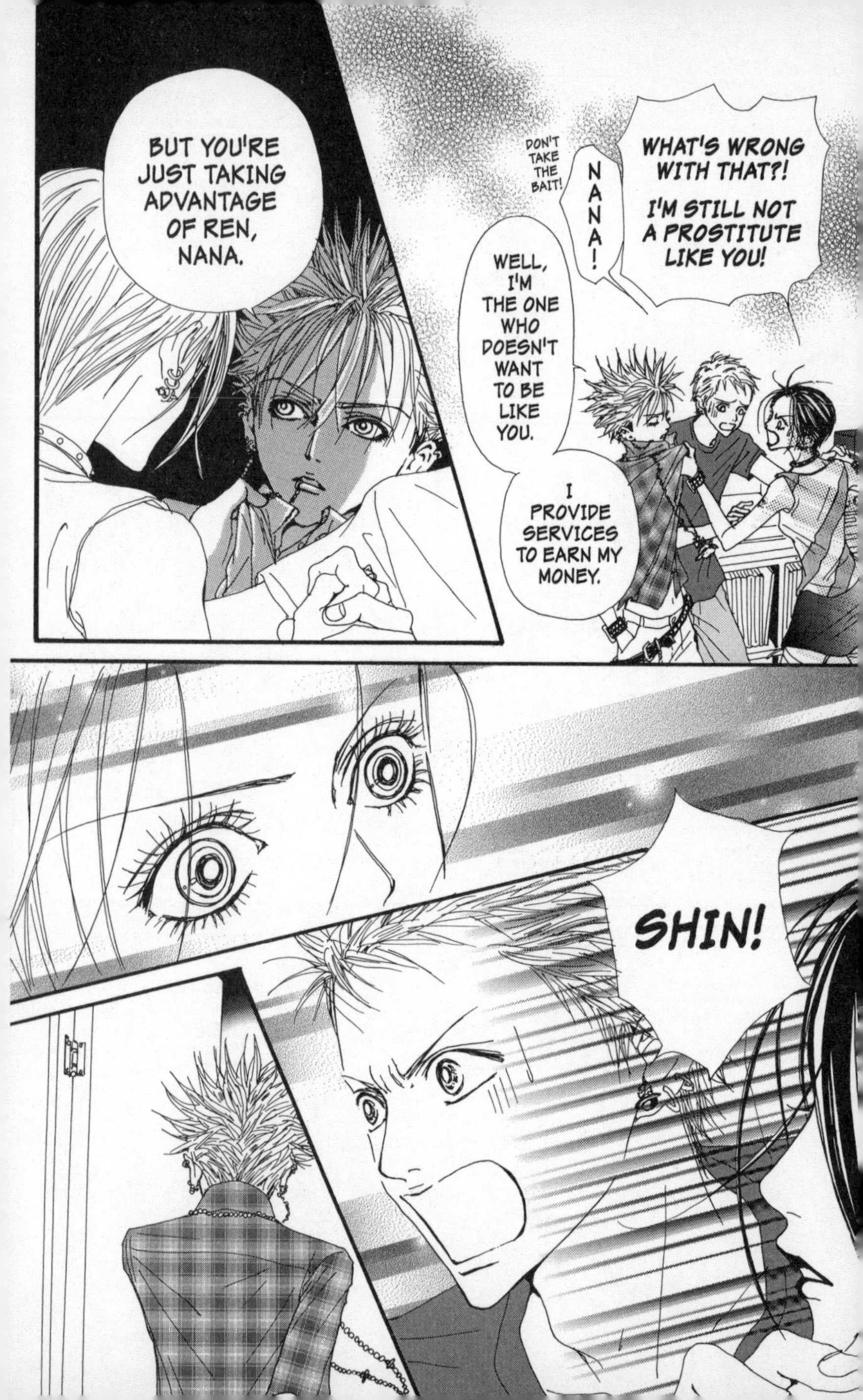
WHAT'S WRONG WITH THAT?! I'M STILL NOT A PROSTITUTE LIKE YOU!
NANA!
DON'T TAKE THE BAIT!
WELL, I'M THE ONE WHO DOESN'T WANT TO BE LIKE YOU.
I PROVIDE SERVICES TO EARN MY MONEY.
BUT YOU'RE JUST TAKING ADVANTAGE OF REN, NANA.
SHIN!

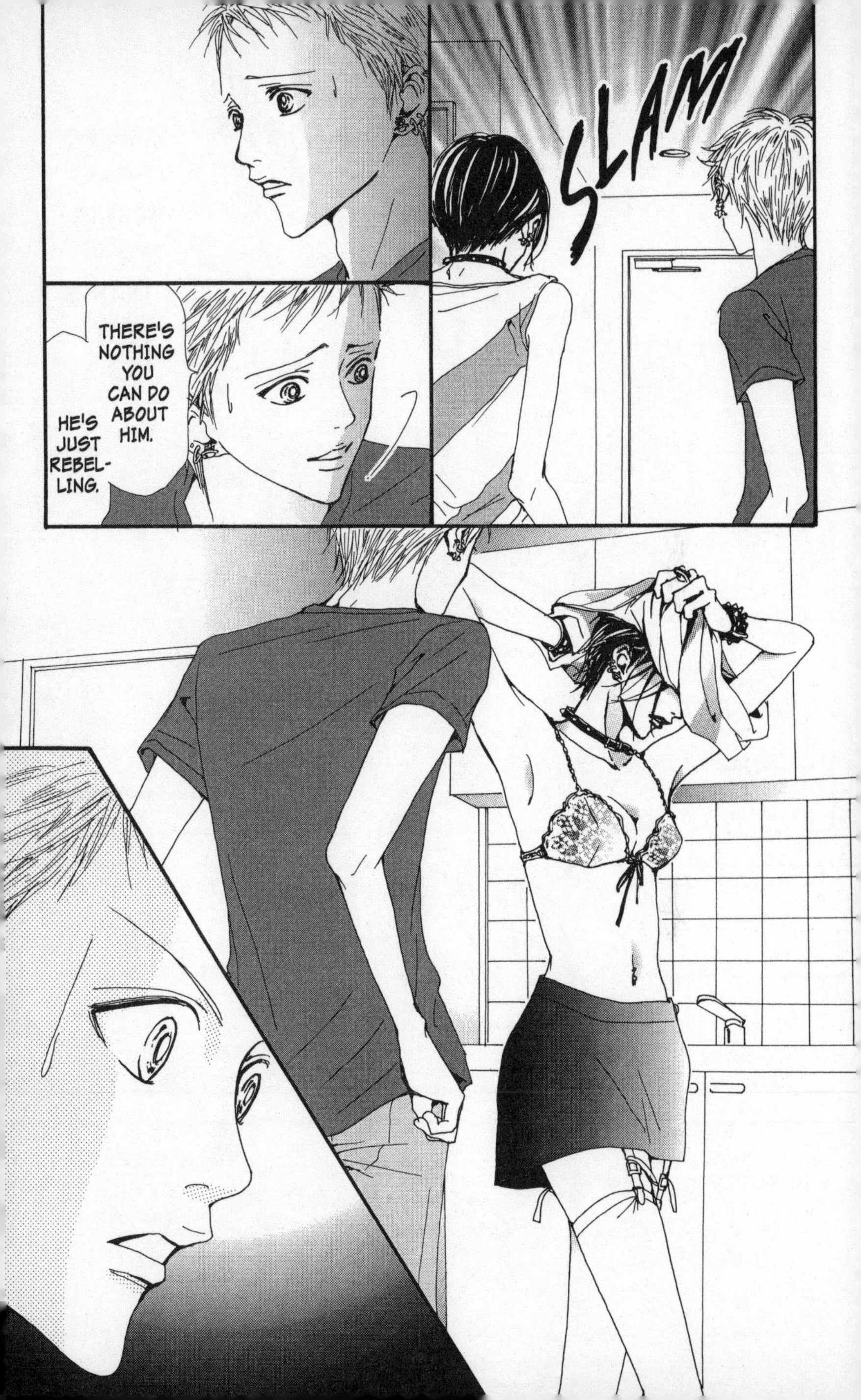
SLAM
THERE'S NOTHING YOU CAN DO ABOUT HIM.
HE'S JUST REBEL-LING.

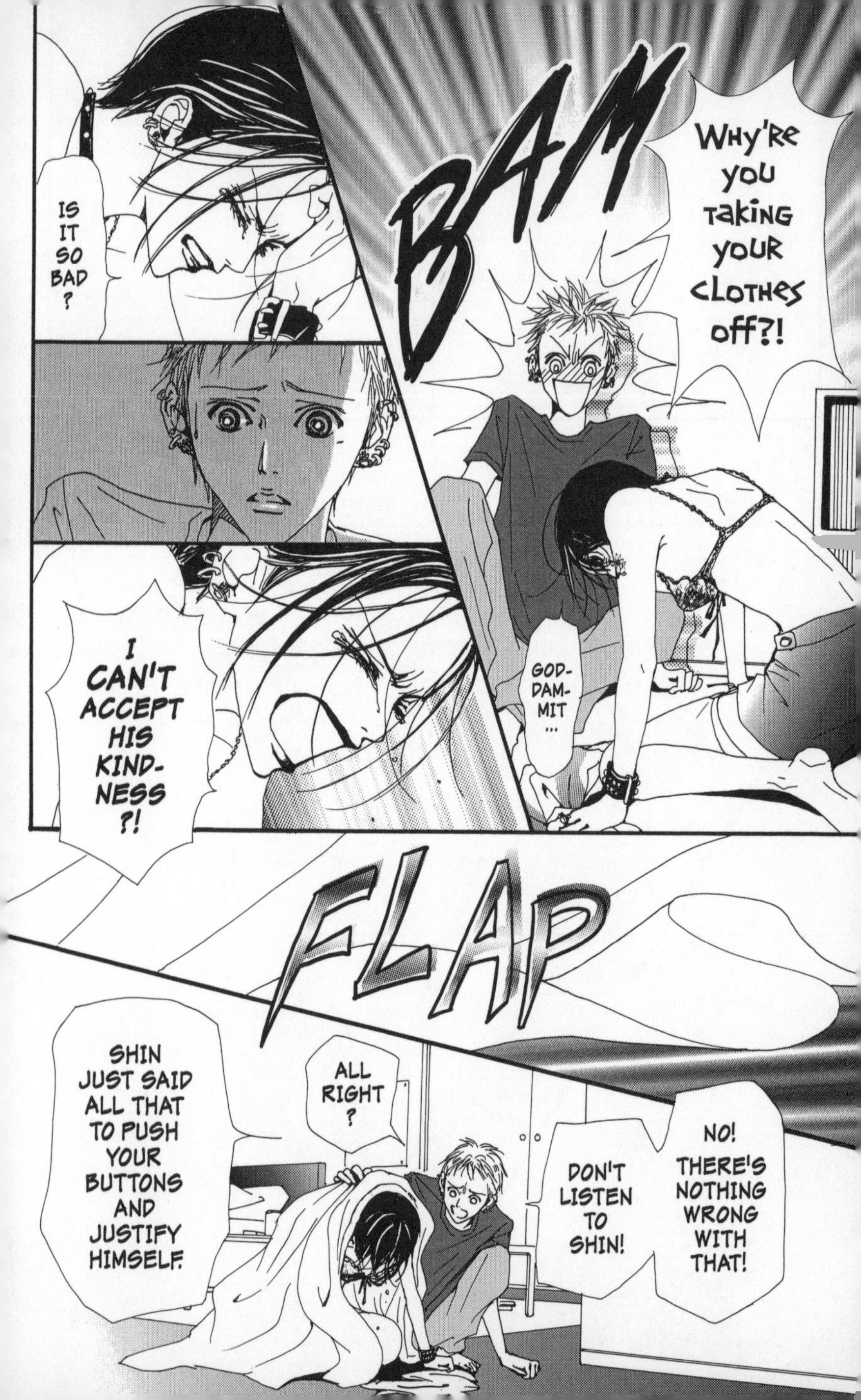
BAM
WHY'RE YOU TAKING YOUR CLOTHES OFF?!
GOD-DAM-MIT...
IS IT SO BAD?
I CAN'T ACCEPT HIS KIND-NESS?!
FLAP
NO! THERE'S NOTHING WRONG WITH THAT!
DON'T LISTEN TO SHIN!
ALL RIGHT?
SHIN JUST SAID ALL THAT TO PUSH YOUR BUTTONS AND JUSTIFY HIMSELF.

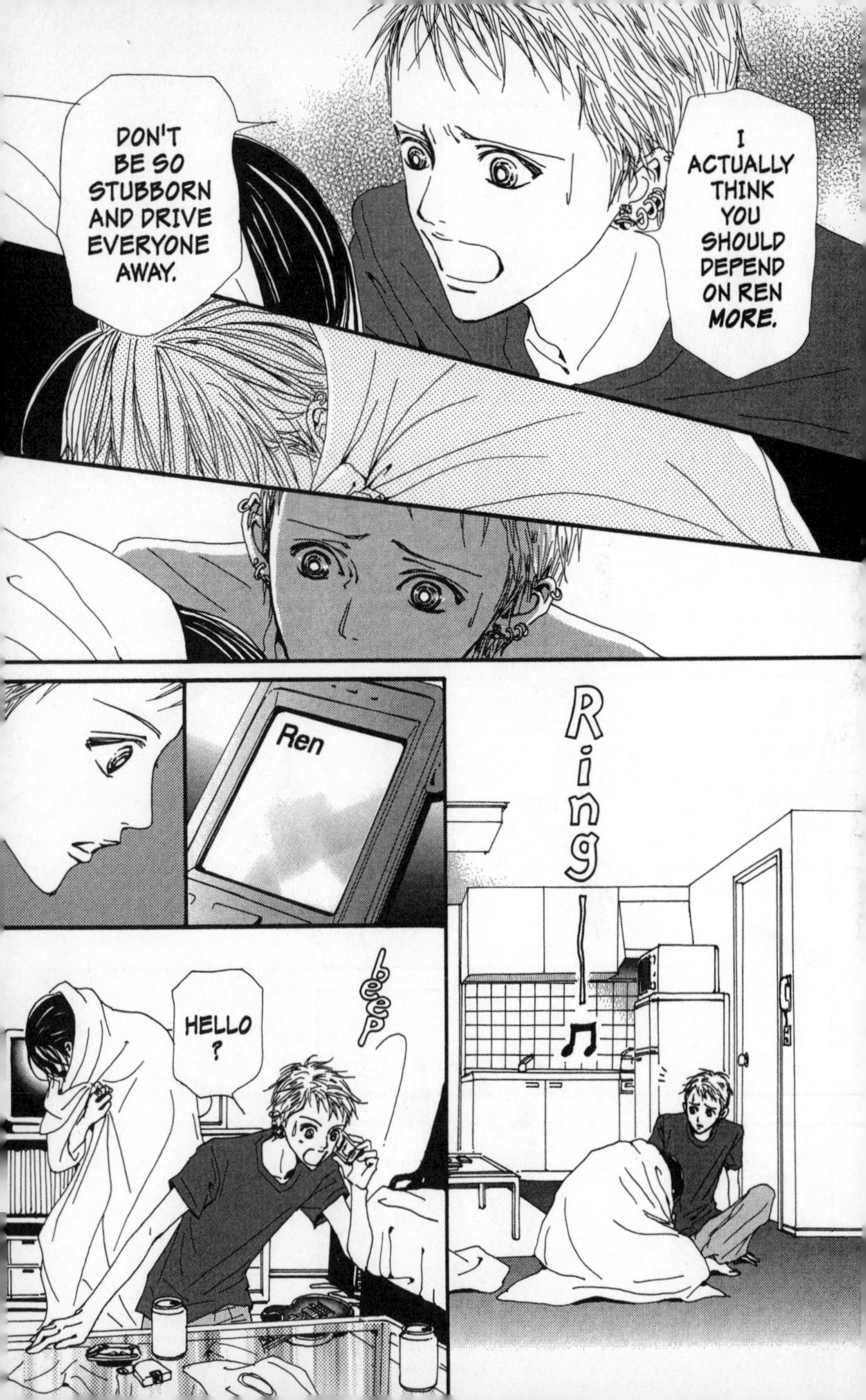

I ACTUALLY THINK YOU SHOULD DEPEND ON REN MORE.
DON'T BE SO STUBBORN AND DRIVE EVERYONE AWAY.
Ring
Ren
beep
HELLO ?

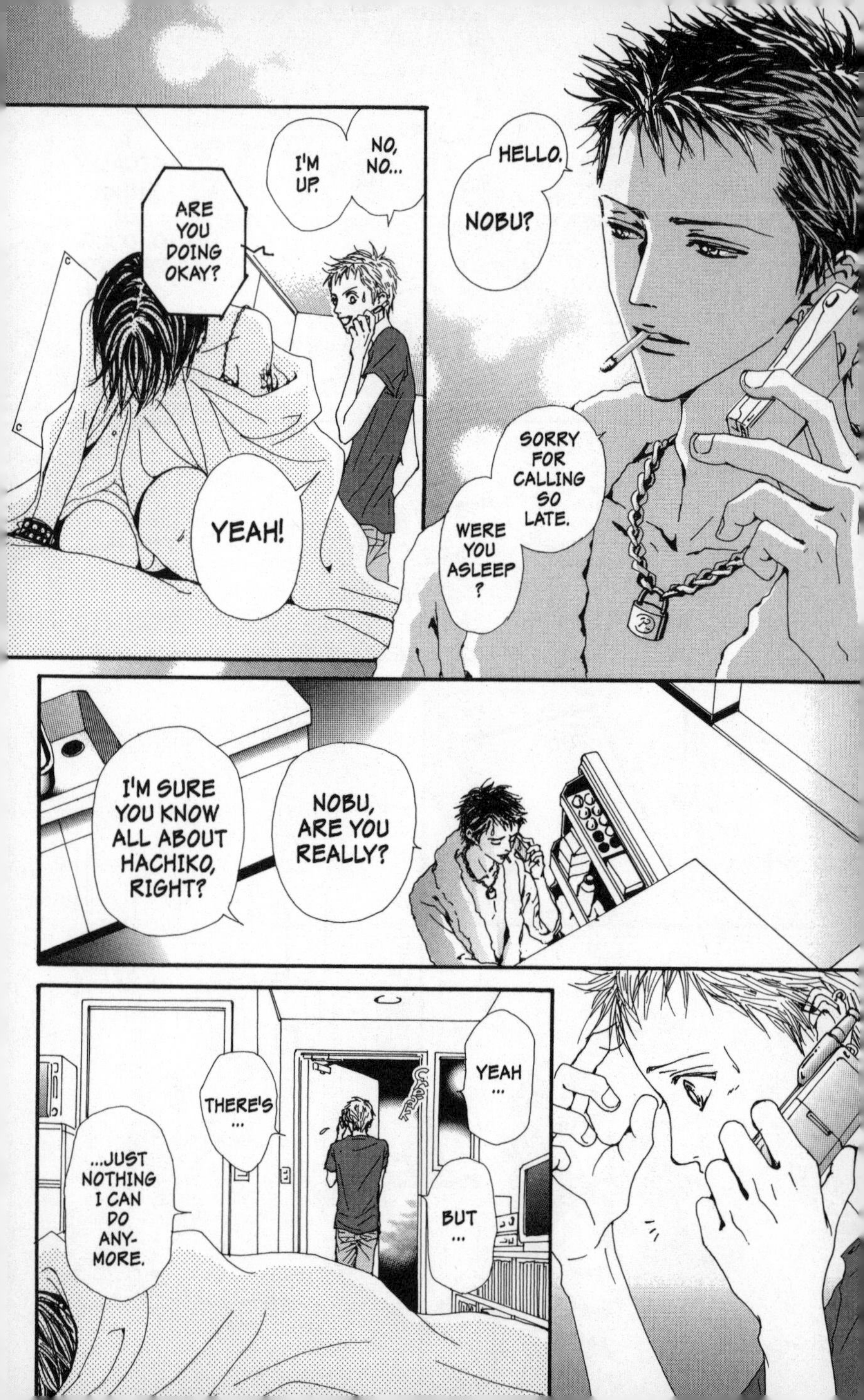
HELLO.
NOBU?
SORRY FOR CALLING SO LATE.
WERE YOU ASLEEP?
NO, NO...
I'M UP.
ARE YOU DOING OKAY?
YEAH!
NOBU, ARE YOU REALLY?
I'M SURE YOU KNOW ALL ABOUT HACHIKO, RIGHT?
YEAH...
BUT...
THERE'S...
...JUST NOTHING I CAN DO ANY-MORE.

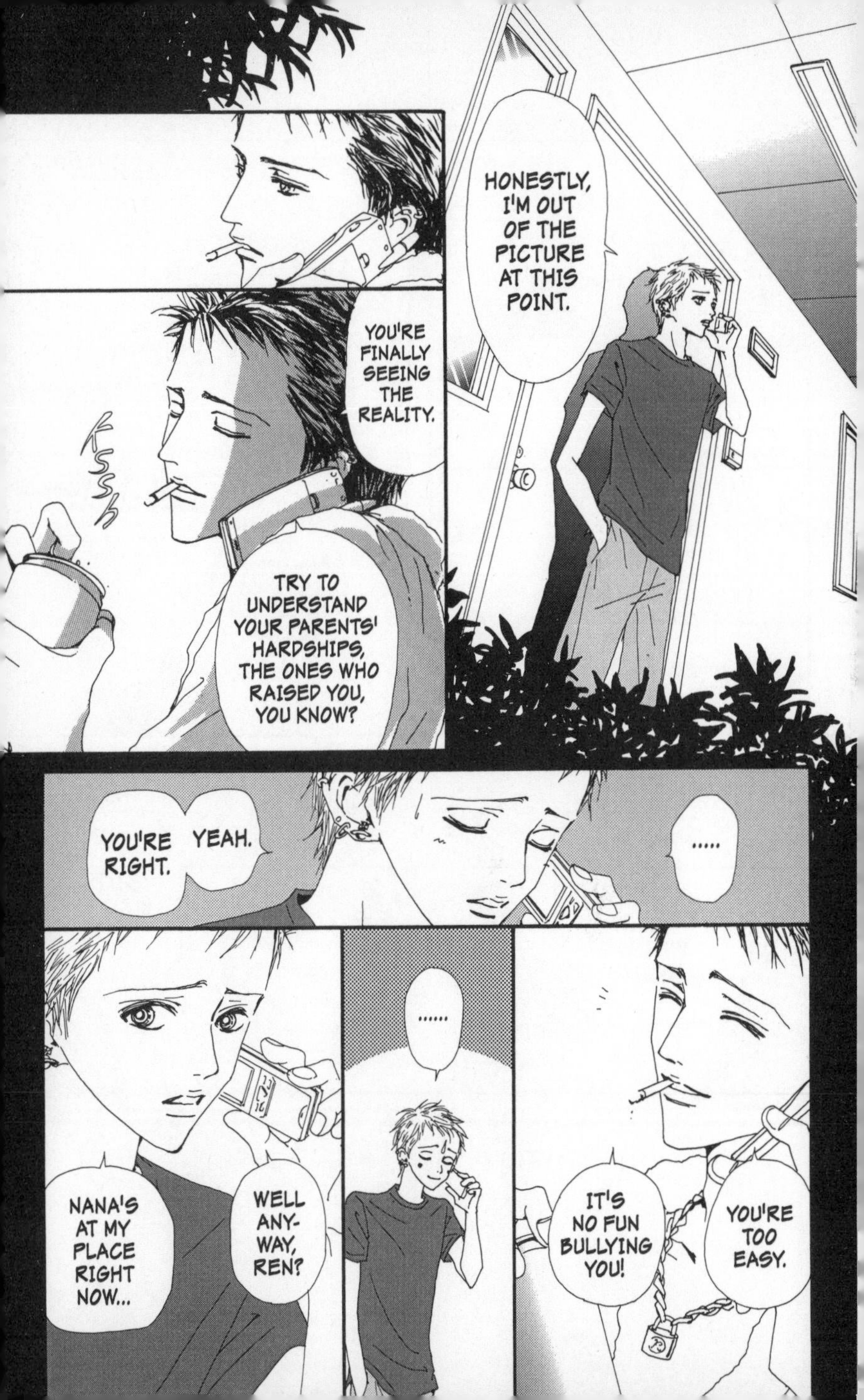
HONESTLY, I'M OUT OF THE PICTURE AT THIS POINT.
YOU'RE FINALLY SEEING THE REALITY.
KSSH
TRY TO UNDERSTAND YOUR PARENTS' HARDSHIPS, THE ONES WHO RAISED YOU, YOU KNOW?
.....
YEAH.
YOU'RE RIGHT.
YOU'RE TOO EASY.
IT'S NO FUN BULLYING YOU!
......
WELL ANY-WAY, REN?
NANA'S AT MY PLACE RIGHT NOW...

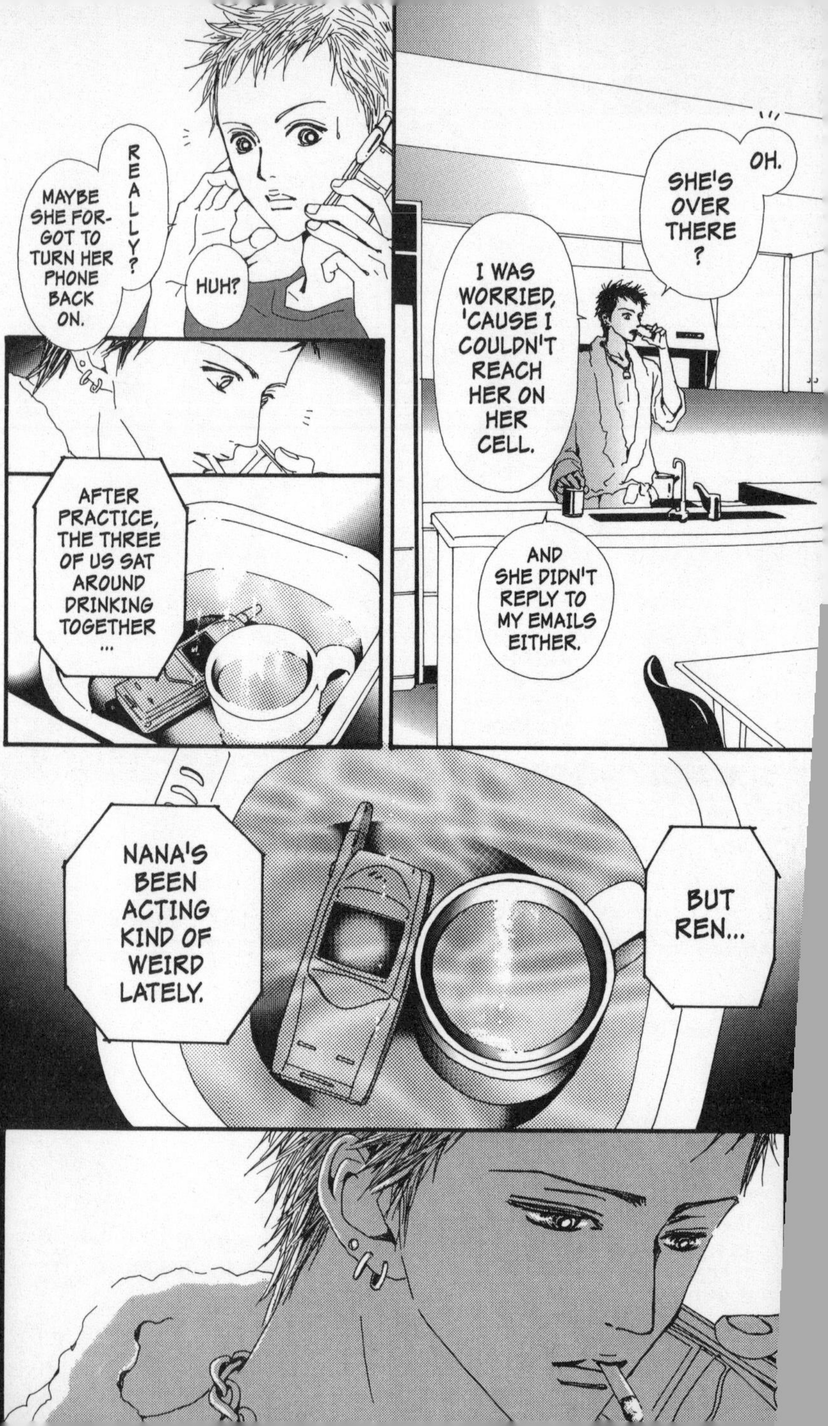
OH.
SHE'S OVER THERE?
I WAS WORRIED, 'CAUSE I COULDN'T REACH HER ON HER CELL.
AND SHE DIDN'T REPLY TO MY EMAILS EITHER.
HUH?
REALLY?
MAYBE SHE FORGOT TO TURN HER PHONE BACK ON.
AFTER PRACTICE, THE THREE OF US SAT AROUND DRINKING TOGETHER...
NANA'S BEEN ACTING KIND OF WEIRD LATELY.
BUT REN...

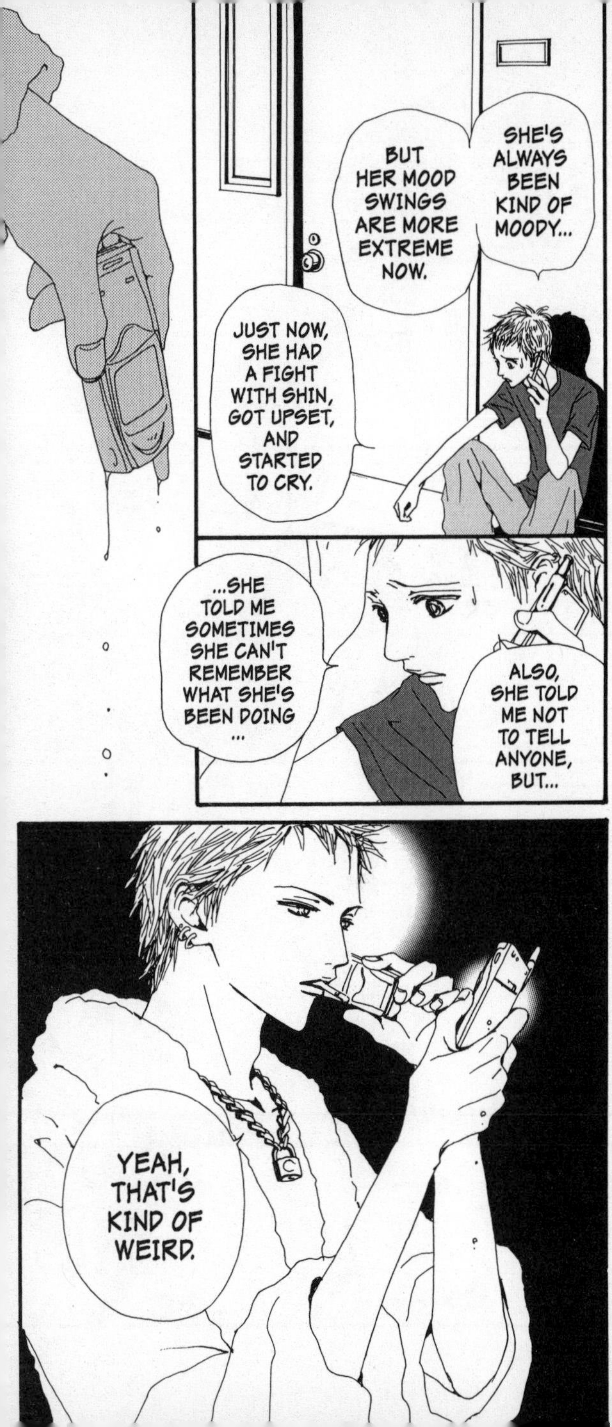
SHE'S ALWAYS BEEN KIND OF MOODY...
BUT HER MOOD SWINGS ARE MORE EXTREME NOW.
JUST NOW, SHE HAD A FIGHT WITH SHIN, GOT UPSET, AND STARTED TO CRY.
ALSO, SHE TOLD ME NOT TO TELL ANYONE, BUT...
...SHE TOLD ME SOMETIMES SHE CAN'T REMEMBER WHAT SHE'S BEEN DOING ...
YEAH, THAT'S KIND OF WEIRD.

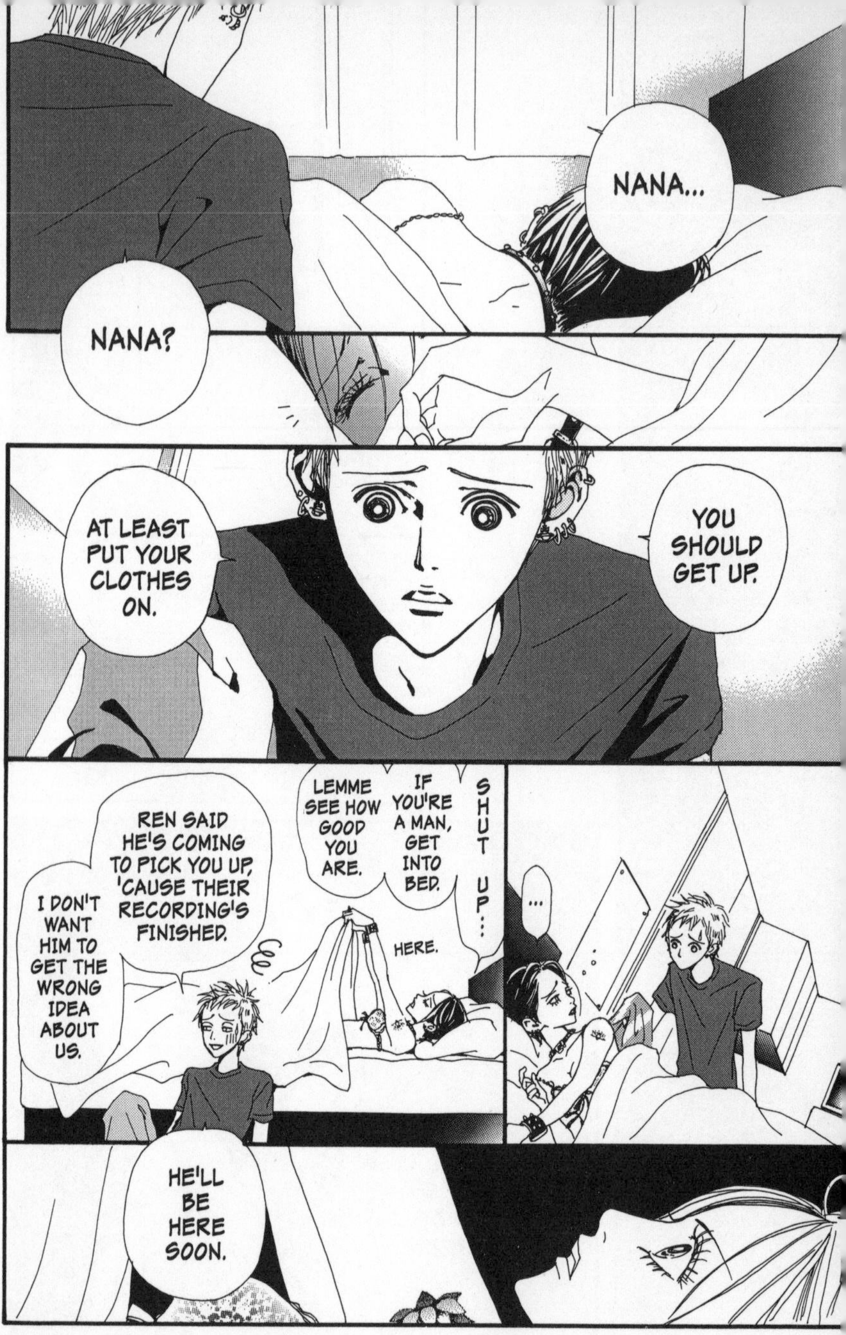
NANA...
NANA?
YOU SHOULD GET UP.
AT LEAST PUT YOUR CLOTHES ON.
...
SHUT UP...
IF YOU'RE A MAN, GET INTO BED.
LEMME SEE HOW GOOD YOU ARE.
HERE.
REN SAID HE'S COMING TO PICK YOU UP, 'CAUSE THEIR RECORDING'S FINISHED.
I DON'T WANT HIM TO GET THE WRONG IDEA ABOUT US.
HE'LL BE HERE SOON.

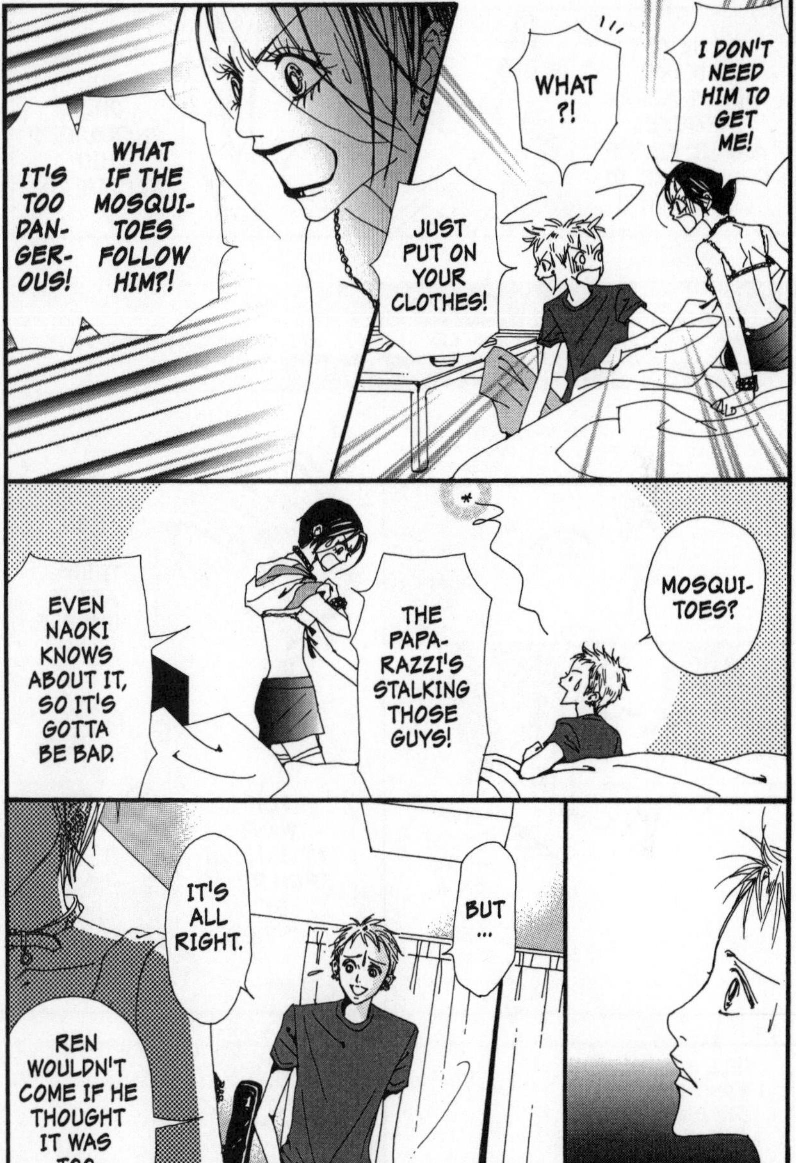
I DON'T NEED HIM TO GET ME!
WHAT?!
JUST PUT ON YOUR CLOTHES!
WHAT IF THE MOSQUI-TOES FOLLOW HIM?!
IT'S TOO DAN-GER-OUS!
MOSQUI-TOES?
THE PAPA-RAZZI'S STALKING THOSE GUYS!
EVEN NAOKI KNOWS ABOUT IT, SO IT'S GOTTA BE BAD.
BUT ...
IT'S ALL RIGHT.
REN WOULDN'T COME IF HE THOUGHT IT WAS TOO RISKY.

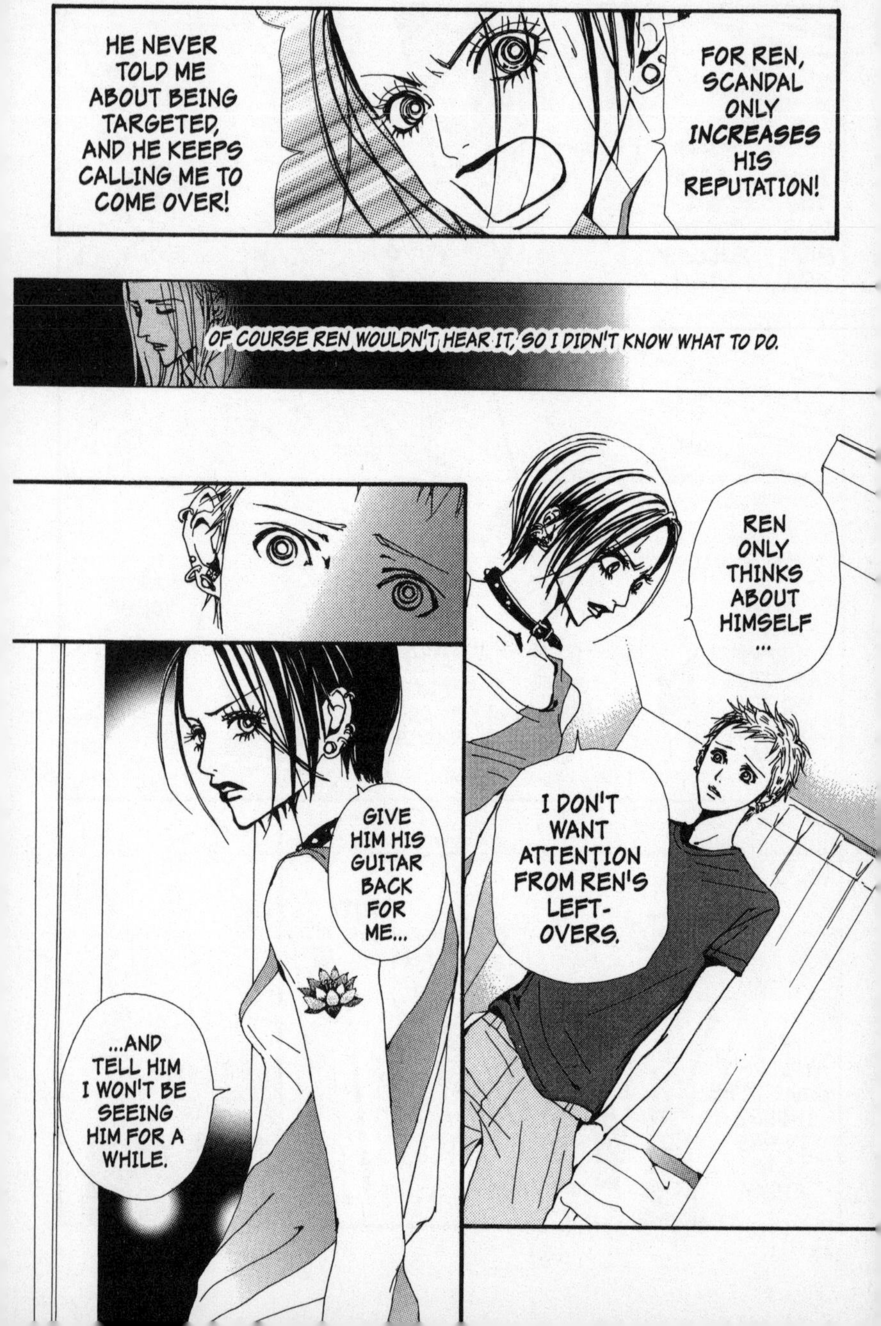
FOR REN, SCANDAL ONLY INCREASES HIS REPUTATION!
HE NEVER TOLD ME ABOUT BEING TARGETED, AND HE KEEPS CALLING ME TO COME OVER!
OF COURSE REN WOULDN'T HEAR IT, SO I DIDN'T KNOW WHAT TO DO.
REN ONLY THINKS ABOUT HIMSELF...
I DON'T WANT ATTENTION FROM REN'S LEFT-OVERS.
GIVE HIM HIS GUITAR BACK FOR ME...
...AND TELL HIM I WON'T BE SEEING HIM FOR A WHILE.

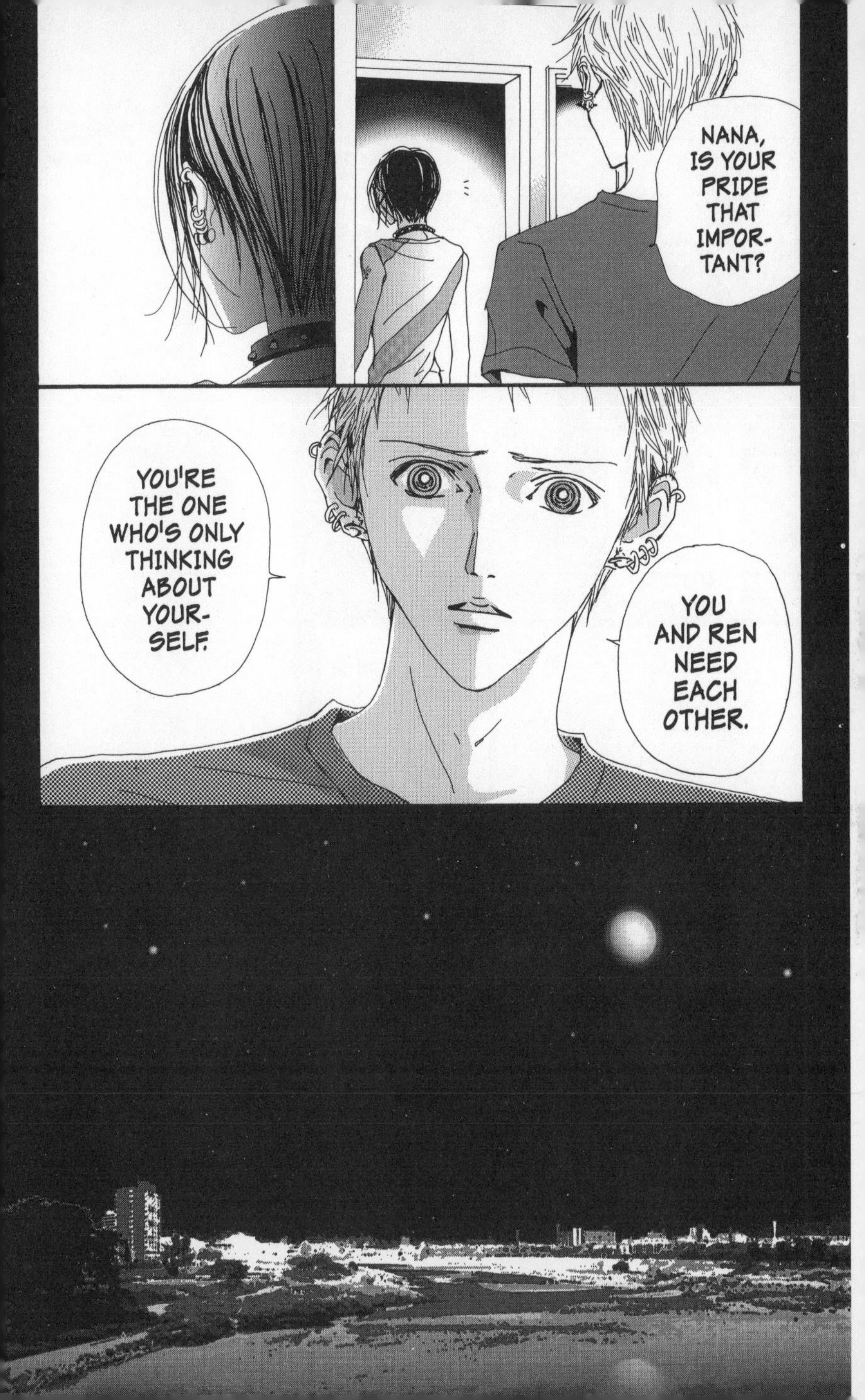
NANA, IS YOUR PRIDE THAT IMPORTANT?
YOU AND REN NEED EACH OTHER.
YOU'RE THE ONE WHO'S ONLY THINKING ABOUT YOURSELF.

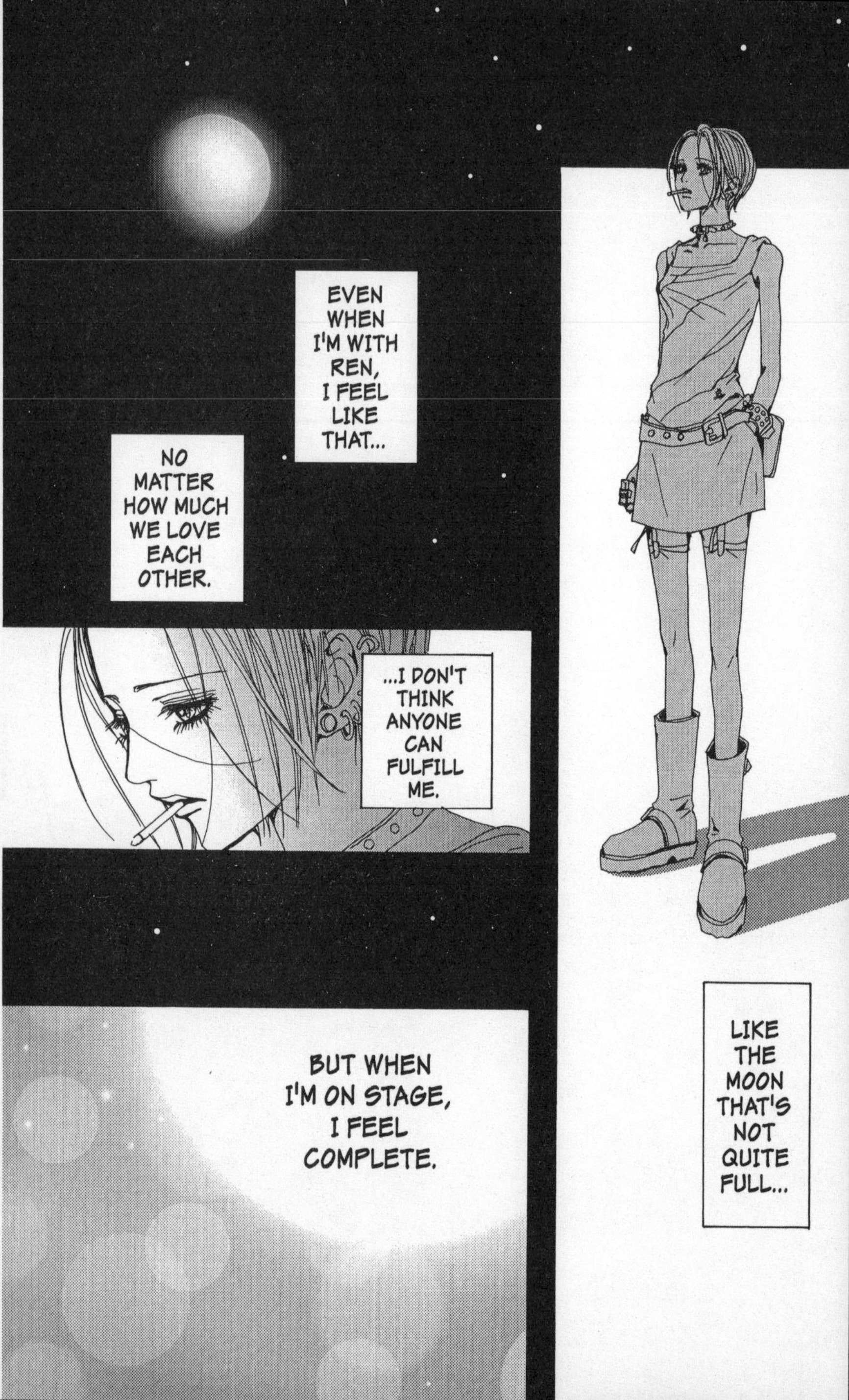
LIKE THE MOON THAT'S NOT QUITE FULL...
EVEN WHEN I'M WITH REN, I FEEL LIKE THAT...
NO MATTER HOW MUCH WE LOVE EACH OTHER.
...I DON'T THINK ANYONE CAN FULFILL ME.
BUT WHEN I'M ON STAGE, I FEEL COMPLETE.

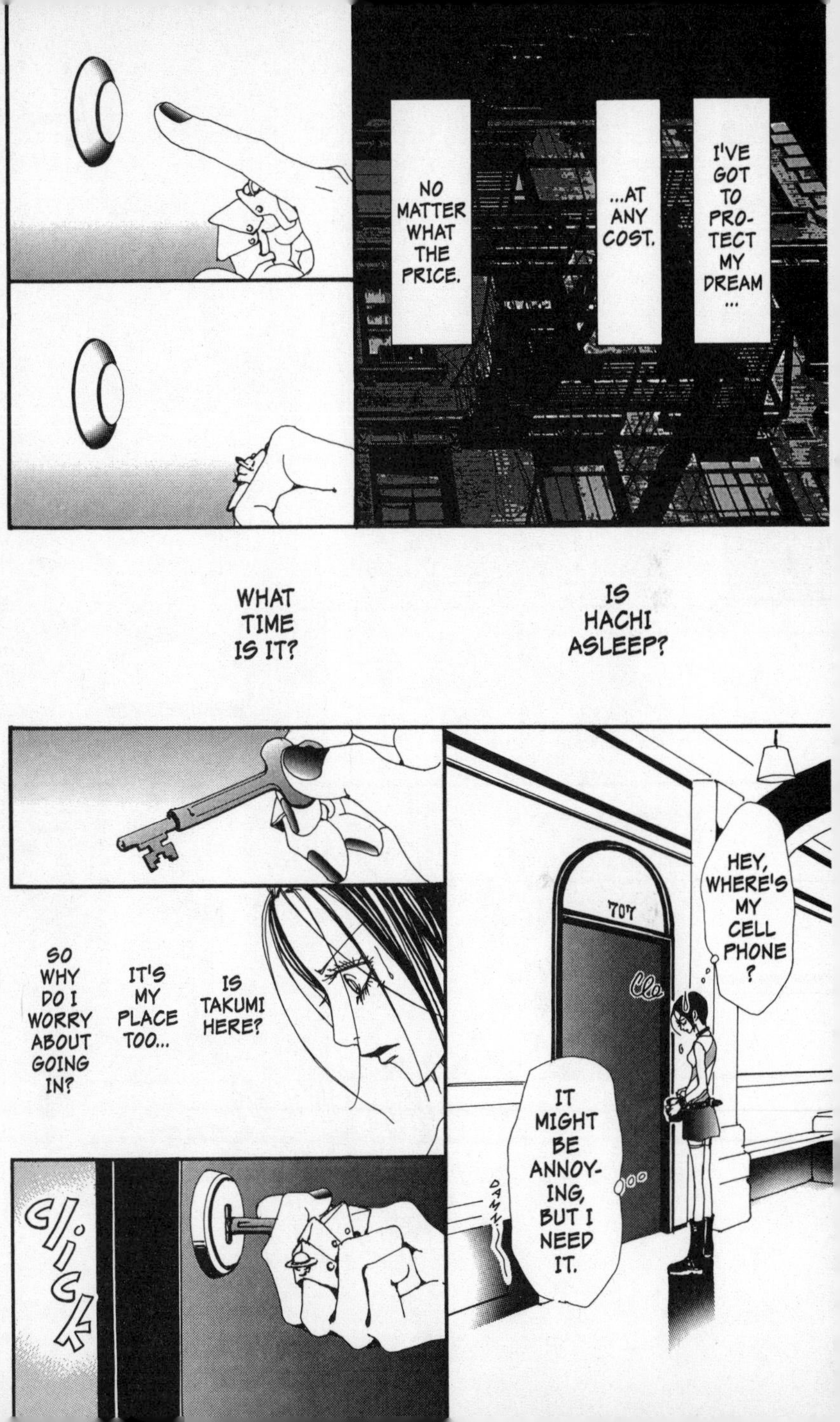
I'VE GOT TO PRO-TECT MY DREAM...
...AT ANY COST.
NO MATTER WHAT THE PRICE.
IS HACHI ASLEEP?
WHAT TIME IS IT?
707
HEY, WHERE'S MY CELL PHONE?
IT MIGHT BE ANNOY-ING, BUT I NEED IT.
DAMN...
IS TAKUMI HERE?
IT'S MY PLACE TOO...
SO WHY DO I WORRY ABOUT GOING IN?
CLICK

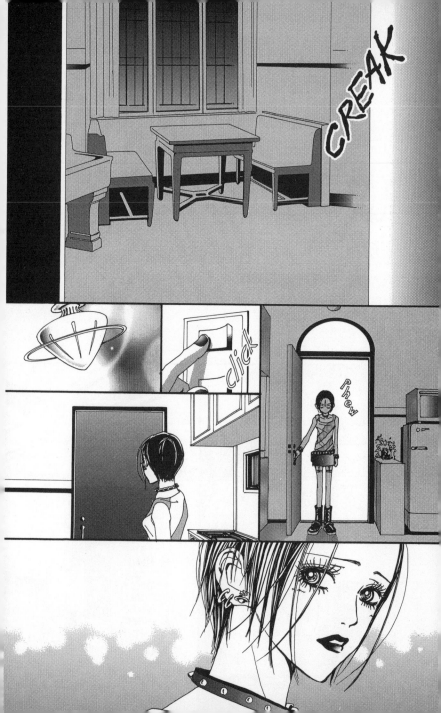

CREAK

click

Phew

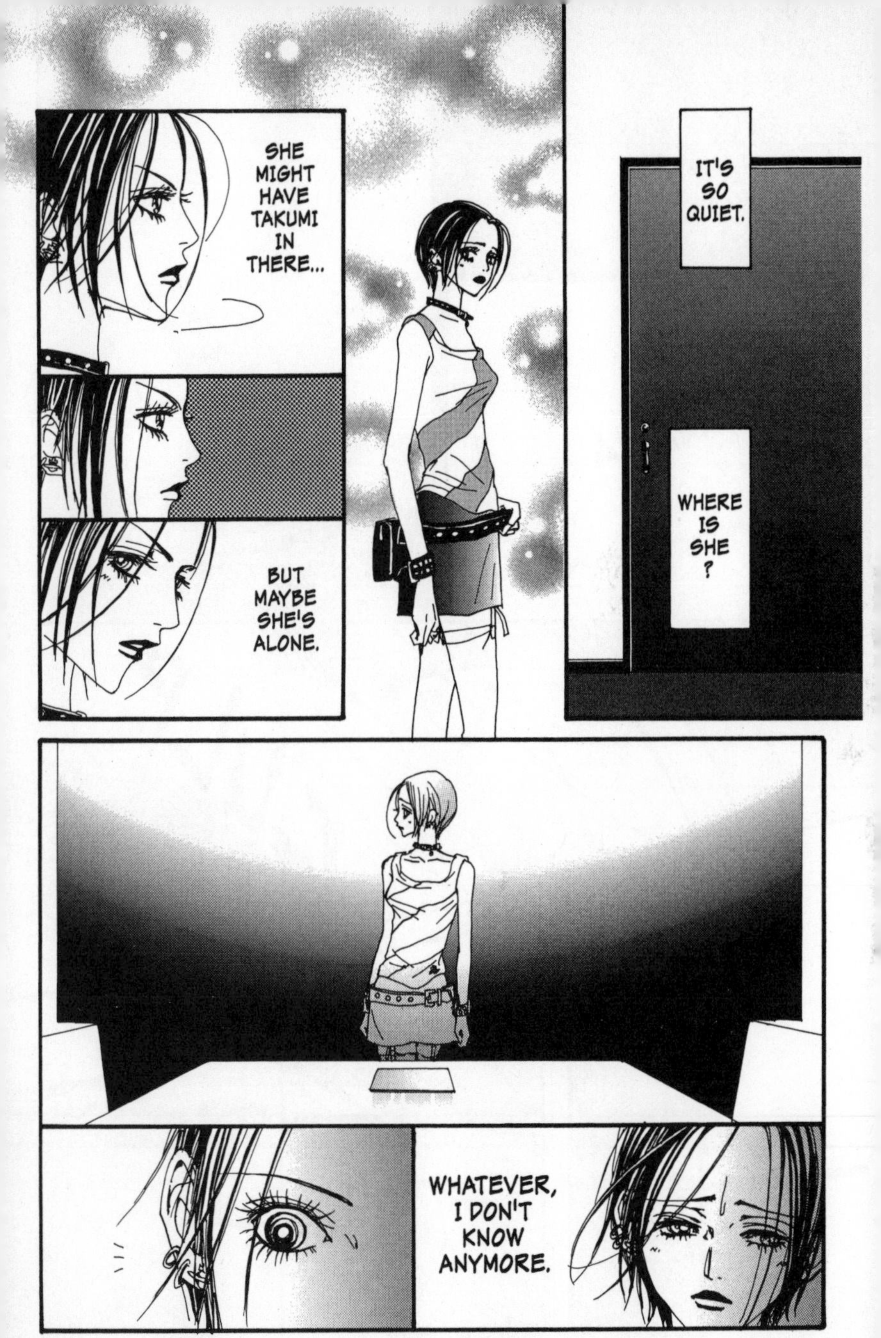
IT'S SO QUIET.
WHERE IS SHE ?
SHE MIGHT HAVE TAKUMI IN THERE...
BUT MAYBE SHE'S ALONE.
WHATEVER, I DON'T KNOW ANYMORE.

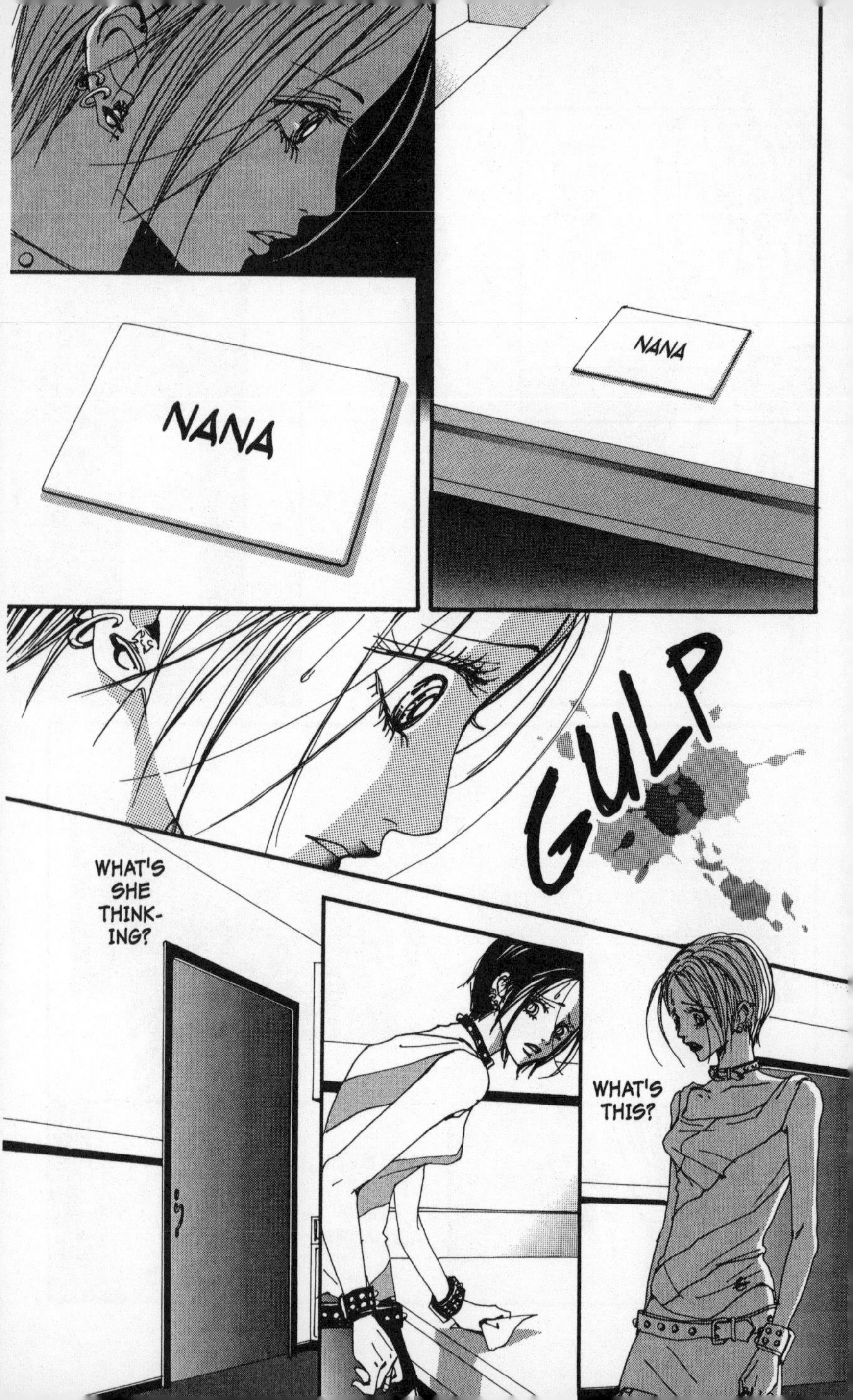
NANA
NANA
GULP
WHAT'S THIS?
WHAT'S SHE THINKING?

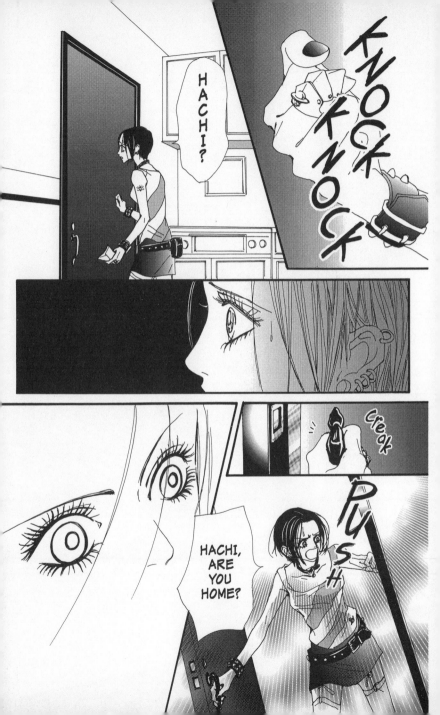

HACHI?

KNOCK KNOCK KNOCK

creak

PUSH

HACHI, ARE YOU HOME?

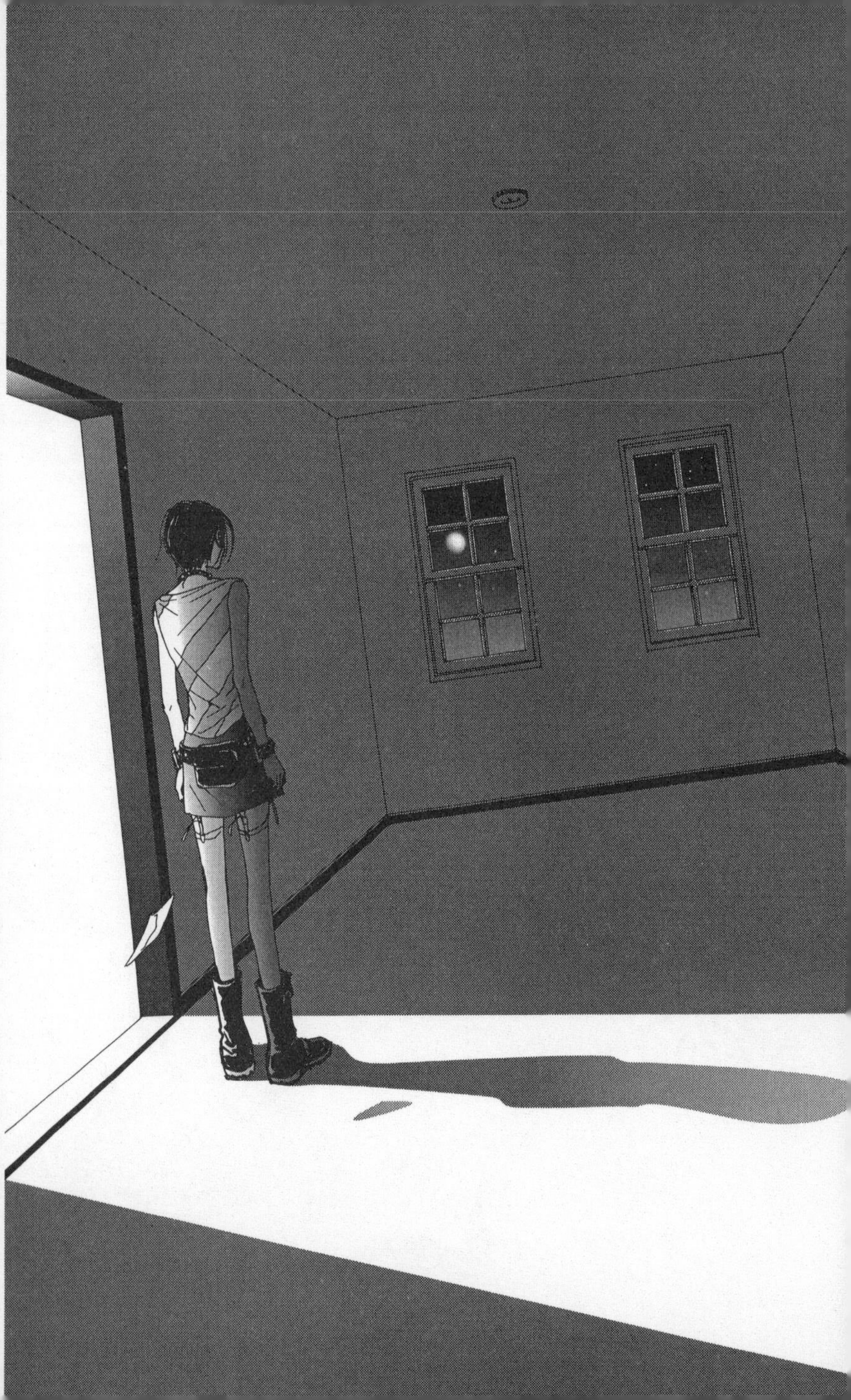

HEY, HACHI...

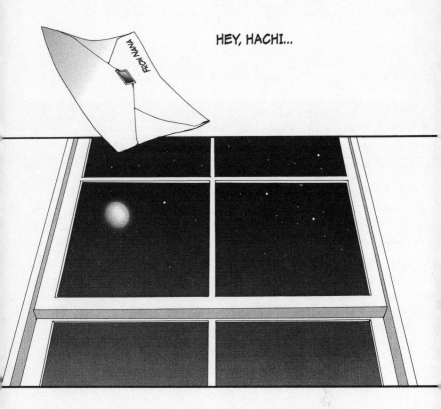

FROM NANA

BACK THEN, WHEN YOU KEPT LOSING YOURSELF IN LOVE...

...MAYBE WE WEREN'T SO DIFFERENT...

...STRUGGLING WITH DESIRES THAT COULDN'T BE FULFILLED.

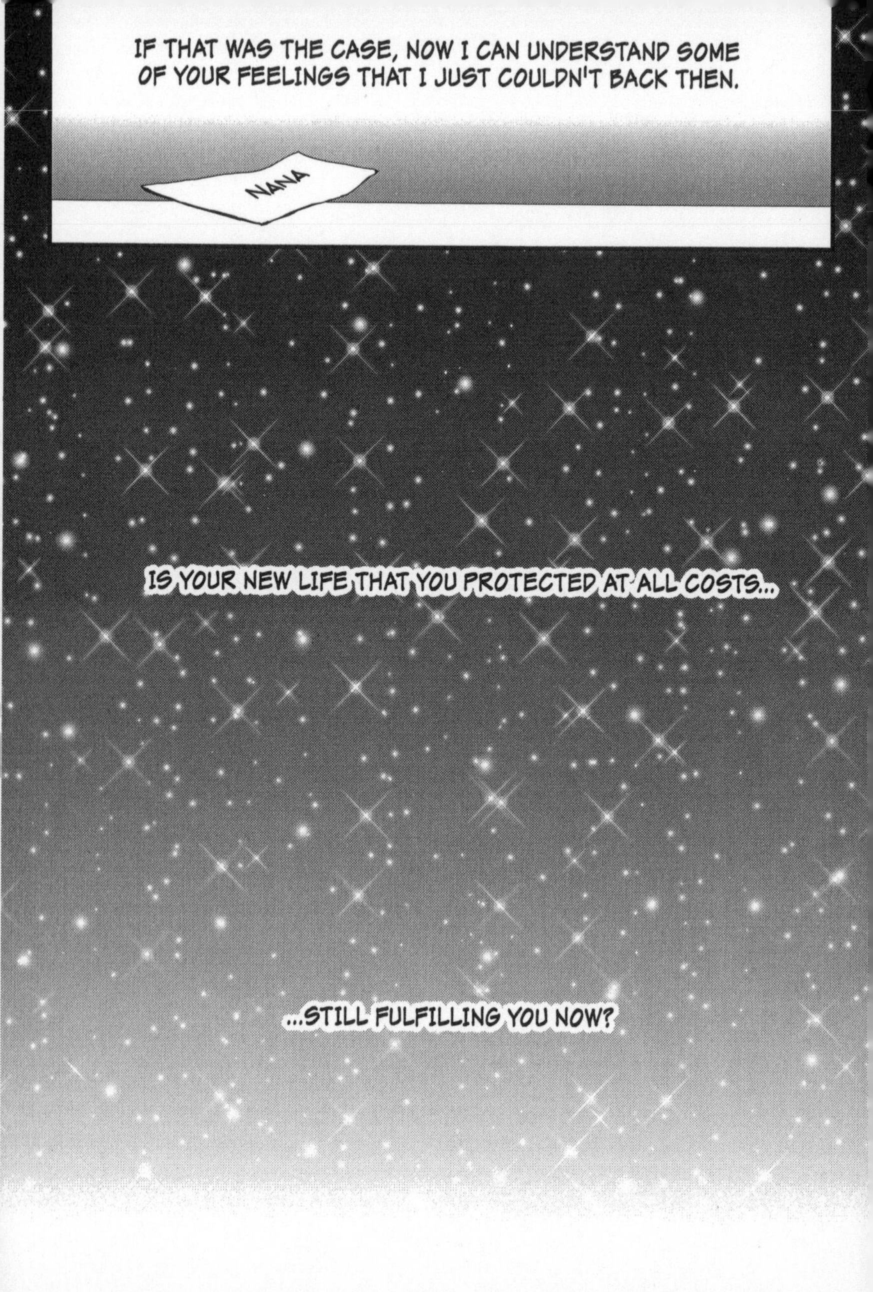
IF THAT WAS THE CASE, NOW I CAN UNDERSTAND SOME OF YOUR FEELINGS THAT I JUST COULDN'T BACK THEN.
NANA
IS YOUR NEW LIFE THAT YOU PROTECTED AT ALL COSTS...
...STILL FULFILLING YOU NOW?

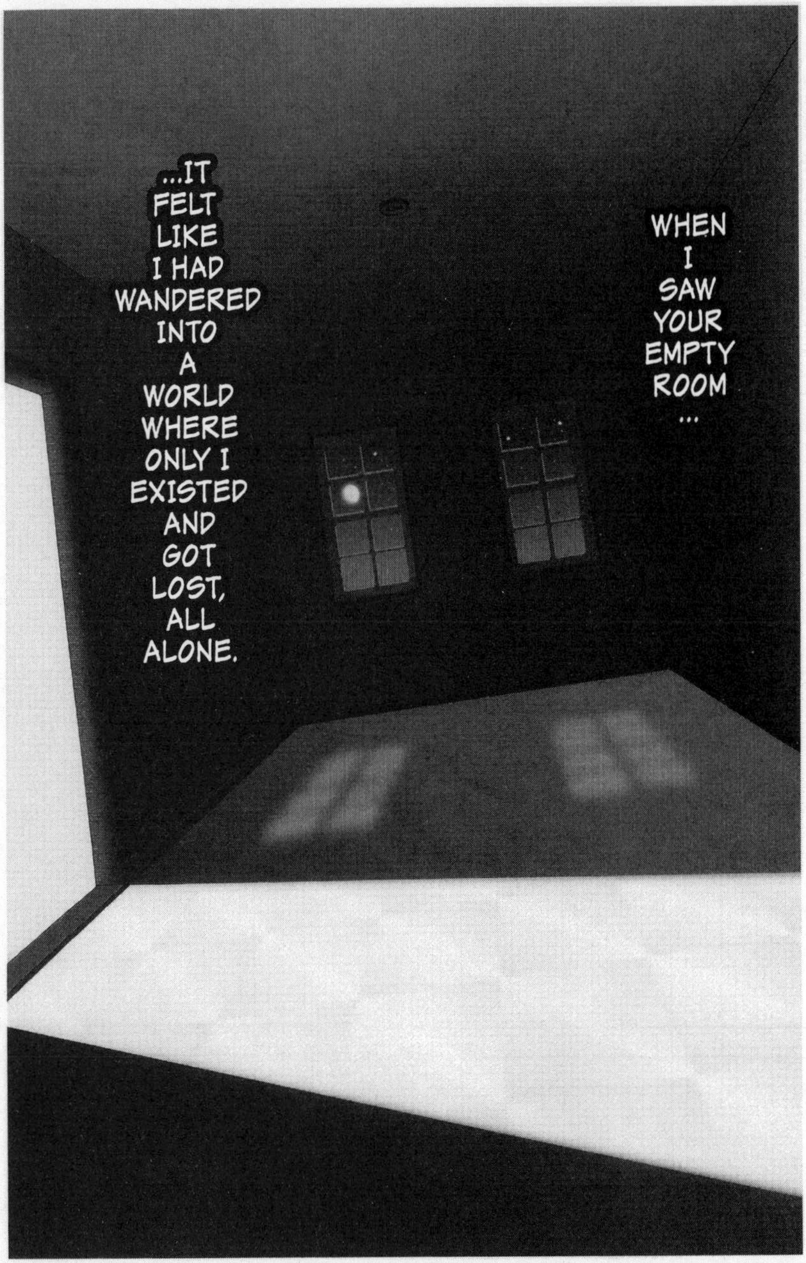
WHEN I SAW YOUR EMPTY ROOM...
...IT FELT LIKE I HAD WANDERED INTO A WORLD WHERE ONLY I EXISTED AND GOT LOST, ALL ALONE.

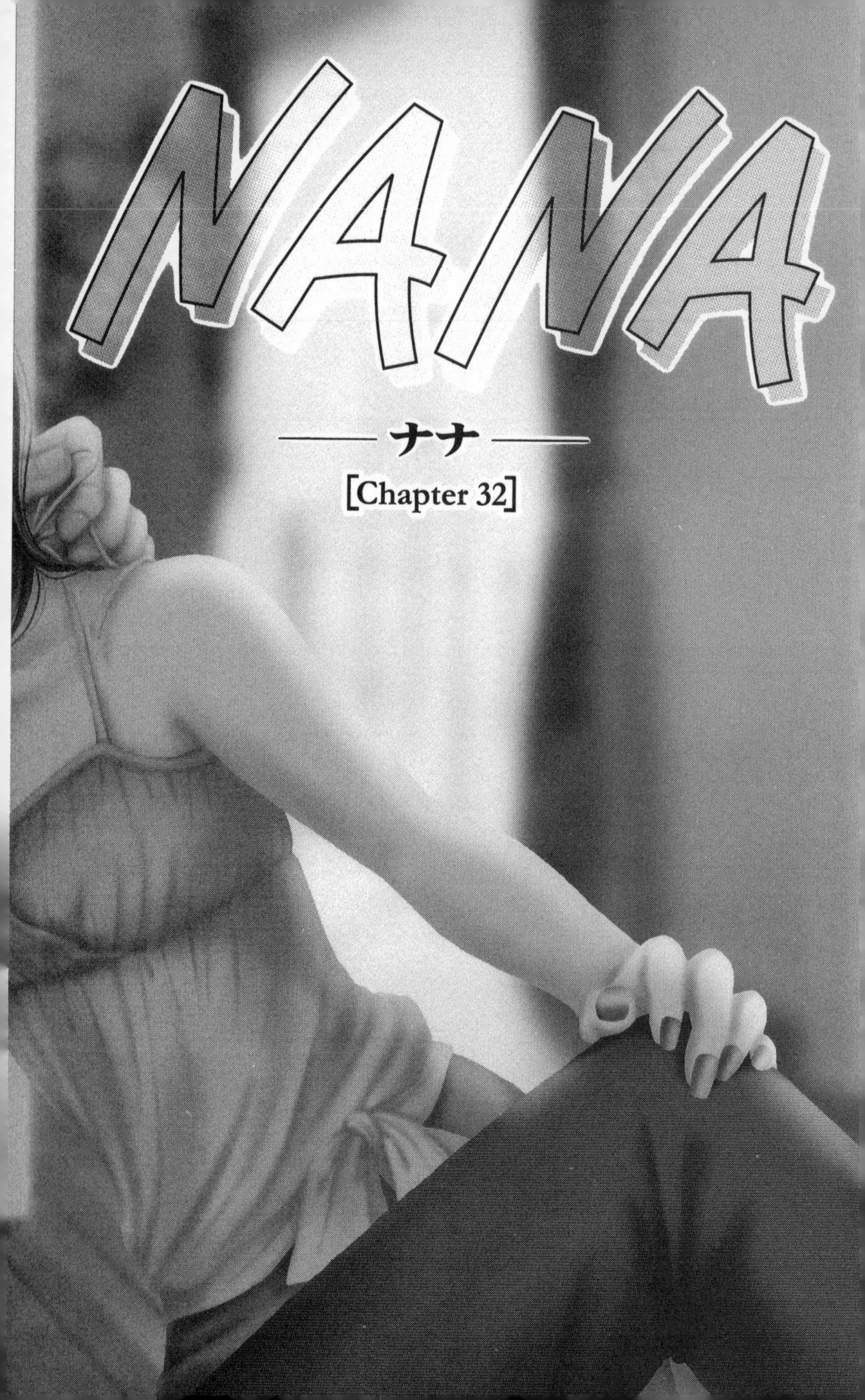
NANA
ナナ
[Chapter 32]

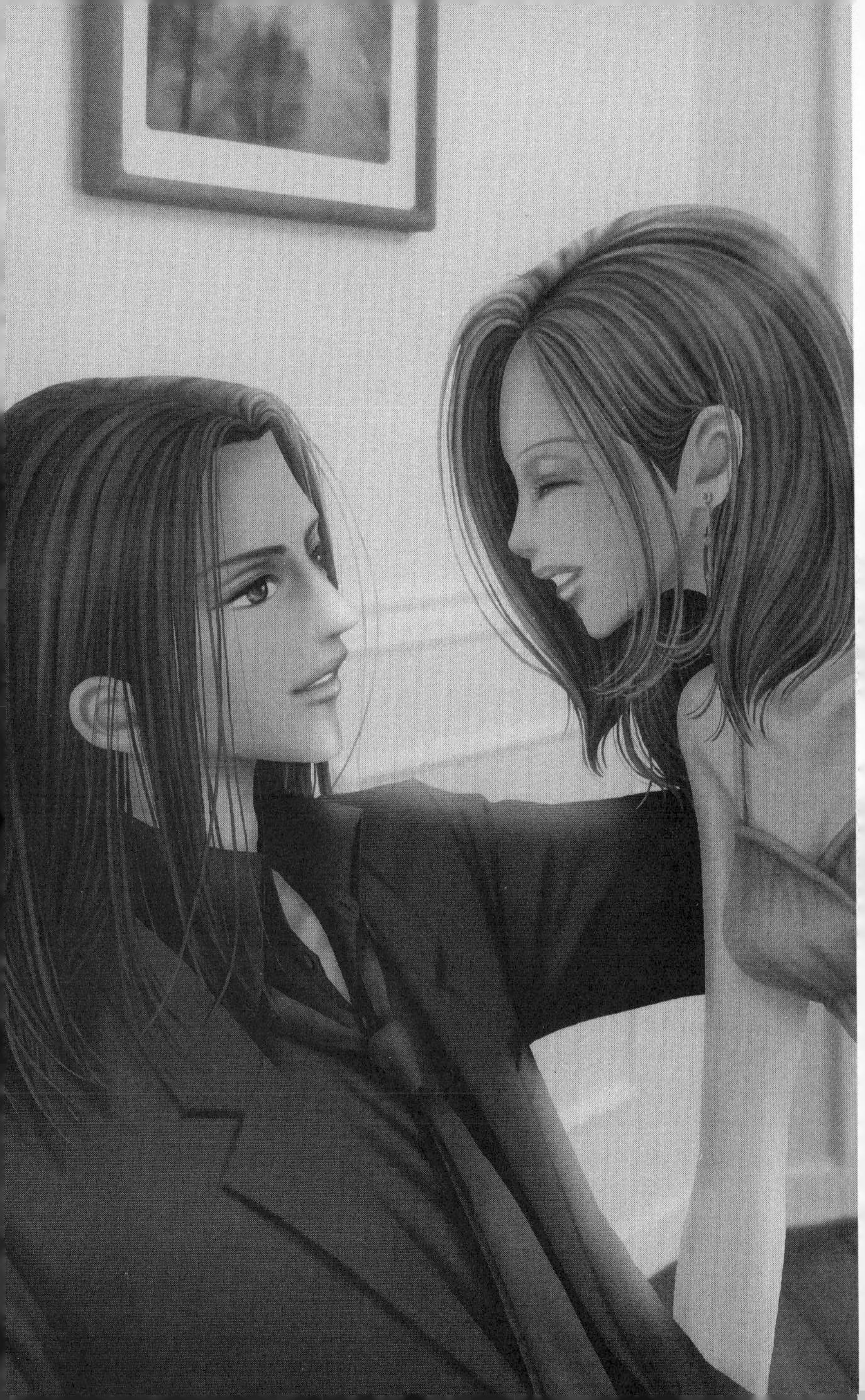

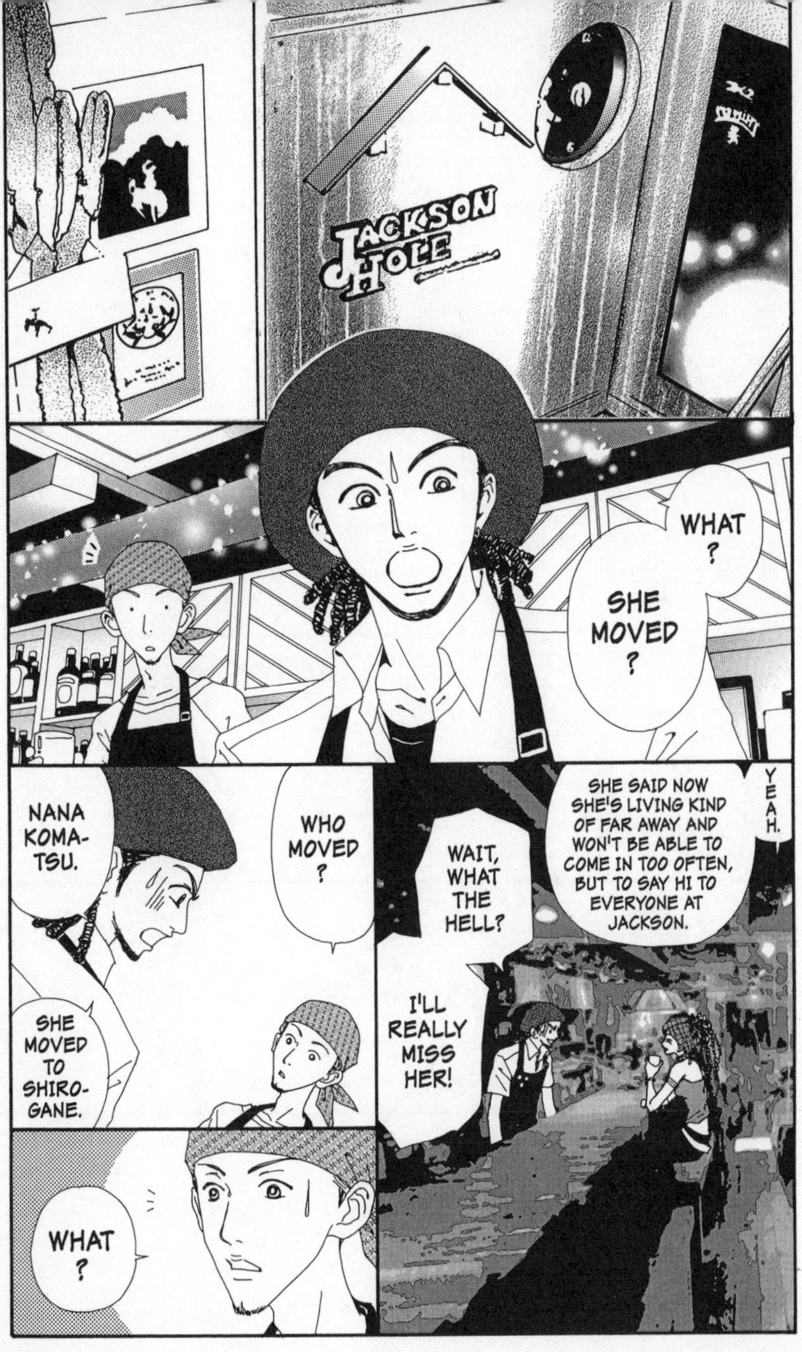
JACKSON HOLE
WHAT?
SHE MOVED?
YEAH.
SHE SAID NOW SHE'S LIVING KIND OF FAR AWAY AND WON'T BE ABLE TO COME IN TOO OFTEN, BUT TO SAY HI TO EVERYONE AT JACKSON.
WAIT, WHAT THE HELL?
I'LL REALLY MISS HER!
WHO MOVED?
NANA KOMATSU.
SHE MOVED TO SHIROGANE.
WHAT?

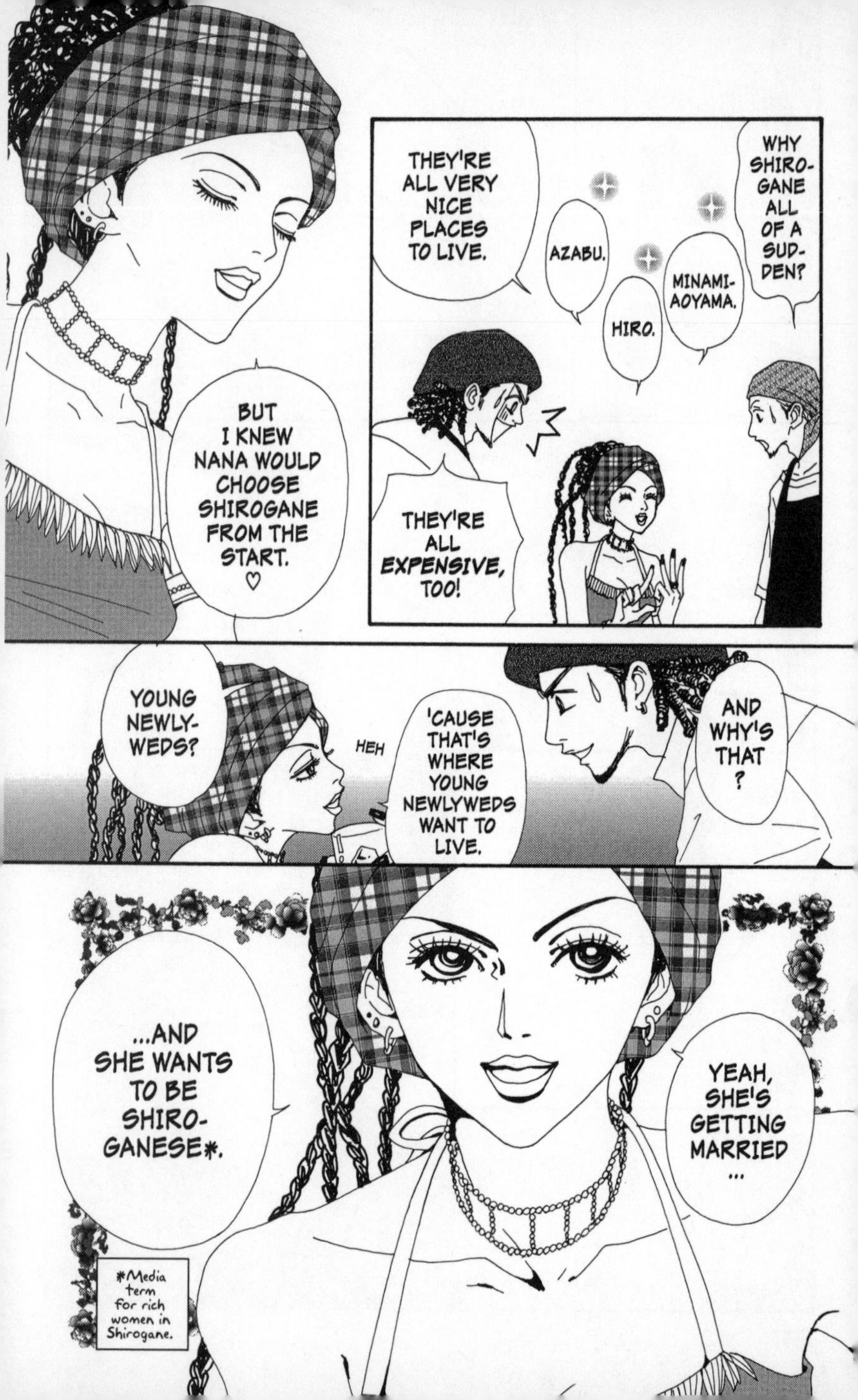
WHY SHIROGANE ALL OF A SUDDEN?
MINAMI-AOYAMA.
HIRO.
AZABU.
THEY'RE ALL VERY NICE PLACES TO LIVE.
THEY'RE ALL EXPENSIVE, TOO!
BUT I KNEW NANA WOULD CHOOSE SHIROGANE FROM THE START. ♡
AND WHY'S THAT?
'CAUSE THAT'S WHERE YOUNG NEWLYWEDS WANT TO LIVE.
HEH
YOUNG NEWLYWEDS?
YEAH, SHE'S GETTING MARRIED...
...AND SHE WANTS TO BE SHIROGANESE*.
*Media term for rich women in Shirogane.

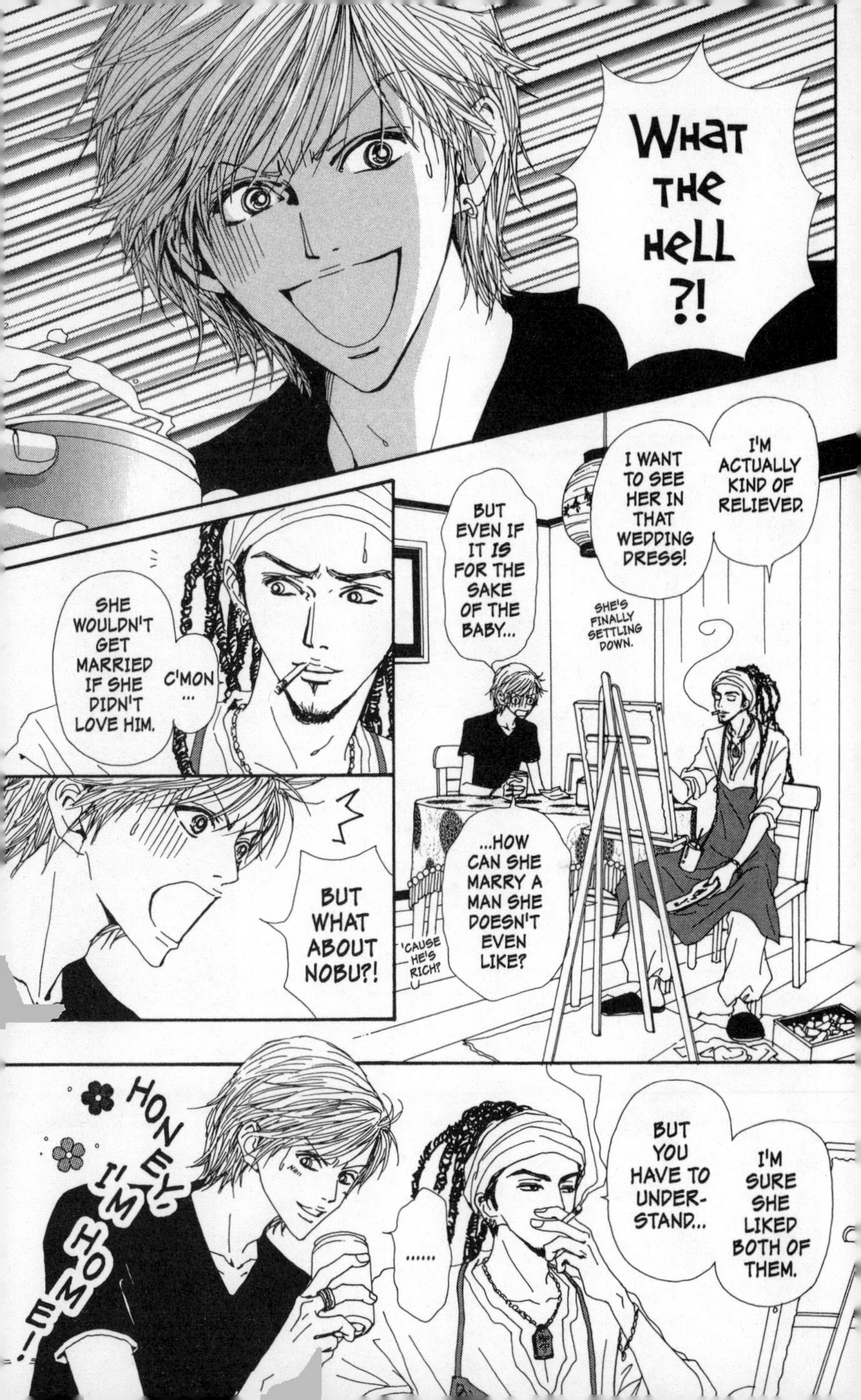
WHAT THE HELL ?!
I'M ACTUALLY KIND OF RELIEVED.
I WANT TO SEE HER IN THAT WEDDING DRESS!
BUT EVEN IF IT IS FOR THE SAKE OF THE BABY...
SHE'S FINALLY SETTLING DOWN.
...HOW CAN SHE MARRY A MAN SHE DOESN'T EVEN LIKE?
'CAUSE HE'S RICH?
C'MON...
SHE WOULDN'T GET MARRIED IF SHE DIDN'T LOVE HIM.
BUT WHAT ABOUT NOBU?!
I'M SURE SHE LIKED BOTH OF THEM.
BUT YOU HAVE TO UNDERSTAND...
......
HONEY~ I'M HOME~!

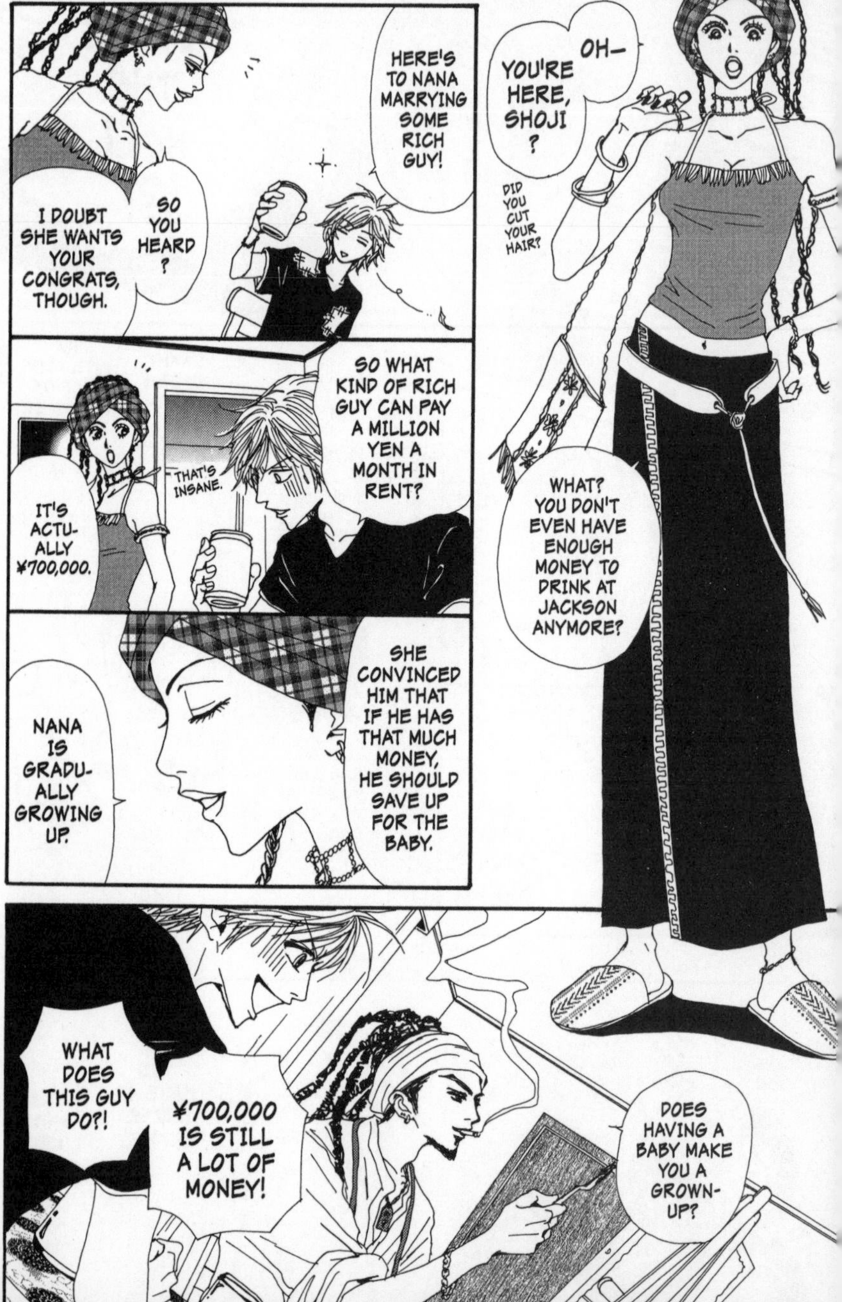
OH—
YOU'RE HERE, SHOJI?
DID YOU CUT YOUR HAIR?
WHAT? YOU DON'T EVEN HAVE ENOUGH MONEY TO DRINK AT JACKSON ANYMORE?
HERE'S TO NANA MARRYING SOME RICH GUY!
SO YOU HEARD?
I DOUBT SHE WANTS YOUR CONGRATS, THOUGH.
SO WHAT KIND OF RICH GUY CAN PAY A MILLION YEN A MONTH IN RENT?
THAT'S INSANE.
IT'S ACTUALLY ¥700,000.
SHE CONVINCED HIM THAT IF HE HAS THAT MUCH MONEY, HE SHOULD SAVE UP FOR THE BABY.
NANA IS GRADUALLY GROWING UP.
DOES HAVING A BABY MAKE YOU A GROWN-UP?
¥700,000 IS STILL A LOT OF MONEY!
WHAT DOES THIS GUY DO?!

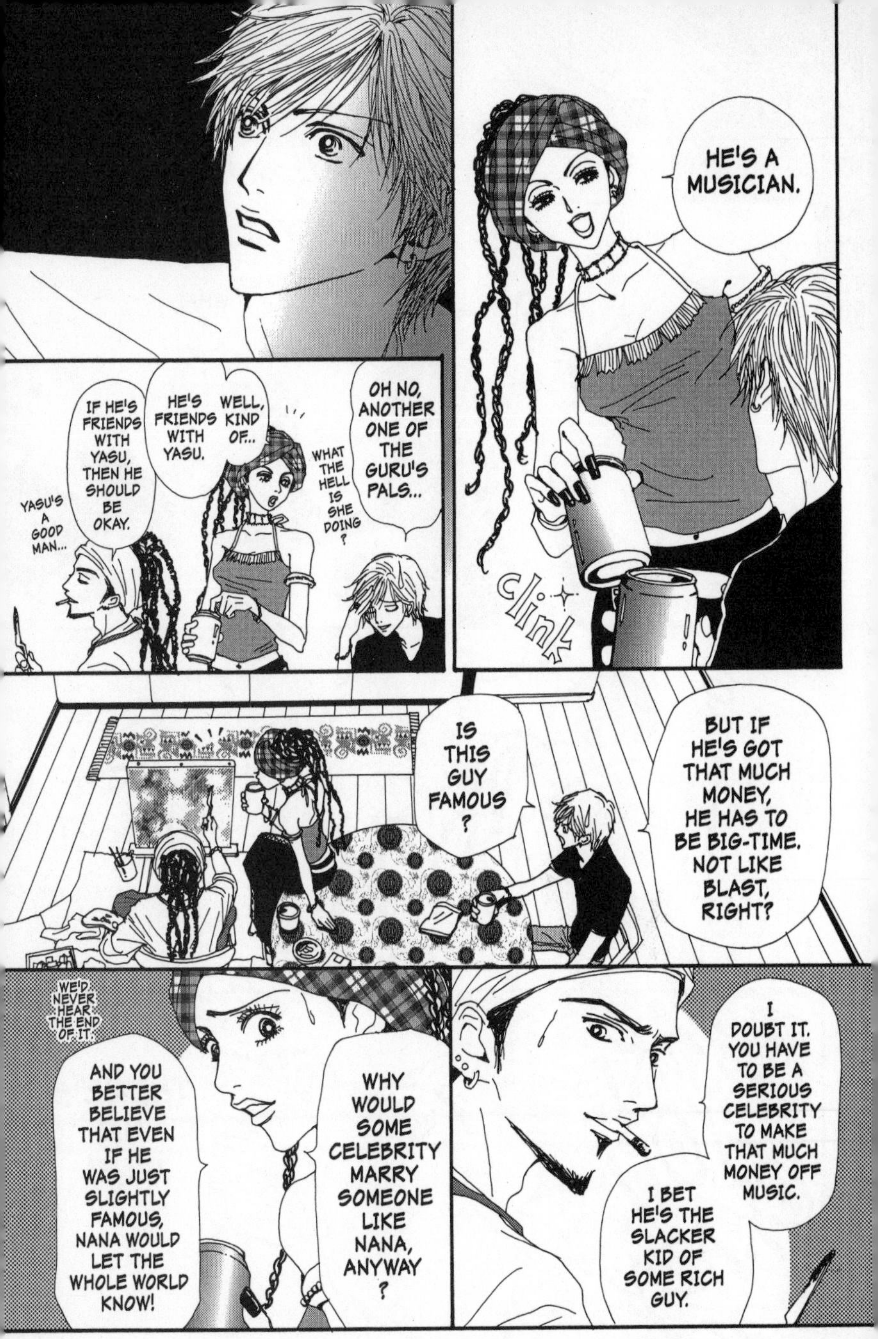
HE'S A MUSICIAN.
clink
OH NO, ANOTHER ONE OF THE GURU'S PALS...
WHAT THE HELL IS SHE DOING?
WELL, KIND OF...
HE'S FRIENDS WITH YASU.
IF HE'S FRIENDS WITH YASU, THEN HE SHOULD BE OKAY.
YASU'S A GOOD MAN...
BUT IF HE'S GOT THAT MUCH MONEY, HE HAS TO BE BIG-TIME. NOT LIKE BLAST, RIGHT?
IS THIS GUY FAMOUS?
I DOUBT IT. YOU HAVE TO BE A SERIOUS CELEBRITY TO MAKE THAT MUCH MONEY OFF MUSIC.
I BET HE'S THE SLACKER KID OF SOME RICH GUY.
WHY WOULD SOME CELEBRITY MARRY SOMEONE LIKE NANA, ANYWAY?
AND YOU BETTER BELIEVE THAT EVEN IF HE WAS JUST SLIGHTLY FAMOUS, NANA WOULD LET THE WHOLE WORLD KNOW!
WE'D NEVER HEAR THE END OF IT.

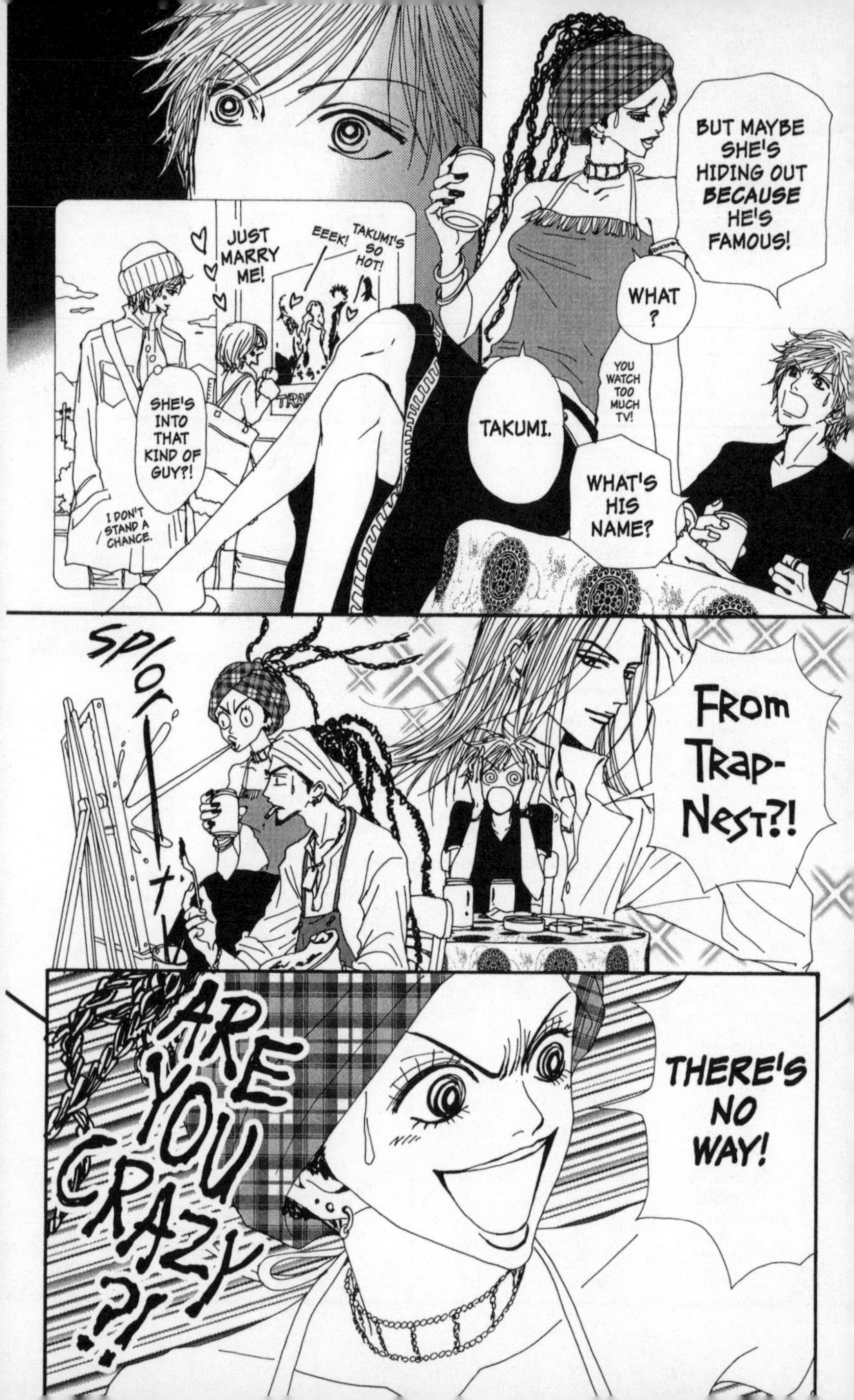
BUT MAYBE SHE'S HIDING OUT BECAUSE HE'S FAMOUS!
WHAT ?
YOU WATCH TOO MUCH TV!
WHAT'S HIS NAME?
TAKUMI.
TAKUMI'S SO HOT!
EEEK!
JUST MARRY ME!
SHE'S INTO THAT KIND OF GUY?!
I DON'T STAND A CHANCE.
From Trap-Nest?!
splort
THERE'S NO WAY!
ARE YOU CRAZY ?!

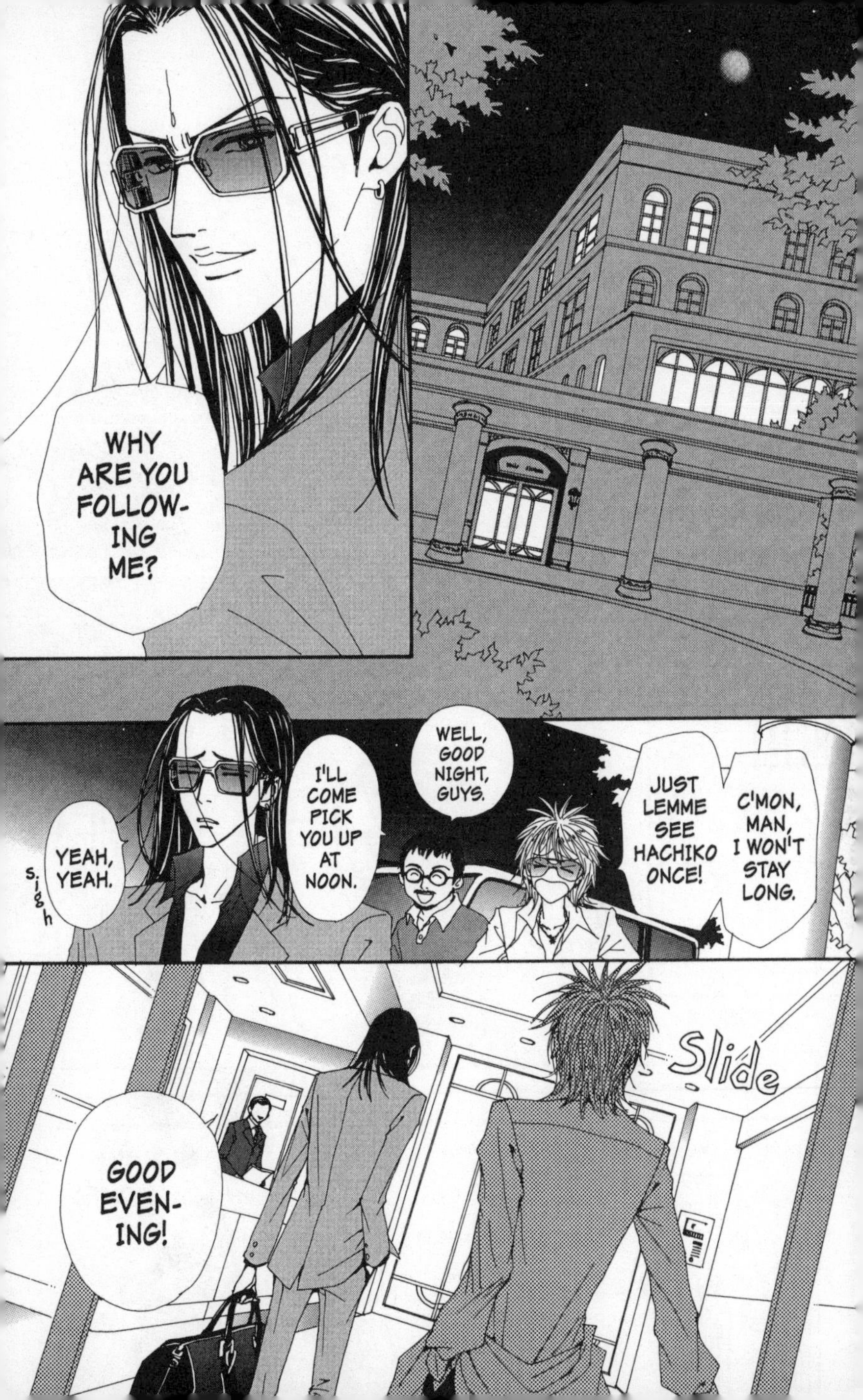
WHY ARE YOU FOLLOW-ING ME?
C'MON, MAN, I WON'T STAY LONG.
JUST LEMME SEE HACHIKO ONCE!
WELL, GOOD NIGHT, GUYS.
I'LL COME PICK YOU UP AT NOON.
YEAH, YEAH.
sigh
Slide
GOOD EVEN-ING!

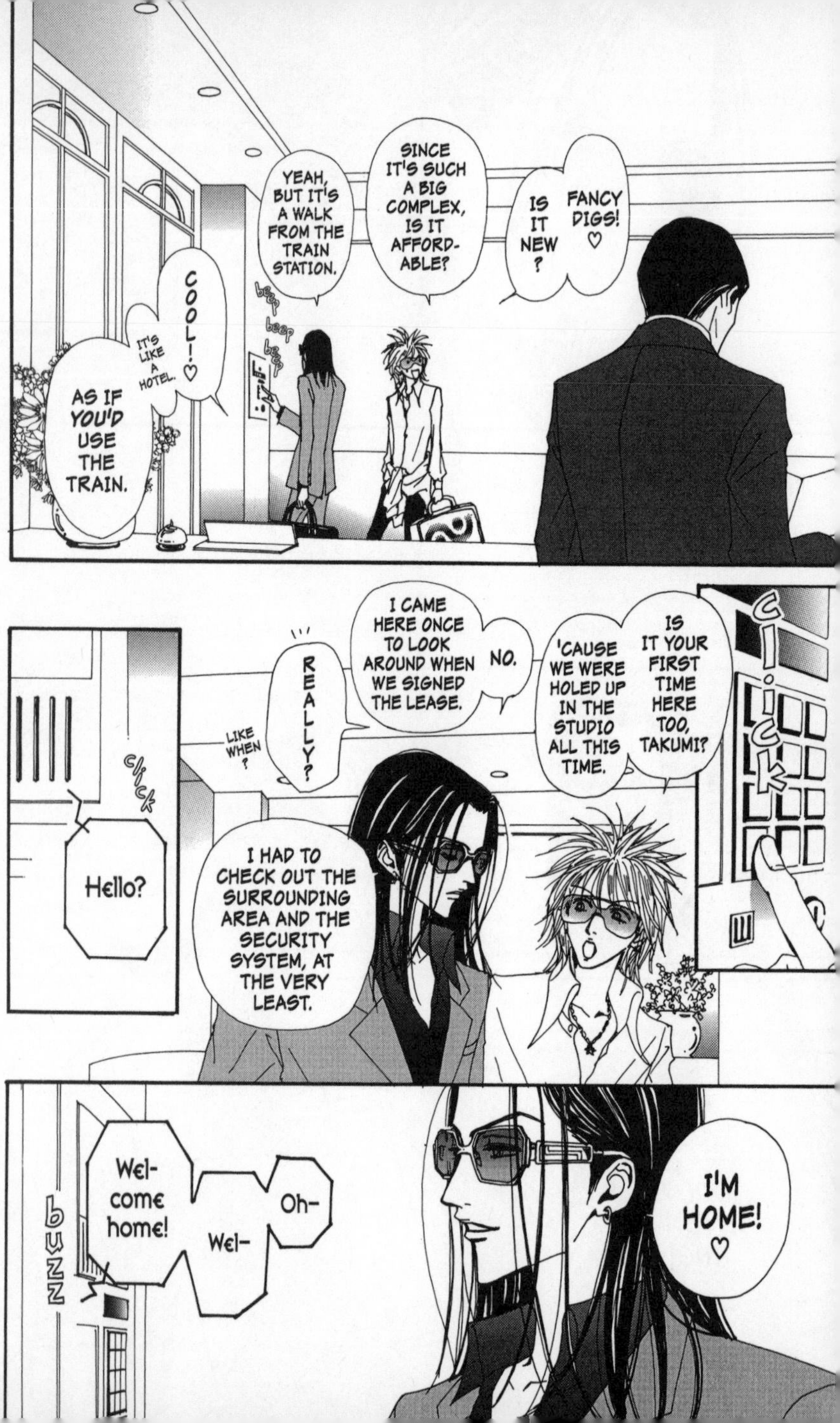

FANCY DIGS! ♡
IS IT NEW?
SINCE IT'S SUCH A BIG COMPLEX, IS IT AFFORDABLE?
YEAH, BUT IT'S A WALK FROM THE TRAIN STATION.
beep beep beep
COOL! ♡
IT'S LIKE A HOTEL.
AS IF YOU'D USE THE TRAIN.
click
IS IT YOUR FIRST TIME HERE TOO, TAKUMI?
'CAUSE WE WERE HOLED UP IN THE STUDIO ALL THIS TIME.
NO.
I CAME HERE ONCE TO LOOK AROUND WHEN WE SIGNED THE LEASE.
REALLY?
LIKE WHEN?
I HAD TO CHECK OUT THE SURROUNDING AREA AND THE SECURITY SYSTEM, AT THE VERY LEAST.
click
Hello?
I'M HOME! ♡
Oh-
Wel-
Welcome home!
buzz

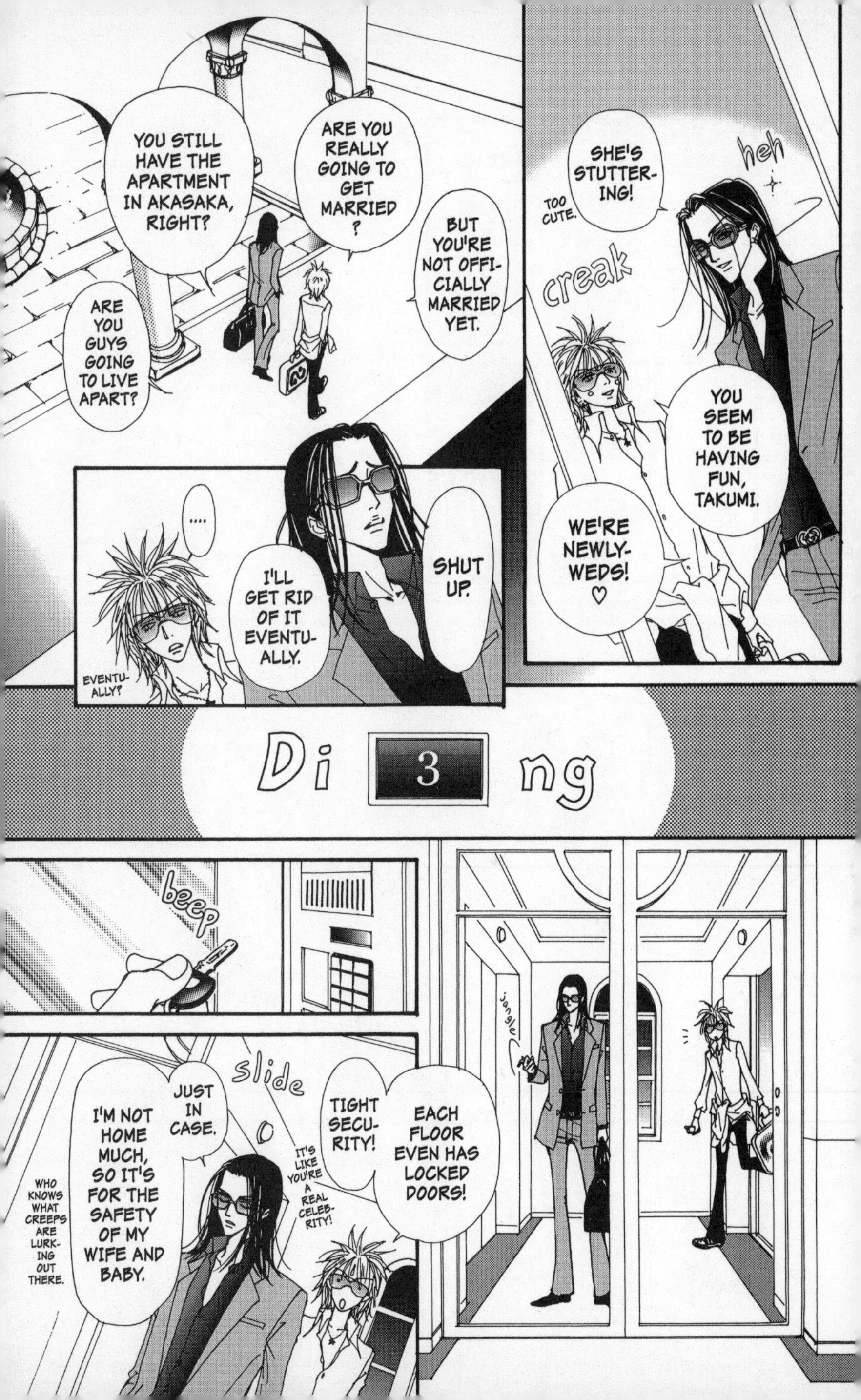
heh
SHE'S STUTTERING!
TOO CUTE.
creak
YOU SEEM TO BE HAVING FUN, TAKUMI.
WE'RE NEWLYWEDS! ♡
ARE YOU REALLY GOING TO GET MARRIED?
BUT YOU'RE NOT OFFICIALLY MARRIED YET.
YOU STILL HAVE THE APARTMENT IN AKASAKA, RIGHT?
ARE YOU GUYS GOING TO LIVE APART?
SHUT UP.
I'LL GET RID OF IT EVENTUALLY.
....
EVENTUALLY?
Di 3 ng
jangle
beep
EACH FLOOR EVEN HAS LOCKED DOORS!
TIGHT SECURITY!
IT'S LIKE YOU'RE A REAL CELEBRITY!
slide
JUST IN CASE.
I'M NOT HOME MUCH, SO IT'S FOR THE SAFETY OF MY WIFE AND BABY.
WHO KNOWS WHAT CREEPS ARE LURKING OUT THERE.

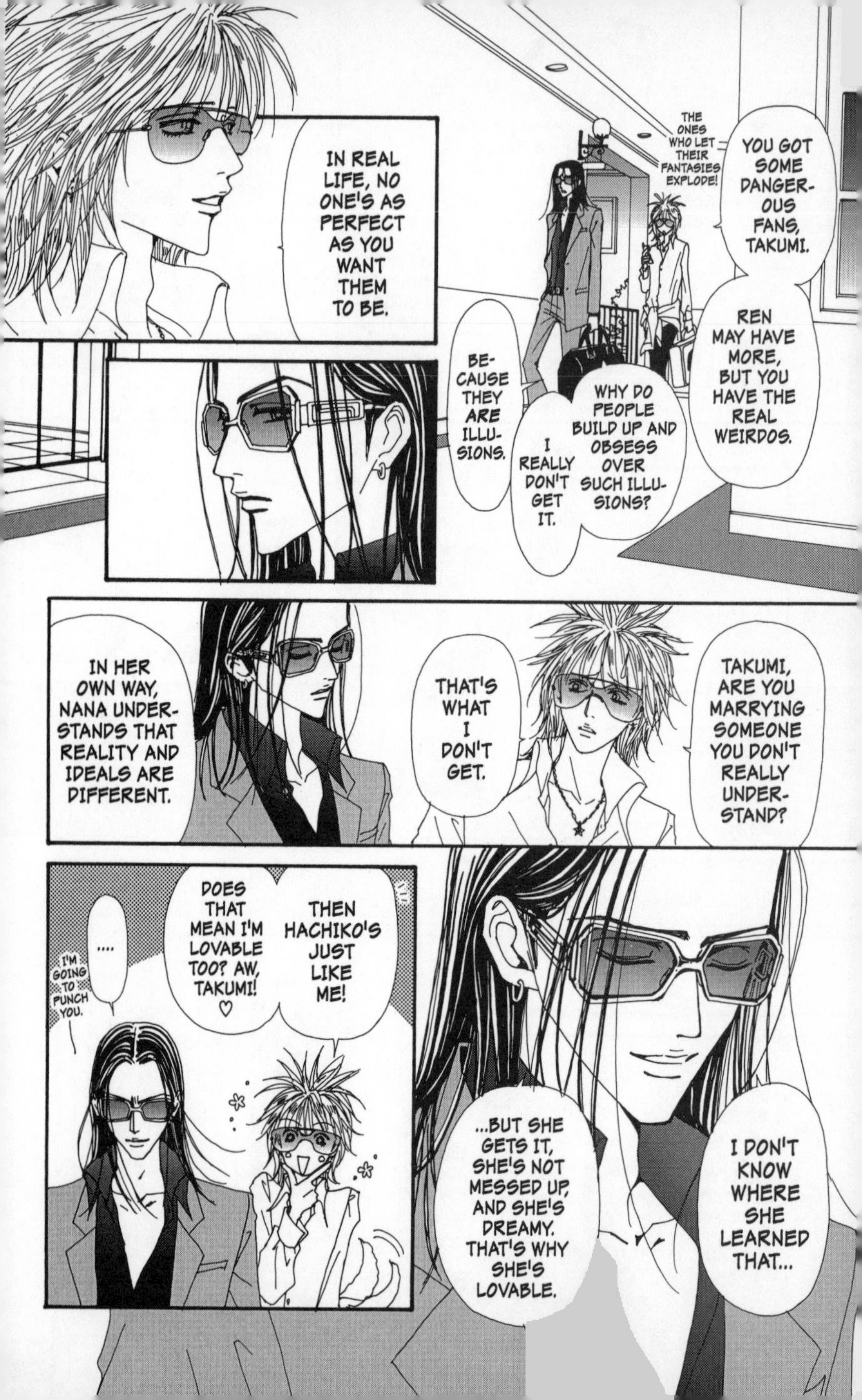
YOU GOT SOME DANGEROUS FANS, TAKUMI.
THE ONES WHO LET THEIR FANTASIES EXPLODE!
REN MAY HAVE MORE, BUT YOU HAVE THE REAL WEIRDOS.
WHY DO PEOPLE BUILD UP AND OBSESS OVER SUCH ILLUSIONS?
I REALLY DON'T GET IT.
BECAUSE THEY ARE ILLUSIONS.
IN REAL LIFE, NO ONE'S AS PERFECT AS YOU WANT THEM TO BE.
TAKUMI, ARE YOU MARRYING SOMEONE YOU DON'T REALLY UNDERSTAND?
THAT'S WHAT I DON'T GET.
IN HER OWN WAY, NANA UNDERSTANDS THAT REALITY AND IDEALS ARE DIFFERENT.
I DON'T KNOW WHERE SHE LEARNED THAT...
...BUT SHE GETS IT, SHE'S NOT MESSED UP, AND SHE'S DREAMY. THAT'S WHY SHE'S LOVABLE.
THEN HACHIKO'S JUST LIKE ME!
DOES THAT MEAN I'M LOVABLE TOO? AW, TAKUMI! ♡
....
I'M GOING TO PUNCH YOU.

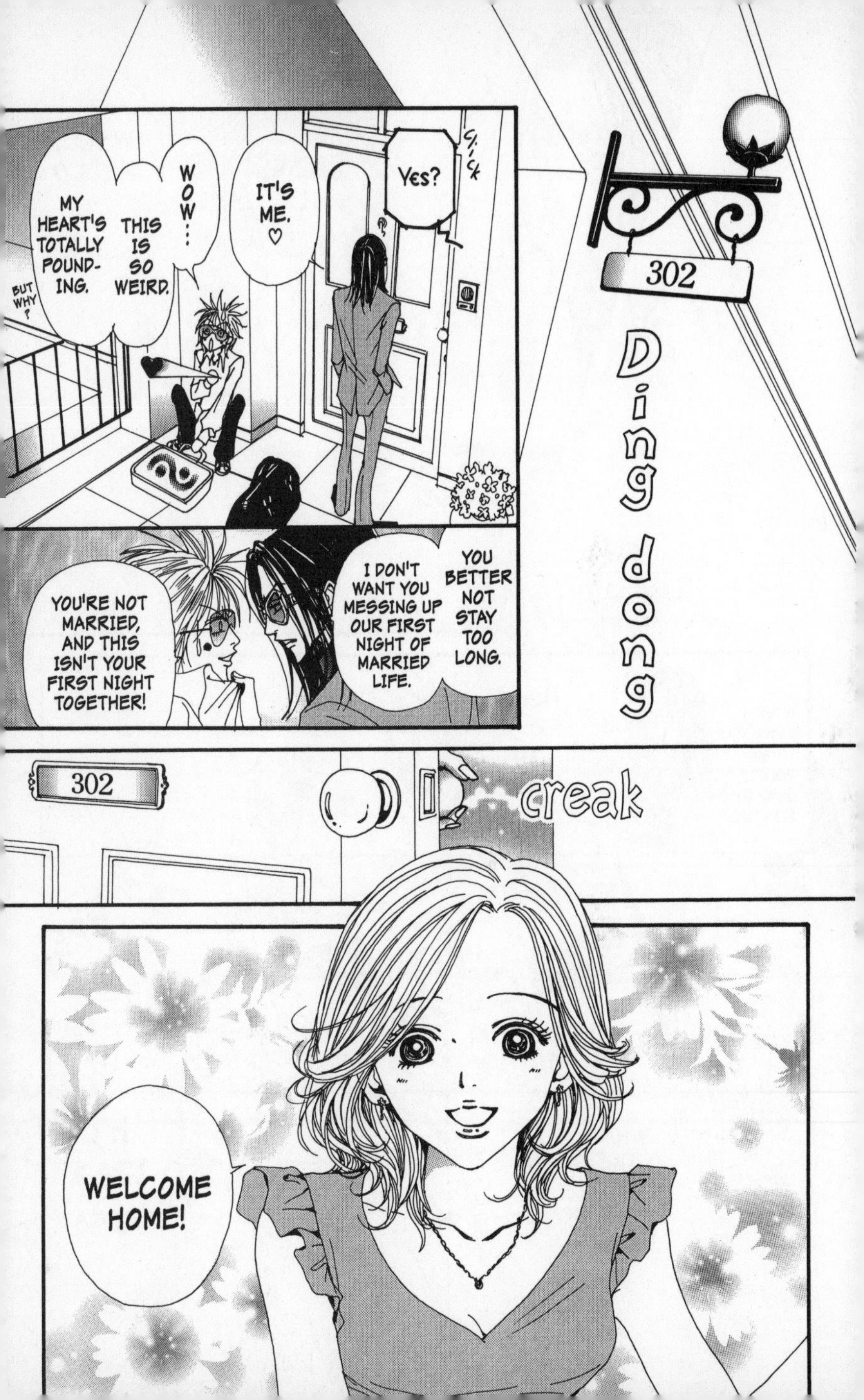
302
Ding dong
Click
Yes?
IT'S ME. ♡
WOW...
THIS IS SO WEIRD.
MY HEART'S TOTALLY POUNDING.
BUT WHY?
YOU BETTER NOT STAY TOO LONG.
I DON'T WANT YOU MESSING UP OUR FIRST NIGHT OF MARRIED LIFE.
YOU'RE NOT MARRIED, AND THIS ISN'T YOUR FIRST NIGHT TOGETHER!
creak
302
WELCOME HOME!

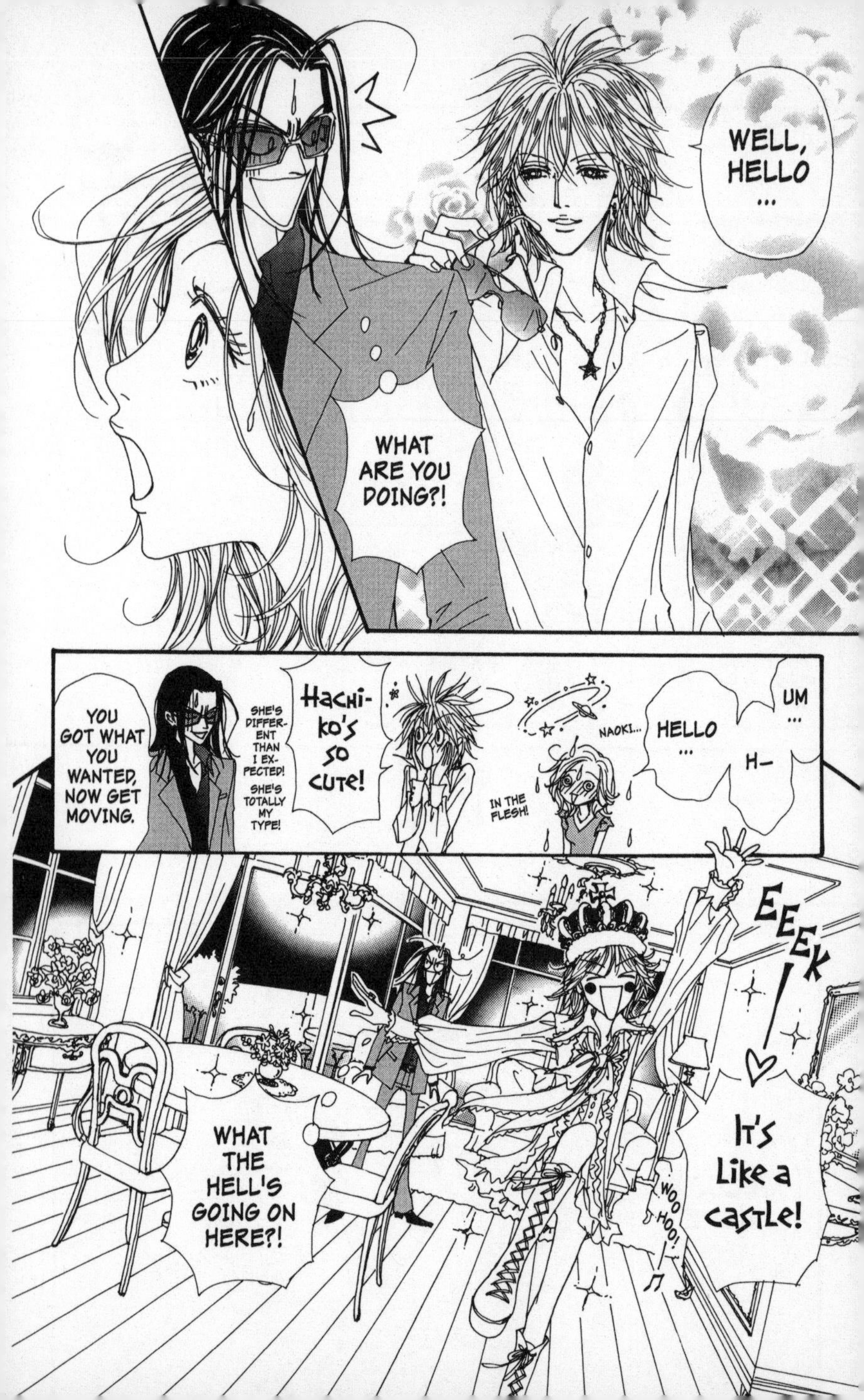
WELL, HELLO ...
WHAT ARE YOU DOING?!
UM ... H—
HELLO ...
NAOKI... IN THE FLESH!
Hachi-ko's so cute!
SHE'S DIFFERENT THAN I EXPECTED! SHE'S TOTALLY MY TYPE!
YOU GOT WHAT YOU WANTED, NOW GET MOVING.
EEEK!
It's like a castle!
WOO HOO!
WHAT THE HELL'S GOING ON HERE?!

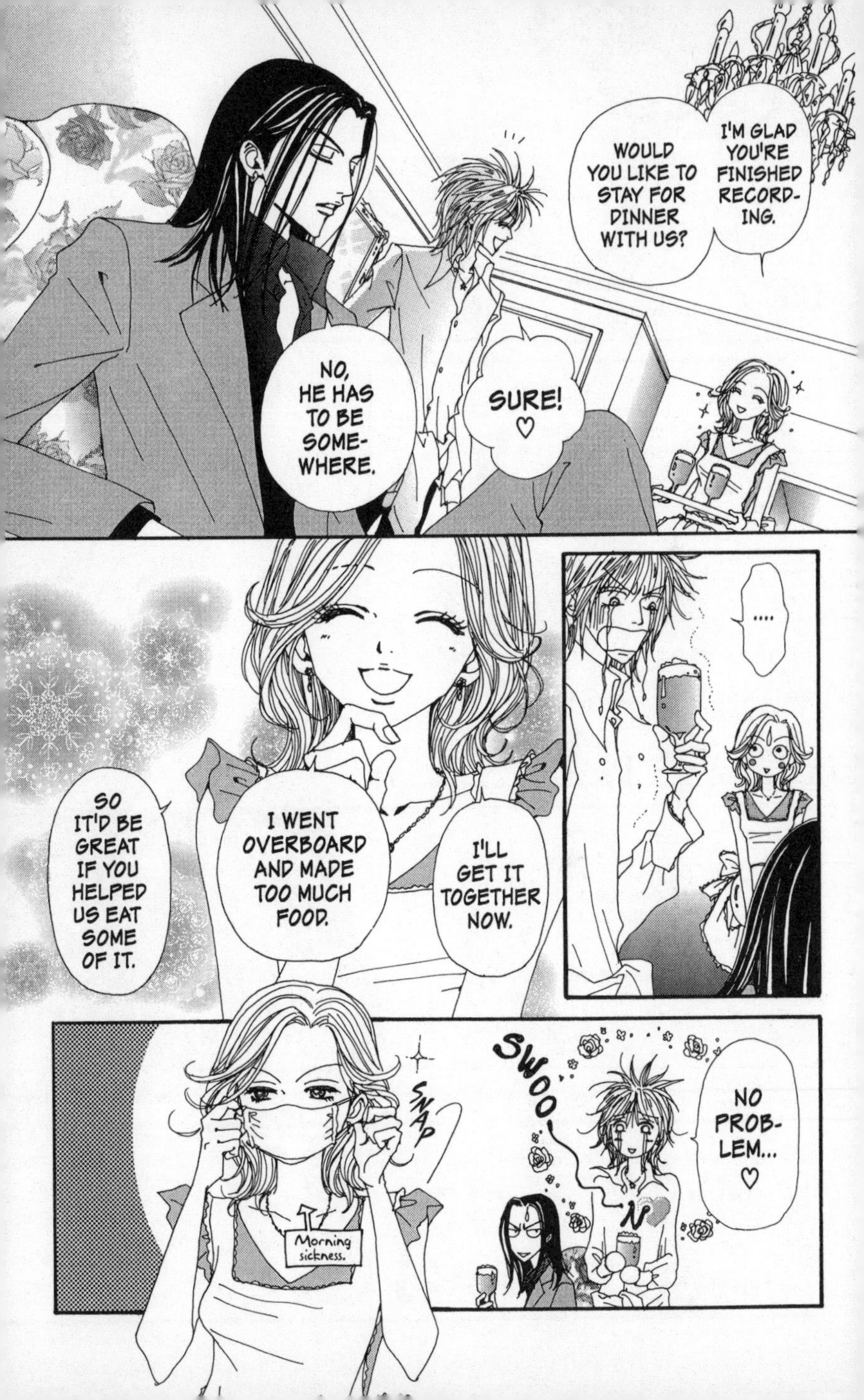
I'M GLAD YOU'RE FINISHED RECORD-ING.
WOULD YOU LIKE TO STAY FOR DINNER WITH US?
SURE! ♡
NO, HE HAS TO BE SOME-WHERE.
....
I'LL GET IT TOGETHER NOW.
I WENT OVERBOARD AND MADE TOO MUCH FOOD.
SO IT'D BE GREAT IF YOU HELPED US EAT SOME OF IT.
NO PROB-LEM... ♡
SWOO
SNAP
Morning sickness.

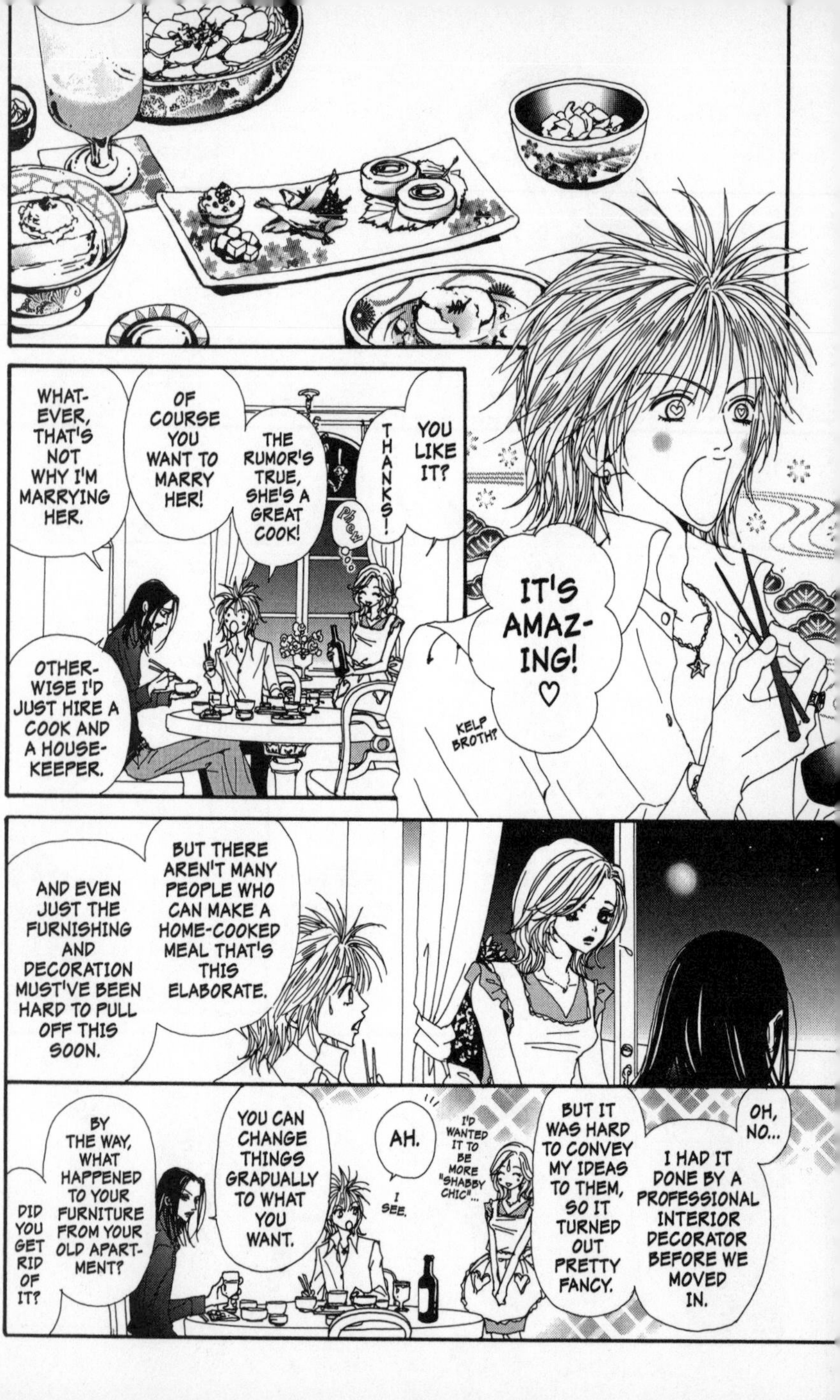
IT'S AMAZ-ING! ♡
KELP BROTH?
YOU LIKE IT?
THANKS!
Phew
THE RUMOR'S TRUE, SHE'S A GREAT COOK!
OF COURSE YOU WANT TO MARRY HER!
WHAT-EVER, THAT'S NOT WHY I'M MARRYING HER.
OTHER-WISE I'D JUST HIRE A COOK AND A HOUSE-KEEPER.
BUT THERE AREN'T MANY PEOPLE WHO CAN MAKE A HOME-COOKED MEAL THAT'S THIS ELABORATE.
AND EVEN JUST THE FURNISHING AND DECORATION MUST'VE BEEN HARD TO PULL OFF THIS SOON.
OH, NO...
I HAD IT DONE BY A PROFESSIONAL INTERIOR DECORATOR BEFORE WE MOVED IN.
BUT IT WAS HARD TO CONVEY MY IDEAS TO THEM, SO IT TURNED OUT PRETTY FANCY.
I'D WANTED IT TO BE MORE "SHABBY CHIC"...
AH.
I SEE.
YOU CAN CHANGE THINGS GRADUALLY TO WHAT YOU WANT.
BY THE WAY, WHAT HAPPENED TO YOUR FURNITURE FROM YOUR OLD APART-MENT?
DID YOU GET RID OF IT?

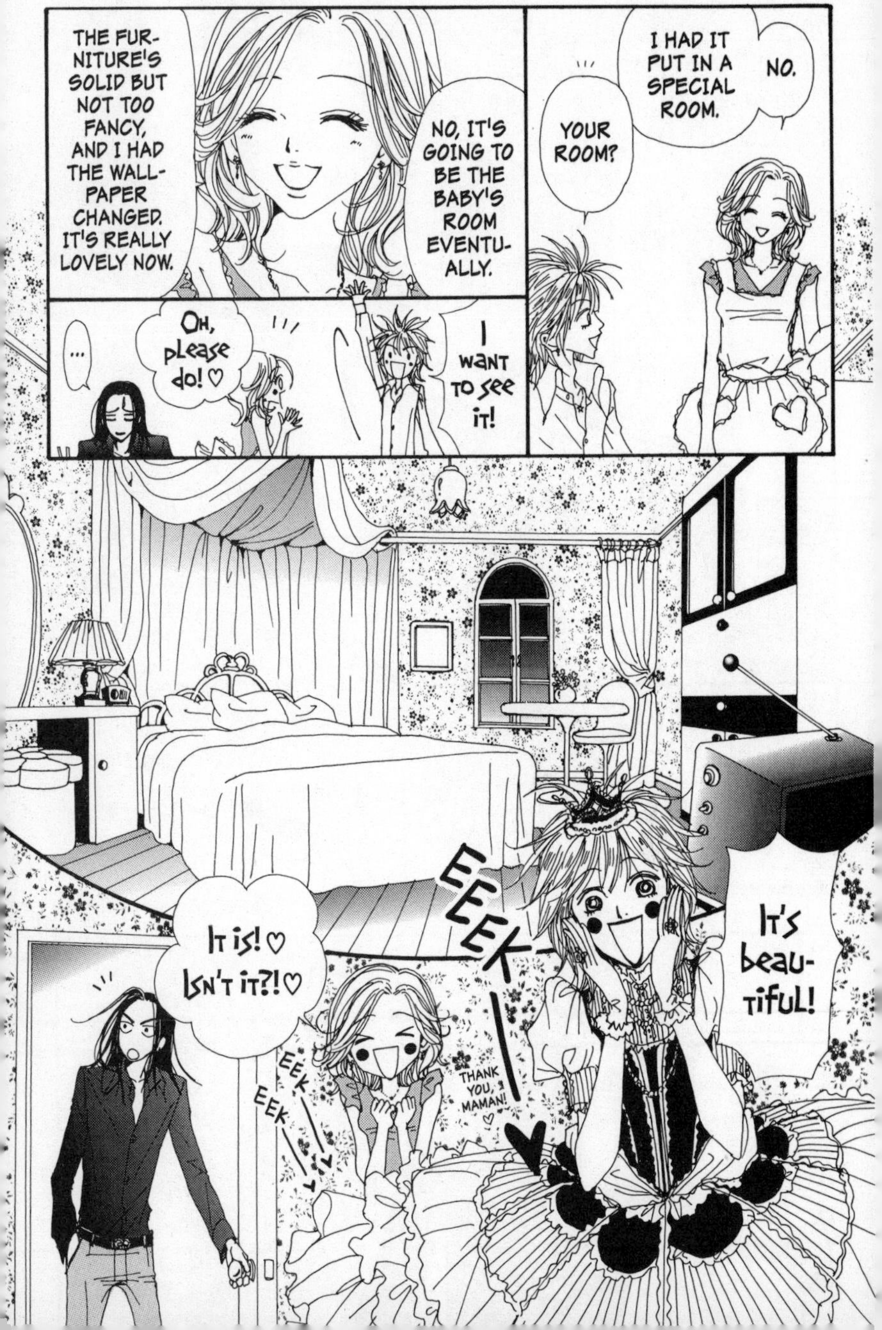
NO.
I HAD IT PUT IN A SPECIAL ROOM.
YOUR ROOM?
NO, IT'S GOING TO BE THE BABY'S ROOM EVENTUALLY.
THE FURNITURE'S SOLID BUT NOT TOO FANCY, AND I HAD THE WALLPAPER CHANGED. IT'S REALLY LOVELY NOW.
I want to see it!
Oh, please do! ♡
...
It's beautiful!
EEEK—
THANK YOU, MAMAN! ♡
It is! ♡ Isn't it?! ♡
EEK
EEK

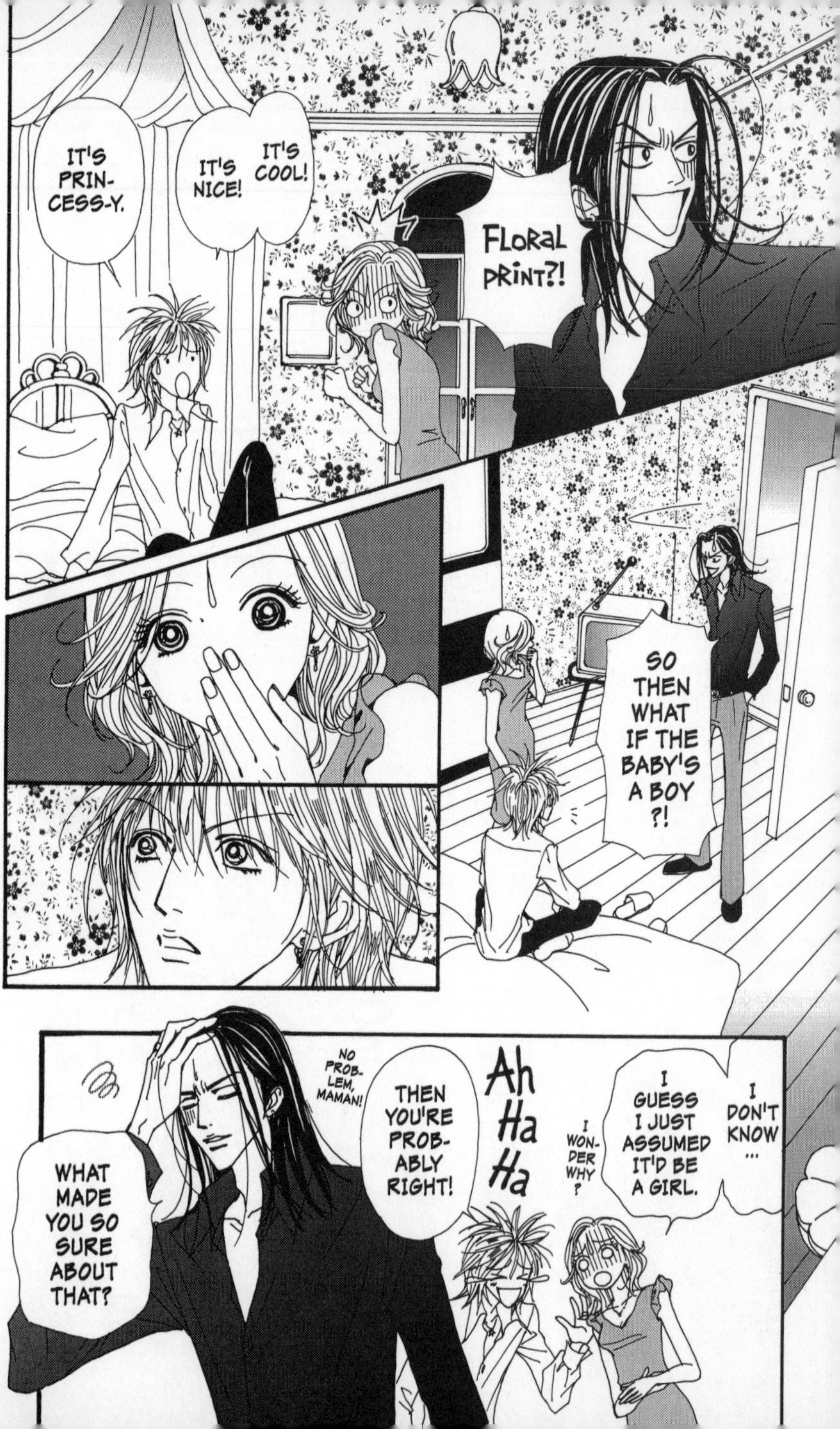
FLORAL PRINT?!
IT'S COOL!
IT'S NICE!
IT'S PRIN-CESS-Y.
SO THEN WHAT IF THE BABY'S A BOY?!
I DON'T KNOW...
I GUESS I JUST ASSUMED IT'D BE A GIRL.
I WONDER WHY?
Ah Ha Ha
THEN YOU'RE PROB-ABLY RIGHT!
NO PROB-LEM, MAMAN!
WHAT MADE YOU SO SURE ABOUT THAT?

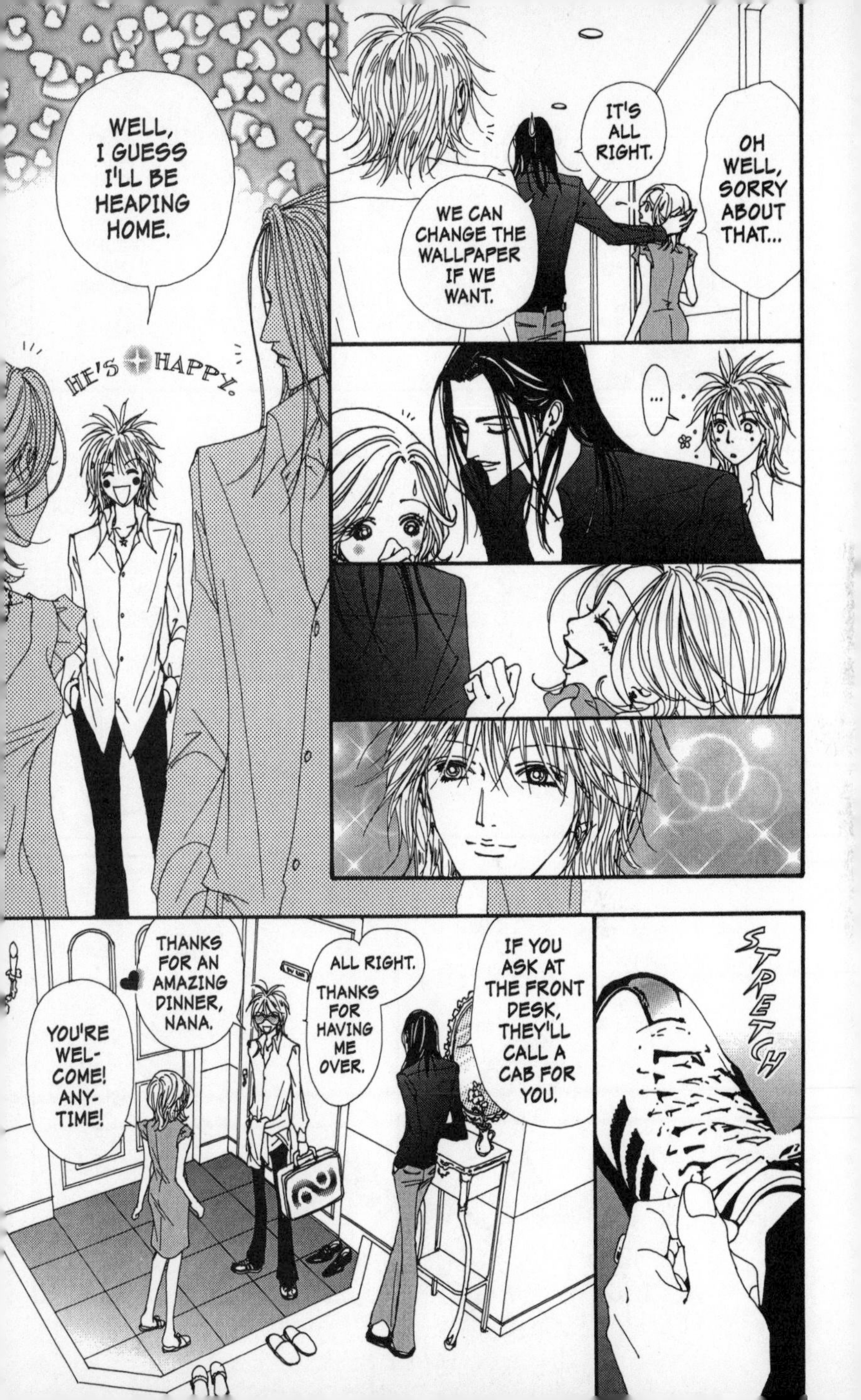

OH WELL, SORRY ABOUT THAT...
IT'S ALL RIGHT.
WE CAN CHANGE THE WALLPAPER IF WE WANT.
...
WELL, I GUESS I'LL BE HEADING HOME.
HE'S HAPPY.
STRETCH
IF YOU ASK AT THE FRONT DESK, THEY'LL CALL A CAB FOR YOU.
ALL RIGHT.
THANKS FOR HAVING ME OVER.
THANKS FOR AN AMAZING DINNER, NANA.
YOU'RE WEL-COME! ANY-TIME!

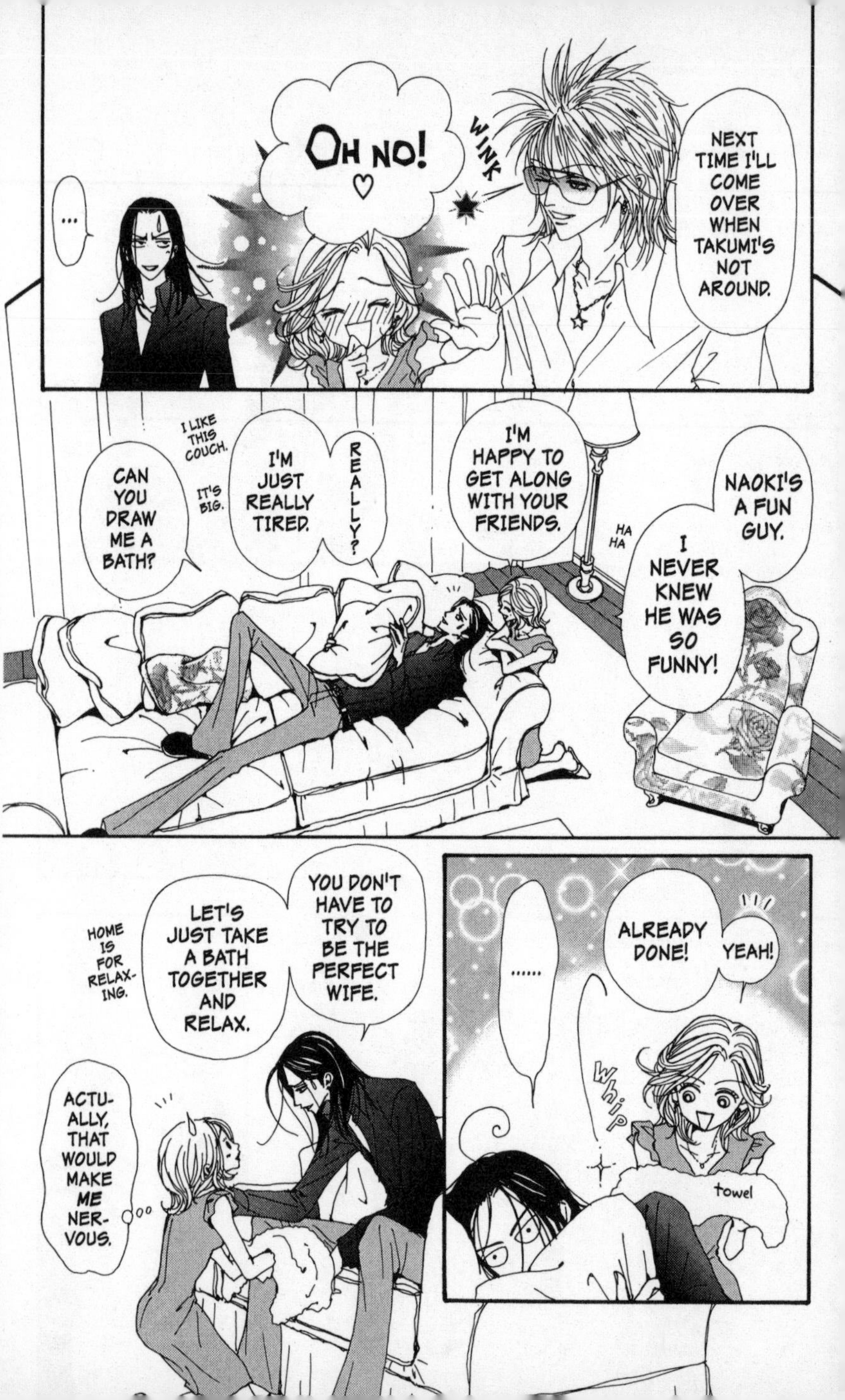
NEXT TIME I'LL COME OVER WHEN TAKUMI'S NOT AROUND.
WINK
OH NO! ♡
...
NAOKI'S A FUN GUY.
I NEVER KNEW HE WAS SO FUNNY!
HA HA
I'M HAPPY TO GET ALONG WITH YOUR FRIENDS.
REALLY?
I'M JUST REALLY TIRED.
I LIKE THIS COUCH.
IT'S BIG.
CAN YOU DRAW ME A BATH?
YEAH!
ALREADY DONE!
Whip
towel
......
YOU DON'T HAVE TO TRY TO BE THE PERFECT WIFE.
LET'S JUST TAKE A BATH TOGETHER AND RELAX.
HOME IS FOR RELAX-ING.
ACTU-ALLY, THAT WOULD MAKE ME NER-VOUS.

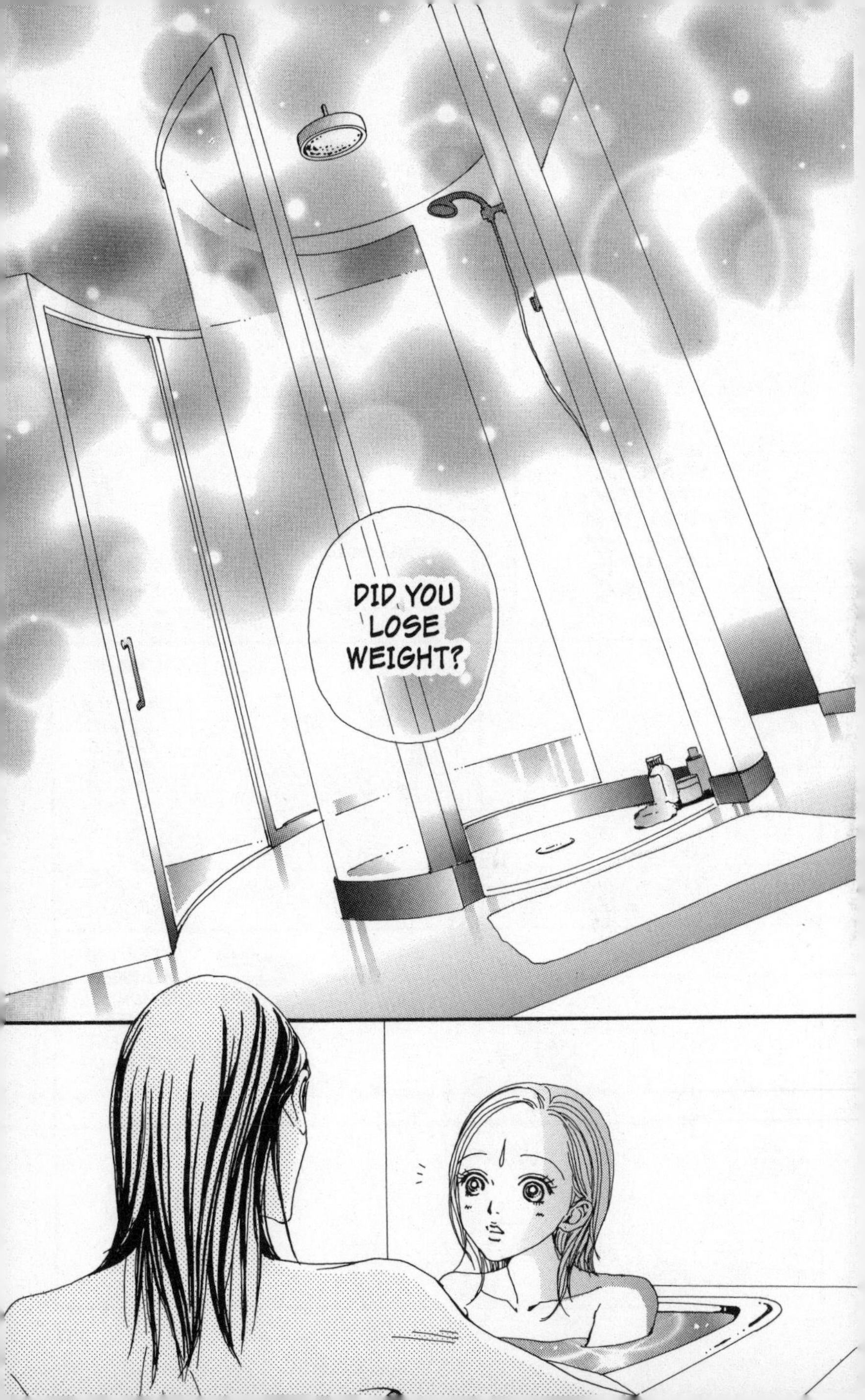
DID YOU LOSE WEIGHT?

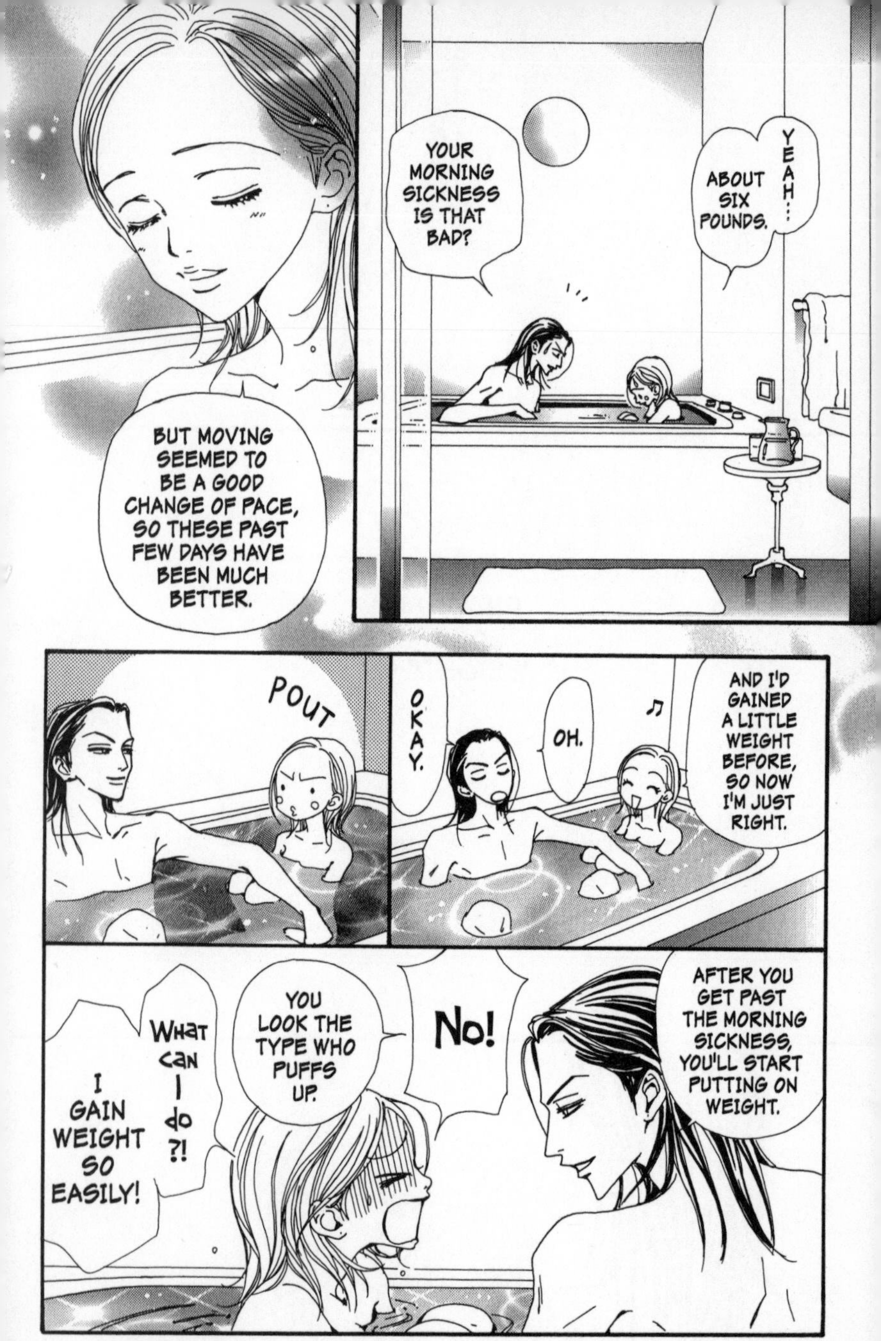

YEAH... ABOUT SIX POUNDS.
YOUR MORNING SICKNESS IS THAT BAD?
BUT MOVING SEEMED TO BE A GOOD CHANGE OF PACE, SO THESE PAST FEW DAYS HAVE BEEN MUCH BETTER.
AND I'D GAINED A LITTLE WEIGHT BEFORE, SO NOW I'M JUST RIGHT.
♪
OH.
OKAY.
POUT
AFTER YOU GET PAST THE MORNING SICKNESS, YOU'LL START PUTTING ON WEIGHT.
No!
YOU LOOK THE TYPE WHO PUFFS UP.
What can I do?!
I GAIN WEIGHT SO EASILY!

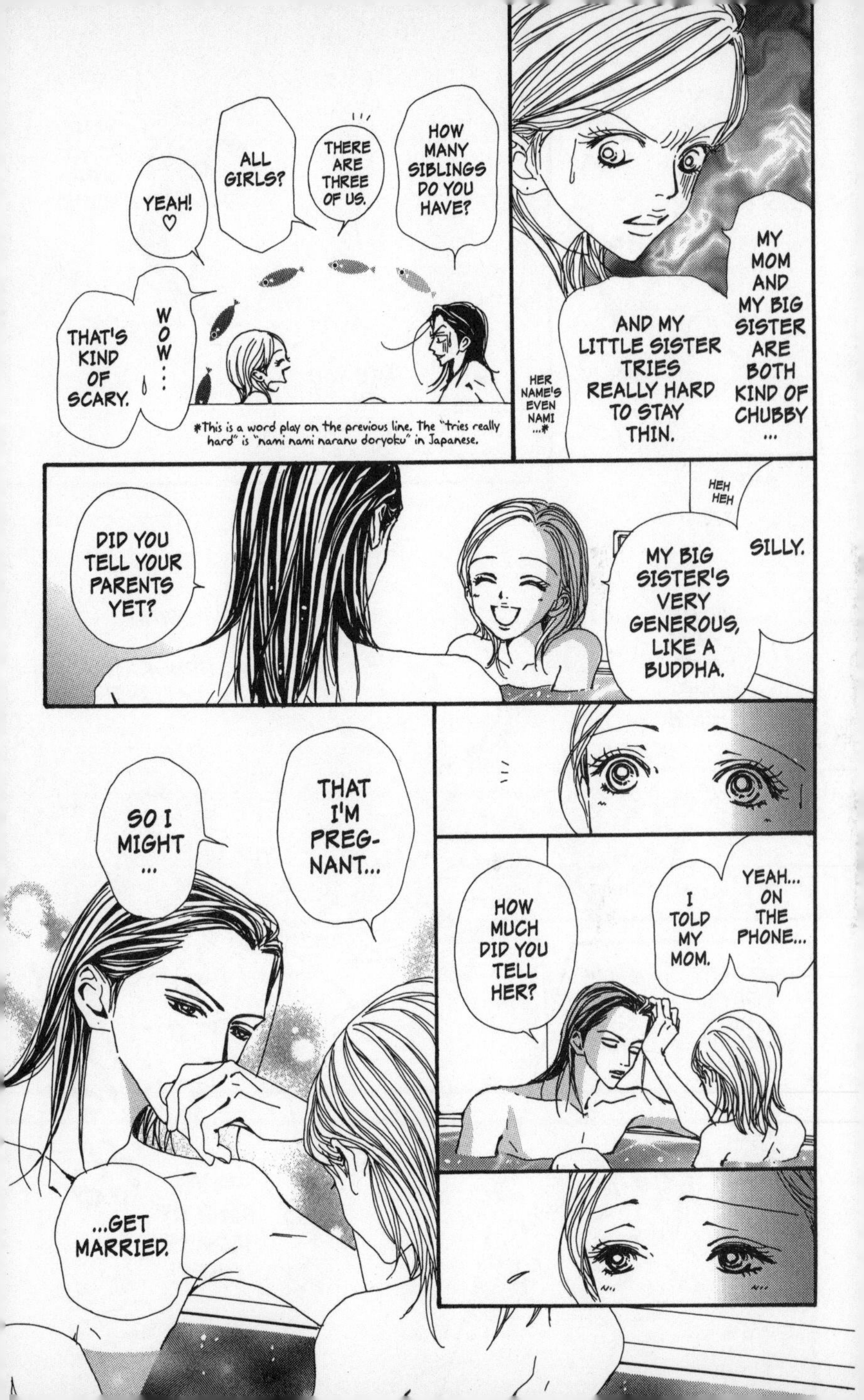
MY MOM AND MY BIG SISTER ARE BOTH KIND OF CHUBBY...
AND MY LITTLE SISTER TRIES REALLY HARD TO STAY THIN.
HER NAME'S EVEN NAMI...*
HOW MANY SIBLINGS DO YOU HAVE?
THERE ARE THREE OF US.
ALL GIRLS?
YEAH! ♡
WOW...
THAT'S KIND OF SCARY.
SILLY.
HEH HEH
MY BIG SISTER'S VERY GENEROUS, LIKE A BUDDHA.
DID YOU TELL YOUR PARENTS YET?
YEAH... ON THE PHONE...
I TOLD MY MOM.
HOW MUCH DID YOU TELL HER?
THAT I'M PREG-NANT...
SO I MIGHT...
...GET MARRIED.

*This is a word play on the previous line. The "tries really hard" is "nami nami naranu doryoku" in Japanese.

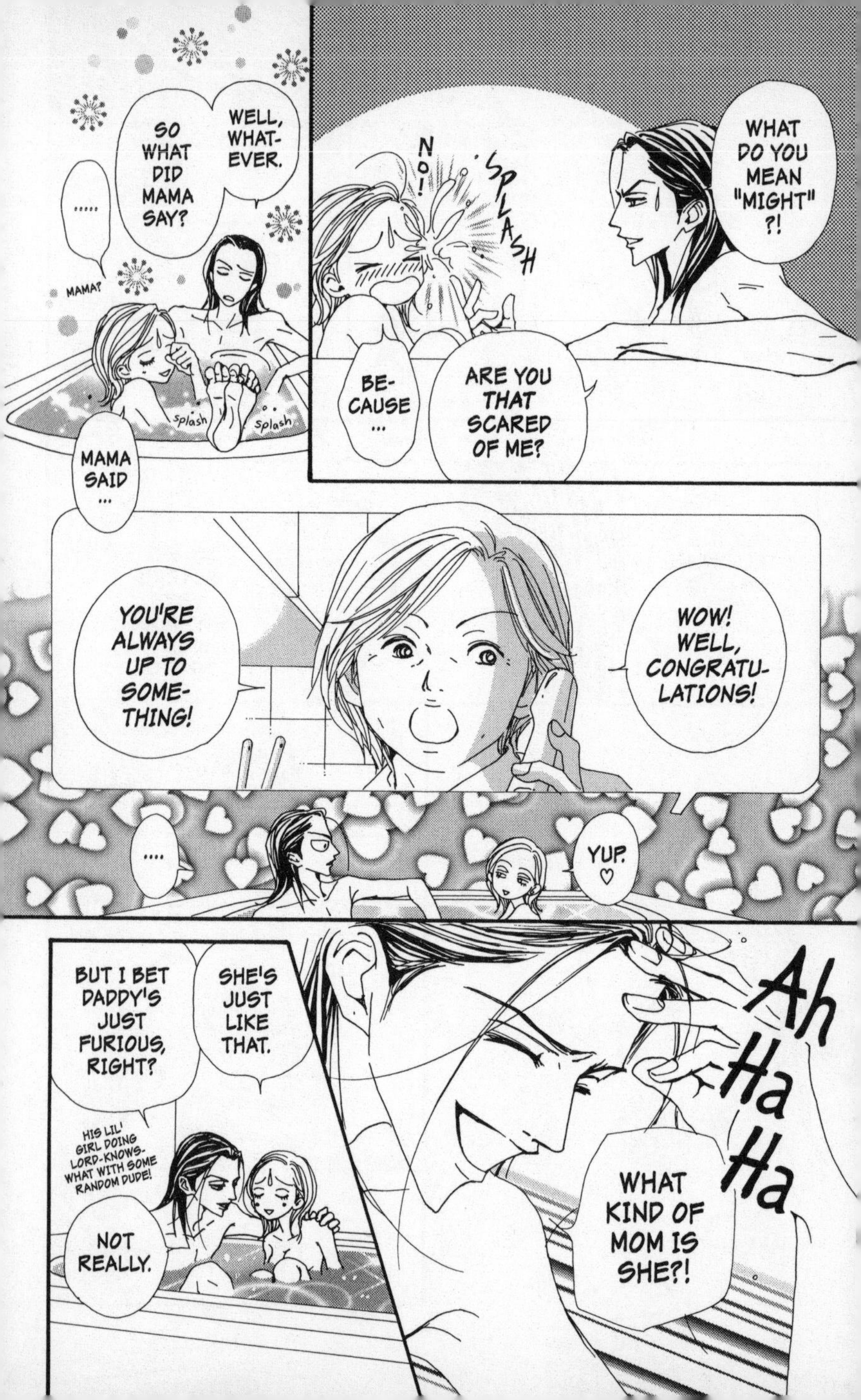
WHAT DO YOU MEAN "MIGHT"?!
NO!
SPLASH
ARE YOU THAT SCARED OF ME?
BE-CAUSE ...
WELL, WHAT-EVER.
SO WHAT DID MAMA SAY?
......
MAMA?
splash
splash
MAMA SAID ...
WOW! WELL, CONGRATU-LATIONS!
YOU'RE ALWAYS UP TO SOME-THING!
YUP. ♡
....
Ah Ha Ha Ha
WHAT KIND OF MOM IS SHE?!
SHE'S JUST LIKE THAT.
BUT I BET DADDY'S JUST FURIOUS, RIGHT?
HIS LIL' GIRL DOING LORD-KNOWS-WHAT WITH SOME RANDOM DUDE!
NOT REALLY.

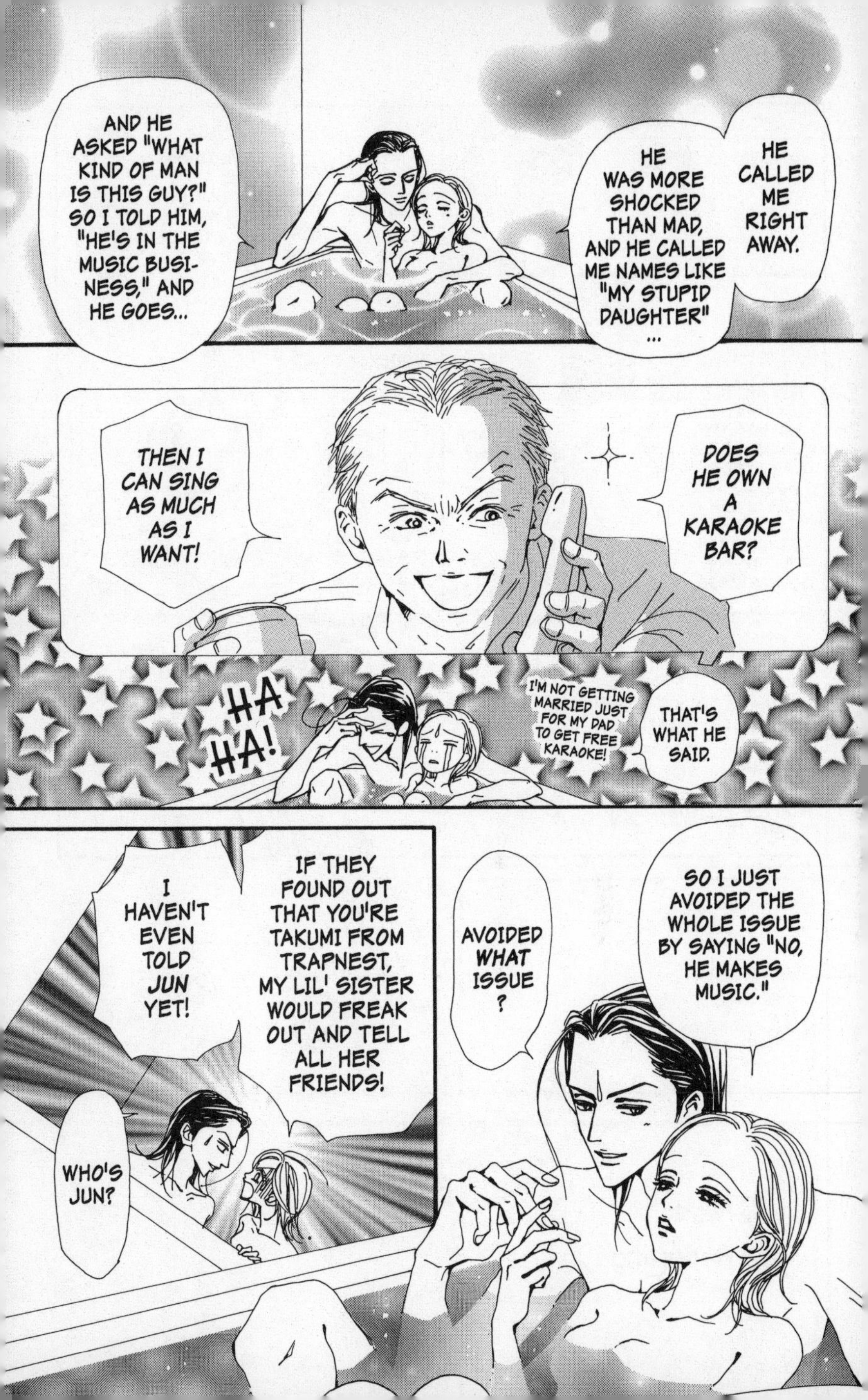
HE CALLED ME RIGHT AWAY.
HE WAS MORE SHOCKED THAN MAD, AND HE CALLED ME NAMES LIKE "MY STUPID DAUGHTER" ...
AND HE ASKED "WHAT KIND OF MAN IS THIS GUY?" SO I TOLD HIM, "HE'S IN THE MUSIC BUSI-NESS," AND HE GOES...
DOES HE OWN A KARAOKE BAR?
THEN I CAN SING AS MUCH AS I WANT!
THAT'S WHAT HE SAID.
I'M NOT GETTING MARRIED JUST FOR MY DAD TO GET FREE KARAOKE!
HA HA!
SO I JUST AVOIDED THE WHOLE ISSUE BY SAYING "NO, HE MAKES MUSIC."
AVOIDED WHAT ISSUE ?
IF THEY FOUND OUT THAT YOU'RE TAKUMI FROM TRAPNEST, MY LIL' SISTER WOULD FREAK OUT AND TELL ALL HER FRIENDS!
I HAVEN'T EVEN TOLD JUN YET!
WHO'S JUN?

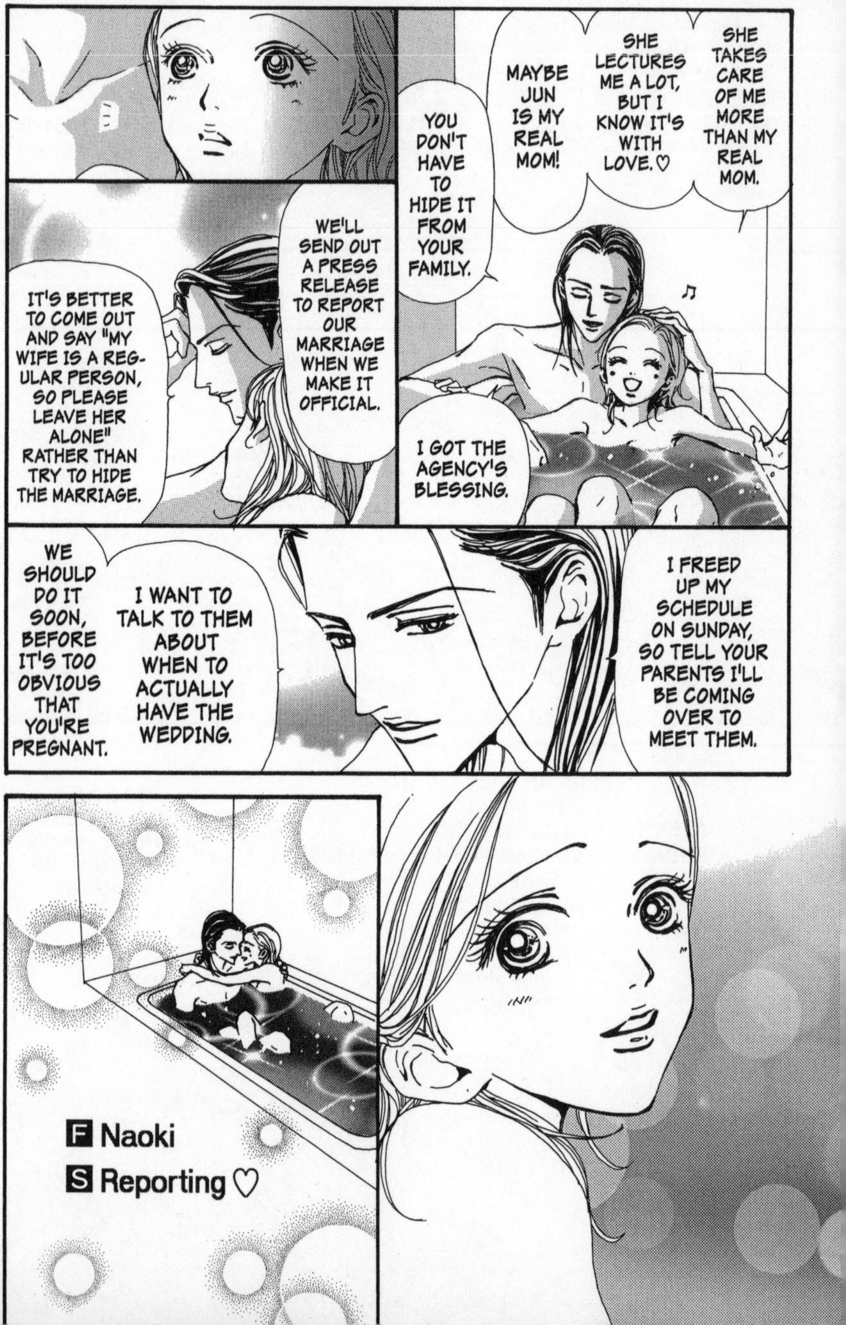
SHE TAKES CARE OF ME MORE THAN MY REAL MOM.
SHE LECTURES ME A LOT, BUT I KNOW IT'S WITH LOVE. ♡
MAYBE JUN IS MY REAL MOM!
YOU DON'T HAVE TO HIDE IT FROM YOUR FAMILY.
I GOT THE AGENCY'S BLESSING.
WE'LL SEND OUT A PRESS RELEASE TO REPORT OUR MARRIAGE WHEN WE MAKE IT OFFICIAL.
IT'S BETTER TO COME OUT AND SAY "MY WIFE IS A REGULAR PERSON, SO PLEASE LEAVE HER ALONE" RATHER THAN TRY TO HIDE THE MARRIAGE.
I FREED UP MY SCHEDULE ON SUNDAY, SO TELL YOUR PARENTS I'LL BE COMING OVER TO MEET THEM.
I WANT TO TALK TO THEM ABOUT WHEN TO ACTUALLY HAVE THE WEDDING.
WE SHOULD DO IT SOON, BEFORE IT'S TOO OBVIOUS THAT YOU'RE PREGNANT.
F Naoki
S Reporting ♡

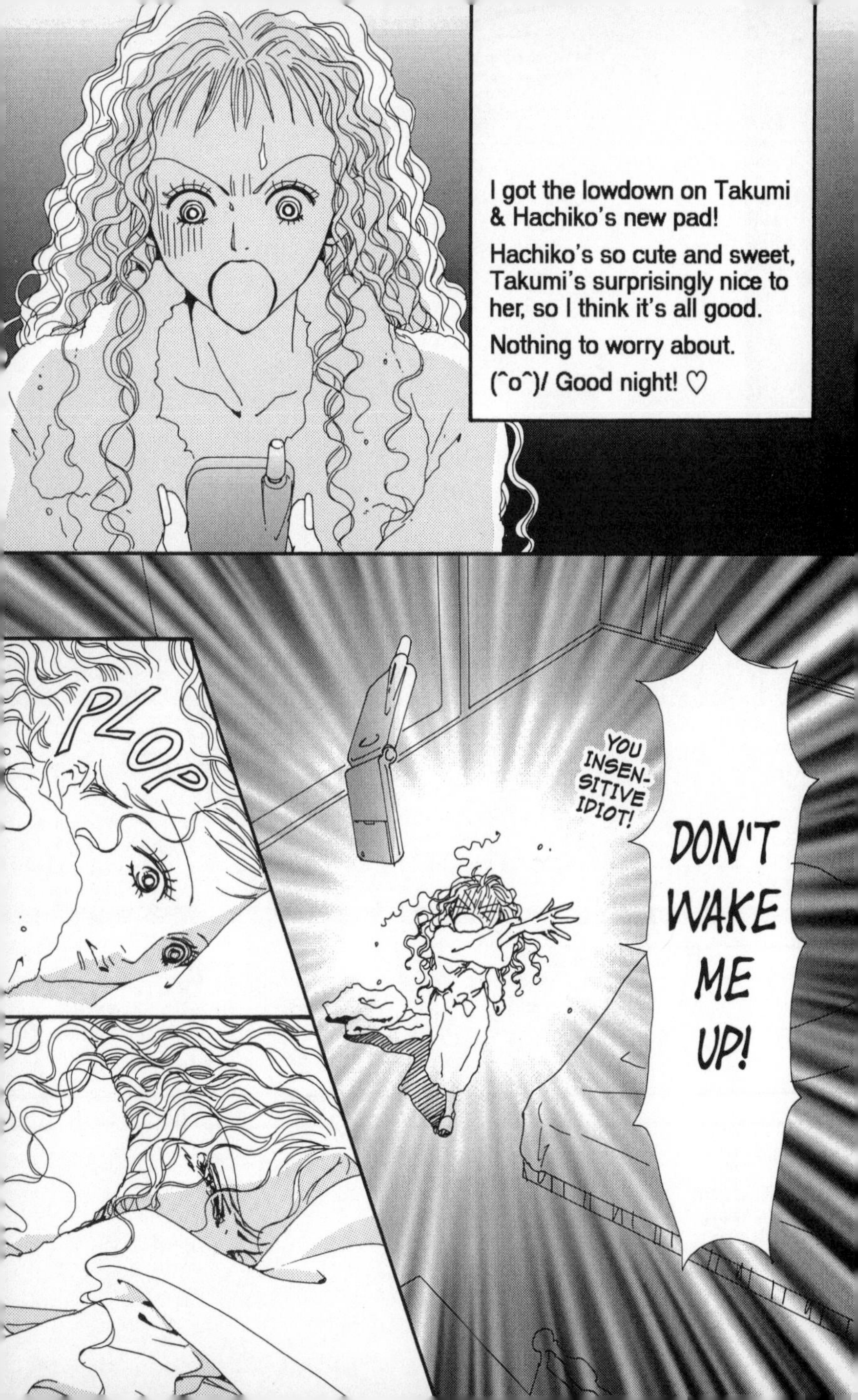
I got the lowdown on Takumi & Hachiko's new pad!
Hachiko's so cute and sweet, Takumi's surprisingly nice to her, so I think it's all good.
Nothing to worry about.
(^o^)/ Good night! ♡
DON'T WAKE ME UP!
YOU INSEN-SITIVE IDIOT!
PLOP

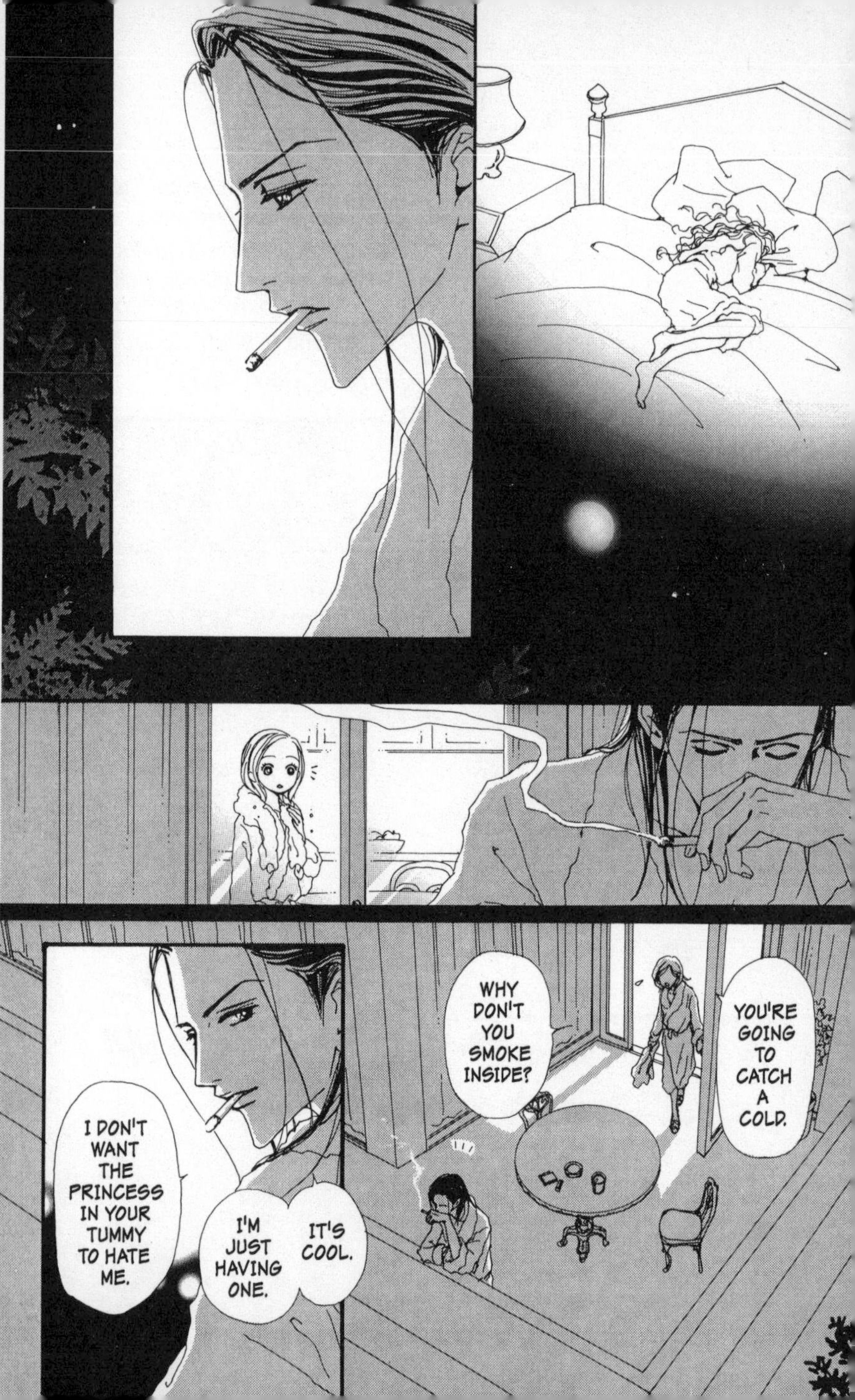
YOU'RE GOING TO CATCH A COLD.
WHY DON'T YOU SMOKE INSIDE?
IT'S COOL.
I'M JUST HAVING ONE.
I DON'T WANT THE PRINCESS IN YOUR TUMMY TO HATE ME.

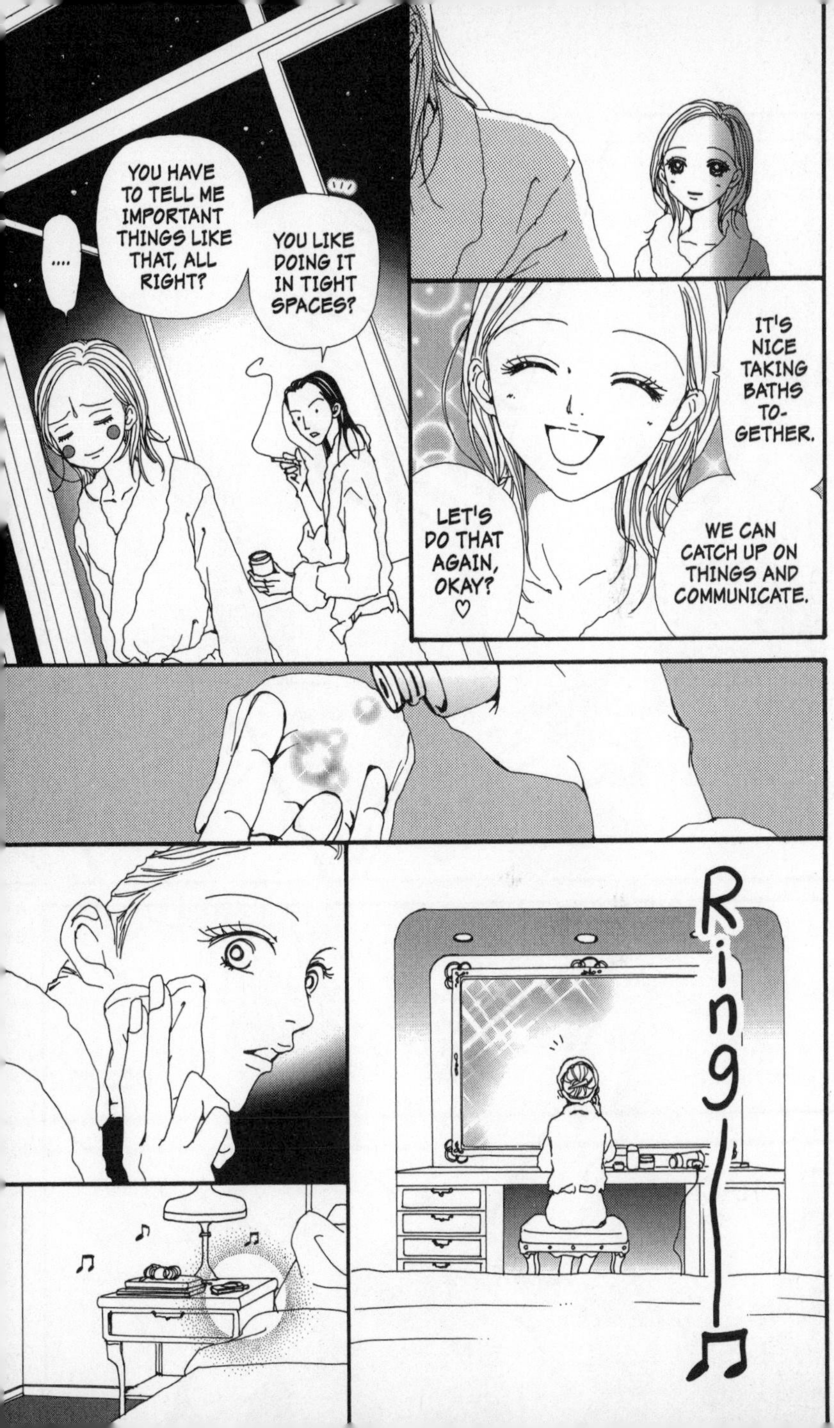
IT'S NICE TAKING BATHS TO-GETHER.
WE CAN CATCH UP ON THINGS AND COMMUNICATE.
LET'S DO THAT AGAIN, OKAY? ♡
YOU LIKE DOING IT IN TIGHT SPACES?
YOU HAVE TO TELL ME IMPORTANT THINGS LIKE THAT, ALL RIGHT?
....
Ring— ♫

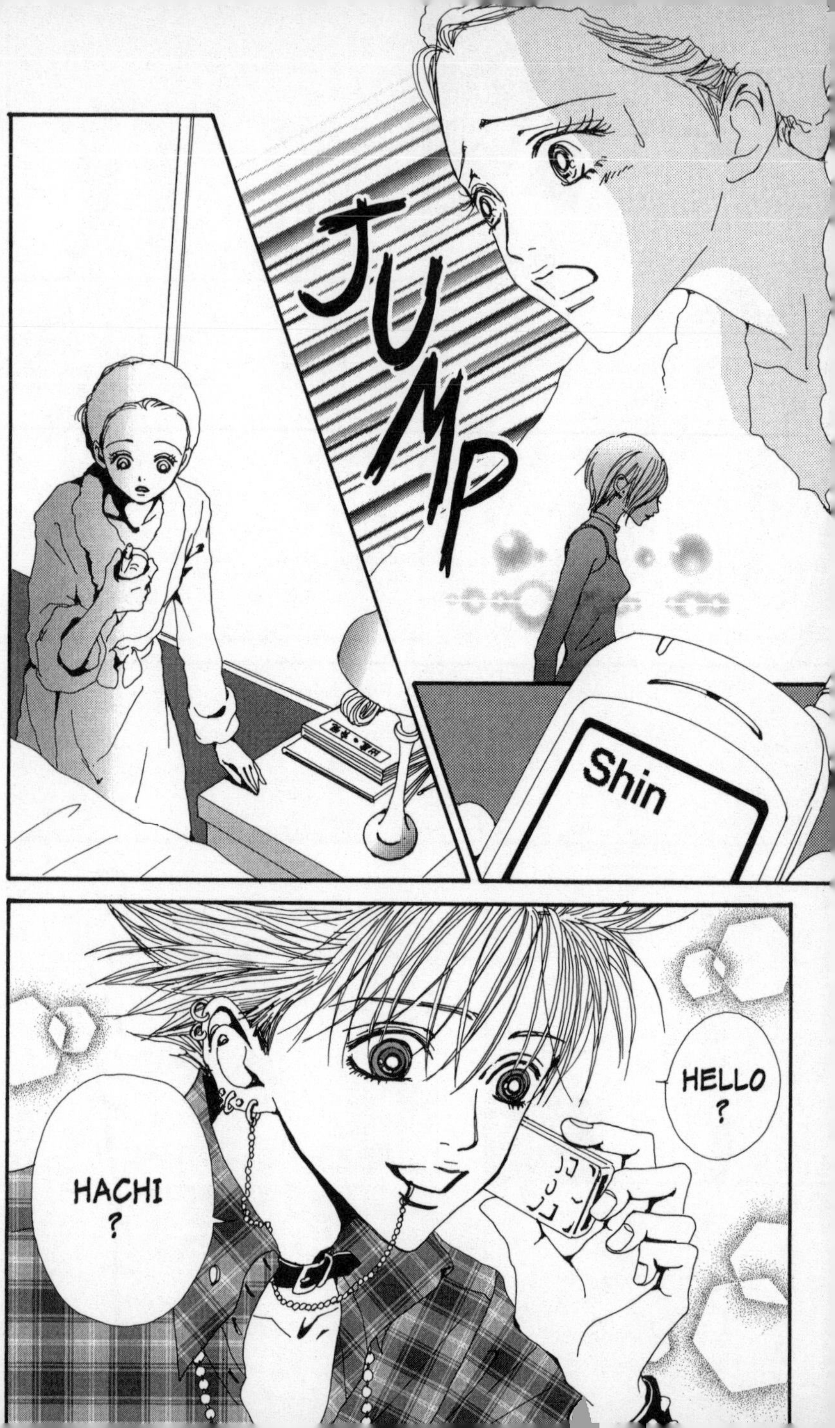
JUMP
Shin
HELLO?
HACHI?

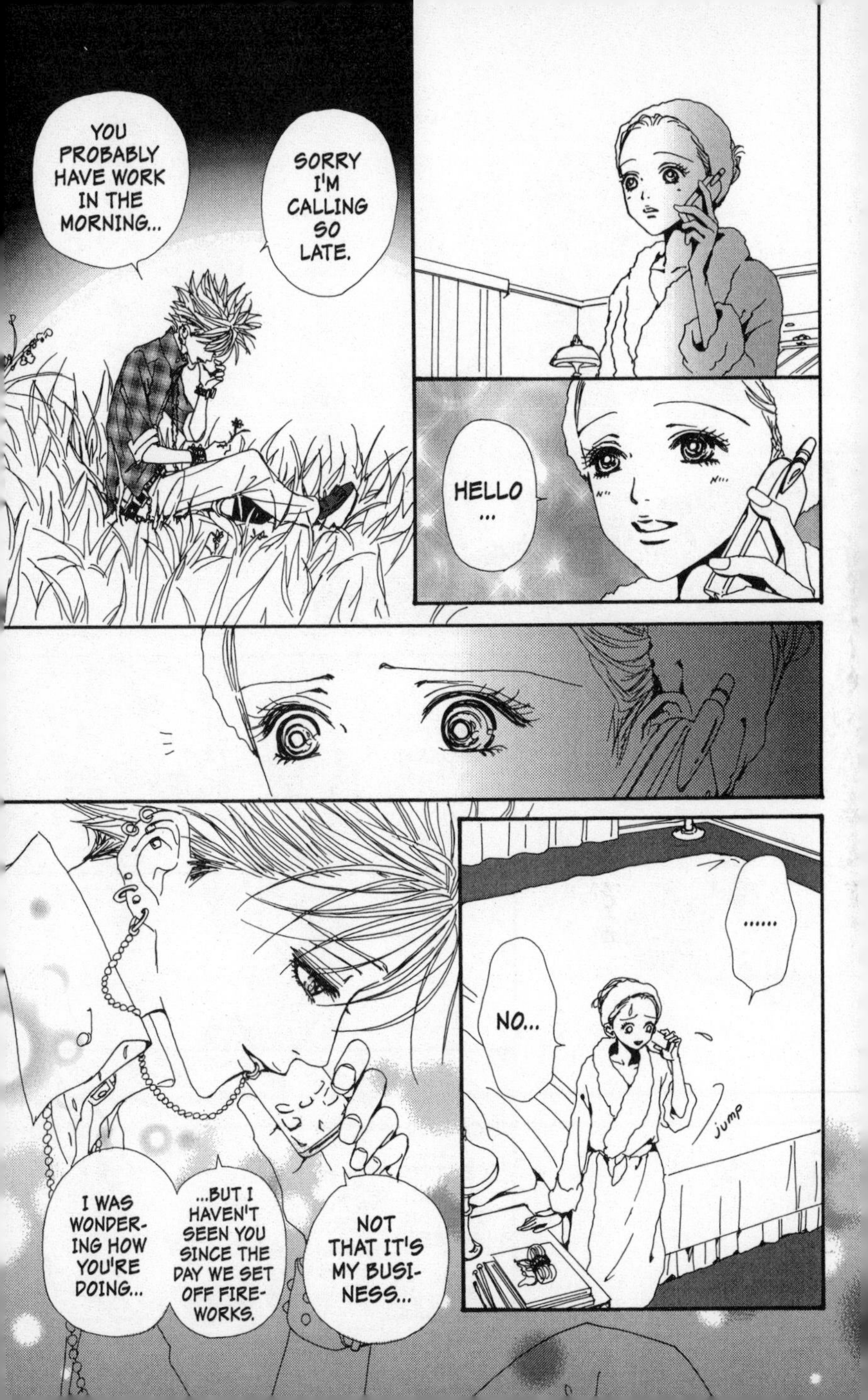
HELLO ...
SORRY I'M CALLING SO LATE.
YOU PROBABLY HAVE WORK IN THE MORNING...
......
NO...
jump
NOT THAT IT'S MY BUSINESS...
...BUT I HAVEN'T SEEN YOU SINCE THE DAY WE SET OFF FIREWORKS.
I WAS WONDERING HOW YOU'RE DOING...

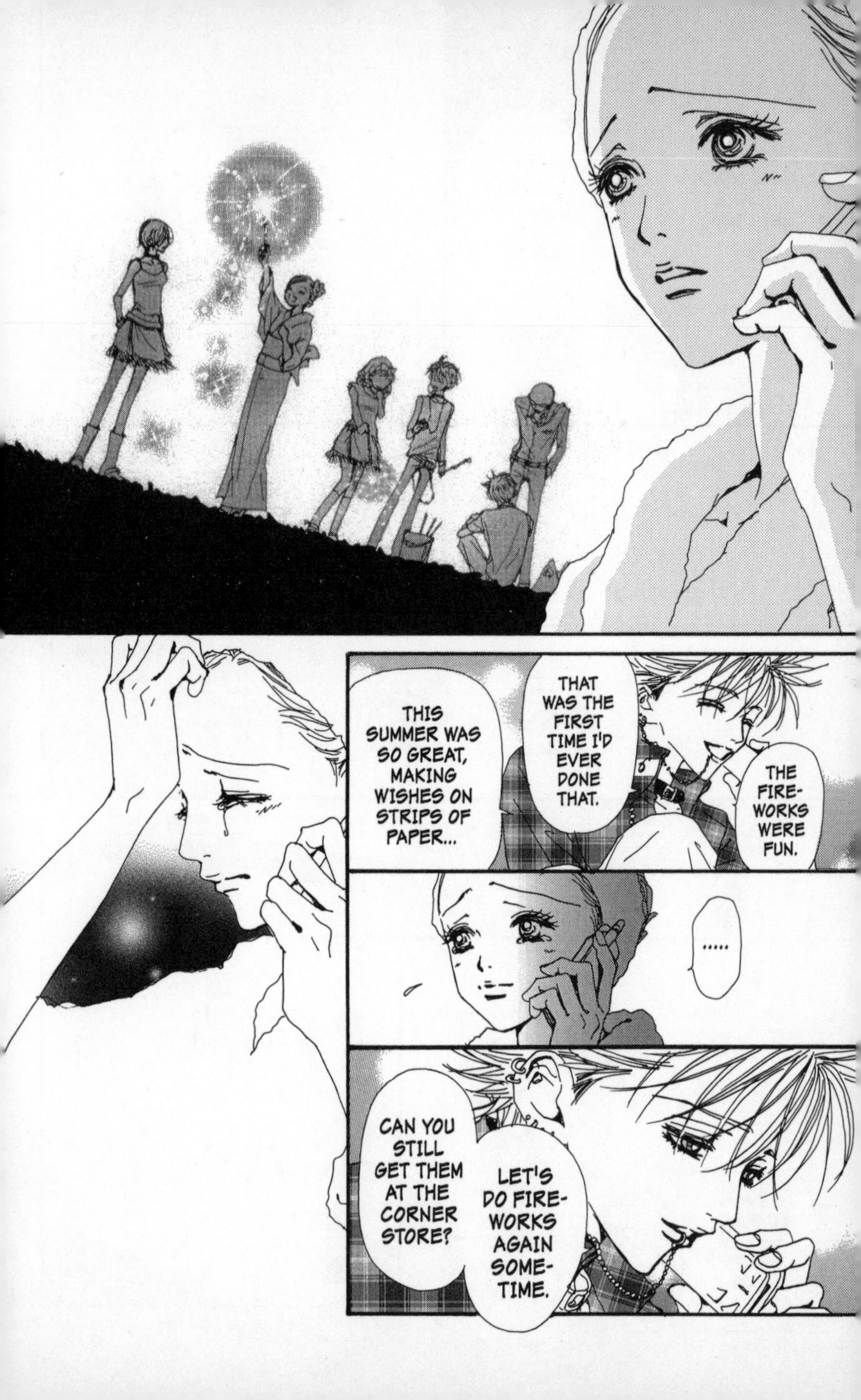
THE FIREWORKS WERE FUN.
THAT WAS THE FIRST TIME I'D EVER DONE THAT.
THIS SUMMER WAS SO GREAT, MAKING WISHES ON STRIPS OF PAPER...
......
LET'S DO FIREWORKS AGAIN SOMETIME.
CAN YOU STILL GET THEM AT THE CORNER STORE?

I'M A TRAITOR...

I CAN'T HANG OUT WITH YOU GUYS ANYMORE...

I'M SORRY, SHIN...

ABOUT WHAT?

NO MATTER WHAT HAPPENS, I'M ALWAYS ON YOUR SIDE.

Creak

DO YOU KNOW WHERE THE HAIR DRYER IS?

NANA...

......

beep

GOOD NIGHT!

I'M SORRY, JUN.

FOUND IT.

DID JUN GIVE YOU ANOTHER LECTURE?

WHAT HAPPENED?

......

I JUST GOT A LITTLE HOMESICK.

NEVER, EVER MENTION THAT NAME AGAIN.

EVEN NOBU HAS A THING OR TWO HE DOESN'T WANT TO TALK ABOUT.

SO THAT'S WHAT'S HAPPENED.

beep

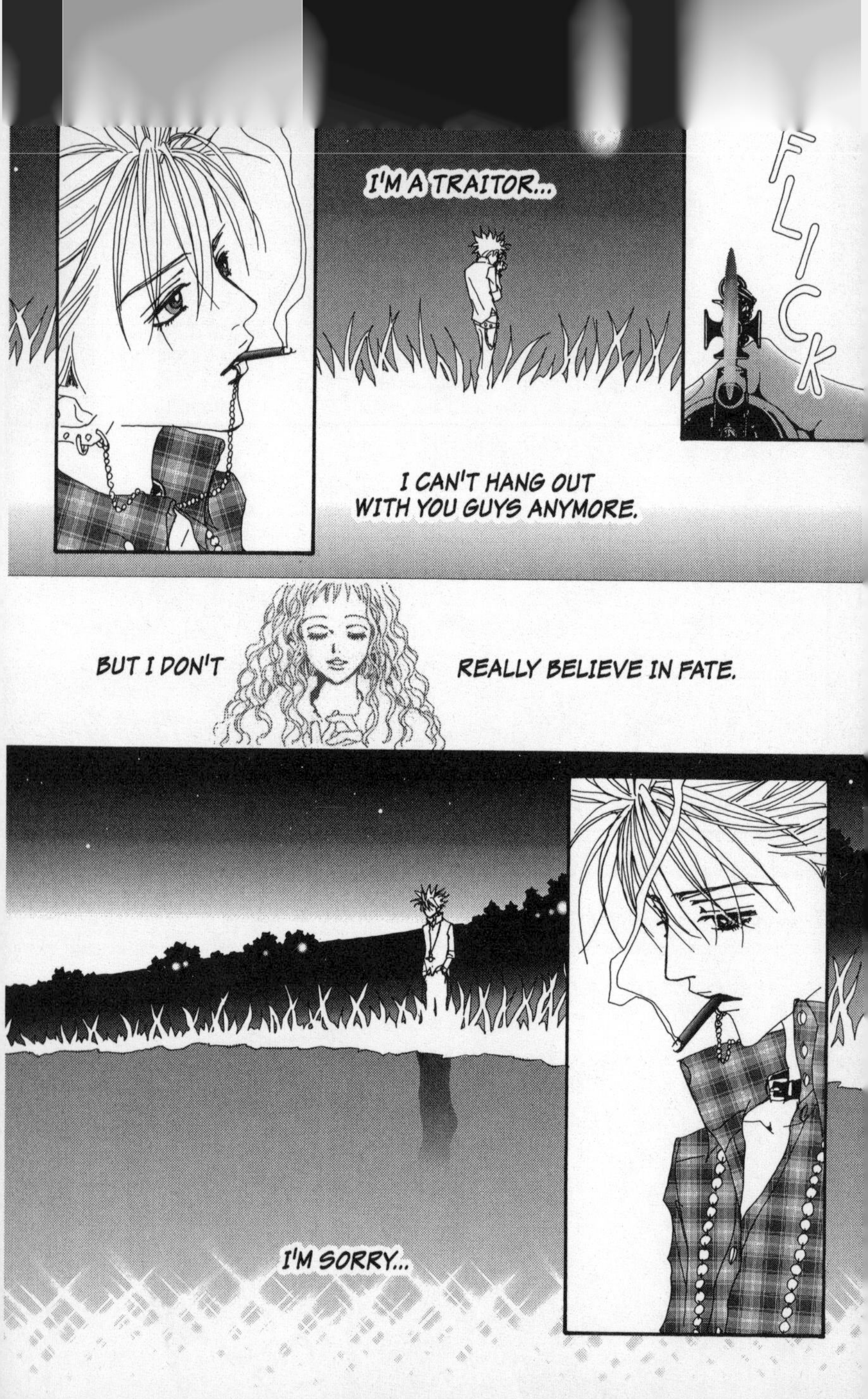
FLICK
I'M A TRAITOR...
I CAN'T HANG OUT WITH YOU GUYS ANYMORE.
BUT I DON'T
REALLY BELIEVE IN FATE.
I'M SORRY...

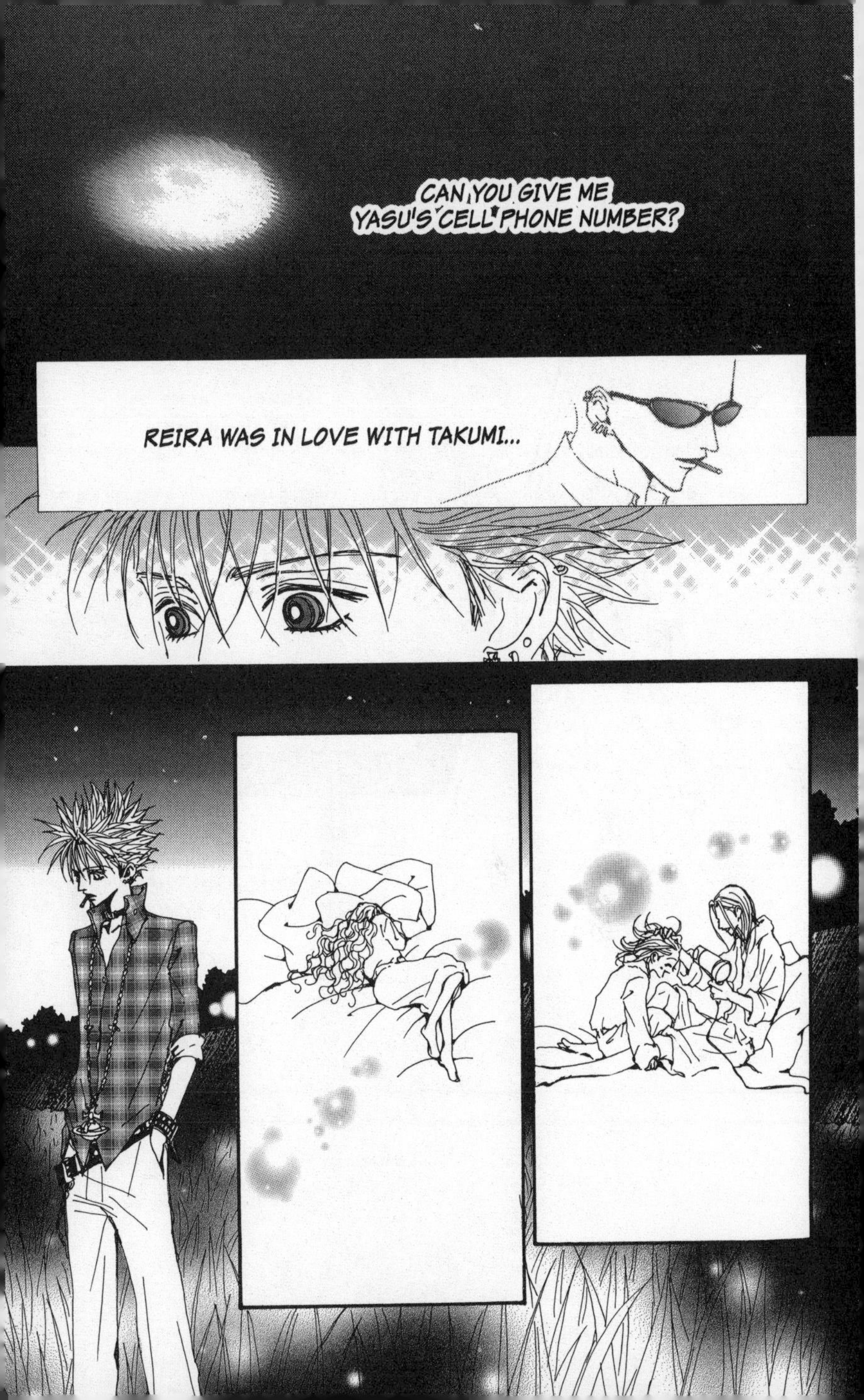
CAN YOU GIVE ME YASU'S CELL PHONE NUMBER?
REIRA WAS IN LOVE WITH TAKUMI...

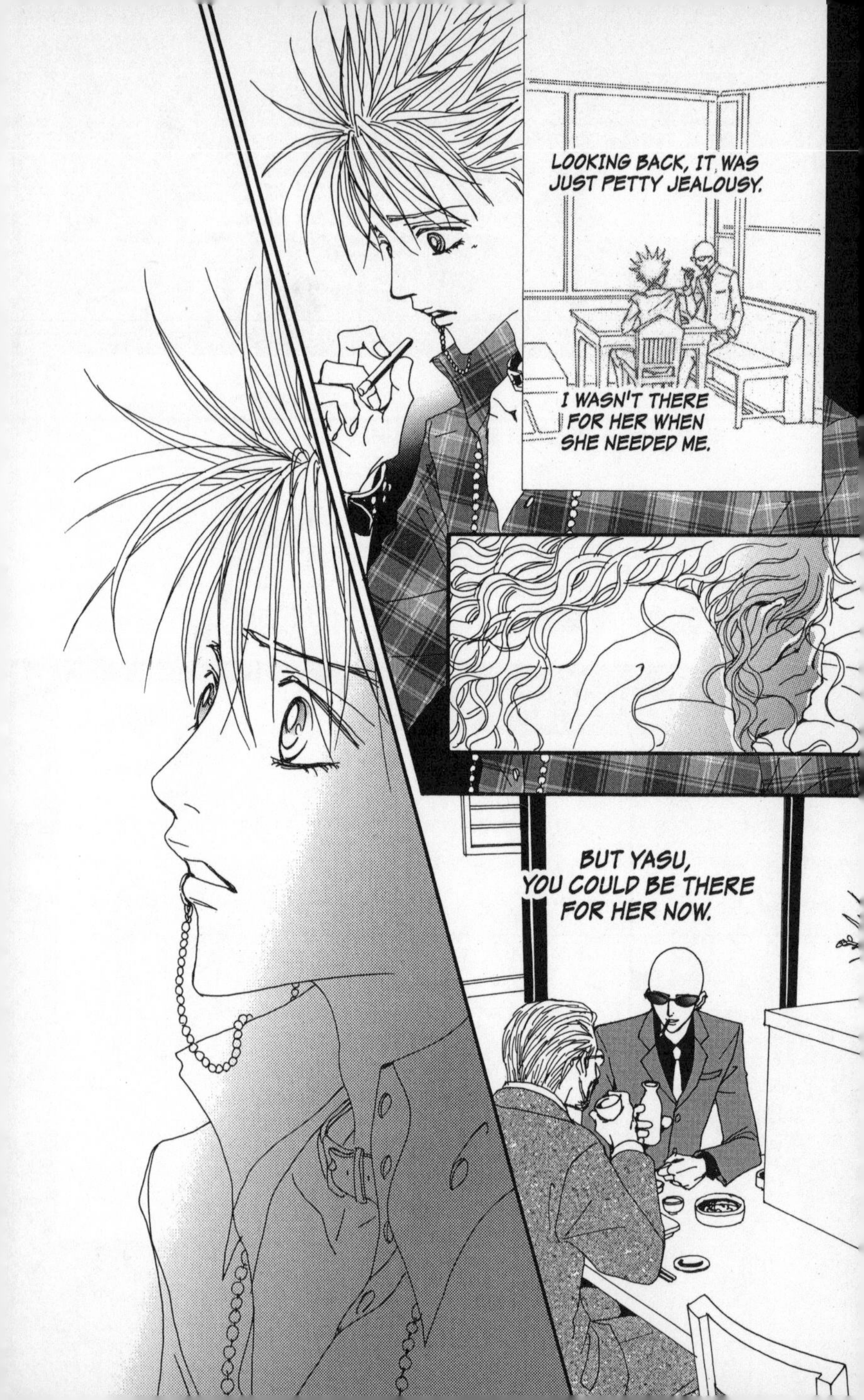
LOOKING BACK, IT WAS JUST PETTY JEALOUSY.
I WASN'T THERE FOR HER WHEN SHE NEEDED ME.
BUT YASU, YOU COULD BE THERE FOR HER NOW.

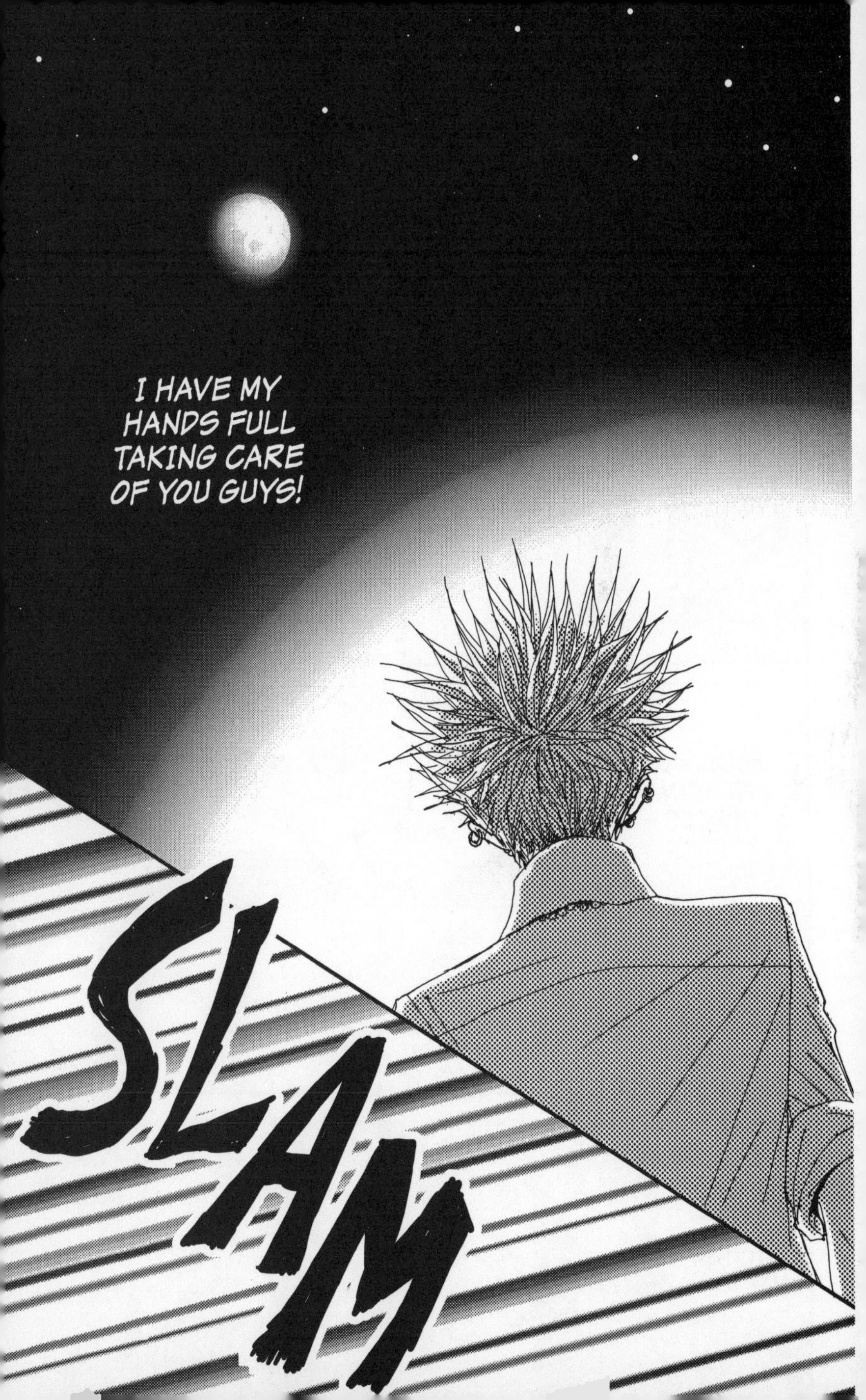
I HAVE MY HANDS FULL TAKING CARE OF YOU GUYS!
SLAM

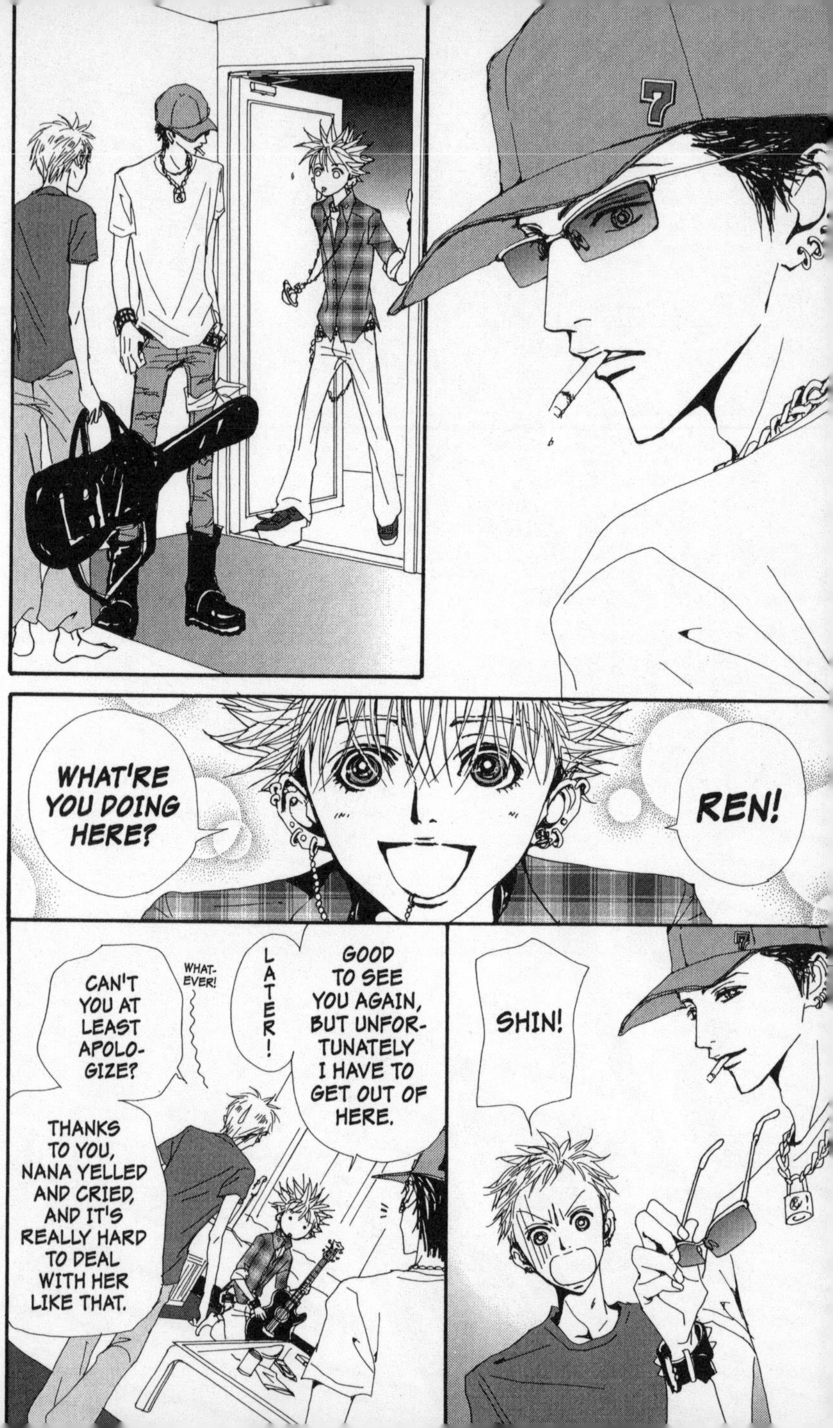
REN!
WHAT'RE YOU DOING HERE?
SHIN!
GOOD TO SEE YOU AGAIN, BUT UNFORTUNATELY I HAVE TO GET OUT OF HERE.
LATER!
WHATEVER!
CAN'T YOU AT LEAST APOLOGIZE?
THANKS TO YOU, NANA YELLED AND CRIED, AND IT'S REALLY HARD TO DEAL WITH HER LIKE THAT.

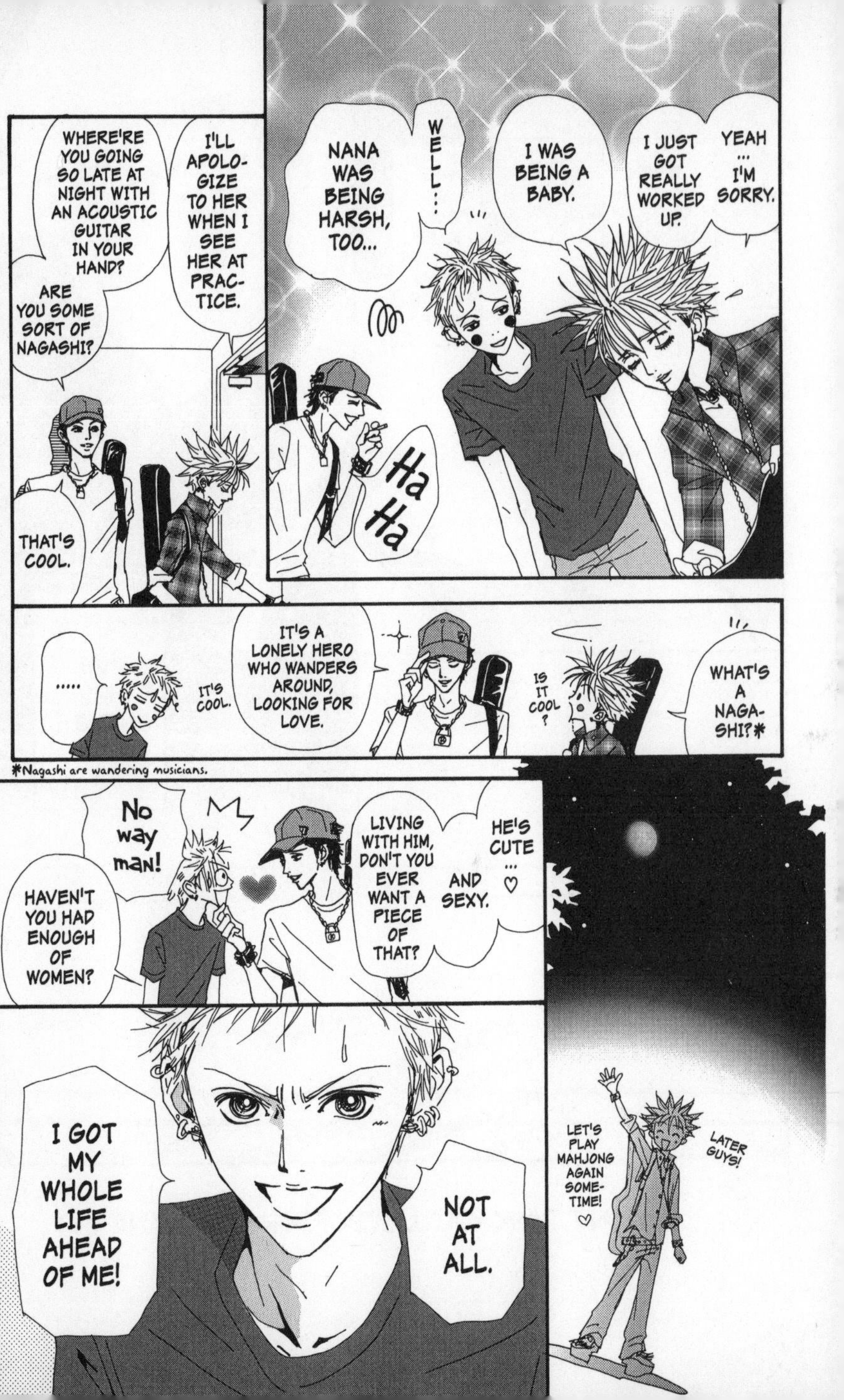
YEAH... I'M SORRY.
I JUST GOT REALLY WORKED UP.
I WAS BEING A BABY.
WELL...
NANA WAS BEING HARSH, TOO...
Ha Ha
I'LL APOLOGIZE TO HER WHEN I SEE HER AT PRACTICE.
WHERE'RE YOU GOING SO LATE AT NIGHT WITH AN ACOUSTIC GUITAR IN YOUR HAND?
ARE YOU SOME SORT OF NAGASHI?
THAT'S COOL.
WHAT'S A NAGASHI?*
IS IT COOL?
IT'S A LONELY HERO WHO WANDERS AROUND, LOOKING FOR LOVE.
IT'S COOL.
.....
LATER GUYS!
LET'S PLAY MAHJONG AGAIN SOMETIME! ♡
HE'S CUTE... ♡
AND SEXY.
LIVING WITH HIM, DON'T YOU EVER WANT A PIECE OF THAT?
No way man!
HAVEN'T YOU HAD ENOUGH OF WOMEN?
NOT AT ALL.
I GOT MY WHOLE LIFE AHEAD OF ME!

*Nagashi are wandering musicians.

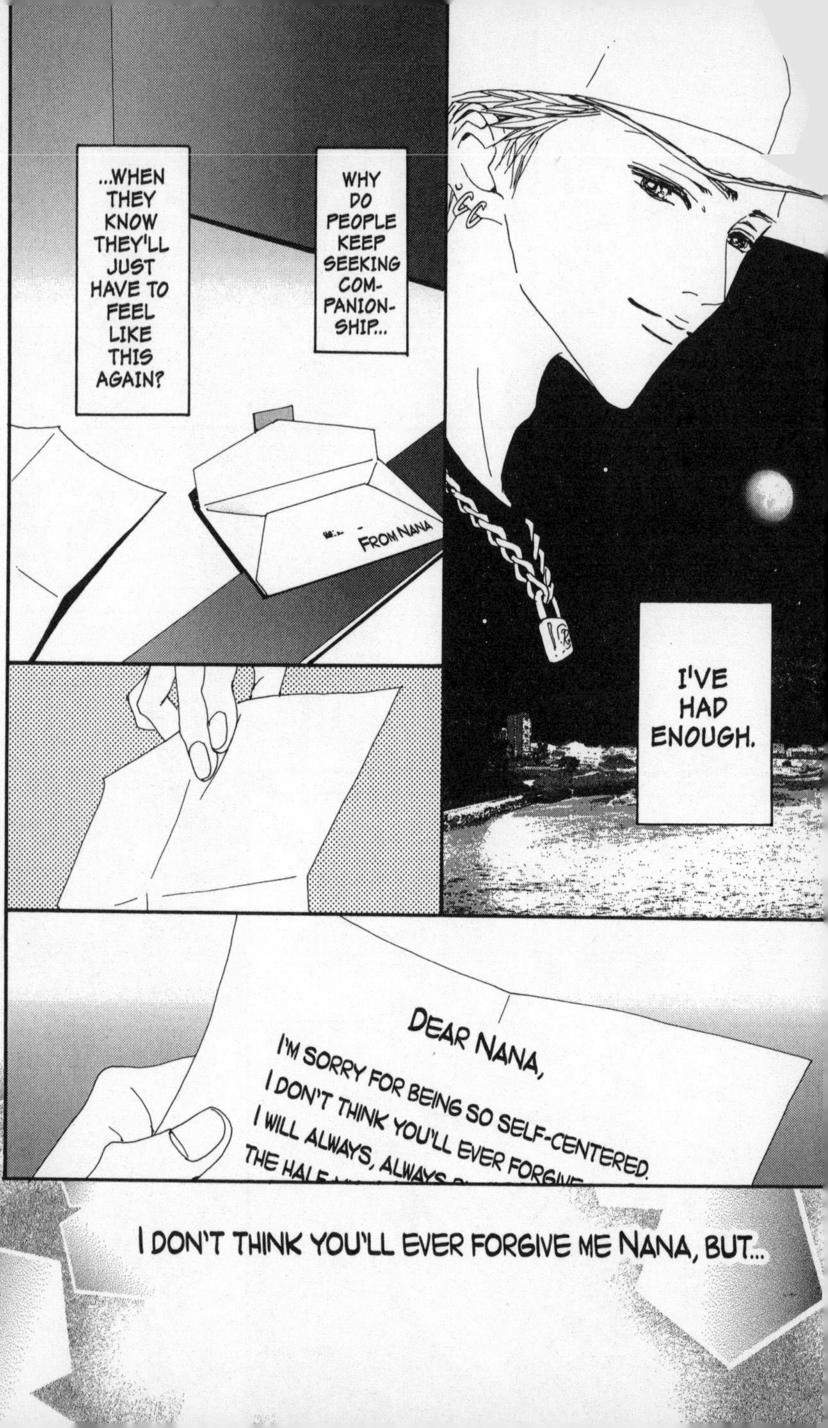
I'VE HAD ENOUGH.
WHY DO PEOPLE KEEP SEEKING COMPANIONSHIP...
...WHEN THEY KNOW THEY'LL JUST HAVE TO FEEL LIKE THIS AGAIN?
FROM NANA
DEAR NANA,
I'M SORRY FOR BEING SO SELF-CENTERED.
I DON'T THINK YOU'LL EVER
I WILL ALWAYS,
I DON'T THINK YOU'LL EVER FORGIVE ME NANA, BUT...

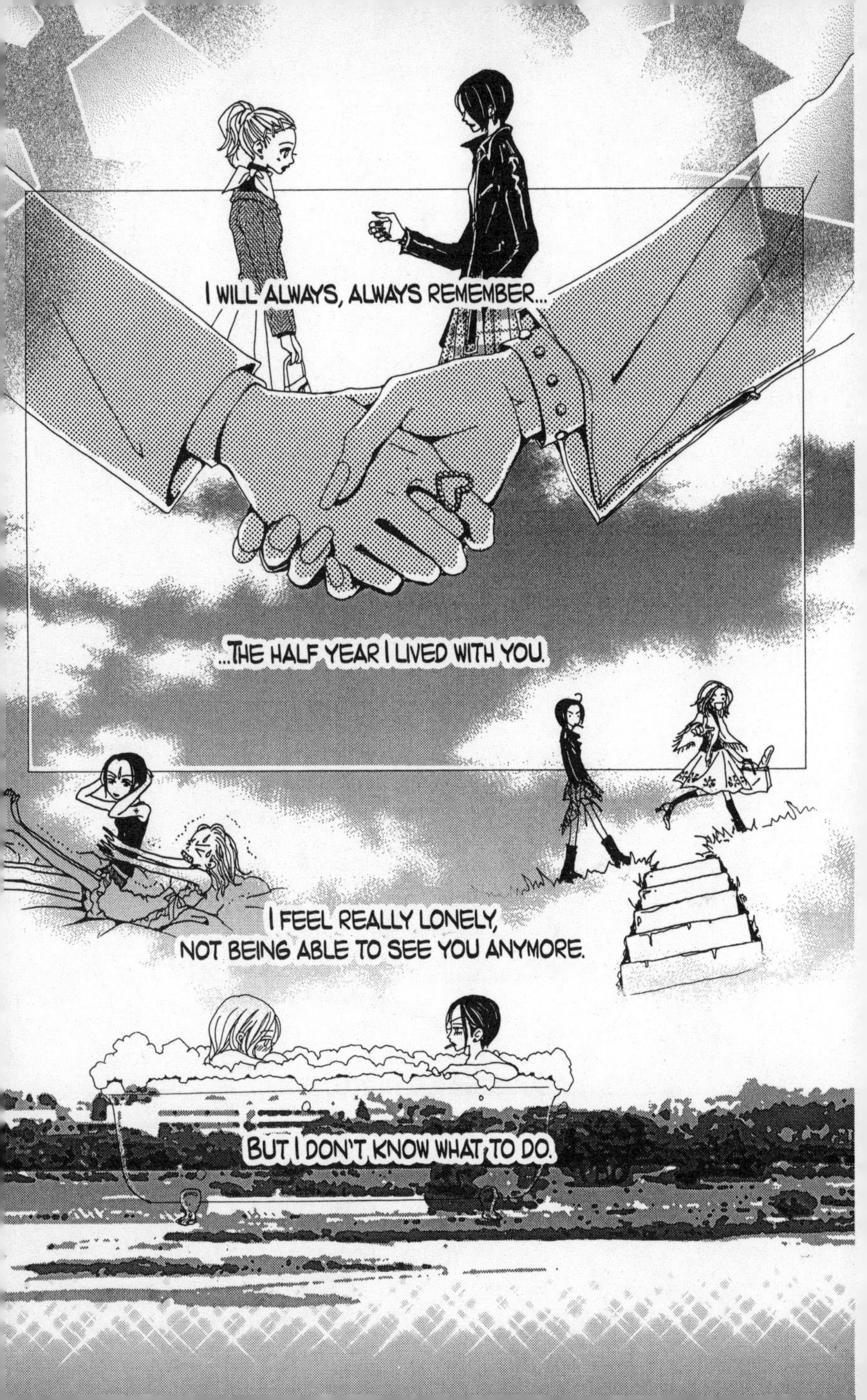
I WILL ALWAYS, ALWAYS REMEMBER...
...THE HALF YEAR I LIVED WITH YOU.
I FEEL REALLY LONELY, NOT BEING ABLE TO SEE YOU ANYMORE.
BUT I DON'T KNOW WHAT TO DO.

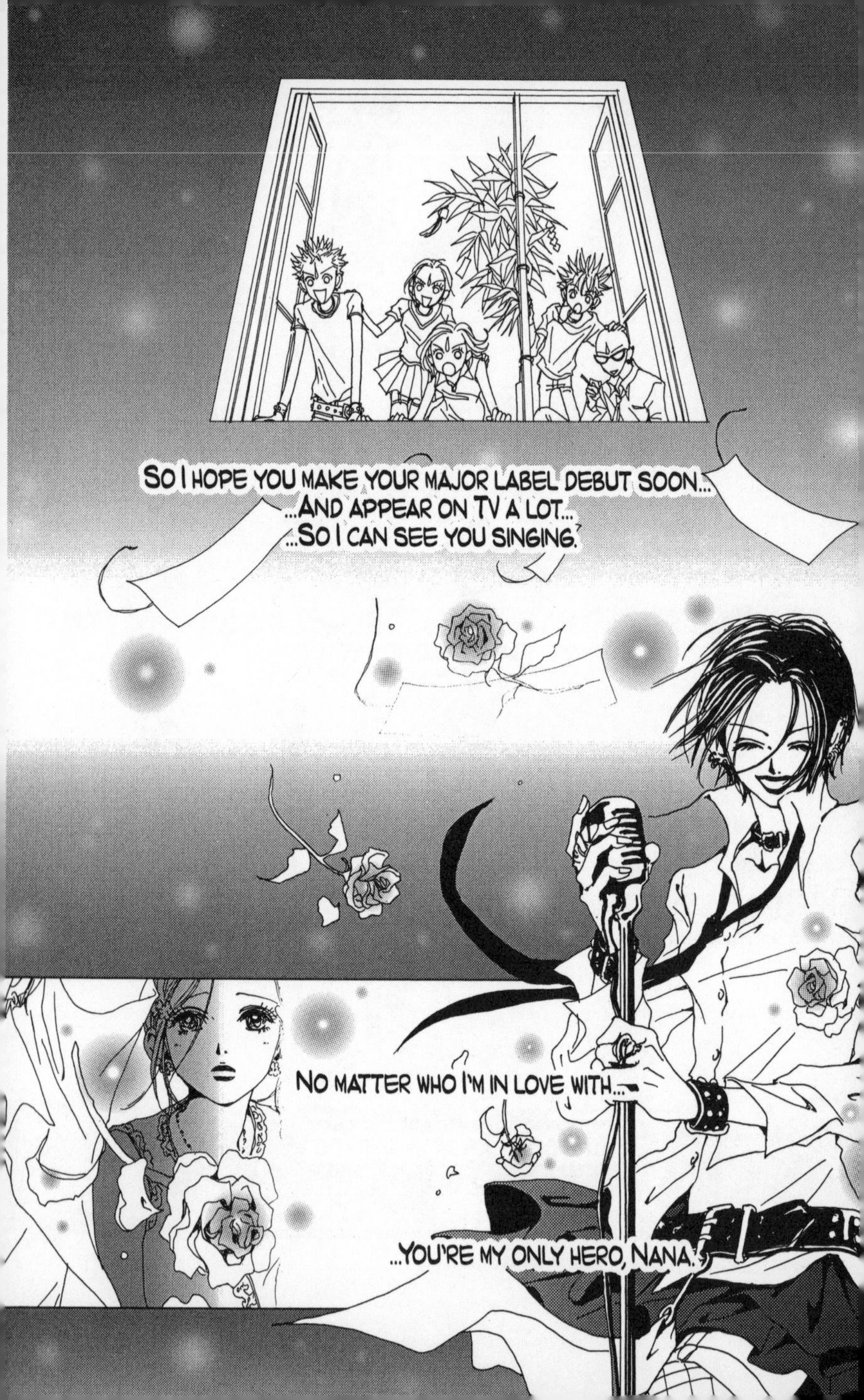
SO I HOPE YOU MAKE YOUR MAJOR LABEL DEBUT SOON...
...AND APPEAR ON TV A LOT...
...SO I CAN SEE YOU SINGING.
NO MATTER WHO I'M IN LOVE WITH...
...YOU'RE MY ONLY HERO, NANA.

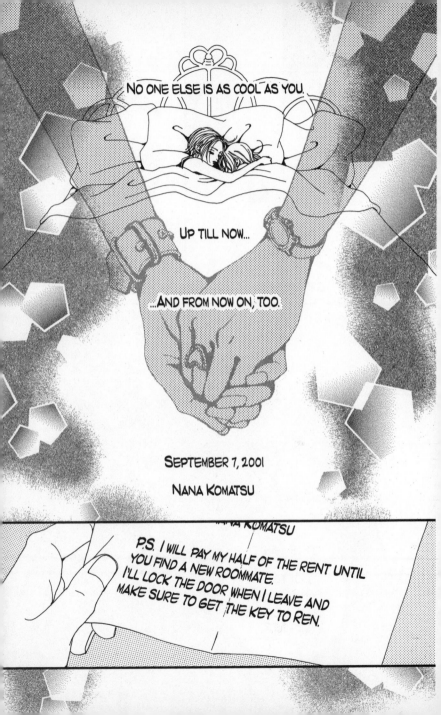

NO ONE ELSE IS AS COOL AS YOU.

UP TILL NOW...

...AND FROM NOW ON, TOO.

SEPTEMBER 7, 2001

NANA KOMATSU

P.S. I WILL PAY MY HALF OF THE RENT UNTIL YOU FIND A NEW ROOMMATE. I'LL LOCK THE DOOR WHEN I LEAVE AND MAKE SURE TO GET THE KEY TO REN.

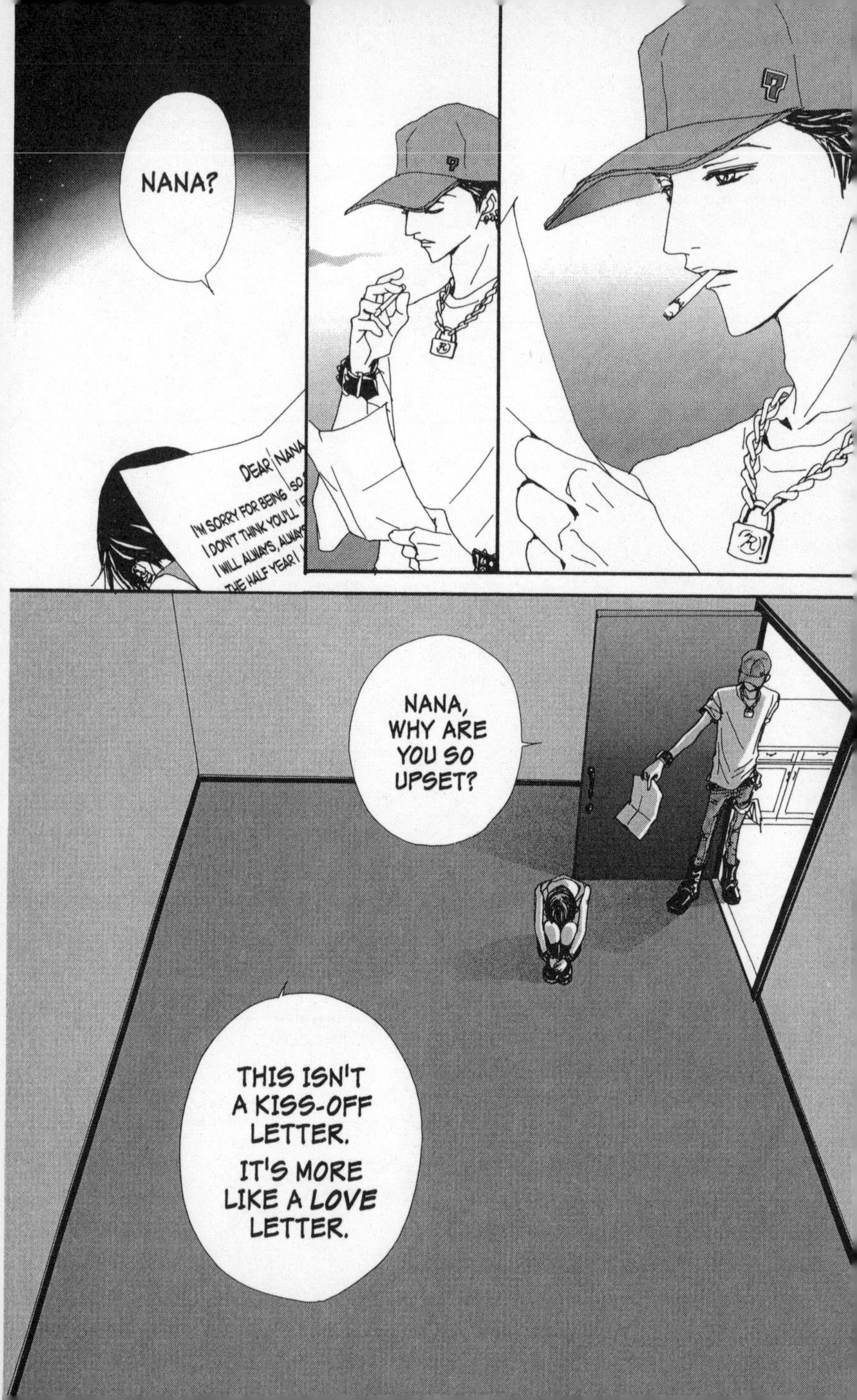
NANA?
DEAR NANA
I'M SORRY FOR BEING SO
I DON'T THINK YOU'LL
I WILL ALWAYS, ALWAYS
THE HALF YEAR I
NANA, WHY ARE YOU SO UPSET?
THIS ISN'T A KISS-OFF LETTER.
IT'S MORE LIKE A *LOVE* LETTER.

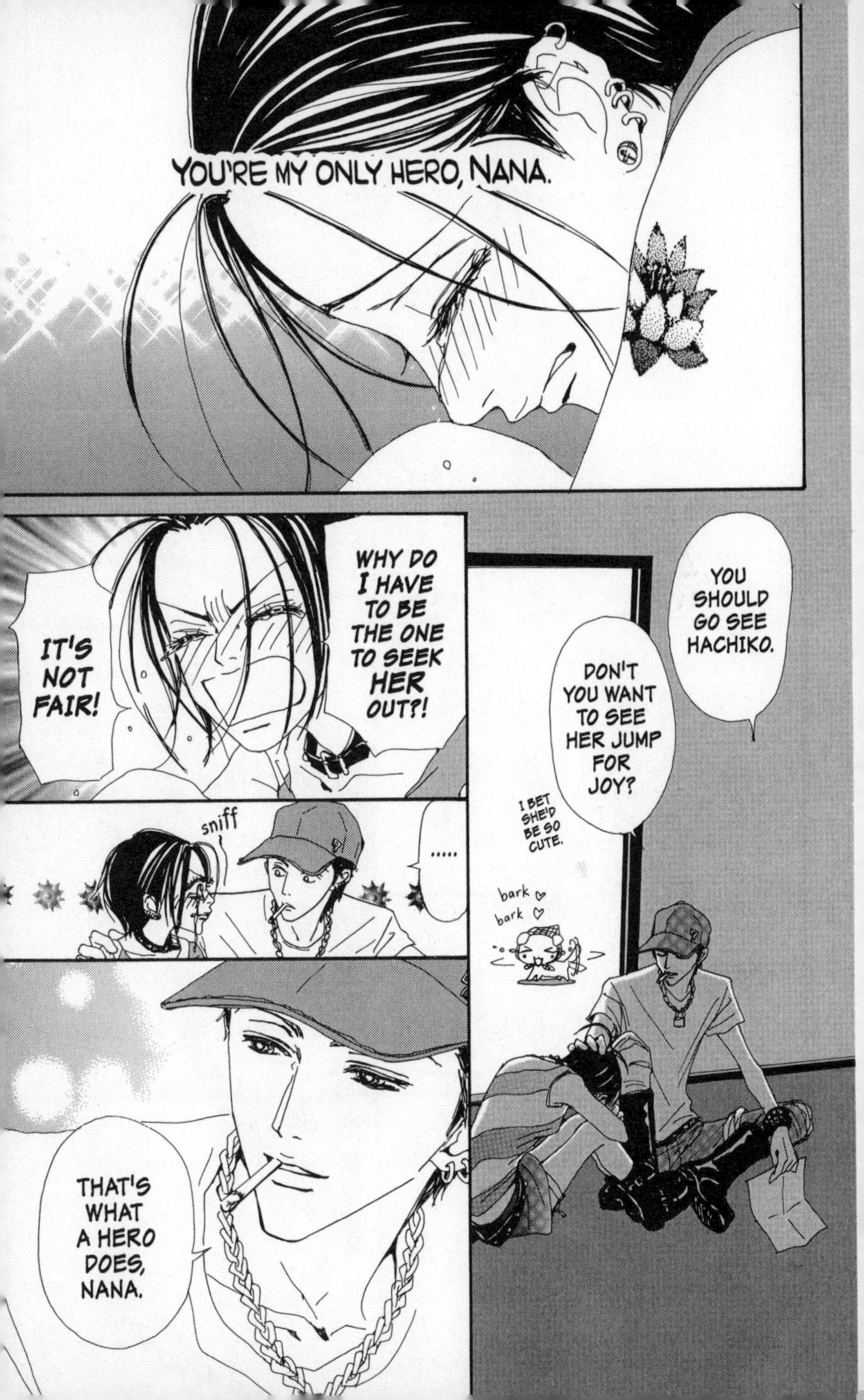
YOU'RE MY ONLY HERO, NANA.
YOU SHOULD GO SEE HACHIKO.
DON'T YOU WANT TO SEE HER JUMP FOR JOY?
I BET SHE'D BE SO CUTE.
bark
bark
WHY DO I HAVE TO BE THE ONE TO SEEK HER OUT?!
IT'S NOT FAIR!
.....
sniff
THAT'S WHAT A HERO DOES, NANA.

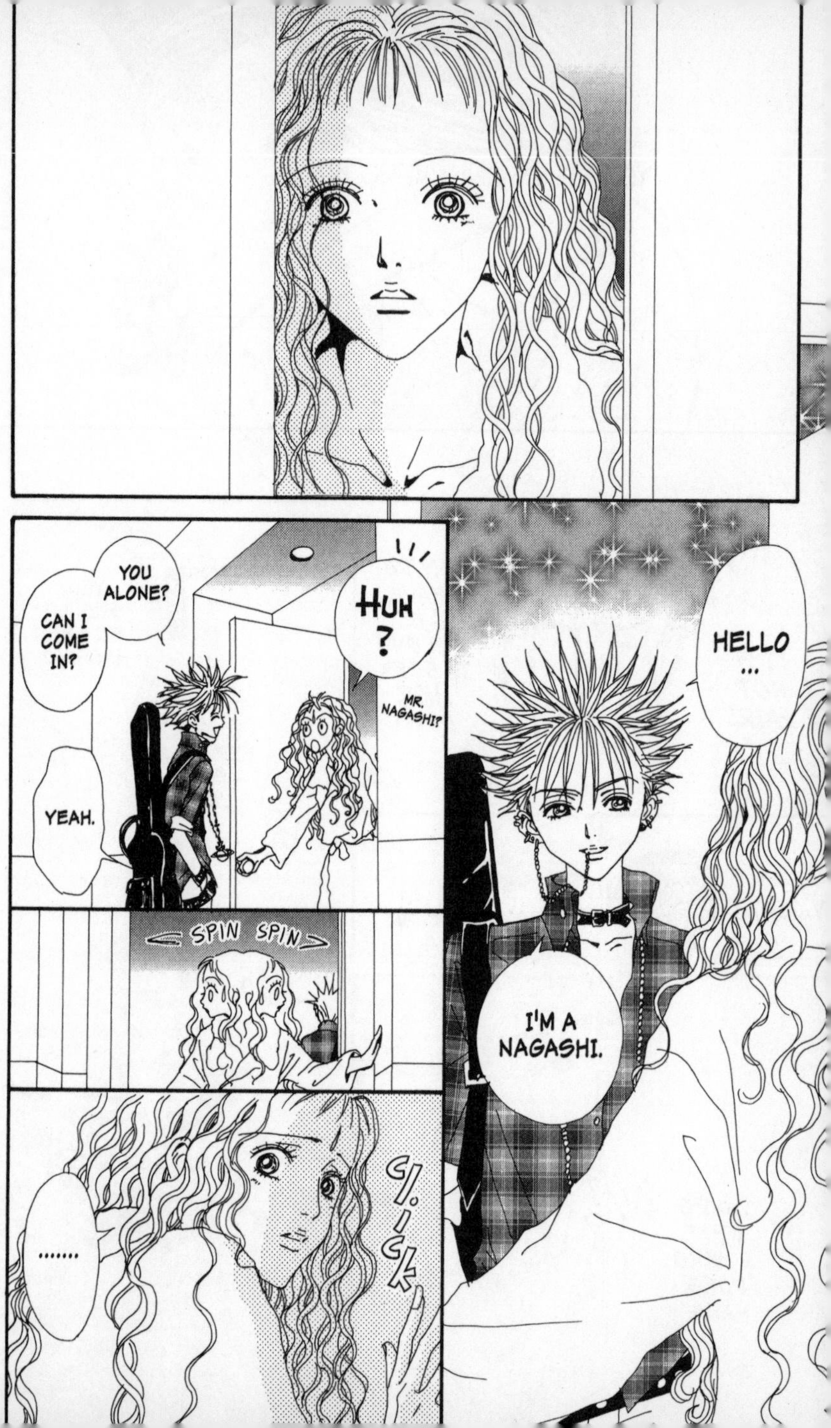
HELLO ...
I'M A NAGASHI.
HUH?
MR. NAGASHI!?
YOU ALONE?
CAN I COME IN?
YEAH.
SPIN SPIN
CLICK
....

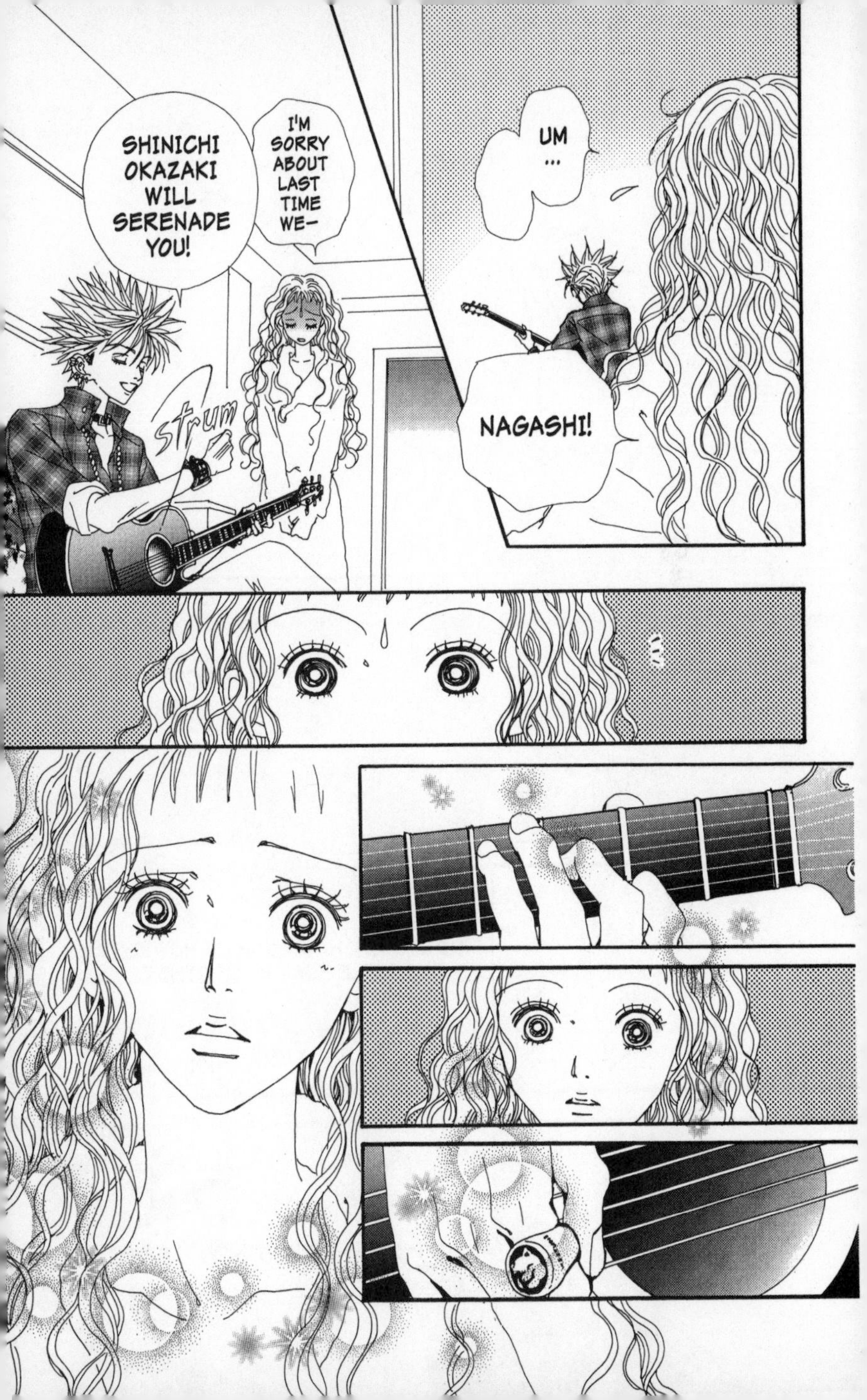
UM ...
NAGASHI!
I'M SORRY ABOUT LAST TIME WE—
SHINICHI OKAZAKI WILL SERENADE YOU!
strum

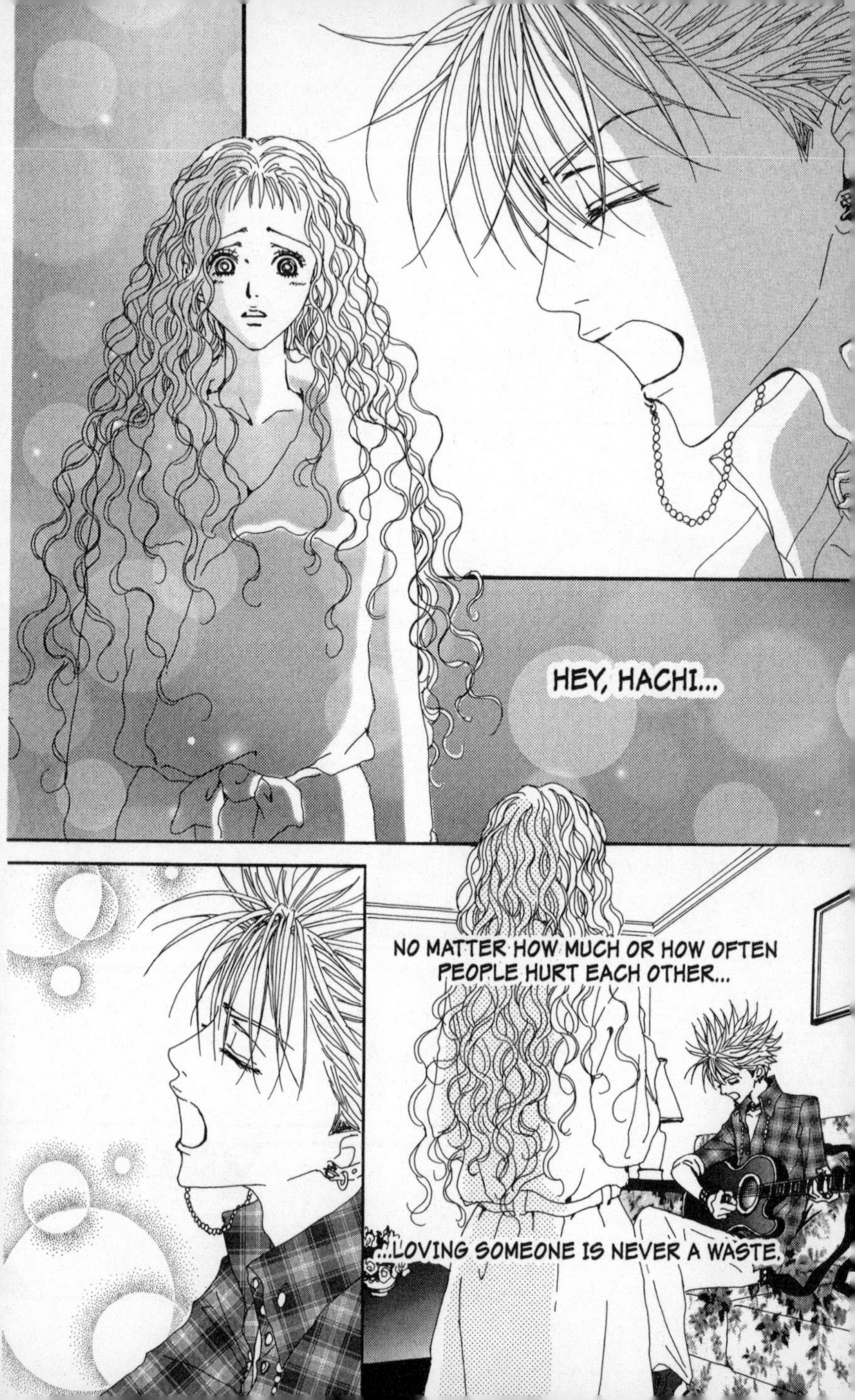
HEY, HACHI...
NO MATTER HOW MUCH OR HOW OFTEN PEOPLE HURT EACH OTHER...
...LOVING SOMEONE IS NEVER A WASTE.

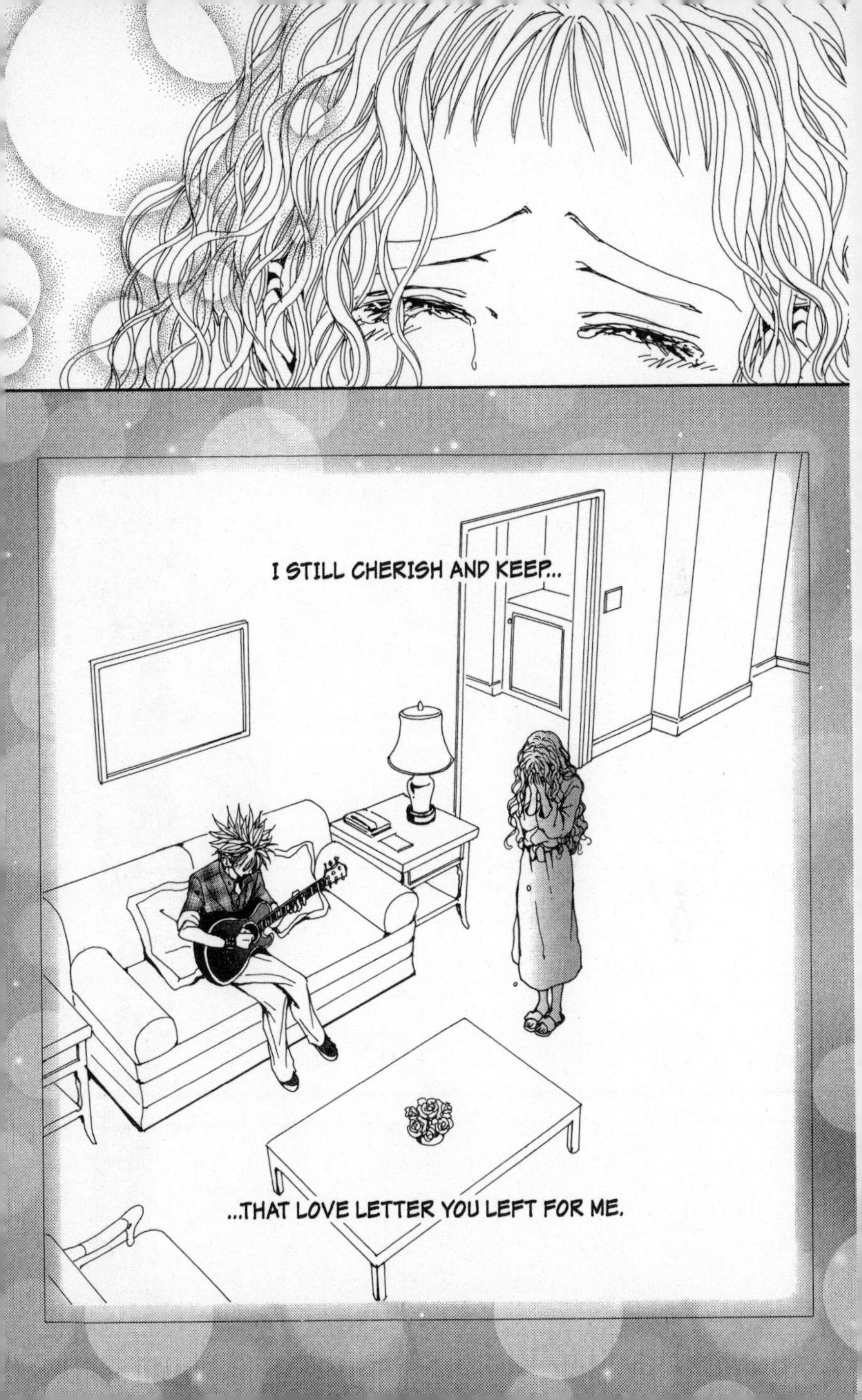
I STILL CHERISH AND KEEP...
...THAT LOVE LETTER YOU LEFT FOR ME.

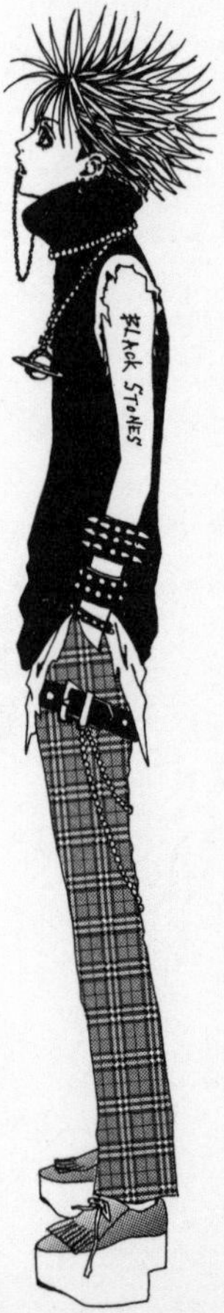
BLACK STONES

Bonus Page

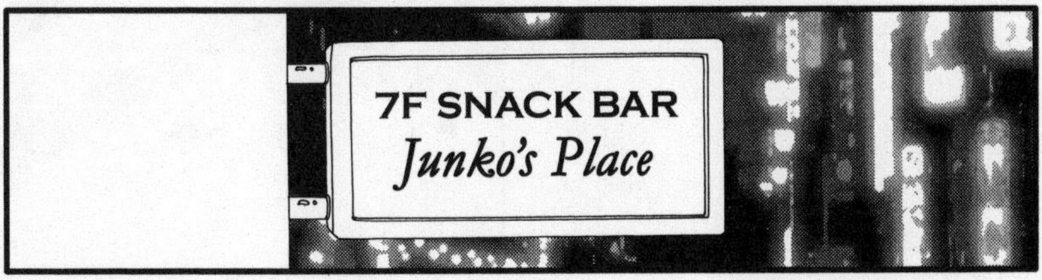
7F SNACK BAR
Junko's Place

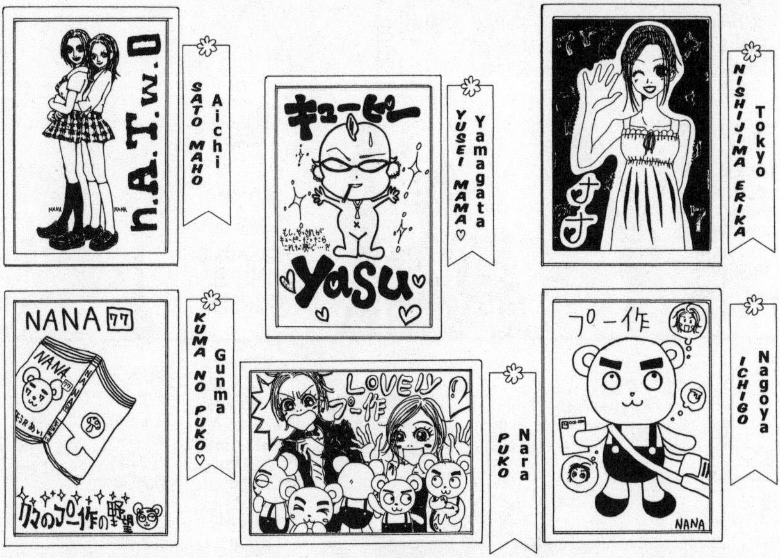
Tokyo
NISHIJIMA ERIKA
キューピー
Yasu
Yamagata
YUSEI MAMA ♡
h.A.T.w.D
NANA
NANA
Aichi
SATO MAHO
プー作
NANA
Nagoya
ICHIGO
LOVELY
プー作
Nara
PUKO
NANA 77
Gunma
KUMA NO PUKO ♡

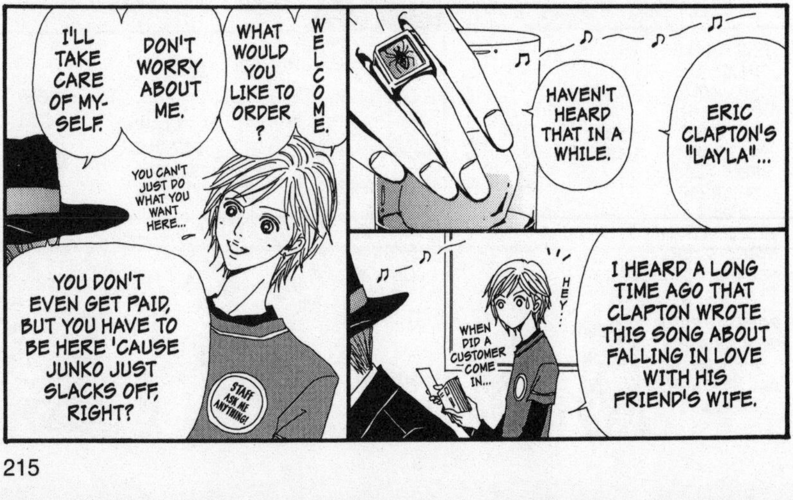
ERIC CLAPTON'S "LAYLA"...
HAVEN'T HEARD THAT IN A WHILE.
I HEARD A LONG TIME AGO THAT CLAPTON WROTE THIS SONG ABOUT FALLING IN LOVE WITH HIS FRIEND'S WIFE.
HEY...
WHEN DID A CUSTOMER COME IN...
WELCOME.
WHAT WOULD YOU LIKE TO ORDER?
DON'T WORRY ABOUT ME.
I'LL TAKE CARE OF MY-SELF.
YOU CAN'T JUST DO WHAT YOU WANT HERE...
YOU DON'T EVEN GET PAID, BUT YOU HAVE TO BE HERE 'CAUSE JUNKO JUST SLACKS OFF, RIGHT?
STAFF ASK ME ANYTHING!

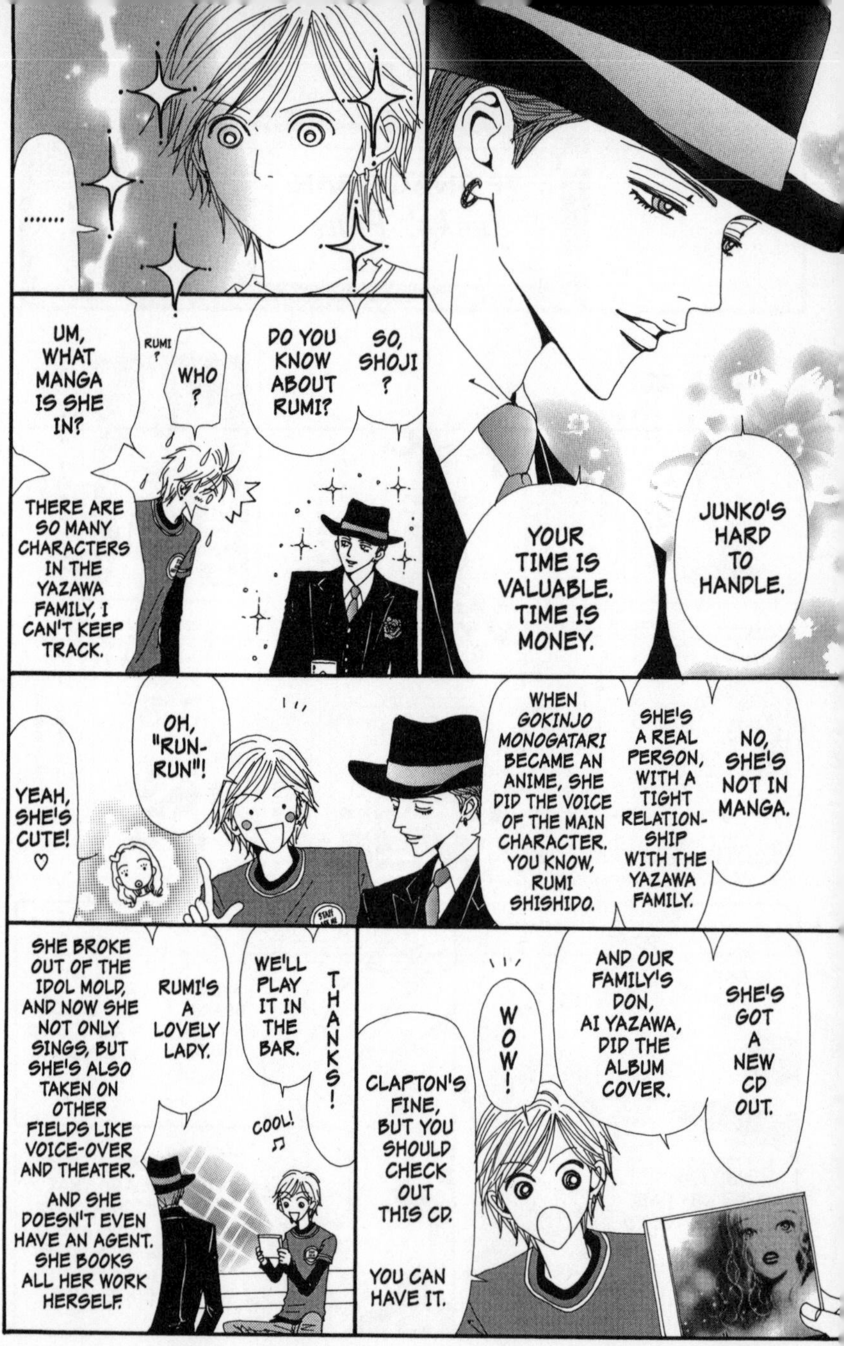
JUNKO'S HARD TO HANDLE.
YOUR TIME IS VALUABLE. TIME IS MONEY.
....
SO, SHOJI?
DO YOU KNOW ABOUT RUMI?
WHO?
RUMI?
UM, WHAT MANGA IS SHE IN?
THERE ARE SO MANY CHARACTERS IN THE YAZAWA FAMILY, I CAN'T KEEP TRACK.
NO, SHE'S NOT IN MANGA.
SHE'S A REAL PERSON, WITH A TIGHT RELATIONSHIP WITH THE YAZAWA FAMILY.
WHEN GOKINJO MONOGATARI BECAME AN ANIME, SHE DID THE VOICE OF THE MAIN CHARACTER. YOU KNOW, RUMI SHISHIDO.
OH, "RUN-RUN"!
YEAH, SHE'S CUTE! ♡
SHE'S GOT A NEW CD OUT.
AND OUR FAMILY'S DON, AI YAZAWA, DID THE ALBUM COVER.
WOW!
CLAPTON'S FINE, BUT YOU SHOULD CHECK OUT THIS CD.
YOU CAN HAVE IT.
THANKS!
WE'LL PLAY IT IN THE BAR.
COOL! ♫
RUMI'S A LOVELY LADY.
SHE BROKE OUT OF THE IDOL MOLD, AND NOW SHE NOT ONLY SINGS, BUT SHE'S ALSO TAKEN ON OTHER FIELDS LIKE VOICE-OVER AND THEATER.
AND SHE DOESN'T EVEN HAVE AN AGENT. SHE BOOKS ALL HER WORK HERSELF.

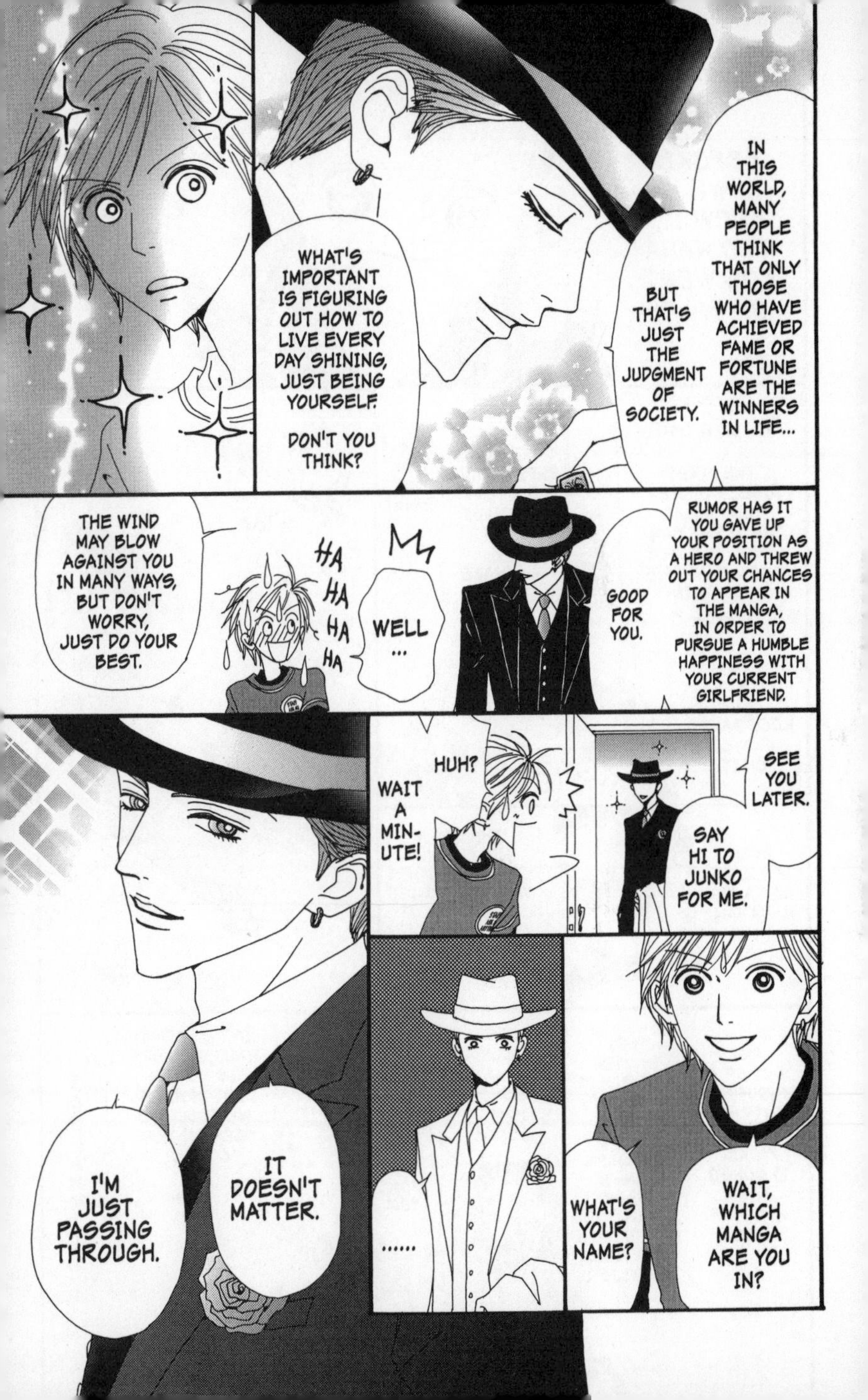
IN THIS WORLD, MANY PEOPLE THINK THAT ONLY THOSE WHO HAVE ACHIEVED FAME OR FORTUNE ARE THE WINNERS IN LIFE...
BUT THAT'S JUST THE JUDGMENT OF SOCIETY.
WHAT'S IMPORTANT IS FIGURING OUT HOW TO LIVE EVERY DAY SHINING, JUST BEING YOURSELF.
DON'T YOU THINK?
RUMOR HAS IT YOU GAVE UP YOUR POSITION AS A HERO AND THREW OUT YOUR CHANCES TO APPEAR IN THE MANGA, IN ORDER TO PURSUE A HUMBLE HAPPINESS WITH YOUR CURRENT GIRLFRIEND.
GOOD FOR YOU.
WELL...
HA HA HA HA
THE WIND MAY BLOW AGAINST YOU IN MANY WAYS, BUT DON'T WORRY, JUST DO YOUR BEST.
SEE YOU LATER.
SAY HI TO JUNKO FOR ME.
HUH?
WAIT A MIN-UTE!
WAIT, WHICH MANGA ARE YOU IN?
WHAT'S YOUR NAME?
......
IT DOESN'T MATTER.
I'M JUST PASSING THROUGH.

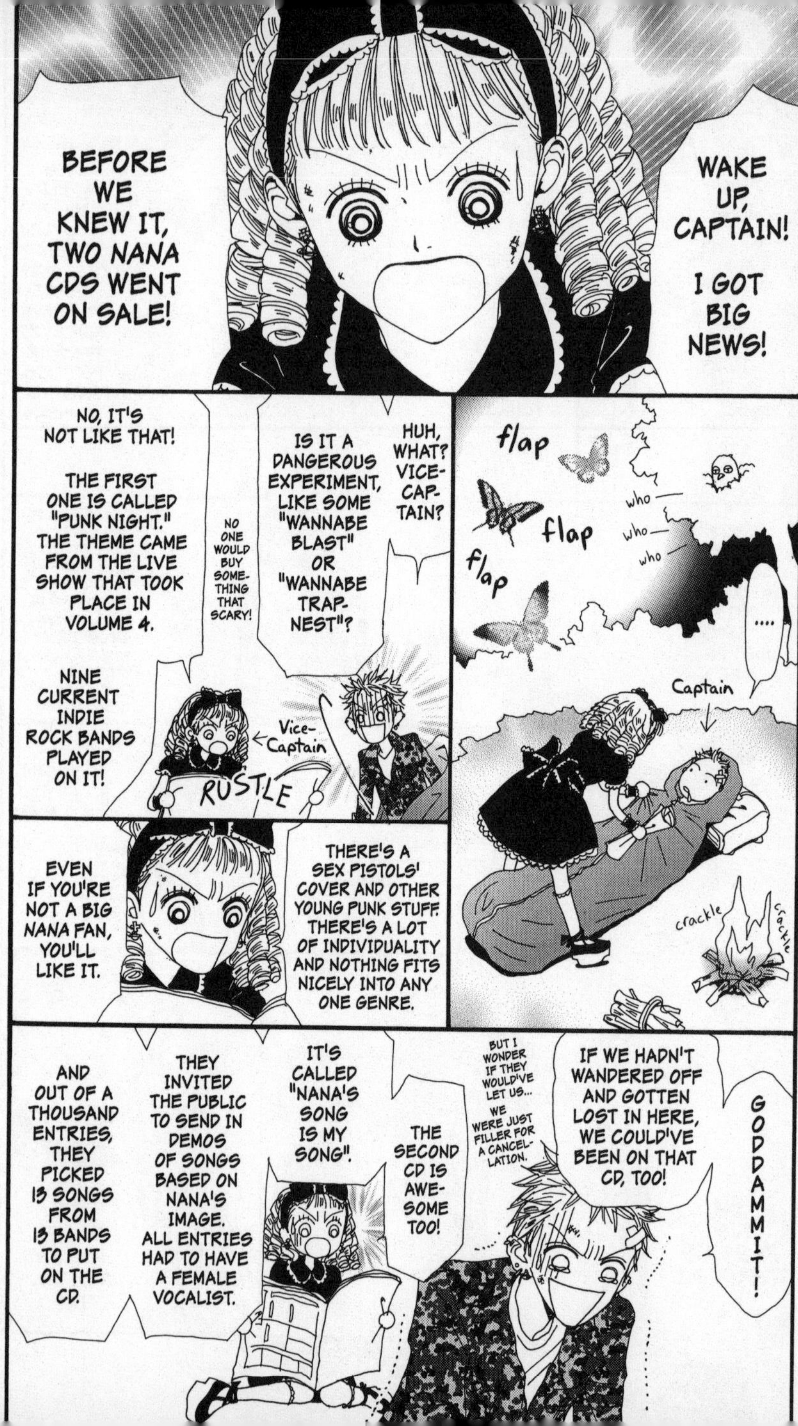
WAKE UP, CAPTAIN!
I GOT BIG NEWS!
BEFORE WE KNEW IT, TWO NANA CDS WENT ON SALE!
flap
flap
flap
who — who — who —
....
Captain
crackle crackle
HUH, WHAT? VICE-CAPTAIN?
IS IT A DANGEROUS EXPERIMENT, LIKE SOME "WANNABE BLAST" OR "WANNABE TRAPNEST"?
NO ONE WOULD BUY SOMETHING THAT SCARY!
NO, IT'S NOT LIKE THAT!
THE FIRST ONE IS CALLED "PUNK NIGHT." THE THEME CAME FROM THE LIVE SHOW THAT TOOK PLACE IN VOLUME 4.
NINE CURRENT INDIE ROCK BANDS PLAYED ON IT!
Vice-Captain
RUSTLE
THERE'S A SEX PISTOLS' COVER AND OTHER YOUNG PUNK STUFF. THERE'S A LOT OF INDIVIDUALITY AND NOTHING FITS NICELY INTO ANY ONE GENRE.
EVEN IF YOU'RE NOT A BIG NANA FAN, YOU'LL LIKE IT.
GODDAMMIT!
IF WE HADN'T WANDERED OFF AND GOTTEN LOST IN HERE, WE COULD'VE BEEN ON THAT CD, TOO!
BUT I WONDER IF THEY WOULD'VE LET US... WE WERE JUST FILLER FOR A CANCELLATION.
THE SECOND CD IS AWESOME TOO!
IT'S CALLED "NANA'S SONG IS MY SONG".
THEY INVITED THE PUBLIC TO SEND IN DEMOS OF SONGS BASED ON NANA'S IMAGE. ALL ENTRIES HAD TO HAVE A FEMALE VOCALIST.
AND OUT OF A THOUSAND ENTRIES, THEY PICKED 13 SONGS FROM 13 BANDS TO PUT ON THE CD.

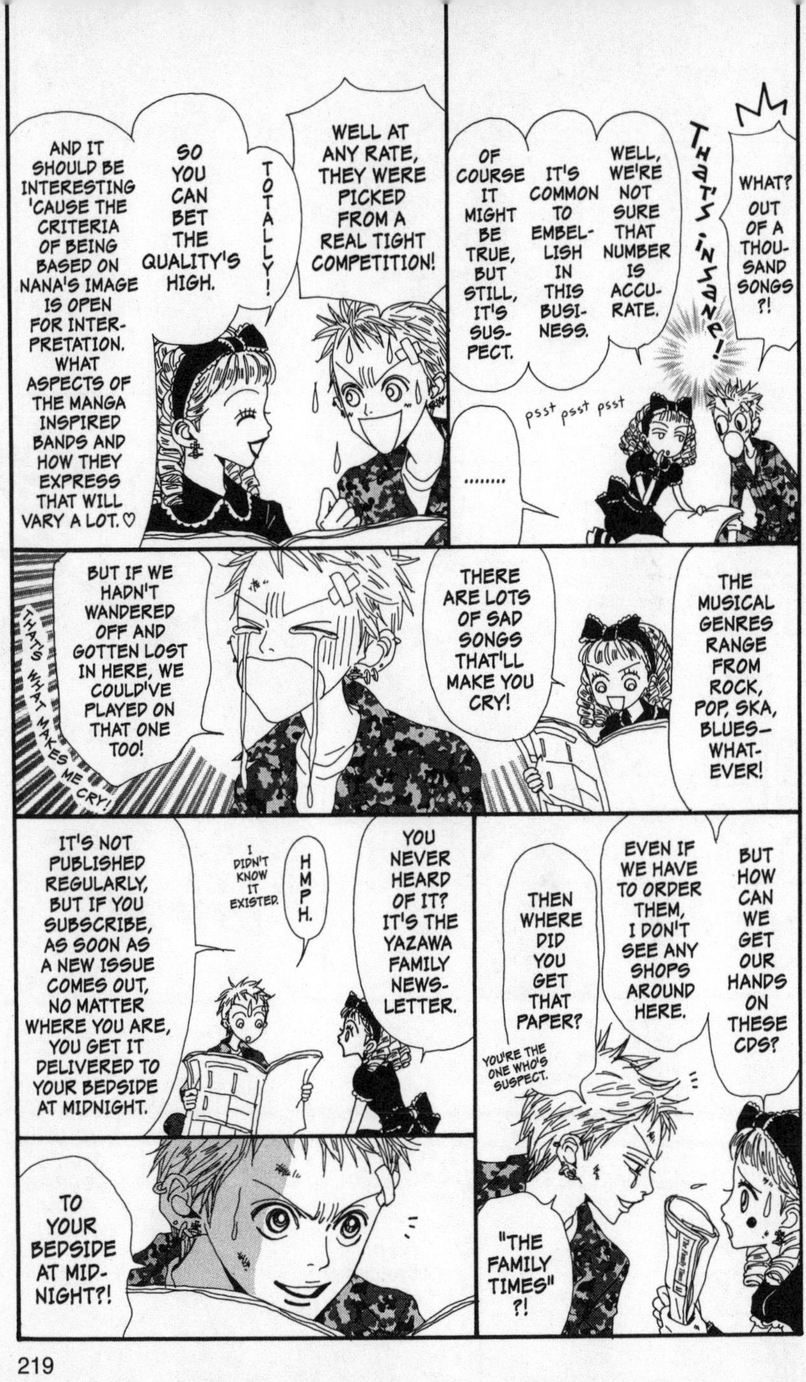

WHAT? OUT OF A THOUSAND SONGS?!
THAT'S INSANE!
WELL, WE'RE NOT SURE THAT NUMBER IS ACCURATE.
IT'S COMMON TO EMBELLISH IN THIS BUSINESS.
OF COURSE IT MIGHT BE TRUE, BUT STILL, IT'S SUSPECT.
....
psst psst psst
WELL AT ANY RATE, THEY WERE PICKED FROM A REAL TIGHT COMPETITION!
TOTALLY!
SO YOU CAN BET THE QUALITY'S HIGH.
AND IT SHOULD BE INTERESTING 'CAUSE THE CRITERIA OF BEING BASED ON NANA'S IMAGE IS OPEN FOR INTERPRETATION. WHAT ASPECTS OF THE MANGA INSPIRED BANDS AND HOW THEY EXPRESS THAT WILL VARY A LOT.♡
THE MUSICAL GENRES RANGE FROM ROCK, POP, SKA, BLUES— WHATEVER!
THERE ARE LOTS OF SAD SONGS THAT'LL MAKE YOU CRY!
BUT IF WE HADN'T WANDERED OFF AND GOTTEN LOST IN HERE, WE COULD'VE PLAYED ON THAT ONE TOO!
THAT'S WHAT MAKES ME CRY!
BUT HOW CAN WE GET OUR HANDS ON THESE CDS?
EVEN IF WE HAVE TO ORDER THEM, I DON'T SEE ANY SHOPS AROUND HERE.
THEN WHERE DID YOU GET THAT PAPER?
YOU'RE THE ONE WHO'S SUSPECT.
"THE FAMILY TIMES"?!
YOU NEVER HEARD OF IT? IT'S THE YAZAWA FAMILY NEWSLETTER.
HMPH.
I DIDN'T KNOW IT EXISTED.
IT'S NOT PUBLISHED REGULARLY, BUT IF YOU SUBSCRIBE, AS SOON AS A NEW ISSUE COMES OUT, NO MATTER WHERE YOU ARE, YOU GET IT DELIVERED TO YOUR BEDSIDE AT MIDNIGHT.
TO YOUR BEDSIDE AT MIDNIGHT?!

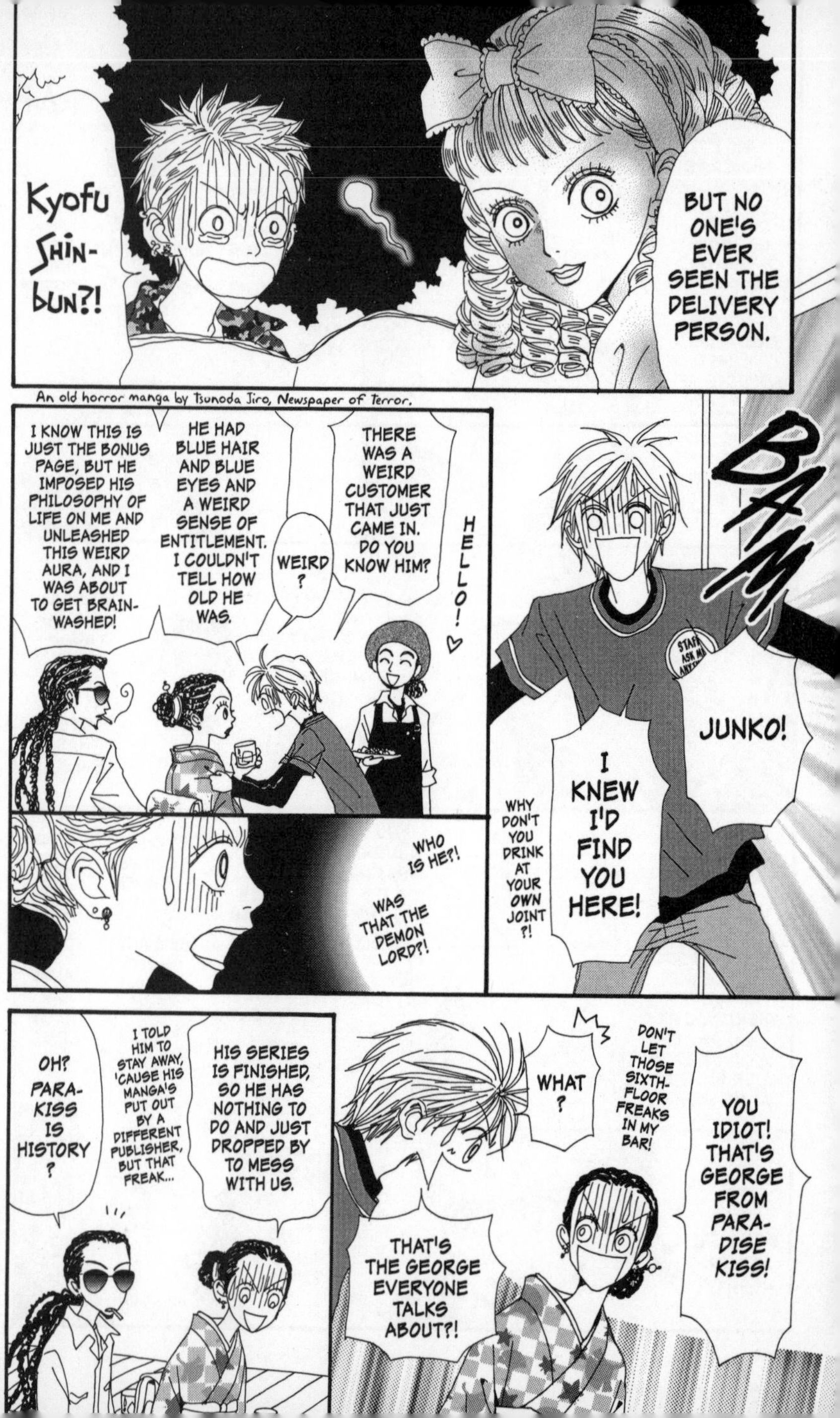
BUT NO ONE'S EVER SEEN THE DELIVERY PERSON.
Kyofu Shin-bun?!
An old horror manga by Tsunoda Jiro, Newspaper of Terror.
BAM
JUNKO!
I KNEW I'D FIND YOU HERE!
WHY DON'T YOU DRINK AT YOUR OWN JOINT?!
HELLO!
THERE WAS A WEIRD CUSTOMER THAT JUST CAME IN. DO YOU KNOW HIM?
WEIRD?
HE HAD BLUE HAIR AND BLUE EYES AND A WEIRD SENSE OF ENTITLEMENT. I COULDN'T TELL HOW OLD HE WAS.
I KNOW THIS IS JUST THE BONUS PAGE, BUT HE IMPOSED HIS PHILOSOPHY OF LIFE ON ME AND UNLEASHED THIS WEIRD AURA, AND I WAS ABOUT TO GET BRAIN-WASHED!
WHO IS HE?!
WAS THAT THE DEMON LORD?!
YOU IDIOT! THAT'S GEORGE FROM PARA-DISE KISS!
DON'T LET THOSE SIXTH-FLOOR FREAKS IN MY BAR!
WHAT?
THAT'S THE GEORGE EVERYONE TALKS ABOUT?!
HIS SERIES IS FINISHED, SO HE HAS NOTHING TO DO AND JUST DROPPED BY TO MESS WITH US.
I TOLD HIM TO STAY AWAY, 'CAUSE HIS MANGA'S PUT OUT BY A DIFFERENT PUBLISHER, BUT THAT FREAK...
OH? PARA-KISS IS HISTORY?

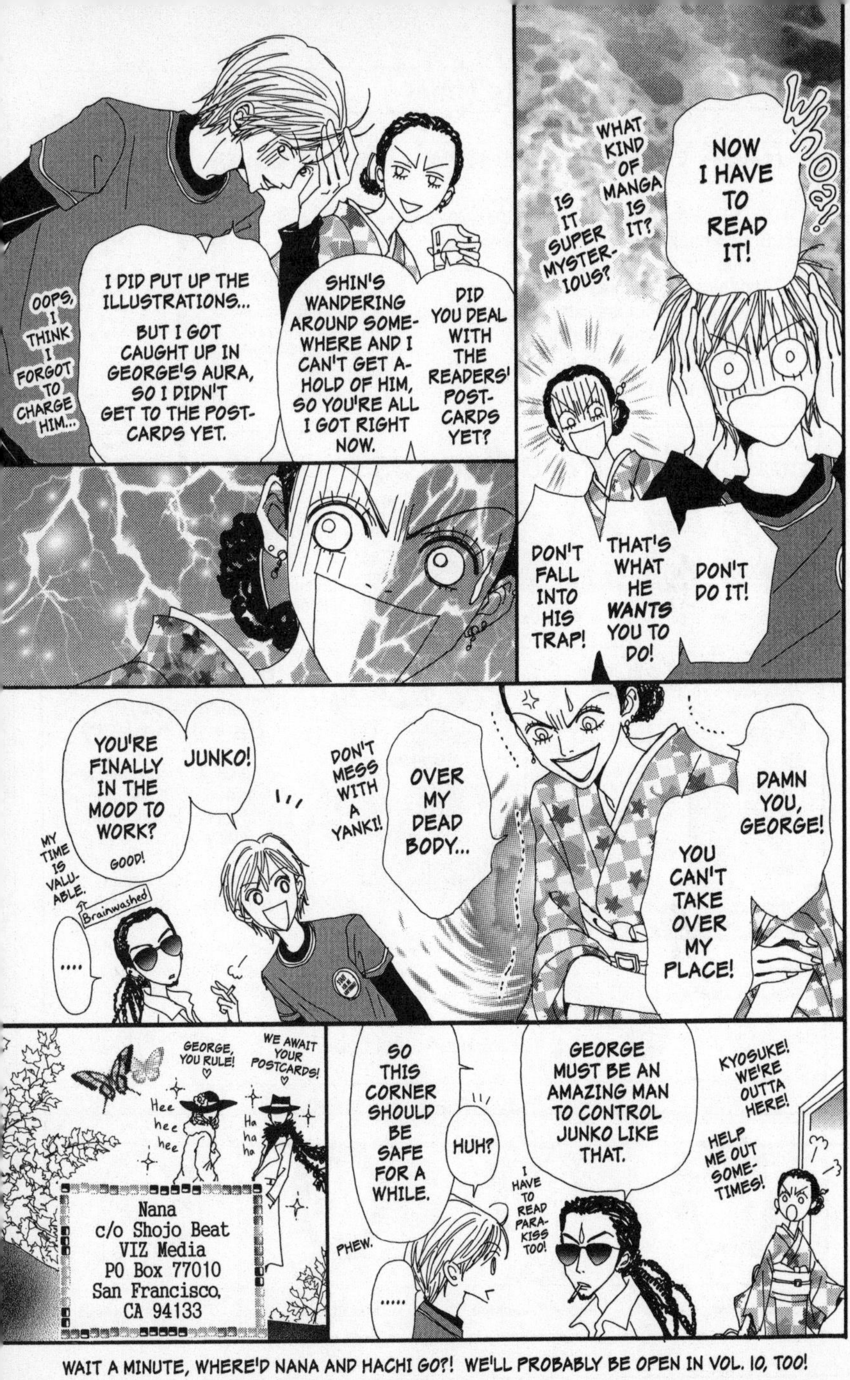
WHOA!
NOW I HAVE TO READ IT!
WHAT KIND OF MANGA IS IT?
IS IT SUPER MYSTERIOUS?
DON'T DO IT!
THAT'S WHAT HE WANTS YOU TO DO!
DON'T FALL INTO HIS TRAP!
DID YOU DEAL WITH THE READERS' POSTCARDS YET?
SHIN'S WANDERING AROUND SOMEWHERE AND I CAN'T GET A-HOLD OF HIM, SO YOU'RE ALL I GOT RIGHT NOW.
I DID PUT UP THE ILLUSTRATIONS...
BUT I GOT CAUGHT UP IN GEORGE'S AURA, SO I DIDN'T GET TO THE POSTCARDS YET.
OOPS, I THINK I FORGOT TO CHARGE HIM...
DAMN YOU, GEORGE!
YOU CAN'T TAKE OVER MY PLACE!
OVER MY DEAD BODY...
DON'T MESS WITH A YANKI!
JUNKO!
YOU'RE FINALLY IN THE MOOD TO WORK?
GOOD!
MY TIME IS VALUABLE.
Brainwashed
....
KYOSUKE! WE'RE OUTTA HERE!
HELP ME OUT SOMETIMES!
GEORGE MUST BE AN AMAZING MAN TO CONTROL JUNKO LIKE THAT.
I HAVE TO READ PARAKISS TOO!
HUH?
SO THIS CORNER SHOULD BE SAFE FOR A WHILE.
PHEW.
.....
WE AWAIT YOUR POSTCARDS!
Ha ha ha
GEORGE, YOU RULE!
Hee hee hee
Nana
c/o Shojo Beat
VIZ Media
PO Box 77010
San Francisco,
CA 94133

WAIT A MINUTE, WHERE'D NANA AND HACHI GO?! WE'LL PROBABLY BE OPEN IN VOL. 10, TOO!

NANA Vol. 9 on Sale Now! It's too Long!

It's 1.5 times as thick as usual! It's really worth a read!
But it's hard to open! And it's expensive!
It's too thin to use as a pillow!
And the story's depressing!
I don't care about the extra story at the end!
The extra pages are stupid!
But it's 1.5 times as thick!

What the hell?!

< Compared to our own product >

The Family Times

Nov. 14, 2003

The sequel to *Gokinjo Monogatari* **Paradise Kiss** is finished!

Shodensha   Five volumes   ¥857 + tax each

"The ending doesn't make sense!"

Lots of complaints! Too self-absorbed!

On sale the 26th of every month!

NANA extras sometimes enclosed in the magazine!

http://cookie.shueisha.co.jp/

Mekke!

Various "Blast" tour swag on sale!

http://mekke.shueisha.co.jp/

Rumi Roll

¥2,500 (without tax)
Label: CD RECORDS
Released by: UK Project

http://UKPROJECT.COM/

Rumi Shishido's new album on sale now! ♡

The original indie idol and our family's idol Runrun's first album in four years is finally out!

Produced by Takahiro Matsumoto (SPARKY).

Composers include the super-foxy Mitsuhiro Oikawa (Mitchy)!

Even if you have to special order it, get it!

🐾 **"Have You Seen Me?"** 🐾

Misato Uehara (alias?)	**Nobuo Terashima**	**Nana Osaki**	**Nana Komatsu**

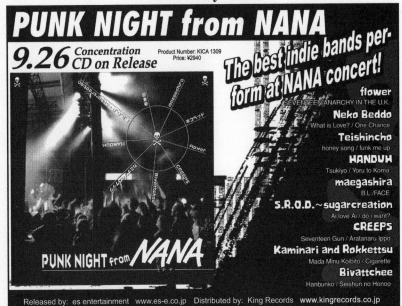

PUNK NIGHT from NANA

9.26 Concentration CD on Release

Product Number: KICA 1309
Price: ¥2940

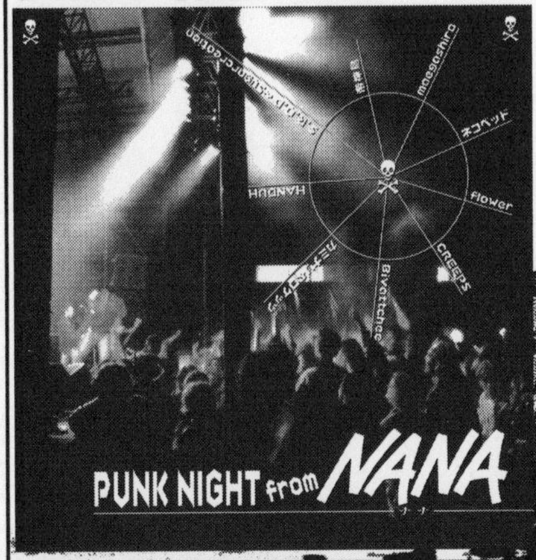
maegashira
ネコベッド
flower
CREEPS
Bivattchee
HANDUH
PUNK NIGHT from NANA

The best indie bands perform at NANA concert!

flower
SEVENTEEN/ANARCHY IN THE U.K.

Neko Beddo
What is Love? / One Chance

Teishincho
honey song / funk me up

HANDUH
Tsukiyo / Yoru to Koma

maegashira
B.L./FACE

S.R.O.D.~sugarcreation
Ai love Ai / do i want?

CREEPS
Seventeen Gun / Aratanaru Ippo

Kaminari and Rokkettsu
Mada Minu Koibito / Cigarette

Bivattchee
Hanbunko / Seishun no Honoo

Released by: es entertainment www.es-e.co.jp Distributed by: King Records www.kingrecords.co.jp

NANA's song is my song

On sale Nov. 6, 2003 ABCA-5027 ¥2500 (tax incl.) **Best seller!**

We invited musicians to submit interpretations of "the musical world of NANA" and chose 13 acts with female singers.

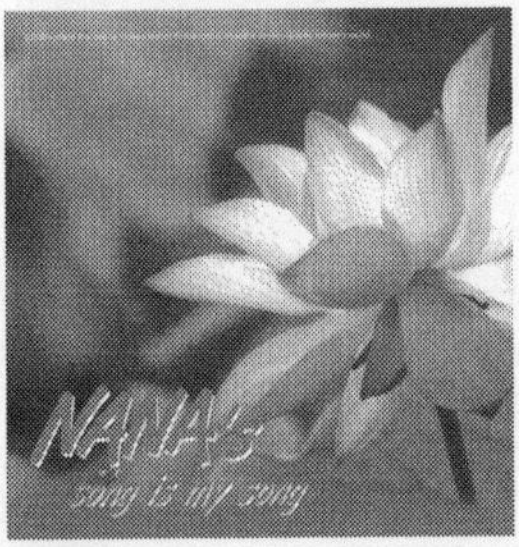
NANA's song is my song

[Studio-recorded Songs]

1. Maaburu / Battle Bomb Rounge
2. Kimi no Namae / SAVAGE GENIUS
3. Rakuen no Tobira / Burukapu
4. Shin-ai / Chihiroizu
5. Lotus Blues / Olive
6. Thanks / Bama☆sister
7. Toi / Buruu Furoggu
8. Not be mine / GREEN BEAR
9. Kanaderu Kami / RK ROSEBUD
10. NO TITLE / Yamaoka Chiharu
11. Mayonaka no Asu / Kakimoto Nanae
12. MY WAY / REALIZE POWER WAVE
13. Atashi no Hana / Ann

momo grapes

Released by: AMJ/Momo+Grapes Distributed by: King Records
Send all inquiries to: Momo+Grapes Company Co. Ltd.
101-0021 Chiyoda Bldg. 2F, 5-2-13 Sotokanda, Chiyoda-ku, Tokyo
Tel: 03-5807-5054 FAX: 03-5807-5954 http://www.momogre.com

☆ All products listed in our newsletter actually exist!

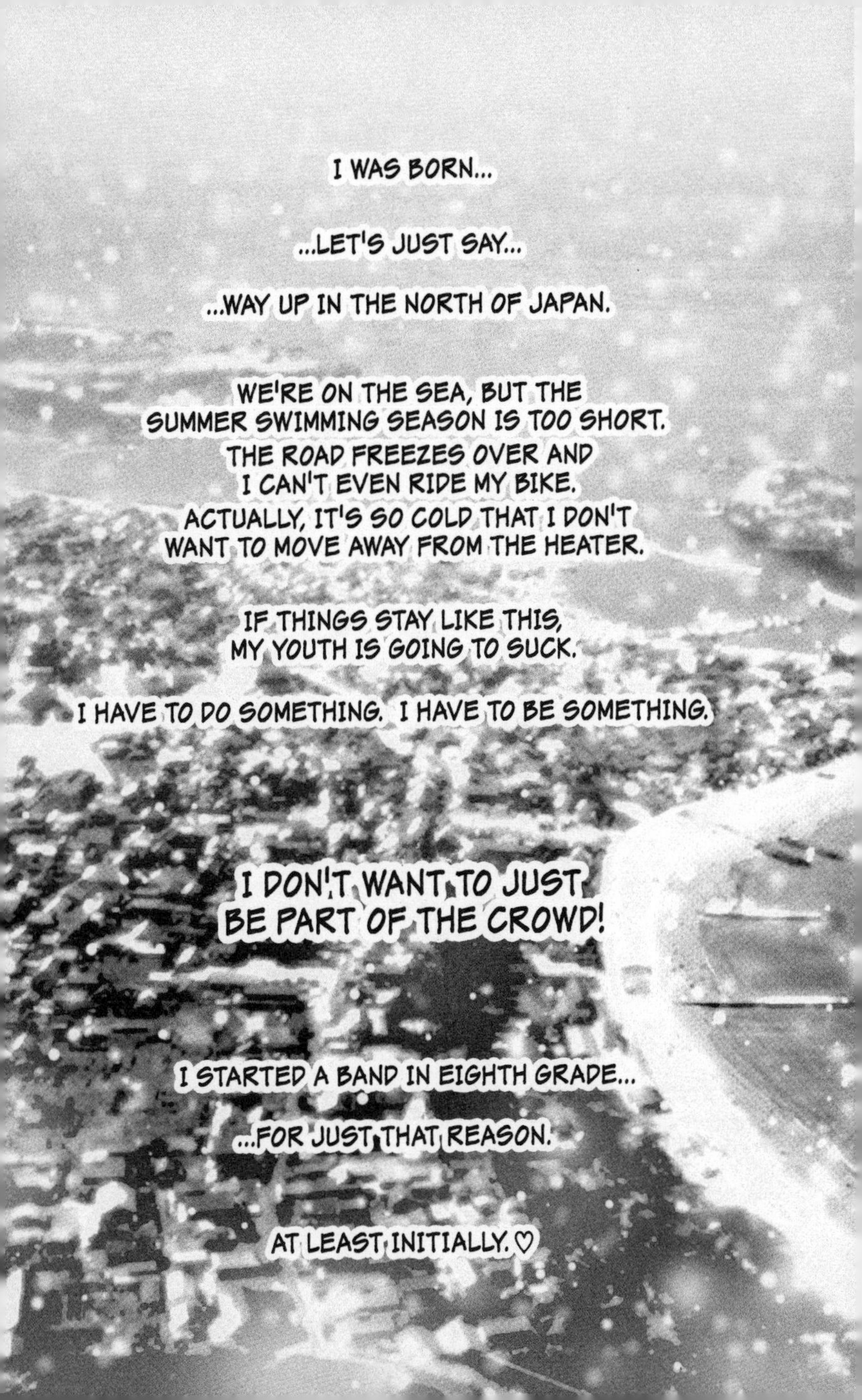
I WAS BORN...
...LET'S JUST SAY...
...WAY UP IN THE NORTH OF JAPAN.
WE'RE ON THE SEA, BUT THE SUMMER SWIMMING SEASON IS TOO SHORT.
THE ROAD FREEZES OVER AND I CAN'T EVEN RIDE MY BIKE.
ACTUALLY, IT'S SO COLD THAT I DON'T WANT TO MOVE AWAY FROM THE HEATER.
IF THINGS STAY LIKE THIS, MY YOUTH IS GOING TO SUCK.
I HAVE TO DO SOMETHING. I HAVE TO BE SOMETHING.
I DON'T WANT TO JUST BE PART OF THE CROWD!
I STARTED A BAND IN EIGHTH GRADE...
...FOR JUST THAT REASON.
AT LEAST INITIALLY.♡

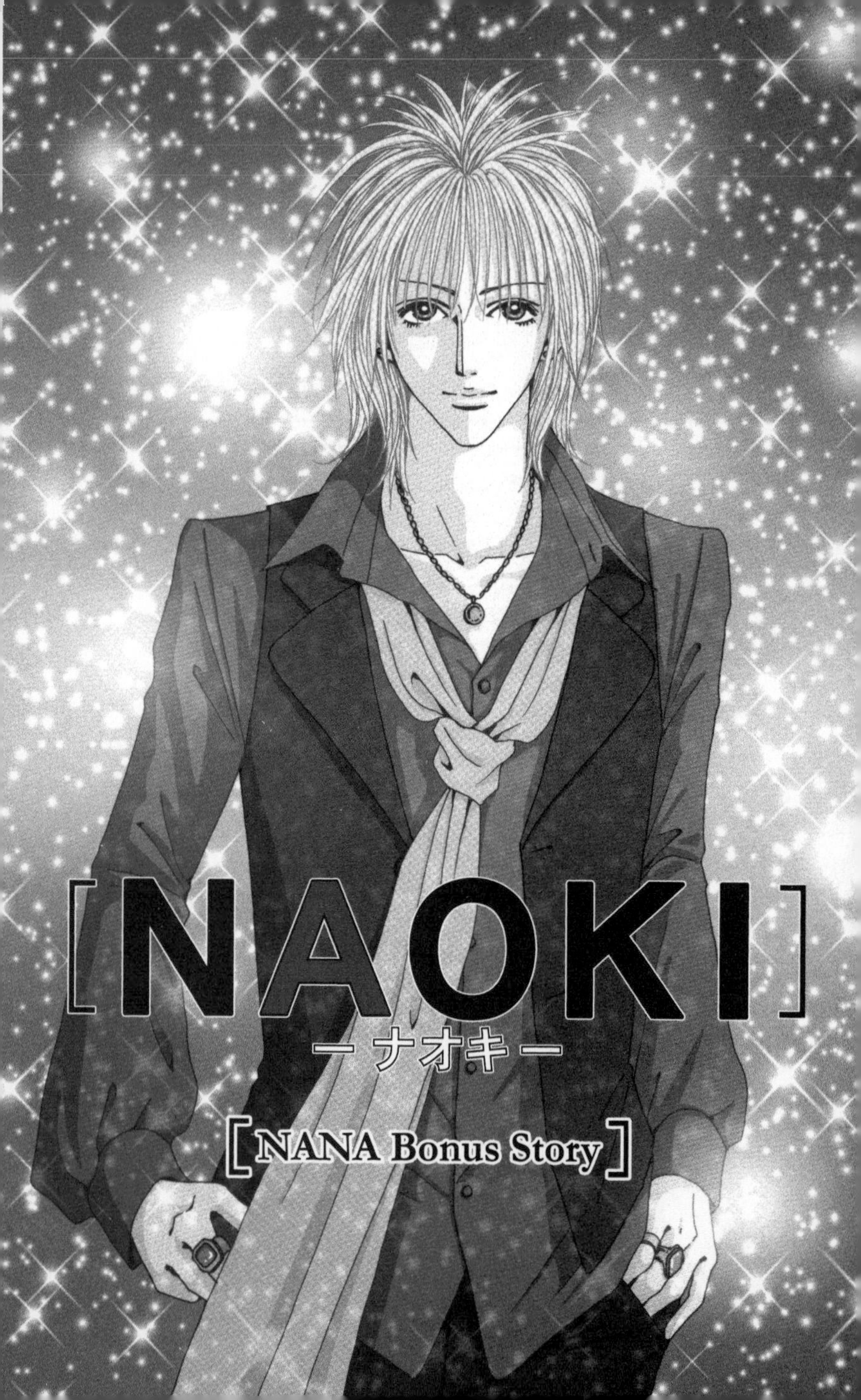
[NAOKI]
ーナオキー
[NANA Bonus Story]

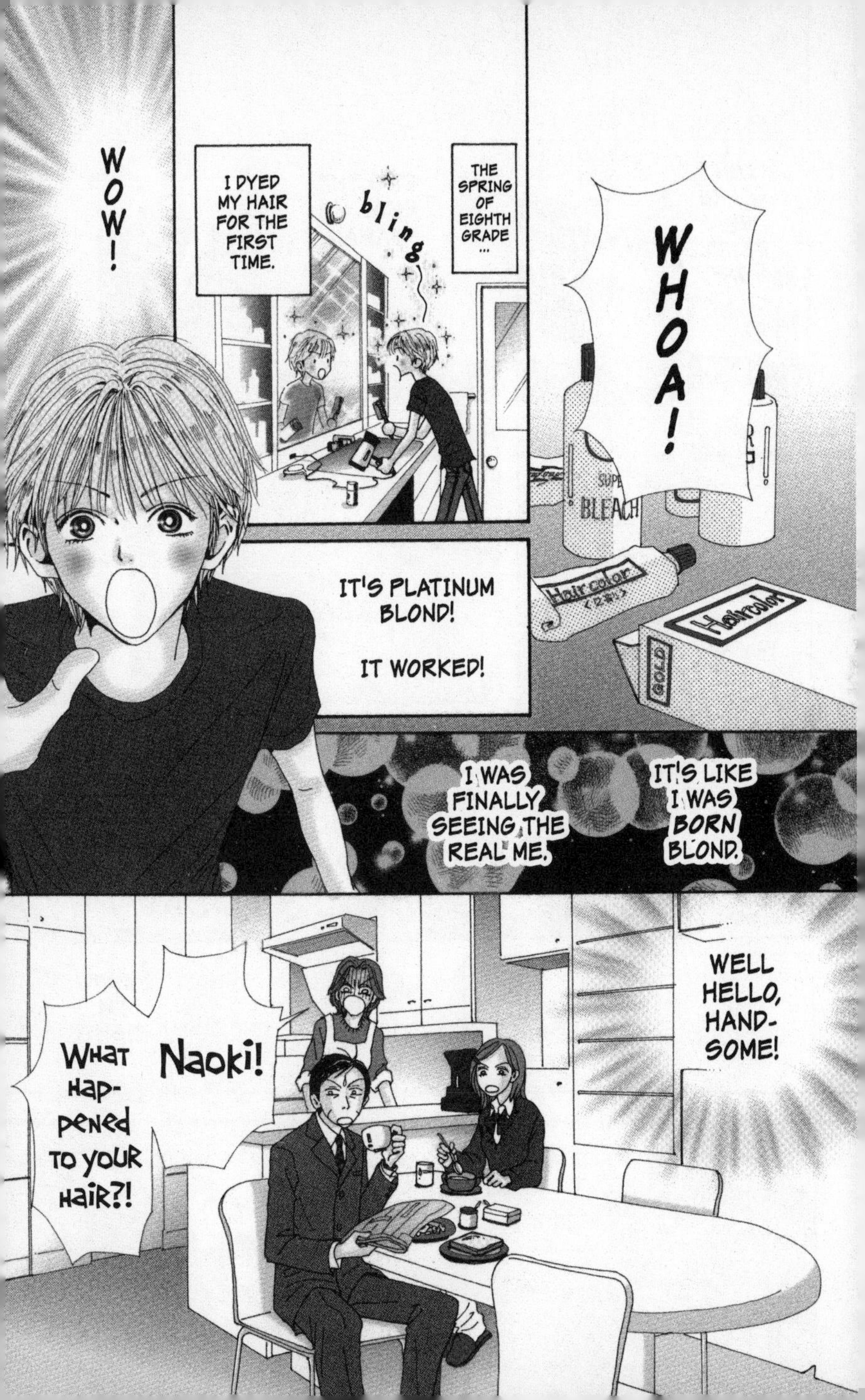
THE SPRING OF EIGHTH GRADE...
I DYED MY HAIR FOR THE FIRST TIME.
bling
WHOA!
BLEACH
Hair color
Haircolor
GOLD
IT'S PLATINUM BLOND!
IT WORKED!
WOW!
IT'S LIKE I WAS BORN BLOND.
I WAS FINALLY SEEING THE REAL ME.
WELL HELLO, HANDSOME!
Naoki!
WHAT HAPPENED TO YOUR HAIR?!

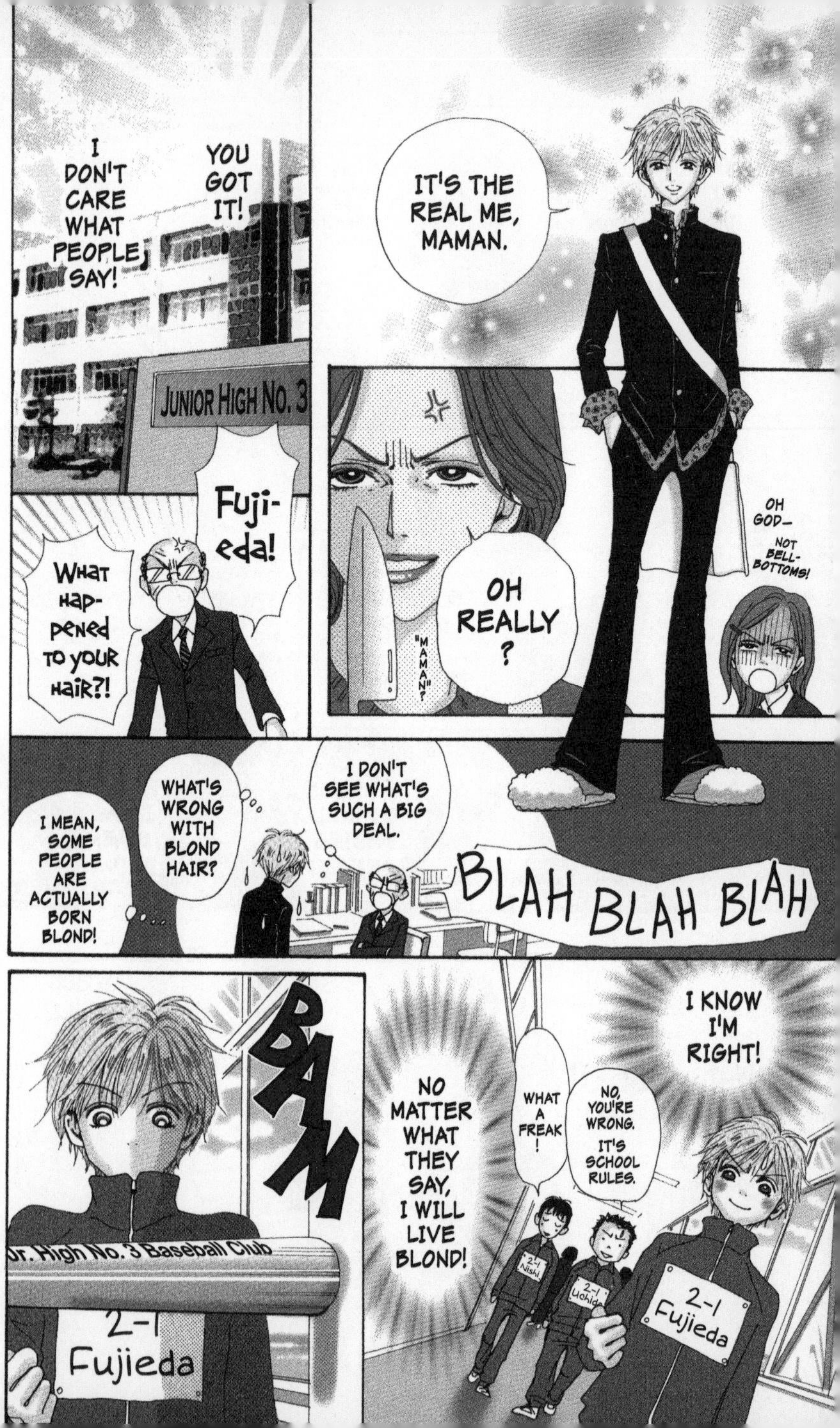
IT'S THE REAL ME, MAMAN.
OH REALLY?
"MAMAN"?
OH GOD— NOT BELL-BOTTOMS!
YOU GOT IT!
I DON'T CARE WHAT PEOPLE SAY!
JUNIOR HIGH No. 3
Fuji-eda!
What hap-pened to your hair?!
BLAH BLAH BLAH
I DON'T SEE WHAT'S SUCH A BIG DEAL.
WHAT'S WRONG WITH BLOND HAIR?
I MEAN, SOME PEOPLE ARE ACTUALLY BORN BLOND!
I KNOW I'M RIGHT!
NO, YOU'RE WRONG. IT'S SCHOOL RULES.
WHAT A FREAK!
NO MATTER WHAT THEY SAY, I WILL LIVE BLOND!
2-1 Fujieda
2-1 Uchida
2-1 Nishi
BAM
Jr. High No. 3 Baseball Club
2-1 Fujieda

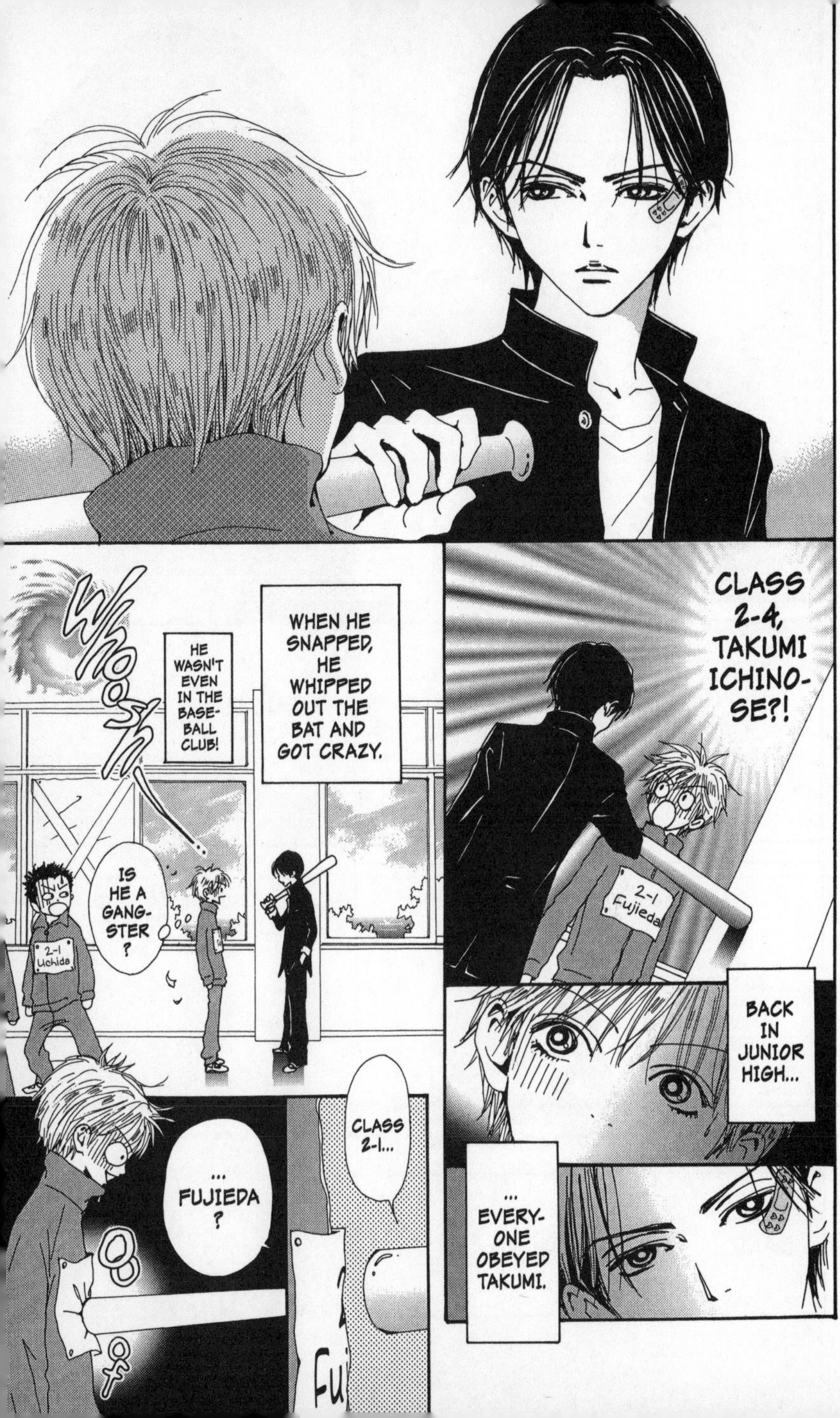
CLASS 2-4, TAKUMI ICHINOSE?!
2-1 Fujieda
BACK IN JUNIOR HIGH...
... EVERYONE OBEYED TAKUMI.
WHEN HE SNAPPED, HE WHIPPED OUT THE BAT AND GOT CRAZY.
HE WASN'T EVEN IN THE BASEBALL CLUB!
WHOOSH
IS HE A GANGSTER?
2-1 Uchida
CLASS 2-1...
... FUJIEDA?
Oof

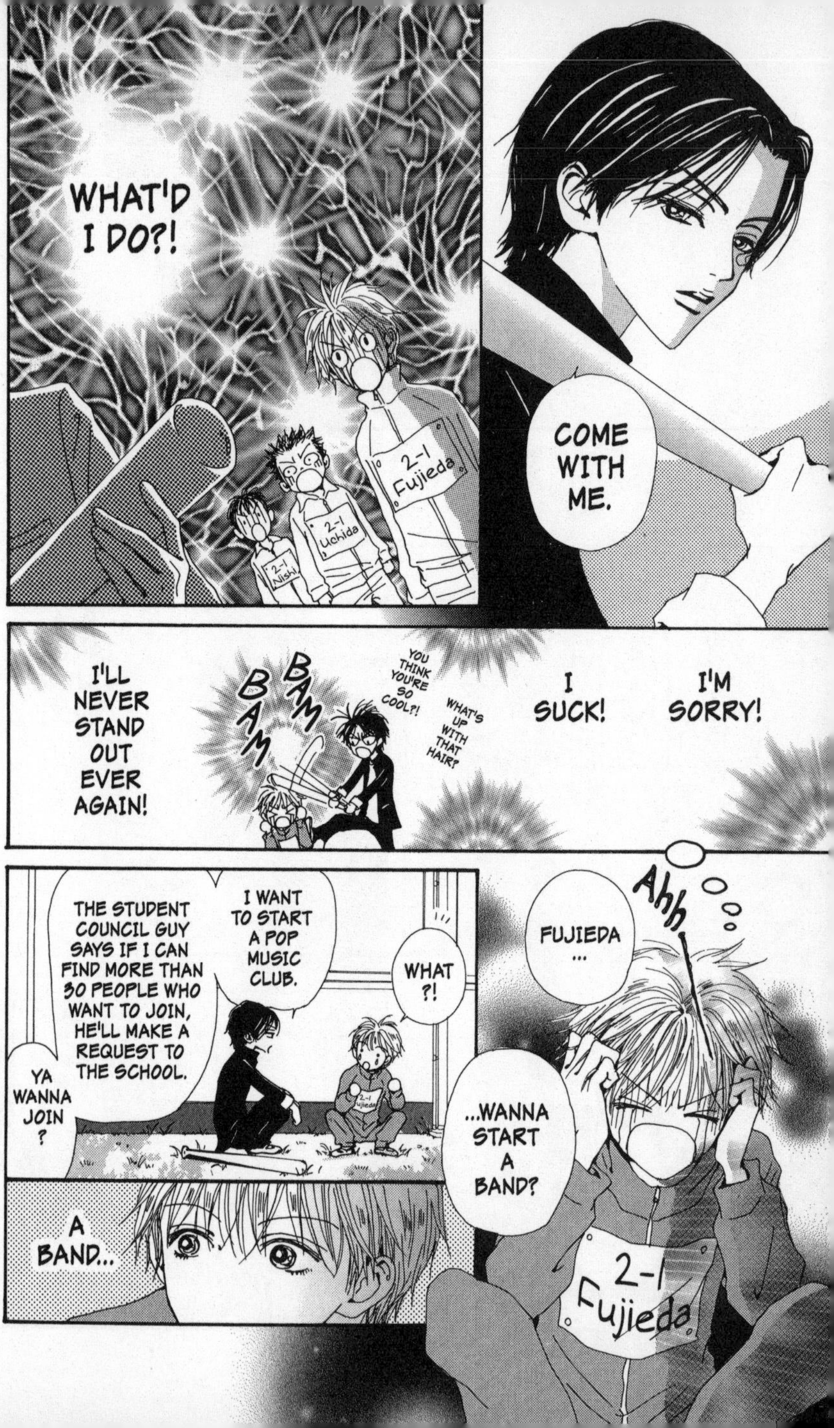
COME WITH ME.
WHAT'D I DO?!
2-1 Fujieda
2-1 Uchida
2-1 Nishi
I'M SORRY!
I SUCK!
WHAT'S UP WITH THAT HAIR?
YOU THINK YOU'RE SO COOL?!
BAM
BAM
I'LL NEVER STAND OUT EVER AGAIN!
Ahh
FUJIEDA ...
...WANNA START A BAND?
2-1 Fujieda
WHAT ?!
I WANT TO START A POP MUSIC CLUB.
THE STUDENT COUNCIL GUY SAYS IF I CAN FIND MORE THAN 30 PEOPLE WHO WANT TO JOIN, HE'LL MAKE A REQUEST TO THE SCHOOL.
YA WANNA JOIN ?
2-1 Fujieda
A BAND...

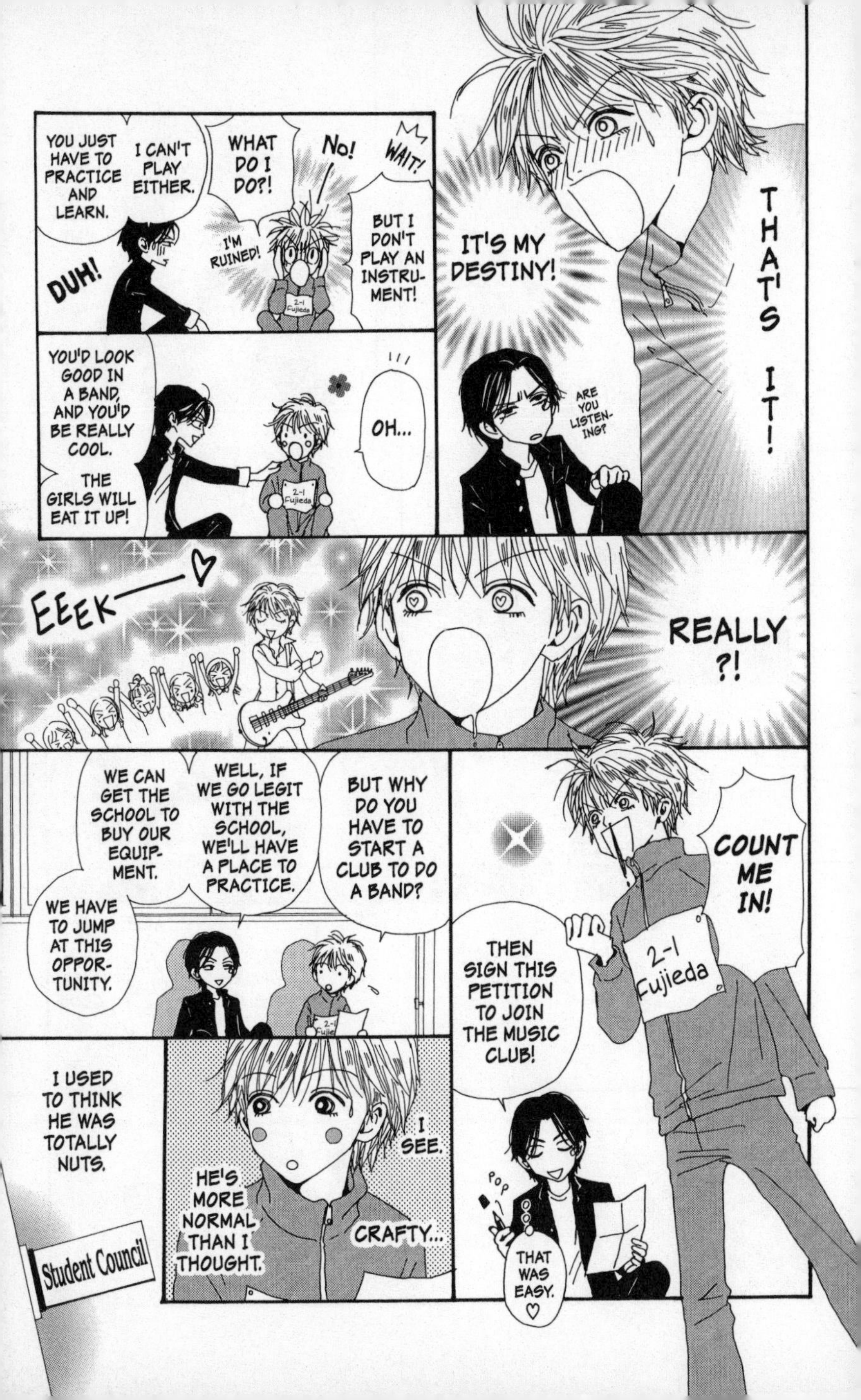
THAT'S IT!
IT'S MY DESTINY!
ARE YOU LISTENING?
WAIT!
No!
BUT I DON'T PLAY AN INSTRUMENT!
WHAT DO I DO?!
I'M RUINED!
I CAN'T PLAY EITHER.
YOU JUST HAVE TO PRACTICE AND LEARN.
DUH!
2-1 Fujieda
OH...
YOU'D LOOK GOOD IN A BAND, AND YOU'D BE REALLY COOL.
THE GIRLS WILL EAT IT UP!
2-1 Fujieda
REALLY ?!
EEEK—♥
COUNT ME IN!
2-1 Fujieda
THEN SIGN THIS PETITION TO JOIN THE MUSIC CLUB!
POP
THAT WAS EASY. ♡
BUT WHY DO YOU HAVE TO START A CLUB TO DO A BAND?
WELL, IF WE GO LEGIT WITH THE SCHOOL, WE'LL HAVE A PLACE TO PRACTICE.
WE CAN GET THE SCHOOL TO BUY OUR EQUIPMENT.
WE HAVE TO JUMP AT THIS OPPORTUNITY.
I SEE.
CRAFTY...
HE'S MORE NORMAL THAN I THOUGHT.
I USED TO THINK HE WAS TOTALLY NUTS.
Student Council

SOMEONE'S HERE FOR YOU!

YASUSHI!

OH NO ... ICHINOSE ...

IS THE PRESIDENT IN?

Takagi

I GOT 30 NAMES ON THIS PETITION.

1-2	Reika Soritsawa♡	2-5	
2-4	Hiroshi WATANABE	1-6	
2-3	Hideto Sato	1-8	
2-2	Makoto Kiroshita	2-4	M
-1	Mitsunori Kishi	2-4	Hana
5	Suouru Ono	1-2	Isao Wada
	Kuniaki Kojima	2-1	Masataka Kubo
	Kioh	1-5	

I'M DEPENDING ON YOU, TAKAGI.♡

♪....

HE WAS SERIOUS?

OH ...

...FOR THE POP MUSIC CLUB?

I KNEW HE'D SAY THAT.

ACADEMIC CLUBS ARE NOT A JOKE!

ARE YOU KIDDING ME?!

A POP MUSIC CLUB?

PLEASE TRY TO CONSIDER IT IN THIS LIGHT...

232

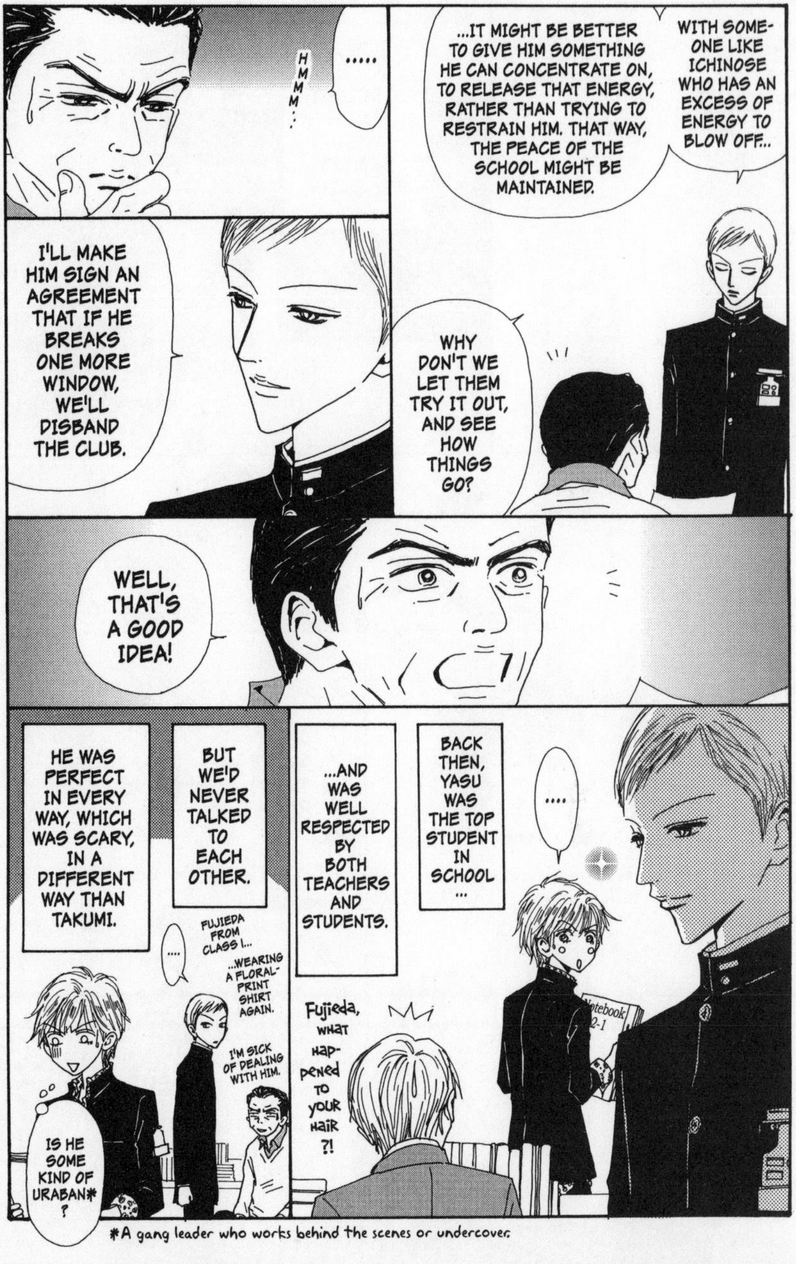
WITH SOME-ONE LIKE ICHINOSE WHO HAS AN EXCESS OF ENERGY TO BLOW OFF...
...IT MIGHT BE BETTER TO GIVE HIM SOMETHING HE CAN CONCENTRATE ON, TO RELEASE THAT ENERGY, RATHER THAN TRYING TO RESTRAIN HIM. THAT WAY, THE PEACE OF THE SCHOOL MIGHT BE MAINTAINED.
......
HMMM...
WHY DON'T WE LET THEM TRY IT OUT, AND SEE HOW THINGS GO?
I'LL MAKE HIM SIGN AN AGREEMENT THAT IF HE BREAKS ONE MORE WINDOW, WE'LL DISBAND THE CLUB.
WELL, THAT'S A GOOD IDEA!
BACK THEN, YASU WAS THE TOP STUDENT IN SCHOOL...
....
...AND WAS WELL RESPECTED BY BOTH TEACHERS AND STUDENTS.
Fujieda, what hap-pened to your hair?!
BUT WE'D NEVER TALKED TO EACH OTHER.
HE WAS PERFECT IN EVERY WAY, WHICH WAS SCARY, IN A DIFFERENT WAY THAN TAKUMI.
FUJIEDA FROM CLASS I...
...WEARING A FLORAL-PRINT SHIRT AGAIN.
I'M SICK OF DEALING WITH HIM.
....
IS HE SOME KIND OF URABAN*?

*A gang leader who works behind the scenes or undercover.

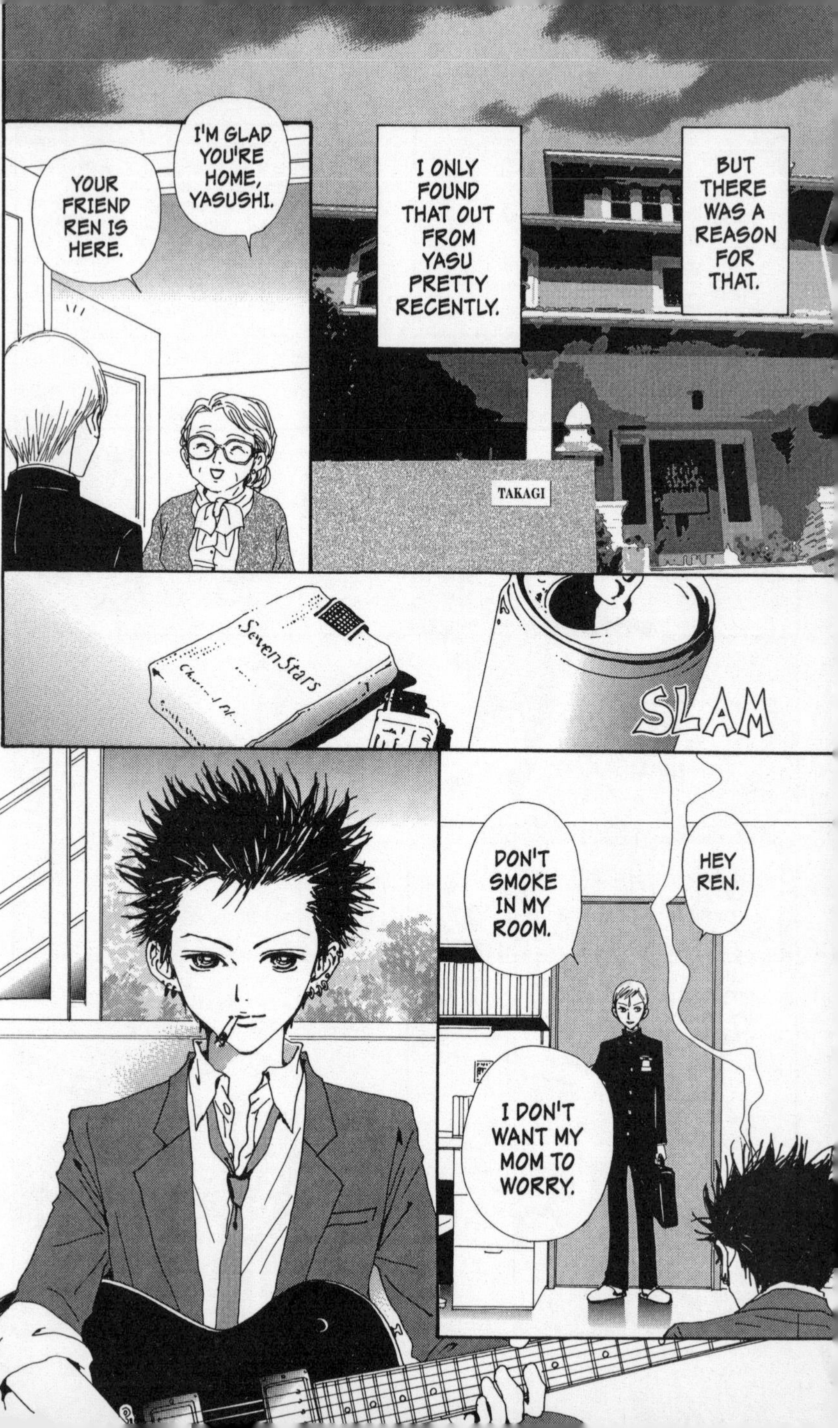
BUT THERE WAS A REASON FOR THAT.
I ONLY FOUND THAT OUT FROM YASU PRETTY RECENTLY.
TAKAGI
I'M GLAD YOU'RE HOME, YASUSHI.
YOUR FRIEND REN IS HERE.
Seven Stars
SLAM
HEY REN.
DON'T SMOKE IN MY ROOM.
I DON'T WANT MY MOM TO WORRY.

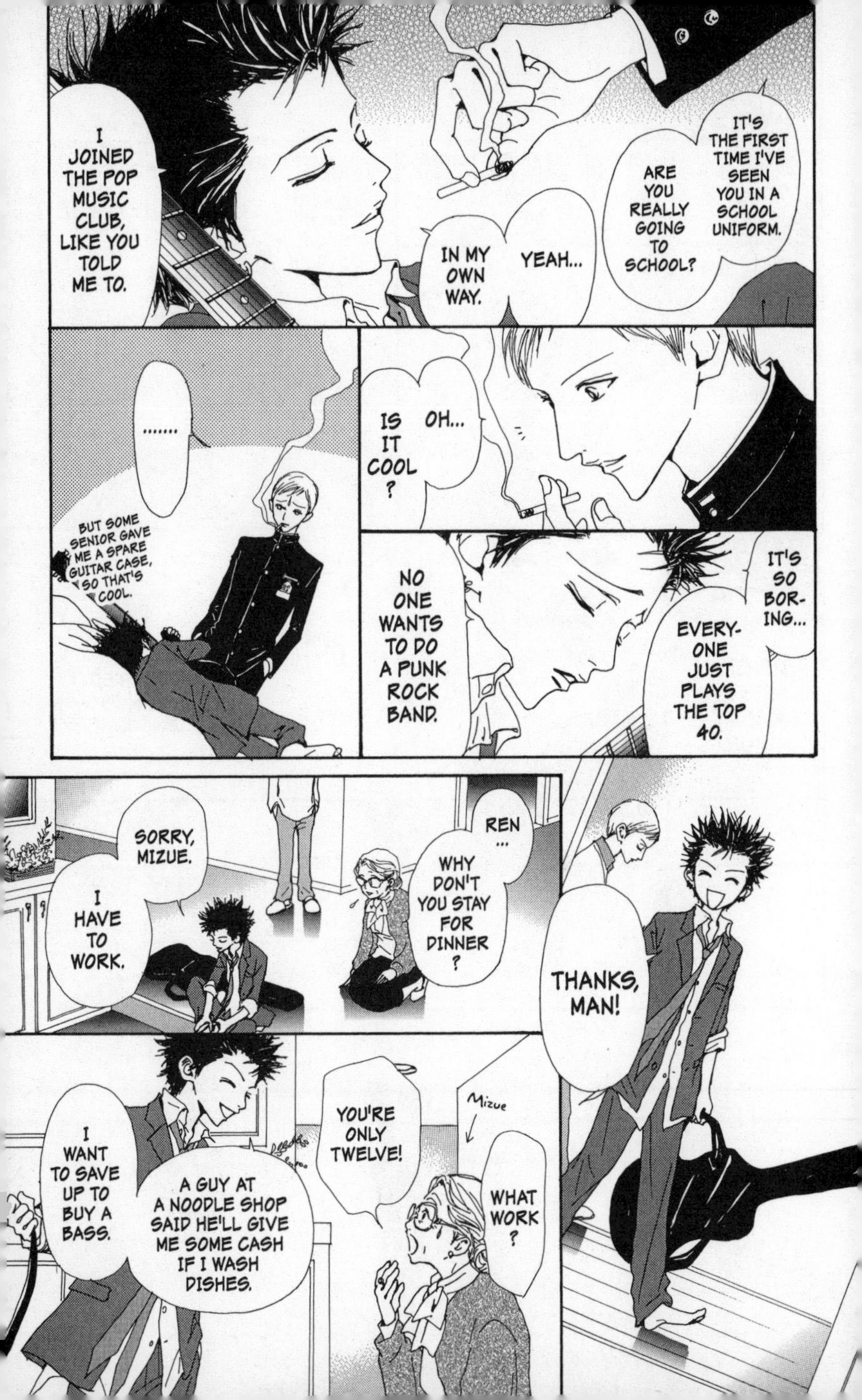
IT'S THE FIRST TIME I'VE SEEN YOU IN A SCHOOL UNIFORM.
ARE YOU REALLY GOING TO SCHOOL?
YEAH...
IN MY OWN WAY.
I JOINED THE POP MUSIC CLUB, LIKE YOU TOLD ME TO.
OH...
IS IT COOL?
IT'S SO BORING...
EVERYONE JUST PLAYS THE TOP 40.
NO ONE WANTS TO DO A PUNK ROCK BAND.
....
BUT SOME SENIOR GAVE ME A SPARE GUITAR CASE, SO THAT'S COOL.
THANKS, MAN!
REN...
WHY DON'T YOU STAY FOR DINNER?
SORRY, MIZUE.
I HAVE TO WORK.
WHAT WORK?
Mizue
YOU'RE ONLY TWELVE!
A GUY AT A NOODLE SHOP SAID HE'LL GIVE ME SOME CASH IF I WASH DISHES.
I WANT TO SAVE UP TO BUY A BASS.

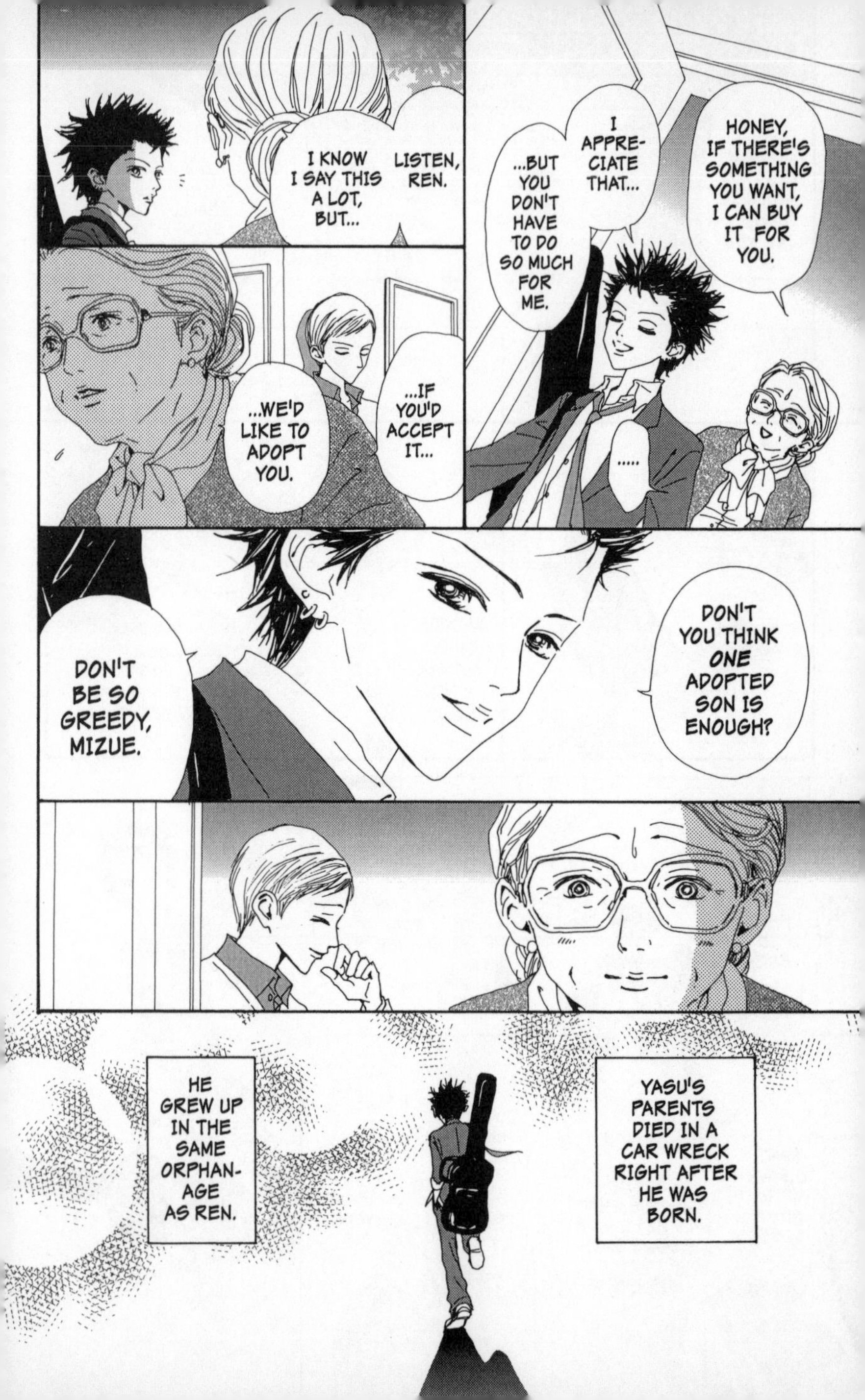
HONEY, IF THERE'S SOMETHING YOU WANT, I CAN BUY IT FOR YOU.
I APPRECIATE THAT...
...BUT YOU DON'T HAVE TO DO SO MUCH FOR ME.
.....
LISTEN, REN.
I KNOW I SAY THIS A LOT, BUT...
...IF YOU'D ACCEPT IT...
...WE'D LIKE TO ADOPT YOU.
DON'T YOU THINK *ONE* ADOPTED SON IS ENOUGH?
DON'T BE SO GREEDY, MIZUE.
YASU'S PARENTS DIED IN A CAR WRECK RIGHT AFTER HE WAS BORN.
HE GREW UP IN THE SAME ORPHANAGE AS REN.

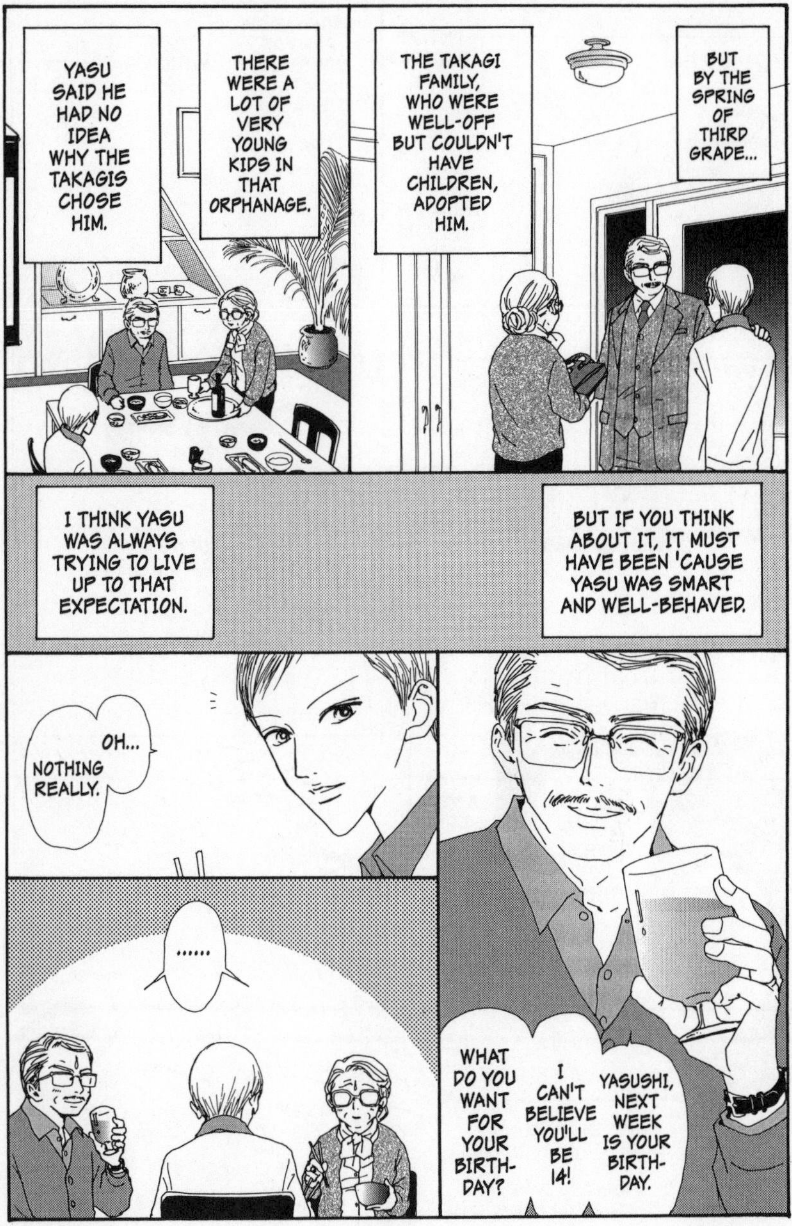
BUT BY THE SPRING OF THIRD GRADE...
THE TAKAGI FAMILY, WHO WERE WELL-OFF BUT COULDN'T HAVE CHILDREN, ADOPTED HIM.
THERE WERE A LOT OF VERY YOUNG KIDS IN THAT ORPHANAGE.
YASU SAID HE HAD NO IDEA WHY THE TAKAGIS CHOSE HIM.
BUT IF YOU THINK ABOUT IT, IT MUST HAVE BEEN 'CAUSE YASU WAS SMART AND WELL-BEHAVED.
I THINK YASU WAS ALWAYS TRYING TO LIVE UP TO THAT EXPECTATION.
YASUSHI, NEXT WEEK IS YOUR BIRTH-DAY.
I CAN'T BELIEVE YOU'LL BE 14!
WHAT DO YOU WANT FOR YOUR BIRTH-DAY?
OH... NOTHING REALLY.
......

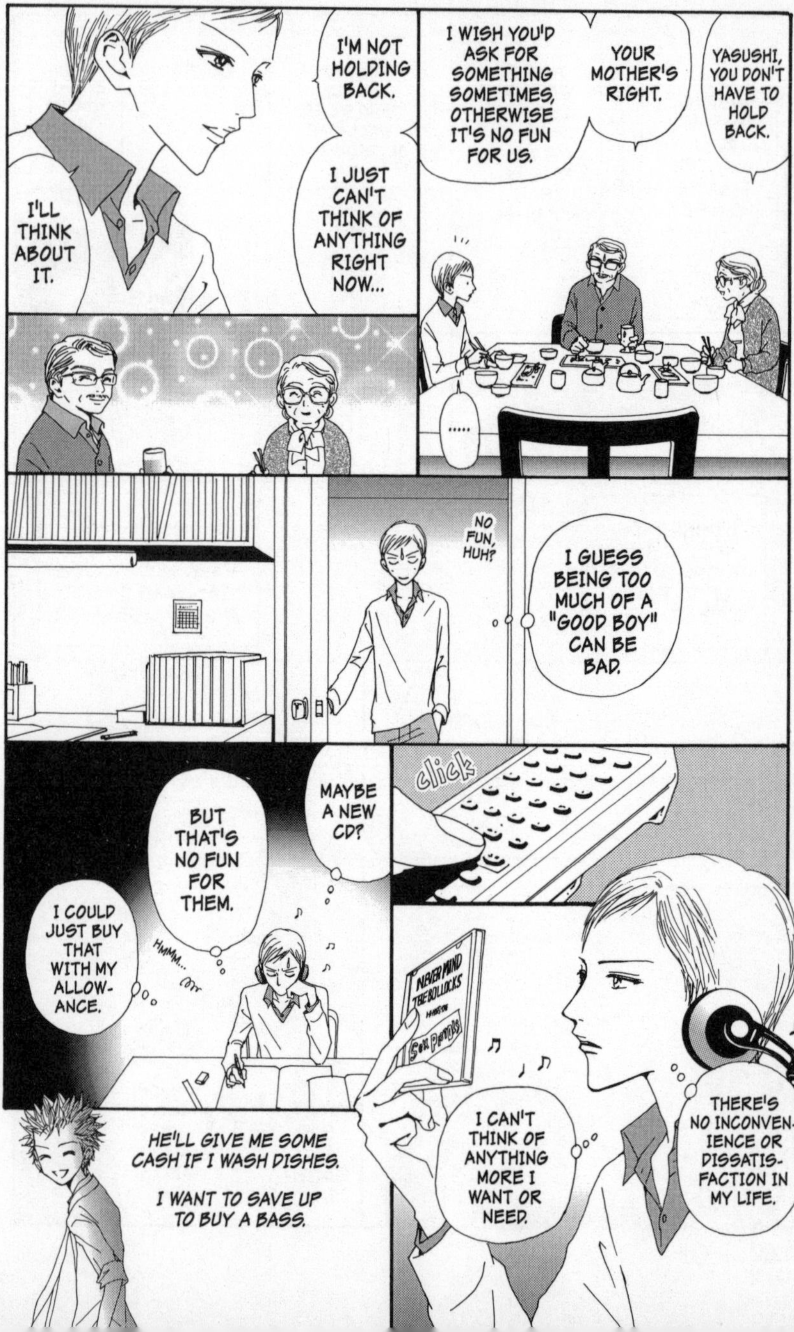
YASUSHI, YOU DON'T HAVE TO HOLD BACK.
YOUR MOTHER'S RIGHT.
I WISH YOU'D ASK FOR SOMETHING SOMETIMES, OTHERWISE IT'S NO FUN FOR US.
......
I'M NOT HOLDING BACK.
I JUST CAN'T THINK OF ANYTHING RIGHT NOW...
I'LL THINK ABOUT IT.
NO FUN, HUH?
I GUESS BEING TOO MUCH OF A "GOOD BOY" CAN BE BAD.
click
NEVER MIND THE BOLLOCKS
SEX PISTOLS
THERE'S NO INCONVENIENCE OR DISSATISFACTION IN MY LIFE.
I CAN'T THINK OF ANYTHING MORE I WANT OR NEED.
MAYBE A NEW CD?
BUT THAT'S NO FUN FOR THEM.
HMMM...
I COULD JUST BUY THAT WITH MY ALLOWANCE.
HE'LL GIVE ME SOME CASH IF I WASH DISHES.
I WANT TO SAVE UP TO BUY A BASS.

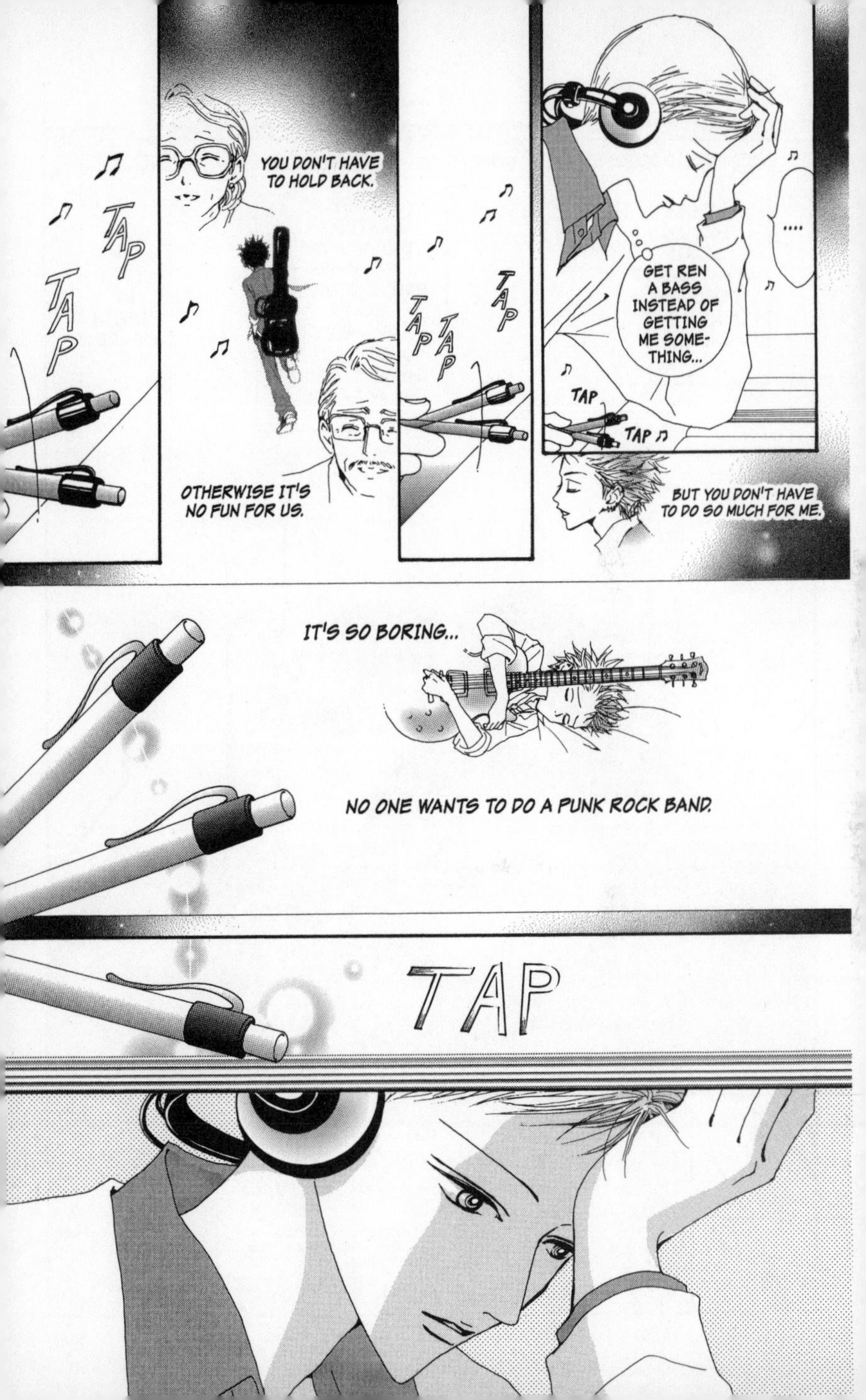
....
GET REN A BASS INSTEAD OF GETTING ME SOMETHING...
TAP
TAP
BUT YOU DON'T HAVE TO DO SO MUCH FOR ME.
TAP
TAP
TAP
YOU DON'T HAVE TO HOLD BACK.
OTHERWISE IT'S NO FUN FOR US.
TAP
TAP
IT'S SO BORING...
NO ONE WANTS TO DO A PUNK ROCK BAND.
TAP

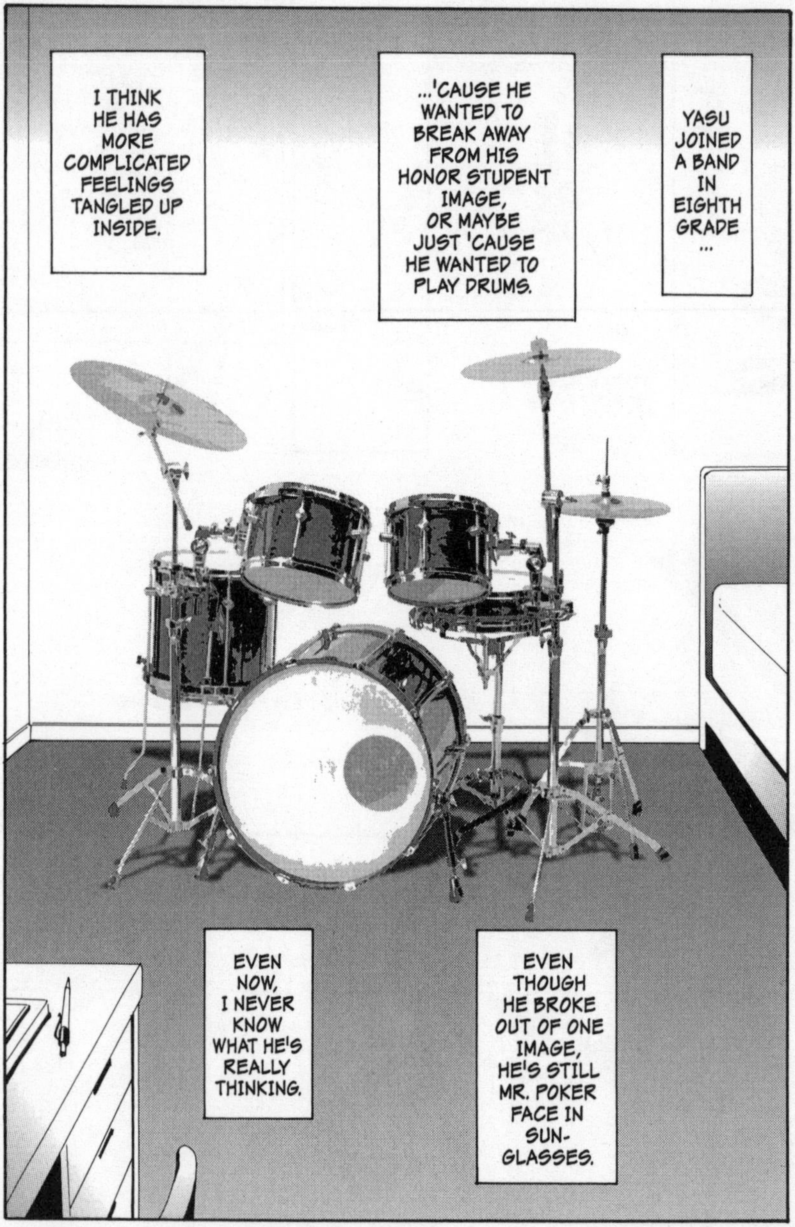
YASU JOINED A BAND IN EIGHTH GRADE ...
...'CAUSE HE WANTED TO BREAK AWAY FROM HIS HONOR STUDENT IMAGE, OR MAYBE JUST 'CAUSE HE WANTED TO PLAY DRUMS.
I THINK HE HAS MORE COMPLICATED FEELINGS TANGLED UP INSIDE.
EVEN THOUGH HE BROKE OUT OF ONE IMAGE, HE'S STILL MR. POKER FACE IN SUN-GLASSES.
EVEN NOW, I NEVER KNOW WHAT HE'S REALLY THINKING.

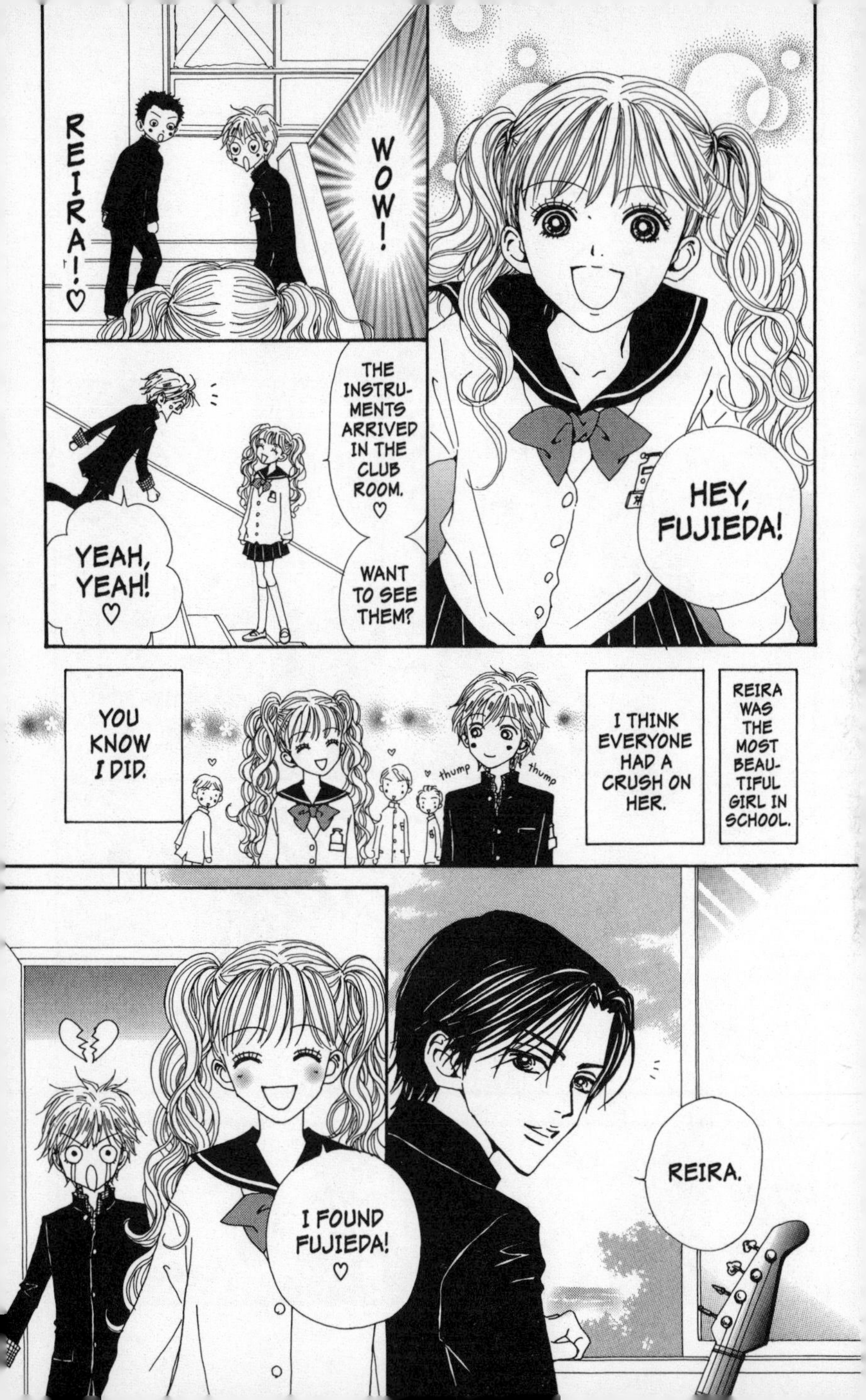
HEY, FUJIEDA!
WOW!
REIRA!♡
THE INSTRUMENTS ARRIVED IN THE CLUB ROOM. ♡
WANT TO SEE THEM?
YEAH, YEAH! ♡
REIRA WAS THE MOST BEAUTIFUL GIRL IN SCHOOL.
I THINK EVERYONE HAD A CRUSH ON HER.
thump thump
YOU KNOW I DID.
REIRA.
I FOUND FUJIEDA! ♡

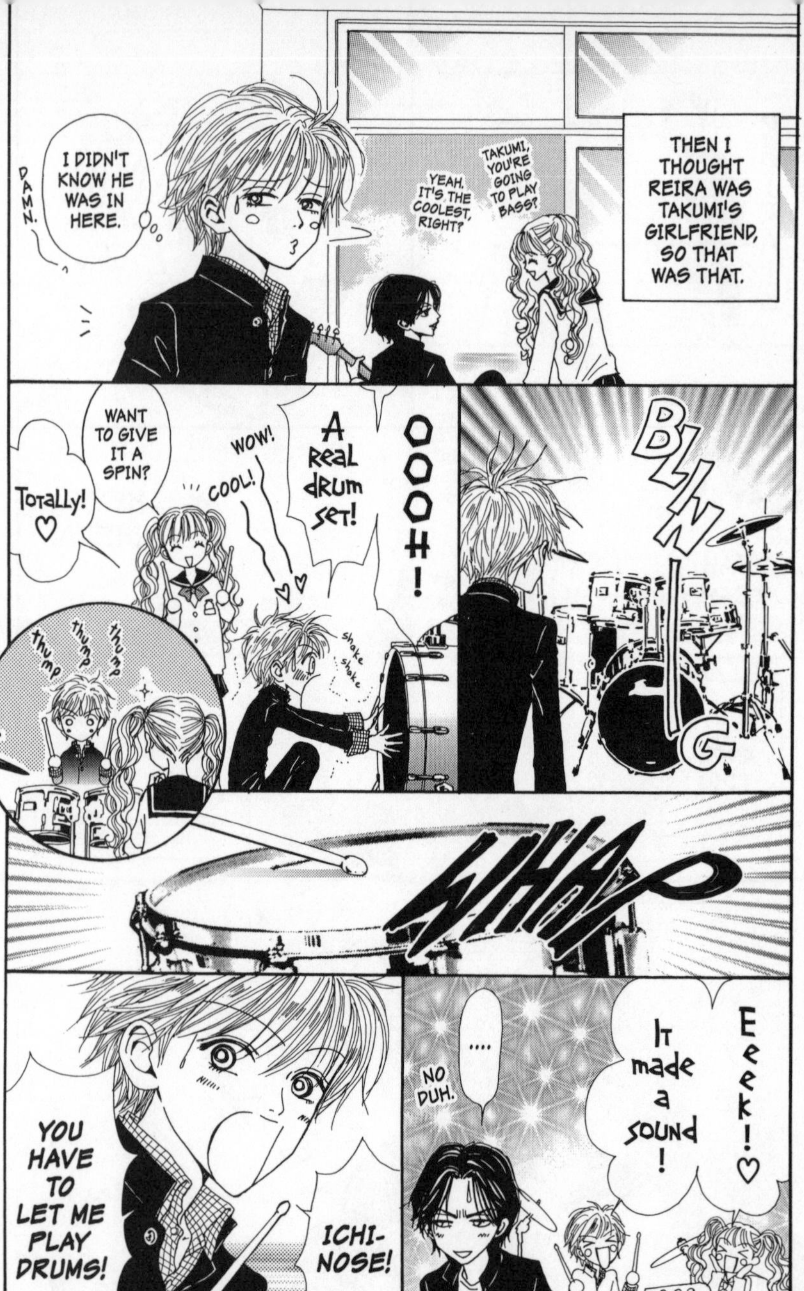
THEN I THOUGHT REIRA WAS TAKUMI'S GIRLFRIEND, SO THAT WAS THAT.
TAKUMI, YOU'RE GOING TO PLAY BASS?
YEAH. IT'S THE COOLEST, RIGHT?
I DIDN'T KNOW HE WAS IN HERE.
DAMN.
BLING
OOOOH!
A real drum set!
WOW!
COOL!
shake shake
WANT TO GIVE IT A SPIN?
Totally! ♡
thump thump thump
WHAP
Eeek! ♡
It made a sound!
....
NO DUH.
ICHI-NOSE!
YOU HAVE TO LET ME PLAY DRUMS!

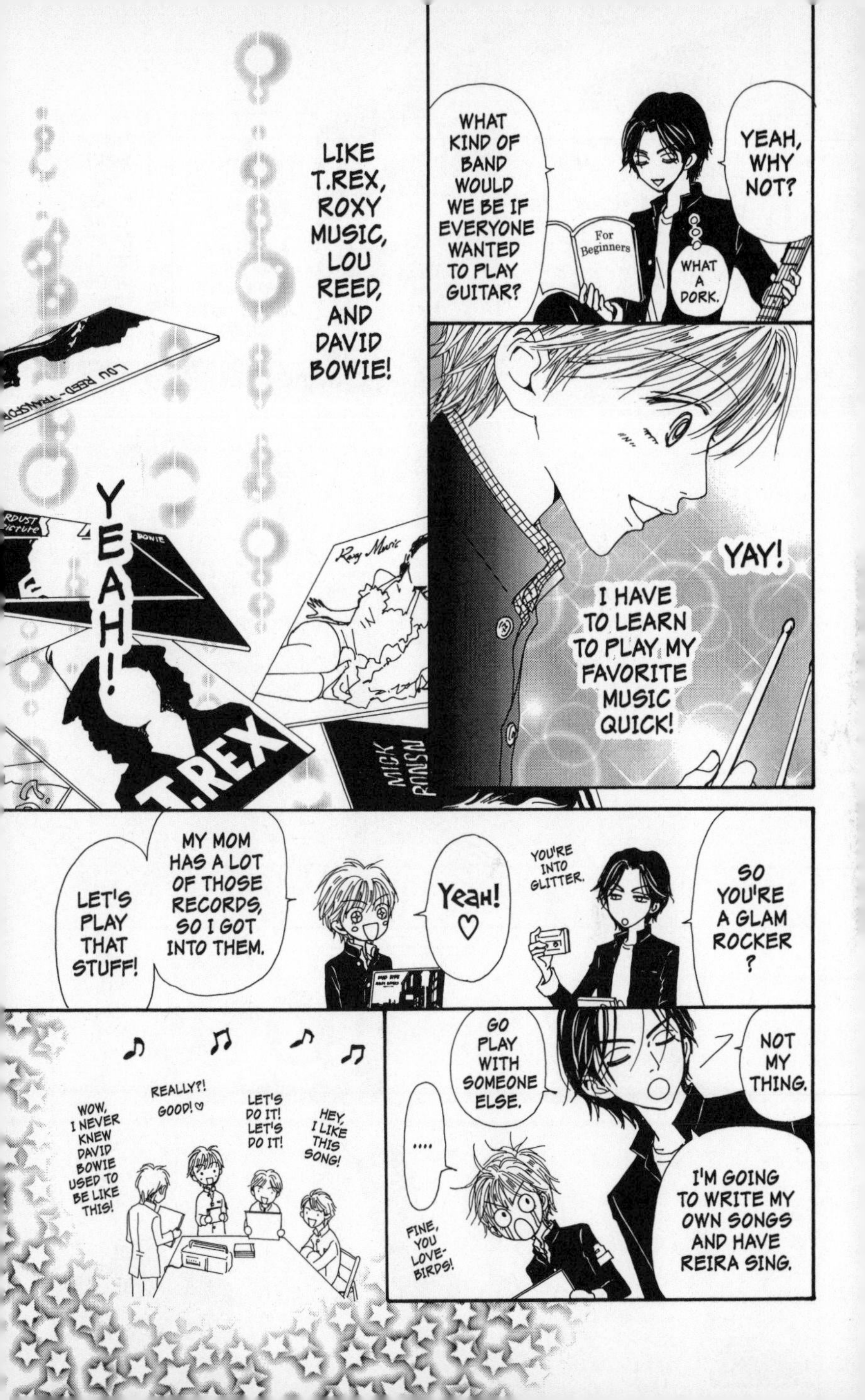
YEAH, WHY NOT?
WHAT KIND OF BAND WOULD WE BE IF EVERYONE WANTED TO PLAY GUITAR?
For Beginners
WHAT A DORK.
YAY!
I HAVE TO LEARN TO PLAY MY FAVORITE MUSIC QUICK!
LIKE T.REX, ROXY MUSIC, LOU REED, AND DAVID BOWIE!
YEAH!
Roxy Music
T.REX
SO YOU'RE A GLAM ROCKER?
YOU'RE INTO GLITTER.
Yeah! ♡
MY MOM HAS A LOT OF THOSE RECORDS, SO I GOT INTO THEM.
LET'S PLAY THAT STUFF!
NOT MY THING.
GO PLAY WITH SOMEONE ELSE.
I'M GOING TO WRITE MY OWN SONGS AND HAVE REIRA SING.
....
FINE, YOU LOVE-BIRDS!
HEY, I LIKE THIS SONG!
LET'S DO IT! LET'S DO IT!
REALLY?! GOOD! ♡
WOW, I NEVER KNEW DAVID BOWIE USED TO BE LIKE THIS!

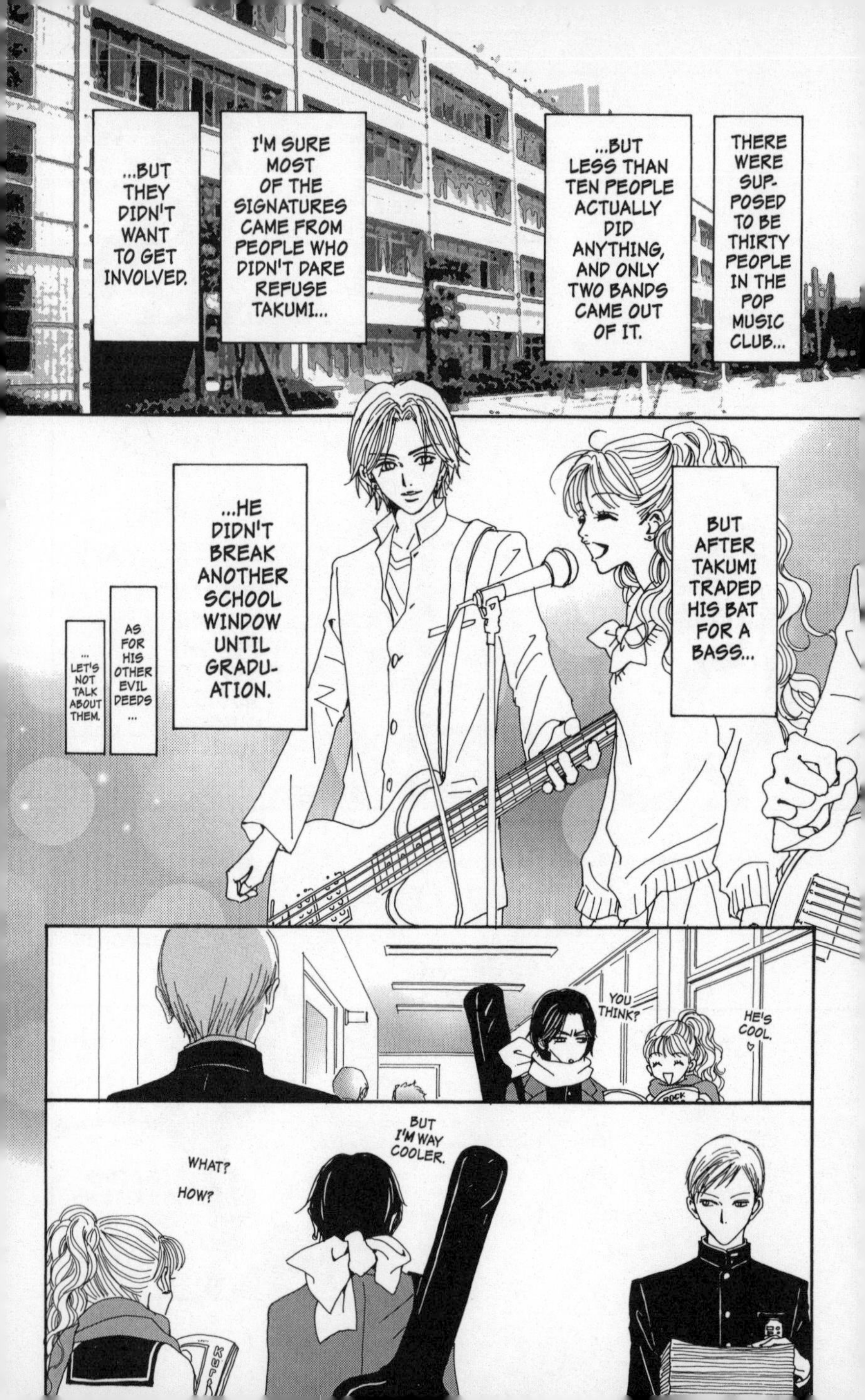
THERE WERE SUP-POSED TO BE THIRTY PEOPLE IN THE POP MUSIC CLUB...
...BUT LESS THAN TEN PEOPLE ACTUALLY DID ANYTHING, AND ONLY TWO BANDS CAME OUT OF IT.
I'M SURE MOST OF THE SIGNATURES CAME FROM PEOPLE WHO DIDN'T DARE REFUSE TAKUMI...
...BUT THEY DIDN'T WANT TO GET INVOLVED.
BUT AFTER TAKUMI TRADED HIS BAT FOR A BASS...
...HE DIDN'T BREAK ANOTHER SCHOOL WINDOW UNTIL GRADU-ATION.
AS FOR HIS OTHER EVIL DEEDS...
...LET'S NOT TALK ABOUT THEM.
HE'S COOL.
YOU THINK?
BUT I'M WAY COOLER.
WHAT?
HOW?

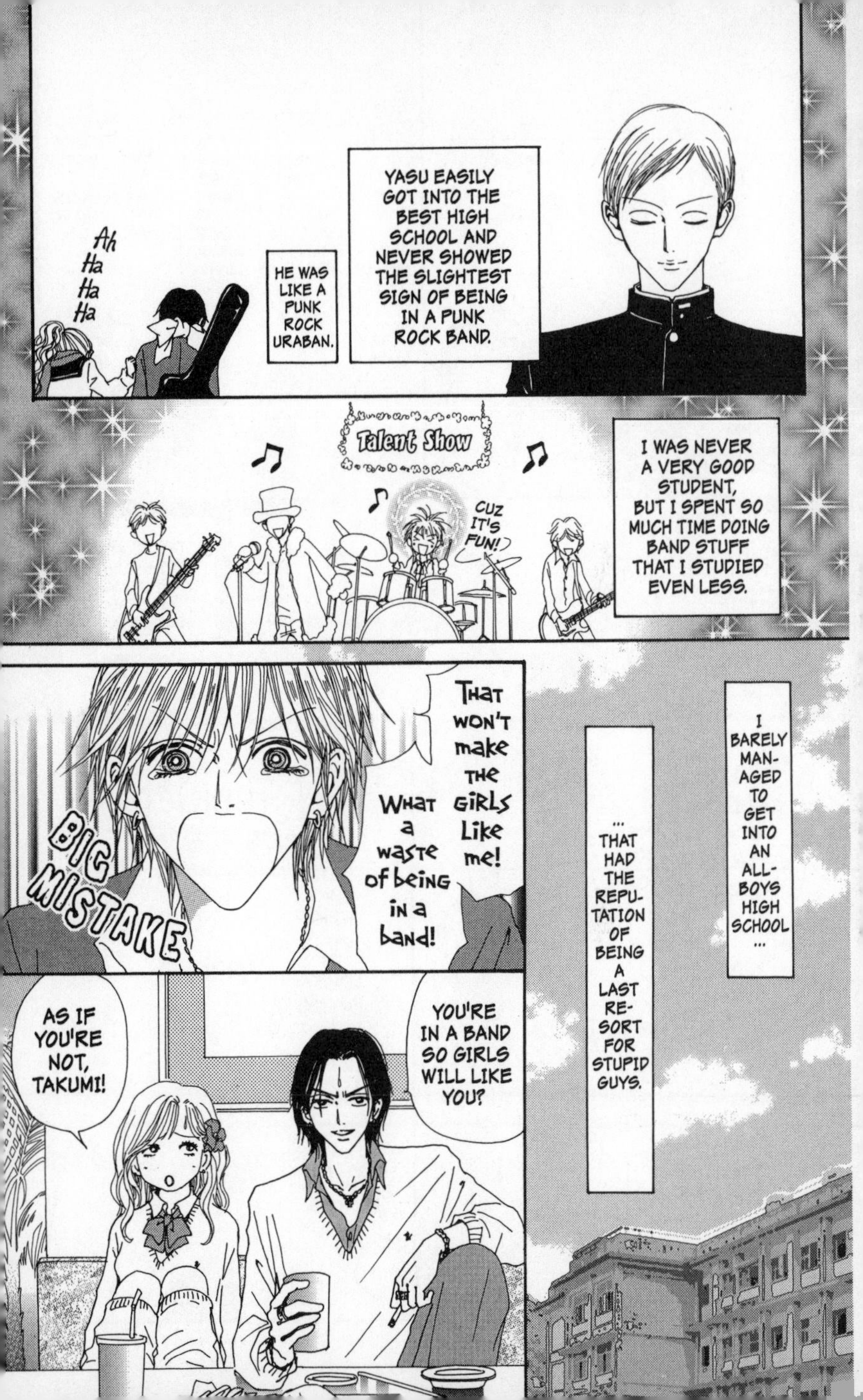
YASU EASILY GOT INTO THE BEST HIGH SCHOOL AND NEVER SHOWED THE SLIGHTEST SIGN OF BEING IN A PUNK ROCK BAND.
HE WAS LIKE A PUNK ROCK URABAN.
Ah Ha Ha Ha
I WAS NEVER A VERY GOOD STUDENT, BUT I SPENT SO MUCH TIME DOING BAND STUFF THAT I STUDIED EVEN LESS.
Talent Show
CUZ IT'S FUN!
I BARELY MAN-AGED TO GET INTO AN ALL-BOYS HIGH SCHOOL ...
... THAT HAD THE REPU-TATION OF BEING A LAST RE-SORT FOR STUPID GUYS.
That won't make the girls like me!
What a waste of being in a band!
BIG MISTAKE
YOU'RE IN A BAND SO GIRLS WILL LIKE YOU?
AS IF YOU'RE NOT, TAKUMI!

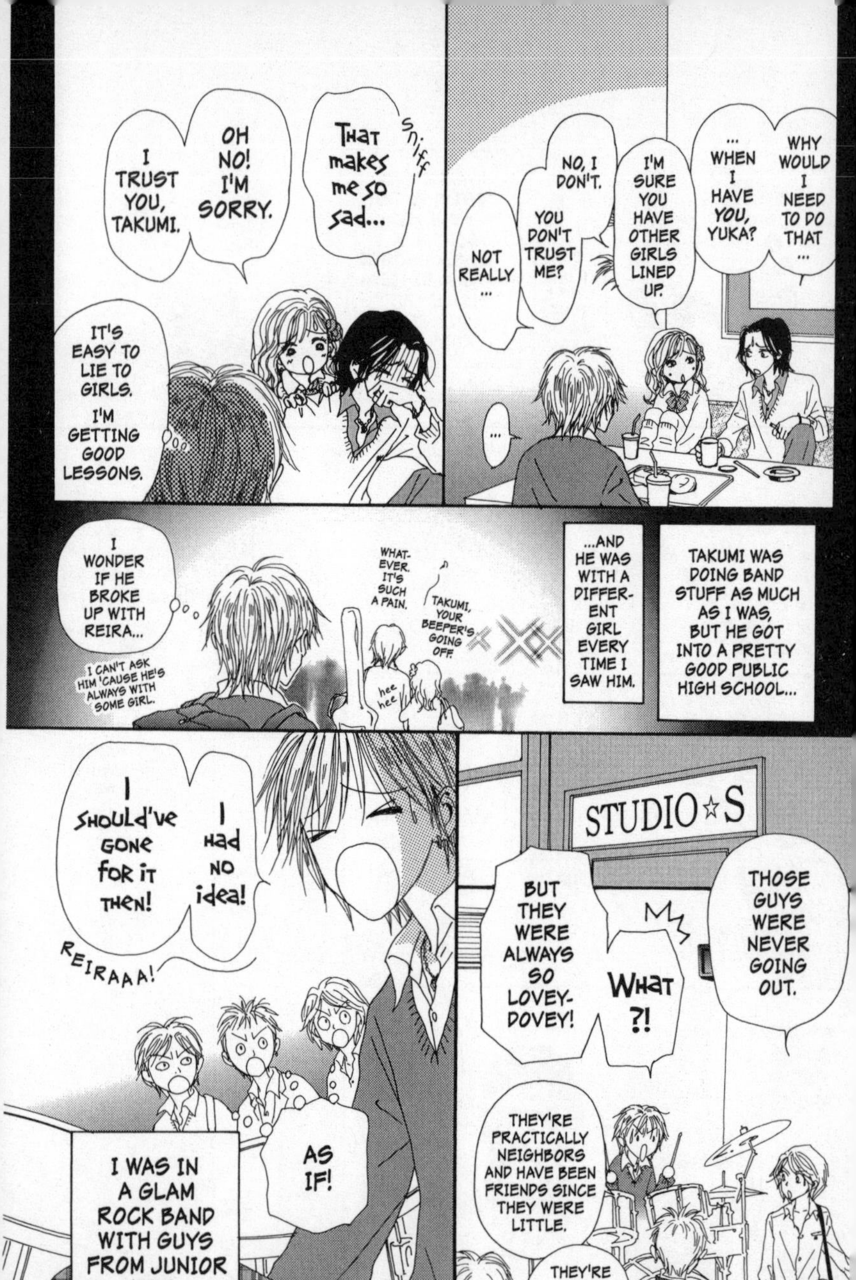
WHY WOULD I NEED TO DO THAT...
...WHEN I HAVE YOU, YUKA?
I'M SURE YOU HAVE OTHER GIRLS LINED UP.
NO, I DON'T.
YOU DON'T TRUST ME?
NOT REALLY...
...
sniff
That makes me so sad...
OH NO! I'M SORRY.
I TRUST YOU, TAKUMI.
IT'S EASY TO LIE TO GIRLS.
I'M GETTING GOOD LESSONS.
TAKUMI WAS DOING BAND STUFF AS MUCH AS I WAS, BUT HE GOT INTO A PRETTY GOOD PUBLIC HIGH SCHOOL...
...AND HE WAS WITH A DIFFERENT GIRL EVERY TIME I SAW HIM.
TAKUMI, YOUR BEEPER'S GOING OFF.
WHATEVER. IT'S SUCH A PAIN.
hee hee
I WONDER IF HE BROKE UP WITH REIRA...
I CAN'T ASK HIM 'CAUSE HE'S ALWAYS WITH SOME GIRL.
STUDIO☆S
THOSE GUYS WERE NEVER GOING OUT.
WHAT?!
BUT THEY WERE ALWAYS SO LOVEY-DOVEY!
THEY'RE PRACTICALLY NEIGHBORS AND HAVE BEEN FRIENDS SINCE THEY WERE LITTLE.
THEY'RE LIKE BROTHER AND SISTER.
I had no idea!
I should've gone for it then!
REIRAAA!
AS IF!
I WAS IN A GLAM ROCK BAND WITH GUYS FROM JUNIOR HIGH...

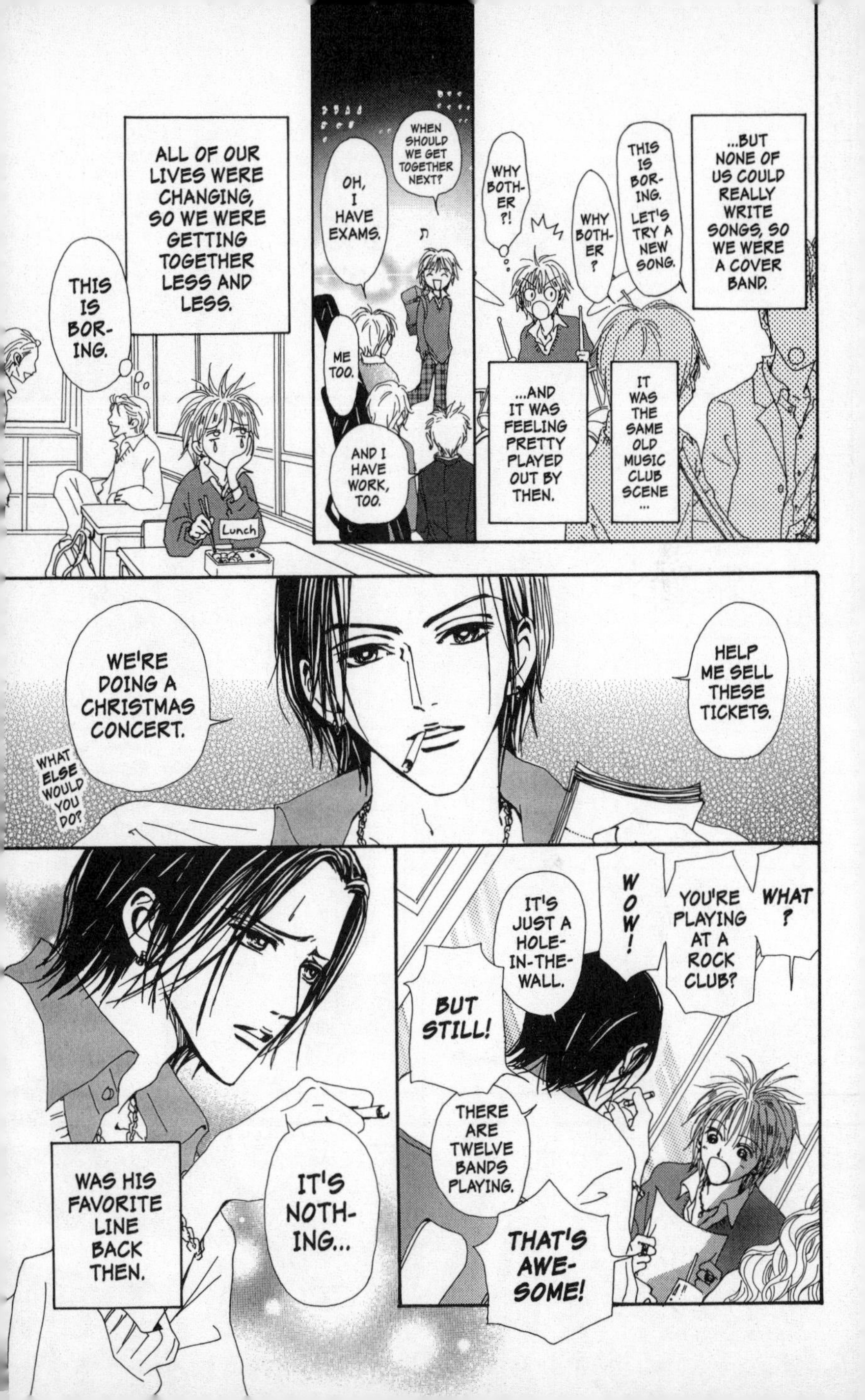
...BUT NONE OF US COULD REALLY WRITE SONGS, SO WE WERE A COVER BAND.
THIS IS BOR-ING. LET'S TRY A NEW SONG.
WHY BOTHER?
WHY BOTHER?!
IT WAS THE SAME OLD MUSIC CLUB SCENE...
...AND IT WAS FEELING PRETTY PLAYED OUT BY THEN.
WHEN SHOULD WE GET TOGETHER NEXT?
OH, I HAVE EXAMS.
ME TOO.
AND I HAVE WORK, TOO.
ALL OF OUR LIVES WERE CHANGING, SO WE WERE GETTING TOGETHER LESS AND LESS.
THIS IS BOR-ING.
Lunch
HELP ME SELL THESE TICKETS.
WE'RE DOING A CHRISTMAS CONCERT.
WHAT ELSE WOULD YOU DO?
WHAT?
YOU'RE PLAYING AT A ROCK CLUB?
WOW!
IT'S JUST A HOLE-IN-THE-WALL.
BUT STILL!
THERE ARE TWELVE BANDS PLAYING.
THAT'S AWE-SOME!
IT'S NOTH-ING...
WAS HIS FAVORITE LINE BACK THEN.

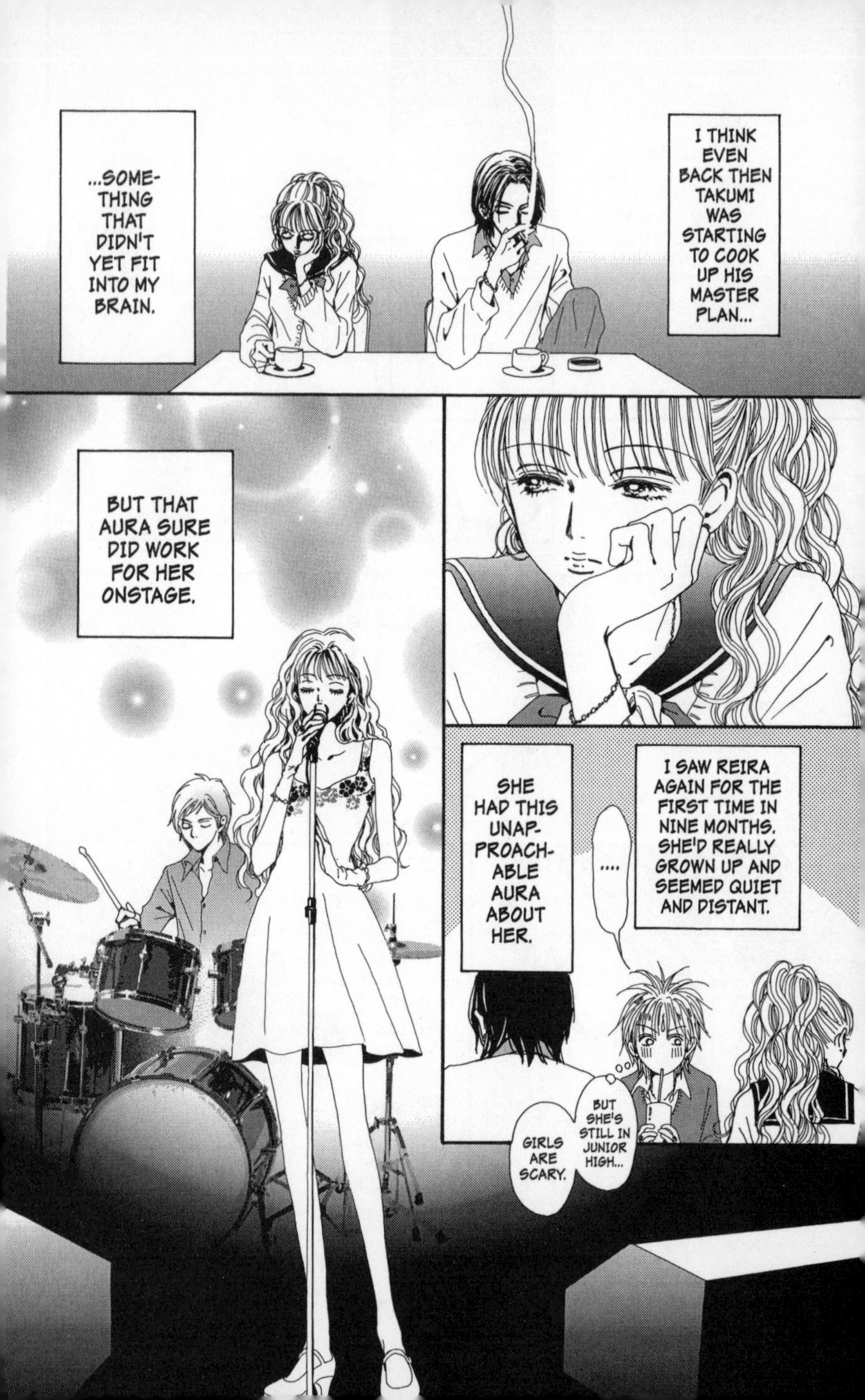
I THINK EVEN BACK THEN TAKUMI WAS STARTING TO COOK UP HIS MASTER PLAN...
...SOME-THING THAT DIDN'T YET FIT INTO MY BRAIN.
I SAW REIRA AGAIN FOR THE FIRST TIME IN NINE MONTHS. SHE'D REALLY GROWN UP AND SEEMED QUIET AND DISTANT.
....
SHE HAD THIS UNAP-PROACH-ABLE AURA ABOUT HER.
BUT SHE'S STILL IN JUNIOR HIGH...
GIRLS ARE SCARY.
BUT THAT AURA SURE DID WORK FOR HER ONSTAGE.

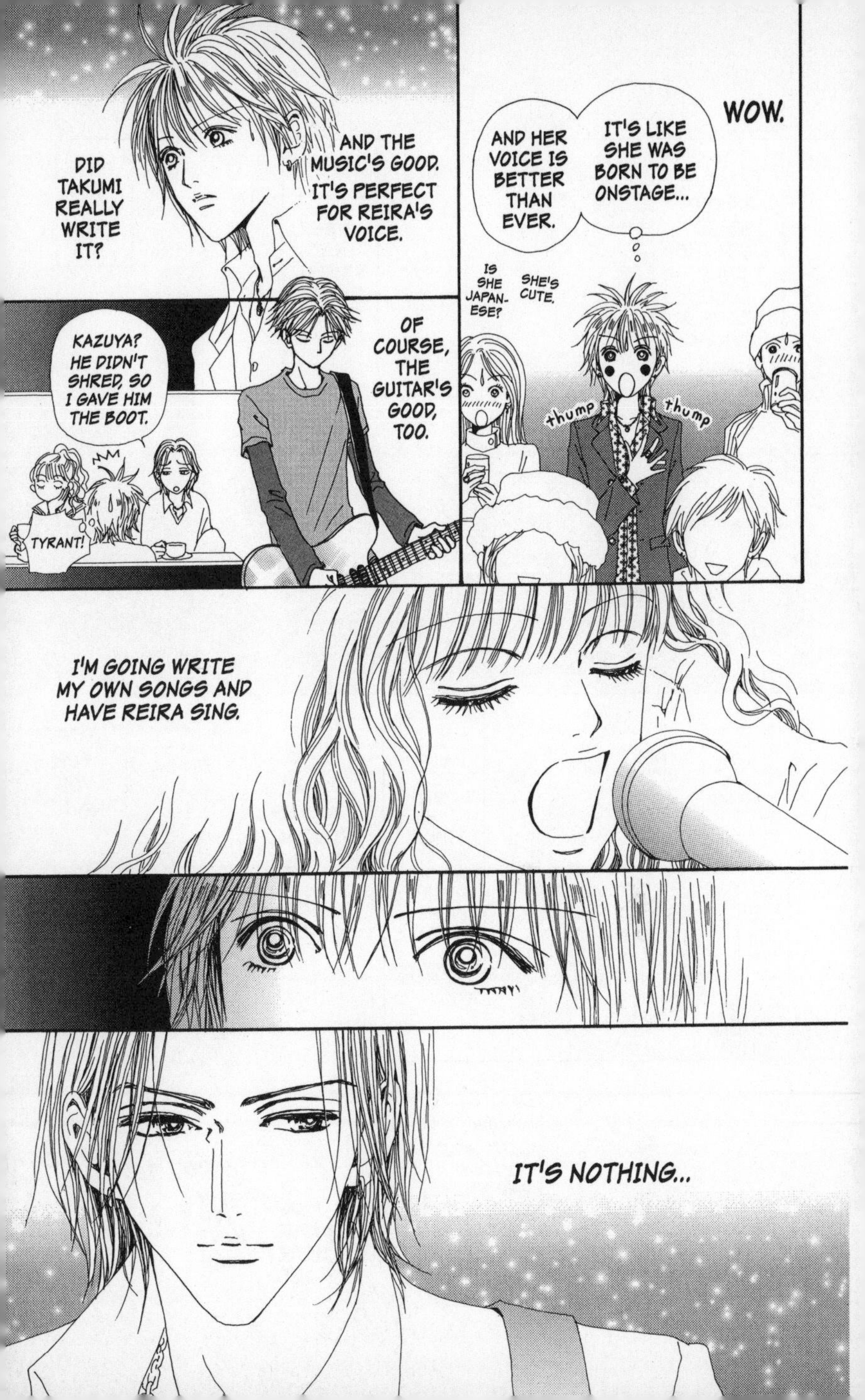
WOW.
IT'S LIKE SHE WAS BORN TO BE ONSTAGE...
AND HER VOICE IS BETTER THAN EVER.
SHE'S CUTE.
IS SHE JAPAN-ESE?
thump thump
AND THE MUSIC'S GOOD. IT'S PERFECT FOR REIRA'S VOICE.
DID TAKUMI REALLY WRITE IT?
OF COURSE, THE GUITAR'S GOOD, TOO.
KAZUYA? HE DIDN'T SHRED, SO I GAVE HIM THE BOOT.
TYRANT!
I'M GOING WRITE MY OWN SONGS AND HAVE REIRA SING.
IT'S NOTHING...

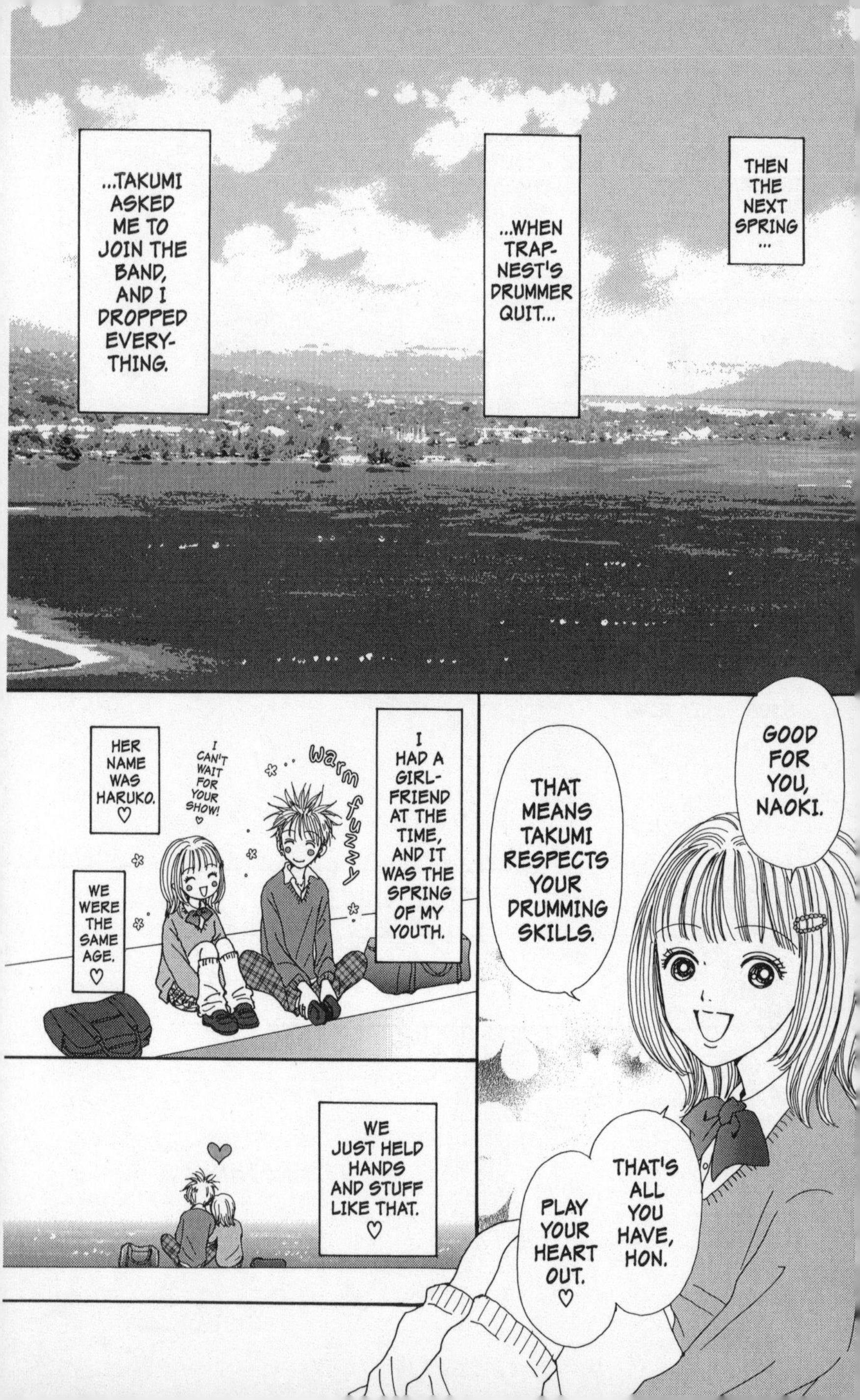
THEN THE NEXT SPRING...
...WHEN TRAP-NEST'S DRUMMER QUIT...
...TAKUMI ASKED ME TO JOIN THE BAND, AND I DROPPED EVERY-THING.
GOOD FOR YOU, NAOKI.
THAT MEANS TAKUMI RESPECTS YOUR DRUMMING SKILLS.
THAT'S ALL YOU HAVE, HON.
PLAY YOUR HEART OUT. ♡
I HAD A GIRL-FRIEND AT THE TIME, AND IT WAS THE SPRING OF MY YOUTH.
warm fuzzy
I CAN'T WAIT FOR YOUR SHOW! ♡
HER NAME WAS HARUKO. ♡
WE WERE THE SAME AGE. ♡
WE JUST HELD HANDS AND STUFF LIKE THAT. ♡

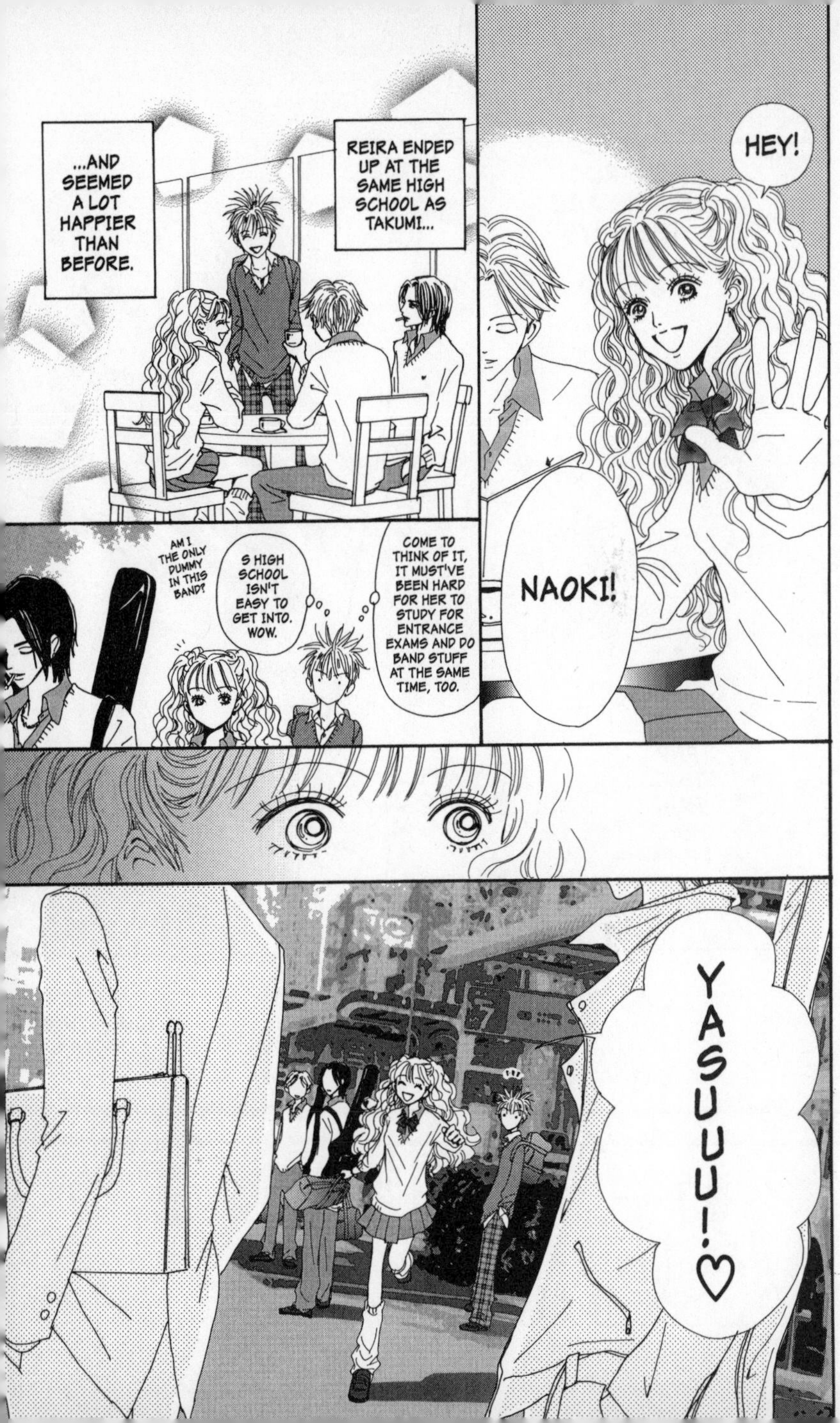
HEY!
NAOKI!
REIRA ENDED UP AT THE SAME HIGH SCHOOL AS TAKUMI...
...AND SEEMED A LOT HAPPIER THAN BEFORE.
COME TO THINK OF IT, IT MUST'VE BEEN HARD FOR HER TO STUDY FOR ENTRANCE EXAMS AND DO BAND STUFF AT THE SAME TIME, TOO.
S HIGH SCHOOL ISN'T EASY TO GET INTO. WOW.
AM I THE ONLY DUMMY IN THIS BAND?
YASUUU!♡

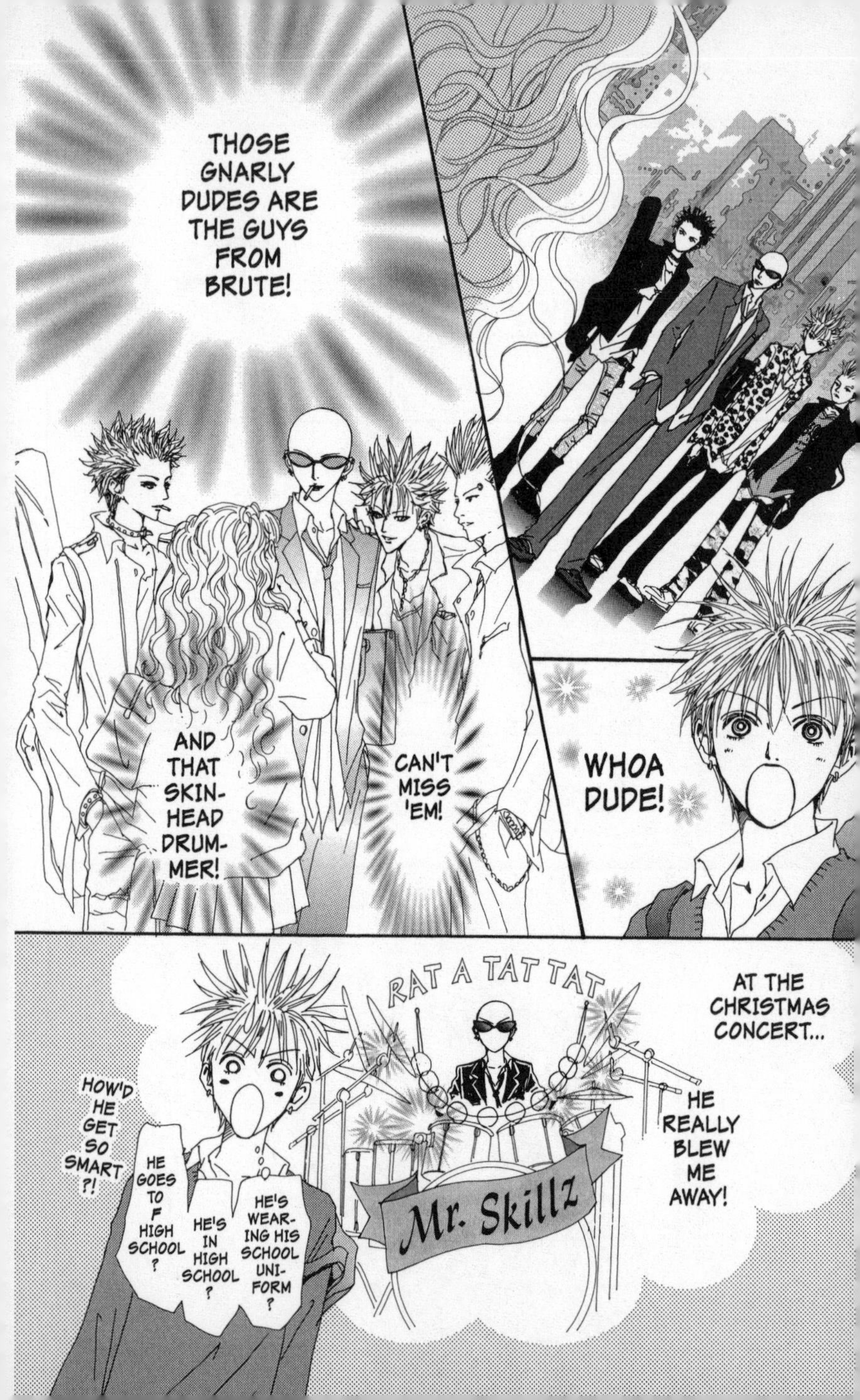
WHOA DUDE!
THOSE GNARLY DUDES ARE THE GUYS FROM BRUTE!
CAN'T MISS 'EM!
AND THAT SKIN-HEAD DRUM-MER!
AT THE CHRISTMAS CONCERT...
RAT A TAT TAT
HE REALLY BLEW ME AWAY!
Mr. Skillz
HE'S WEAR-ING HIS SCHOOL UNI-FORM?
HE'S IN HIGH SCHOOL?
HE GOES TO F HIGH SCHOOL?
HOW'D HE GET SO SMART?!

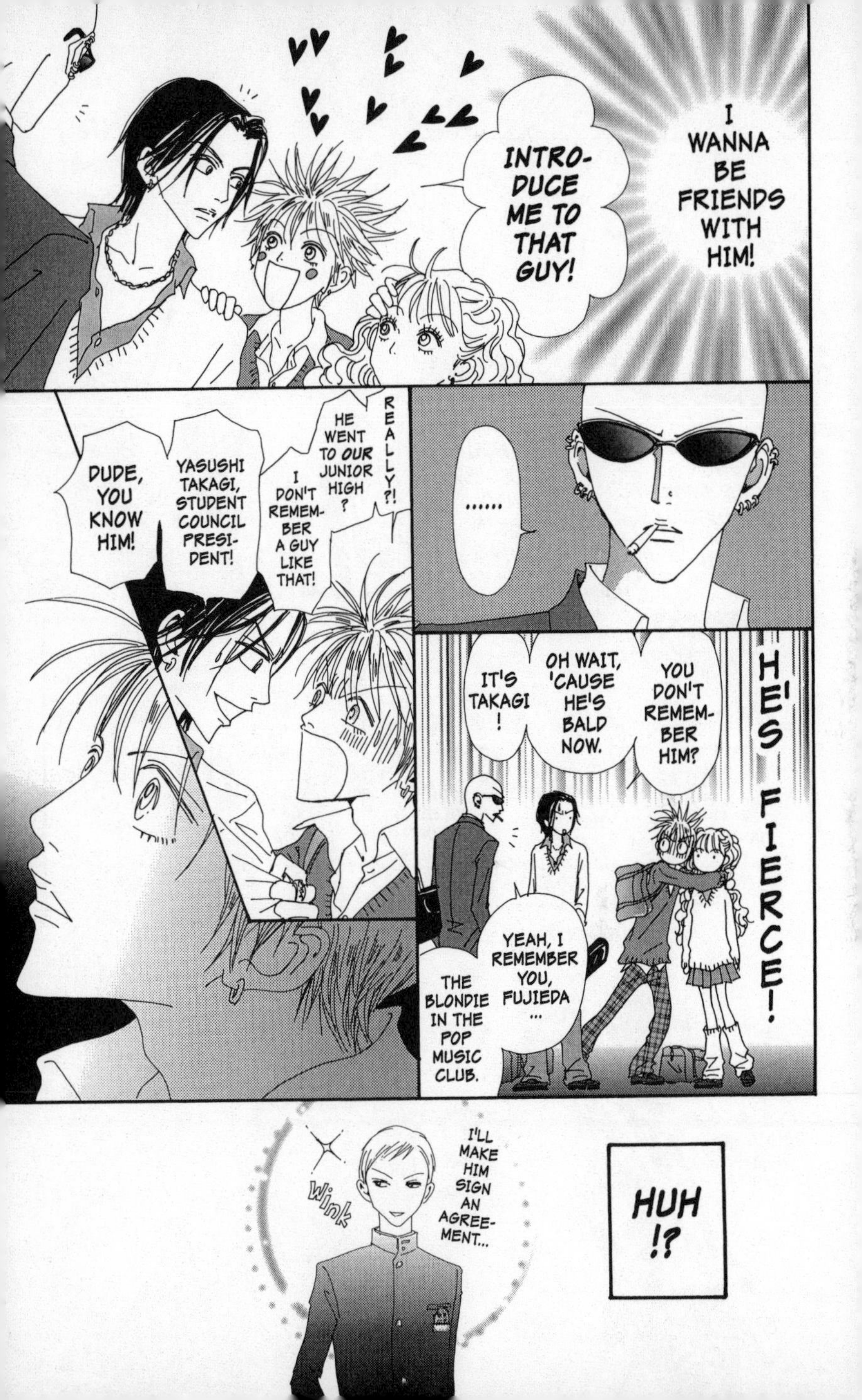
I WANNA BE FRIENDS WITH HIM!
INTRO-DUCE ME TO THAT GUY!
......
HE'S FIERCE!
YOU DON'T REMEM-BER HIM?
OH WAIT, 'CAUSE HE'S BALD NOW.
IT'S TAKAGI!
YEAH, I REMEMBER YOU, FUJIEDA...
THE BLONDIE IN THE POP MUSIC CLUB.
REALLY?!
HE WENT TO OUR JUNIOR HIGH?
I DON'T REMEM-BER A GUY LIKE THAT!
YASUSHI TAKAGI, STUDENT COUNCIL PRESI-DENT!
DUDE, YOU KNOW HIM!
HUH!?
Wink
I'LL MAKE HIM SIGN AN AGREE-MENT...

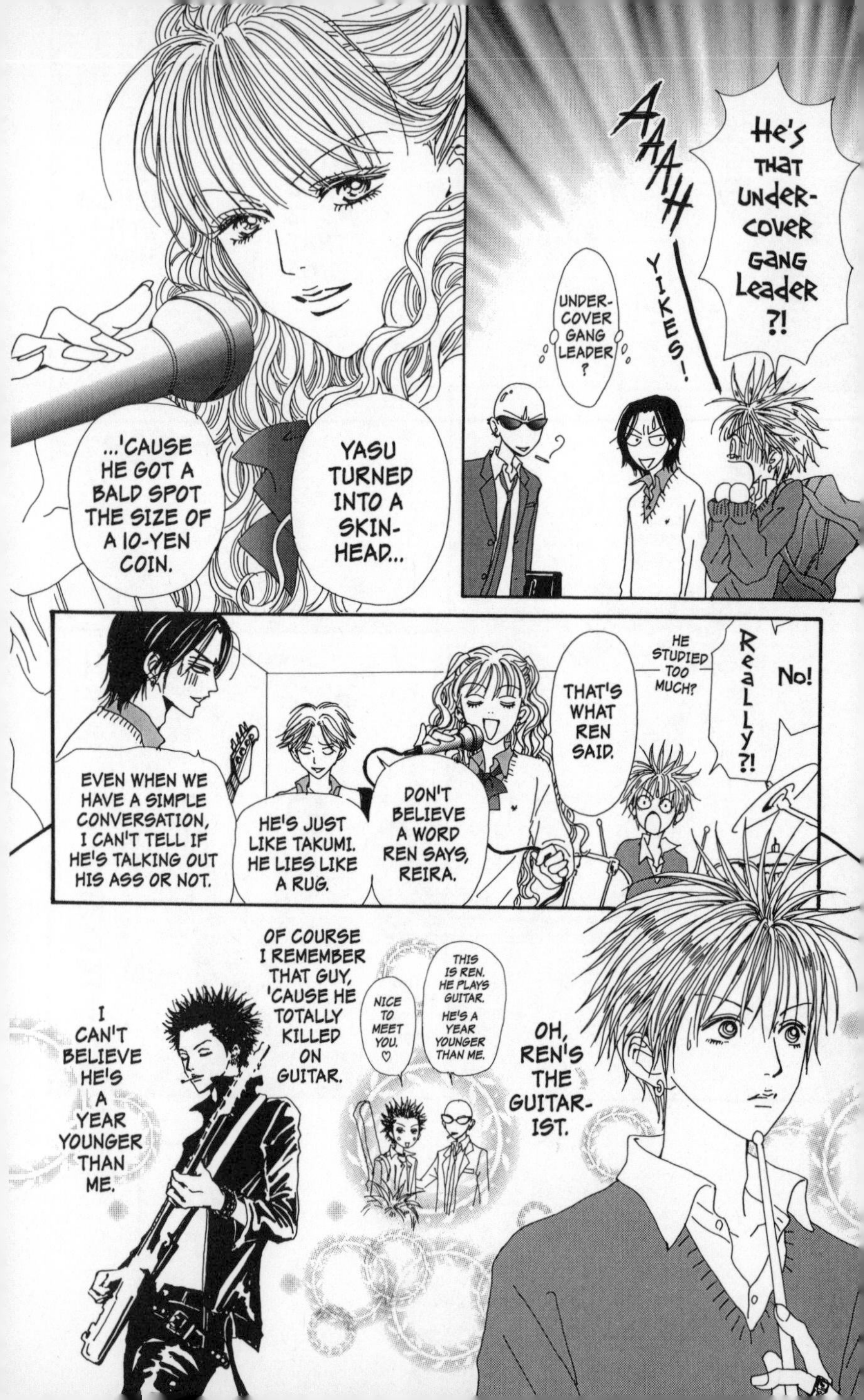
He's that under-cover gang Leader?!
AAAHH
YIKES!
UNDER-COVER GANG LEADER?
YASU TURNED INTO A SKIN-HEAD...
...'CAUSE HE GOT A BALD SPOT THE SIZE OF A 10-YEN COIN.
No!
Really?!
HE STUDIED TOO MUCH?
THAT'S WHAT REN SAID.
DON'T BELIEVE A WORD REN SAYS, REIRA.
HE'S JUST LIKE TAKUMI. HE LIES LIKE A RUG.
EVEN WHEN WE HAVE A SIMPLE CONVERSATION, I CAN'T TELL IF HE'S TALKING OUT HIS ASS OR NOT.
OH, REN'S THE GUITAR-IST.
THIS IS REN. HE PLAYS GUITAR. HE'S A YEAR YOUNGER THAN ME.
NICE TO MEET YOU. ♡
OF COURSE I REMEMBER THAT GUY, 'CAUSE HE TOTALLY KILLED ON GUITAR.
I CAN'T BELIEVE HE'S A YEAR YOUNGER THAN ME.

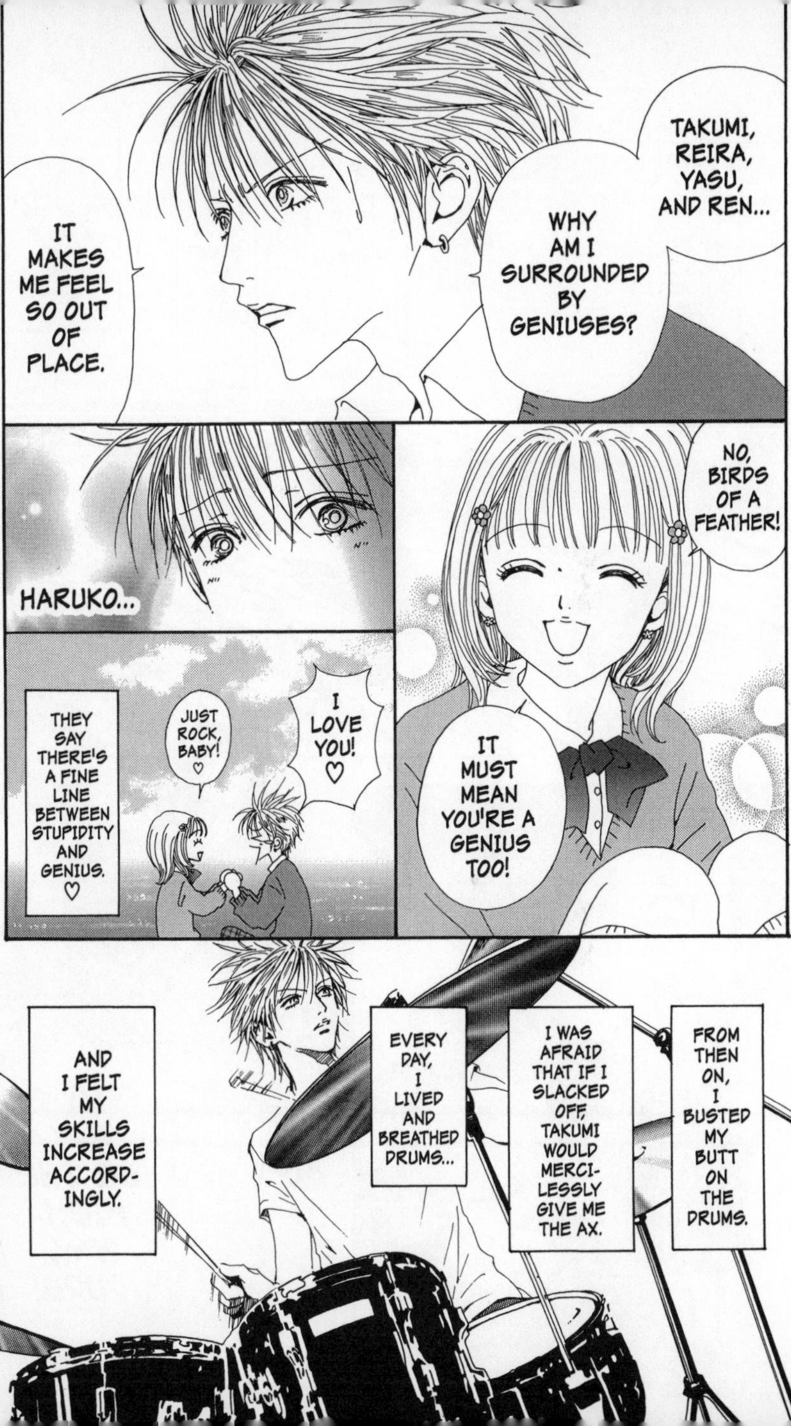
TAKUMI, REIRA, YASU, AND REN...
WHY AM I SURROUNDED BY GENIUSES?
IT MAKES ME FEEL SO OUT OF PLACE.
NO, BIRDS OF A FEATHER!
IT MUST MEAN YOU'RE A GENIUS TOO!
HARUKO...
I LOVE YOU! ♡
JUST ROCK, BABY! ♡
THEY SAY THERE'S A FINE LINE BETWEEN STUPIDITY AND GENIUS. ♡
FROM THEN ON, I BUSTED MY BUTT ON THE DRUMS.
I WAS AFRAID THAT IF I SLACKED OFF, TAKUMI WOULD MERCILESSLY GIVE ME THE AX.
EVERY DAY, I LIVED AND BREATHED DRUMS...
AND I FELT MY SKILLS INCREASE ACCORDINGLY.

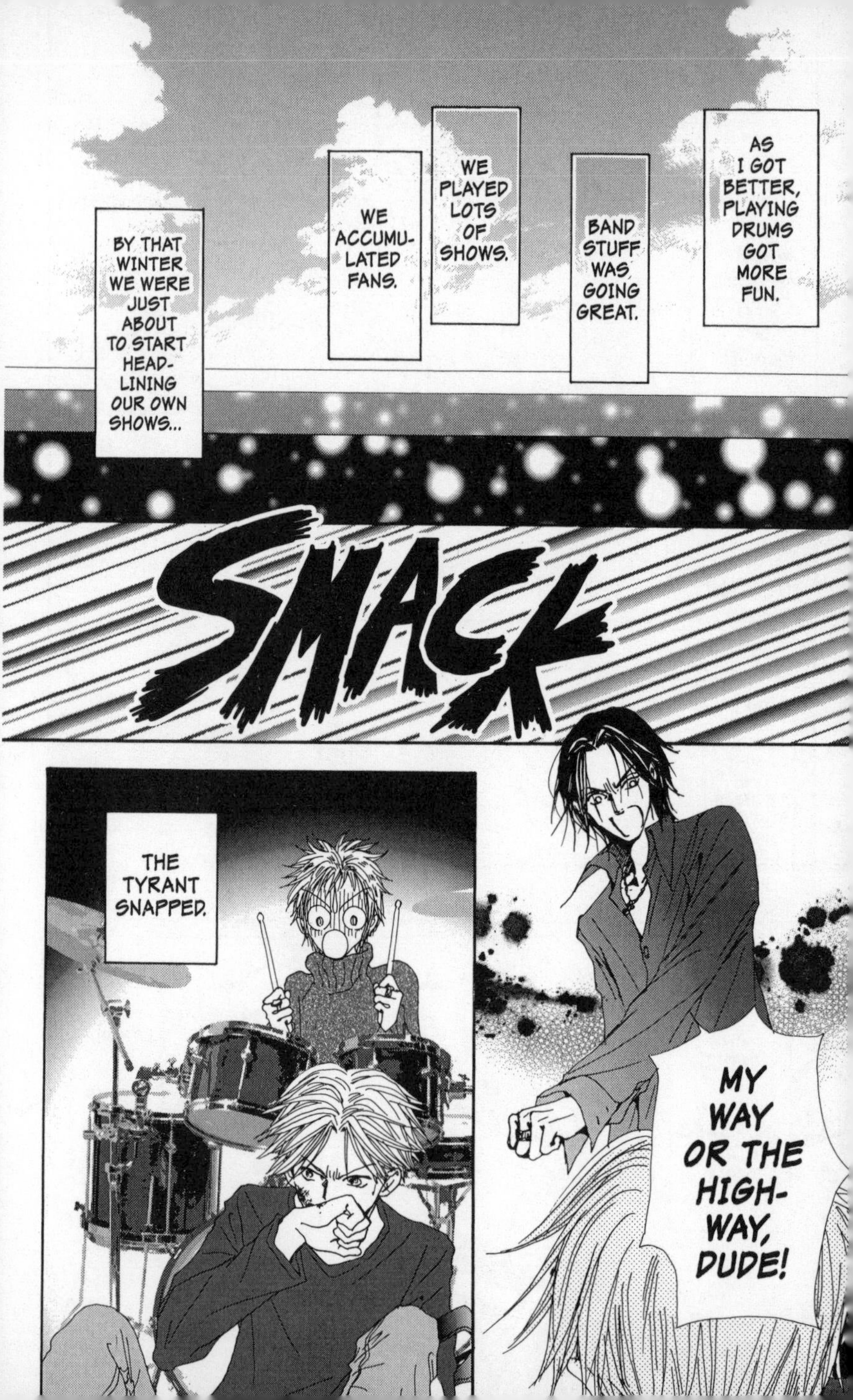
AS I GOT BETTER, PLAYING DRUMS GOT MORE FUN.
BAND STUFF WAS GOING GREAT.
WE PLAYED LOTS OF SHOWS.
WE ACCUMULATED FANS.
BY THAT WINTER WE WERE JUST ABOUT TO START HEAD-LINING OUR OWN SHOWS...
SMACK
MY WAY OR THE HIGH-WAY, DUDE!
THE TYRANT SNAPPED.

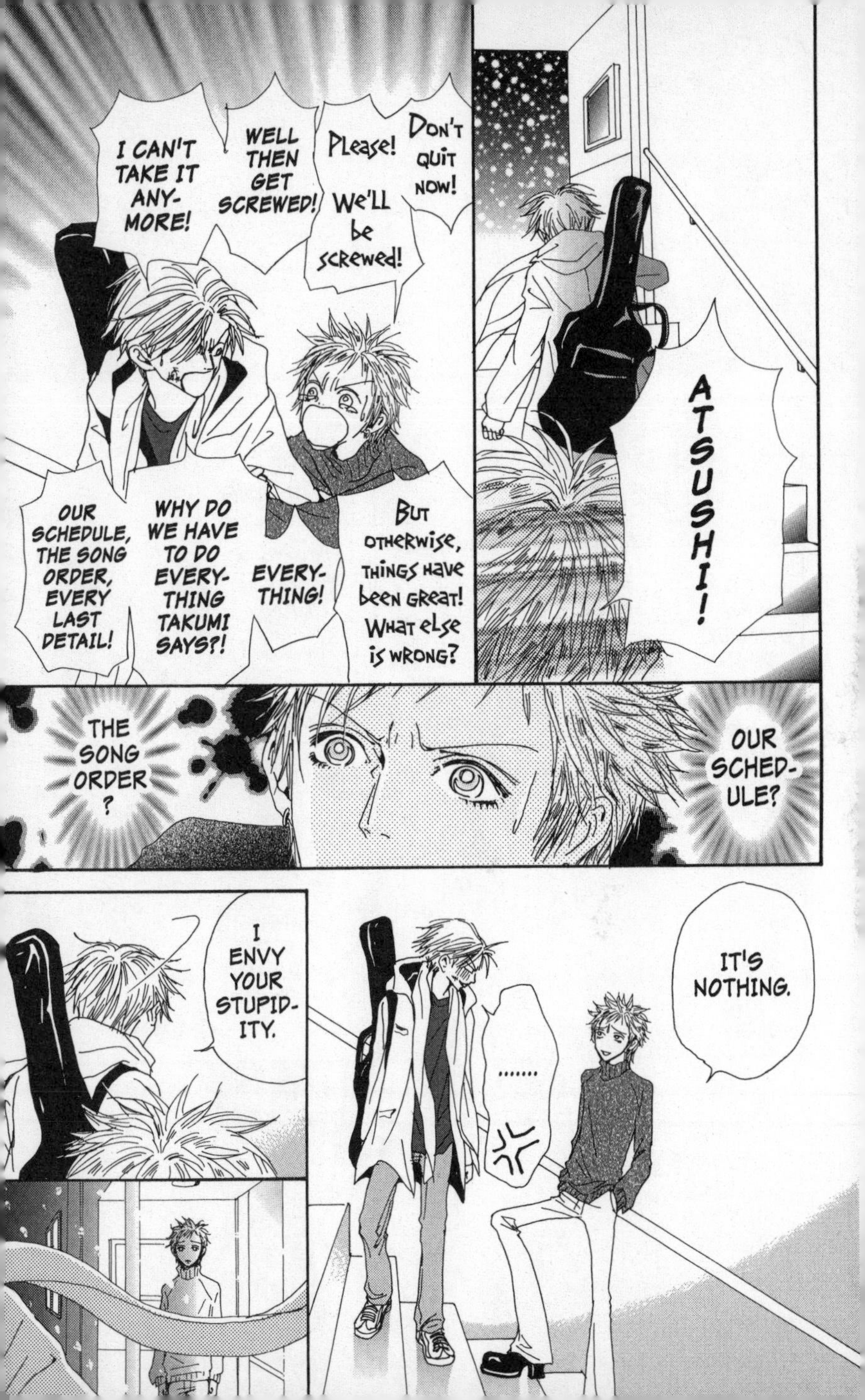
ATSUSHI!
Don't quit now!
Please! We'll be screwed!
WELL THEN GET SCREWED!
I CAN'T TAKE IT ANYMORE!
But otherwise, things have been great! What else is wrong?
EVERYTHING!
WHY DO WE HAVE TO DO EVERYTHING TAKUMI SAYS?!
OUR SCHEDULE, THE SONG ORDER, EVERY LAST DETAIL!
OUR SCHEDULE?
THE SONG ORDER?
IT'S NOTHING.
....
I ENVY YOUR STUPIDITY.

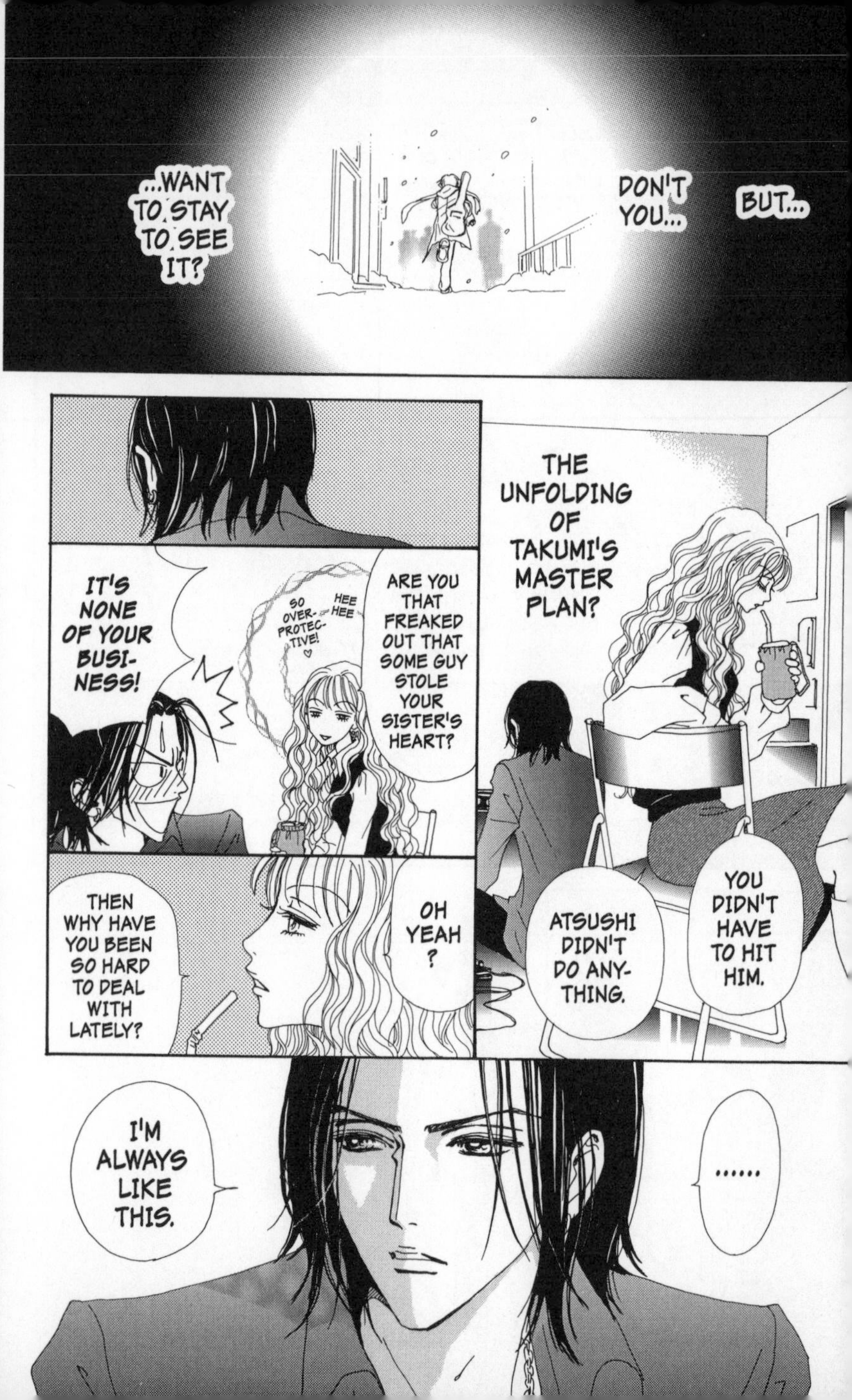
BUT...
DON'T YOU...
...WANT TO STAY TO SEE IT?
THE UNFOLDING OF TAKUMI'S MASTER PLAN?
YOU DIDN'T HAVE TO HIT HIM.
ATSUSHI DIDN'T DO ANYTHING.
ARE YOU THAT FREAKED OUT THAT SOME GUY STOLE YOUR SISTER'S HEART?
HEE HEE
SO OVER-PROTEC-TIVE! ♡
IT'S NONE OF YOUR BUSI-NESS!
OH YEAH?
THEN WHY HAVE YOU BEEN SO HARD TO DEAL WITH LATELY?
......
I'M ALWAYS LIKE THIS.

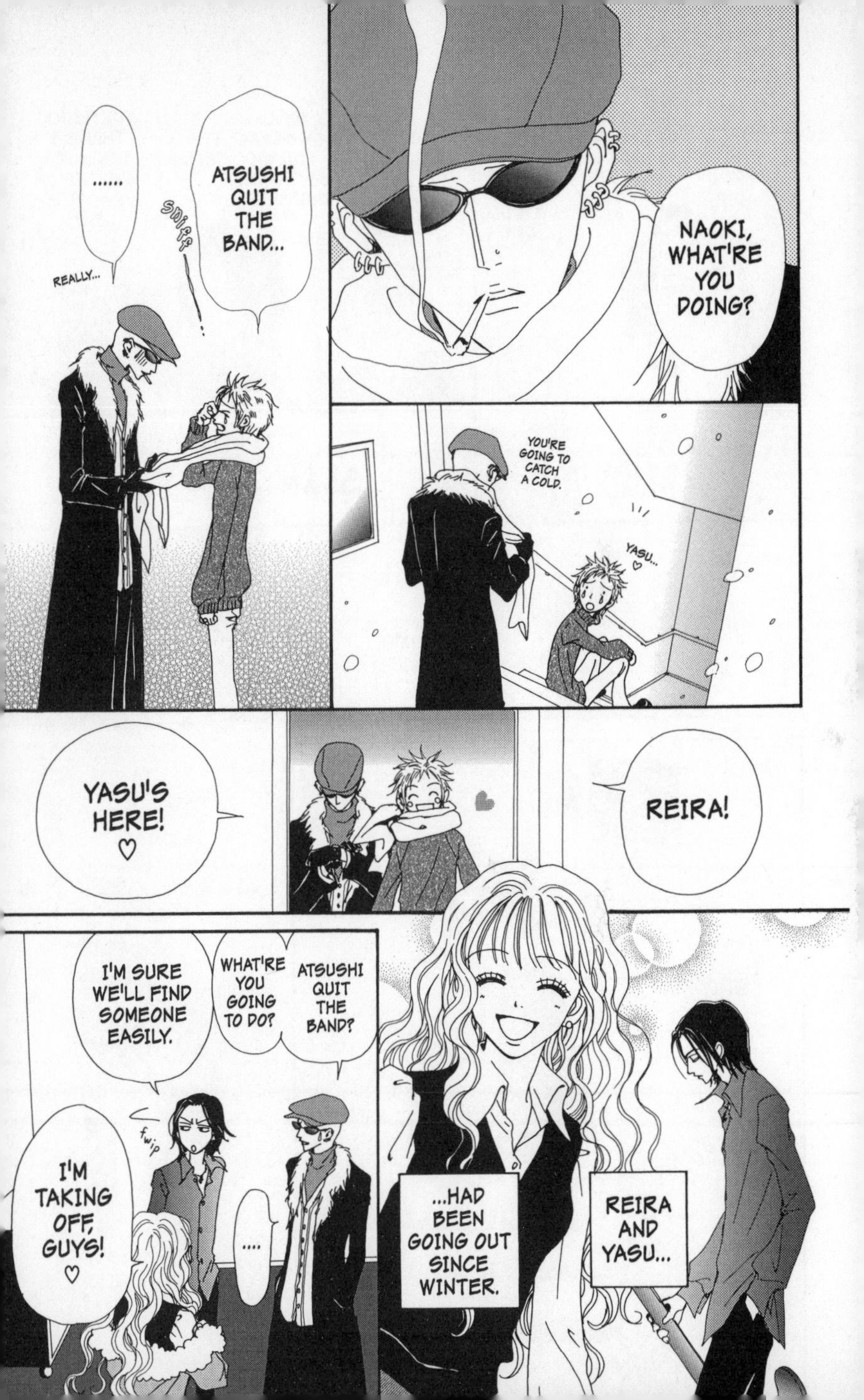
NAOKI, WHAT'RE YOU DOING?
YOU'RE GOING TO CATCH A COLD.
YASU... ♥
ATSUSHI QUIT THE BAND...
SNIFF
......
REALLY...
REIRA!
YASU'S HERE! ♡
REIRA AND YASU...
...HAD BEEN GOING OUT SINCE WINTER.
ATSUSHI QUIT THE BAND?
WHAT'RE YOU GOING TO DO?
I'M SURE WE'LL FIND SOMEONE EASILY.
fwip
....
I'M TAKING OFF, GUYS! ♡

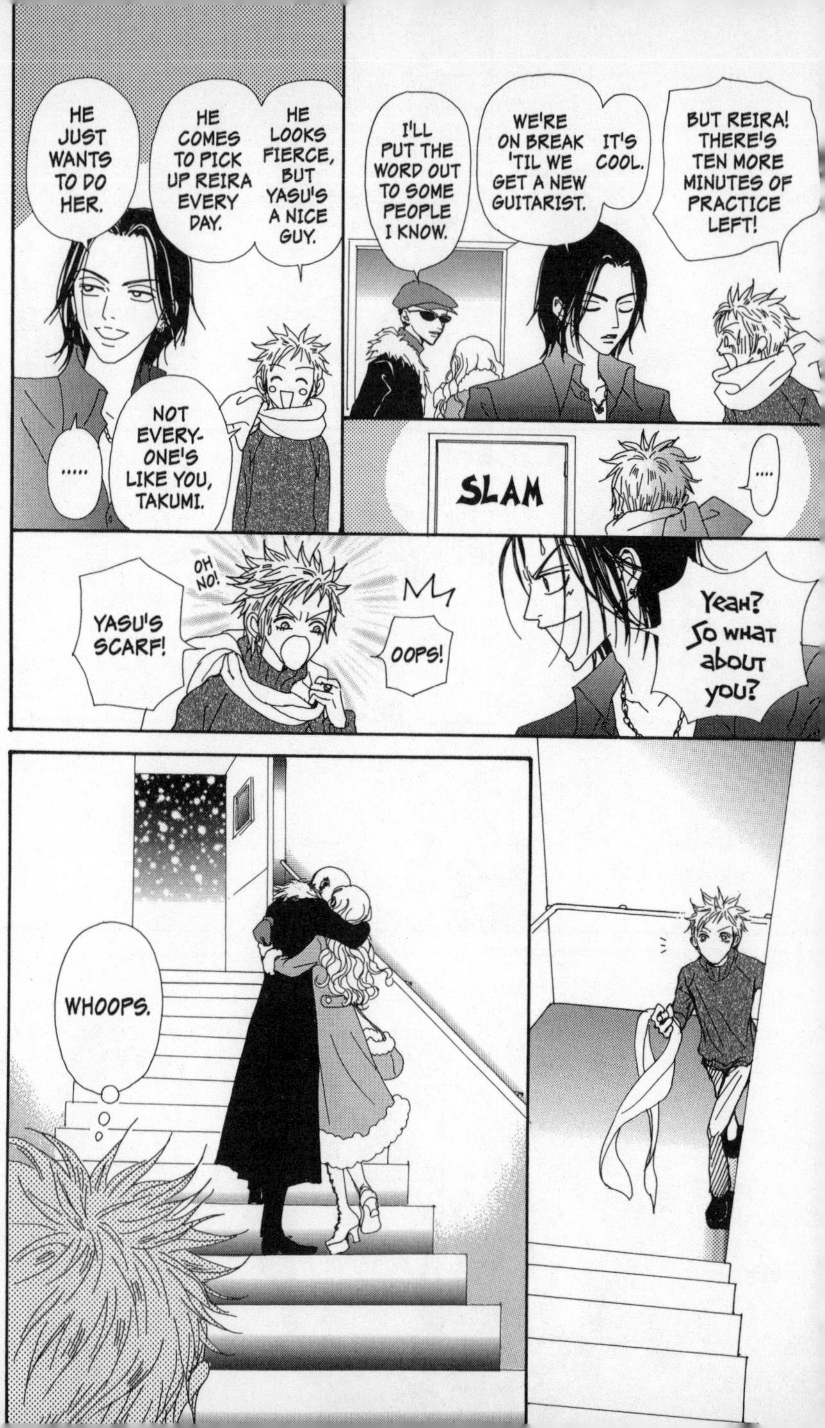
BUT REIRA! THERE'S TEN MORE MINUTES OF PRACTICE LEFT!
IT'S COOL.
WE'RE ON BREAK 'TIL WE GET A NEW GUITARIST.
I'LL PUT THE WORD OUT TO SOME PEOPLE I KNOW.
....
SLAM
HE LOOKS FIERCE, BUT YASU'S A NICE GUY.
HE COMES TO PICK UP REIRA EVERY DAY.
HE JUST WANTS TO DO HER.
NOT EVERYONE'S LIKE YOU, TAKUMI.
.....
Yeah? So what about you?
OOPS!
OH NO!
YASU'S SCARF!
WHOOPS.

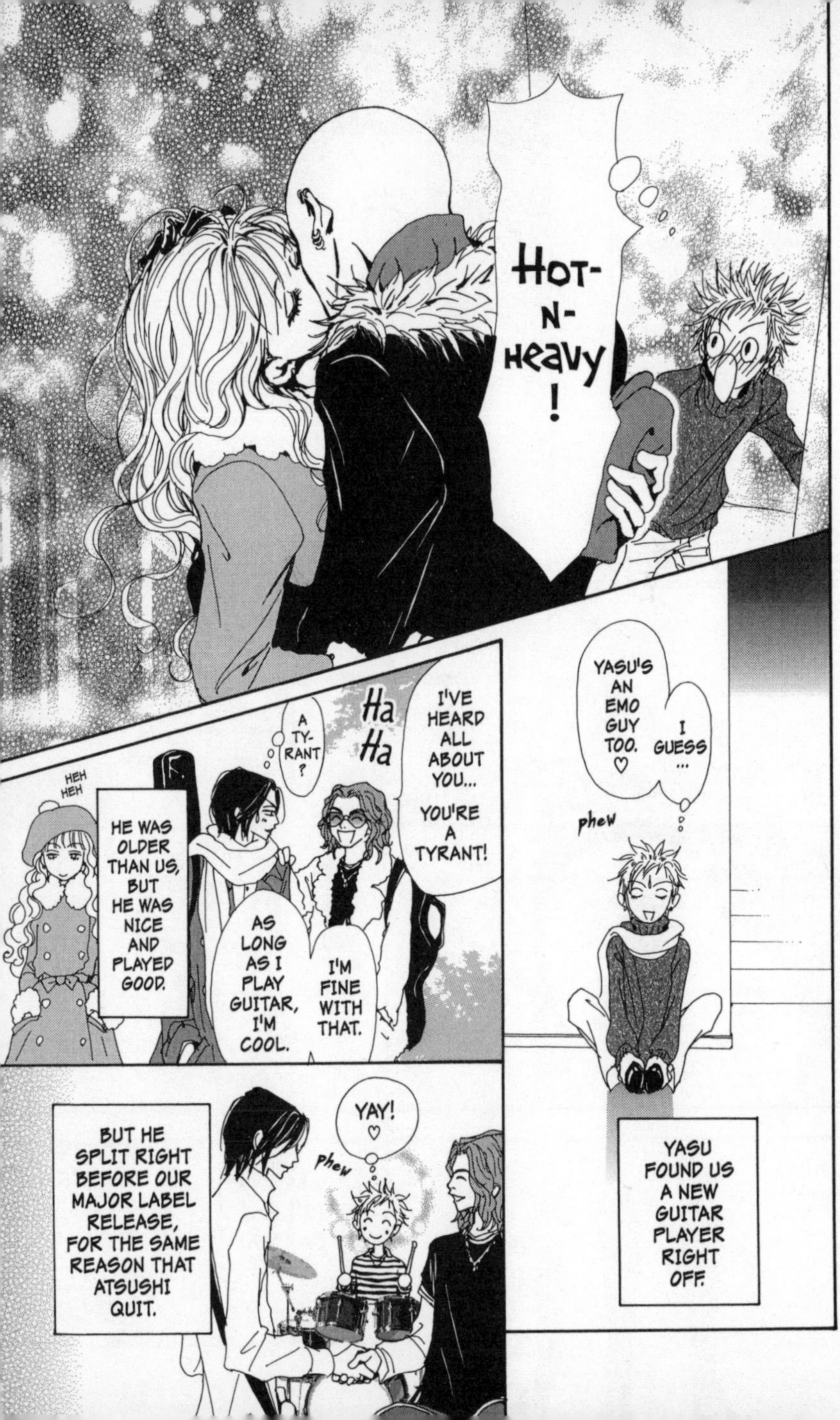
HOT-N-HEAVY!
YASU'S AN EMO GUY TOO. ♡
I GUESS...
phew
YASU FOUND US A NEW GUITAR PLAYER RIGHT OFF.
I'VE HEARD ALL ABOUT YOU... YOU'RE A TYRANT!
Ha Ha
A TY-RANT?
HEH HEH
AS LONG AS I PLAY GUITAR, I'M COOL.
I'M FINE WITH THAT.
HE WAS OLDER THAN US, BUT HE WAS NICE AND PLAYED GOOD.
YAY! ♡
phew
BUT HE SPLIT RIGHT BEFORE OUR MAJOR LABEL RELEASE, FOR THE SAME REASON THAT ATSUSHI QUIT.

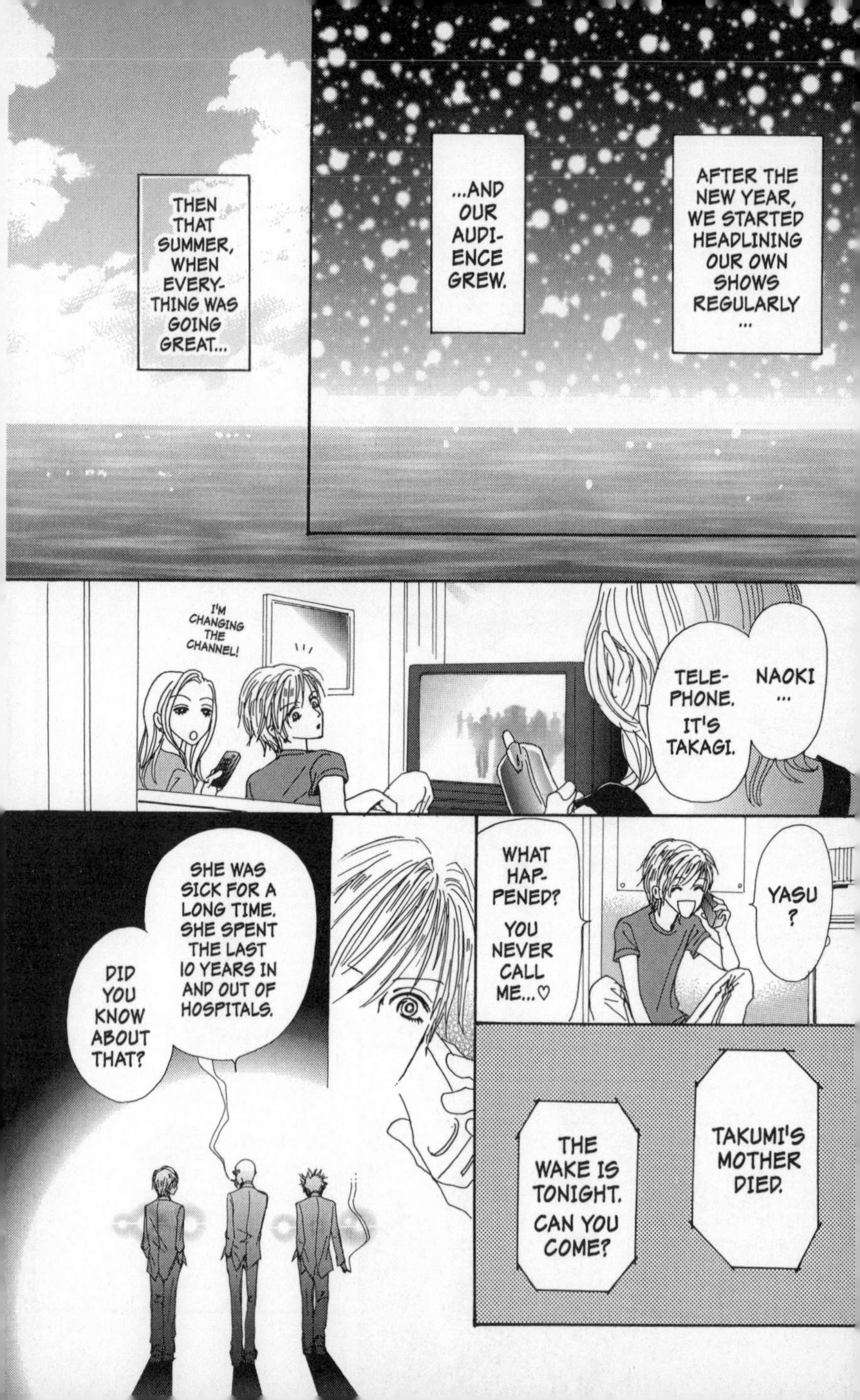
AFTER THE NEW YEAR, WE STARTED HEADLINING OUR OWN SHOWS REGULARLY...
...AND OUR AUDIENCE GREW.
THEN THAT SUMMER, WHEN EVERYTHING WAS GOING GREAT...
NAOKI...
TELEPHONE. IT'S TAKAGI.
I'M CHANGING THE CHANNEL!
YASU?
WHAT HAPPENED? YOU NEVER CALL ME...♡
TAKUMI'S MOTHER DIED.
THE WAKE IS TONIGHT. CAN YOU COME?
SHE WAS SICK FOR A LONG TIME. SHE SPENT THE LAST 10 YEARS IN AND OUT OF HOSPITALS.
DID YOU KNOW ABOUT THAT?

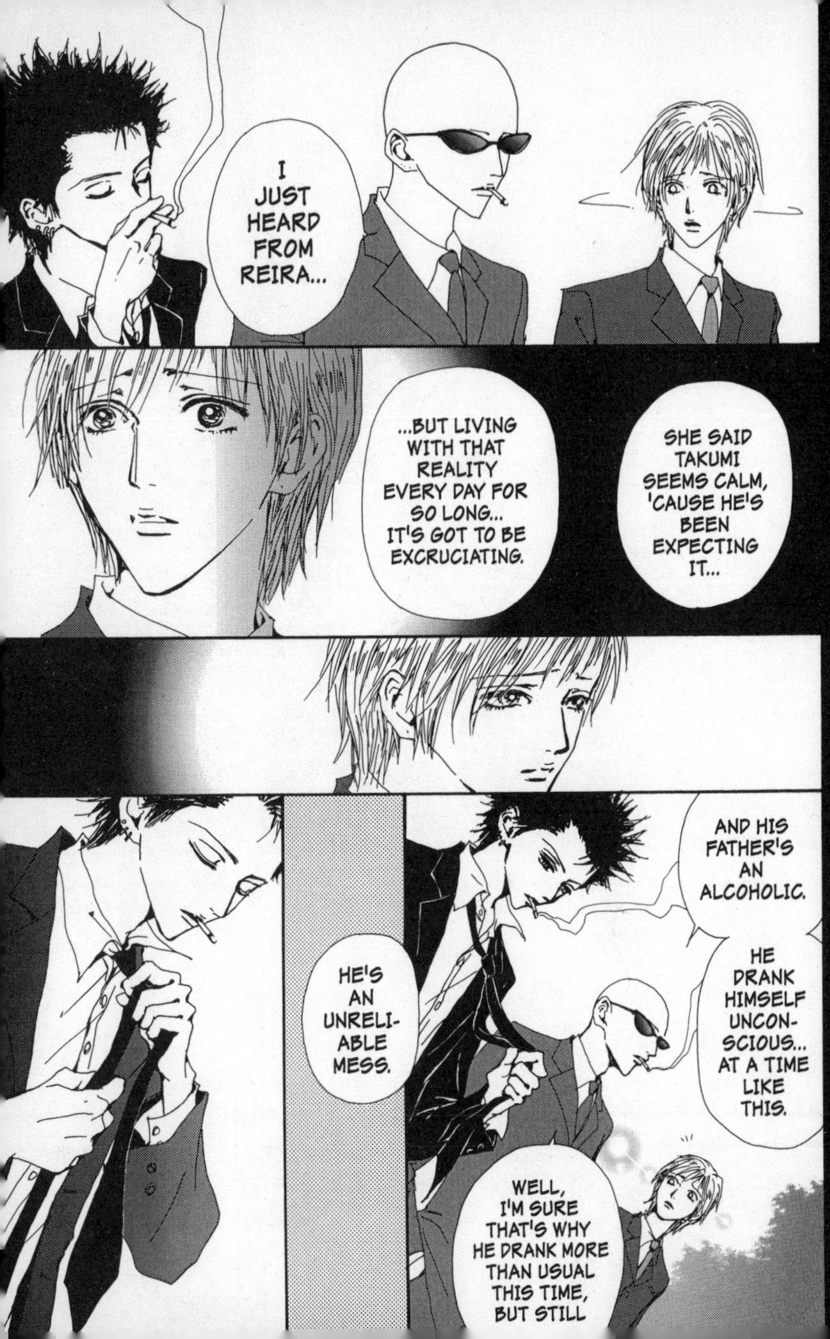
I JUST HEARD FROM REIRA...
SHE SAID TAKUMI SEEMS CALM, 'CAUSE HE'S BEEN EXPECTING IT...
...BUT LIVING WITH THAT REALITY EVERY DAY FOR SO LONG... IT'S GOT TO BE EXCRUCIATING.
AND HIS FATHER'S AN ALCOHOLIC.
HE DRANK HIMSELF UNCONSCIOUS... AT A TIME LIKE THIS.
HE'S AN UNRELIABLE MESS.
WELL, I'M SURE THAT'S WHY HE DRANK MORE THAN USUAL THIS TIME, BUT STILL

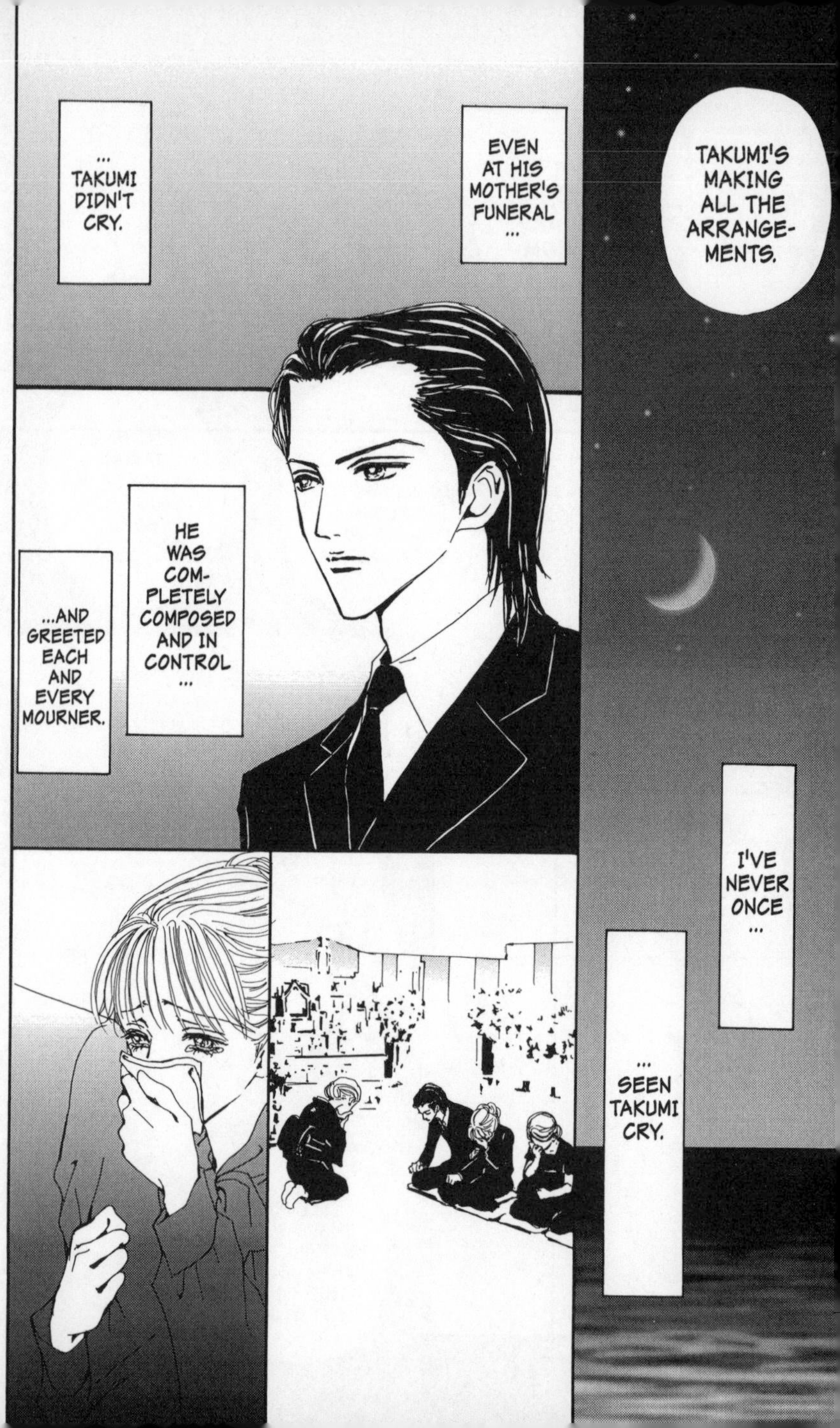
TAKUMI'S MAKING ALL THE ARRANGE-MENTS.
I'VE NEVER ONCE ...
... SEEN TAKUMI CRY.
EVEN AT HIS MOTHER'S FUNERAL ...
... TAKUMI DIDN'T CRY.
HE WAS COM-PLETELY COMPOSED AND IN CONTROL ...
...AND GREETED EACH AND EVERY MOURNER.

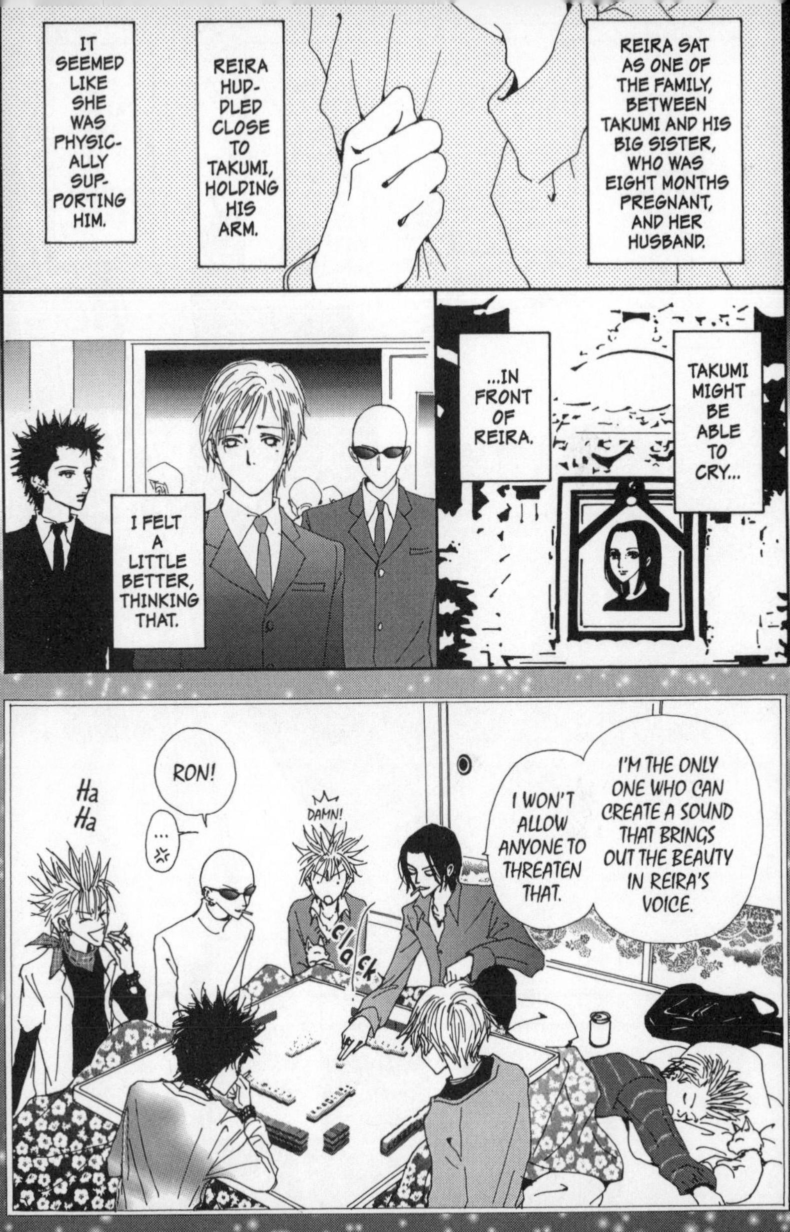
REIRA SAT AS ONE OF THE FAMILY, BETWEEN TAKUMI AND HIS BIG SISTER, WHO WAS EIGHT MONTHS PREGNANT, AND HER HUSBAND.
REIRA HUD-DLED CLOSE TO TAKUMI, HOLDING HIS ARM.
IT SEEMED LIKE SHE WAS PHYSIC-ALLY SUP-PORTING HIM.
TAKUMI MIGHT BE ABLE TO CRY...
...IN FRONT OF REIRA.
I FELT A LITTLE BETTER, THINKING THAT.
I'M THE ONLY ONE WHO CAN CREATE A SOUND THAT BRINGS OUT THE BEAUTY IN REIRA'S VOICE.
I WON'T ALLOW ANYONE TO THREATEN THAT.
DAMN!
CLACK
RON!
...
Ha Ha

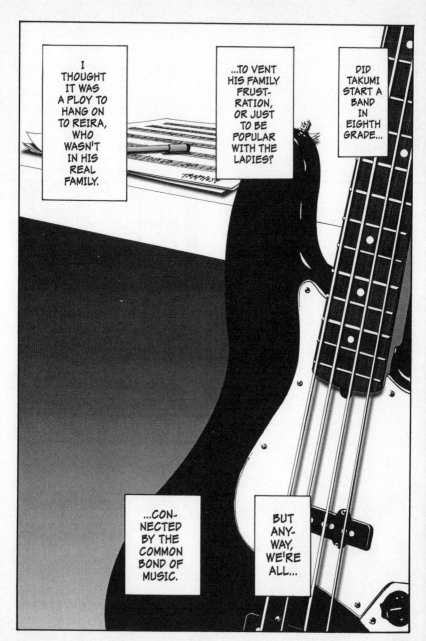

DID TAKUMI START A BAND IN EIGHTH GRADE...

...TO VENT HIS FAMILY FRUSTRATION, OR JUST TO BE POPULAR WITH THE LADIES?

I THOUGHT IT WAS A PLOY TO HANG ON TO REIRA, WHO WASN'T IN HIS REAL FAMILY.

BUT ANYWAY, WE'RE ALL...

...CONNECTED BY THE COMMON BOND OF MUSIC.

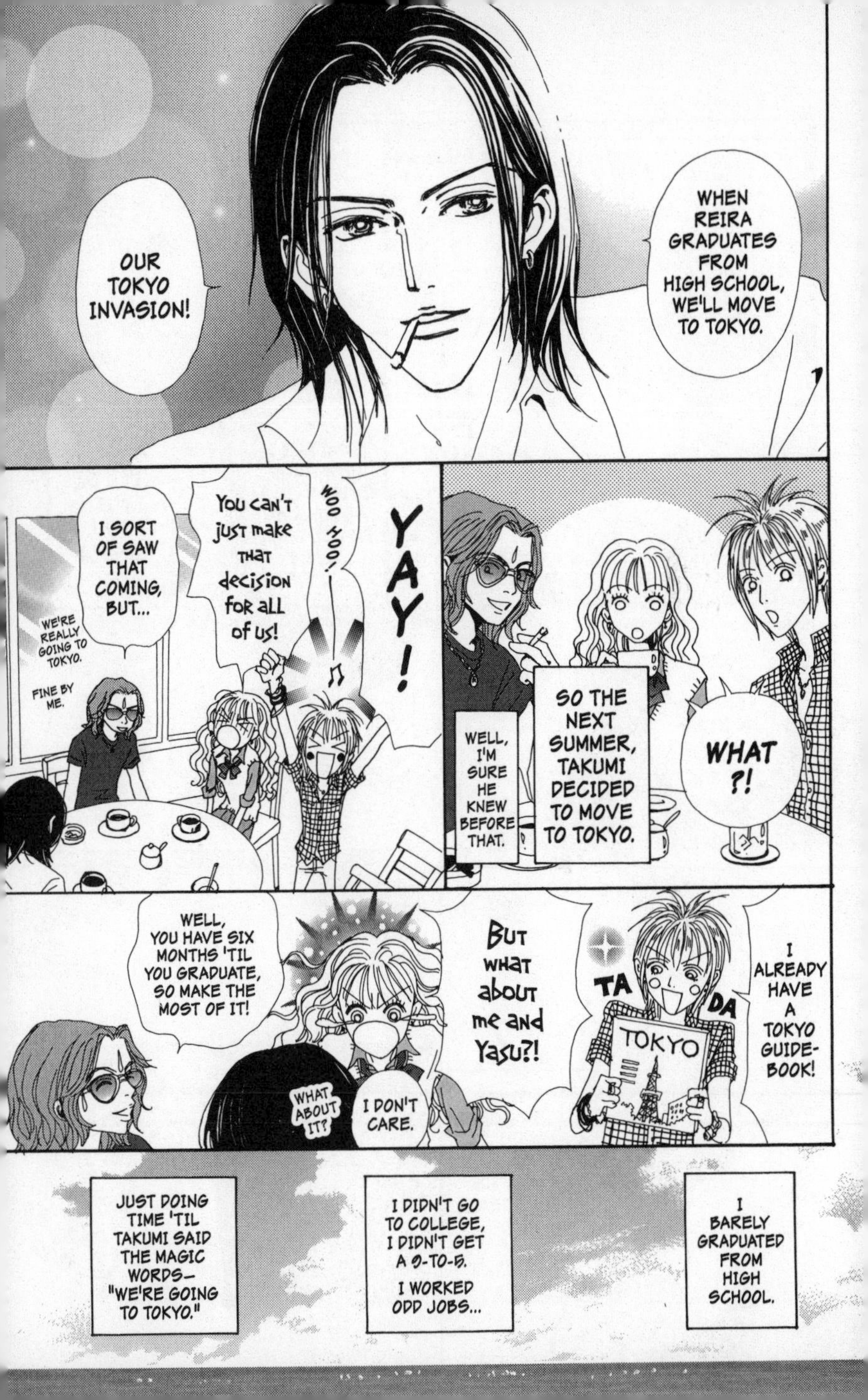
WHEN REIRA GRADUATES FROM HIGH SCHOOL, WE'LL MOVE TO TOKYO.
OUR TOKYO INVASION!
SO THE NEXT SUMMER, TAKUMI DECIDED TO MOVE TO TOKYO.
WHAT?!
WELL, I'M SURE HE KNEW BEFORE THAT.
YAY!
WOO HOO!
You can't just make that decision for all of us!
I SORT OF SAW THAT COMING, BUT...
WE'RE REALLY GOING TO TOKYO.
FINE BY ME.
I ALREADY HAVE A TOKYO GUIDE-BOOK!
TA DA
TOKYO
But what about me and Yasu?!
I DON'T CARE.
WHAT ABOUT IT?
WELL, YOU HAVE SIX MONTHS 'TIL YOU GRADUATE, SO MAKE THE MOST OF IT!
I BARELY GRADUATED FROM HIGH SCHOOL.
I DIDN'T GO TO COLLEGE, I DIDN'T GET A 9-TO-5.
I WORKED ODD JOBS...
JUST DOING TIME 'TIL TAKUMI SAID THE MAGIC WORDS— "WE'RE GOING TO TOKYO."

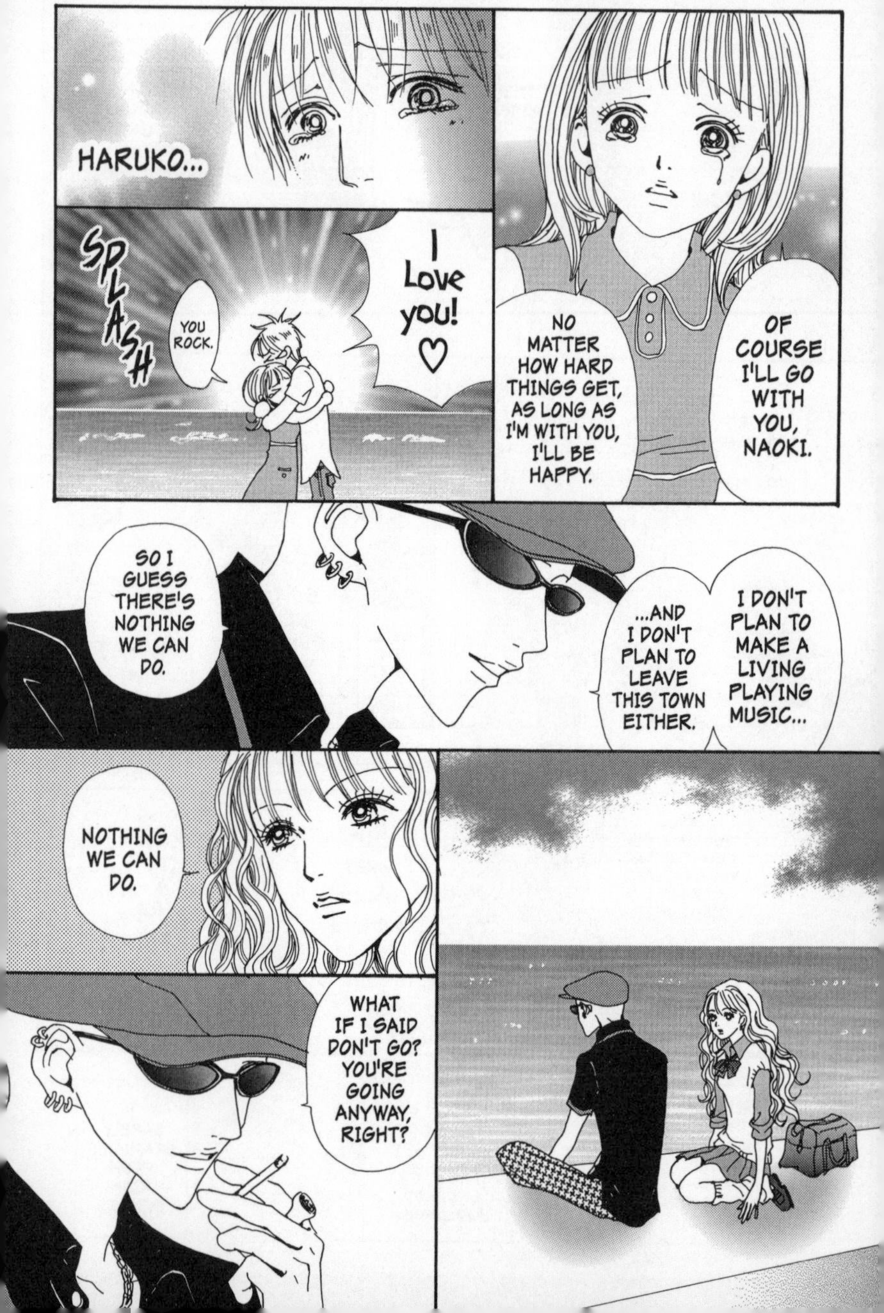
OF COURSE I'LL GO WITH YOU, NAOKI.
NO MATTER HOW HARD THINGS GET, AS LONG AS I'M WITH YOU, I'LL BE HAPPY.
HARUKO...
I Love you! ♥
YOU ROCK.
SPLASH
I DON'T PLAN TO MAKE A LIVING PLAYING MUSIC...
...AND I DON'T PLAN TO LEAVE THIS TOWN EITHER.
SO I GUESS THERE'S NOTHING WE CAN DO.
NOTHING WE CAN DO.
WHAT IF I SAID DON'T GO? YOU'RE GOING ANYWAY, RIGHT?

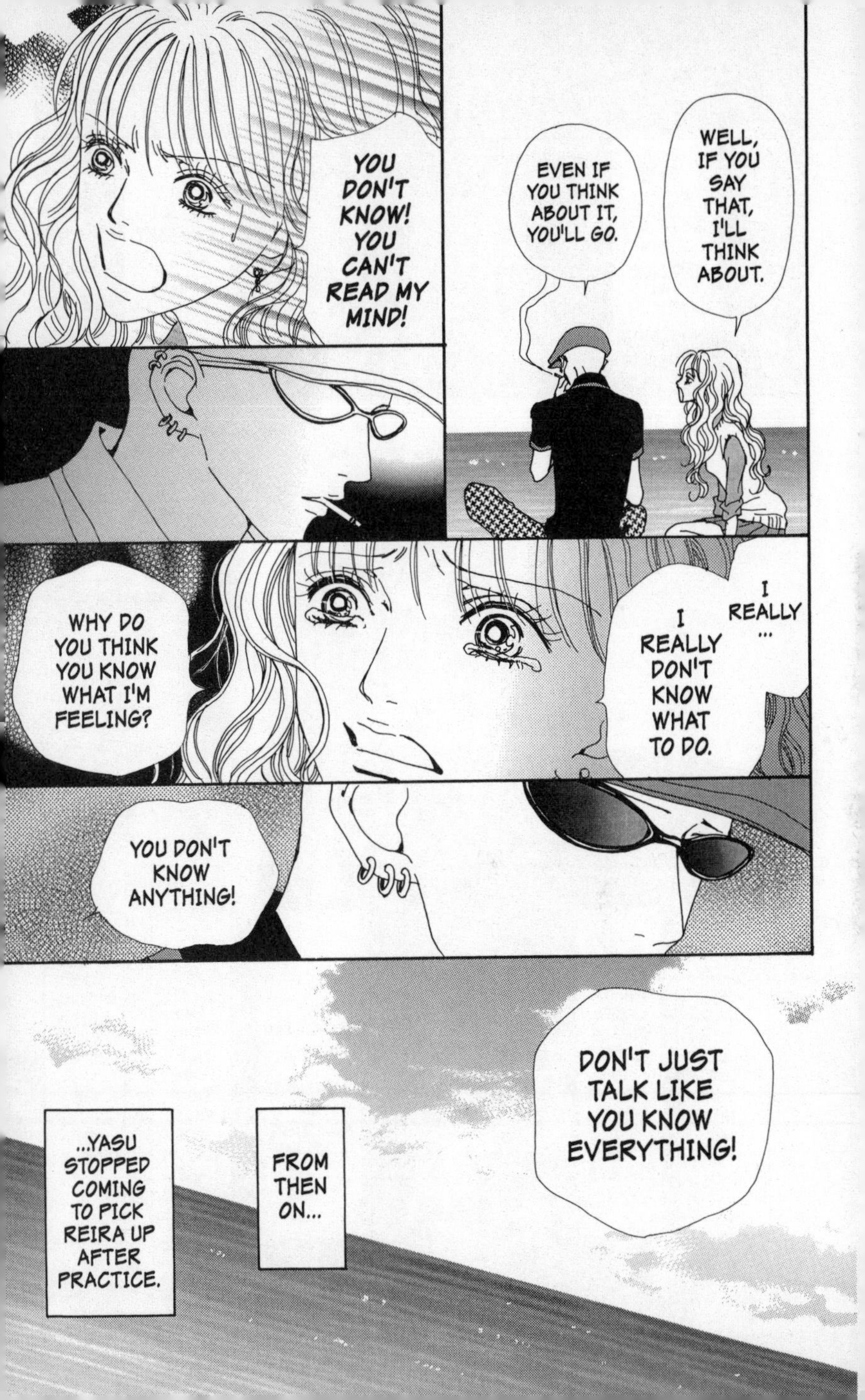
WELL, IF YOU SAY THAT, I'LL THINK ABOUT.
EVEN IF YOU THINK ABOUT IT, YOU'LL GO.
YOU DON'T KNOW! YOU CAN'T READ MY MIND!
I REALLY...
I REALLY DON'T KNOW WHAT TO DO.
WHY DO YOU THINK YOU KNOW WHAT I'M FEELING?
YOU DON'T KNOW ANYTHING!
DON'T JUST TALK LIKE YOU KNOW EVERYTHING!
FROM THEN ON...
...YASU STOPPED COMING TO PICK REIRA UP AFTER PRACTICE.

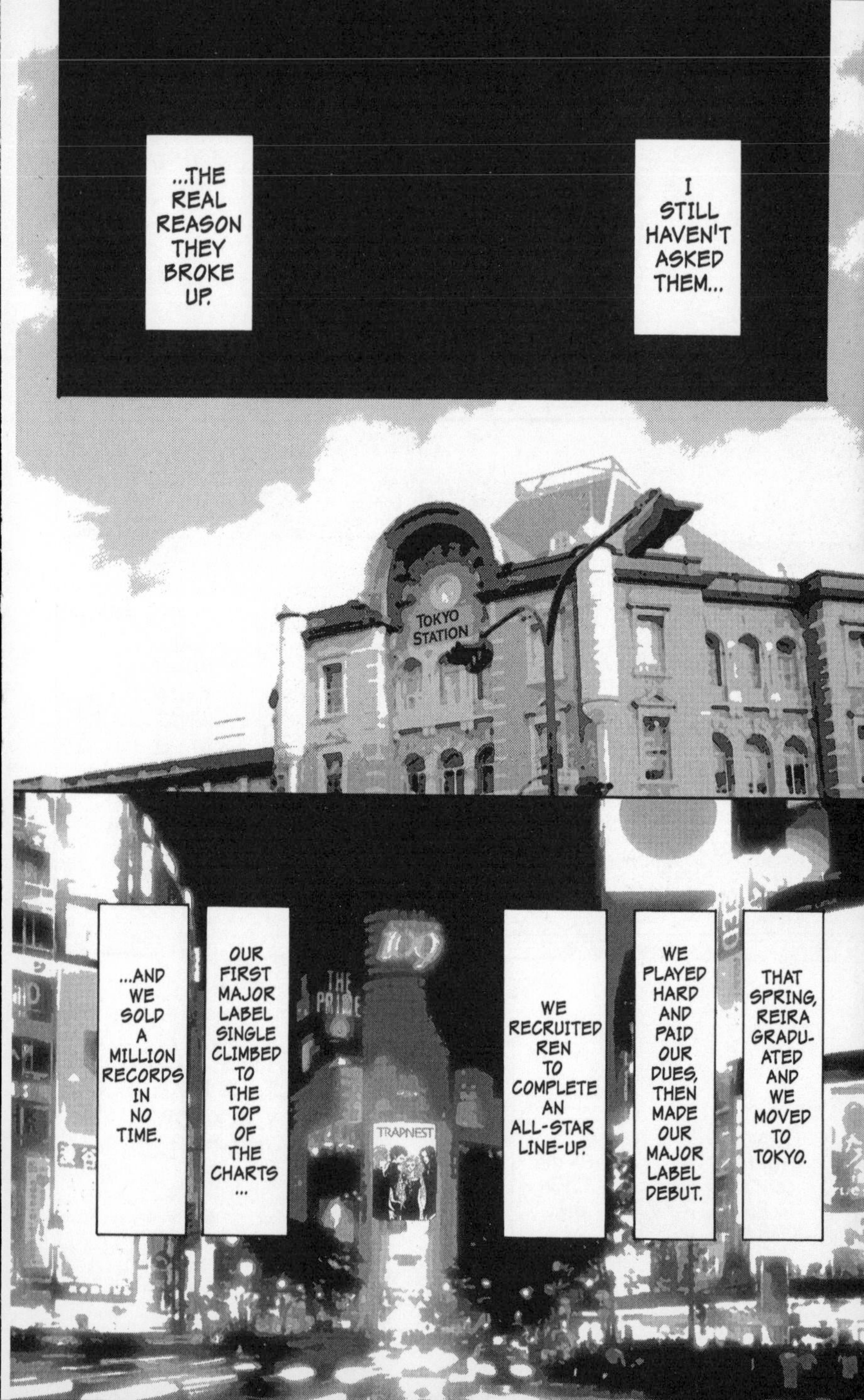
I STILL HAVEN'T ASKED THEM...
...THE REAL REASON THEY BROKE UP.
TOKYO STATION
THAT SPRING, REIRA GRADU-ATED AND WE MOVED TO TOKYO.
WE PLAYED HARD AND PAID OUR DUES, THEN MADE OUR MAJOR LABEL DEBUT.
WE RECRUITED REN TO COMPLETE AN ALL-STAR LINE-UP.
THE PRIME
TRAPNEST
OUR FIRST MAJOR LABEL SINGLE CLIMBED TO THE TOP OF THE CHARTS...
...AND WE SOLD A MILLION RECORDS IN NO TIME.

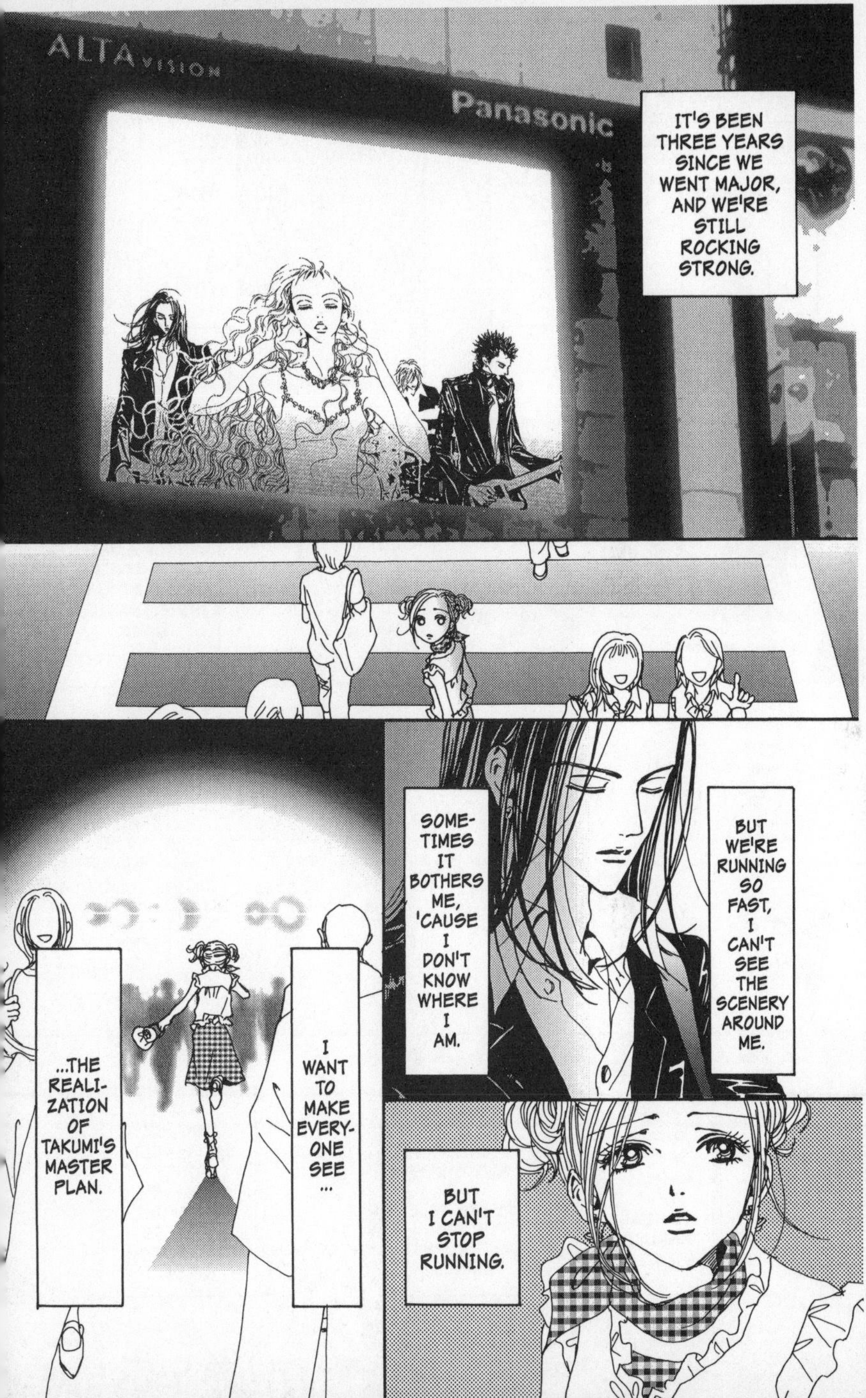
ALTA VISION
Panasonic
IT'S BEEN THREE YEARS SINCE WE WENT MAJOR, AND WE'RE STILL ROCKING STRONG.
BUT WE'RE RUNNING SO FAST, I CAN'T SEE THE SCENERY AROUND ME.
SOMETIMES IT BOTHERS ME, 'CAUSE I DON'T KNOW WHERE I AM.
BUT I CAN'T STOP RUNNING.
I WANT TO MAKE EVERYONE SEE...
...THE REALIZATION OF TAKUMI'S MASTER PLAN.

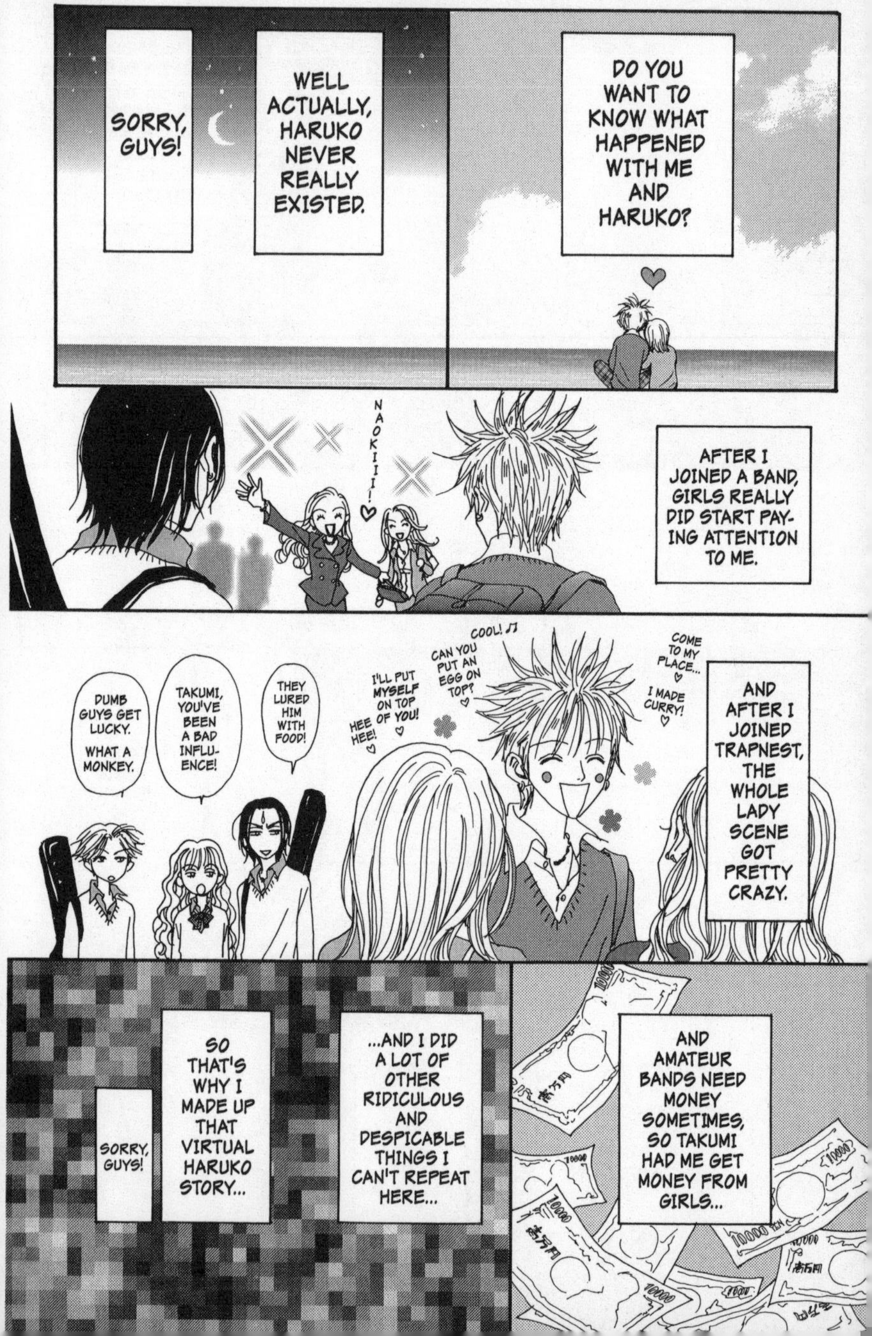
DO YOU WANT TO KNOW WHAT HAPPENED WITH ME AND HARUKO?
WELL ACTUALLY, HARUKO NEVER REALLY EXISTED.
SORRY, GUYS!
AFTER I JOINED A BAND, GIRLS REALLY DID START PAYING ATTENTION TO ME.
NAOKIII!
AND AFTER I JOINED TRAPNEST, THE WHOLE LADY SCENE GOT PRETTY CRAZY.
COME TO MY PLACE...
I MADE CURRY!
COOL!
CAN YOU PUT AN EGG ON TOP?
I'LL PUT MYSELF ON TOP OF YOU!
HEE HEE!
THEY LURED HIM WITH FOOD!
TAKUMI, YOU'VE BEEN A BAD INFLUENCE!
DUMB GUYS GET LUCKY.
WHAT A MONKEY.
AND AMATEUR BANDS NEED MONEY SOMETIMES, SO TAKUMI HAD ME GET MONEY FROM GIRLS...
...AND I DID A LOT OF OTHER RIDICULOUS AND DESPICABLE THINGS I CAN'T REPEAT HERE...
SO THAT'S WHY I MADE UP THAT VIRTUAL HARUKO STORY...
SORRY, GUYS!

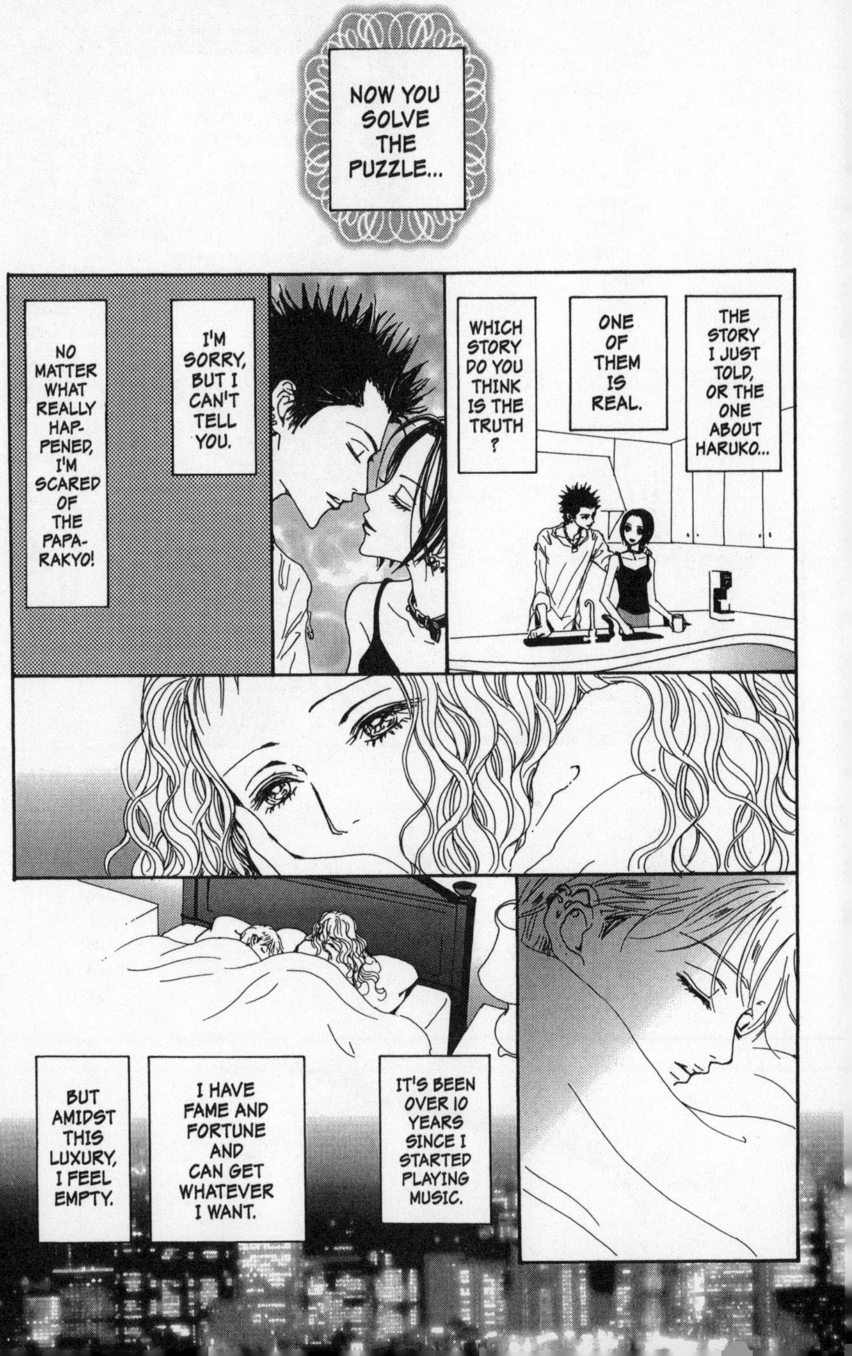
NOW YOU SOLVE THE PUZZLE...
THE STORY I JUST TOLD, OR THE ONE ABOUT HARUKO...
ONE OF THEM IS REAL.
WHICH STORY DO YOU THINK IS THE TRUTH?
I'M SORRY, BUT I CAN'T TELL YOU.
NO MATTER WHAT REALLY HAP-PENED, I'M SCARED OF THE PAPA-RAKYO!
IT'S BEEN OVER 10 YEARS SINCE I STARTED PLAYING MUSIC.
I HAVE FAME AND FORTUNE AND CAN GET WHATEVER I WANT.
BUT AMIDST THIS LUXURY, I FEEL EMPTY.

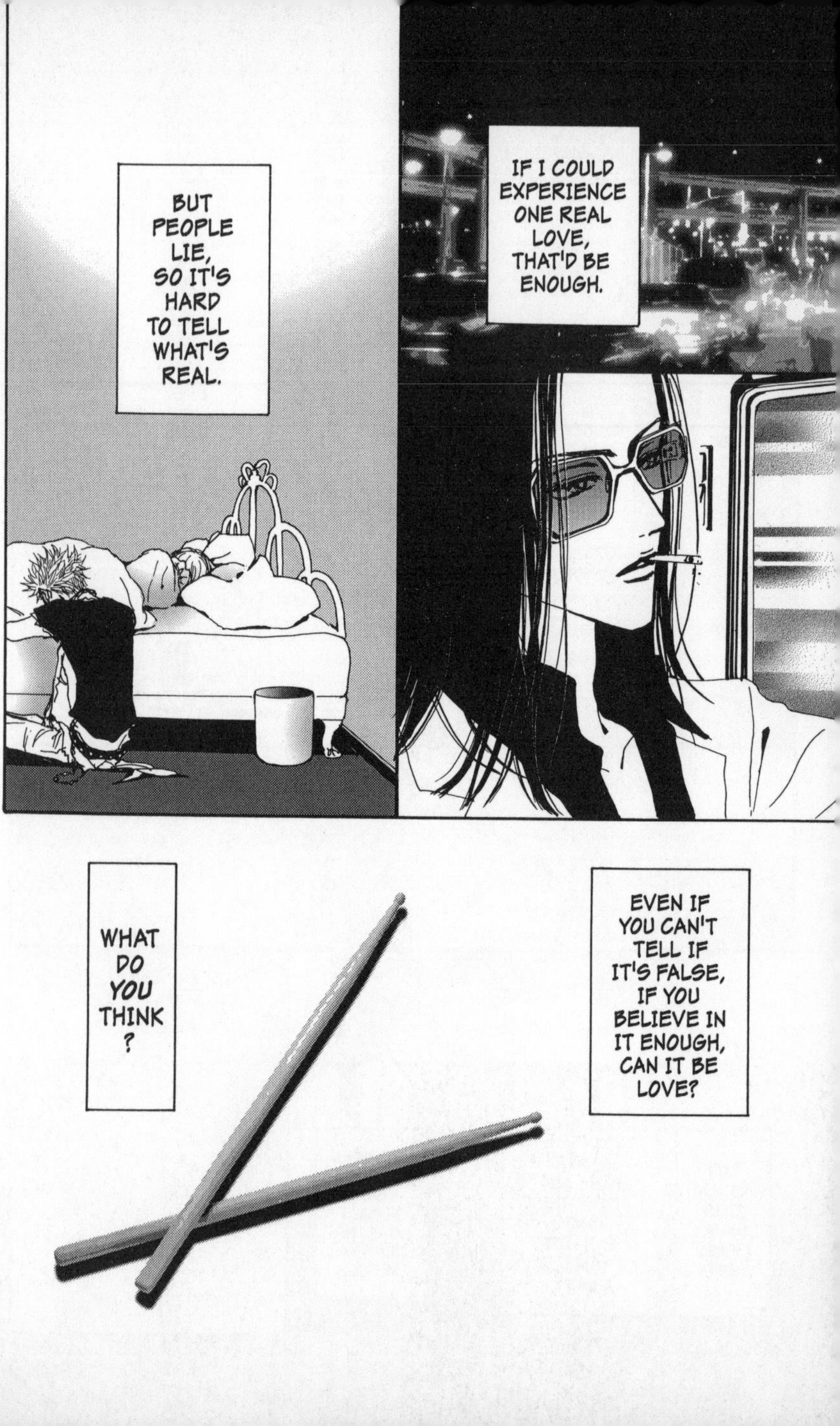
IF I COULD EXPERIENCE ONE REAL LOVE, THAT'D BE ENOUGH.
BUT PEOPLE LIE, SO IT'S HARD TO TELL WHAT'S REAL.
EVEN IF YOU CAN'T TELL IF IT'S FALSE, IF YOU BELIEVE IN IT ENOUGH, CAN IT BE LOVE?
WHAT DO *YOU* THINK ?

One day, I realized I had to write a bonus story. I was talking to my editor about it (Let's do a story about the history of Trapnest!) when Naoki swooped down triumphantly, shouting "Then I'm the star!" The day will come when he gets his place in the sun. You really don't know what's going to happen next in this manga! ☺ —Ai Yazawa

Ai Yazawa is the creator of many popular manga titles, including *Tenshi Nanka Janai* (I'm No Angel) and *Gokinjo Monogatari* (Neighborhood Story). Another series, *Kagen no Tsuki* (Last Quarter), was made into a live-action movie and released in late 2004. American readers were introduced to Yazawa's stylish and sexy storytelling in 2002 when her title *Paradise Kiss* was translated into English.

Nana has become the all-time best-selling shojo title from Japanese publishing giant Shueisha, and the series even garnered a Shogakukan Manga Award in the girls category in 2003. A live-action *Nana* movie was released in Japan last year.

NANA
VOL. 9

Shojo Beat Edition

STORY AND ART BY AI YAZAWA

English Adaptation/Allison Wolfe
Translation/Tomo Kimura
Touch-up Art & Lettering/Sabrina Heep
Cover Design/Courtney Utt
Interior Design/Julie Behn
Editor/Pancha Diaz

Printed in the U.S.A.

Published by VIZ Media, LLC
P.O. Box 77010
San Francisco, CA 94107

10 9 8 7 6 5 4 3
First printing, March 2008
Third printing, October 2015

www.viz.com www.shojobeat.com

RATED M FOR MATURE

PARENTAL ADVISORY
NANA is rated M for Mature and is recommended for mature readers. This volume contains strong language and sexual situations.
ratings.viz.com

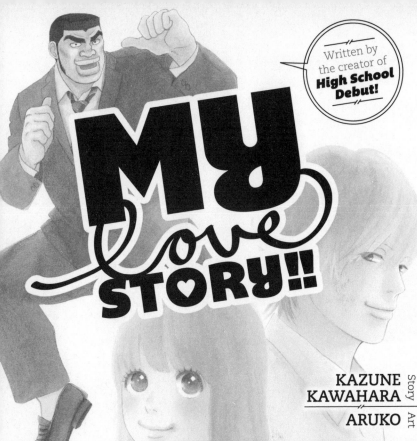

Written by the creator of **High School Debut!**

MY love STORY!!

KAZUNE KAWAHARA — Story

ARUKO — Art

Takeo Goda is a GIANT guy with a GIANT *heart*

Too bad the girls don't want him!
(They want his good-looking best friend, Sunakawa.)

Used to being on the sidelines, Takeo simply stands tall and accepts his fate. But one day when he saves a girl named Yamato from a harasser on the train, his (love!) life suddenly takes an incredible turn!

www.viz.com   www.shojobeat.com   RATED TEEN ratings.viz.com

ORE MONOGATARI!! © 2011 by Kazune Kawahara, Aruko/SHUEISHA Inc.

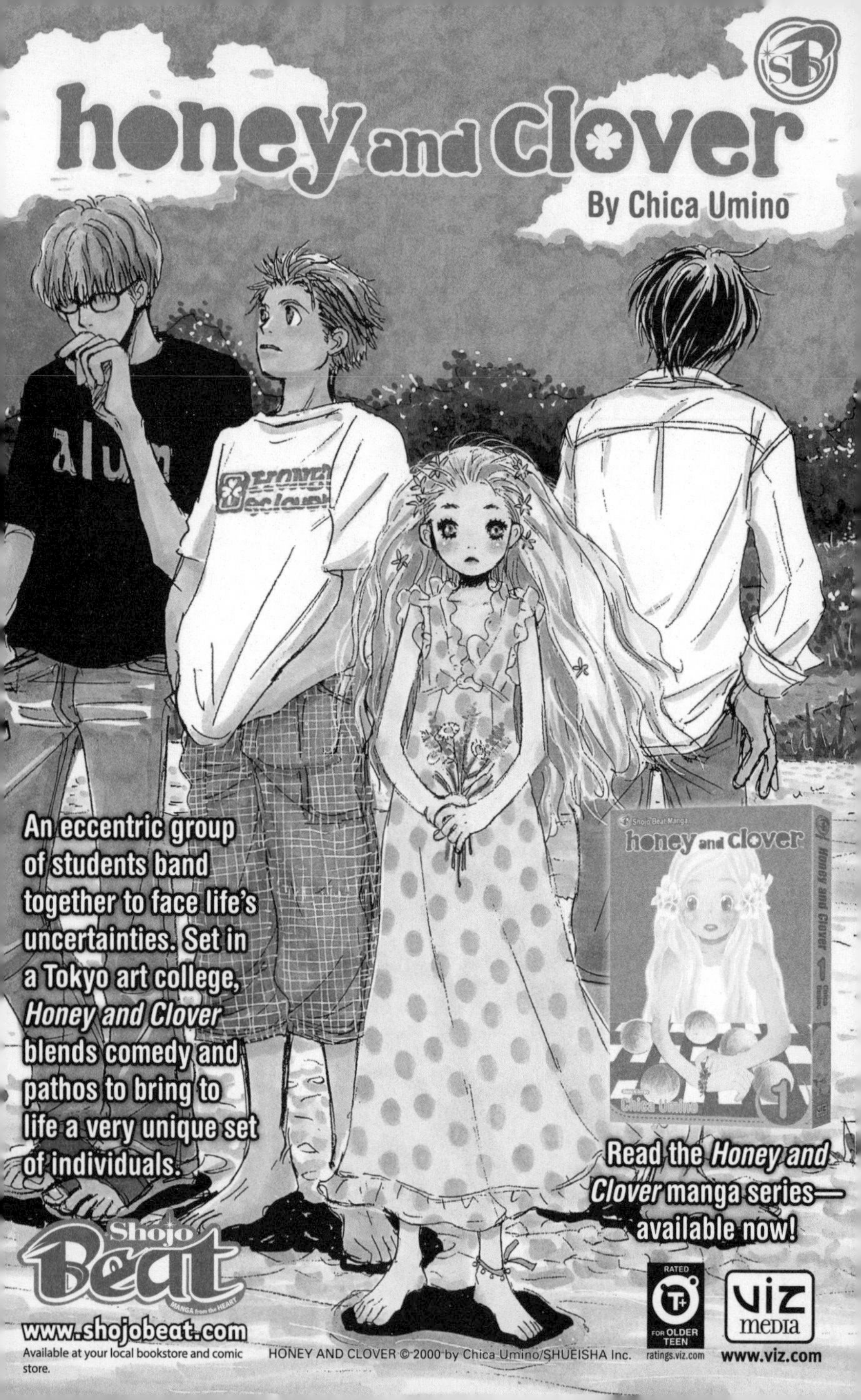
honey and clover
By Chica Umino
An eccentric group of students band together to face life's uncertainties. Set in a Tokyo art college, *Honey and Clover* blends comedy and pathos to bring to life a very unique set of individuals.
Read the *Honey and Clover* manga series—available now!
Shojo Beat
www.shojobeat.com
Available at your local bookstore and comic store.
HONEY AND CLOVER © 2000 by Chica Umino/SHUEISHA Inc.
RATED T+ FOR OLDER TEEN
ratings.viz.com
viz media
www.viz.com